EX · LIBRIS

Short story writer and novelist Owen Marshall has written, or edited, twenty-three books to date. Awards for his fiction include the PEN Lillian Ida Smith Award twice, the *Evening Standard* Short Story Prize, the American Express Short Story Award, the New Zealand Literary Fund Scholarship in Letters, Fellowships at the universities of Canterbury and Otago, and the Katherine Mansfield Memorial Fellowship in Menton, France. He received the ONZM for services to Literature in the New Zealand New Year Honours, 2000. In 2002 the University of Canterbury awarded him the honorary degree of Doctor of Letters and in 2005 appointed himself an adjunct professor. His novel *Harlequin Rex* won the Montana New Zealand Book Awards Deutz Medal for Fiction in 2000, and in 2006 his short-story collection *Watch of Gryphons* was shortlisted for the same prize.

Owen Marshall was born in 1941, has spent almost all his life in South Island towns, and has an affinity with provincial New Zealand.

National Library of New Zealand Cataloguing-in-Publication Data

Marshall, Owen, 1941-
Short stories —Selections.
Owen Marshall selected stories / Owen Marshall ; Vincent O'Sullivan, editor.
ISBN 978-1-86941-958-5
I. O'Sullivan, Vincent. II. Title.
NZ823.2—dc 22

For more information about our titles go to www.randomhouse.co.nz

A VINTAGE BOOK
published by
Random House New Zealand
18 Poland Road, Glenfield, Auckland, New Zealand

Random House International
Random House
20 Vauxhall Bridge Road
London, SW1V 2SA
United Kingdom

Random House Australia (Pty) Ltd
Level 3, 100 Pacific Highway
North Sydney 2060, Australia

Random House South Africa Pty Ltd
Isle of Houghton
Corner Boundary Road and Carse O'Gowrie
Houghton 2198, South Africa

Random House Publishers India Private Ltd
301 World Trade Tower, Hotel Intercontinental Grand Complex
Barakhamba Lane, New Delhi 110 001, India

First published 2008

ISBN 978 1 86941 958 5

Cover and text design: Anna Seabrook
Cover image: *Cookhouse* by Grahame Sydney, 2001. Oil on linen. 760mm x 1020mm. Private
collection.
Printed in China by Everbest Printing Co Ltd

Owen Marshall

selected stories

Edited by Vincent O'Sullivan

V

Contents

hat his body is occupied with as much as his mind (including
 dog with his bare hands). Or consider how in several stories
 establish the reality of their world not only by talking with
her. This is done as well by how they relate as workers, the
, which a workplace doubles as emotional bullring. 'Iris' as
309 Hollandia' as finely balanced pathos; these are the kind
es that scotch once and for all the occasional comment that
l is less effective when writing about women. He writes less
bout them than he does about men, but that is a different

shall knows a lot about how things are done, how various
es are pursued. He knows how work shapes and reveals the
 woman who does it. He notices how physical effort, whether
 or by choice, defines. The conviction he brings to story-
is from that kind of depth. If a man is an accountant we
vhat it is like to do accounts. We see and feel how a teacher
, a mechanic fixes motors, a cleric comforts, a pervert gets on
erverting. More than any other of our writers, he has taken
 imaginative franchise on a particular kind of New Zealand
stly South Island — life, much as there is a David Malouf
sland, or a Tim Winton Western Australia. His world by and
ay be one we are familiar with. But how it is distilled, how
smantled and re-presented to us, is a matter of novelty and
e, technical adroitness and penetration.
 often been struck by how differently New Zealand's two
hort story writers go about their business. Marshall — I am
g a little here — may admire Katherine Mansfield, but does
rticularly like her stories. One isn't surprised. Mansfield's
ament, as we know it from her letters and notebooks,
nds almost everything in her fiction: that glancing brush with
 her hovering refusal to insist or underline, the inheritance
-impressionism that often defines her. She disliked the idea
on working towards a moral point as much as Marshall is

Introduction

I

Even when a publisher allows you sixty a
choose the 'best' stories from a writer you g
out to be a tall order. The ones that have alw
particular favourites easily pick themselves.
the increasingly delicate business of balancing
Marshall's stories take in, with doing justice to
go into their making.

No New Zealander has written anywhe
stories, although their sheer quantity has no
what makes them unique. What reading then
that 'Marshall country' is a distinctive and co
much like the one we live in day by day, and y
'copy'. What his stories add to it is a remarkabl
more than we usually see in characters who lo
at our troubled best and our recognisable wor
so distinctive and appealing in these stories, l
seem a slightly odd angle to come from. But
centre of how Marshall tells a story.

When I think of how these narratives dra
of how few writers tell you quite so convin
characters *do* for a living. Take the strange a
'Tomorrow We Save the Orphans', where th
us most works as night-watchman in a larg
separate his emergence as a personality from

hour,
killing
wome
each c
ways
satire,
of sto
Marsh
often
matte

Ma
activit
man o
for pa
telling
know
teache
with
out a
— m
Quee
large
it is c
surpr
I'v
finest
guess
not
temp
comr
even
of pc
of fic

Introduction

Even when a publisher allows you sixty as a round number, to choose the 'best' stories from a writer you greatly admire can turn out to be a tall order. The ones that have always stayed with you as particular favourites easily pick themselves. After that, it becomes the increasingly delicate business of balancing the variety that Owen Marshall's stories take in, with doing justice to the range of skills that go into their making.

No New Zealander has written anywhere near so many short stories, although their sheer quantity has nothing much to do with what makes them unique. What reading them brings home to you is that 'Marshall country' is a distinctive and compelling place, pretty much like the one we live in day by day, and yet by no means a mere 'copy'. What his stories add to it is a remarkable clarity. We are shown more than we usually see in characters who look like us, talk like us, at our troubled best and our recognisable worst. To touch on what is so distinctive and appealing in these stories, I begin with what may seem a slightly odd angle to come from. But it is something at the centre of how Marshall tells a story.

When I think of how these narratives draw you in, I think too of how few writers tell you quite so convincingly what it is their characters *do* for a living. Take the strange and marginally sinister 'Tomorrow We Save the Orphans', where the figure who interests us most works as night-watchman in a large factory. You cannot separate his emergence as a personality from what he does hour by hour, what his body is occupied with as much as his mind (including killing a dog with his bare hands). Or consider how in several stories women establish the reality of their world not only by talking with each other. This is done as well by how they relate as workers, the ways in which a workplace doubles as emotional bullring. 'Iris' as satire, '309 Hollandia' as finely balanced pathos; these are the kind of stories that scotch once and for all the occasional comment that Marshall is less effective when writing about women. He writes less often about them than he does about men, but that is a different matter.

Marshall knows a lot about how things are done, how various activities are pursued. He knows how work shapes and reveals the man or woman who does it. He notices how physical effort, whether for pay or by choice, defines. The conviction he brings to story-telling is from that kind of depth. If a man is an accountant we know what it is like to do accounts. We see and feel how a teacher teaches, a mechanic fixes motors, a cleric comforts, a pervert gets on with perverting. More than any other of our writers, he has taken out an imaginative franchise on a particular kind of New Zealand — mostly South Island — life, much as there is a David Malouf Queensland, or a Tim Winton Western Australia. His world by and large may be one we are familiar with. But how it is distilled, how it is dismantled and re-presented to us, is a matter of novelty and surprise, technical adroitness and penetration.

I've often been struck by how differently New Zealand's two finest short story writers go about their business. Marshall — I am guessing a little here — may admire Katherine Mansfield, but does not particularly like her stories. One isn't surprised. Mansfield's temperament, as we know it from her letters and notebooks, commands almost everything in her fiction: that glancing brush with events, her hovering refusal to insist or underline, the inheritance of post-impressionism that often defines her. She disliked the idea of fiction working towards a moral point as much as Marshall is

Contents

nature. Mumsie has been nagging him to fix a broken door.

> *'All right, Mumsie,' he said, 'I'll come and do it now,' but*
> *he stayed sitting there, his hands on the table, his face*
> *still once more, and only his eyes jit jittering as bugs do*
> *sometimes in warm evening air.*

Once you've taken these stories on board, you'll have more than a fair idea of what 'Marshall country' is like, day by day, bedroom by bedroom. They encompass its preferences and personalities, its terrain and its aspirations, its narrowness and its imaginative ploys in transcending it. And as well as its ordinary decencies, should you want a take on what goes wrong when a deeply secular community grates on its limitations, Marshall is your man for that as well.

II

Marshall has never been perturbed by that handful of academic theorists who would love to call the shots for what creative writers actually do. For a time there in the eighties and nineties, critics who doubled as cultural boundary riders often over-estimated writing that stroked their political agendas, much as they undervalued what did not. Mere male pakeha 'realists' came in for something of a drubbing. Part of this was almost a terror of aesthetic judgement, a deep reluctance to think there could be 'significant' writing about what the fashion of the moment happened not to crave. The assessing of literature became politics conducted by other means.

Marshall has always outflanked the kind of naïve categorising that caged him as simply 'social realist'. It was rather too easy to forget that 'realism', as a genre a writer chooses to work in, is in itself neither more nor less imaginative or 'writerly' than fantasy, symbolism, post-modernism or any other mode. That by far the greater part of good fiction still occurs within that category tells you how extensive and various its possibilities are. The mistake in thinking that Marshall came along simply as yet another inheritor of what Frank Sargeson attended to sixty or seventy years back is easily enough countered by reading half a dozen stories. Marshall's 'realism' in that traditional sense consistently catches the nuances of what is local and regional. But to note that is only to begin. What makes his stories impressive beyond the depictions we acknowledge as 'the very thing' comes down to what he does sentence by sentence, the glinting reach of his metaphor, the compelling turns of phrase. And how much depends on their comic flair, the deftness of their wit, the extent to which he rings the changes on vernacular speech. (Look at 'The Language Picnic' for a brilliant send-up of those who fancy Kiwi lingo covers all occasions.)

And what of that unmistakable moral groundswell that is almost a constant in Marshall's fiction? That quiet but firm template that a story insists is part of its implied 'world view'? This is something far more generous, far less judgmental, than anything you would call a mere set of rules. It is more perhaps what you might think of as a consistent cast of mind, as the stories unravel how and why we humans behave this way or that; how personality is defined by the social niche we inhabit and the choices we make. Sometimes the characters are aware of these complexities. If they are not, you find that the author's voice may take you aside, confiding what it is good and necessary for you to know, while the turns of the narrative justify that confidence. Yet clearly something else is involved, a disposition, you could say, that is the author's as much as the story's. In Marshall's fictional universe there is a deep conviction, beyond its appearance in any particular story and pervasive throughout so many, that the daily business of living is, among so much else, a coming to terms with disappointment and loss. It is a matter of what suffices. What sets this so far beyond casual despondency brings us back to the verve with which a story is told, its sly comic slant, the bite and élan

Contents

nature. Mumsie has been nagging him to fix a broken door.

> *'All right, Mumsie,' he said, 'I'll come and do it now,' but*
> *he stayed sitting there, his hands on the table, his face*
> *still once more, and only his eyes jit jittering as bugs do*
> *sometimes in warm evening air.*

Once you've taken these stories on board, you'll have more than a fair idea of what 'Marshall country' is like, day by day, bedroom by bedroom. They encompass its preferences and personalities, its terrain and its aspirations, its narrowness and its imaginative ploys in transcending it. And as well as its ordinary decencies, should you want a take on what goes wrong when a deeply secular community grates on its limitations, Marshall is your man for that as well.

II

Marshall has never been perturbed by that handful of academic theorists who would love to call the shots for what creative writers actually do. For a time there in the eighties and nineties, critics who doubled as cultural boundary riders often over-estimated writing that stroked their political agendas, much as they undervalued what did not. Mere male pakeha 'realists' came in for something of a drubbing. Part of this was almost a terror of aesthetic judgement, a deep reluctance to think there could be 'significant' writing about what the fashion of the moment happened not to crave. The assessing of literature became politics conducted by other means.

Marshall has always outflanked the kind of naïve categorising that caged him as simply 'social realist'. It was rather too easy to forget that 'realism', as a genre a writer chooses to work in, is in itself neither more nor less imaginative or 'writerly' than fantasy, symbolism, post-modernism or any other mode. That by far the greater part of good fiction still occurs within that category tells you how extensive and various its possibilities are. The mistake in thinking that Marshall came along simply as yet another inheritor of what Frank Sargeson attended to sixty or seventy years back is easily enough countered by reading half a dozen stories. Marshall's 'realism' in that traditional sense consistently catches the nuances of what is local and regional. But to note that is only to begin. What makes his stories impressive beyond the depictions we acknowledge as 'the very thing' comes down to what he does sentence by sentence, the glinting reach of his metaphor, the compelling turns of phrase. And how much depends on their comic flair, the deftness of their wit, the extent to which he rings the changes on vernacular speech. (Look at 'The Language Picnic' for a brilliant send-up of those who fancy Kiwi lingo covers all occasions.)

And what of that unmistakable moral groundswell that is almost a constant in Marshall's fiction? That quiet but firm template that a story insists is part of its implied 'world view'? This is something far more generous, far less judgmental, than anything you would call a mere set of rules. It is more perhaps what you might think of as a consistent cast of mind, as the stories unravel how and why we humans behave this way or that; how personality is defined by the social niche we inhabit and the choices we make. Sometimes the characters are aware of these complexities. If they are not, you find that the author's voice may take you aside, confiding what it is good and necessary for you to know, while the turns of the narrative justify that confidence. Yet clearly something else is involved, a disposition, you could say, that is the author's as much as the story's. In Marshall's fictional universe there is a deep conviction, beyond its appearance in any particular story and pervasive throughout so many, that the daily business of living is, among so much else, a coming to terms with disappointment and loss. It is a matter of what suffices. What sets this so far beyond casual despondency brings us back to the verve with which a story is told, its sly comic slant, the bite and élan hour, what his body is occupied with as much as his mind (including killing a dog with his bare hands). Or consider how in several stories women establish the reality of their world not only by talking with each other. This is done as well by how they relate as workers, the ways in which a workplace doubles as emotional bullring. 'Iris' as satire, '309 Hollandia' as finely balanced pathos; these are the kind of stories that scotch once and for all the occasional comment that Marshall is less effective when writing about women. He writes less often about them than he does about men, but that is a different matter.

Marshall knows a lot about how things are done, how various activities are pursued. He knows how work shapes and reveals the man or woman who does it. He notices how physical effort, whether for pay or by choice, defines. The conviction he brings to story-telling is from that kind of depth. If a man is an accountant we know what it is like to do accounts. We see and feel how a teacher teaches, a mechanic fixes motors, a cleric comforts, a pervert gets on with perverting. More than any other of our writers, he has taken out an imaginative franchise on a particular kind of New Zealand — mostly South Island — life, much as there is a David Malouf Queensland, or a Tim Winton Western Australia. His world by and large may be one we are familiar with. But how it is distilled, how it is dismantled and re-presented to us, is a matter of novelty and surprise, technical adroitness and penetration.

I've often been struck by how differently New Zealand's two finest short story writers go about their business. Marshall — I am guessing a little here — may admire Katherine Mansfield, but does not particularly like her stories. One isn't surprised. Mansfield's temperament, as we know it from her letters and notebooks, commands almost everything in her fiction: that glancing brush with events, her hovering refusal to insist or underline, the inheritance of post-impressionism that often defines her. She disliked the idea of fiction working towards a moral point as much as Marshall is

Introduction

Even when a publisher allows you sixty as a round number, to choose the 'best' stories from a writer you greatly admire can turn out to be a tall order. The ones that have always stayed with you as particular favourites easily pick themselves. After that, it becomes the increasingly delicate business of balancing the variety that Owen Marshall's stories take in, with doing justice to the range of skills that go into their making.

No New Zealander has written anywhere near so many short stories, although their sheer quantity has nothing much to do with what makes them unique. What reading them brings home to you is that 'Marshall country' is a distinctive and compelling place, pretty much like the one we live in day by day, and yet by no means a mere 'copy'. What his stories add to it is a remarkable clarity. We are shown more than we usually see in characters who look like us, talk like us, at our troubled best and our recognisable worst. To touch on what is so distinctive and appealing in these stories, I begin with what may seem a slightly odd angle to come from. But it is something at the centre of how Marshall tells a story.

When I think of how these narratives draw you in, I think too of how few writers tell you quite so convincingly what it is their characters *do* for a living. Take the strange and marginally sinister 'Tomorrow We Save the Orphans', where the figure who interests us most works as night-watchman in a large factory. You cannot separate his emergence as a personality from what he does hour by of its perceptions, the acceptance that what we read is close enough to life for us to be absorbed in much the same way.

A stoic humanism is one way you could describe Marshall's take on experience. Yet there is another shadowy presence. I mean it totally as a compliment, and an artistic one at that, when I say how often he brings to mind the great tradition of English and American fiction whose moral ancestry is unmistakably Protestant, although by now a Protestantism relieved of dogmatic weight. It is there in what you could call the sternness of the stories, the certainty of where their values lie. So many, especially those about adolescents and loners, are accounts of individual testing, of initiations into a darker wisdom than where they began. There is the insistence that an act carries with it, always, an ethical trail. 'Watch very carefully,' as we might imagine a magician advising, 'there may well be a moral hidden under the Jack.' What his forbears would have put down to Original Sin, Marshall, with equal insistence, and rather more humour, uncovers as depravity shorn of its theological fleece.

It is part of that clear-eyed, unsentimental inheritance to call shit for what it is. Which is also as good a way as any to describe the compulsive, perverted energy exposed in a story like 'The Rule of Jenny Pen', or the small meannesses and diluted malice in dozens of others. If Marshall is good at touching quite what it is that our suburban or rural lives take seriously, and what the limitations to that seriousness may be, he's as much of a dab hand when it comes to what most threatens simple decencies.

I quite expect that another editor choosing sixty of Marshall's stories might finish up with at least half that are different from the ones I've selected here. There are many that could well be represented which leave probability behind and let fantasy rip, or stories that are driven by the sheer gusto of language. There is at least one masterpiece of this kind which, if pressed, I'd put among his finest half-dozen narratives. 'The Divided World' riffs and descants by setting up oppositions with exuberant linguistic play. Its listing of opposites, that balancing of what one of his more solemn characters might even call 'the wise harvest of experience', is a mix of smart one-liners, *ersatz* insights, satiric scorn, seen-it-all cynicism, comic inventiveness — and of course, that 'wise harvest' by the cartload. What holds the piece together in an almost liturgical way is the insistent yet richly varied rhythm of its sentences. Only a very good writer could bring it off, only a sustained comic current keep it afloat. I can't think of any New Zealand writer other than John Clark who manages that kind of wit, or has the quirkiness of eye and voice to keep up the performance between its confiding opening chant, 'The world is divided between you and me, you and me babee, you and me,' and its neatly echoing conclusion that you had better get it right, for you've only got one shot: 'The world is divided between you and me, you and me for a time, you and me.'

For quite a long time as I read Marshall's stories, I knew there was an aspect to them that I could not quite find the word for. Then it occurred to me that he is one of those writers who makes you aware of the rich tradition of the genre he is writing in, even when what he does is very much his own. To think of writers as diverse as Hawthorne or O'Connor, H.E. Bates or Hemingway, as one comes to the end of Marshall, is not because his stories derive from theirs, but because of what they have in common: that same commitment to getting their time and their people right, with a rightness that is both moral perspective, and aesthetic choice. To be convincingly part of that tradition is also to extend it.

As legal counsel like to put it, I am happy, after calling sixty witnesses, to rest my case.

Supper Waltz Wilson

Supper Waltz loved oysters, and in the season he had them for his tea whenever his mother was on the afternoon shift. About half-past four, after we'd been playing along the cliffs, or wandering in the town, he'd buy his oysters. He couldn't wait any longer. If the rest of us had any money we'd buy some too, and walk up to the shelters over-looking the bay. Winter is the time for oysters, and from the shelters we would watch the leaden waters of the harbour, and the heat from the oysters and chips would make our noses run. Pongo, Graeme, Supper Waltz, and I. Supper Waltz didn't just eat his oysters; he ravished them. First he would tear off the batter, then hold the steaming oyster by its frill and bite cruelly into its centre with his sharp teeth. Sometimes, as a conscious indulgence, he'd eat two at once, growling with pleasure deep in his throat. It was another occasion on which we realised that Supper Waltz had a heightened perception of the world.

Children take their own situation as the universal one when they're young. My father dominated our family as naturally as a pyramid does the sands. That's why I always found the Wilson household disconcerting, I suppose. Mr Wilson was a butcher, but years ago he'd had a revelation from the Lord telling him not to work anymore, and his religious conviction never wavered afterwards. He always seemed to be in his room. Scores of times I was at the Wilsons', and if Mr Wilson was mentioned he was almost always in his room. If he wasn't then he was in the lavatory singing hymns. He knew all the words, and never had to go dum-de-dah or some-such in places. He didn't seem to have much of an ear, though, and it wasn't good to listen to. Once he was singing, and Supper Waltz's eldest brother was in the kitchen. 'Arse arias again today, Mum,' he said, and Mrs Wilson threw down the carrot she was scraping into the sink, and began to laugh. The carrot splashed up water on to her face, and the drops ran like tears as she laughed. Supper Waltz laughed a lot too, and I joined in the way you do when you're not sure why.

Mrs Wilson worked in the woollen mills. She often seemed to be just coming, or just going. A very matter-of-fact woman, Mrs Wilson. Tall and strong, lacking any graces. When she cycled up the rise to the house, she didn't get off and wheel the bike the way other women did, but stood up on the pedals, using her weight and strength like a man, pushing right up to the gate. Pongo's and Graeme's mothers usually said hello to me, or asked about my parents, but I don't remember Mrs Wilson saying anything at all to me — except the once. A hard woman if she wanted to be I guess, Mrs Wilson. Wherever Supper Waltz got his looks it wasn't from his mother. They had the same eyes, though. The same restless, flickering eyes, like light through the wings of a bird in a cage.

Most grown-ups didn't like Supper Waltz. They were used to youngsters who were socially clumsy, and submissive to authority. The Reverend Mr Weir called him a smart aleck and barred him from the Boys' Brigade, and old Raymond detested him. Adults didn't understand the fierce vision of Supper Waltz's world, and they resented his unspoken contempt of their ways. The square of the hypotenuse, the 1832 Reform Act, were as dead leaves to Supper Waltz, and only art interested him. Old Raymond loved to ridicule him. 'And how many, Wilson, did you say you got for the test? Speak up lad. You got nothing! Well, perhaps that explains why I couldn't hear anything, Wilson. I didn't hear any mark because you didn't get any mark. Not a one, lad.' Raymond with his broken teeth and first class honours degree, had to get his own back. I understand it better now. Raymond hated Supper Waltz because he neither needed nor desired anything that Raymond had, and they both knew it.

Girls knew that Supper Waltz was different too. Supper Waltz seemed old in the ways of the world. As fifth formers it wasn't easy for most of us to be the ladies' man. Pongo had a face as round and as innocent as a child's. Baby Brother, the girls called him. Supper Waltz never missed out at a teenage dance; Supper Waltz was a parochial legend of our youth. He went home with sixth form girls, and some even that had left school. Girls came looking for Supper Waltz, some without knowing why and blushing because of it. Some girls hated Supper Waltz, they said — afterwards. Supper Waltz rarely danced in the early part of the evening. He'd hang around the door, smoking, talking, watching who went in and who went out. We'd nudge one another and snigger when the supper waltz was announced. I don't think I ever saw Supper Waltz refused by a girl.

Supper Waltz had an understanding of women all right. Like the time I wanted to go out with Alice Hume. She was at the private girls' school. She wore a short, green skirt in the hockey games, and the inside of her thighs was flat and smooth. It used to give me a headache just watching her. Supper Waltz and I waited for her as she went to church, and I asked her to see me the next weekend. I thought she was going to say yes, but finally she went off laughing with the others without giving an answer. She had a rather longer dress on that day but I still got a headache. Supper Waltz didn't joke about her or anything. We went into the golf course nearby and hunted for balls to sell. After a while I asked him why Alice Hume hadn't said she'd go out with me. Supper Waltz had no trouble with the answer. 'It's the Fair Isle jersey,' he said. 'No girl will make a date with you in a Fair Isle jersey.' My mother had given me the jersey for my last birthday. I thought of it as part of my best clothes. 'It's a kid's jersey, Hughie, see?' said Supper Waltz frankly 'Girls think a lot about that sort of thing.' Supper Waltz was right of course. With some of my money from potato picking I bought a denim top, and I did my hair without a part before I asked Alice Hume again. I never told Supper Waltz about her thighs and my headaches, but the day she agreed to go out with me Supper Waltz watched her walk away and said, 'She has really good legs, you know, really good legs', and he seemed pleased for me in a brotherly way.

It might seem that Supper Waltz was always the leader, and that I was just tagging along all the time, but it wasn't really like that. There were ways in which Supper Waltz depended on me. With adults, for example, Supper Waltz let me do most of the talking. Even old Raymond said on my report that I was a straightforward, sensible boy. He meant predictable, I think. I was in the cricket team by the fifth form, and bigger than most of the others. I kicked Wilderborne in the back when he picked on Supper Waltz in the baths enclosure. Both Pongo and Graeme were better than Supper Waltz at some things too; Graeme was dux in the end. We all lacked the vision of Supper Waltz though. The world was sharper, brighter for him, and the meaning always clear. Once Supper Waltz, Graeme and I went camping in the Rangitata Gorge, and came down the rapids on lilos. The water was a good deal rougher than we thought. Graeme got thrown off his lilo and smashed two teeth out on the rocks. I went on only because I couldn't stop. I felt sure I was going to drown. Supper Waltz loved it. Each time he bobbed up from the spray and turmoil of the water, he laughed and stared about as if born anew. He wanted to go down again but Graeme and I wouldn't. That night, lying in the pup tent among the lupins, Supper Waltz told us that each time he'd come up from beneath the water the world seemed a different colour. Crimson the last time; after the longest spell under when his lilo capsized, everything was crimson he said. Graeme and I said nothing. The revelation rather embarrassed us and, besides, Graeme's mouth was too sore for him to speak.

Another time a group of us went into the reserve to do some geography fieldwork with Scotty, and at the edge of one of the gullies was a cast sheep. It lay on its side at the verge of some blackberry bushes, and the flat circle of its rotation was stained with urine and droppings. The sheep's black rubber lip twitched, and its eyes bulged with mild perplexity at its own fate. Some of the class tried to stand it up, but each time it just swayed there a moment before falling stiffly on the same side, flattened like the underneath of a scone. Scotty told everybody to leave it alone, but even as we worked our way through the blackberry into the gully, we could hear the sheep's hoarse, strained breathing. Wilderborne said he was going to come back after school and give it the works.

Once out of the sight and sound of it most of us could forget the sheep, but it persisted in Supper Waltz's mind. He was very quiet, and when the others were looking at some shell fossils in the limestone, I saw him crying. That would have surprised old Raymond and Mr Weir; anyone who thought Supper Waltz was so tough. He had a lot of emotion in him, did Supper Waltz. He could stand up to old Raymond and the head without a change of expression, but train whistles and morepork calls in the dark would haunt him for hours.

When I think of what happened to his father, and about Supper Waltz going away, I think of the evening I heard Mr Wilson talking about his voices. That was months before, but I always imagine him going mad right after I saw him in the kitchen. Recollection is apt to sandwich such things up, and there's a type of logic in it, I suppose. I'd climbed into Supper Waltz's window, and was sitting on his bed reading until he finished his tea. Then I heard Mr Wilson talking, and I went along the passage and stood there, looking in on the angle to the lighted kitchen. I very rarely saw Mr Wilson, and with me in the dark and him in the light I got a good chance. He was younger and softer looking than his wife. He had a pale, smooth face like a schoolteacher's or a parson's. He had youthful, fair curls, and yet his fingers were stained with nicotine, and his stomach folded softly over his belt.

'I heard the voice again today,' he said earnestly.

'Did you?' said Mrs Wilson. Her tone was the mild encouragement of a mother to her child, and she continued to iron rapidly from the cane basket on the table.

'Prepare for leadership, it said. Keep yourself ready for the test.' Mr Wilson ran his hand through his bright, metallic curls, and as they sprang back I half expected them to jangle. He seemed to be addressing a larger audience than Supper Waltz and Mrs Wilson. Like Supper Waltz he was small, and he had the strut of a small man as he walked about the kitchen. 'I will turn a righteous sword in the guts of this poor world before I'm finished,' he said. Despite the falseness of the words he said it with conviction. 'It was the voice to the left of me. That's always the strongest voice, the one to the left of me, and it doesn't hurt, not that one. I've got a feeling my leadership is near, Melanie.' That had the strangest sound of all — Melanie, Mrs Wilson as Melanie — and although no one could see me I smiled sheepishly.

Mrs Wilson and Supper Waltz didn't find it remarkable however. 'Good,' said Mrs Wilson. She ran over a shirt-collar quickly, her thumb anticipating the iron along its length with practised ease. Supper Waltz was eating bread and cold meat, his eyes turning upwards like a sheepdog's with satisfaction as he ate.

'Everything will be sorted out then. I'll have my proper place then. I'm ready for the work.' The thought of his great work and its immediacy seemed to lift Mr Wilson. He went abruptly through to the lavatory, and there began to sing about the land of Canaan. In his absence, as in his presence, the kitchen went on as before: Mrs Wilson ironing urgently and Supper Waltz eating his meat sandwiches as if he would never stop.

The day months afterwards, the day after it happened, was a Wednesday and Supper Waltz wasn't at school. It was a hot day and I thought he'd probably bunked to be in the sun. Supper Waltz often took days off, and if the teachers checked up on him he'd produce notes that he'd written himself, but signed by his father. I imagined Mr Wilson signing them in his room, or on the toilet seat, as he waited for his call. Supper Waltz never explained to me why that one duty was performed by his father, when all else had been resigned to Mrs Wilson. I suspected that his mother never knew when he hadn't been at class. She came up to the school once, though, summoned after Supper Waltz and old Raymond had a confrontation in the film room. We were in one of the front rooms, and I saw her arrive, pedalling right up the sweep of the drive, and she left her bike leaning on the hydrangeas by the steps to the school office. She blew her nose in a businesslike way on what looked like half an old teatowel, and strode up the steps like a man. One or two of the boys close to the window laughed, but Supper Waltz and I didn't let on we knew who it was.

But that Wednesday, after it must have happened, I was sitting in Raymond's room when the first assistant came in. Old Raymond always made a show of rapport with his boys when there was another master in the room. 'Pop outside with Mr Haldane, Williams,' and he patted my shoulder as I passed. 'When the door was closed Haldane stood in the corridor for a moment, gazing absently down at the worn lino, and then up at the paper pellets that had been chewed and flicked on to the yellow ceiling. Most boys respected Haldane, although he wore some of the worst clothes in the school, and caned with distant severity.

'Stuart Wilson,' he said, and for just a moment I didn't think of Supper Waltz. None of us called him Stuart. 'You're his best friend, I understand.' It made me feel rather good, that; to be singled out by Haldane as Supper Waltz's best friend. It was a form of recognition in its way. 'You know the family quite well. You're there quite often?' I told him I was. Haldane looked at me as if he were wondering how much of me was still boy and how much had grown up. I think he decided to be cautious. 'Stuart's father isn't well, and there's been a bit of an accident at their home. Mrs Wilson wants you to go round and see if you can help. Stuart's rather upset. Have you got a bike? You needn't be back before afternoon school.' As I started off down the corridor he added, 'And Williams, use your common sense, won't you, lad. Don't tittle-tattle other people's problems all round the school, will you.' That disappointed me a bit, for after all I was Supper Waltz's best friend.

I remember that someone had twisted the dynamo bracket on my bike right into the spokes, and it broke off as I was straightening it. I felt odd biking alone in the sun down that street, always crowded before. In three blocks I passed only a mother and her push-chair. I was young enough to be amazed by the realisation that other people live different lives. It was like that all the way to Supper Waltz's place, hardly a car, hardly a sound, with just a few women around Direens' store, and a little kid crying at the top of Manuka Drive because his trike had overturned in the gutter.

I must have been to the Wilsons' hundreds of times, yet I felt shy arriving there then, during school time, and having been sent for. Mrs Wilson was sitting at the kitchen table, moving the butter dish round and round with her finger. 'Come in, Hughie,' she said. I don't think she'd ever used my name before. 'Sit down. We've had trouble here, Hughie.' She was a direct woman, Mrs Wilson. Her left hand was in plaster, and the fingertips stuck out from the end of it like pink teats. With her other hand she kept moving the butter dish on the red formica table. 'Stuart's father's had a breakdown and has had to go to hospital.'

'Oh.' I watched the butter dish revolve, and wondered about Mr Wilson's Canaan.

'The point is Stuart's run off. I haven't seen him since last night. Do you know where he could be?'

'No.'

'He's fond of you, Hughie. He might come to see you. He's very upset. But you're his friend.'

'Supper Waltz and I have always been friends,' I said. 'Always will be.' Mrs Wilson smiled, either at the nickname, or the claim of eternity; a man's smile, which divided her lined face.

'Bit of a charmer with the girls, from what I hear,' she said.

'With everyone. I mean they all like him.' I was trying to please with that admittedly. Teachers and parsons didn't like Supper Waltz, and some girls didn't — afterwards. Supper Waltz put his tongue in their mouths when he kissed them.

'His father was a popular man. He had a gift of imagination, that man, but not the character to go with it.' It wasn't as cruel a judgement as it sounded, for Mrs Wilson still had a half-smile, and she stopped moving the dish for a moment, 'He was national president of the Master Butchers' Federation when he was twenty-eight.' Mrs Wilson looked past me, and it was unusual to see her at rest. 'Then he began to listen to the morepork,' she said quietly after a time, and leant her head on her knuckles as the smile died. No one could call Mrs Wilson a dreamer, though, and she was soon practical again. She got up, and cleared her throat by spitting into the sink. 'I'm going back to work this afternoon,' she said. 'I'll have to leave a note in case Stuart comes home when I'm away. You'll let me know, Hughie, won't you, if he comes to see you? Don't let him do anything silly.' It seemed my day for being treated as an adult, and I tried not to be self-conscious. Mrs Wilson came out to see me leave, and as we talked by the wash house she busied herself by pulling at the twitch in the garden with her good hand. When I rode away the bleak whiteness of the plaster on her other hand caught the sun, and I saw also in the house next door a woman watching Mrs Wilson from behind the curtains.

I slept in the upstairs sunporch, and on the Wednesday night Supper Waltz woke me by pitching clods up at the window. I was annoyed at first, because whenever he did that I had to clean the glass and sills before Mum saw the mess in the morning. Then it came back to me about Mr Wilson and the trouble. I swung out of the window, let myself hang down by the arms at full stretch, then dropped into the garden below. It was after twelve, and Supper Waltz and I went into the garage and turned on the bench light, as we always did when he came round late. He had some oysters and chips, and we ate them in silence, Supper Waltz treating each oyster as a sacrifice of significance. He didn't say anything much for a long time. He wanted the reassurance of habit; to test some part of the old way and find it the same.

'Dad's a loony,' he said finally, turning his face from the light. 'He's a bloody loony. They took him off last night.' Even though it was Supper Waltz's dad, and I felt sorry for them both, I couldn't help being curious about the way it had been. 'Howling like a wolf or something, you mean?' said Supper Waltz when I asked him. 'Nothing like that. He was going out with no clothes on, to start his mission for Christ. He broke Mum's arm in the door when she tried to stop him. Said his time was come. His time had come all right.' Supper Waltz showed a depth of cynicism that aged him. 'You can say that again. He locked himself in the lav, Hughie, when they came, kept shouting and singing. In the lav, eh? Jesus!' Supper Waltz laughed in a harsh, pent-up way, and the tears showed in the light of the bench bulb. The paper on his knee shook with his laughter, and the few chips that we had left, because of their black eyes, danced in the salt.

It seemed fitting in a way, Mr Wilson locking himself in the lavatory. It had always been a refuge for him. I didn't say that to Supper Waltz; instead I told him that his mother was waiting for him to go home. 'No,' he said, 'I'm not going home. I'll write to her in a day or two. Tell her that. Tell her I'm all right and so on, but not what I'm going to do.'

'What are you going to do?'

'I'm off up to Christchurch tonight. Danny's got a job for me in Lyttelton. As soon as I can I'll be on one of the big overseas ships. You know, European ports and all that.' Supper Waltz's brothers were all seamen, as if united in some quest. He had a period of bravado, and got carried away describing all the things he was going to do as a sailor, but I knew he was churned up inside. It showed in his restlessness, and the flickering eyes like light through the wings of a bird in a cage.

Before he went I crept back upstairs, and got eleven shillings for him. It was all I had, but I gave him the two flat tins of Abdullah cooltip as well. I always kept them to smoke on weekend nights when I went out. I turned out the garage light, and went with Supper Waltz down the street a bit so we wouldn't be heard outside the house. Supper Waltz kept talking urgently about all the things that lay before him. I think that, once started, he was more set on convincing himself than me. Although I was his best friend, and he'd come to me, I felt for the first time there in the dark street that Supper Waltz had already gone. He'd cast off from the rest of us, and was on his way. He'd made the break. The exhilaration of it seemed to separate us. 'See you, Hughie. Wish me luck, Hughie.' His fierce mood drove him running down the pavement, until he was lost in the shadows of the trees around the orphanage.

If it had been me, or Graeme, or Pongo, they would soon have caught us, but I didn't think they'd catch Supper Waltz if he didn't want them to. Supper Waltz knew the way of the world. Supper Waltz would look after himself, you bet, I told myself.

Keep running, Supper Waltz, don't let the morepork get you.

A Southland Girl

The road to the Heads wound along the backbone of the land, and although the slope was not sheer on either side, green paddocks dipping over the flanks and trees around the solitary homesteads, yet Tinsley felt dizzy. The sea was three boundaries, and over its intensity his eyes slid without purchase. He felt that if he looked too long, he would be sucked from the peninsula into the flat horizon of the sea. The wind was only moderate by coastal standards, but it had that special momentum of wind unchecked across a thousand miles of ocean. Not a gusting, straining wind, but a constant and insolent pressure like the palm of a hand on his chest. Tinsley could feel it alter its point of pressure as he turned off the gravel road to the Heads, and began descending the track to Witham's. He held the big Ariel in second, and the drag of the engine was sufficient to slow him. As he dropped lower, the small spurs of the peninsula rose up around him and the vertigo of the top road passed. The abstract totality of the ocean was hidden, and on the stony beach below Witham's he could hear real waves, and see the swirling kelp beds at the point.

Unlike most of the farmhouses of the peninsula, Witham's was not weatherboard and red iron roof. It was a comparatively modern house made of small aggregate blocks, tinted unpleasant shades of blue and pink, it had a netting fence all round to keep out the stock, but there was no garden apart from residual ornamental firs, burnt on the seaward side by the salt winds. Farther away were the sheds, yards, and trucking ramp, all on such a slope that Tinsley had the impression that one good kick would send the lot on to the beach below.

Tinsley couldn't find an area flat enough to take the stand of the heavy motorbike, and so he leant it on the timber supports of the shearing shed. George Witham was fixing the fence at the creek above the beach. Tinsley made his way towards him over the sloping ground contoured with sheep tracks. The grass was a prosperous green, but Tinsley knew it was a sham. The peninsula country lacked necessary trace elements, leached by continual dampness. George had a post each side of the small creek, and was hanging a baton on netting between them. When the creek flooded, the baton and netting would swing back with the current and allow rubbish to pass underneath instead of building up on the fence and tearing it out. George was attaching the baton with staples and green baling twine when Tinsley arrived.

'No fog today, George.'

'Fog or bloody wind. We only have the two alternatives here. Today it's wind.' George put some more staples in his mouth, and lifted one foot out of the creek mud before the boot went under. He wore old, pin-stripe suit trousers and a sports coat with the pocket torn away. His face was weathered but not careworn, the lines of youth simply more deeply etched, and his hair stuck innocently up from the crown of his head as a schoolboy's does, though he was fifty-odd. He was one of Tinsley's original clients and Tinsley knew his nature.

'I hear Godsall next door has sold up. Couldn't make a go of it,' said Tinsley. George's lined face lightened. Misfortune was his only form of humour. 'Left most of his money with the stock firm, they say. Didn't come out of it with much.' George nodded, and actually smiled, showing wet galvanised staples in the spaces where teeth were missing. 'Have you seen the new chap yet? I thought I might call on him later.'

George cupped his hand and emptied his mouth of staples. 'Selwyn Hamilton,' he said. 'Comes from mid-Canterbury way. Doesn't look a farmer's arsehole to me.' George smiled again, drew the other boot from the mud and sought firmer ground.

'This fire of yours, George, I'd better take a look at it. The sooner the paper work's done, the sooner we can pay out.'

'The east side of the hay shed. I've left it just as it was when we put it out. I'd say the best part of a hundred bales. You have a look for yourself, and then go up to the house. The wife's out but my niece is staying with us, a Southland girl, she'll make us a cup of tea.' As George turned back to the fence he noticed a fishing-boat setting cray-pots off the point. The small boat seemed to be having difficulty with its engine. 'Might be in trouble,' said George, brightening, but as they watched the engine caught, and the boat moved out again. The crewman leant on the cabin, smoking. George put staples in his mouth once more, and Tinsley walked back over the sloping paddock to the yards.

He inspected the charring in the shed and agreed with George's estimate. In his book he wrote some notes to use on the claim form, and then went uphill to the house. He didn't hear the piano until he was inside the gate, for he was upwind and the sound was swept away towards the summit road. It was fluent and authoritative playing, and Tinsley thought it a record or cassette. He couldn't imagine Mrs Witham playing the piano. Tinsley knew nothing of music; the only record he had ever bought was a collection of film themes, and he'd given that to his brother when he left home. But as he stood there by the pale pink and blue blocks of Witham's house, seeing the waves surge up the beach, and the flat stones scuttle like crabs back to the sea, he felt the music sharp and fresh pass like a shiver through him.

Tinsley's knock at the door was answered by a call, and he went in, closing the door firmly against the pressure of the wind. There was no-one in the kitchen, but past the sliding doors to the living-room he could see a girl at the piano. She wore jeans and a yellow skivvy top, and her fair hair swung gently as she played. In the dulling conformity of that room, its two-tone tufted suite, nest of coffee-tables, and setter dogs in bas-relief on the fire-guard, she eclipsed her setting with natural individuality, and drove back banality to the corners of the room.

She turned her head and told him to sit down. Tinsley didn't go into the room, but took one of the kitchen chairs and sat by the sliding doors to listen. He was surprised how rapidly she played, and had the fancy that the girl was working quickly and skilfully like a juggler to keep it all in the air above them, dancing and colourful.

'Godowsky,' she said when the piece was finished. 'I told myself that I was going to play it right through. I didn't mean to be rude.'

'It was great.'

'What did it make you feel?' The girl had a round face, and her eyebrows were thin and arched. Tinsley thought the jeans she was wearing were probably boys', for they were very tight at the hips, but too big at the waist. She watched him seriously as though she valued his opinion. It made him feel selfconscious, and he was annoyed with himself because of it.

'I'm not much on music I'm afraid,' he said.

'What you mean is you're shy about discussing it.'

'What I mean is what I said. I don't know enough about music to discuss it. It's not one of my interests.' Tinsley found himself ruffled, not so much at her question and his ignorance, as the situation of arguing with the girl before he had met her. It unsettled him.

'I know quite a lot about music,' she said. 'I'm completing a music degree. Music's so important to me, I expect everybody else to be just as interested. I think we're all like that; each with our own obsession. Don't you?' Tinsley wasn't going to answer that without returning to what should have been done first.

'My name's Wade Tinsley. I'm your uncle's insurance rep. George said to come up to the house for morning tea.'

'What's your obsessive interest?' she asked earnestly, and she leant forward on the swivel piano-stool to watch him.

It was an odd and trivial stalemate, broken by George Witham's arrival from the paddocks. George struggled on the doorstep for a time to get his boots off, then came through into the kitchen. 'You've met Heather then,' he said as a statement, and as the girl put on the jug for tea she smiled at Tinsley; nothing coquettish, but an open smile at the paradox of human relationships.

As they drank the tea, and Tinsley prepared the claim form, George looked idly at the paper. 'Another clothing firm gone phut,' he said with mild satisfaction. 'Three teenagers killed on the motorway. Nobody ever learns.' Witham ran his finger around the inside of his mouth, as if suspecting that a last staple remained there, and then drained his cup with a gulp. 'I can't see things getting any better,' he said, and brightened at the thought.

Witham and Heather went down to the sheds when Tinsley left. George was on his way back to the fence, but the girl had no other reason than to watch Tinsley go. As he turned the motor-bike to face up the hill it overbalanced, pulling him with it so that he nearly fell. Heather and George laughed and for the first time Tinsley recognized a family similarity. 'Is there any flat piece at all on this bloody farm of yours, George?' he asked with mock bitterness.

'None at all,' said Witham contentedly and went off to his work.

'You're not hurt, are you?' Her eyelashes were darker than her hair, and her upper arms were round and smooth. 'Sorry I laughed but it looked quite funny. Why don't you have a car? It seems strange to have a bike for business?'

'Are you completing a degree in that too? Studying occupational transport patterns?' For all her apparent forwardness she was easily rebuffed, but Tinsley watched her flush without a sense of victory.

'No need to be nasty,' she said.

Tinsley felt compelled, as a form of oblique apology, to answer her question. 'My family had an agency for British bikes,' he said.

'I've got used to having motor-bikes, I suppose; I don't usually fall over them.'

'I like all the chrome bits. Would you take me up to the turnoff?' She clasped him firmly as they started off, and on the way up Tinsley left the track, sweeping up and down the grassy bank along the side, giving voice to the easy power of the four cylinders.

At the top road he halted. The flat sea was a vacuum on three sides, and the insistent salt wind sucked away his breath. They sat overlooking Witham's farm; so foreshortened by the incline that the house seemed to be set in the sea itself, and the sheds to have slipped to the beach as Tinsley had imagined. Heather told him she had no lectures on Fridays, and often came to Witham's for weekends, to reduce boarding costs. The wind raised goose-pimples on her round arms, and blew the hair back from her face. She had broad shoulders to match her hips; small breasts, set rather low. Tinsley found himself looking often at girls' breasts and legs since his marriage broke up.

'I had a letter yesterday,' she said, 'from my boyfriend. Saying we were finished.'

Tinsley accepted the almost impersonal frankness. 'Why was that?'

'He's found someone else I suppose. He kept on about getting married, but I wasn't sure. On and on all the time about getting married; now he's found someone else.'

'I used to be married,' said Tinsley. It was as if another person was speaking. Tinsley could not believe he was telling a stranger about his life. 'I was married for six years. I learnt the difference between men and women; men accept their isolation, women see the world as an extension of themselves.'

'I don't know much about people. My boyfriend and I never seemed to be honest with each other. When I saw you come today I made up my mind I was going to be honest with you, whoever you were.' She smiled at him again, as if pleased with her resolution, and how she had stuck to it. They watched each other for a moment without speaking, both aware that the game grew harder not easier as they knew more of each other. 'Will you come out and see me again?' Ten years before he would have taken the invitation in only one way; he would have drawn her into the pines and kissed her as a prelude, but he had grown more cynical. He had suffered the outcome of such things blithely begun.

'How old are you?' he asked.

'Twenty.'

'I'm thirty-four. If I came out again what would we do? Talk of the intricacies of human relationships, or make love in one of George's hedges?'

'Tell me something honest before you go then,' and she waited, looking up at him. Her eyes were grey, and her smile put two new-moon creases at the corners of her mouth.

'I don't like looking at the sea from up here. It makes me giddy.'

She laughed and looked round the three sides of ocean as though to test his fear. 'I love it,' she said. 'Tell me something else.'

'I never knew a round face could be beautiful,' and he wondered if he should kiss her after all.

'No sexy stuff. If you come out again, I'll play more Godowsky for you.'

'I don't suppose I'll be along the peninsula for a while.' He put on his helmet, and she retreated a step or two as he started the bike.

'Goodbye,' she shouted over the engine noise, and Tinsley raised his hand. Through the tinted perspex of his full visor helmet the picture of her was subdued, and he felt sorry for her and for himself. Sorry that life doesn't resemble thoughts about life, and that things change.

Each return to his flat gave Tinsley the fleeting impression of having walked in a chronological circle, and caught up with his own past. It was one of the dangers of living alone. The paper was a pale tent on the carpet where he had dropped it, the open marmalade jar sat next to the toaster on the bench, and through the door to the bedroom the wrinkled sheets of his unmade bed caught the late afternoon sun. Even the vacant easy-chair and blank television set held their angles of the night before. Tinsley spent a few minutes not so much tidying as moving his belongings about to reassure himself that the day had passed.

He grilled himself some sausages, leaving the oven light on in the darkened room so that he wouldn't forget them as he made his phone calls. She was still in his mind though, the Southland girl. The people he had met later in the day were not substantial, but Heather and Witham's farm, even the fearsome sea, were as clear as ever. He could see her thin, arched eyebrows, and feel her arms in casual embrace as they rode up to the turn-off. Tinsley told himself he should have taken what he could get. His wife would be amused to find him thinking of another woman. 'Aren't you a fine one?' she would say. 'The playboy of the western world.' She prided herself on such literary allusions. She had attended a course on modern drama at the polytech, and had almost the full set of abridged novels from the *Reader's Digest*. She liked the uniformity of height they made along the bookcase shelves.

He watched the sausages spitting at the oven light, and even as he affirmed the conclusion not to go to Witham's again, he knew he would.

There was fog on the peninsula when he went back with George Witham's cheque. Fog so heavy that the gravel on the road was wet, and the road materialised out of the mist only yards before him, and was lost only yards behind. Tinsley seemed to be travelling the same section with drooping grass verges again and again. Some sheep, the same colour as the fog, scampered in front of him before thinking to turn off, and stood stupidly pressing against the wire fence as he passed. The fog confused Tinsley's sense of distance, and he was on the point of stopping, wondering if he had overshot, when he came to the turn-off. Mist billowed up the track, muffling the sound of his motor-bike, and cutting off any sight of the sea, although he could hear the waves on the beach below Witham's sheds.

George was making repairs on his woolpress, the wood waxy-brown from the oil of generations of fleeces. 'Bloody top won't swing away cleanly,' said George, and he gave the press a warning kick.

'How's Selwyn Hamilton getting on next door?'

'Struggling,' said George with a pleasure devoid of malice. 'Footrot's giving him a real hammering.'

'Fog's thick today, George.'

'You'll see it'll get worse. Then it will blow from the southeast for about three days. It's either wind or fog on the peninsula, you know that, Wade.'

Tinsley gave George the cheque, and they talked about the stubborn imperfections of the press. Tinsley said he might go up to the house and say hello to Heather. 'I wouldn't,' said George. 'They're dressmaking up there; bits and pieces all over the place.' But Tinsley went up all the same.

Mrs Witham came to the door. She was a tall, calm woman whose apparent serenity may have been a reflection of inner contentment, or simply unresponsiveness. Behind her, amid the spread patterns and material in the living room, Heather was kneeling. It warmed him to see the welcoming pleasure in her face. Despite the feeling between them, Tinsley had to play the stranger and stand before Mrs Witham while they made talk so small that it disappeared altogether after a time.

Later Heather and Tinsley went out for a walk together. The girl took boots and parka from the porch, and Tinsley put on his coat. They looked in at the shearing-shed door. 'Don't hide in there all day, Uncle,' Heather said. 'Come up and help us with the dressmaking later on.' George grumbled a reply, but his tone showed that he was pleased with the attention. Tinsley and Heather went down the steep track to the shingle beach. George was right; the mist was thickening into drizzle, drifting in from the sea, the drops so fine they rested unbroken like tiny bubbles on the fabric of Tinsley's coat. The stones grated beneath their feet as they walked, and then Tinsley deliberately trod on the kelp pods, instead of bursting they squeaked and slid away. Each wave sprang fully formed through the fog and cast itself at the beach.

'Tell me something honest now we're alone,' she said.

'Did you think I'd come back to see you?'

'I hoped you would.'

'I felt absurd up there with Mrs Witham. As if I should make some declaration of intent.'

'You're a pessimist. Did you know that? And scratch a pessimist and you find an idealist underneath.' Such glib generalisation in anyone else would have annoyed Tinsley. But she was probably right. He couldn't remember anything in the last few years that had turned out better than he had expected. The wooden man, his wife had called him, because his temperament was so even. She had not recognised that polarity so characteristic of marriage: the more extravagant her own fluctuation of mood and experience, the more resigned and watchful he became, curbing in himself the qualities in her that disconcerted him.

'Are you a moody person?' he said.

'Impulsive sometimes, but not moody. I'm not dependent on what happens outside as long as I've got my music.'

Her fair hair was just beginning to cling in the dampness, and her face was smooth in its seriousness. He had the selfish idea that even if it didn't work out between them, perhaps he could make love to her before it was over. That would be something, and he had grown accustomed to compromise, even in anticipation. But he wanted there to be trust. They talked out the things they felt they had to share, even his marriage, and Tinsley was surprised how shrewd the girl was in her comments, and how much blame she made him admit without blaming him herself. He complained half-seriously that their understanding was becoming very analytical, but she said firm ground was necessary to dance upon. Tinsley told her things he hadn't told anyone for a long time, and felt better for it. They stood by the point where Tinsley and George Witham had seen the fishing-boat on his last visit to the peninsula. In the pearl light the rolling kelp beds weren't brown, but a visceral mustard. 'There's always risk with honesty,' she said without pretension, 'but you've got to try don't you? You've got to believe that you can really get to know people, and that it's worthwhile to do so. Not much point otherwise.' It was mundane the way she put it, but Tinsley knew she was right. There wasn't much point otherwise, as she said.

Tinsley met her often after that. He'd go down to the university when she had finished her lectures, or pick her up at the place where she boarded. They went to the movies sometimes. Neither of them seemed to feel any need to be in with a group. Sometimes Heather cooked for him in his flat, and sometimes he ran her out to Witham's on Fridays, or back on Sundays. Having justified their love to himself Tinsley never thought there might be others who couldn't accept it. He had grown out of the habit of considering other people's personal feelings. In early winter Mrs Witham rang him up, and told him that he wasn't welcome on the peninsula any more.

Only a week or so later Heather's parents came to see him.

He was doing his washing, and thought at first they were clients that the insurance office had directed to his address. The concern that had driven them to come, plus the embarrassment they felt, was released in their anger. Mrs Preston's hands twisted and worried at her handbag as she talked shrilly at Tinsley, letting out all the things she had been brooding on. Yet although the rush of words had an element of rehearsal, she couldn't express herself as she wanted to, and her anger rose. Her husband stood grimly beside her, and in the few pauses that she allowed he repeated, 'Just stop messing around with her. Understand?' Although his wife was George Witham's sister, Mr Preston bore the greater likeness; a brotherhood of farmers. His brown, seamed face was perplexed above the constriction of a tie, and the tops of his ears were scaly with repeated sunburn.

Their anger depressed Tinsley. He tried to tell them how he felt about Heather, but it only brought on a greater shrillness and incoherence from Mrs Preston, and a more ominous emphasis from Heather's father. Tinsley realized that as the threat to their daughter's happiness he could have no right on his side, so he stood in the doorway of his flat still holding the soap packet, and listened in silence to all the reasons why Heather and he didn't belong together. About his failed marriage, his age, his job, the effect on her musical career, even his motor-bike. Tinsley had considered most of these himself at one time or another, but he was unable to match the simple conviction of Heather's parents.

When Mrs Preston had finally spent herself, she stood panting, trying to think of anything she had not already repeated several times. It was the moment of greatest embarrassment for all three, for after such passion the platitudes of leavetaking were inappropriate; yet Tinsley didn't wish to close the door in their faces without a word, and the Prestons groped for something on which to go.

'Well then,' Mrs Preston said, 'Now you see.'

'Just stop messing around with her. Understand,' said Mr Preston again.

They began to retreat awkwardly, Mrs Preston still half-facing him as if she regarded Tinsley as too dangerous to turn her back on.

He took the company car down to meet Heather the next morning, and he watched the students on their way home, looking as withdrawn and harassed as any other group at the end of a working day. Heather stood out from the others, as one who is cherished always stands out. Her fair hair was bound back from her face, and the heavy material of her long skirt swirled from her hips.

'Godowsky,' she said, 'I really love him.'

'And Bruckner and Kodaly.' Tinsley smiled as her aura filled the car. He knew the names of her favourites without any understanding; they might just as well have been the names of Italian foods that she loved and which he had never tried.

In the flat he told her about the visit from her parents, trying to make it sound funny, to escape the hurt. First about Mrs Witham, then Mr and Mrs Preston. 'Everybody seems so sure that they know what's best. I wish I did.'

'It's time we went away,' said Heather. She turned off the light. In the dull glow of the heater she began to undress, slipping the heavy skirt over her hips when the side zip was undone, and peeling off her jersey vigorously like a boy. Because she was broad-shouldered her breasts seemed small when she was clothed, but naked and with her arms in front of her body as she sat before the heater, they were full and tilted, the nipples stained like wine corks and the bra lines still traced on the pale skin. In contrast with her hair and skin, which seemed to gather in what light there was, Tinsley's darkness was accentuated, and even the black hairs on his stomach lay close like pencil lines. His skin refused the heater's light, and seemed all shadow, darkest over his shoulders and the muscles which flexed above his shoulder blade as he leant forward.

'Let's go away then,' he said, and the glowing element caught the lines of his face in a pattern, a *moko* almost, of resignation.

The next week Tinsley rode out along the headland one last time to get her; into the insolent pressure of the wind, and not wanting to look directly at the vacuum of the sea. The gulls whipped past with their wings locked, and though the helmet prevented him from hearing them, he knew their cynics' cries.

He was early at the top of the track, and he walked into the windbreak on George's side of the road. The line was only a few trees thick, and most of them had branches, twisted and broken, which had wept resin onto the rough bark. Tinsley sat on the fallen pine-needles just far enough in to be hidden from the farmhouse below, and looked over the sloping paddocks of George Witham's land. On the surface it was a reassuring sight, sheep and fences, earth and sky, all in their places; even the turnips right side up, the leaves with their veins exposed to the wind. But Tinsley had lost his boyhood trust in the benevolence of nature, and saw rather an isolating preoccupation with its own rotation of growth and decay. He was aware that as his powers of affection had lessened, he no longer had the conviction to sustain the existence of other people when he was alone.

Yet she came. He saw her first just above the house, then she reappeared on the gully track much closer. She walked with a purpose, swinging an overnight bag. She didn't seem consciously defiant, just convinced of her right to make her own way. Tinsley watched her smooth, round face, and the womanly curve of her hips as the wind blew her dress close. As they met and held hands neither could talk about the significance of what they were doing. 'Tell me something honest,' she said.

'I hate the sea.' Before they put on their helmets he looked once more directly out over the sea, and felt it yaw before him. 'It's the mockery of it,' he said. 'We won't ever live by the sea.'

'I always thought you people loved the ocean. Vikings of the sunrise and all that.'

'Someday I'll tell you what the sea really is,' he said. He turned the bike around and swept along the summit road, and Heather behind him turned her face to one side and leant against his back. If Tinsley looked only ahead he could see the bulk of the land rise up before them.

The Tsunami

I remember it was the day of the tidal wave from Chile. 'A tsunami,' Peter had said again, angrily, as we stood by the bench at breakfast. 'Nothing to do with the tide, nothing at all. A tsunami's a shock wave.'

Yet there it was in the paper of the night before; all about the Chilean tidal wave and how it was expected to be up to twenty-five feet high, and might sweep right over low-lying areas. Peter was doing a third unit of geography, and he took it as academic affront that even the newspaper talked about the tsunami as a tidal wave instead of a tsunami. Toby and I agreed, of course.

'A tsunami, right,' we said, but we still thought of it as the tidal wave. In all of us is the perversity to resist correction.

We had tacitly decided that the tidal wave would be a big thing in our day. This wasn't a compliment to Chile, or the wave. As students we found almost every day some preoccupation to shield us from our studies. Even now I have a fellow feeling when I read of prisoners who tamed cockroaches, or devised whole new political systems in their heads to pass the time. Thoreau knew that most of mankind understand a prisoner's world.

The newspaper said that the wave was expected between noon and two p.m., and over the radio there were warnings to farmers and property-owners to be prepared. It was a compelling notion: the great wave sweeping majestically across thousands of miles of ocean, to fall with thunderous devastation on our New Zealand. It quite captured the imagination of the city, and before midday the cars were streaming out to the coast.

We bought pies and a half-gallon jar of apple wine on our way to the estuary. 'A carafe, you mean,' said the pale man in the bottle-store loftily. He still used hair cream and we mocked him as we went on.

'A carafe, you mean. Oh quite, quite.' We passed the jar of wine from one to another, regarding it quizzically and twisting our faces to suggest the features of the pale bottle-store man.

By twelve-thirty the cars were parked in rows along the beach frontages, and their occupants belched comfortably and waited for something to happen. Many people were down on the beach, impatient for the tidal wave to come. Peter's logical mind was outraged. 'My God, look at these people,' he said. 'If the tsunami does come it'll kill thousands, thousands of them.' He gave a shrill laugh of exasperation and incredulity. But Toby and I were delighted; it accorded with the youthful cynicism we cultivated at the university. We drove up the hill and parked in a children's play area, with swings, see-saws, and a humpty-dumpty among the grass. We took our apple wine and round pies, and sat with humpty-dumpty on his wall, looking down over the houses on to the crowds along the estuary and beach. Toby stuck out his corduroy legs in delight at the unsought demonstration of human nature acted out before him.

'Look at them, Peter,' he kept saying, and drew further joy from the resentment with which Peter watched the crowd press forward to the tsunami.

Another car drove on to the playground, and a couple got out and stood with their backs supported by the grille, looking down upon the sea. Then the man wandered closer, and I recognised Leslie Foster. He sat on a swing with his hands hanging between his knees. He had a thin, Spanish face, with a beard to suit it, and his shoulders were slightly hunched in that typical way I recalled from the years we were at school together. At school at the same time would be a better description. He and I had mutual friends, but we never found any ease in each other's company. I never trusted his sneering humour, and he considered me something of a milksop, I think. Yet at university we gave each other greater recognition, for there our common background, always taken for granted before, was something of a link.

I went over and sat on the bleached, wooden seat of the other swing. I stretched my legs to pass the puddle in the rut beneath. 'How are things?' I said. He turned his head and gave his quirking, Spanish smile. 'I don't think that tidal wave's coming,' I said.

'Bloody tidal wave. Who needs it?' he said.

We talked idly for a time, but every topic seemed to release the same bitterness, and he didn't even pretend to listen to anything I said. He would screw up his eyes impatiently, and rock back on the swing. 'She wanted to come out here today,' he broke in. 'It wasn't my idea.' We both looked over at the woman still standing at the front of the car and staring out to sea. As if she realised she was the topic of our conversation, she glanced back at us, then came over towards the swings. Les introduced her grudgingly as Mrs Elizabeth Reid, his landlady.

'Nice to meet friends of Les,' she said. I wouldn't guess at her age, but she wasn't a girl. She had a lot of flesh on her upper arms and shoulders, and her hips swept out like a harp. 'I like a run in the car,' she said. 'Blows the cobwebs out and that, don't you think?' Les screwed up his eyes, and gave his mocking, lop-sided smile. 'I wanted to go down by the beach with everyone else, but Les wouldn't.' She paused and then said, 'It's late,' as if the tidal wave were a train or bus delayed by departmental inefficiency. 'It's a run out, though, isn't it? A chance to have a breather.' She had an unpleasant voice: ingratiating, but with a metallic edge.

'Yes. Chance to have a breather,' repeated Les, mocking the idiom, but she didn't seem to realise it. She went off to sit in the car out of the breeze, and have a cigarette. Les and I were left swaying on the worn seats of the playground swings. 'Chance to have a breather,' said

Les again, with morose emphasis. 'Well, I suppose that's fair enough. You'd laugh if I told you. If I told you what she's sprung on me today.' I didn't ask. I wasn't really interested in any of his confidences, but I knew he was going to tell me anyway. It was something to do with his loneliness, I suppose; picking on me just because I was there and we had been to the same school. 'She's pregnant, the lovely lady. She told me on the way out.' He rocked back and forth, setting loose a distorted image in the water beneath the swing.

'You could get something done, I suppose.'

'Not easy,' he said, with a sneer at my vagueness, and the ignorance of facts that it revealed. 'Anyway, she feels that marriage is the best answer. She's divorced, but thinks in terms of marriage.' I made a feeble reply about how nice she seemed, and how things had a habit of working out. Les ignored it completely. 'I'll have to leave varsity. I can't see myself getting by in fulltime study with her and a kid.'

'I suppose so.' It did seem a waste. Les was a clever student. Even at school he'd been a clever beggar, and he'd had straight As since then.

'I can't blame her for it happening.' I admired him for saying that. In his own crabbed way he'd always seen things as they were. He was honest with himself. 'She's rather a passive person, really,' he said. 'Likes to talk more than anything else. It started last year. when she went on a citrus fruit diet. I used to go into the bathroom and joke about it when she stood on the scales with a towel round herself. Sometimes I'd put a foot deliberately on the scales, and she would laugh and jab back with her elbows.' Les was going to say more, then he broke off with a barking laugh. 'Funny how these things get started,' he said, and he pushed out with his legs to get the swing going again as a sign he'd finished talking about the seduction of his landlady.

I hadn't wanted to hear about it, but personal revelations impose an obligation, and I asked him if he wanted some apple wine. 'Love it,' said Les, and he came with me back to the wall on which sat the patient humpty-dumpty, smiling in the face of his imminent fall and the tsunami. Les knew Toby, and I introduced him to Peter.

'I don't think the tsunami will persist across all that ocean,' said Peter.

'The what?' said Les.

'The tidal wave. He means the tidal wave,' put in Toby and I.

'That bloody thing,' said Les with belittling contempt, looking not out to sea, but towards the car and his landlady. He tipped the apple wine down his throat without appearing to swallow. We could hear its unimpeded gurgle as it went down, and we began to drink more rapidly to keep up. Les cast a malaise over our group, interrupting the established pattern of our relationships. He was interested only in his own problems, and our wine.

His impatience seemed to extend to the people along the foreshore below. The tsunami had not come; promises of something different had failed once again. Some people began to leave for the city, and only those with nothing they wished to return to remained. A few roared their cars across the asphalt frontage of the beach, while others stood in the sand-dunes and pelted beer bottles with stones.

When the wine was finished, Les said he'd better take his landlady home. I walked part of the way towards the car with him to show a fitting sense of comradeship for a fellow old boy whose secret I shared. By now he wished he hadn't told me, of course, and not being able to say just that, he got in some remark about how heavy I was. I saw him cross the rough grass of the playground, walking in his round-shouldered, rather furtive way. I felt no loyalty whatsoever, and told Toby and Peter as soon as I rejoined them. We watched Les and Mrs Reid having a last look down to the beach. She was talking, and waved a hand dismissively towards the ocean. Her strong hips and jutting breasts seemed to accentuate Leslie's stooped concavity.

'Serve him right. Serve him damn right,' said Toby. It wasn't a moral judgement, rather a reference to all those nights on which Les had returned to his landlady, and Toby had fretted his time away with cards and bitter study.

Les and Mrs Reid drove quite close to regain the road. I could see her mouth opening and closing quickly as she talked to him, and Les glanced at me as they passed. It was his own smile, though, inwardly directed and not for me. His tilted, Spanish smile which he still wore as he turned the car again and began to drive down the hill. Elizabeth Reid had turned sideways somewhat in the seat, the better to watch him as she talked, and her mouth opened and closed effortlessly. It was a recollection which I found hard to shake off as we ourselves left. Peter was in a good humour because the tsunami had failed as he had predicted, but the unwanted glimpse of Leslie Foster's life had chilled my mood, and Toby's too in a different way. He sat silently, holding the empty wine flask between his knees, and reflecting on his unwilling celibacy.

Before tea, as I prepared the vegetables, I listened to a government seismologist on the radio explaining why the tidal wave hadn't come. I suppose he was a different seismologist from the one the papers had quoted the day before. I called out to the others to say it was on the news about the tidal wave not coming.

'Tsunami,' said Peter.

'Right.'

'The tsunami certainly came for old Les Foster, though, didn't it? Talk about shock wave,' said Toby. How we laughed at that. Toby and Peter came into the kitchen so we could see one another as we laughed, and better share the joke. All youth is pagan, and we believed that as the gods were satisfied with their sport, the rest of us were safe awhile. 'Came for old Les all right, the tsunami.' Even as I laughed I saw again Les and his landlady as they drove away, and that inward smile upon his face. As a drowning man might smile, for they say that at the very end the water is accepted, and that the past life spins out vividly. In Leslie's case it may well have been the future rather than the past he saw.

Descent from the Flugelhorn

It was the third in a series of summer droughts. North Otago must be as bad for droughts as anywhere in the country, I guess. In March the landscape lay stretched and broken like the dried skin of a dead rabbit, shrunken away from the bones and sockets. The pale yellow clay showed through the tops of the downs like hip bones, and even the willows along the bed of the Waipohu Stream had the blue-grey of attrition.

Wayne Stenning and I were selling raffle tickets so that the club could have new jerseys for the season. All over the district we went, and despite the cost of the petrol it was worth it. Most we called on had some connection with the club, and even if they didn't directly, then as country people they identified with the district name and gave anyway. Usually they bought whole books, not single tickets, which made the tripping about worthwhile. Wayne and I had been at it most of the afternoon and we were cutting over the old quarry road to call at a last few houses. The dust was bad. Some people had oiled the road outside their gates, but it didn't seem to do much good. In any case you couldn't see where the dust had settled, for everything was much the same colour.

Wayne was pleasant company, always ready with a joke, or a laugh at somebody else's. He'd been training most of the summer. Keen as mustard he was, and with some cause. Last season he made the local representative side and got his name in the rugby almanac's list of players from lesser unions worth watching. He had the right build for a prop — not all that tall, but his chest was so thick that his clothes hung out all round and made him look fat, which he wasn't.

I hadn't realised that Bernie Dalgety lived on that road, but we turned into a farm and found him at the yards, drafting sheep. I'd met him a few times at the gun club. He took three books. The only drawback was that Wayne got some grease on his slacks when we sat on the drill, waiting for Bernie to get the money. Wayne said they were his best trousers and his wife would be peeved. He hadn't been married long. He couldn't stay worried, however, and told Bernie the joke about the librarian and the lion tamer. He did a bit of running on the spot, too, before we got back into the car — said he'd been having some trouble with cramp in the thigh muscles. Bernie and I told him the cause of that and he laughed, but said he was serious. I hadn't begun any training myself. I'd reached the stage at which the most usual adjective applied to my game was 'experienced'. Anyone who sticks with the game reaches that point eventually — a sort of watershed after which you're no longer capable of improving, and it takes cunning to disguise the fact that you've gone back.

We nearly missed the place after Dalgety's. It was in a fold of the downs, and well back from the road. New farmhouses go for a view: prominence before all else. The old houses of the district seem to have been sited chiefly with the idea of escaping the wind. There was no cattlestop and no name on the letter-box. Wayne opened the gate and told me he'd close it and run up after me. Needed the exercise, he said, so I went on. The drive wasn't used much, I could tell, for the dry grass in the centre strip scratched and flurried underneath the car as I drove. I could see Wayne in the rear vision mirror, jogging easily along, doing a few quick knees-ups from time to time. He let his arms hang loosely and flapped his hands to ensure relaxation. Our coach was very keen on relaxation; he trained anyone who would turn up three hours a night in the name of relaxation.

The house was of old-fashioned dark brick. It had bay windows that bulged outwards and heavy, green tiles. The shrubs and trees must once have been in ordered harmony with the house, but in old age had attained a freakish disproportion. Shattered pines along the south side reached over the tiles and mounds of their needles lay in the guttering. The path to the front door was obstructed by the growth of a giant rhododendron, mostly wood, but with a few clusters of leaves that defied the drought. The tall macrocarpa hedge down the other side had been cut so often that there was little foliage, rather a series of massive, convoluted branches that seemed barely contained in the rectangular shape the years had imposed on them.

Wayne and I avoided the rhododendron and walked along the concrete path towards the back door. At the far corner of the house was a sunporch that had been glassed in comparatively recently, for its large panes contrasted with the windows of the rest of the house. Wayne stopped suddenly at the corner, and I stumbled into him from behind. 'There's someone in there,' he said. 'We can ask him.' We stood a little foolishly by the glass doors and looked in. The place was well chosen, for despite the hedge the late afternoon sun was a warm pressure on the backs of our heads, and suffused the room with an amber glow. The rich and heavy light was liquid, and its slow current bore dust that glinted and eddied, dissipating the shape of the dark dresser and falling like a fragile veil in front of the old man who sat facing us.

The old man was dressed, but over his clothes he wore a pink candlewick dressing-gown, and in front of the cane chair he sat in, his zipped leather slippers stuck out, shiny and without the wrinkles of wear. Something in their positioning made it seem they had been placed by someone else, rather than the random result of movement. A green towel lay across his lap and his hands rested there, the fingers curled and trembling slightly. 'Hello,' said Wayne. He said it uncertainly, because he felt odd speaking through the closed door, yet he couldn't keep looking in at the old man only a few feet away without saying something. There was no coarseness of age in the old man's face, no warts, enlarged pores or tufts of hair. He seemed to have passed the time of excrescences and, like driftwood, only the essential shape and grain remained. His head and face were entirely smooth, polished even, the skin in the amber of the afternoon sun responding with a slight sheen.

'Don't think the old coot heard me,' said Wayne softly, and he turned his face away to snigger uneasily. The old man's neck did not stand up from his collar, or the folds of the candlewick dressing-gown. Instead it protruded parallel with the ground like the neck of a tortoise, and so his head, to keep his abstracted gaze level, was tilted back. His head and neck were not directly forward, however, but rested more along the line of his left shoulder.

When I was a boy I had a favourite marble with a coloured spiral at the centre of the glass. Gradually the surface got crazed; little pits and star bruises appeared on the glass until it was clouded and the coloured spiral had lost its vividness. The old man's eyes were like that, and the lower lids had fallen away somewhat, revealing moist red linings that emphasised the bruised opaque eyes, and contrasted with the pale sheen of his skin.

Wayne would have opened the door, but the old man was alone in the room and there didn't seem much point. We carried on round the house until the back door, where we knocked and waited. After seeing the old man Wayne needed reassurance of his youth. He performed several jumps from the crouch, leaping towards the tiled roof and patting the guttering. No one came to the door in answer to our knocks, or Wayne's acrobatics. 'Strange sort of an outfit,' he said. 'There must be someone else about, surely.' We were going to leave when there was a lot of noise from hens, and moving round the end of the hedge we saw a woman feeding white leghorns on the bare ground in front of the farm sheds.

She was a big woman in cardigan and dark stockings despite the heat. She came heavily towards us, the last hens falling off behind her when they realised she had no more grain. In one hand was an old milking bucket half-filled with eggs, and she leant to the other side against the weight. At a distance she didn't look so old, but when she was close, though the strength was still there, the age was more apparent: rosettes of pigment stained her skin, and as she set the bucket down before us the swollen joints of her fingers clasped on the handle had difficulty releasing, nearly pulling the bucket over.

'We're selling raffle tickets on behalf of the Waipohu rugby club. For new jerseys.' Wayne seemed to assume that all old people were deaf, and he shouted into her face.

'Where have you been?' she said in reply. Wayne didn't know how to answer that, but she meant what other people in the district had we visited, and as we told her the ones we could remember, she murmured 'Yes, yes,' as if the familiar names established our authenticity. Her voice was flat and worn, but steady enough. She came back with us to the house, refusing to have the bucket carried for her. 'Dad would like to see you,' she said. 'I'll take a ticket for Dad.' Dad must have been her husband, not her father, yet the term she adopted for convenience in family times had stuck. Culland was the name she wanted on the ticket. I wrote it for her, because she said she found writing difficult. Watching her swollen fingers attempting to get money from her purse, we could understand. That was later, though. First she left the eggs at the back door, and took us through the dark, wainscoted hall to the sunroom to see Dad.

The old man hadn't shifted, but we approached him from a different angle and, like a figurine, his aspect altered. He'd been a big man once, but his shoulders seemed folded and the pink candlewick fell away loosely. 'These young people are from the Waipohu rugby club, Dad,' said Mrs Culland as we sat along the window seat, the sun behind us again, the golden dust drifting once more before the old man's face. 'Selling raffle tickets, Dad,' she said. Wayne nodded his head and chuckled, as if selling raffle tickets was a good joke he wanted the old man to share. Mrs Culland said nothing for some time. She forgot us and had a rest, breathing slowly and massaging the joints of each finger in turn.

'Well,' said Wayne brightly, in a manner that preceded comments about really being on our way and so on. Neither responded. Mrs Culland continued to rest, and the old man's terrapin neck and head remained extended, his eyes unblinking, and his hands trembling on the green towel. The mainspring of the world seemed to have run down, and time was held back in the amber warmth of the sunroom. The macrocarpa shadows stole further across the dry lawn, and the sound of Mrs Culland's coarse, swollen hands as she rubbed them together was like the sighing of a distant sea. Even Wayne stopped fidgeting and sat resigned, reading again the prizes listed on the raffle books he held. Three days at Mount Cook in the off-season, or the cash equivalent, was first prize.

'Dad played rugby,' said Mrs Culland. 'Not here though — in Southland. All his family played.'

'Great game,' said Wayne a little patronisingly, and flexed the heavy muscles of his outstretched leg.

'Played for the South Island twice,' she said in her flat voice. 'Booby Culland everyone called him then.' She pronounced it as a title and, heaving herself up, went to the dresser and returned with a photo of her husband in the South Island team.

'South Island,' said Wayne in an altered voice. The transience of it all seemed to catch him. Booby Culland's photo showed the arrogance of youth and strength. Guiltily, Wayne looked from the photo to the old man and quickly away again. 'Lock,' he said.

'That's right,' said Mrs Culland.

'Line-out specialist, I suppose.'

'Yes.'

Mrs Culland leant forward from the window seat, and held the old man's nearer arm, so that for a moment the hand stopped trembling. 'We're talking about football, Dad,' she said. 'Football.' The old man opened his mouth slightly, but if he wanted to speak he was prevented by his top dentures, which slipped down, exposing a swollen seam of artificial gum, as if he were bringing something up.

Mrs Culland released his arm matter-of-factly and pushed his chin up. But briefly his opaque, bruised eyes focused in revelation; for an instant the prisoner could be seen from the shadows and behind the bars. 'Football, Dad,' she said again.

He tried once more. 'Descent from the Flugelhorn.' His voice was almost identical to that of his wife — worn and even, as if she had adopted the practice of ventriloquism.

'No, Dad, football. You know.'

'Descent from the Flugelhorn,' he repeated, and his eyes turned away. A thin skein of spittle ran from his mouth down the pink chenille of his left shoulder, touching it with amber spangles in the sunlight. Mrs Culland pushed his chin up again.

'He was very keen on music,' she said, in a form of explanation. 'As he got older and the boys took over the property, he turned to music.' There was another pause, and we sat subdued in the unrepentant sun of the summer drought.

'Lived for his football, though, as a young man. No doubt about that. They all did in his family but Booby Culland was the best of them. Played in the provincial side fifty-one times and was made captain for Southland on the day of his last game.' Wayne took it as a blow more than anything else. He still held the photo and he cast about for other things to rest his gaze upon apart from the old man. 'I'll show you the jersey,' said Mrs Culland. I tried to tell her it wasn't necessary but she had become accustomed to following her own will and went off into the rest of the house.

'Jesus, it's hot in here,' said Wayne. 'We'd better push off soon. There are other places yet and we don't want to be too late.'

As we waited the old man gave three sharp, inward breaths, and then, as if something had given way at the centre of him, his shoulders folded still further. His big translucent hands gripped the green towel in his lap, and one foot extended on the wooden floor of the porch so that the soft sole of the leather slipper squeaked as it moved. There seemed to be no breathing out. 'Jesus,' said Wayne.

The old man looked much the same, but his posture gradually slackened, and although his neck still lay along his shoulder, his face turned down and lost its level gaze. 'Jesus,' said Wayne, and stood with his hands into fists as I tried to feel the old man's pulse.

Mrs Culland thought he'd just had a turn when she came back but, when she realised he was dead, she let the jersey slide into his lap with the towel, and began to stroke the smooth grain of his head. She didn't weep, she didn't even sit down; she stood beside him and it seemed as if her flesh had settled more heavily as her cupped hands moved clumsily over his head. We asked if we could help, but she said she could get in touch with everyone by phone. 'I did pay you, didn't I?' she said, and when she was satisfied of that she let us go. We never thought to use the sunroom door — perhaps it didn't open, anyway. We went out the back door, and as we passed the windows on our way to the car neither of us looked in.

Wayne called jerkily to me that he would run on a little, and I didn't hurry after him. If he wanted the chance to run it out then I didn't mind. Sooner or later he'd find it didn't work with everything. I let the car idle down the drive, the grass rustling beneath the chassis. Wayne had gone a fair way. As I shut the gate I could see him up the road, running hard along the grass verge. He ran a mile or so, and when I found him he had reached the dip and was sitting below a willow in the dry streambed. As I got out of the car I could hear him crying, and I went over and sat with him, the fine willow roots draped like hessian down the bank behind us.

The light began to change, but the evening was still hot, with no promise of rain. Homecoming magpies began their harsh calls in the trees around us, and a Land-Rover came through, travelling towards Culland's, rolling out dust clouds that we could barely see, but that had their own flinty taste. Wayne had stopped crying, and dug with a twig in the sand and leaves. 'Sorry about that,' he said. He gave a rather shy smile. 'Do you think everyone gets the feeling some time or other that they've passed themselves going the other way?'

'Yes.'

It was all we had to say about it, and it was enough. It doesn't always help to tease things out, to dissect our experiences like school days' frogs. As we stood up to go the magpies began a great racket, and some flew off in protest, the wingbeats whistling in the still air. 'I've ruined these tweeds of mine,' said Wayne. As well as the oil stain he'd torn them along the upper seams, where the sweat had made them grip as he ran.

'Put them down to experience,' I said as we went back to the car, and he smiled again at that. He hoped his wife would understand, he said.

The Master of Big Jingles

I know what it's called now, it's called fennel. Knowing the name doesn't make it what it was, however. I see it rarely now. It peers occasionally from the neglected and passing sections, like the face of a small man over the shoulders of others in a crowd. Its fronds are the pale green of hollow glass, and it has a look of pinched resignation, as if it can foresee the evolutionary course before it.

When Creamy Myers and I were young, it was in its prime. There were forests of it pressing in on the town, and it reared up confidently in waxy profusion. The rough strip below the bridge was its heartland, and there Creamy and I had our hut. We could reach it by tunnel tracks from the riverbank, and the fence. We built it in the summer that ended our Standard Four year, and in the summer after that we renewed it in our friendship. The year we finished primary school we restored it again. We cut out the tunnel tracks as usual, so narrow that the top foliage showed no tell-tale gap, and even Rainbow Johnston wouldn't find them. We evicted the hedgehog and its loosely balled nest from the hut, and spread new sacks to mark our occupation. In a biscuit tin we kept the important things, wax-heads, shanghais, tobacco, fishing lines and the tin of cows' teat ointment I found on the bridge.

Fennel is the great home of snails: it is their paradise, nirvana and happy hunting ground. The matchless abundance of the snails was a fascination to us, and a symbol of the place itself. The snails were the scarabs of our own hieroglyphic society, and the snail hunt was the most satisfying of our rituals. From the length, breadth and depth of the river terrace we took them. From time to time one of us would return, and lift his shirt from his trousers, to tumble the catch into the biscuit tin. When we had a massed heap of them, perhaps a hundred and fifty or more, we would sit in the hut and anoint them. We used the cows' teat vaseline, rubbing it on the shells to darken the pattern and make them shine. We would lie the snails in handfuls among the fennel, just off the sacks, and in the penumbral green light. As we watched the snails would begin their ceremonial dispersal: large and small, sly and bold, all with the patterns of their shells waxed and gleaming. Scores of snails, each with its own set angle of direction. The gradual, myriad intersection of the planes of their escape through the fennel was like an abacus of three dimensions.

The friendship of Creamy and myself was the smallest and strongest of several circles. We often played with Arty and Lloyd, and there were other faces that we expected at other times. If we went swimming at the town baths, for instance, we joined up with the Rosenberg twins. They didn't seem to do much else but swim. But sometimes when Creamy and I were sick of what the others were doing, or after school when we'd rather be alone, then we'd make our signal, just a movement of the head, that meant we'd meet later at the hut. The hut was something apart from the rest of the world. In its life were only Creamy and me. As long as we agreed, our word was law; and no conventions but our own were followed.

I remember just when Creamy told me about going to Technical. We'd had a snail hunt, and were sitting by the river to wash. Creamy had his shirt off, and the snail tracks glistened on his chest. The linear droppings, inoffensively small, clung there too. 'Dad told me I'm not going to Boys' High after all,' he said. 'He's sending me to Tech.' Creamy's voice was doubtful, as if he wasn't sure whether it marked an important decision or not.

'But I thought we were all going to High?'

Creamy leant into the shingle of the river. He supported himself on his arms, and lifted first one hand, then the other to wash his chest. 'Dad said if I'm going into the garage with him, I need the Tech courses. He doesn't go much on languages and stuff.' Creamy had a broad, almost oriental face, and his upper lip was unusually full. It sat slightly over the bottom lip, and gave his face an expression of thoughtful drollery.

'I suppose after school we'll be able to do things together just the same. Maybe it's just like being in different classes at the same school.' I had a premonition, though, that Creamy's father had done something which would harm us.

'I did try to get Dad to change his mind,' said Creamy. He said it almost as if he wanted it recorded, lest some time in the future he might be blamed for not putting up more of a fight. Creamy flexed his arms, and recoiled out of the water with easy grace. He pulled the back of his trousers down, and showed the marks of a hiding. 'I did try,' said Creamy, and his upper lip quirked a little at the understatement.

'I don't see why it should make that much difference.' I could say that because it was weeks away in any case. When you are thirteen, nothing that is weeks away can be taken seriously. Creamy and I controlled time in those days. We could spin out one summer's day for an eternity of experience.

'Maybe I'll play against you in football,' said Creamy speculatively.

'I'll cut you down if you do.' We smiled, and Creamy skipped stones across the surface of the river with a flick of his wrist. The sun dried the water from us, and snapped the broom pods like an ambush on the other side of the river. Already I was surprised at my innocence in thinking that all my friends must go like myself to the High School.

Time made no headway against us that summer, not while we were together. But then my family went on holiday to the Queen

Charlotte Sounds, and I returned to find the world moved on. The new term was before us, and Creamy was indeed going to the Tech, and I to the High.

I didn't see Creamy after school during the first week, and on Saturday when we went after lizards on the slopes behind the reservoir, we didn't wear uniform. But the next Tuesday we met at the hut, and the nature of our division was apparent. Although I should have expected it, Creamy's Tech uniform was a blow. His grey trousers to my navy blue, his banded socks and cap, distinct in a separate allegiance. Creamy was never deceived by outward appearance. A smile spread out under his full upper lip, and creased his tanned face. 'I see you've lost your knob, too,' he said, and lightly touched the top of his cap.

'The fourth formers tore them off. Initiation,' I said.

'Same with us.' It was typical of Creamy that he should notice first about our uniforms a subtlety we had in common, whereas I couldn't help seeing us from the outside. Even my friendship with Creamy hadn't given me a totally personal view. Creamy didn't mention the uniforms again. We left our caps with our shoes and socks in the hut, and waded in the river to catch crayfish. As long as we maintained the old life separate from the new, then both could exist. It was like those studies I did at High School, about the primitive societies existing for hundreds of years, and then collapsing when the white man came. Creamy and I couldn't change much in the old way, because our ideas came from different sources that year. Sooner or later the white man would come; the white man comes one way or another to all the pagan societies of our youth.

I never sat down to think it out but, if I had, it must have seemed that as Creamy and I had held our friendship through the end of that summer, and the first term at our new schools, then there was no reason why we shouldn't go on. That wasn't the way of it, however. In the winter months I didn't see much of Creamy. The days were short, and the rugby practices we went to almost always came on different nights. I made new friends too, like big Matthew and Ken Marsden. When I was with Creamy, I sometimes found myself assuming that he knew all about High, and then halfway through some story I'd realise that it must have been meaningless to him. Creamy never showed any impatience. Creamy had a natural and attractive courtesy. He would sit there smiling, his expanding lip faintly frog-like, and say, 'He sounds a real hard case,' or, 'I wish I'd seen that.' Unless I asked him, he never said much about Tech. The odd thing perhaps about sport, or the time he saw Rainbow Johnston smash the windows in the gym. Rainbow was the baron of all our childhood fiefdoms. He had a job at the pie cart in the evenings, and made more money by stealing milk coupons. Birds stopped singing when Rainbow came past. He knew how to twist an arm till the tears came, did Rainbow; and it was said he made little kids put their hands in his trousers.

In the third term, when it became summer again, we began going back to the river. Not just Creamy and me anymore, though, for I'd grown accustomed to spending my time with Matthew and Ken. The first time I took them to the hut, Arty was with us too. Arty knew Creamy from primary school, but Matthew and Ken didn't. I could see them measuring themselves against Creamy as the afternoon went on. Creamy didn't seem to mind. Creamy liked a challenge in his own unassuming way. Creamy could stand measurement beside anyone I knew.

The mentality of youth is able to unhook its jaws like a snake, and swallow whole antelopes of experience. Youth is a time for excess: for breaking through the ice to swim, for heaping up a mountain of anointed snails from the fennel, for sledging until your hands are bleeding from the ropes, and sunstroke smites you down. Youth is a time for crazes: hula-hoops and underwater goggles, bubble gum and three-D cardboard viewers.

But that year it was knucklebones. The year when Creamy and my new High School friends met, it was knucklebones.

Knucklebones had risen obscurely, like an Asian plague, and swept as an epidemic through our world — brief and spectacular. Creamy excelled at knucklebones, of course: Creamy was insolently good at knucklebones. Like chickens about a hen, the knucklebones grouped and disbanded, came and went around Creamy's hand. Creamy had begun with plastic knucklebones. The soft drink colours of the pieces would rise and fall, collect and separate, at Creamy's behest. He won an aluminium set in the Bible class competition. The aluminium ones were heavier and didn't ricochet. Creamy was even better with the aluminium ones. Cutting cabbages, camels, swatting flies, clicks, little jingles, through the arch, goliath, horses in the stable; Creamy mastered them all.

Creamy's expression didn't change when Ken challenged him to knucklebones. He seemed interested in my new friends. His fair hair hung over his forehead, and his complex face was squinting in the sun. Ken was good at knucklebones, as good as me, but he wouldn't beat Creamy, I knew. Creamy was a golden boy, and it's useless to envy those the gods have blessed. Ken and he went right through knucklebones twice without any faults. 'What do you think is the hardest of all?' said Creamy. Ken considered. He pushed the knucklebones about the ground with his finger as he thought.

'I reckon big jingles,' he said.

'Ten big jingles on the go,' said Creamy. 'I challenge you to ten big jingles without a fault.'

'You go first then,' said Arty. 'You go first and if you make a mistake then Ken wins.'

'All right,' said Creamy. The injustice of it didn't seem to worry him. He started out as smoothly as ever, allowing no time for tension to gather. His rhythm didn't vary, and his broad face was relaxed.

'That's good going,' said Matthew when Creamy had finished, and Ken had failed to match him.

'They're small though, these aluminium ones.' Arty seemed jealous of the praise. 'Smaller than real or plastic knucklebones. It's a big advantage to have them smaller in big jingles.'

'Stiff,' said Creamy.

Later in the afternoon we found ourselves fooling about by the bridge. Along the underside of the bridge was a pipe which Creamy and I sometimes crossed to prove we could do it. 'Creamy and I often climb across that,' I told the others. They looked at it in silence.

'Shall we do it now?' said Matthew at last. He thought he was strong enough to try anything.

There's no dichotomy of body and spirit when you're young. Adults see the body as an enemy, or a vehicle to be apprehensively maintained. There's just you, when you're young; flesh and spirit are indivisible. For Creamy and I then, for all of us in youth, any failure in body was a failure of the spirit too. Creamy went first. As always when he was concentrating, his lunar upper lip seemed more obvious, the humorous expression of his face more pronounced, as though he were awaiting the punch line of some unfolding joke. He leant out, and took hold of the pipe. He moved his grip about, as a gymnast does to let his hands know the nature of the task, then he swung under the pipe, and began hand over hand to work his way to the central bridge support. He used his legs as a pendulum, so that the weight of his body was transferred easily from one hand to the other as he moved. When he reached the centre support Creamy rested in the crook of its timbers, and looked down to the river.

Then he carried on, hanging and swaying below the pipe, becoming smaller in silhouette against the far bank as he went.

'Seems easy enough,' said Arty.

'You go next then,' said Ken.

Arty measured the drop between Creamy's swaying figure and the river beneath. 'I would,' he said. 'I would, but I've got this chest congestion. I see the doctor about it.'

'Sure.'

Matthew could only think about one thing at a time, and as he was busy watching Creamy he found himself next in line for the pipe. The rest of us, by slight manoeuvrings, had got behind him. 'It's me then,' said Matthew. He took a grip and his body flopped down beneath the pipe, and stopped with a jerk. His upstretched arms were pulled well clear of his jersey and his hands were clamped on to the pipe. The crossing was an exercise in sheer strength for Matthew. He pulled himself along clumsily and his legs hung down like fenceposts below his thick body. I went next. I didn't want Arty in front of me in case he froze, and I couldn't get past. The few feet just before the central support were the worst, for if I looked down there I could see the concrete base of the timber supports on which I'd fall, instead of into the water. I used to count the number of swings I made just there; one, two, three, four, until I was able to put my feet on the wooden supports. The second half wasn't so bad, because at the end, if you were tired, you could drop off on to the grassy bank which rose up towards the underside of the bridge.

Arty and Ken didn't go over at all. Arty pretended he'd seen a big trout in the hole beneath the bridge, and he and Ken went down and poked under the bank with a stick. When we came back over the bridge, we couldn't see any big trout in the hole. 'Want to go over the pipe again?' said Creamy mildly.

'That's hard work, that.' Matthew was always honest.

'Good, though,' said Creamy.

As we scuffed about in the shingle at the end of the bridge, a horse and rider came past. The horse paused and, with flaunting tail, deposited vast rolls of waste. Matthew watched the horse with awe. 'I bet horses are the biggest shitters around,' he said.

'No, in proportion guinea pigs are far greater shitters,' said Creamy.

'Guinea pigs?'

'Yeah, in proportion they are.'

'Rabbits are good shitters,' said Arty.

'I don't see how anything could beat horses and elephants,' said Ken. As an ally he weakened Matthew's argument. The rest of us recognised the subtlety of Creamy's reasoning.

'Guineas are by far the best shitters in proportion.' Creamy knew he was right. 'Imagine a guinea pig as big as a horse. Now there would be a shitter.'

'Yeah,' said Matthew in wonder, and capitulation.

We had a swim, and threw fennel spears at each other during the rest of the afternoon. We forgot about the time, and Ken's sister came looking for him. She left her bike by the road, and came down to the fence, calling out for Ken. 'You've got to come home,' she said. Her breasts caused furrows across the material of her blouse.

'Have you been eating too much, or something,' said Arty. We had a good laugh at that witticism. 'Turning into a moo-vie star,' continued Arty, pleased with his reception. He tucked his thumbs into his shirt, and paraded before her and us.

'Oh, get lost,' she said. She began to go back up the bank towards the road. 'You'd better come, Ken. You know what'll happen,' she said.

'Hubba hubba, ding ding, look at the tits on that thing,' we sang.

'Watch out for Rainbow Johnston,' I called out.

'Hey, Rainbow, here she is.'

'Quick, Rainbow.'

For the first time Ken's sister seemed flustered. She looked back along the riverbank, and then hurried on to her bike. I don't know why I called out about Rainbow. Perhaps, in looking at her smooth legs and breasts, I found some part of Rainbow in myself, some desire to reach out and pinch her, or twist her arm, or worse.

Ken stayed a little longer, trying to show he wasn't afraid of being late, but we soon all began straggling back down the road. Creamy and I walked the last part together. 'I'm looking forward to the full summer,' I said. Creamy agreed. He played with his knucklebones, and whistled as he walked, his upper lip funnelling out and creating a very clear, penetrating whistle. His shoes, worn by water and grass during the afternoon, were almost white at the toes. Creamy stopped whistling, and asked me if Ken and Matthew were the two I liked best at High School. I told him I quite liked them.

'I'm getting sick of Arty,' said Creamy thoughtfully. 'You know that. I'm finding Arty pretty much of a pill.'

'So am I,' I said. Creamy tossed his aluminium knucklebones up and down again in the palm of his hand. We were nearly at the street where Creamy turned off. 'You didn't mind Ken and Matthew being there?' I asked him.

Creamy didn't give any glib answer. He walked on for a while.

'I suppose it's selfish to just have one or two friends,' he said. 'I suppose as you get older, you meet more and more people and make friends with them. Only I don't seem to find as many as you. There's an awful lot like Arty.'

As Creamy went off home, I thought about that. For the first time I realised that, despite being good at everything, Creamy didn't have that many friends. Being good at everything was in itself a disadvantage even. That's what was the matter with Arty. He resented Creamy's ability. Somewhere, sometime, he'd like to see Creamy take a fall.

The next Saturday I went again. Ken couldn't come, but Matthew and Arty did. I hadn't seen Creamy, but I thought he'd be there. He had another Tech boy with him. None of us knew him. He had eyebrows that grew right across the top of his nose. I'd never seen anyone with one long eyebrow like that before. His name was Warwick Masters. When he thought something was funny, he let his head fall forward, bouncing on his chest, and gave a snuffling laugh on the indrawn breath.

Creamy and I hadn't had any snail hunts that summer. No decision was made not to, we just didn't do it. As third formers we were growing out of snail hunts, and into more fitting things like knucklebones, and calling hubba hubba, ding ding, at Ken's sister. Yet the way Warwick treated the snails made me so angry I could feel my throat becoming tight. 'Christ Almighty,' said Warwick, 'look at these snails.' He reached into the fennel walls of the hut, and plucked out the snails. 'Just look at these snails, will you.' He let his head bounce on his chest, and gave his idiotic, sucking laugh. He arranged a line of them by the wall, then smashed each one with his fist. The shells cracked like biscuits, and what was left of the snails seemed to swell up in visceral agony after Warwick's fist was lifted. Creamy made no attempt to stop him. He hardly seemed to notice what he was doing.

'Don't do that,' I said to Warwick.

'Bloody snails.'

'It only makes a mess in the hut.'

'Stiff,' said Warwick. 'That's really stiff.'

'Just leave them alone.'

'Yeah?'

'Yeah.'

'Yeah?'

'Yeah.' The verbal sparring quickened into a semblance of humour, and Warwick bounced his head and laughed.

'Anyway,' said Arty, 'I don't think you Tech guys should come to the hut.'

'It's always been my hut too,' said Creamy seriously. Three summers are an accepted eternity when one is young.

'Its got to be either Tech or High ground,' said Matthew. He liked things simple for his own peace of mind. 'All the places got to be either Tech or High.' Matthew's simplicity had found the truth. All the places that mattered in our town were either High or Tech ground. The territories were marked, and only the adults in their naivety were unaware. My father never understood why I wouldn't take the short cut through the timber yard on my way to school.

'This side of the bridge is ours,' said Arty.

'But it's closest to the Tech swimming hole.'

'Stiff.'

Warwick picked up some of the squashed snails and quickly wiped them down Arty's face, then crashed away through the fennel a few paces, and stood bouncing his head and snorting. Creamy's subtle and unique face creased with delight, but he made no movement. Arty flung the remaining mess of snails at him, and urged Matthew to grab him. 'Grab him, Matthew, grab him.' Creamy dodged Matthew's first clumsy attempt. He seemed as if he were about to say something, but Arty got in first. 'High on to Tech,' he shouted.

'Yeah,' I heard myself say, but without reason. It seemed to come from a surface part of me, and not deeper where I thought things out. Creamy slipped from the hut, and stood with Warwick.

'For today you mean,' he said, smiling. Creamy loved a battle.

'For always,' said Arty. Arty was pleased that at last he had something over Creamy. Creamy was Tech, and the rest of us were High. Creamy was quicker, stronger, better at knucklebones and swinging under the bridge, a true friend, but he was Tech. Arty, like most weak people, enjoyed advantages he couldn't himself create. 'For always. No more Tech farts on the bank. Fight you for it.'

It was three on to two, but that didn't worry Creamy. He had a sense of occasion, though, did Creamy. If it had to be Tech against High after all, then it should be done on a fitting scale. 'Thursday night then,' said Creamy. His full upper lip expanded as he thought about it, and his eyes took on the visionary look with which he regarded his schemes. A look that hinted at the appreciation of more colours than existed in the spectrums of the rest of us. 'On Thursday after school we'll have the full fight between Tech and High for the bank. You get all you can, and we'll meet you. All out war.'

'I don't know,' said Arty. 'Maybe we should set rules and numbers.' Arty's brief moment of initiative was over; Creamy had, as always, taken control.

'All out war,' he repeated, and Warwick's head bounced and his laugh sounded through the fennel.

'Is it really all out war?' I said. I could see Creamy's face not many paces away, but he didn't answer. 'All out?' I said. Creamy's face was relaxed and droll, so difficult to read.

'Full scale,' cried Warwick. 'Tech against High.' And still Creamy didn't answer.

'We'll win easily,' said Matthew. 'We can round up a dozen or more easily.'

'Look out for Rainbow Johnston, that's all,' called Warwick. He went off, laughing, to follow Creamy, who had turned away and begun walking towards the fence below the bridge.

I watched Creamy climb up to the road with Warwick, and I knew it had happened. I knew that him going to Tech and me going to High had ruined our friendship after all. I looked at Arty and Matthew standing by the hut, and I knew that neither of them was half the friend that Creamy had been. 'Do you think they'll really get Rainbow?' said Arty hollowly.

'I've heard things about Rainbow. I think we need plenty of guys.' Matthew's slow logic was depressing.

'Can we get enough, though?' said Arty.

'Jesus, Arty,' I said, 'will you stop moaning.'

That week at school we started getting as many allies as we could. Arty wrote the names down at the back of his pad. He had two lists — one headed possibles and one headed probables, like trial teams. There were some names in the possibles that I hardly knew. Not even all the probables were at the gate after school on Thursday, though. Arty himself didn't show up until we were just about to go. We told him he was trying to get out of it. 'No I'm not. I'm coming, of course I'm coming. I just had to put off other things, that's all. What do you think of this stick?' Arty had a short piece of sawn timber. He hit it against the fives courts, and then tried not to show that he'd jarred his hand. 'I reckon I'm ready,' he said.

We began walking towards the river, but a car drew up over the road, and the man driving it called out to Arty. It was Arty's father. Arty went over and talked with him, then came partly back.

'Wouldn't you know it,' he said. 'I've got to go up to the hospital for my tests. It has to be tonight.' With Arty's father watching from the car, it wasn't any use saying much. 'Maybe the Tech will be there again tomorrow night. I'll be right for tomorrow.'

'Sure,' said Ken. Arty walked over the road quickly. As he got into the car he let his stick slip on to the roadway.

'He rang his dad,' said Lloyd. 'That's what he did.' Arty couldn't meet our eyes as the car pulled away.

'What a dunny brush he turned out to be,' said Matthew and we laughed. I was on the point of telling them what Creamy had said about Arty. Creamy had him picked all right, then I remembered that Creamy had become the enemy.

That left seven of us. Matthew, Ken, Lloyd, Buzz Swanson and the Rosenbergs. And me, of course. As we got closer to the bridge, I had a strange feeling that our group was becoming smaller, although the number remained the same. Ken was walking beside me, and I saw how frail he was. His legs were so thin they seemed swollen at the knees to accommodate the joints. He had little, white teeth that looked as if they were his first set. Even as Ken smiled at me, I thought to myself that he was going to be useless. I didn't want to be by Ken when we were fighting. I'd keep by Matthew. Matthew's dirty knees were comfortingly large, and he plodded on resolutely. 'Perhaps we should scout around first, and find out how many of them there are,' I said to Matthew.

'I've got to be home by half past five,' said Ken. I bet you do, Ken, I bet you do, I thought. I resolved that not only would I stick with Matthew when it started, I'd make sure Ken wasn't protecting my back. I had some idea it was going to be like the musketeers of Dumas, us back to back against the odds of the Tech boys.

We stood on the raised road leading up to the bridge, and looked over the bank from the fence, across the frothing fennel to the greywacke shingle of the riverbed, where the larger stones crouched like rabbits in the afternoon sun. Creamy stepped out from the cover of the willows two hundred yards away. He raised one arm slowly and lowered it again. It caught the significance of our presence, as a hawk becomes the sky. It had nothing to do with friendship, or compromise: it was a sign of recognition. It was a sign of deeper cognisance too, in that we were there. Unlike Arty and the others on the list, we had come. So Creamy acknowledged our equality of hostility.

Life was drama when we were young. The power of it made Lloyd's voice shake when he reminded us to keep together as we broke our way through the fennel. Creamy watched us coming for a bit, then disappeared behind the willows. 'Where are they?' said Ken. They were below the bank, where the terrace met the riverbed. As if to answer Ken's question, they began throwing stones which snicked through the fennel.

'Let's head for the willows,' I said. The Tech harried us as we went. I could hear Warwick's indrawn laugh, and I had a desultory stick fight with a boy who used to be in cubs with me. The Rosenberg twins were the best fighters on our side. They probably had the least notion as to why we were there in the first place, but they were the best fighters all right. They seemed to fight intuitively as one person, four arms and four feet. They rolled one Tech kid over the bank, and winded him on the shingle below. Matthew seemed unable to catch anyone to fight in this sort of guerrilla warfare. Nobody took him on, but he was too slow to take on anybody himself. He kept moving towards the willows, and we skirmished about him.

I think the whole thing might have petered out, if Rainbow hadn't come. Even in an all out fight there were rules: you knew that no one would deliberately poke anything in your eye, or hold your head under water longer than you could hold your breath. Rainbow was different. He liked to hurt people, did Rainbow. He stepped up on to the bank by the willows, and halted our forward progress. He had a thick stick. 'So it's Tech against High,' said Rainbow. His features were gathered closely on his round head, like sprout marks on a coconut. He held the stick in front of Ken, and Ken stopped. The rest of us did nothing. We did nothing not just because Rainbow Johnston was a fifth former, but because he was Rainbow Johnston. And deep down we were glad he'd picked on Ken, and not on us.

'I'm pax,' said Ken. It was the best he could think of, and its incongruity set the Tech guys laughing.

'Pax!' said Rainbow bitterly. 'We don't have any pax between Tech and High.' He drew back his stick, and speared it out at Ken, catching him on the side of the chest. Ken fell on his back, and as his head hit the soft grass his hair flopped away from his face, making him seem even younger.

'Ah, Jesus,' said Ken, and he got up and felt his side where he'd been struck. He laughed shakily and picked up his own stick in a show of defiance. Then he dropped his stick again, and began to cry. He slumped down on his knees and held his side. He arched his back and squeezed his eyes closed with the pain.

'We've won,' said Creamy, before anyone else could think of a reaction to what had happened. Rainbow motioned with his stick towards the rest of us. 'We've won,' repeated Creamy quietly. 'You can stay and play in the hut, Rainbow.' Creamy had found the right note as ever. With the fight declared over, Rainbow felt a bit ashamed to be with third formers. He vaulted over the sagging willow trunk on to the riverbed, and slouched off upstream. 'See you, Rainbow,' said Creamy.

'Yeah,' said Rainbow.

Ken was still crying. There was some blood showing through his shirt from the graze, and Matthew and I helped him up. We began to go back to the bridge through the fennel. 'They can't come here again, Creamy, can they?' called out Warwick. 'It's Tech now.'

'They can't come here again,' said Creamy. His face was the same, relaxed, and with the upper lip creating the impression of incipient humour. He didn't speak with any special triumph.

We broke down the fennel in our retreat, paying no attention to the tunnels Creamy and I had made. I was glad Tech had won. I joined in the talk about the injustice of Rainbow being there, but I was glad they'd won. It gave a more general explanation for the end of our friendship — Creamy's and mine. There couldn't be any personal betrayal when it was a matter of Tech and High, a commitment to a cause. Ken was still crying, but with greater artifice as his sense of heroism grew. He leant to one side, and he held his shirt out so it wouldn't stick to his graze. The fennel fronds were like miniature conifers, smaller and smaller, each in the join of the other as marsupial embryos in a pouch. The oddly coastal smell of the crushed fennel was all about us. 'I don't know that we lost, not really fair and square,' said Matthew. 'If Rainbow hadn't been there I mean.' They could say what they liked, but for myself I knew I'd lost all right. And it was worse that, as I climbed from the fennel, up onto the road, I could understand what it was I'd lost, and why.

Mr Van Gogh

When he went into hospital our newspaper said that Mr Van Gogh's name was Frank Reprieve Wilcox, and that was the first time I'd ever heard the name. But I knew Mr Van Gogh well enough. He came around the town sometimes on Sunday afternoons, and he would excuse himself for disturbing you and ask if there were any coloured bottles to carry on the work of Mr Vincent Van Gogh. Whether you gave him bottles or not, it was better never to enquire about his art, for he would stand by any back door on a Sunday afternoon and talk of Van Gogh until the tears ran down his face, and his gabardine coat flapped in agitation.

Only those who wanted to mock him, encouraged him to talk. Like Mr Souness next door who had some relatives from Auckland staying when Mr Van Gogh came, and got him going as a local turn to entertain the visitors. 'Was he any good, though, this Van Gogh bugger?' Mr Souness said, nudging a relative, and, 'But he was barmy, wasn't he? Admit it. He was another mad artist.' Mr Van Gogh never realised that there was no interest, only cruelty, behind such questions. He talked of the religious insight of Van Gogh's painting at Arles, and his genius in colour symbolism. He laughed and cried as he explained to Mr Souness's relations the loyalty of brother Theo, and the prescience of the critic Aurier. They were sufficiently impressed to ask Mr Van Gogh whether they could see his ears for a moment. Mr Souness and his relations stood around Mr Van Gogh, and laughed so loud when it was said, that I went away from the fence without watching any more. Mr Van Gogh was standing before the laughter with his arms outstretched like a cross, and talking all the more urgently. Something about cypresses and the hills of Provence.

Mr Van Gogh had a war pension, and lived in a wooden bungalow right beside the bridge. The original colours of the house had given up their differences, and weathered stoically to an integration of rust and exposed wood. The iron on the roof was stained with rust, and looked much the same as the corrugated weatherboards. The garden was full of docks and fennel. It had two crab apple trees which we didn't bother to rob.

Mr Van Gogh didn't appear to have anything worth stealing. He used to paint in oils, my father said, but it was expensive and nothing ever sold, so he began to work in glass. No one saw any of his artwork, but sometimes when he came round on Sundays, he'd have a set of drinking glasses made out of wine bottles, or an ashtray to sell made out of a vinegar flagon. My father was surprised that they were no better than any other do it yourself product.

Although he had no proper job, Mr Van Gogh worked as though the day of judgement was upon him. He used his attached wash-house as a studio, and on fine days he'd sit in the doorway to get the sun. There he'd cut and grind and polish away at the glass. He would even eat in the doorway of the wash-house as he worked. He must have taken in a deal of glass dust with his sandwiches. Often I could see him as I went down to the river. If I called out to him, he'd say 'Good on you', still working on the glass, grinding, cutting, polishing. If I was by myself I'd watch a while sometimes before going down to the river. One piece after another, none of them bigger than a thumbnail. A sheet of glass sheds the light, he said. They had to be small to concentrate the light. Some of the bits were thick and faceted, others so delicate he would hold them to the sun to check. Mr Van Gogh liked to talk of individual paintings as he worked — the poet's garden, street in Auvers, or starry night. He stored the different colours and shapes in cardboard boxes that said Hard Jubes on the sides. Yellow was difficult, the colour of personal expression, Mr Van Gogh said, but so difficult to get right in glass. He bought yellow glass from Austria, but he'd never matched Van Gogh's yellow. He never thought so much of his yellow glass, he said, even from Austria.

Mr Van Gogh wasn't all that odd-looking. Sure, he had old-fashioned clothes — galoshes in winter and his gabardine coat with concealed buttonholes, and in summer his policemen and firemen braces over grey workshirts. But he was clean, and clean-shaven. His hair was long, though, and grey like his shirts. He combed it back from his face with his fingers, so that it settled in tresses, giving him the look of a careworn lion.

Because my father was a parson it was thought he should be responsible for Mr Van Gogh and other weird people. Mr Souness said that it was just as well that my father had something to occupy his time for the other six days of the week. Ministers get some odd people to deal with, I'd say. Reggie Kane was a peeping tom who had fits whether he saw anything or not, and Miss O'Conner was convinced that someone was trying to burn down her house at night, and she used to work in the vegetable garden in her nightdress. Our family knew Mr Van Gogh wasn't like the others, though most people treated him the same. My father said that Mr Van Gogh's only problem was that he'd made a commitment to something which other people couldn't understand. My father had a good deal of fellow-feeling for Mr Van Gogh in some ways. Mr Van Gogh would've been all right if his obsession had been with politics or horse-racing. He wouldn't have been a crackpot then.

Two or three times Mr Van Gogh came to our house to use the phone. He'd stand quietly at the door, and make his apologies for bothering us. He was ordering more yellow glass from Austria perhaps, or checking on his pension. Mr Van Gogh's humility was complete on anything but art. He was submissive even to the least deserving. On art, though, he would have argued with Lucifer, for it was his necessity and power. It was what he was. His head would rise with his voice. He would rake back his grey hair, and for a moment the backward pressure would rejuvenate his face before the lines could appear again, the plumes of hair begin a faint cascade upon his forehead. He could be derisive and curt, fervent and eloquent, but people didn't understand. A naked intensity of belief is an obscene exposure in ordinary conversation. It was better not to start him off, my mother said.

When the council decided to make the bridge a two-lane one, Mr Van Gogh's house had to come down. The engineers said that the approaches to the new bridge would have to be at least twice the width of the bridge itself, and Mr Van Gogh's house was right next to the old bridge. Even the house next to Mr Van Gogh's would probably have to go, the consultant thought. Mr Van Gogh took it badly. He stuck up the backs of the letters the council wrote, and sent them back. He wouldn't let anyone inside to value the house. He wouldn't talk about compensation. The council asked my father to get Mr Van Gogh to see reason. My father said he was willing to try and explain the business, but he didn't know if he could justify it. The council didn't seem to recognise the distinction.

As far as I know, Mr Van Gogh never let anyone into his house. Even my father had to stand on the doorstep, and Mr Van Gogh stood just inside the door, and there was a blanket hanging across the hall behind him to block off the sight of anything to a visitor at the door. My mother said she could imagine the squalor of it behind the blanket. An old man living alone like that, she said.

My father did his best. So did the council and the Ministry of Works, I suppose. They selected two other houses to show Mr Van Gogh, and a retirement villa in the grounds of the combined churches' eventide home, but he wouldn't go to see them. He became furtive and worried. He'd hardly leave his house lest the people come and demolish it while he was away. The council gave Mr Van Gogh until the end of March to move out of his home. Progress couldn't be obstructed indefinitely, they said. Mr Souness looked forward to some final confrontation. 'The old bugger is holding up the democratic wishes of the town,' he said. He thought everyone had been far too soft on Mr Van Gogh.

In the end it worked out pretty well for the council people. Mrs Witham rang our house at teatime to say she'd seen Mr Van Gogh crawling from the wash-house into his front door, and that he must be drunk. My father and I went down to the bridge, and found Mr Van Gogh lying on his back in the hallway, puffing and blowing as he tried to breathe. 'It's all right now,' said my father to Mr Van Gogh. What a place he was in, though. For through that worn, chapped doorway, and past the blanket, was the art and homage of Mr Van Gogh. Except for the floor, all the surfaces of the passage and lounge were the glass inlays of a Van Gogh vision. Some glass was set in like nuggets, winking as jewelled eyes from a pit. Other pieces were lenses set behind or before similarly delicate sections of different colours to give complexity of toning. The glass interior of Mr Van Gogh's home was an interplay of light and colour that flamed in green, and yellow, and prussian blue, in the evening sun across the riverbank. Some of the great paintings were there: *Red Vineyard*, *Little Pear Tree*, *View of Arles with Irises*, each reproduced in tireless, faithful hues one way or another.

Mr Van Gogh lay like clay in the passage, almost at the lounge door. I thought that I was looking at a dying man. I blamed all that glass dust that he'd been taking in for years, but my father said it was something more sudden. He pulled down the blanket from the hall, and put it over Mr Van Gogh to keep him warm, then went down the path to ring the ambulance. The blanket hid Mr Van Gogh's workshirt and firemen's braces, but he didn't look much warmer. His face was the colour of a plucked chicken with just a few small veins high on his cheeks. Very small, twisted veins, that looked as if they didn't lead anywhere. I stood there beside him, and looked at his work on the walls. The yellow sun seemed to shine particularly on the long wall of the lounge where Mr Van Gogh had his own tribute to the man we knew him as. In green glass cubes was built up the lettering of one of the master's beliefs — 'Just as we take the train to Tarascon or Rouen, we take death to reach a star' — and above that Mr Van Gogh's train to Tarascon and a star rose up the entire wall. The cab was blue, and sparks of pure vermilion flew away. It all bore no more relation to the dross of glasses and ashtrays that Mr Van Gogh brought round on Sundays, than the husk of the chrysalis to the risen butterfly.

My father came back and waited with me in the summer evening. 'It has taken years to do, years to do,' he said. 'So many pieces of glass.' The fire and life upon the walls and ceiling defied Mr Van Gogh's drained face. He'd spent all those years doing it, and it didn't help him. It rose like a phoenix in its own flame, and he wasn't part of it anymore, but lay on his back and tried to breathe. All the colour, and purpose, and vision of Mr Van Gogh had gone out of himself and was there on the walls about us.

Both the St John's men were fat. I thought at the time how unusual it was. You don't get many fat St John's men. They put an oxygen mask on Mr Van Gogh, and we all lifted him on to the stretcher. Even they stood for a few seconds, amazed by the stained glass. 'Christ Almighty,' said one of them. They took Mr Van Gogh away on a trolley stretcher very close to the ground.

'What do you think?' asked my father.

'He won't necessarily die,' said the St John's man. He sounded defensive. 'He's breathing okay now.'

Mr Van Gogh went into intensive care. The hospital said that he was holding his own, but Mr Souness said he wouldn't come out. He said that it was his ticker, that his ticker was about to give up on him. Anyway there was nothing to stop the council and the Ministry of Works from going ahead. People came from all over the town to see Mr Van Gogh's house before they pulled it down. There was talk of keeping one or two of the pictures, and the mayor had his photograph in the paper, standing beside the train to Tarascon and a star. But the novelty soon passed, and the glass was all stuck directly to the walls with tile glue. The town clerk said there were no funds available to preserve any of it, and it was only glass anyway, he said. Someone left the door unlocked, and Rainbow Johnston and his friends got in and smashed a lot of the pictures. Mr Van Gogh's nephew came from Feilding, and took away the power tools.

My father and I went down to the river to see the house demolished. With Mr Van Gogh's neighbours, Mr Souness and the linesmen who had disconnected the power, we waited for it to come down. There were quite a few children too. The contractor had loosened it structurally, and then the dozer was put through it. The dozer driver's mate wore a football jersey and sandshoes. He kept us back on the road. Mr Van Gogh's place collapsed stubbornly, and without any dramatic noise, as if it were made of fabric rather than timber. The old walls stretched and tore.

Only once did my father and I get a glimpse of Mr Van Gogh's work beneath the weathered hide of the house. Part of the passage rose sheer from the wreckage for a moment, like a face card from a worn deck. All the glass in all its patterns spangled and glistened in yellow, red and green. Just that one projection, that's all, like the vivid, hot intestines of the old house, and then the stringy walls encompassed the panel again, and stretched and tore. The house collapsed like an old elephant in the drought, surrounded by so many enemies.

'Down she comes,' cried the driver's mate, and the driver raised his thumb and winked. There was a lot of dust, and people backed away. Mr Souness kept laughing, and rubbed his knuckles into his left eye because of the dust.

'All the time Mr Van Gogh spent,' I said to my father. 'All that colour, all that glass.'

'There'll always be a Mr Van Gogh somewhere,' my father said.

The Charcoal Burners' Dream

At reception I felt I belonged still to the outside world. I could breathe the exhaust fumes from the passing traffic in the street outside, and there was an undeniably healthy man in a post office smock sorting letters with one of the reception nurses. As I was taken down the corridor, however, and up the stairs, the smell closed in; a uniquely institutional fragrance of antiseptics, medication, polishes — and resignation.

I was taken to the far end of Men's Surgical Two, almost to the balcony room, and I put my case on the bed and stood awkwardly before the veterans of the ward. There was a sparrow in the balcony room, and Nurse McKerrow wanted it let out. Colin and Jimmy chased it as best they could from one side of the room to the other, but only one window would open, and the sparrow slammed instead into the closed panes, becoming more dazed and bloody. Chris was in the next bed to mine. 'Oh, for Christ sake,' he said and he cast his yellow hair from his face impatiently. 'Can you move about much?' he asked me. 'Throw a towel over it then, please, and let it out.' I went into the balcony room, and the next time the sparrow struck the glass I dropped the towel over it, and then released it through the open window. The bird half fell, half fluttered the three storeys into the hospital garden below. A trim pebble garden like a cemetery, with waxy camellias in a row.

Colin and Jimmy reluctantly came back to their beds, and I got out my pyjamas and dressing-gown to change. Nurse McKerrow

said I could pull the curtain screen, but I knew the impression that
would create. I had to prove my anatomy, as well as my pyjamas,
to be suitably nondescript. Chris watched me, propped up on his
pillows. His almost yellow hair hung limply, like a transplanted
tussock. When I was in my pyjamas, Chris considered I had formally
joined them, and I was introduced to those close to my bed, Jimmy,
Colin, Richard and Chris himself. Throughout the afternoon
those less immediate in the ward were mentioned as they brought
themselves to notice by refusing to eat, having a good-looking visitor,
or being on the surgery list for the next day. Each was identified
by his complaint as a suffix title. Arthur Prentice spine fusion, old
Mr Webster prostate. Chris himself was bowel. He said the word
bowel in the tone of voice a man might use for an ex-wife. A tone of
intimacy and betrayal all at once.

Colin talked most to me that first day, superficial things, of course,
about the hospital routine and the All Black tour, the headlines in
the paper and the difficulty of making small businesses pay. That was
Colin's line, small businesses. The sort of things you would expect
two strangers in bed to discuss. I was to find, however, that there
wasn't any more to Colin than the first superficial contact. When I
left hospital he still talked about the All Blacks and small businesses
with the same conformity. Colin was the tribal New Zealander, for
whom the greatest horror is to be different from what he imagines
the majority to be.

Chris didn't talk much the first day, but I was aware of an aura of
goodwill. In the morning, after Mr Millar had gone, and the others
were having breakfast, Chris noticed me lying quietly. He told me
what a good bone surgeon Mr Millar was, and how well known he
was for it. I wasn't allowed to eat anything before the operation. I
had trouble in my knee: bone disease in the knee cap, and cartilages
to come out as well. Chris watched as Nurse McKerrow shaved and
bathed my knee before the operation. When it was so smooth and
pink that it shone, she gave me a jab of something. I remember Chris

saying, 'Pentathol. My favourite magic carpet. As good as a night with Nurse McKerrow — almost.' Colin and Jimmy laughed, and Nurse McKerrow smiled with her eyes.

'Send in the trolley,' I said extravagantly. 'I'm ready for the trolley', and I wondered why the others laughed so hard.

The pain kept me from sleeping much the first two or three nights after the operation, despite the stuff they gave me. At night the ward was not completely dark, because of the light spilling from the sister's office. It dwindled down the ward, and didn't reach into the balcony room. But from where I was, looking back along the rows of beds towards the light, I could see pretty well once I got used to it. Old Mr Webster coughed a lot without waking up, and the radiators stood along the wall, on the lino, like piano accordions. I had plenty of time for thinking on those long nights. Lying there, looking along the beds towards the office, and with enough pain to banish any inner deceit, I had enough time for thinking all right. Chris talked to me sometimes to take my mind off the pain. I was too selfish to realise then that he was awake for the same reason. That's when he first told me about the Liberal Mythology. Never let yourself get sucked in by the Liberal Mythology, he said. He saw it in the way I talked about my best friend who came to see me shortly after the operation. I told Chris how close we were, and how I'd known him over thirty years. 'The Liberal Mythology,' said Chris.

'What?'

'All this about searching out kindred souls. It's all part of the Liberal Mythology. You have as your friends who you can get as your friends, just as you have as your wife who you can get for your wife. Don't kid yourself any other way. It doesn't make them any less precious, but it's the truth of it. Take Jimmy there: he'd like to be friends with you, and marry Nurse McKerrow. Right?' We looked across at Jimmy. He lay asleep, with one arm over his face. 'How much choice has Jimmy really got?' said Chris. I couldn't think of any form of rebuttal, except saying that I wasn't the same as Jimmy.

'Only a matter of degree, for you and me,' said Chris.

During the day Chris helped me with my exercises. At first he'd just tell me how far I was getting my heel off the bed, as I lay on my back and tried to lift the leg. Later he'd rest his hand gently on the top of my foot to give me more weight to lift as the knee became stronger. 'You've got it beaten, Hugh, that's sure enough,' he'd say.

Anything that jarred my leg was the worst: knocking it with the crutch, or catching the toe on a rug, would bring an instant sweat. Hopping was out; progress was a matter of deliberate smoothness. On the fourth day I slipped while in the toilet and got wedged in the corner amid my crutches. My bad leg pressed against the lavatory bowl. I should have called out in a calm voice of suppressed pain to tell the nurse what had happened. It never occurred to me to do any such thing. I lay there, giving a very quavering and sustained squeal, like that of a girl. The sustained squeal was best, because any deep breath was enough to alter the unbearable pressure on my leg. The ward enjoyed it when I was carried back ignominiously from the toilets.

I began to get better rapidly, though. After a fortnight or so, Chris and I were able to go up to the geriatric wing and watch television at night. We weren't allowed to use the lift, so it meant a stiff climb and a rather furtive hobble along the dim corridors. The television was left on in the geriatric dayroom, right through until closedown. Sometimes Jimmy would come with us, occasionally a patient from some other ward, but usually just Chris and me. And the locals, of course. There were several geriatrics whose beds were regularly pushed into the dayroom at night, not because they liked television, but because they disturbed the others if left in the ward. Mind you, they may have enjoyed television. Chris said it's easy to be dogmatic when speaking for those who can't speak for themselves.

Puck and the Wrestler were our most consistent viewing companions. The Wrestler's skin was too large for him, and flowed around the few fixed features of his face. Only on the top of his head was it tight. His eyes were circular, and ringed with creases like those of a parrot. The Wrestler had regressed to some time of persistent physical endeavour, and reiterated it all in a monologue of quiet despair. 'That's a good hold, Bob. Ah yes. Ah yes. Ah Bob, Bob, that's a good hold. I'll pin your shoulders yet. But that's a good hold, Bob. Ah yes.' The Wrestler never moved, and his voice was drab in tone, but behind it somewhere was an epic of pain and fortitude, and underlying submission as if he fought with life itself. Puck provided less of a window. Most of the time he sat as primly as Whistler's mother, his hands demurely on the folded sheets. But from time to time he would give his own cry. It was the sound a contented chicken makes in the yard when the afternoon sun is hot, the dust dry and a breeze in the pines by the woolshed. Poo-oo-ook. You know the sound. A sound of drawling enquiry in a rising inflexion. Puck caught it perfectly. He did it most when everything was quiet: late at night when there was something subdued on the television or, even better, when it had finished. Then, as Chris and I prepared to leave, we would hear him. 'Poo-oo-ook. Poo-oo-ook', gathering the sunshine, the dry, grey dust, and the pine trees about himself. We called him Puck because of Kipling's *Puck of Pook's Hill*. It was the most successful joke I ever made with Chris, mentioning Puck of Pook's Hill. His soft, even laugh went on and on, until he started swearing at me because I'd made his bowels hurt.

Nurse Hart was the night nurse on the geriatric ward. She seemed to feel the responsibility of it deeply. Unlike the physios and Nurse McKerrow, she wasn't immediately good-looking, and she was very quiet. She had legs, though, said Chris. Chris was quick to notice those girls who had legs. Nurse Hart's legs were long and graceful, growing more rounded to the thighs. Nurse Hart liked Chris and me to be in the dayroom watching television, in case something went wrong with her patients.

The physios were the best-looking girls in the hospital, except for Nurse McKerrow. All of us agreed the physios were the best, though, apart from Jimmy, we couldn't think of any explanation for it. Jimmy thought it was because they liked massaging people, and we knew that was just the inevitable expression of Jimmy's mind. 'All that rubbing and gripping,' said Jimmy slyly. 'The good-looking ones like to do it the most.' Jimmy was in for some sort of club foot, but he wasn't very Byronic. He had a cramped, impoverished face, and acquaintance disclosed a mind of similar character. He collected magazines of nudes, and laid them on the bed when the nurses came, in what he considered a subtle declaration of intention. From the balcony one day we watched Jimmy playing with his transistor. He found a woman's voice on one channel, and lay twisting the volume knob back and forth so that it sounded as if the woman was panting.

'Poor little bastard,' said Chris. Colin would have laughed, but Chris saw the poverty in Jimmy rather than the humour.

The Reverend Metcalf came to see us on Wednesday. Wednesday was his hospital day. I haven't anything against clergymen as such, not as such, but Chris and I disliked the Reverend Metcalf. He wore a look of infinite understanding and superiority. He had a rich, well-modulated laugh, tinged with pathos to hint at the load of revelation he bore. He would lay out his modulated laugh as a tapestry, while his eyes strayed to other beds, or the face of his digital watch. He was a vicarious vicar: a walking crucifixion, full of suffering yet having experienced no pain. I watched Chris regard the Reverend Metcalf as he left. 'The Liberal Mythology again?' I said.

'The Liberal Mythology.' Chris moved restlessly in his bed, stirred by the appearance once more of his old adversary. 'Life and death are the religious divisions in the Liberal Mythology,' he said. 'Now the reality of it, Hugh, the reality, is different.' Chris loved the word reality. The way he said it gave it weight and sheen, a soundness. 'The reality is the cycle of growth and decay.'

'And life after death?' I asked, because I couldn't quite see what he was getting at.

'How can the personality survive death, when it can't always survive life? That's it, all right. Take Puck, or the Wrestler: there's not much left to gather, is there? The Liberal Mythology deals in theory, see Hugh. You have life, and you have death: you have the prime of functioning personality, you have its perpetuation in spirit. It's a very comforting thing, the Liberal Mythology and being a theory it doesn't concern itself with the complications of transition.' Chris rolled over carefully. He put a pillow beneath his groin, and hung his head over the bed in his favourite position to rid himself of flatulence. 'There's a bit of the pattern of the lino further down that looks like a giraffe,' he said. His yellow hair drooped away from his neck, and I was dismayed to see how the bones stood out beneath the skin.

Perhaps it was because he was losing so much weight that Chris had to have another operation. You don't know with bowels, mind. Mr Millar came to see him again, and told him he was to have another operation. The rest of us on our beds looked across to him to see how he was taking it. 'I'm having my operation Tuesday, Nurse McKerrow. Give me a kiss.' It was unashamed blackmail, and both he and Nurse McKerrow laughed. She looked quickly down the ward, then bent over Chris. She kissed him, and Chris made no attempt to encircle her with his arms, but with one finger traced a line down her side, sweeping slowly over her hip before dropping his hand to the bed again. 'Tell Mother I died happy,' said Chris, and Jimmy cried out excitedly as we laughed, and said he wanted a kiss too. Nurse McKerrow went back up the ward. She looked as if she had received as much as she had given.

The night before his second operation, Chris came up to the geriatrics' television with me. We sat with Puck and the Wrestler, and watched a film about a donkey that talked. Chris couldn't sit still; he leant on his chair more than he sat on it, and he lay on Puck's bed with him for a while. Nurse Hart brought us coffee, and tried to share with us her fears concerning old Mrs Sanderson in the main ward. Later, when the donkey was winning the war for the Allies, Nurse Hart came back crying, and told us that Mrs Sanderson had tried to swallow her handkerchief and choked to death. Chris and I went into the darkened ward, and pushed Mrs Sanderson out to wait for the hospital orderlies. Mrs Sanderson's wispy hair stood up from her head, as if in her death she had frightened herself as well as Nurse Hart.

After the orderlies had come and gone, Nurse Hart remained in the dayroom with us for comfort. She stood by Chris's chair and tried not to be upset. Chris held her hand and talked to her. Gradually her head came down towards the chair, until she rested her forehead on the top of Chris's head. Her hair covered part of his face, and she didn't speak, though Chris continued to talk in his reduced but definite way. It was a scene of reassurance. The Wrestler and I were quiet, although I was not unaware, and Puck seemed to realise that the mood of the dayroom was particularly calm. 'Poo-oo-ook,' he said tentatively. 'Poo-oo-ook,' and the sunshine of it, and the sighing pine trees, gathered around us.

Chris was a lot worse after the second operation. He didn't seem to be able to pull himself right back to complete participation. The pain made him restless, and sometimes impatient. When I looked at him, and he wasn't aware of it, his face was full of a strange enquiry. As if he were getting smaller and smaller inside himself and could hardly see out of his own eyes. He didn't come up to the television anymore at night. Nurse Hart asked me how he was, and when I told her that he wasn't so good, she looked even more nervous than usual. She was afraid one of the geriatrics might have a turn, she said. Two died the week before, she said.

Chris liked to read poetry with me, and often on warm afternoons we would sit in chairs in the balcony room, and talk of poetry. I pushed for Dylan Thomas, and though Chris liked him well enough, he wouldn't have him in first place. He said that Thomas was the storm, but that Frost was the clarity after the storm. He may be right, the more I come to think of it. Other afternoons we would just sit and look over the hospital grounds towards the city. On those occasions we'd talk only when things cropped up: like the charcoal burners' dream, for instance, when Chris and I saw a primary school class crocodiling past towards the library. 'When I was a boy I believed in the stories read to me about the charcoal burners' dream,' said Chris. 'Those poor but sturdy charcoal burners who would share their bread and cheese in the forest with anyone who needed it. No matter how the odds were stacked against them, the charcoal burners believed that if they were brave and kind, then things would work out in the end. And so they always did.'

'I haven't read a story like that for a long time,' I said.

'Neither have I,' said Chris.

He kept trying, though. He had all the guts in the world; well, metaphorically, of course, his lack of it in the other way was the problem. On a Wednesday, when the Reverend Metcalf had gone, but the false tapestry of his laugh still lingered, Chris undressed Nurse McKerrow. 'Nurse McKerrow,' said Chris seriously. 'Why have you taken off your cap? I thought that was against the regulations?' Nurse McKerrow instinctively touched her cap, then went on washing old Mr Webster. 'Nurse McKerrow, you shouldn't take off your stockings in the ward. Not here, Nurse McKerrow.' Colin looked from one to the other, his face sagging because he was so busy trying to realise what was going on that he forgot to keep any expression on his face. Chris drew the blanket up towards his head. 'Not your uniform. My God, Nurse McKerrow, you can't take off your uniform in front of us all.' Jimmy began to laugh. Nurse McKerrow looked across at Chris, and they held each other's glance like a sliver of sunlight from one side of the ward to the other. 'Lovely Nurse McKerrow,' said Chris in a mocking voice of no mockery, 'you have nothing on at all. Nothing at all. How could you be so shameless.'

'Nothing at all,' squealed Jimmy.

'Nothing at all,' said Chris quietly, and smiled at her across the ward.

'You are the biggest fool,' said Nurse McKerrow, smiling with her eyes.

'I see Nurse McKerrow with nothing on at all,' said Chris.

And so he did, and she knew he did and didn't mind, while Colin couldn't understand, and said, 'What's this all about? Bloody Chris Palmer's going mad again.' Even if Nurse McKerrow had taken all her clothes off, Colin wouldn't have seen what Chris saw because he didn't have that searing, blue spark of imagination that Chris had. That searing, blue spark that burnt away the flux and the dross, and allowed Chris to see reality as it was, and as he wished it to be, both at the same time. And Chris knew the difference between them: that was the price for seeing both, I suppose. The blue spark that gave the light was corrosive, eating away at the bowels of things.

Chris was never bored with life. He hated what he saw at times, but he was never bored with life. He was on a higher voltage than any of the others. When I compared him with the bland conformity of Colin and Richard, or the shrunken appreciation of the world that was Jimmy's, then I couldn't understand why it was that Chris was dying, why the doctors were cutting his bowel up piece by piece. I wasn't prepared to change places with Chris myself, but if I'd had the power I would have let Jimmy or Colin, any of the others in the ward, die in place of Chris. I'm not afraid to admit it. Like Chris I'm not in the grip of the Liberal Mythology any longer: I don't believe in the charcoal burners' dream. If God had given me the power, I would have said, give Jimmy or Colin the bowel. I could have said it firmly. It doesn't matter how many times we talk about people being equal, it's not true. Some people are worth a dozen of the rest of us. The way perhaps one pohutukawa is worth a dozen tea-tree bushes. You don't like the idea, but I'll say it again. Some people are worth a dozen of the rest of us.

On Chris's last afternoon I was playing poker with Richard. Chris hated cards. Cards is just killing time, he used to say. He hated even to be near people playing cards, as if the trivial and repetitious talk as the cards were played prevented him from reading, or thinking. The ward was warm and quiet. Nurse McKerrow was laughing and talking in the office, and old Mr Webster had his transistor on to listen to the cricket. Chris stood in the balcony room by the windows, his fair hair drab in the sunlight. When I looked up again, he had opened the window and was sitting on the sill itself, facing back towards us. That surprised me, for he didn't like sitting on anything hard. I picked up a red jack, I remember, a red jack which pleased me because it gave me a straight, and when I looked up again Chris was gone. Jimmy was pointing and crying out.

To walk without crutches I had the habit of counting the steps. It helped me to be deliberate, and to anticipate the discomfort. So I counted from one to eleven as I walked into the balcony room. The garden was a long way down, the garden into which I'd released the bird on the day I arrived. Chris lay by the camellias, his blue dressing-gown distinct. His flight through the air had pushed up the legs of his pyjamas, and his long, white ankles showed amid the camellia bushes.

Nurse McKerrow phoned downstairs, and a doctor and orderlies came out into the garden. Nurse McKerrow tried to lead me away from the window, but I stayed. I watched the doctor's urgency replaced by resignation, and saw one of the orderlies shake his head. Colin began to construct his emotional defence. 'It must have been an accident,' he said. 'Oh my God, what a thing to see. A fall, an accident like that.' I didn't answer him, but I thought it was the old Liberal Mythology all over again: the charcoal burners' dream.

Usually I won't let myself dwell on it now I'm well. But sometimes when I catch a whiff of some antiseptic, or see those old-style radiators, like the piano accordions that stood along the wall in Men's Surgical Two, then I think of Jimmy, of Puck, of Nurse McKerrow, and of Chris. I have a feeling that they're all still there;

that the mood of resignation and reality is waiting for me, waiting for the end of the charcoal burners' dream.

Cabernet Sauvignon
with My Brother

I walked the last two miles to my brother's place. I was lucky to have hitched as close as I did. Along the flat through Darfield and Kirwee early in the morning I'd done a good deal of walking, but then a tractor repair man took me to within two miles. He told me he'd been working on the hydraulics of a new Case harvester which cost eighty thousand dollars.

I love the accumulated heat of the Canterbury autumn. When you rest on the ground you can feel the sustained warmth coming up into your body, and there are pools of dust like talcum powder along the roads. It's not the mock tropicality of the Far North, but the real New Zealand summer. It dries the flat of your tongue if you dare to breathe through your mouth. After spending the vacation working on the coast, I was happy to be back in Canterbury.

My brother Raf lived on seventeen hectares of gravel close to West Melton. He had been a tutor in economics at Lincoln, but resigned on a matter of principle. He said it was a form of hypocrisy to pretend to any skill in financial affairs, when the best salary he could command was that of a tutor. Raf said that the most important things to achieve in life were privacy and revenue. At West Melton on seventeen hectares he had privacy, but the income was precarious. Raf's best crop was manoeuvres. He said he received a small but consistent return from manoeuvres. The army paid him for access to the riverbed. Heavy manoeuvres was the better paying crop he said, but harder on the ground.

As I walked up the natural terrace to Raf's place, the heat shimmer on the riverbed was already beginning. The stones in Raf's paddocks didn't seem to have become any less numerous. I noticed that because last time I visited my brother, he told me that ploughing only brought them up, and that picking them off was uneconomic. Raf believed that if the ground were grazed naturally, and just a little super added from time to time, then worm action would increase the height of the soil until the stones were eventually covered right over. He said he read a report of French research on it in Brittany. Raf had a knack of finding theoretical justification for his lifestyle.

He was working on his motorbike when I arrived. It was an old Norton 500 cc, an enormous single-pot machine, and his only form of transport. With it he towed a trailer large enough for ten bales of hay. He left the front tube hanging from the tyre, and came down the track to meet me. 'Ah, Tony,' he said, and took me by the shoulder. 'I hoped to see you before the term began.' His blue eyes seemed bleached from the sun, and his hair and eyebrows were nearly white. 'I told myself you'd come,' he said. Although he was my brother, he was about fourteen years older than me: we were more like uncle and nephew in some ways. I was aware of the emphasis and undisguised pleasure in his voice. 'I've got quite a lot of beer at the moment,' he said proudly. 'I sold another dozen lambs last week.' To have revenue to share, as well as privacy, made him feel his hospitality was complete.

'I can't stay the night. Lectures start tomorrow. I should have been in today, really.'

'Well, we've the day together then,' said Raf, 'and you'll get out sometime during the term.'

I went with Raf into his house, and he put into his pygmy fridge as many bottles of beer as it would hold. The kitchen floor had a slant, and when the fridge was operating the vibration caused it to creep from the wall, inch by inch. I could see it, as we sat at the table with our coffee, shuffling up to Raf's shoulder like a prototype robot. 'It takes about seven minutes to reach the table,' said Raf. He tolerated it because it never broke down, just had to be pushed back to the wall every seven minutes. 'I have to switch it off when I go outside,' he said.

Raf felt no obligation to ask about our parents. Not that he disliked them; it was his way of showing that his friendship with me was apart from any other connection between us. He knew I'd tell him anything that he should know. 'You seem happy here still,' I said.

'Happiness is related to the level of expectation,' said Raf, and he pushed back the fridge. 'To be the mayor of Wellington, or the second richest farmer in Southland, is a gnawing futility if you can only be satisfied by being Prime Minister. Our education system should be directed to inculcating as low an expectation as possible in every child, and then most of them could grow up to be happy.' Raf's spur of the moment principle paid no heed to envy, but then he was working from the premise of his own nature. My brother was one of the minority who didn't compare themselves with others. He was self-sufficient in his ideas and ambitions. He enjoyed simple things like being able to produce a meal for me from his property. We went outside, taking some beer with us and I helped Raf to fix the front tube. As we did so he laid out his plans for our lunch. 'If only we'd had rain,' he said, 'then there would have been mushrooms. I've been spreading the spores year by year. Now I get cartons-full at times and take them in to sell. Everything's right for them now except the rain.'

'I'm not all that fussed on them anyway,' I said, just so that he wouldn't feel my level of expectation had been high.

'I've been saving some rabbits, though, down by the pines. And I've got plenty of eggs and vegetables. We could have chook, but fresh game is better.' Raf thought we should cull the rabbits before we had too much beer, and we went off over the stones and brown grass of his seventeen hectares towards the pines. 'You're doing accounting and economics, aren't you,' he said.

'Law. I'm doing law.'

'I found there wasn't much privacy in economics. I should say that law would be much the same: more revenue probably, but no privacy.' Raf stopped, and enjoyed the privacy of his land for a moment. The small terraces and scarps vibrated in the heat. The bird calls were outnumbered by the muted sound of firing from the West Melton butts. 'I've been thinking of going out of sheep into Angora goats,' said Raf. 'I read an article saying they're much more profitable per head, ideal for smaller properties. Three rabbits?' He tagged on about the rabbits after a pause, when we had started to walk towards the pines again. 'Is one and a half rabbits enough for you?'

'Fine.'

'I've been keeping an eye on these. There's nearly a dozen here. I've been looking forward to a special occasion so I could use some.' Raf walked in an arc behind the pines, so that we would come from the broken slope where there was gorse and briar. He shot two rabbits quickly with the twelve-gauge, and then had me walk through the pines and flush another out to make the three.

Raf and I sat on the front step of his house, and he cleaned the rabbits, as I peeled the potatoes. He went over the various ways in which the rabbits could be combined with the other food we had. We ate those rabbits several times over before we had lunch. They were good at last, though, with potatoes, pumpkin, cheese sauce, boiled eggs and beer. Repletion made Raf even more relaxed and thoughtful. 'You get plenty of girls at the university, I suppose,' he asked me. For the first time there was a hint of dissatisfaction in his voice. 'Girls don't seem much interested in privacy. I had a woman out here before Christmas. She did a lot of screenprinting. She seemed to like it here for several weeks, but then she began to mope. She said she found the landscape oppressive. She wasn't a very tall girl, but big where it mattered, mind you.' My brother was at a loss to explain why anyone should prefer the city. 'I have to go into

Christchurch now,' he said. There was a note of grievance. He saw it as a lack of consideration, the screenprinting girl choosing to go back to town.

'Maybe it's the old house,' I said. 'Women have higher expectations there, I suppose.'

'I bought a new bed for us. A brass one, original. It cost me a fat lamb cheque. She hated anything artificial: plastic, vinyl, nylon, veneers, anything like that.' There certainly wasn't much of such material in Raf's house. Almost everything looked pre-war. Even the walls were tongue and groove. 'She was a nice girl in many ways,' Raf said.

In mid-afternoon a visitor came. 'It's McLay,' Raf said. 'He's bought the big place up the road. I forgot all about him. He's come to look at my bore and pump.' McLay was a farmer of self-importance: one of those men who walk in a perfectly normal manner, but whose evident conceit makes them appear to swagger. He parked his European car at an angle which best displayed its lines, and his sense of complacency grew as he came closer to the house.

'Seen better days I'd say,' he said, and he tapped with his shoe at the decayed boards close to the ground along the front of the house. 'I like a place in permanent materials myself,' he said. 'Always have, always will.' Raf was never defensive about his property. He considered it too much of a blessing to need its weaknesses concealed.

'Most of the exterior is shot,' he said frankly. 'We had rabbit for lunch.' McLay was somewhat baffled by that, and suffered a subtle loss of initiative.

McLay would have taken his car to the pump, but Raf said it was easier if we sat in the trailer behind the Norton. McLay found it difficult to maintain his dignity there. He sat very upright, with one hand on the side to limit the bouncing, and with the other he tried to repel Raf's greasy tools, which clattered around us. Raf had one bore sunk into the gravel, and he ran off water to his troughs. When he reached the place he switched off the motorbike, and sat there enjoying the sun. 'Never seems to run dry, this bore,' he said. 'It's with the river being so close, I suppose.' McLay had scrambled from the trailer, and was wiping his wrist on the grass to clean it, after warding off Raf's grease-gun. He felt a need to dissociate himself from Raf's scale of farming.

'I'll need to put in perhaps a dozen of these bores,' he told me. 'I've three hundred and fifty hectares, you see, and I hope to irrigate from them as well.'

'I only need to run it for an hour or so each day,' said Raf. He lifted the rusted kerosene tin that protected the motor.

'Mine will have to be electric, with remote switches. I won't be able to spend all day mucking about with petrol engines,' countered McLay. Raf wound up the starting cord, and pulled with no result. 'Gives a bit of trouble, does it?' said McLay. Raf tried again and again. The only result was one cough, which flicked the starting cord up to give Raf a stinging blow across the face. McLay gave an understanding laugh. 'Pity it's not Briggs and Stratton. They're the only small motor, I always say. I think you've flooded it.' Raf seized the choke, fully extended it, and bent it across the motor. McLay was quiet. Two veins began to swell beneath the skin of my brother's forehead. They made an inverted Y the colour of a bruise. He tried twice more with the cord, attempts of elaborate calmness, then he went to the trailer and brought back the crowbar. He systematically beat the four-stroke motor until the cooling fins had coalesced with the cylinder head, until the various attached parts had broken away. The crowbar made a solid crump, crump sound of impact, and the pipe from the bore rattled in its housing. Some of Raf's sheep stopped grazing to regard him for a while then resumed feeding. McLay had an uneasy smile, and his eyes switched furtively back and forth from Raf to me.

By the time Raf had finished, the veins in his forehead had subsided, and he wiped the sweat away with a sense of achievement. 'Never underestimate the perversity of objects,' he said. 'Never let them get away with it. A switch won't function, a fitting or tool won't work, then before you know — open revolt. Don't give an inch. Did you hear what I said, McLay? Never underestimate the perversity of objects.'

'I'd better be on my way now,' said McLay. There was an increasing air of placating wariness about him, as he realised the full extent of my brother's eccentricity.

'I'm going to use a windmill here,' said Raf. 'I should really have fitted one long ago. We're going to have to get back to wind power a lot more in this country.'

McLay rode back in the trailer without attempting to speak against the noise of the Norton, and when we reached the house he went off with a minimum leave-taking. 'An odd sort of chap. Didn't you think?' Raf said. There was no irony apparent in his voice.

Raf brought out more beer, and we sat again on the front step to drink it. The rural delivery car went past his gate without stopping. 'At Lincoln,' he said, 'the postman was a woman. She used to pedal about in yellow shorts, and her legs were very strong and brown.' He paused, and then said, 'So very brown,' in a wistful way. 'She used to like me making puns about her having more mail than she could deal with. I have to go to Christchurch now.' The inconvenience of it rankled. 'I thought I might have had a letter from the Agriculture Department with information about goats,' he said. 'I intend those to be my two priorities this year: goats and the windmill.'

My brother's prevalent attitude to life was one of convinced cheerfulness, yet the non-arrival of the department's letter concerning the goats, and the poignant recollection of the Lincoln post girl's legs, had brought him as close to depression as I had ever seen him. The drink too, I suppose. We'd had quite a lot to drink. I felt it was a good time to tell him of my present. 'I brought you a present.'

'Thank you.'

'Cabernet sauvignon. It's only New Zealand, but it's a medal winner, and four years old. I remembered you liked it best.'

The secret of Raf's joy in life was his appreciation of all the pleasures, irrespective of scale. He got up from the step in excitement. 'What a day!' he said. I got the bottle from my pack, and we had an uncorking ceremony. Raf put the bottle on the step to breathe and warm. 'We won't have any more beer now until after the wine,' he said. 'We don't want to be unable to appreciate it. Afterwards it doesn't matter.'

'I'll have to go at six or seven. I don't want to have to hitch into Christchurch in the dark.'

'Right. I'd take you in, but I've only got one helmet, and the lights on the bike aren't going.'

Raf seemed to have forgotten his disappointment about the goats and other things. His thin face was alive with speculative enterprise again. 'What to have with the cabernet?' he said. 'We can't drink a good wine with just anything.' The full sophistication of a mind which had achieved honours in economics was given to the problem, and while the world grappled with the exigencies concerning inflation, corruption, guerrilla warfare, spiritual degeneration and environmental pollution, Raf and I sat amidst his seventeen quiet hectares at West Melton, and discussed the entourage for our cabernet. My brother was a great believer in immediate things.

We had peas and baked potatoes, tinned red cabbage and corn. We ate it from plates on our knees, as we sat on the front step. Raf talked to me of his experiences on the continent, and how bad the vin ordinaire was in the south of France. He had some good wine glasses, and we raised them to the evening sun to admire the colour of the wine. Raf invited me to forget university, and join him on his goat and windmill farm. 'Economics is a subject that destroys an appreciation of spiritual things,' said Raf.

'Law. I'm doing law.'

'Same thing,' said Raf. 'Probably worse.' He became so carried away in trying to persuade me of the deadening nature of formal studies, that he absent-mindedly kept the last of the cabernet sauvignon for himself, and so I fell back on beer. 'If you'd seen some of the places I have — Bangkok, Glasgow, Nice — then the value of privacy would be clear to you. Space brings the individual dignity, Tony. Herd animals are always the least attractive. Have you noticed that? I think that's one of the main reasons I want to move from sheep to goats. Goats have individuality, it seems to me.'

'A goat suits a name.'

'That's my point.' Raf sat relaxed on the step, his shingle land spreading away before him.

Just on twilight Raf took me down to the West Melton corner on the Norton. He drove carefully, conscious of the drink we'd had. 'Come out and see me soon,' he said. 'I meant what I said about forgetting economics, and joining me here to live.' I watched him ride off, without lights, and cautious of the power of the motorbike. I could hear it long after he was out of sight, and I imagined my brother riding up his track, over the stones, towards his disreputable house. To resist the maudlin effects of the wine and the beer, I lay down in the long grass, out of sight of the road. I rested my head on my pack, and slept for an hour or so.

So I ended up hitchhiking into the city in the dark after all. I was lucky, though, for after walking a few minutes, I was picked up by a dentist and his daughter. Her name was Susan. We talked about cars, and I tried not to breathe on Susan, lest she think me a typical boozy student. The dentist said he'd been having trouble trying to get the wheels balanced on his Lancia. 'Never underestimate the perversity of objects,' I said. The dentist liked that, and so did Susan. They had an appreciation for a turn of phrase. Raf would have enjoyed its reception. It isn't often that incantations are effective beyond the frontiers of their own kingdom.

Prince Valiant

There's some ugly country in New Zealand, don't let them tell you it's not so. Some of it is the country we are trying to form in our own image, perhaps. The Sinclair property was part of it. Bush had been taken off the slopes years before, and the soil was slumping into the gullies, the outwash spoiling what river flats there'd been. Eight and a half thousand hectares of land in an agony of transition. And Sinclair's place was only one of several just the same.

Sinclair had his priorities right. Money for super, then for his stock, then for his family. The country there just died without topdressing every other year. It was no use asking for anything to be done about the shearers' quarters. Over the four seasons that I could remember, nothing had been improved. The wall above the stove was still blistered bare of paint from the oven fire we had in the first year I went. The bunks had only slats, and palliasses with a smell of mildew and string. Under the bottom bunk by the door was a pile of *National Geographic* magazines with the covers torn off. I could look up from the glossy artificiality of winter in Vermont, or West Irian religious rites, and see the scoured track to the yard. Dog kennels with the beaten ground to the extension of the chains, and a tide mark beyond each of a hundred mutton bones. The bones stuck from the ground like defective teeth. No one ever came from the *National Geographic* to see it all, even when it was summer in Vermont.

I joined the others at Sinclair's. The gang didn't come up to full strength until well into the summer. I spent several months on forestry work at Dargaville, and started shearing again when they moved up country. Cathro still ran things. We had a fresh roustabout, but Neddy was the only new shearer. Neddy was younger than the rest of us: all elbows, knees, and eyes of a level intensity if you bothered to notice. Neddy was a good shearer. Tall, so that he suffered in the back, but flowing in his style and with the ability to calm sheep with his grip. Top-class shearers have that. Others, like Norman and Speel Harrison, transfer their impatience so the sheep will struggle if they can. I've seen Speel brain them with the handpiece when his temper was up.

Neddy wasn't disliked, and his shearing ability was recognised. He was easy and without malice. His laugh and brief replies were at once obliging and dismissive. He never drew close into the group. Perhaps it was his subtle lack of deference, or a companion's realisation, after a time with Neddy, that he considered one person very much like another and placed no great store on any, least of all himself.

Neddy was the one we called Prince Valiant, because of his car. It was a Chrysler Charger. He had it resprayed while they were working at the place before Sinclair's. A metallic green of gloss and iridescence. For some reason he'd never replaced the bumpers, and the brackets stuck out like small antlers at the charge. In scroll work on each side were the words Prince Valiant. The letters were chrome yellow with black edging, and a lance was the underline, piercing the letters.

So he was Prince Valiant, you see. At times there was something of a sneer in its use. The car was thought a pretension by the Harrisons and Sinclair. Neddy didn't seem to mind. He spent a lot of time on his car. He had twin speakers mounted by the back window, and a line of clammy little monsters hanging suspended there. They were green and purple, the colours of cloudy jellies. He had a file box in the front passenger's footwell, and he kept all his country and western tapes there. People like Willie Nelson and Whitey Schaeffer, Efram Nathan and Webb Pierce. Often during breaks, or after lunch,

Neddy would go and sit in his car with the door open. He'd play his tapes, drink beer and gaze over Sinclair's raddled land.

Neddy talked to me only once about the car. I was sorting and oiling some combs, and he was making himself new sack slippers. A few deft tucks, and some stitches with the bag needle. 'I like to drive,' he said. 'I like to drive at night. Close everything up, turn on the music, and drive. At night what's outside could be anywhere. It just falls away behind. The music and me in there driving. It's a whole world.' He looked at me quickly with intent eyes. The laugh he gave disparaged himself, lest my reply should do it. Neddy had been expelled from school. He couldn't get the hang of it, he told me. All the time he was at school, Neddy felt he was getting pushed around and, having no sense of the existence of other people, he couldn't see any reason for being pushed around. Neddy's family hadn't done much by him, I gather. Cathro knew a bit about it. All I ever heard from Neddy was a comment in the shed when the Harrisons used the bale stencil to brand the roustabout's backside. He said his father had used a hot clothes iron on his mother.

Another thing which kept Neddy a bit apart was the intensity of his interest in a girl in Te Tarehi. It had been going on most of the summer, Cathro said. No matter where they were working, every second or third night Neddy went all the way down to Te Tarehi to see his girlfriend. He'd put on his blue slacks and stock boots after tea, and that would be the last of him until the Charger came rumbling back up the track. Norman and Speel complained about being woken up when Neddy came into the quarters late, so several times when Neddy had had more beer than usual, he just switched off the car, and slept right there. I've come out before breakfast and seen him lying asleep, his polished stock boots dangling from his ankles, and his face pressed into the crease at the back of the seat.

Neddy's girlfriend was a source of undeclared envy. Speel and I resented being left with a pile of *National Geographics* without covers, and a monologue from his brother about the Social Credit philosophy. Speel tried to convince himself that Neddy's girlfriend in Te Tarehi wasn't worth it. He said he'd met someone who knew her: that she was flat-chested and the town bike. Neddy would carry on getting ready, waxing his stock boots, or taking his blue slacks from the newspaper underneath his palliasse. 'Bite your arse,' he'd say with a smile. The less Neddy said about his girl in Te Tarehi, the more desirable she became.

We were due to finish the last mob at Sinclair's on a Friday. On Thursday evening Neddy came out again ready for town. The ends of his hair were wet because he'd been cleaning his face. His blue slacks had pewter buttons on the back. In one hand he held three beer bottles by their necks like chickens. He laid them along the bench seat on the passenger's side. Sinclair had come down to catch him. 'You could do a job for me, Prince Valiant,' he said. Sinclair was pleased to demonstrate his familiarity with the joke. 'If you can get your mind off shagging, that is.' Sinclair tried to take some paper from his trouser pocket, but the trousers were too tight, and the pocket opening was pressed flat. 'It's a note for the Wrightson's agent.' Sinclair squirmed and swore. 'You'll need to go to his house. The office will be shut.'

'I won't be going that way'

'There's only one way to Te Tarehi, for God's sake!' Sinclair gave a burst of laughter, drawing the others into laughter too. Neddy made himself comfortable in his car. He switched on a tape. Sinclair had the folded sheet at last from his pocket, and he came confidently towards Neddy's open window.

'Bite your arse,' said Neddy gently, and the Charger moved away. The misshapen creatures jiggled in the back window, the posts of the yards made a pattern of reflections in the green, metallic paint.

'Bastard,' said Sinclair. He went into the quarters to find Cathro and complain. 'Cathro, Cathro,' he called.

The Charger didn't come back during the night. Before we started next morning Cathro rang the two other homesteads in the district, in case Neddy had broken down, but they knew nothing. Then, after ten, Mr Beaven rang back. Neddy's car had been seen in a gully on the Ypres Creek turn-off, and Neddy was dead.

Cathro and I drove up. Mr Beaven and his head shepherd were there. They were waiting for the constable from Te Tarehi. The car had missed the corner and struck the yellow creek bank. From the road there seemed to be no damage. The metallic paint was untouched beneath the fine dust that the dew had set. But when we climbed down we found the Charger had struck with force. Mr Beaven and his man had covered Neddy and the dash with a rug from the back seat. His legs lay in a restful pose partly out of the door. I could see from the soles of his stock boots, how little wear they'd had. The flaccid monsters hanging in the back window jostled each other in the wind.

It was an intrusion to wait alongside the car. We went back up to the road and waited for the police. We leant on Mr Beaven's car and talked. 'He's been driving around here night after night,' said Mr Beaven. 'We keep seeing the lights from the homestead, along Kelly's Cut, the through road, and here as well. At times we've passed him on the road coming up. A green Chrysler without bumpers. He must have been covering a hundred miles or more a night, just cruising round.'

'Listening to his music,' said Cathro. 'Neddy loved to be by himself, listening to his music as he drove. The boys called him Prince Valiant.'

'I saw that on the car,' said Mr Beaven. 'All doo-dahed up all right.' Cathro didn't say anything about Neddy girlfriend in town, the girl that each of us had imagined according to his own expectation, and who had no other life.

Those nights Neddy had left us, he'd fired up on beer and music, driving along the top roads. It didn't say much for our company, but then ugly country breeds ugly people, I suppose. Even so, the death of someone you don't know well can have its acid, for without the protection of emotion there's a clarity in what is bleak and random. As we sat and waited in the morning, I thought of Neddy driving alone, with his dashlights, the monsters, the songs of Whitey Schaeffer and Webb Pierce. And, in the darkness, that poor country slipping by.

Thinking of Bagheera

'You don't much care for pets, I know,' says my neighbour. She smiles bleakly across the patio, and sips my Christmas sherry. She is pleased to be able to categorise me so utterly. It won't do to try to tell her of Bagheera, though what she says brings him back to me.

The cat was not even mine, but had been bought for my younger sisters. They soon excluded him from their affections, however. My sisters preferred those possessions which could be dominated. Compliant dolls who would accept the twisting of their arms and legs, and easily cleaned bright, plastic toys. The cat went away a lot, and had for them a disconcerting smell of life and muscle.

My father named the cat Bagheera. My father had a predilection for literary allusion, to use his own phrase. Not that I heard him use it about himself. He was referring to Mr McIntyre, his deputy. I remember my father talking about Mr McIntyre to Mum; pausing to preface his remarks with a disparaging smile, and saying that Mr McIntyre had a predilection for literary allusion. I caught the tone although I couldn't understand the words. There was blossom on the ground that evening, for as he said it I looked out to the fruit trees, and saw the blossom blowing on the ground. Pink, apricot blossom, some lying amid the gravel of the drive, a fading tint towards the garage.

In the evening Bagheera and I would go for a walk. We agreed on equality in our friendship. We would maintain a general direction, but take our individual digressions. In the jungle of the potato rows or sweet corn I would hide, waiting for him to find me, and rub his round head against my face.

The cat brought trophies to the broad window sill of my bedroom. Thrush wings, fledglings, mice and once a pukeko chick. My father hated the mess. He always drove the cat from the window when he saw it there. Yet often at night, waking briefly, I would look to the window and Bagheera would be there, a darker shape against the sky, his eyes at full stretch in the dusk. I was the only one in the family who could whistle him. It was a loyalty I would sometimes abuse just to impress my friends. Within a minute or two he would appear, springing suddenly from the roof of the sheds, or gliding from beneath the red currant bushes at the bottom of the garden. Beauty is not as common in this world as the claims that are made for it. But Bagheera's black hide flowed like deep water, and his indolent grace masked speed and strength. At times I would put my face right up to him to destroy perspective, and imagine him a full-size panther, see the broad expanse of his velvet nose, and his awesome Colgate smile.

In December Bagheera got sick. For three days he didn't come despite my whistling. We were having an end-of-term pageant at school and I was a wise man from the east, so I didn't have much time to look for him. But the day after we broke up, I heard Bagheera under the house. I talked to him for more than an hour, and he crawled bit by bit towards me, yet not close enough to touch. I hated to see him. He had scabs along his chin, his breathing made a sound like the sucking of a straw at the bottom of a fizz bottle. He wouldn't eat anything and just lapped weakly at the water I brought, before he backed laboriously again into the darkness under the house.

Each time I looked, his eyes would be blazing there, more fiery as his sickness grew, as if they consumed his substance.

My father decided to take Bagheera to the vet. He brought out Grandad's walking stick and said that he'd hook the cat out when I called him within reach. How easily the cat would normally have avoided such a plan. My father pinned Bagheera down, and tried to drag him closer. Bagheera rolled and gasped before he managed to free himself and creep back among the low piles. He knocked an empty tin as he went. It was the tin from the pears I had stolen after being strapped by my father for fishing in my best clothes. When the walking stick failed my father lost interest in the cat.

He had given him his chance and after that he put the matter out of his mind. My father possessed a very disciplined mind. I couldn't forget, though, for Bagheera had become my cat. At night I would look sometimes to the window, but his calm presence was never there, and instead I kept thinking of his eyes in the perpetual darkness beneath the house. Beseeching eyes that waited for me to fulfil the obligation of our friendship.

I asked my father to shoot Bagheera. To put him out of his misery, I said. It was a common enough expression, but my father had no conception of misery in others. I imagine he saw it, in regard to people at least, as the result of incompetence, or lack of drive. But I kept on at him. I said that Bagheera might spread infection to my sisters, or die under the house and cause a smell in the guest rooms. These considerations, which required no empathy, seemed to impress my father. He refused to fire under the house, though, he said. I'd have to coax Bagheera out where he could get a safe shot. He wasn't supposed to shoot at all within the borough limits, he said. At the time I didn't fully realise the irony of needing my father to kill Bagheera. I was the only possible go-between.

My father came out late in the afternoon, and stood with the rifle in the shade of the grapevine trellis, waiting for me to call Bagheera out. I felt the hot sun, unaccustomed on the back of my knees as I lay down. It was about the time that Bagheera and I would often take our walk, and I called him with all the urgency and need that I could gather. Even the pet names I used, even those, with the sensitivity of boyhood and my father standing there, for I would spare nothing in my friendship. Bagheera came gradually, his black fur dingy with the dust of the foundations, and the corruption within himself. I could hear his breathing, the straw sucking and spluttering, I could see his blazing eyes level with my own. To get him to quit the piles, and move into the light, was the hardest thing. I was aware of my father's impatience and adult discomfort with the situation.

'Move away from it,' he said, when Bagheera was at the veranda steps and trembling by the saucer of water. My father raised the .22, with which he never missed. No Poona colonel could have shown a greater sureness of aim. My sisters grouped at the study window to watch, their interest in the cat temporarily renewed by the oddity of his death.

The shot was not loud, a compressed, hissing sound. Bagheera arched into the air, grace and panther for a last time, and sped away across the lawn into the garden. Just for one moment he raced ahead of death, just for one moment left death behind, with a defiance that stopped my breathing with its triumph. 'I wouldn't think anyone heard the shot at all,' said my father with satisfaction. The saucer lay undisturbed, and beside it one gout of purple blood. Don't tell me it wasn't purple, for I see it still, opalescent blood beside the freshly torn white wood the bullet dug in the veranda boards.

I didn't go to find the body among the currant bushes. Instead I went and lay hidden in the old compost heap, with the large, rasping pumpkin leaves to shade me, and the slaters questing back and forth, wondering why they'd been disturbed. My father and mother walked down by the hedge and I heard my father talking of Bagheera and me. 'I find it hard to understand,' he said. 'He seemed determined to have it shot. Sat there for ages cajoling it out to be shot. And after the attachment he seemed to have for it, too. He's a funny lad, Mary. Why couldn't he leave the wretched thing alone?' My father's voice had a tone of mixed indignation and revulsion, as if someone had been sick on the car seat, or one of his employees had broken down and cried. But I remembered Bagheera's release across the lawn, and thought it all worthwhile. He'd done his dash all right.

I lay in the evening warmth, and watched a pumpkin flower only inches from my face. The image of the pumpkin flower was distorted in the flickering light and shade beneath the leaves. The gaping, yellow mouth and slender stamen nodded and rolled like a processional Chinese dragon: the ones they have at weddings, and funerals.

Requiem in a Town House

Mr Thorpe came off sixteen hundred hectares of hill country when he finally retired, and his wife found a town house for them in Papanui. Town house is a euphemism for a free-standing retirement flat, and retirement flat is a euphemism for things best left so disguised.

Mr Thorpe made no complaint to his wife when he first saw the place of his captivity. She had accepted a firmament of natural things for forty years, and he had promised her the choice of their retirement. Yet as the removal men brought those possessions which would fit into the new home, Mr Thorpe stood helplessly by, like an old, gaunt camel in a small enclosure. Merely by moving his head from side to side he could encompass the whole of his domain and, being long-sighted by nature and habit, he found it hard to hold the immediate prospect of their section in focus.

It wasn't that Mr Thorpe had come to the city determined to die. He didn't give up without a struggle. He was a farmer and a war veteran. He went to church on Sundays with his wife, and listened to the vicar explaining the envelope donation system. He joined the bowling club, and learned which side had the bias. But he could not escape a sense of loss and futility even amid the clink of the bowls, and he grew weary of being bullied by the swollen-chested women at afternoon tea time.

Mrs Thorpe developed the habit of sending her husband out to wait for the post. It stopped him from blocking doorways, and filling up the small room of their town house. He would stand at the letter-box, resting his eyes by looking into the distance, and when the postman came he would start to speak. But the postman always said hello and goodbye before Mr Thorpe could get anything out. There might be a letter from their daughter in Levin, a coloured sheet of specials from the supermarket, or something from the *Readers' Digest* which he had been especially selected to receive. It wasn't the same as being able to have a decent talk with the postman though.

The town house imposed indignities on Mr Thorpe: its mean conception was the antithesis of what he had known. To eat his meals he must sit at what appeared to be a formica ironing board with chrome supports. It was called a dining bar. After a meal Mr Thorpe would stand up and walk three paces to the window to see the traffic pass, and three paces back again. He would look at the knives in their wall holders, and wonder at his shrunken world. He had to bathe in a plastic water-hole beneath the shower. His arthritis prevented him from washing his feet while standing, and he had to crouch in the water-hole on his buttocks, with his knees like two more bald heads alongside his own. He thought of the full-length metal and enamel bath on the farm. Sometimes he went even further back, to the broad pools of the Waipounae River in which he swam as a young man. The bunched cutty grass to avoid, the willows reaching over, the shingle beneath. The turn and cast of the water in the small rapids was like the movement of a woman's shoulder, and the smell of mint was there, crushed along the side channels as he walked.

In the town house even the lavatory lacked anything more than visual privacy. It was next to the living room: in such a house everything, in fact, is next to the living room. Mrs Thorpe's bridge friends could hear the paper parting on its perforations, and reluctantly number the deposits. Mrs Thorpe would talk more loudly to provide distraction, and her husband would sit within the resounding hardboard, and twist his face in humiliation at the wall.

The hand-basin was plastic, shaped like half a walnut shell, and too shallow to hold the water he needed. The windows had narrow aluminium frames which warped in his hand when he tried to open them. The front step was called a patio by the agent, and the wall beside it was sprayed with coloured pebbles and glue.

The section provided little comfort for Mr Thorpe. The fences separating his ground from his neighbours' were so vestigial that he found it difficult not to intrude. One evening as he stood in the sun, like a camel whose wounded expression is above it all, he was abused by McAlister next door for being a nosy old fool. Mr Thorpe was enjoying the feel of the sun on his face, and thinking of his farm, when he became aware that he was facing the McAlisters as they sunbathed on a rug. Mrs McAlister had a big stomach, and legs trailing away from it like two pieces of string. 'Muttonheaded old fool,' McAlister said, after swearing at Mr Thorpe over the fence. Mr Thorpe turned away in shame, for he was sensitive concerning privacy. 'Oiy. Go away you nosy old fool,' shouted McAlister.

After that Mr Thorpe unconsciously exaggerated his stoop when he was in his section, to reduce the amount of his body which would appear above the fences, and he would keep his eyes down modestly as he mowed the apron lawn, or tipped his rubbish into the bag.

He tried walking in the street, but it was too busy. The diesel trucks doused him with black fumes, and most of the children used the footpath to ride bikes on. The pedestrian lights beckoned him with Cross Now, then changed to Don't Cross whenever he began.

Mr Thorpe took to sleeping in the garage. In the corner was a heavy couch that had been brought in from the farm, but wouldn't fit in the house. It was opposite the bench on which he'd heaped his tools and pots of dried-up paint. At first he maintained a pretence of occupation between bouts of sleep, by sorting screws, nails, tap washers and hose fittings into margarine pottles. As his despair deepened he would go directly to the couch, and stretch out with his head on the old, embroidered cushion. It was one place in which he didn't have to stoop. He had an army blanket with a stripe, for he had begun to feel the chill which is of years, not weather. There he would lie in the back of the garage; free from the traffic, the McAlisters, and the confines of his own town house. He had always been able to sleep well, and in retirement he slept even better. He was granted the release of sleep.

Mr Thorpe would lie asleep with his mouth open, and his breath would whine and flutter because of the relaxed membranes of his mouth and throat. His face had weathered into a set configuration, but it was younger somehow when he slept. His wife played bridge in the living room with her friends, or watched programmes of glossy intrigue. Mr Thorpe lay in the garage, and revisited all the places from which he had drawn his strength. Age is a conjuror, and it played the trick of turning upside down his memory, so that all he had first known was exact and fresh again, and all the things most recent were husks and faded obscurity. Mr Thorpe talked with his father again, soldiered again, courted again; yet when he was awake he forgot the name of the vicar with whom he shook hands every Sunday, and was perplexed when asked for the number of his own town house. Waking up was the worst of all. Waking from the spaciousness and immediacy of past experience, to the walls of his small bedroom closing in, or the paint pots massing on the garage bench.

'He sleeps all the time, just about,' Mrs Thorpe told the doctor, and Mr Thorpe gave a smile which was part apology for being able to sleep so well. 'He must sleep for sixteen or seventeen hours of the twenty-four sometimes. He sleeps most of the day in the garage.'

'Ah, he's got a hideaway then,' said the doctor. He used a jocular tone, perhaps because he was afraid of the response to any serious enquiry. Let sleeping dogs lie is a sound enough philosophy. 'You need more sleep when you're older,' said the doctor. He'd forgotten that the last time Mrs Thorpe came on her own account, he'd told her that old people don't need as much sleep.

'And he hasn't got the same energy anymore. Not the energy he once had. His interest in things has gone. Hasn't it, Rob?' Mr Thorpe smiled again, and was about to say that he missed the farm life, when his wife and the doctor began to discuss the medication he should have.

He never did take any of the medicine, but after the visit to the doctor he tried briefly to interest himself in being awake, for his wife's sake. He sat in front of the television, but no matter how loud he had it, the words never seemed clear. There was a good deal of reverberation, and laughter from the set seemed to drown out the lines before he caught their meaning. He could never share the contestants' excitement over the origin of the term *deus ex machina*.

A dream began to recur. A dream about the town house in Papanui. In the dream he could feel himself growing larger and larger, until he burst from the garage and could easily stand right over the house, and those of his neighbours. And he would take the town house, all the pressed board, plastic and veneers, and crush it as easily as you crush the light moulded tray when all the peaches have been eaten. Then in his dream he would start walking away from the city towards the farmland. He always liked that best in his dream. He was so tall that with each stride he could feel the slipstream of the air about his head, and the hills came up larger with every step, like a succession of held frames.

He told his wife about the dream. She thought it amusing. She told him that he never could get the farm out of his head, could he. She said he should ask McAlister if he would like to go fishing.

In the dream Mr Thorpe never reached the hills; he never actually reached where he was walking to so forcefully. But he seemed to be coming closer time by time. As he drew nearer, he thought it was the country that he knew. The hills looked like the upper Waipounae, and he thought that he would soon be able to hear the cry of the stilts, or the sound of the stones in the river during the thaw, or the flat, self-sufficient whistle made by the southerly across the bluffs at the top of the valley.

The Late Call

The city glinted behind the harbour, and high above the level of the water. The harbour woolstores were low, and beyond them the men walking back along the wharves could have seen the street lights, and the neons green and red, and the cars in lines towards the city. But the men going back to work in the evening didn't turn to look; the car horns far-off and shouts of young people were not important to them. The noise and the lights from the city only made the wharves seem darker, and were distanced by the blackness of the sea; diminished by blue stars in the winter sky.

There was only one ship working a late call, and in ones and twos the men came from the bridge over the railway or the carpark, towards it. They had their hands in their pockets, and their shoulders were hunched against the still air. As they went out along the wharf there was water not rock fill beneath the heavy timbers, and the footsteps were louder and began to echo.

Colin came from the walk-bridge by himself. He wore a tartan jacket zipped to the throat, and a woollen cap. Like the others he had his chin down against the cold, his hands in his pockets. He had his hook over his shoulder, and the wooden handle lay on his chest. He walked steadily, his steps beginning to echo as he went further out. He walked as if he would have been content to keep right on walking, past the meat boat with the late call and on towards the sea and the small, blue stars of the winter sky. He may have done it, may just have done it, but he was overtaken.

'There's no friggin' rush,' Paul said. 'The work will always be there.'

'Hi,' said Colin.

'One thing. It can't be any bloody colder in the wagon or the hold than it is outside.'

'You're right.' They walked closer to the boat. The strung loading lights didn't have the suffusing glow of a summer night, but were crimped, white icicles. 'At least you had a hot meal. Living close enough,' said Colin.

'Shit,' said Paul. He gave the laugh hard cases give against themselves when they know they've done it again. 'Never went home, did I?' he said. 'Stayed and boozed at the Cook. I forgot to ring home even. Jesus Christ.'

'Yeah,' said Colin. 'Well.'

The union men were the aristocracy of the shift; anyone else was just a seagull, no matter how regular. The wharfies kept jobs like tally-clerk and winchman to themselves. As of right they took the break before the end of a shift, so they could leave early. Mac looked at Colin. 'You, shithead,' he said. 'You and your mate into the bloody wagon.' Colin looked past the cold loading lights and said nothing. He climbed into the wagon and put his gloves on. Paul and he arranged the chute in the middle of the wagon which was already cleared. 'Start those bastards coming,' said Mac from below. Colin and Paul began taking carcasses and slipping them down the chute to the all-weather loader. They worked on opposite sides, each gradually retreating into his end of the wagon. The carcasses were hard and hollow; the belly flaps like plywood to Colin's gloved hands. Each carcass was half-thrown, half-guided onto the chute, where it glissaded down to the loader. Paul wasn't able to keep to a rhythm of delivery with Colin.

'Jesus Christ,' said Paul. He swayed a bit as if the wagon were in motion on the rails. 'I'm sorry but I'm pissed a bit you see. I'm pissed a bit on an empty stomach. I only had a few lousy chips.'

'Hey, you useless shitheads!' cried Mac. 'What do you think you're at in there? Send them down evenly. You just about smashed my hand between them. These shitheads. These seagulls.'

'It's this bloody chute, Mac,' said Paul. He winked at Colin and mouthed an obscenity from the depth of the wagon. He tried to concentrate on his work.

A rhythm of work was an advantage in the wagon. It kept up body heat. Colin breathed shallowly so that the air didn't reach deep into his lungs. Each breath was white for a moment before his face. On the wagon walls frost dewlaps had built up like fungus lying in undulating lines which were revealed as the layers of meat were removed. Delicate, pure frost forms, and sometimes as Colin bent to take the hard flesh of a lamb he saw the finest points of light, winter stars in the ice palaces along the wagon walls.

'Okay, shithead,' said Mac. 'Have a turn on the loader. Jesus, I've seen bloody women toss better meat than you two,' He came into the wagon, and coughed and spat onto the wagon wall.

'Some of those women would be used to handling meat though,' said Paul. It put Mac in a good humour.

'Right,' he said. 'You're right, shagger,' and laughed and spat again.

Feeding carcasses into the escalating loader was the easiest stint of all; not enough to keep Colin warm. He was glad of the distraction when he had to help Mac set up another chute in the wagon, to reach into the ends. They needed three men in the wagon then; the third at the junction of the chutes, turning the carcasses for the slide to the loader. Colin was the turner for Mac and his mate. The lambs seemed weightless in Mac's hands. He wasn't big, but he knew the balance point of things by practice, and the carcasses rose and flipped and turned and slid with grace and of their own volition, quite detached from Mac, who spat and swore and talked. And he slipped a lamb to a hand which appeared in the briefly open door on the other side of the wagon; a side hidden in deep shadow and desolate before the sea. No one made any comment. 'Shitheads,' said Mac loudly, and in a non-specific way, to emphasise his authority. Colin smiled down at Paul by the loader. Paul seemed to be brimming over with the beer he'd drunk instead of going home. His lips gleamed wetly, moisture shone in his eyes and seeped around his nose. 'Any of you shitheads see something funny?' said Mac.

'Not really,' said Colin.

'Not really my arse. Not really my bloody arse. You shitheads.'

As he worked in the doorway Colin could see the loading lights reflected on the rails set in the wharf, and the breathing movement of the ship's side. He heard without interest the noise of people and cars a long way off. A light winked at the end of the breakwater, and the small, night-frosted stars shone steadily back. From somewhere at the stern of the ship water ran constantly into the sea. The loader was new and quiet; its metal sides trembled and the white carcasses rose up to the deck out of sight.

Three ship girls came past during Colin's break. They had warm coats, but short skirts. Mac stopped work to watch them. 'Some lucky bastard rides tonight,' he said. He called to them. 'Hey girls, you don't have to go any further than here! Come on over here!'

'Right. Yes, Jesus,' said Paul, He wiped his wet mouth. One girl stood boldly for a moment, enjoying the attention. She parted her coat and put her hands on her hips.

'It takes hard cash,' she said.

'Hard. I'll give you hard. Jesus,' said Mac. Old Chevy Williams began chattering his broken teeth as he laughed, and Paul's moist eyes enlarged. 'Anything girl, anything,' said Mac.

'No,' she said. 'I know you wharfies. Your hands are too bloody cold.' She laughed and followed her friends.

'What do you think, shithead?' said Mac to Colin.

'It wasn't a cold hand I had in mind.'

'Too true. Not cold at all by Jesus, hah.' Mac was reluctant to let the subject go. Old Chevy had started work again. His teeth no longer chattered.

'A piece of arse,' he said nostalgically. 'I liked a piece of arse.' The others began barracking his impotence.

To shunt off an empty wagon and replace it with a full one was an undertaking which taxed the resources of the railway system. The railway men said little in response to the cheerful abuse of the shift: mostly they looked away as they rode the brake levers of the wagons. During the delay Colin sat on a bollard at the edge of the lights, and smoked a cigarillo. Chevy came and scrounged one, as was a wharfie's prerogative. Hands in pockets, and jacket collars up as a protection from the cold air drifting in from the sea, they smoked. Old Chevy held his cigarillo in the centre of his lips like a chimpanzee, and coughed companionably from the side of his mouth. Colin raised his heels, and jiggled his legs. He could hear the seawater slopping amongst the piles: the heavy ropes to the ship alternately lifted and slackened as dark lines against the sky. 'Can't be more than an hour to knocking off,' said Chevy. The cigarillo waggled in his mouth.

'How long have you been working on the wharves, Chevy?' Old Chevy worked his chin up and down on the question.

'We used to put them aboard a sling-load at a time. You needed skills to work here at one time.' He walked quietly away to forestall any further questions. He coughed a bit to lessen the abruptness of his departure.

'Hey, shitheads. Stop pulling yourselves and let's get these bastards loaded,' said Mac. The new wagon was ready. He pointed to Colin. 'You and your mate for the bloody wagon again, and keep it even flow this time.' The opened wagon revealed a wall of frozen lamb in muslin shrouds. Getting the first few dozen out to clear a platform was the worst job. Paul fumbled with the top row, and a carcass slid past his arms and struck him on the side of the head as it fell. The other men laughed and swore.

'Jesus,' said Paul. There was blood on his ear. A graze hurts in the cold.

'Useless bastard,' said Mac. With a neat movement he trapped the bouncing carcass under one boot. 'Have you been on the piss, you useless bastard?'

'Hardly any for Christ's sake,' said Paul. 'It's the way it's stacked here. It's all to hell at the top here Mac, honest.'

'Yeah,' said Mac. 'So you say.'

It was better once space had been cleared for a trestle. Paul tried to keep a regular flow down the chute, alternating with Colin. With alcoholic seriousness he copied Colin's rhythm. The bright blood was like a stud on his ear lobe.

Colin didn't mind loading meat. The repetition became timeless, and closed him off from what was happening to other people. Each lamb was as the last; each row diminishing then seemingly complete again. The sound of the carcasses on the chute, his boots on the wagon floor, his breath in the frozen air. The intricate frost patterns as he bent into the wagon; and when he turned again a glimpse of the loading lights streaked against the sky.

The break before the end of shift was taken as of right by Mac and his mate. Old Chevy was the only wharfie left to finish with the seagulls. As he went, Mac called to Colin: 'Close up the wagon, shithead, when it's finished. Then you're done. Don't let your pissed mate go playing silly buggers either.' The four who were left cleaned the wagon out well before nine. Chevy watched the doors being closed and the chutes stacked. He called up something to those on deck, and then coughed as a farewell before disappearing into the darkness. Colin and Paul walked to the buildings at the entry to the wharf, and turned off and climbed the walk-bridge over the railway line. Colin put his wet leather gloves in the top pocket of his jacket. The cold air from the sea moved quietly into the city beside them; drawn from the darkened fusion of ocean and sky across the harbour and up into the lights, the streets, and the people.

'There's work for several days,' said Paul. 'You're all right. Mac likes you, but I probably won't get back on come Monday because I got pissed.'

'They'll want ten or twelve gangs on Monday for those overseas ships,' said Colin.

'But there'll be four times that number wanting work. And I didn't go home at tea.' Paul twisted his face up at the thought of the consequences. 'Jesus, I'm going to cop it there.' Colin had nothing to say. Paul laughed the laugh he used when he had decided again to do the thing he'd regret. 'Let's go to the Cook before closing,' he said. 'Jesus, might as well now. Have a bloody feed and warm up and that. Sink a few and warm up.'

'I've got to get back,' said Colin. They walked one more block, coming into the shops at the north end of the city.

'See you Monday then,' said Paul, 'Jesus it's cold.' He turned in towards the noise and lights: unmistakably a working man amongst the people dressed for the Friday. His boots gave him a rocking motion as he walked. He was thinking of the Cook. Already he had forgotten Colin, as he had forgotten his wife. Experience had taught him to put the past and the future out of his mind.

Colin cut across the inner city. People jostled and giggled; the cars flowed past, motorbikes accelerated amongst them. The windows shone out, giving an illusion of warmth. There was a sense of expectancy which he couldn't share. Like a late arrival at a party he felt distanced from the mood. He took with him through the streets the impersonality of the harbour; the habits of an environment with no obvious seduction; the memory of the frost and carcasses, men who were not friends, and of the blue, needle points of the stars in a winter sky.

Kenneth's Friend

At the north side, towards the point, the shore was rocky. When the tide was going out I liked to search the ponds for butterfish and flat crabs like cardboard cut-outs, sea snails with plates instead of heads, and flowing anemones in pink and mauve. Once Kenneth let a rock fall on my hand there on purpose, after I told him I didn't want to spend the morning making papier-mâché figures. He said it was an accident, of course, but I knew he meant it. The rock had a hundred edges of old accretions, and cut like glass. I sat and waited for the sun to stop the cuts bleeding. I thought about Kenneth and me, and how I came to be there at all.

I had good friends when I lived in Palmerston North, friends that experience had shown the value of, but when we shifted to Blenheim I didn't have time to make friends before the holidays. I liked Robby Macdonald best. He and I became close later, but Kenneth seemed to attach himself to me in those first weeks. Perhaps he felt it gave him at least a temporary distinction to be seen with the new boy. He came home with me often after school, and lent me *Crimson Comet* magazines. At Christmas-time he invited me to go with his family to their holiday home in Queen Charlotte Sound. His father was a lawyer and mayor of the town. My mother was pleased I'd been invited, and for sixteen days too. She gave me a crash course on table manners and guest etiquette. I had a ten-shilling note in an envelope, so that I could buy something for Kenneth's parents before I left.

The house had a full veranda along the front, facing out towards the bay. We used to have meals there and, standing out like violin music from among the talk of the Kinlethlys and their guests, I could hear the native birds in the bush, and the waves on the beach. It was a millionaire's setting in any country but ours, though Mr Kinlethly was a lawyer and mayor of the town admittedly. Glow-worms too: there were glow-worms under the cool bank of the stream. At night I crept out to see them, hanging my head over the bank, and with my arms in the creek to hold me up. The earth in the bush was soft and fibrous: I could plunge my hands into it without stubbing the fingers. The sand of the small bay was cream where it was dry, and yellow closer to the water. There was no driftwood, but sometimes after rough weather there would be corpses of bull kelp covered with flies, and filigree patterns of more fragile seaweed pressed in the sand.

What Kenneth wanted, I found out, wasn't a friend, but someone to boss about. A sort of young brother, without the inconvenience of his sharing any parental affection. With no natural authority at school, Kenneth made the most of his position at the bay. Each night before we went to bed, Kenneth enjoyed the privilege of choosing his bunk and so underlined his superiority. He might bounce on the top bunk for a while, then say that he'd chosen the bottom one; he might wait until I'd put my pyjamas on one of them, then he'd toss my pyjamas off and say he'd decided to sleep there himself. He liked to play cards and Monopoly for hours on end, or work on his shell collection. Whenever we had a disagreement as to what we should do, Kenneth would say that I could go home if I didn't like it. I think in a way that's what Kenneth wanted — for me to say that I wanted to go home, that I couldn't stick it out. He didn't understand how much the bay offered me, despite its ownership. Kenneth's parents didn't know we disliked each other. We carried on our unequal struggle within the framework of their expectations. We slept together, and set off in the mornings to play together. We didn't kick each other at the table, or sulk to disclose our feud. His parents were always there, however, as a final recourse: the reason I had to come to heel and follow him back to the house when he saw fit, or help him catalogue his shells in the evening instead of watching the glow-worms.

The Kinlethlys seemed to take their bay for granted, corrupted by the ease and completeness of their ownership. Mr Kinlethly was away more days than he was there, and at night he shared the family enthusiasm for cards. I never saw him walk into the bush, and he went fishing only once or twice as a sort of tokenism. There was no doubt he was pleased with the place, though. He liked visitors so that they could praise it, and I heard him telling Mrs Kinlethly that the property had appreciated seven hundred percent since he purchased it. Mrs Kinlethly had some reservations, I think. She wouldn't allow any uncleaned fish near the house. She said the smell lingered. We would gut them at the shore, washing the soft flaps of their bellies in the salt water, and tossing their entrails to the gulls. Mrs Kinlethly gave us what she called the filleting board, and we would scale and dismember the blue cod and tarakihi in the ocean they came from: the filleting board between Kenneth and me, our feet stretching into the ripples. Mrs Kinlethly seemed sensitive to the smell of fish. When the wind was strong from the sea, blowing directly up to the house, she said it smelled of fish. It didn't really. It carried the smell of kelp, sand-hoppers, mussels, jetty timber, island farms, distant horizons, and fish.

One wall of Kenneth's room was covered with the display case for his shells, and our bunks were on the opposite side. I thought the collection interesting at first: the variety of colours and shapes, the neatly typed documentation. Each entry seemed to have one sentence beginning 'This specimen . . .'. Mr Kinlethly wrote them out, and Kenneth proudly typed them on the special stickers, which I got to lick. 'This specimen a particularly fine example from the northern coast of Sabah'. 'This specimen a gift from Colonel

L. S. Gilchrist following a visit to our bay' or 'This specimen one of the few examples with mantle intact'. The collection seemed to admirably satisfy the two Kinlethly requirements concerning possessions — display and investment.

My dislike of the shells began when I had sunstroke. Kenneth and I had been collecting limpets on the rocks, and I forgot to wear a hat. The sun on the back of my neck all morning was too much for me. I lay on the bottom bunk, and tried not to think of the bowl Mrs Kinlethly had placed on a towel by the bed. The family considered it rather inconsiderate of me to get sick. After all, I was there to keep Kenneth amused, not to add to Mrs Kinlethly's workload. I lay there trying not to be a bother, and hearing Kenneth's laugh from the veranda. In the late afternoon Mr Kinlethly brought a guest back from Picton, and they came in to see the shells. 'A friend of Kenneth's,' said Mr Kinlethly as my introduction. I was bereft of any more individual name at the bay. It was always 'Kenneth's friend'. 'I think he's been off colour today,' said Mr Kinlethly. 'Now here's one in particular, the *Cypraea argus*.'

'Oh yes.'

'And *Oliva cryptospira*.'

'Strikingly formed, isn't it?'

'*Cassis cornuta*.'

I wanted to be sick. The nerves in my stomach trampolined, and saliva flooded my mouth. The mixing bowl on the towel seemed to blossom before me. Mr Kinlethly was in no hurry. 'Most in this other section were collected locally,' he said. 'Kenneth is a very assiduous collector, and also people around the Sounds have become aware of our interest. A surprising number of shells come as gifts.' Despite myself I looked over at the shells. Many of them seemed to have the sheen of new bone; like that revealed when you turn the flesh away from the shoulder or knuckle of a newly killed sheep. I had to discipline myself, so that I wasn't sick until Mr Kinlethly and his visitor had left the room. The shells were always different for me after that.

The Kinlethlys had a clinker-built dinghy. It had a little bilge water in it that smelled of scales and bait. They had their own boatshed for it even, just like a garage, with folding doors so that the dinghy could be pulled in, and a hand-winch at the back of the shed to do it with. The dinghy was never put in the shed while I was there. Kenneth said they left it out all summer. We used to pull it up the sand a way, and then take out the anchor and push one of the flukes in the ground in case of a storm or freak tide. Using the dinghy was probably the best thing of all. When we went fishing I could forget the boring times, like playing Monopoly, and helping Kenneth with his shells. I could look down the woven cord of the hand line, seeing how the refraction made it veer off into the green depths, and I could listen to the water slapping against the sides of the dinghy. Closer to shore the sea was so clear that I could see orange starfish on the bottom, and the sculptured sand-dunes there, the sweeping outlines formed by the currents and not the wind. Flounder hid there, so successfully that they didn't exist until they moved, and vanished again when they stopped, as some magician's trick.

Wonderful things happened at the bay, even though I was only Kenneth's friend. Like the time we were out in the dinghy and it began to rain. The water was calm, but the cloud pressed lower and lower, squeezing out what air remained between it and the sea, and then the rain began. I'd never been at sea in rain before. The cloud dipped down into the sea, and the water lay smooth and malleable beneath the impact of the drops. The surface dimpled in the rain, and the darkest and closest of the clouds towed shadows which undulated like stingrays across the swell. 'I never think of it raining on the sea,' I said to Kenneth. 'Imagine it raining on whole oceans, and there's no one there.'

'Bound to happen,' said Kenneth. He couldn't see why I was in no hurry to get back.

'I always think of it raining on trees, animals, the roofs of cars,' I said weakly. I couldn't share with Kenneth the wonder that I felt.

Kenneth had no respect for confidences. That evening at tea, when Mrs Kinlethly told the others how wet he and I had got in the dinghy, Kenneth said that I'd wanted to stay out and see the rain. 'He didn't know that rain fell on the sea as well as on the land,' said Kenneth. That wasn't the whole truth of it, but it was no use saying anything. I just blushed, and Mrs Kinlethly laughed. Kenneth's father said, 'Sounds as if we have a real landlubber in our midst', in a tone which implied he wasn't a landlubber. I learnt not to talk to Kenneth about anything that mattered.

On the Thursday of the second week there were dolphins again at the entrance of the bay. I admired dolphins more than anything else. They seemed set on a wheel, the highest point of which just let them break the surface before curving down into the depths. I imagined they did a complete cartwheel down there in the green water, then came sliding up again, like a sideshow. 'There's dolphins out at the point,' said Mr Kinlethly. Mr and Mrs Thomson and their two unmarried daughters were with us on Thursday.

'I've never seen dolphins,' said Mrs Thomson.

'Quite a school of them,' said Mr Kinlethly. He decided that his guests must make an expedition in the dinghy to see the dolphins. Mrs Kinlethly wouldn't go, but the Thomsons settled the dinghy well down in the water and there wasn't room for both Kenneth and me.

'There's not room for both the boys,' said Mrs Kinlethly. Kenneth didn't care about the dolphins, but he wasn't going to let me go. He called out that he wanted to go, and his father hauled him aboard.

'Kenneth's friend can come another time,' said Mrs Thomson vacuously, and the dinghy pulled away clumsily. I waded out a bit, and kicked around in the water to show I didn't care, but I could see Kenneth with his head partly down watching me, waiting to catch my eye, and with the knowing little grin he had when he knew I was hurt. The dinghy angled away towards deeper water, the bow sweeping this way then that, with the uneven rowing of Mr Kinlethly and Mr Thomson.

'Dolphins, here we come,' I heard Kenneth shouting in his high voice.

That finished it for me, not missing out on the dolphins, but Kenneth going merely because he knew I wanted to. I'd taken a good deal because, after all, I was just a friend of Kenneth's invited for part of the holidays, but I was beginning to think myself pretty spineless. I thought of my Palmerston friends, and the short work they'd have made of Kenneth. I left Mrs Kinlethly watching the dinghy leave the shelter of the bay to reach the dolphins at the point. I went up to the house, across the wide, wooden veranda and into Kenneth's room. From the bottom bunk I took a pillowcase, and began to fill it with shells from Kenneth's collection. I tried to remember the ones he and his father liked best, the ones most often shown to visitors: *Pecten maximus*, *Bursa bubo*, and *Cassis cornuta*, the yellow helmet. The heavy specimens I threw into the bag, and heard them crunch into the shells already there. Once I was committed to it, the enormity of the crime gave it greater significance and release. Whatever outrage the Kinlethlys might feel, whatever recompense they might insist on, Kenneth would understand: he'd know why it was done, and what it represented in terms of him and me.

I took the shells up the track into the bush, and I sat above the glow-worm creek and threw the shells into the creekbed, and into the bush around it. Most disappeared without sound, swallowed up in the leaves and tobacco soil. The yellow helmet stuck in the cleft of a tree, and as I sat guiltily in the coolness and heard the ocean in the bay, it didn't seem incongruous to me, that *Cassis cornuta* set like a jewel in the branches. The bush was a good imitation of an ocean floor, or so I could imagine it anyway.

A sense of drabness followed the excitement of rebellion. I came down to the house, and replaced the pillowcase. Without a plan I began to return to the beach, scuffling in the stones and listening to the sound of the sea. Mrs Kinlethly came up the path towards me. I thought she must have found out about the shells already, and her response was more than anything I'd expected. She walked with her hands crossed on her chest, as if keeping something there from escaping, and her tongue hung half out of her mouth. It was an obscenity worse than if she'd opened her dress as she came. I tried not to look at her face, and I felt the muscles of my arms and shoulders tighten, like at school just before I was strapped. Mrs Kinlethly passed so close to me that I heard the leather of her sandals squeaking, but she didn't stop or say anything. She went up the steps, and the house swallowed her up in complete silence. I couldn't work out what was happening. I sat down there by the path and waited. I looked out towards the bay and the drifting gulls, letting the wind bring the associations of the sea up to me.

Mr Kinlethly came up next, without his trousers and with everything else wet. Instead of his hair being combed across his head as usual, it hung down one side like ice-plant, and the true extent of his baldness was revealed. 'The dinghy went over. Kenneth's gone,' he shouted at me forcefully and looked about for others to tell. He seemed amazed that there was just me by the path in the sun, and the birds calling in the bush behind the house. His eyes searched for the crowds that should have been there to receive such news. When I made no reply, he turned away despairingly. 'Kenneth's gone. I must get to the phone,' he shouted at the monkey-puzzle tree by the veranda, and he strode into the house. His coloured shirt stuck to his back, and on the ankle of one white leg were parallel cuts from the rocks.

The house filled rapidly after Mr Kinlethly made his phone calls, until there were enough people even for him: relatives from both sides of the family, friends, and folk from the next bay. Two policemen from Picton came, quiet men who kept out of the house and began the search for Kenneth. I rang my father when I could, and asked him to pick me up at the turn-off by four o'clock. My mother had made it very clear to me about thanking the Kinlethlys before I left, but the way it was I couldn't bring myself to say anything. I just packed my things, and walked up to the road to wait for my father. I was up there by mid-afternoon, and I climbed up the bank above the road and sat there waiting. I hadn't had anything to eat since breakfast. I could see right over the bay, and although the house was hidden by the foreshortened slope and the bush, I could see the boatshed like a garage at the edge of the sand. Where the dinghy had capsized at the point, the chop was visible, occasional small, white crests in the wind.

The Divided World

The world is divided between you and me, you and me babee, you and me. The world is divided between those who laugh on the inward, and those on the outward breath; between those who say at this point in time, and those who say that it does appear to be the case.

The world is divided between the superstitious, and the unimaginative; between those who love men, and those who love women; between those who have witnessed Bjorn Borg's top-spin, and those who have lost the chance; between the exemplary, and the few of us who are left.

The world is divided into those who appreciate Jane Austen, and fools. The world is divided between the apathy of ignorant youth, and the despair of incorrigible old age. The world is divided between those who blame Lucifer, and those who blame a lack of dietary fibre; between mediocrity and its own evolution; between the over-worked, and the unemployed; between those who have a daughter, and those denied the greatest blessings.

The world is divided between those who say they adore the country and never go there, and those who say they hate the city and never leave it. The world is divided in the beginning, on all sides, and before God. The world is divided between those we betray, and those who betray us; between those who wake in the darkness with tears, and those too drugged to dream; between those who will not stand a dripping tap, and those who are moderate men. The world is divided among those who deserve it, but not often and not enough.

The world is divided between those who realise their own value, and those who think they may still amount to something; between those who prefer quiz shows, and those who still await their frontal lobotomy; between the old which has lost its edge, and the new which has not been tested; between indecision and hypocrisy, between feeble vacillation and energetic error; between cup and lip. The world is divided between those who understood the significance of Randolph Scott, and the new generation.

The world is divided between those who know nothing smoother than satin, and those who know a woman's thigh. The world is divided between the meek who will inherit the earth, and the strong who will dispossess them of it; between those who believe that they are essentially alone, and those who will be convinced with time; between Sadducees and Pharisees, Hannibal and Hasdrubal, Shaka and Dingane, Dracula and the Wolfman.

The world is divided between those who make a profession of software and prosper, and those who say they recall garlands, mole-catchers and stone walls. The world is divided between silver spoons, and macrocarpa childhoods; between the appalling and the appalled; between consenting adults; between the devil, and the deep big C; between honest toiling forwards, and flashy temperamental backs; between those who help others, and those prepared to let nature take their course.

The world is divided between those who have owned a Triumph 2000, and philistines; between those who have had sex, and those prepared to give it another try; between those who remember the old school haka, and those who attend no reunions even in the mind. The world is divided between those who have a favourite corduroy coat, and those with no affection for habit. The world is divided between those who maintain the distinction between further and farther, and those who compromise with usage; between those who have attended universities, and those who have been inwardly disappointed in other ways; between animals who know only joy and pain, and we who can visualise our own deaths. The world is divided between those who can roll their tongues, and those with more archaic genes. The world is divided between those who should know better.

The world is divided between the Greeks and their gods, and the Trojans who would otherwise have won; between the Green Mountain Boys, and the Black Mountain Boys; between those who gargle in a stranger's bathroom, and those with acquired delicacy; between the undiscerning undistinguished undeserving mass, and us. The world is divided into the states of Jeopardy and Paranoia, Halidom and Dugong, Condominium and the Tribal Lands, all of these, none of these. The world is divided between those who try themselves, and those who seek a less corrupt judge.

The world is divided between those who are tolerant and wise, and their husbands. The world is divided between those in authority, and those resentful of it; between those who are white, and those whose virtues are not so immediately apparent; between those who face the world with a religion, and those who wish to but have only irony in its place. The world is divided between those who have shifted to the North Island, and those passed over for promotion; between one thing and another if distinctions should be made; between tolerant contempt of the artist, and awe of the Cactus and Succulent Society's president. The world is divided between a lawyer and his client, but not equally or *per se*.

The world is divided between those people whose character is known, and those from whom something may still be expected. The world is divided between rancour and disgust, idolatry and idiocy, ballet and bidet, Sordello and Bordello, Bishop Blougram's and Prufrock's apologies. The world is divided between the first and the last; between a man and a woman; between sun and moon; stoics and epicureans; scholards and dullards; the fragrance of mint in the riverbeds and desolate clay. The world is divided between Lucky Jims, and those who see no humour in it; between professed intentions, and the things we would wish undone; between nostalgic falsehood, and anticipatory regret; between dreams of avarice, and visions of self-esteem.

The world is divided between the vices of free will, and the virtues of necessity; between those who know where be Wold Jar the tinker, and those cast into darkness; between those who delight in games, and those who lack even that saving grace; between Tyrannosaurus Rex, and civilised marriages; between New Zealanders, and those people with a culture; between our adult selves, and the blue remembered hills.

The world is divided between those who boast of their climate, and those who rejoice in secret that a cold wind isolates a landscape. The world is divided between those who accept the division, and those who instigated it; between books on the Royal Family or gardens, and the remaining ten percent of publishers' products; between those who are proud, and those who have lost their self-respect and so become the most dangerous of men. The world is divided on the merits of everything; on all questions raised (at this point in time). The world is divided between optimism and Mr Weston's good wine; between those who see, and those who understand between confiding voluble people, and those we wish to know; between those on the inside looking out, and those on the outside looking in.

The world is divided between men who despise others for being what they are, and women who despise them for what they are not. The world is divided between those anxious concerning the physical, and those in terror of the mind; between those who love sausages and onions, and those who are effete; between the people we always suspected, and the butlers who did it; between idlers, and those who work hard all their lives to be able to do nothing when they die.

The world is divided between the few now, and the great majority on the other side. The world is divided above all, while we sleep, beneath our noses, and before we notice. The world is divided as we are all divided. The world is divided between you and me, you and me for a time, you and me.

The Seed Merchant

Father very worse, the telegram read. I had it folded in my pocket during the flight south. The wording itched in my mind, and the irritation diverted my worry. I imagined my mother being told that both very and much were an unnecessary expense, and agreeing without caring to cut one out. I was mowing the lawn when it came. I caught a flight so soon afterwards that in the hair of my wrist were fine pieces of cut grass, held out from the skin. At such times the senses are capable of meticulous observation. Birdy Watson was thirteen when he tried to climb the cenotaph, fell off and killed himself. As the taxi passed I saw, far above the stone figures, the ledge that Birdy reached, and the concrete steps below that broke him on his fall. Even his nickname had not saved him. The town had grown rapidly, the driver told me, though it held no progeny of Birdy's or of mine.

My father had rallied by the time I reached him. You will recognise the terminology. He had rallied surprisingly well, the doctor said. So my father was able to return home and wait a little longer. He lay in his own bed, and as I talked first in the hall with my mother and sister, I could hear him clearing his throat as he waited to welcome me. A questing smile as he tried to see in my face a picture of himself before I could disguise it. He clasped my hand rather than shook it, and looked away, asked about Susan and the children as a defence against his own predicament. The rowan trees by the fence were in berry amidst the fingered leaves, and I could see the hardwood chopping block where roosters had been sacrificed. All of us had lived together in the place, yet each had a separate experience of it: in the same way we share life, I suppose.

'Lately I've often thought of things to say to you,' my father said. 'No one argues about books anymore. No one cares. It's all politics and entertainment now, you see.'

'Reading and writing are too slow for them,' I said.

My father nodded against the pillow. 'Even in sport,' he said. 'Even in sport all they're interested in is finishes, and the money.'

I sat in the cane chair by the window and talked with my father. I hadn't been there long before he mentioned Ivy. He asked if I remembered her, and said what a close friend of my mother's she'd been. He turned his head and looked at the window with flat eyes, the symptom of the inverted vision of memory. The skin lay loosely on the tendons of his neck, and stubble was salt and pepper beneath his jaw-line. After a time he said, 'You remember Ivy.' He took my silence as forgetfulness. 'You stayed with her at times as a boy. You mustn't forget Ivy. People used to take her and your mother as sisters. Did you know that?'

Ivy must have been thirty odd when I stayed with her. She laughed a lot. There was always reason for a laugh at things, even though she did have her mother to look after. The trams came right past their house. Over thirty years ago. The noise and smell of the trams on the street straight through to the square. Ivy and her mother made painted eggs of wood. Ivy was a nurse as well at a private hospital, but I remember them sitting with trays of eggs. The old woman sanded the eggs wet and dry. She had a slight moustache. Ivy painted them: several coats and then designs and varnish. Patterns like Fair Isle, or hooped colours, or little circles like the seeds of silver birch. I don't know what they were for: darning, or paperweights, or to be valued for their own sake perhaps, on a mantelpiece in deep blue and gold.

'She came sometimes to stay with us. A great friend of your

mother's.' And of my father. 'You remember staying there now?' he said. Yes, I remembered things that had a new interpretation with the years. Like the seed merchant. Some friend was with Ivy. They laughed in the bedroom as Ivy finished dressing to go out, and the trams rattled past to the square. I was to remain behind with the old lady, and fill the coal scuttle from time to time. Ivy called to me from her room. The two of them were laughing again. How they were laughing, and there was powder smudged on the dark polish of the duchess, and underclothes on the bed like the limp, pink petals of a rose. Ivy stopped me with her hand, and brushed the hair from my forehead.

'This is Frank's boy,' she said. Her friend started to laugh. 'Oh stop it,' said Ivy, laughing herself, and swaying back to ease the effort of the laughter. She brushed my hair again to show she wasn't meaning to laugh at me.

'How is your father? How is the seed merchant?' said Ivy's friend. Her top teeth were slightly buck, yet white and of a size.

'He's not a seed merchant,' I said. 'He works for the paper.'

'Oh, Ivy always told me he was,' she said.

'He proved to be, by God!' said Ivy.

I was disappointed not to be going with them into the city, for at night the noise and lights of the tram blurred its outline, fusing the tram with the other colours and movement of the city night.

My father slept a good deal. I spent much of each day working in the section which had been neglected because of his illness. I cleared and levelled several garden plots, and put them down in grass. I lacked the resignation of my mother and sister to sit and talk quietly in the living room with his medicines on a tray, while they waited for him to wake. Each task served to exorcise some small ghost of time past, trivial familiars that were in wait within the simplest things. My father's fishing rod above the garage door, and the breadboard shaped like a pig.

Sport was my father's realm as a journalist. He was given his own column when I was in the fourth form, and stayed so long in the hotel that my brother and I divided his scallops between us, and enjoyed the celebration on his behalf. I read to him about sport, and wildlife, which was his other interest. For years he said that he would write a book on that great man Anthony Wilding, but it was never done. 'Ivy married, you know,' he said. 'Went to live in Tasmania, but it didn't last.' We were quiet for a time. My father seemed to want me to remember Ivy, and I did, but not in his way. 'It didn't last,' my father said. 'She came back to New Zealand again, but we never saw her.' Ivy took me to the pictures in the square at night. On the tram I stood by the driver and watched him use the solid metal levers in place of a steering wheel. The noise, and the lights of the square in the distance. Ivy bought chocolates loose in a bag, and she laughed with the manager, who looked at the front of her dress. She told me that she used to go to the pictures often with my mother when they were nurses together. I hadn't thought about Ivy for a long time before coming to see my father: the trams, the painted wooden eggs, the seed merchant. Sitting with my father I realised more clearly that my age had prevented me from knowing Ivy as she was to a man, though even then I was conscious I think of warmth, fluidity of movement, and laughter both generous and knowing. 'They were fine lasses, those two. Ivy and your mother. A lot of people thought they were sisters,' said my father. I had no clear recollection of my mother at Ivy's age. We make present appearance retrospective for those close to us. 'You were only a boy,' said my father, recalling not so much my age then, as his own. Frank the snappy dresser and journalist perhaps.

'Trams ran right past her gate,' I said. 'Right past and rattling on down into the square.'

'I know.'

'And Ivy's old mother who was always cold, always sitting over the fire or heater.'

'Of course. Old Mrs Ransumeen. But she was deaf, you remember.

Yes, that's right. Ivy's mother, Mrs Ransumeen. She didn't sleep well, but she was rather deaf.' My father laughed quietly. I couldn't remember the old lady being all that deaf. My father's laugh was even and subdued. It seemed the laugh of a younger man, just that once.

I asked my mother about Ivy one afternoon. My father had fallen asleep while I read aloud from his articles on Anthony Wilding. He started to weep in his sleep: the tears soaked into the white, cotton pillow, yet he lay without sound or movement, apart from his breathing. I hope never to see that again. I told my mother that he asked about Ivy quite often. She said he never mentioned Ivy to her. She'd known Ivy longer than the rest of us, but then perhaps a friend's view of Ivy was not what my father wanted.

The wind was strong outside. It set up a persistent and familiar whine around one of the protruding barge-boards. 'Could you cut back the twisted willow by the study again sometime?' my father said. 'The branches rub on the side of the house in the wind, and the leaves block the guttering.'

'You cut it down years ago,' I told him. He was quiet for a time, smiling.

'What an old fool I've become,' he said. 'Jesus, just an old fool. Even my sense of taste is playing up. I get a sudden taste of onions or marmalade when I'm lying in bed. It makes me sick at times, the taste of things I haven't eaten, suddenly there in my throat.' Ivy's mother had kept clearing her throat all the time — arp, arp, arp. Indignities come with age, it seems. She used to wet the eggs to give them a last buffing with a leather cloth. She always reminded us to check the coal bin before we left her alone in the winter. I don't think my brother ever went to stay with Ivy, it was always me.

Ivy took me to the knick-knack and souvenir shop by the river once. She had her eggs in a shoe box, each wrapped in tissue. She took some out to impress the shopkeeper, and spread them on the counter, and moved them with her fingers to show how even, bright and smooth they were. He touched each in turn after she had, his hands following hers. Ivy laughed, making the eggs brighter than ever on the counter, and her dress rustled on her stockings. I wonder if he knew better than I did what use they were, and I wonder why I never thought to ask her.

My father had become a noisy breather, not snoring, but the air forced in and out, whispering in his nose, resounding in his chest, so that the mechanism by which life is sustained was always emphasised. His thoughts turned back, and I couldn't follow him all the way. We started out as equals, with the same perspective in that at least we were adults, but as we went back my sight became that of a boy, while he remembered Ivy as a man. I don't know if my father realised that, or what he expected of me. Any interpretation of what we knew as a child is dangerous. 'I took them both to the Industries Fair once,' he said. 'I was working for the old *Herald* and had complimentary tickets. There was a demonstration of working machinery from the woollen mills, and a glass blower who made goblets and ships as you watched. Your mother and Ivy wore dresses with puffed sleeves.' My father paused. 'The skin that girls had then,' he said. I had a vision of my father then as in his old photos, with a soft brim hat, and two-tone shoes. With a smooth, thin face, and one hand in his pocket.

These questions and offerings of Ivy occurred among many other things not relevant to them in my talks with my father, but the reiteration was not in my imagination, I thought. I told my sister that in a way it embarrassed me, for I wasn't sure what was required. I was going to tell her of the seed merchant, but closed my mouth on it. She is a shrewd and handsome woman, my sister. About the age that Ivy had been, when I think of it. She said that he had a history with Ivy, odd expression, but that it was the time back he wanted, not just Ivy. She said the ache was for the time of it: Ivy and our mother like sisters, and he himself as he was. My sister may be right, and I too insensitive to understand. Perhaps my father did in fact see Ivy as the image of what they both were, my mother and her: even the image of what all three were then. He never knew Ivy old, never saw her since he knew her, and she had never seen him old.

My father would sweat a lot sometimes as he lay in bed. Not on his face, but at the base of his neck, the pit where neck met chest, and the sweat would glisten there with the movement of his chest and the forced breathing. When I went down to the living room my mother would ask me if he was awake. Ivy's mother fell asleep in front of the fire in the evenings. Ivy placed a patterned tea cosy on her head, and we laughed without noise, or malice. 'We lost touch with her after her marriage broke up and she came back. Even that we heard about through someone else,' my father said. 'Like a sister to your mother, like a mother to you.'

'I remember her better when I stayed with her, than when she came to visit us.'

'It was different,' my father said.

My father asked me to clean out the desk in his study, and yes, I found one of Ivy's eggs lying with Forest and Bird annual reports, typewriter ribbons, dry fountain pens and pieces of kauri gum. The egg was royal blue, with gold and red rosettes. Still shiny, but old-fashioned in a way I couldn't pick. The decoration gave a false impression of jewelled solidity, for when I lifted up that Trojan egg it lay lightly in my hand, as if already hatched. I could see faint cracks in the paint, which compensated for the drying of the wood through many years. The tram-lines were shiny in the street outside Ivy's house, as if someone from the council polished the top surface. On a hot day the sun caught the lines for blocks ahead, and the trams shook and shimmered all the more in the currents of heat. Ivy used to push my hair off my forehead, and make a part using her own comb. I felt ashamed of the egg in a way. I put it in my pocket as I stood in the study, and my fingers caught on the edges of the telegram still there. Father very worse, it said, and it was true again.

The Paper Parcel

For a long time I thought everybody could see the future in the way I could myself: an expectation based upon desire. The dream logic of the mind. Even though events were often very different, it was the reality I blamed and not the vision. The reality failed to match the vision, which was the first and greater view. The actual encroached, but expectation drew off, and set up again upon the high ground of the future.

I remember asking Dusty Rhodes what he thought being in a submarine was like. I dunno, he said, I dunno do I, until I've been in one. What a way to live. He didn't know any better. He was spared any disillusion at least. No matter how many times it happened, I felt a sense of loss and betrayal when things proved other than I had seen them. Not different only, but also less in fitness and in unity.

Like the fancy dress ball, for instance. I was twelve when the senior classes had a fancy dress ball to end the year. It was a strict convention that you had to have a partner in advance. Anyone not paired off would hold his hand in fire rather than turn up that night. As far as I knew I had only three attributes to attract the opposite sex. I was the second fastest runner in the school, I was top in maths and I had blue eyes. Dusty Rhodes was fastest boy, I never beat him, although sometimes I dreamt I might. I became accustomed to despair, and his greasy hair in front of me as we ran race after race. Dusty drowned in the Wairau the next year, by the berth of the coaster which used to come over from Wellington and up the river. For years I had a guilt that I might have wished it. I was second fastest in the school to Dusty. I used to boast to the others that my legs just went that fast without any effort from the rest of me. To enhance this I had the habit of looking sideways as I ran, as if to see the cars on the road to the bridge, and escape the boredom of my automatic legs. Being top of maths was the second thing, and quite beyond my control. I was always top and never had an explanation for it. I was fearful I would lose the trick of it. And the blue eyes. There were only four boys with blue eyes in the class, and Fiona McCartney told Bodger that she liked blue eyes best. The class had been singing beautiful, beautiful brown eyes, and Bodger asked her which she preferred. Fiona McCartney blushed and said blue eyes, and the other girls giggled. I didn't forget that. I was beginning to store up points of knowledge about girls. Fiona McCartney was the oracle about such things at that school.

So those were the advantages I had going for me, and I exploited them to the full in the weeks before the fancy dress dance. I never ran so often or so fast. I was closer to first and further from third than ever before. I turned my head to the side with casual indifference and the old legs went with a will. I took to answering more maths questions in class, and fluked most of them right, and I used to widen my eyes when I was close to girls so that the blue of them would be more conspicuous.

Fiona McCartney passed a message to me saying she wanted to see me by the canteen at playtime, and when she came we went over by the sycamores and railings. She put one hand on the railing and swung her right foot in an arc on the grass. She glanced at her friends by the canteen and considered she had set a good scene. I widened my eyes at her, and held my breath without realising it. She told me that she wouldn't be going to the dance with me. I hadn't asked her, but she knew she was every boy's choice and was letting me down gently. As I was the second fastest and so on, she realised my expectations. I felt dizzy, then remembered to breathe out again. She said I'd have no trouble getting someone to go with. The girls had been talking, she said. She said the girls had been talking and she put the tip of her tongue between her teeth and smiled. I smiled back and widened my eyes as if I were aware of what girls said.

It made me more anxious, though, Fiona saying that, especially when we started having dancing practices. I wondered which of the girls had partners arranged already, for I wanted to avoid the humiliation of asking them. Kelly Howick saved me the trouble. At the third practice she said to me that I wasn't much of a dancer, and was I going to the fancy dress night. I said that I thought that I probably would. Casually I said it, and looked to the side as if I were running. I widened my eyes too, which wasn't much good when I was looking away. Are you listening? she said. In the past I'd thought about Kelly mainly as the girl most likely to keep me from fluking top in maths. She was top in most things. She had definite breasts, though, and was pretty. Only a certain matter-of-fact manner prevented her from being more like Fiona McCartney. It came to me that she was willing to be my partner. Only later did it also occur to me that she and her friends had made the decision without my presence being required. I will be your partner if you like, she said. She didn't need an answer. She seemed pleased for me. She smiled at me, and at her friends, as we moved awkwardly to the dancing instructions of Bodger and Miss Erikson.

I'd had my share of success in life. Top of maths and running, as I've said, and trials for the under-thirteen reps, but in that school hall I felt for the first time the heady stuff of sexual preferment. Kelly Howick had sought me out. I looked with contempt upon the others in the hall: Dusty Rhodes who could only run fast, and Bodger with the sweat stains on his shirt. For the first time I perceived myself in the mirror of the feminine eye; I was filled with casual arrogance and power, I was aware of a new dimension to life. My head kept nodding indolently as we danced, and my shoulders shrugging in some instinctive male response.

The knowledge of sexual magnetism was a novelty. I felt I should be able to tap it for other purposes. The day after the dancing practice I raced Dusty again. I felt the new power within me and was resolved to express it in my running also. I would bury him. In fact it made not an inch of difference. I still had to run behind Dusty, his hair bobbing. And he didn't even have a partner to the dance. It was a shock to discover that the power generated by sexual preferment was not directly transferable to athletic performance.

In my mind I was quite sure how the fancy dress dance would be. Sure, I had been let down somewhat in the past by the failure of events to conform with my directions, but I wasn't responsible for that. I saw Kelly and myself always in the centre of the hall, always in the better light, and somehow slightly larger than our classmates. I would dance, or stand quietly and attract the attention of other girls because of my blue eyes, and a certain calmness of manner. Kelly would be constantly asking my opinion, and I would be giving it with easy finality. Instead of the lucky spot waltz there would be quizzes on tables, or a sprint the length of the hall and back when Dusty happened to be outside.

Kelly Howick talked to me during practices. I made the adult discovery that some people are ugly. I'd had the foolish idea that there were no common standards of appearance. Now I began to realise otherwise. Collie Richardson, for example, who told the best jokes in the school. He had a very small upper lip. It was like a little skirt, and his gums and teeth were always exposed beneath it. Once I realised he was ugly I never liked his jokes as much again.

At the practices Kelly took over my instruction. She gave an individual repetition of what Bodger and Miss Erikson kept saying. You've not got much rhythm, have you, she said. Me! Second fastest and with automatic legs. In other circumstances it would have irritated me, but in the complacency of preferment I let it pass. I just looked aside and widened my eyes at Fiona McCartney. Certain things about girls have to be tolerated for the overall benefit.

I skidded on loose stones by the sycamores next day and put a long graze along my left forearm. Mrs Hamil put iodine on it and Kelly was quite concerned. It won't show on the night, will it? she said. What are you going to wear anyway? What's your outfit like? Her saying that made my arm begin to throb. The blood seeped out into beads despite the iodine. I hadn't done anything about a costume. The priority of getting a partner had obscured all other aspects of the dance. I asked my mother about it that night, and she said that's nice, a costume party is nice. Sure, we'll think of something. And my father made jokes for his own amusement about being cloaked in ignorance, or dressed in a little brief authority. I could tell they didn't have the right view of the ball at all, that they were thinking of it as some party, some kids' thing.

Tony Poole said his parents were hiring a full cowboy outfit with sheepskin chaps, bandanna and matched revolvers. Dusty's parents were pretty poor. I thought he wouldn't have much to wear even when he did arrange a partner. But he said his cousin had a Captain Marvel costume which had been professionally made. What is it you're going as? Kelly asked me again. I started questioning my mother once more. What was she going to do for me? Kelly was going as Bo Peep. What about my costume, I said to my mother. Oh, we'll rustle up something don't you worry, she said. But I did. The more casual and unperturbed she was, the more I worried.

Finally my mother said she thought I should go as a parcel. A parcel, Jesus. She remembered someone at the New Year's party as a parcel, and he was a great hit. It was a cheap costume too, she said. A parcel, Jesus. It was the originality of it that intrigued her, she said. Anyone could go as a policeman or a musketeer; people grew tired of seeing them. The parcel left only head and limbs out, she said, and I could make up a giant stamp with crayons, and over my parcel body have stickers saying Fragile, London, This Side Up, Luxemburg, Handle with Care. The parcel was set to torpedo my night with Kelly Howick. Bo Peep Kelly with her beginning breasts and braided hair, and me as a brown paper parcel with a stamp done in crayon.

There was a sense of inevitability about the parcel. I tried to persuade my mother that I should go as something else. I said I wouldn't wear it, but the parcel became part of me before I ever saw it, something irrevocable and humiliating before I was even dressed in it.

The dance was supposed to start at eight. It said so on the printed sheet I brought home. Nobody arrives at a dance on time, though, my mother said. She never realised how little adult convention applies to the young. It said eight o'clock on the sheet, didn't it? Why would it say that if it didn't mean it? Nobody comes to a dance till later my mother said. It's just how it's done. But I saw eight o'clock written. I knew everyone would be there. Anthony Poole in his cowboy outfit, and Kelly as Bo Peep.

On that Friday I didn't run well. Dusty beat me without hardly trying, and although I looked away as I ran, I was having a hard time to keep ahead of Ricky Ransumeen in third place. My automatic legs were being affected. I thought a good deal about that because it seemed unfair. When I was selected by Kelly, when desirability was conferred on me, although the power was great, it hadn't made me any faster, as I told you. But on that last day, as I turned my head in studied casualness, instead of the flowing leaves of the sycamores by the fence, I saw myself in a parcel costume with a crayon stamp. Just for a moment there in the stippled leaves and keeping pace with me was a *doppelgänger* in a parcel. I lacked rhythm as I ran, I lacked a full chest of air, my automatic legs made demands.

It wasn't until after tea that my mother even began the parcel. I had to wear my swimming togs so no clothes would show below the parcel. The brown paper strips were wrapped around me like nappies, and round and round my chest, and holes cut for my head and arms. I was tied with twine and with a yellow ribbon in a bow at the front. Over my heart was stuck the crayoned stamp, huge and serrated. Other oblong stickers were plastered on with flour-

and-water paste. This Side Up, Handle with Care, On Her Majesty's Service, Do Not Rattle. I was finally packed by eight o'clock, and set off on my bike for the school assembly hall. I tried to sit up straight on the seat so that the parcel wouldn't crinkle too much. The wrapping made noises as I rode, and the greasy blue and red head on the stamp grinned in the setting sun. I told myself that the parcel was really quite clever and would go down well. I could only half believe it, yet I never seriously thought about not going. The power of sexual preferment was enough to transform me. It would make difference distinction, and nonconformity audacity. To be with Kelly Howick would be sufficient to defeat the parcel.

They had started, of course. I knew it. The sheet had said eight o'clock after all. The light from the hall spilled out into the soft summer evening. The noise of the band and the dancing slid out with the light, and echoed in the quad. Bodger patrolled the grounds, alert for vandalism, or lust. Late, said Bodger. He looked at my costume and said no more. As I went in he was still there on the edge of the light and the noise, and with the blue evening as a backdrop. He had his hands behind his back, and he swayed forward on his toes. Hurry up then, said Bodger. I slipped in round the edge of the door, and worked my way over to the boys' side. Tony Poole had a curled stetson, sheepskin chaps, checked shirt and six-guns with matching handles. He came back from seeing Fiona McCartney to her seat. Toomey was a fire chief with a crested helmet that glittered, and a hatchet at his belt. Dusty's Captain Marvel insignia was startling on his chest, and his cloak was cherry rich and heavy. And I was a parcel. A brown paper parcel with bare legs and sandshoes. A brown paper parcel that crinkled when I moved. A brown paper parcel with a stamp drawn up in red and blue. It wasn't right: not for the second fastest runner in the whole school, not for the top maths boy, and the one preferred by Kelly Howick. What the hell is that you're wearing? said Dusty. Wouldn't you like to know, I said.

I went over to claim Kelly when the music began for the next dance. It was a foxtrot. I had learnt both sorts of dance. A waltz was where you took one step to the side every now and again, and a quickstep was where you kept forging ahead. A foxtrot is just a slower quickstep. I'm a little late, I said, smiling and nodding. I found that, without meaning to, I was trying to compensate for being a parcel. Kelly's Bo Peep outfit suited her. The bodice with the crossed straps accentuated her breasts, and she had a curved crook. She looked fifteen at least. As we danced I knew that she was looking at the parcel. I heard myself laughing loudly at Captain Marvel who was fighting with a pirate, but Kelly kept looking at my costume. I was going to come as a pirate myself, I said. I had a better pirate outfit than that; a huge hat with skull and crossbones, and an eye-patch. What? she said. I was going to come as a pirate, I said. I can't hear you for all the noise your brown paper makes, Kelly said. It wasn't so, of course. The band was making more noise than the parcel. No, she was giving me the message. Even the way she danced with me was different from other times. She had a dull expression on her face, as if she was doing me a favour by dancing. I tried whirling her around, the way Bodger and Miss Erikson had demonstrated. I nearly fell over, she said. It was a lesson for me in the transience of sexual preferment. It was apparently something that had to be taken advantage of immediately.

I was determined not to mention being a parcel. Not admitting it was some way of keeping the full force of its humiliation from me. I quite like Dusty's Captain Marvel suit, I told Kelly. A bit overdone, but I quite like it. I told Miss Erikson I'd help with supper, she said. It won't be worth you coming over for the next dance because I'll start helping her soon, I think. Sure, sure, I said, we must have the grub on time. The grub on time! I couldn't believe I was saying it. And afterwards I'll probably help with the washing up, Kelly said.

Flour-and-water paste isn't very successful when there's any movement. Some of the stickers were starting to work loose on the brown paper. This Way Up fell on to the dance floor. Handle with

Care came off and I tucked it under the twine. It worked down low on my waist, and Dusty and Ricky Ransumeen started pointing and laughing at its anatomical juxtaposition. I took Kelly back to her side of the hall after the dance. See you then, I said. She slipped among the other girls with a murmur. Who could blame her? As I went back over the floor I could see several of my labels there. Fragile, Via Antwerp, Airmail. Maybe someone would start collecting them and draw attention to them. The parcel was ceasing to be recognisable as such. Without stickers, wrinkled and lopsided after the dancing, it had lost what little illusion of costume it ever had. I was a kid wrapped in brown paper and wearing bathing togs and sandshoes. Ah, Jesus me. Only the stamp over my heart seemed firmly stuck. A mark of Cain in crayon that leered out on all the world, and would not release itself, or me. I was beaten all right. I couldn't maintain any longer my vision of how the night should be. And the withdrawal of sexual preferment had weakened me; my esteem had been eroded. I began to work my way towards the door: a paper parcel through the Batmen, policemen, riverboat gamblers and Indian chiefs. Little Wade Stewart was a Pluto. He came up to me with Fragile. Is this yours? he said kindly Yes, what a dag, isn't it? I said. I kept on moving towards the door, and reached it as the lucky spot waltz was announced.

It felt good outside. The summer dusk, the distanced and impersonal buildings, the lucky spot music fading as I made my way to the bikesheds. Bodger loomed up. I got a bit of a nosebleed, I told him, but as I was by myself he wasn't interested. I rode out of the grounds, and the crinkle of the parcel and the lessening music conjoined down the quiet street. I allowed myself the indulgence of self-pity for a time. I was outside myself, I accompanied myself, I consoled myself, for the bland incomprehension of adults and the loss of sexual status. I felt I had been hard done by, that was the truth. Perhaps there would be a fire in the hall. I imagined the flames leaping from the walls, and the riverboat gamblers and fairy queens put to flight. Faster and faster I biked. I saw the fiery press of the blaze, the terror of my classmates, the impotence of Bodger and Miss Erikson. I stood up on the pedals in the soft, summer night and put on a sprint that would have carried me clear of any possible pursuit. Parcel my arse, I shouted, and louder, parcel my arse. I reckoned that I was about the fastest bike rider at that school. I reckoned that even Dusty Rhodes wouldn't be a patch on me at that. I felt the wind of my flight pushing the brown paper against me as I swept without a light down the blue streets.

There was a light in the living room when I reached home, however. I put the bike away, and looked through the gap between curtain-edge and window-side. My mother was listening to the radio and talking; my father was cleaning his shoes on a newspaper spread by his chair. I had to find some immediate focus for revenge, and they would serve as enemies. I crept into the kitchen and took a packet of my father's cigarettes from behind the clock, and struck a match to inspect the pantry cupboard. Mixed fruit pack, I chose; raisins, candied peel, sultanas, figs, cherries. I took the fruit pack and cigarettes to the woodshed. I sat on the pine slabs in the lean-to there, and ate the fruit mix and smoked my father's Pall Mall. I ripped off the stamp in crayon, and burnt holes in it. I flashed the glowing cigarette against the navy sky, writing Zorro in swift neon. I undid the twine and unwrapped the parcel, burying the pieces in the wood heap. Jesus, I said, so what? Who cares about the dance and being a paper parcel? I was still second fastest in the school, wasn't I? Wasn't I! I sat in my togs and singlet, ate my dried fruit, and watched the smoke curl as shadows from my fingers. Let the world come on, I could take it. And next time it would be different. I could see so clearly the next year's dance, when I would be Napoleon and Fiona McCartney my Josephine. That's how it would be all right.

The Fat Boy

The men coming from the railway yards were the first to notice the fat boy. He stood beneath the overhead bridge, among the cars illegally parked there. He had both hands in the pockets of his short pants and the strain of that plus his heavy thighs made the flap of his fly gape. The fat boy watched the passers-by with the froglike, faintly enquiring look that the faces of fat boys have. The fat boy's hair was amazingly fair and straight; it shone with nourishment; it was straight and oddly medieval.

The men were leaving at twenty past four. It was a conventional extension of the time for washing up that their union had obtained. They resented the fat boy's regard day after day. They were sure that he was stealing from the cars, and it was just as well they were coming past early to watch him, they said. Sometimes they would shout at the fat boy and tell him to get lost, as they walked in their overalls along the black margin of the track past the old gasworks. Seventeen thousand dollars worth of railway property was found missing when the audit was made. The men knew it was outsiders. They remembered the fat boy. The fat kid is the lookout for the ring taking all the stuff, they told the management. Dozens of workers could swear to having seen the fat boy. They went looking for him, but he wasn't to be found beneath the overhead bridge anymore.

Instead the fat boy began to frequent McNulty's warehouse in Cully Street. Even through the cracked and stained windows the staff could see him standing by the side of the building where the bicycles were left. Sometimes he would kick at the clumps of weeds which grew in the broken pavement there, sometimes he would puff his fat cheeks and blow out little explosions of air, sometimes he would just stand with his hands in his pockets and look at the warehouse as if to impress it on his mind. He had a habit of pulling his mouth to one side, as if biting the skin on the inside of his cheek, the way children do. Often in school time he was there. Sometimes even in the rain he was there. The rain glistened on his round cheeks, and seemed to shrink his pants so that the lining turned up at the leg holes. The new girl looked out and said he looked as if he was crying. The owner said he'd make him cry all right. He was sick of ordering him away, the owner said.

McNulty's warehouse burnt down in November. The owner made particular mention to the police of the fat boy, but when McNulty's built again in a better area with the insurance money, the fat boy never appeared. The paper reported what the owner said about the fat boy. The railway men said it was the same fat boy all right. They said the fat kid was somehow tied up in a lot of the crime going on.

The fat boy seemed to be in uniform, but although he was clearly seen by many people there was no agreement as to his school or family. Some said his socks had the blue diamonds of Marsden High, but others said the blue was in the bands of College. The fat boy had thick legs with no apparent muscles, and they didn't narrow to the ankle. If just his legs could have been turned upside down no one would ever know it. When the fat boy lifted his brows enquiringly, one crease would form in the smooth, thick skin of his forehead.

The fat boy seemed to be a harbinger of trouble. The fat boy walked behind old Mrs Denzil on her way home from the shopping centre, and he loitered in the shade of her wooden fence, which was draped with dark convolvulus leaves and its pale flowers. The police maintained a quiet watch on the house for two days in case the fat boy came again. On the third night someone broke into Mrs Denzil's house and tied her upside down in the washtub. Her Victorian cameo brooch was stolen, together with the tinned food she hoarded, and eighty-four-year-old Mrs Denzil was left tied upside down in the tub with a tennis ball in her mouth to block her breathing. Oh, that fat boy, they said; even murder, they said. That fat boy was so much more evil than their own sons. There wasn't anything that the fat boy wouldn't do, was there, they said.

Nigel Lammerton saw the fat boy on the night he was arrested for beating his wife. Lammerton told the police that when he returned from the hotel he saw the fat boy on the porch of his home, and that his wife couldn't explain why. Lammerton said that he saw the fat boy looking in the window at them while they argued, but that when he ran outside the fat boy was gone. It was the fat boy, and the medication that he had been taking, that made him lose control, Nigel Lammerton told the court. Mrs Lammerton agreed with everything her husband said about the fat boy.

The fat boy could not be found for questioning, but then no one had ever known the fat boy to say anything. He just watched. The paper said he was malevolent. No one likes a fat kid staring at them all the time. Lammerton said that everyone was entitled to privacy without a fat kid staring at him. The fat boy had the knack of being where he was least desired.

There was a certain effrontery about the fat boy. He appeared in council chambers during the discussion in committee on a special dispensation from the town planning scheme. The deputy mayor was declaring that no present councillors had any connection with the consortium that had made application. He became aware of the fat boy watching him from the corridor to the town clerk's office. The fat boy's fair hair trembled a little as his mouth stretched in a cavernous yawn and, without taking his hands from his pockets, he tapped with his shoe at the wainscotting, the way boys do. One of the councillors went from the meeting to confront the fat boy, but he must have slipped away through the offices, the councillor said.

The deputy mayor thought that in all of his considerable

experience he had never seen such a sly one as the fat boy. He said that somehow he could never bring himself to trust a fat boy, just never could bring himself to trust one, he said.

The fat boy was seen at the IHC centre the day before Melanie Lamb was found to be pregnant. The air was warm, sparrows chirped beneath the swaying birch catkins and pecked at a vomited pie in the gutter. The fat boy stood before the railings and held one of the iron bars like a staff. The children smiled at him as he watched, and were content in his presence, but the supervisors saw him there and remembered when the doctor said that Melanie was pregnant. The music teacher who lived next door to the Lambs thought it a very significant recollection. He said that when he came to think of it he recalled the fat boy standing in the evenings by the hedge at the rear of Melanie's house. A very fat, ugly boy, the music teacher said, and everyone agreed that such a unique description fitted the fat boy perfectly and must be him. It was a terrible thing, the music teacher said, to think that the fat boy could take advantage of Melanie's handicap, even if she was physically advanced.

More than any of the other things, it was what he did to Melanie Lamb that enabled people to close ranks against the fat boy. They recognised in him a common enemy. Vigilante groups organised from the King Dick and Tasman hotels began searching for the fat boy. Not many days before Christmas they caught up with the fat boy by the gasworks. Artie Compeyson was drowning kittens in the cutting, and saw the fat boy watching, but didn't let on. The fat boy was stolid at the top of the cutting, His pudding face and medieval hair showed clearly in the moonlight and against the grimy storage tanks of the old gasworks. He was still waiting when the vigilantes came, and they surrounded him there in the patches of light and shadow. The fat boy didn't run, or cry out. He watched them converge, his thick legs apart and his hands pushed deep into the pockets of his short trousers. He was sly all right.

They managed to overpower him, they said. Nigel Lammerton,

with his experience as a wife-beater, got in one or two really good thuds on the fat boy's face before he went down, and the music teacher, who had an educated foot, kicked the fat boy between the legs. Everyone knew the fat boy must be made to pay for what he had done.

No one seemed to know what happened to the fat boy's body, and such a body wasn't easy to hide. The moon seemed to go behind cloud just at the time the fat boy fell, and the vigilantes became rather confused after the excitement of the night, and the debriefing at the King Dick and the Tasman. Although the police dragged the cutting, they found only the sack with kittens in it, and five stolen tyres.

Nearly everyone was relieved that the fat boy had been got rid of. God, but he was evil, they said, that fat boy, all the things he did. It didn't bear thinking about, they said. And no one likes a fat boy watching them, you know. They shared, among other things, a conviction that life would be immeasurably better for them all with the fat boy gone.

The Day Hemingway Died

You'll be wary of too much coincidence, I know, but I had been reading a good deal of Hemingway about that time. We weren't doing it in lectures either. The *Faerie Queene* was what we were doing in lectures. The *Faerie Queene* is suitable for university study because people wouldn't read it otherwise. The lecture in the afternoon was on arachnid imagery in Book Two. The lecturer had the habit of lifting his head from his notes and glancing despairingly around the tiered seating, as if he feared we were drawing closer to suffocate him.

It was raining that day, and the streets were softened with it, and the cars hissed by. I rode very slowly because my bike had no front mudguard, and the faster I went the more water the wheel flicked up at me. So I was in the rain longer, but the water coming down was cleaner than that coming up. When the rain began to run down my face, I imagined I was Neanderthal, and persevered with sullen endurance. Cars came from behind, hissing like cave bears as they passed.

Mrs Ransumeen complained if I dripped inside. So I stood in the wash-house and dried off with a pillowcase from the laundry basket. I wriggled my toes and they squelched inside my desert boots. I put my feet down very flat when I went inside, so they wouldn't squelch. 'Don't you leave wet socks in your room,' said Mrs Ransumeen.

'I don't really think Neanderthal was a dead end,' I said. 'More and more research seems to show that they added to the gene pool that carried on.'

'I'm not doing any washing tomorrow. I'm not.'

'It's subjective, I know, but I feel the stirrings of Neanderthal at times. Some atavism of the mind, I guess.'

'Oh, shut your blah,' said Mrs Ransumeen. Her face was like an old party balloon that had been left strung up too long, become small and tired with stretch marks and scar tissue. Yet still more air pressure inside than out. Mrs Ransumeen's face was like that; looking blown up and deflated both at the same time.

'For three pounds ten a week I don't have to listen to your rubbish,' she said. 'And I don't have to pick up wet socks from your room neither. Stop dripping on the floor, will you.'

Mrs Ransumeen had beautiful hair. She had hair that girls would steal for. It was black and heavy. When well brushed it had a secret gleam, like water glimpsed in a deep well. Every woman has something of beauty I suppose.

I went up the stairs, squelching. The party balloon stood at the bottom. 'It's a cold meal,' she said. The rain drifted into the window on the stairway landing. I should've gone back down and had it out with her about one hot meal a day. I owed it to myself, to keep my self-respect. For a moment I thought I could do it.

'Oh well,' I said. 'Yes, okay.' Even Neanderthal genes can be recessive.

Ron's door was open. He was lying on his bed with his hands behind his head. He was grinning at me. As I changed my socks he mocked me through the wall. 'Okay, Mrs Ransumeen. Yes, Mrs Ransumeen. Cold tea, how delightful, Mrs Ransumeen. Let me lick your bum, Mrs Ransumeen.' Ron was an engineering student. He lacked any culture, but had prodigious courage. He even took on the Ransumeens once or twice. Got beaten, but at least he took them on. He had to get worked up to it, mind you, with drink, or the desperation of academic failure. He had no culture, but a certain vision of self, did Ron. He had that hopeless courage that arouses both admiration and pity. In all other ways he was even less than ordinary.

The radio in the kitchen was always on. It was on when we came down for the cold meal. The party balloon liked to listen to the talkback shows. She loved to hear people making fools of themselves. 'Listen to that silly bitch,' she said.

'Arp, barp,' went her husband.

'For God's sake, stop that face-farting all the time,' said Mrs Ransumeen.

'It's natural, isn't it? A natural function, for Christ's sake.' Ransumeen's face was the evasive, plural face of a man who had no self-respect. A face pushed forward by impetuosity without talent, and worn back again by constant disadvantage. It was the face of a man who gets by how he can. It was the face in which you fear to look in case you see yourself.

The radio said that Hemingway had put a shotgun in his mouth and killed himself. 'It's a poor show, that's all, if a man can't express his natural functions in his own home,' said Ransumeen. When it said about Hemingway, each object in my line of sight assumed a derisive clarity. There was first the Belgium sausage sandwich on my plate. Its pink edge peeped like a cat's tongue from the uncut side, and the top piece of bread had a smooth indentation in one corner from a bubble in the dough.

'I saw the old tart next door putting rubbish in our can again,' said the party balloon. The salt and pepper were faceted glass with red plastic tops. The salt had five holes, and two were blocked because of the humidity. What I felt had less to do with Hemingway as a writer, than with the idea that no one cared if he lived or died anyway. There were better writers than Hemingway, but he was the one who died that day. In homes all over the country there would be the news about Hemingway, and no one cared. On the bench was a pie-dish with water in it to soak the burnt apricot on the bottom, and a tube of golden macaroons. The price was marked with felt pen on the cellophane.

'Lincoln is always a hard team to beat in the forwards,' said Ron.

'I'll take all the rubbish I can lay my hands on, and the next time she does it I'll follow that old bitch back and turf it all over her floor.'

'It said Hemingway's dead,' I said.

'Bread,' said Ransumeen. He had his hand out for it.

'Because she lives by herself, she thinks she can do what she likes.'

'And with this rain there'll be a heavy ground all right, and the forwards will tell.'

'I said Hemingway killed himself.'

'Barp, arp. Ah, that's better out than in, as the actress said to the bishop.'

I quite like macaroons actually, but the party balloon never put more than two each on the table. When I'm working I can eat a whole packet easily. The first Hemingway story I ever read was 'Indian Camp'. Hemingway wasn't always beating his chest. Mrs Ransumeen had a broad, yellow ribbon in her hair. When she turned aside to criticise her husband her hair had a sheen so dark there were hints of purple, as had the skin of a Melanesian bishop I heard preach once in Timaru. Sometimes I thought her hair must be false, and that underneath was the real hair that suited an ugly woman. Ron asked if he could have a stronger bulb in his room. He said he couldn't see to do his work, and he had two assignments due that week. 'Oh, you shut up,' said Mrs Ransumeen.

'Yeah,' said Ransumeen. 'You shut your cakehole. You're just a boarder here.' Vulgarity was a natural property of the Ransumeens, and to deplore it was like criticising wetness in water, or the smell of methane.

The salt sloped high left to low right, and the pepper the other way. It must have happened as Mrs Ransumeen carried them to the table gripped by the tops in the fingers of one hand. The cellars tend to angle out when they're carried that way. The butter had Marmite on its top edge like an ink line, and one pendant of water dithered from the cold tap. The radio had finished with Hemingway, and begun on political instability in Italy. It was a lot more important perhaps. I don't know. 'You're not going out tonight,' said the party balloon. Ransumeen gnawed his sandwich and said nothing. It was a silence of hope rather than subterfuge. 'Are you deaf or bloody something?' she said.

'I may have to go out for a bit,' he said. She started on him, but with an underlying boredom from countless victories. Ron and I went upstairs.

Nothing in my room had changed for Hemingway, and the houses outside looked the same as ever. Mould stains always showed up on the roughcast when it rained, and the knuckled camellia bushes moved a little in the drizzle and the wind. Nothing flamed in the sky for Hemingway. Not even an aurora of picadors, or quail in the sun.

Mrs Ransumeen's voice reached a competent fighting pitch. She could sustain it as long as she wished. Her virulence was that of self-pity rather than active hatred. 'And why the hell you can't get some better job anyway I don't know,' she said.

'Ah, for Christ's sake,' said Ransumeen.

'S'obvious you won't get anywhere again. We never get invited anywhere.'

'Who's going to invite us, for Christ's sake?' Ransumeen went out, and left her talking.

'That's right. That's right,' she said. 'You bloody go out. Whether you get back in is another story.' She began banging the dishes in the sink, and talking to the radio again. 'Will you shut your face, I say? Prouting on,' she told the announcer. She traded him for a tidal flow of film themes. She seemed to be banging the utensils in time with them.

It seemed colder in my room as the darkness deepened outside. The bulb of small power grew even dimmer in the cold. Ron came in. He wore two jerseys, which gave him a stomach. 'The troll has turned off our heaters at the switch board,' he said. 'It's unbearable.' His hands were yellow with cold, and his fingernails lilac. Mrs Ransumeen had become quiet below. She had laid the snare and was content to wait. 'We can't put up with it. Why should we? We can't work like this,' said Ron.

'Today I won't stand for it,' I said. Ron was encouraged by my support.

'Let's have it out with her.' Ron had a square, practical face and a feeling for natural justice. 'We'll do something about it. The troll has turned the heat off again and it's the middle of winter.' He swayed and marched on the spot, partly to keep warm and partly in rising militancy.

As we went down together, I felt that the day had to be marked in some way. As the lightning wouldn't strike, some risk was necessary on the day that Hemingway died. Mrs Ransumeen sat with her arms laid before her on the table. The twin bars of the kitchen heater glowed. 'Our heaters are off,' said Ron.

'Yes,' I said. It was a token of our alliance. Mrs Ransumeen's fat arms were dimpled, and spreading on the table as if filled with water.

'So?' she said.

'It's cold,' I whined. Hemingway knew all about the cold.

'It's too cold to work in our rooms,' said Ron.

'Horseshit,' said the party balloon. She began to breathe more noisily through her nose, and she stirred in the chair. She was getting ready to really let go, I thought. Ron and I stood shoulder to shoulder. Then her mood began to change, as visible in its way as a change of weather. Her eyes dulled like the surface of a pond beneath a breeze, and her shoulders settled. Her expression was for a moment surprised as she felt the change spreading from within, the new imperative. Her hands spread out like a starfish and, despite herself, she began to cry. 'Oh, I don't know. I just don't know,' she said. As she cried she lifted her hands and began rubbing her face, smearing the tears from forehead to chin. 'Sometimes I just wish to God I was dead,' she said. 'One lousy thing after another. One lousy day after another. A rented house, and a husband who becomes less and less a man.' She stood up, and her breathing was broken with hiccups from her sobbing. She went over to the fridge and opened it. From the rack behind the door she took eggs one by one and flicked her forearm and wrist to send them against the window, the bench and the cupboards. Her throwing action was restricted, and her defiance half-hearted. The eggs broke with the sound of black beetles being stood on. Mrs Ransumeen seemed to find no relief in doing it, and it shamed us to watch.

It should have been very comic: my landlady throwing eggs in the kitchen on the day that Hemingway died. Yet the thing is that it wasn't in the least funny. On the radio a man explained the importance of mulching shrubs for summer. The party balloon rather dully cast the eggs, and they crushed like beetles. 'Now I've bloody done it,' she said. 'I've started now and I've really done it. He'll notice something when he comes home tonight.'

'Will he ever,' said Ron softly. He was afraid to disturb her apathy. She began to cry again, and her mouth opened into the speechless square that accompanies the onslaught of tears. She closed the fridge door, and stood with one forgotten egg in her hand.

'Horseshit to it all anyway,' she managed to say. The situation was beyond her response. She was struggling with a crisis, the significance of which provided her with no greater means to confront it. Smashing eggs and crying were the only outlets she could think of. Ron and I left her there. We had nothing to offer as a consolation. Contempt and fear were stronger than our pity. We went quietly up the stairs. Ron was uncertain.

'I've never seen her like this before. She's packed up properly.'

That's how it was for me on the day that Hemingway died. I had meant to give it all a humorous gloss, and get in a bit of sex; bed springs and muffled cries. That's what people like in a story. But it remains much as it was. Cold and wet, horseshit and broken eggs, no heat in my room and a landlady I disliked crying aloud in the kitchen.

Another Generation

The patio illumine was the single source of light; diffused through glass, influenced in progress by the colours, textures, shapes of furniture and ornaments until the room was dim hued, an aquarium, and movement met resistance from the liquid air. Lucretia was curled in a corner of the large sofa, and Franc urged his claim. His fingers trailed over her left heel, and he traced the relaxed achilles tendon of her ankle. Please. His voice was thickened by anticipation and aquarium air. You can trust yourself with me. Please. The flesh of his neck had a slight sheen of sweat, attractive in the intimacy of that partial light. We need to, he said. What sort of balance have you got? A hundred, two hundred thousand, both earned and given. Tell me how you keep your money. Tell me all the things you do with it; the ways you calculate the interest; all the forms of investment and return you've found. Tell me again those strange things you do with silver.

Lucretia breathed heavily although at rest; as a pouting fish breathes in conscious satisfaction of life sustained. The ruffles of her blouse flared like gills, and were caught in ripples of merging green light, green shadow, as they moved. She looked through the full-length windows and glass doors to the patio, saw above the mask of garden trees a dusted pattern of stars. You could give me silver coins, said Franc. His fingers continued a play of stops along her heel. It's a thing with you — pure silver coins. You could lay out hundreds in the moonlight, white mounds all pressing down. If you trusted me, if you loved me.

I can't, said Lucretia. As he said silver coins her mouth had opened and eyelids drooped for an instant, but her face was turned away.

Please.

I can't yet, but soon; when we're sure of each other. You know I love you.

How do I know. I don't know, said Franc. His whisper was harsh and close. Lucretia began to weep. Let me give you used notes. He used a lover's voice. All worn notes, warm and worn, the corners frayed like the toes of old slippers, the colours darkened by the alchemy of a thousand palms and purposes. Some have things written on them — names, phone numbers, shopping lists, poetry. They're so old and knowing, like tobacco leaves, with veins of their own life beginning to form again, but old notes are from a tree more ancient even, and with a more persistent fragrance. Used notes at the last are cynical, pleasured, corrupt with all the venal impulse to which they must submit.

Don't, don't, Lucretia murmured.

Please. Just a straight missionary gift then?

I can't: not yet.

Marx, said Franc, jerking his head. He sat up abruptly and began to put on his shoes. Lucretia sobbed beside him. It was a familiar ending between them. A lace snapped because of his impatience, and he swore again — Ricardo. He next spoke calmly, with an effort, ashamed that Lucretia was weeping. I'm sorry. I don't want to upset you, you know that.

We could have sex, she said: an offer of reconciliation.

We can have that anytime, with anyone. It means nothing. A vacant, instinctual rabbiting.

I love you. I want to share the most intense of emotions with you. Franc was eager for agreement, but she was downcast at the injustice yet necessity of her caution. Franc stood in the blurred shadows to put on his jacket. He stroked Lucretia's head; ran one blouse ruffle between thumb and finger to assure her of affection. I've got to go, he said. It's all right. Forget it. I'll ring you tomorrow.

Lucretia's parents were also concerned for her. They talked of it when she had gone upstairs to her room. Her eyes are red. She's been crying, Mrs Rand said.

What is the matter with her these days? Mr Rand's voice was vigorous with worry and impatience. Why does she keep on with him if they can't be happy. I'm Benthamed if I know.

I think Franc's too serious, and she doesn't want to commit herself.

They're not financing each other are they?

Sol!

Well, I don't understand young people these days. Money is all they think about. And there's no bounds of decency or restraint any more you know. They even hang around the banks and share rooms and make suggestions to people coming in and out. It all needs cleaning up. They caress money in full view in the parks, and whistle at the millionaires. Kids miss school to go gambling together, or sniffing mint dyes.

They're just more open about it, I suppose, and you know Franc's quite brilliant at his job. He's on 100,000 a year, and in three super and pension groups. Lucretia says he has seven major forms of security asset, and not all in this country.

I know, yes, I know, said Mr Rand, but it's all so calculating and deliberate now isn't it. So selfish. You and I weren't always moneying when we first married. We didn't talk about it much; we kept our feelings in check. Look at television and video news now; all details of mergers, frauds, extortion, robbery cases and close-ups of the tellers' faces after they've passed over all the money, and interviews with lottery winners and bankrupts before they've a chance to control their emotions. Drooling coverage of self-immolation, people swallowing the new doubloon which precisely blocks the windpipe. It's disgusting. And the Unions with reports of nonexistent wage rounds every month to keep the workers titillated. It debases everything. It does. I'm serious.

It's that financial lodge of yours.

No, I'm serious. From the necessary economic motivation and medium of exchange, money's perverted to a personal buzz. No one remembers its social purpose any more.

Stop worrying, and come to bed. Things change.

I mean it. It's a worrying thing that's happening, said Mr Rand. Where it leads and so on.

Come to bed and I'll tell you how the old man Henessey made all his money, and what he does with it.

You don't know.

I do though.

Aw, come on now, said Mr Rand.

I do though. Mabel Henessey got excited at our share club and told me it all. You wouldn't believe about old man Henessey, and he looks so righteous. I know for sure that sometimes he —. Even though they were alone, Mrs Rand leant ladylike to her husband's ear to impart her story.

Is that a fact, said Mr Rand. Well I'll be Keynesed.

Franc drove late at night from the residential heights of the Rands, to the entertainment section of the city strung along John Stuart Mill Boulevard and Laski Street. All that time with Lucretia in the muted light, the affection, the stalemate. He was still breathing deeply, and he could feel the pulse beat at the sides of his neck. He idled down Laski Street in the indulgence district, one more cruising electric car in a line of them, between the loan shops, parlours, coin halls, speciality stands and dough flick cinemas. Franc parked outside one of the smaller arcades. He rested there, telling himself that he needed the rest, and perhaps might do no more than that. He thought of Lucretia, how her breathing became when she was talking of solid silver, how she was in thrall to the cool, moon metal and would place her tongue between her teeth and gently bite when she saw such coins. He thought of his own father, and what he was making day after day after day. Franc knew his father was behind Pan Globe Enterprises, and that he personally gave bonuses to fifty-three executives one by one in his office each year.

From his car, Franc could see the display of titles in the speciality video shop; hot sellers of the moment. Borrowers and Lenders Be, Mortgage Mistress, What's In Kitty, The Buck Stops Here, and the notorious Cash Me In. He took his thick wallet from the dash locker, and left the car. He was deliberate, yet there was a sense of disappointment in himself within his deliberate mood. Franc ignored the appraising faces of the groups along the arcade frontage. To stand was to suggest interest, and he kept walking, kept his eyes glancing past the faces, until he reached the bankcard vending machines deep in the arcade. The police had grown weary of moving people on, graffiti blossomed on the walls and were interpolated into the intructions themselves, reefs of champagne cans had been built up by the wall and capped with plastic spoons from Jumbo pies. Yet the noise, the movement, the colour and the commerce, kept all tense and defiant.

Like a favourite coral terrace in the reef, the vending wall had its special shoal, its own population, constant, yet ever changing in its pattern, intimate only within itself, yet ever conscious of others watching, twisting out from the vending machines with smiles and body language to be observed, then circling back in to recapture conversation and resume a pose. Franc watched a chunky young man with a Roman fringe. The young man had a gold coin in his hand which was always moving. In obsessive ritual it appeared between each pair of fingers in turn, dipped into the palm, scudded against gravity like a modest, yellow mouse across the back of his hand. Goldy circled out twice from the wall, then came a third time, stood by Franc and performed his easy actions with the coin. He smiled with closed lips to himself, as though he considered Franc was about to say something both humorous and predictable. I want you to give me used notes, said Franc.

Whatever you say, squire. I've a place handy.

I haven't time, said Franc. Just come further into the arcade.

Whatever suits your fancy, squire, said Goldy.

In a recessed doorway to the closed office of an investment counsellor, Franc gave up his thick wallet, and leant his shoulder into the corner to give him support against the onslaught of ecstasy. Goldy ran notes over Franc's face and hands, crinkled them tenderly beside his ear, insinuated them into the slits of his shirt front. Worn, used notes frayed and soiled to the texture of skin, worn as skin, natural as skin, necessary as skin and sin, scented with usury and compromises and enslavements and desires. Tokens of power, each with its colours of face value a dim nationality in the recess of the doorway.

Goldy was at once skilful and contemptuous, and all the time his own gold remained in his hand, rustling mouse-like amongst the paper money. Goldy took the sweat from Franc's forehead with notes as soft as napkins. This is your thing all right, squire, he said. Franc buckled in the corner, breathing as if stabbed.

Talk to me, talk to me, he said. The notes were familiar, like sections of worn sheets, finely creased and tinged with inflicted experience. Goldy gripped some notes and imposed tension until they tore with the sound of a small fire crackling in its grate. Tens were royal blue, twenties rust orange, and others green and yellow: all colours rendered subtle by usage, and barely more than degrees of shadow in the doorway where Goldy and Franc were close together. I said talk to me, said Franc.

Baht, rupee, escudo, chon, the obedient whisper began. Centavos, peso, florins, centime, rial, colon, satung, piaster, lek, schilling, lira, stater, drachma, krona. Some notes crumpled and fell, lay amongst their feet on the tiled floor of the investment counsellor's small portico. Dinars, talents, zloty, aurei, quetzal, crowns, gulden, cedi, shekel, yen, groschen, ruble. Franc's eyes rolled. The white of them caught light from the arcade of indulgences and was tinged with green-blue like the white of a hard-boiled egg. There we are then, squire. The two of them were close together in the deep doorway, and notes like worn tongues, with all the knowing and unknowing language, passed between them.

People in search of mercenary pleasure came back and forth in the arcade. The automatic vending machines clicked obligingly, car horns and insolent cries echoed from the street, a youth sprayed dollar signs and kissed them dry, and the neons in the arcade glowed as living coral in tropical intensity. Opposite Franc's doorway a message in pink incessantly began on the left and ran off to the right again, again. Money Is The Best Charge, it said.

The Frozen Continents

I had never met Beavis before he and I were put on the PEP scheme together. I finished filling in the form promising not to divulge vital and confidential council business which might come my way, and then followed the supervisor to the car. Beavis was already seated. 'This is Beavis,' said the supervisor.

'Typhoon Agnes hit central Philippines on the fifth of November claiming more than eight hundred lives,' said Beavis. 'Five hundred on Panay Island alone, three hundred and twenty-five kilometres south of Manila. Another forty-five killed in Leyte and Eastern Sawar provinces.' The supervisor looked away: I said hello to Beavis.

The PEP scheme was an inside one at the museum because it was winter. Where we were taken, however, it seemed colder than outside. Museums create a chill at the best of times, but in our unused part were ice-floes and penguins. A panorama, the supervisor said. All the penguins were to be handled with care and stored out of harm's way along the wall, but the rest was to be dismantled and carried down to the yard. 'I'll look in tomorrow and see how you're going,' said the supervisor. His nose was dripping in the cold.

'Right,' I said.

'A cold wave at the end of last year claimed at least two hundred and ninety lives in north and east India. Low temperatures and unseasonal fog and rain caused general disruption to air traffic,' said Beavis, with no apparent realisation of irony.

'There's a toilet and tearoom at the west end of the corridor on this floor. Ten-thirty and three-thirty,' said the supervisor. He started coughing as he left.

The ocean was what we began on first. As it was plywood it was difficult to recover any sheets to use again. When the water was gone we would be able to move about freely and take greater care with the ice-floes and penguins. I found it an odd sensation at first, standing waist deep in Antarctica as we dismantled it. I pointed out to Beavis the clear symbolism relating to man's despoliation of the last natural continent and so on. Beavis in reply told me that fourteen people were killed in a stampede when a fire broke out during a wedding ceremony at Unye in the Turkish province of Ordu.

We had the green sea out by ten-thirty. Beavis stood shivering by a window we had uncovered and wiped free of dust. He had his arms folded and a hand in each armpit, and he looked wistfully down on to a square of frosted grass, and the neat gravel boundaries. 'It's time for our tea-break,' I told him.

An outline of a hand in felt pen and a list of instructions concerning the Zip were the only decorations on the cream walls of the tearoom: points about not leaving the Zip unattended when filling and so on. I had it read within the first minute, but then words are always the things I notice. There was one failure in agreement of number between subject and verb, but overall the notice served its purpose. I wasn't as confident in assessing the people. They accepted us with exaggerated comradeship as is the response of people in secure, professional employment when confronted with PEP workers, amputees or Vietnamese refugees. I gave my name and introduced Beavis. Beavis had a classy-looking pair of basketball boots, and the most hair on the backs of his hands that I've ever seen. 'Army worms invaded the Zambezi Valley in the north of Zimbabwe and destroyed maize and sorghum crops over more than one hundred square kilometres of farmland,' he said. The museum staff present became more amiable still.

One girl had seductive earlobes and dark, close curls. I had a vision in which I persuaded her to come with me, in which I bit her ear beneath the curls and we made the earth move, or at least shook Antarctica with some vehemence. Instead, all of us apart from Beavis shuffled and spoke of inconsequential things. Beavis had several cups of coffee, then abruptly told us of the twenty-four bed-ridden people who died in a fire which broke out in an old-people's home near the town of Beauvais. Impressively recounted, it subdued us all. I guiltily enjoyed the warmth from the wall heaters and my tea — before going back to the South Pole.

Antarctica had been built in sections and we tried to get as much clean timber and plywood sheets out as possible. As we worked I explained to Beavis the Celtic influence in modern poetry, and he told me of the bush fires in south-east Australia, and the earthquake, six on the Richter scale, which killed at least twenty people in India's Assam state. Beavis had a clear, well-modulated voice, and he was deft with the hammer and saw as well. I thought that he'd probably been one of those students, brilliant and compulsive, whose brain had spiralled free of any strict prescription. We had a rest after managing to strip off the first hessian and plaster ice-floe. The sun gradually turned the corner of the museum, melting the frost from a section of the lawn. It caused a precise demarcation between green and white, like the pattern of a flag. Beavis looked out too, and pondered.

We got on well, Beavis and I, although he wasn't light-hearted at all. As he was releasing one penguin the torso came away in his hands, and left the bum and webbed feet on the ice. Beavis stumbled back on to the discarded timber, exposing the heavy treads of his basketball boots, but he didn't laugh with me, just rubbed his shins and looked carefully down the corridor as if expecting a visitor. 'There's got to be some natural mortality among penguins,' I said. 'Put it behind the others and it'll hardly show.'

'More than one hundred people drowned when a boat capsized in mid-stream on the Kirtonkhola River near the town of Barisal in Bangladesh,' said Beavis.

I carried armfuls of wood and plaster down to the yard before lunchtime. I experimented with several different routes, partly for variety of experience, partly in the hope of seeing the girl with the dark curls, but she wasn't visible. Somehow I imagined her in the medieval glass and tapestry section rather than in natural history panoramas. I discussed the subject of feminine perfection with Beavis, pointing out the paradox that, in nature as in art, beauty comes not from beauty, but from the combination of the ordinary and the earthly. 'That woman,' I said to Beavis, 'is skin, blood and spittle, that's the wonder of it.' Beavis considered the insight and told me that more than four hundred passengers were killed when a crowded train plunged into a ravine near Awash, some two hundred and fifty kilometres east of Addis Ababa.

Beavis suffered a headache a little before twelve o'clock. I think the cold, and the dust from the penguins, caused it. He sat on a four by four exposed from the display and leant on to the window. His cheek spread out and whitened on the glass. Three times he began to tell me of a tsunami in Hokkaido, but his words slurred into an unintelligible vortex. He burped, and rolled his face on the icy glass. 'It's time for our lunch-break anyway,' I said. He rolled his head back and forth in supplication and whispered ahh, ahh, ahh to comfort himself. The penguins refused to become involved; each retained its viewpoint with fixed intensity. Illness isolates more effectively than absence. I knew Beavis wouldn't miss me for a while, so I went to the small staffroom and made two cups of sweet tea, and brought them and the yellow seat cover back to Antarctica.

The yellow cover draped well around Beavis's shoulders, and he held it together at his chest. He had dribbled on the back of his hand and the black hair glistened there. He sipped his tea, though, and listened while I explained why I had given up formal academic studies, and my plan to use the Values Party to restructure education in New Zealand. I think he was pretty much convinced and I let him sit quietly as I worked. Afterwards he seemed to feel better, because he wiped his face with the yellow cover, and fluffed up his hair. He told me about the Bhopal poisonous gas discharge which caused more than two and a half thousand deaths. 'I remember that one,' I said. There was quite a lot I could say about Bhopal, and I said it as we started on the penguins and ice-floes again. Beavis's preoccupation with recent accidental disasters was a salutary thing in some ways: it minimised our own grievance, made even Antarctica's grip bearable.

The sun made steady progress around the building, and the frost cut back across the lawn with surgical precision. Beavis's affliction passed. I went, in all, eleven different ways down to the yard with remains of the southern continent, but I never saw Aphrodite. I stopped the permutations when a gaunt man with the look of an Egyptologist shouted at me that if I dropped any more rubbish in his wing he'd contact the PEP supervisor.

There's a knack to everything, and Beavis and I were getting the hang of our job. We didn't tear any more penguins after that first one in the morning, yet some of them were soft and weakened, and smelt like teddy-bears stored away for coming generations. I said to Beavis that there'd been too much moisture over the years, and that a controlled climate was necessary for the sort of exhibits which had stuffed birds. 'Torrential rain caused flooding and mudslides which killed eleven people and swept away dwellings on the outskirts of Belo Horizonte in the south-east state of Minas Gerais, Brazil.'

Before three o'clock I remembered to smuggle the seat-cover back to the tearoom, and return our cups. I told Beavis that my estimate was that we'd have the whole panorama cleared out inside four days. PEP schemes lasted three months, therefore obviously a good deal of job variety remained — other panoramas to destroy, perhaps. A nocturnal setting for our kiwis, or an outdated display of feral cat species. Beavis made no reply. He was most moved to conversation by literary and philosophical concerns. It was a credit to him really: he had very little small talk, did Beavis.

Do not turn off at the wall, it said by the Zip in the tearoom. The Egyptologist was there and he bore a grudge. 'We're going to have three months of this then, are we,' he said. 'A gradual demolition of the institution around us.'

'A Venezuelan freighter was washed ashore in Florida during a storm that caused one death and millions of dollars of damage.'

'For Christ's sake,' said the gaunt man.

The girl with the dark curls didn't come in. The tearoom hardly seemed the same place as that of the morning, but I knew from the writing on the wall that it was. As we went away the Egyptologist had a laugh at our expense. Beavis didn't mind: he trailed his hand on the banisters, and made sure he didn't step on any of the triangles in the lino pattern. Circles were safe, it appeared.

The ice age was in retreat before us. I had fourteen penguins arranged in column of route along the wall, and in the grounds two piles grew — one of rubbish and one of reusable timber. We realised that the sun wasn't going to reach our window, and days start to get colder again in winter after four o'clock. I suggested to Beavis that we leave the penguins in the habitat which suited them, and show our initiative by burning the scraps we'd collected in the yard. We could keep warm with good excuse until knock-off time. I didn't want Beavis to suffer one of his headaches again.

We built a small fire on a garden plot, stood close to it for warmth, and watched the smoke ghost away in the quiet, cold afternoon. Beavis enjoyed the job of putting new pieces on the fire, and I listened as he told of the consequences when the Citarum River overflowed into several villages of Java's Bundung region and considered myself lucky. The park trees had black, scrawny branches like roots in the air, as if the summer trees had been turned upside down for the season. Deep hidden in the soil were green leaves and scarlet berries.

The museum rose up beyond the yard and the park, but despite all the windows I couldn't see anyone looking out at all. No one to hear us, no one to join us, no one to judge us. The strip of lawn closest to the museum still kept its frost like a snowfall. It would build there day after day. No one to see Beavis and me with our fire. Beavis delicately nudged timber into the fire with his basketball boots, and watched smoke weave through the tree roots. I pointed out to him that we were burning Antarctica to keep ourselves warm, which was an option not available to Scott and Shackleton. 'More than five hundred died when a liquid gas depot exploded at San Juan Ixhuatepec, a suburb of Mexico City,' said Beavis.

I felt very hungry by the time the hooters went. Beavis and I had missed lunch because of his headache. If he didn't have something soon I thought he might get another attack because of a low blood-sugar level. My own blood-sugar level was pretty low, it seemed to me. We left the fire to burn itself out, and went three blocks down to the shops. I had enough money for two hot pies, and when I came out of the shop I saw Beavis sitting on the traffic island watching the five o'clock rush. Some people walked, some trotted. Some of the cars had Turbo written on their sides, and some had only obscure patterns of rust, but they all stormed on past Beavis who was as incongruous there as among the penguins. His lips were moving. I suppose he was reminding the world of earthquakes in Chile, or of an outbreak of cholera in Mali.

I was surprised how satisfied most of the people were, but good on them, good on them. How should they know that the frozen continent was to be found right here in the midst of our city after all.

Valley Day

Every second month Brian went with his father on the Big Kick. They drove up the valley, and the minister took services at the little church of Hepburn and at the Sutherlands' house. One midday service at Hepburn going up, one in the afternoon at Sutherlands', then the evening drive home. In the autumn the long sun would squint down the valley and the shadows blossom from hedges and trees, and slant from the woodwork of buildings in angles no longer true.

One sermon did the trick on the Big Kick, with only the level of formality altered to suit the circumstances. The minister was relaxed despite the hours of driving, and treated it as a gallant expedition for his son's sake. 'Off on the Big Kick again, eh,' he said. 'The Big Kick.' The scent of the hot motor, taste of finest, stealthy dust, sight of the valley floor paddocks all odd shapes to fit the river flats and, higher in the gullies sloping back, the bush made a stand. Few farmhouses, fewer cars to be met, and dust ahead a clear warning anyway.

Brian had his hand in the airflow, and used it to feel the lift on his palm. He assessed the road. Each dip, each trit-trotting bridge, places he would set his ambushes. Hurons or Assyrians swarmed out to test his courage, while his father practised parts of the sermon or recited Burns and then murmured in wonderment at such genius. Brian made the air take some of the weight of his hand, and he kept his head from the window when a small swamp of rushes and flax was passed in case there were snipers hiding there.

'Will the one-armed man from the war be there?' he said.

'Mr Lascelles. Don't draw attention to it.'

'It happened in the war.'

'His tank was hit, I believe. The arm was amputated only after a long struggle to save it: not until he was back in New Zealand. I visited him in hospital I remember.'

'You can still feel your fingers when you've got no arm,' Brian said. 'They itch and that. If someone stood on where they would be then you'd feel the pain.'

'No,' said his father, but the boy kept thinking it. He saw a cloud a long way off like a loaf of bread, and the top spread more rapidly than the bottom, and both were transformed into an octopus.

Hepburn was a district rather than a settlement. The cemetery was the largest piece of civic real estate, and the greatest gathering of population that could be mustered in one place. Mrs Patchett had nearly finished cleaning the church. She was upset because a bird had got in and made a mess, and then died by the pulpit. She said there were holes under the eaves. Even such a small church maintained its fragrance of old coats and old prayers, of repeated varnish and supplication, and insects as tenants with a life-cycle of their own. The air was heavy with patterns of the past: shapes almost visible, sounds brimming audible. An accumulated human presence: not threatening, instead embarrassed to be found still there, and having no place else to go. There were seven pews down one side, and six on the other. Down the aisle stretched two parallel brass carpet crimps, but no carpet in between. One stained window, all the rest were plain, a blood poppy amidst green and blue, dedicated to the Lascelles brothers killed within three days of each other in the Great War.

Brian took the bird out on the dust shovel. It left just a stain on the boards behind the pulpit. He threw the bird above the long grass: it broke apart in the air, and the boy closed his eyes lest some part of it fly back into his face. He brought his father's Bible, soft and heavy, from the car, and the travelling communion tray with the rows of small glasses set like glass corks in the holes, and the bottle full of the shed blood of Christ.

'Don't wander off then,' said his father. 'Don't get dirty, or wander off. Remember we'll be going with one of the families for lunch.' The boy was watching a walnut tree which overshadowed the back of the church, and ranks of pines behind. He found a place where, Indian-like, he was hidden, but could look out. He crossed his legs and watched the families begin to arrive. The Hepburn church no longer had a piano, and the man with the piano accordion came early to practise the hymns required. 'Rock of Ages', and 'Turn Back O Man'. He was shy, very muscular, and prefaced everything he played or said with a conciliatory cough. Fourteen other people came as the piano accordion played. Fourteen adults and six children. Brian watched the children linger in the sunlight, before trailing in behind their parents. The one-armed Mr Lascelles came. Even to Brian, Mr Lascelles didn't look old. He wasn't all that many years back from the war, and he laughed and turned to other people by the cars as if he were no different. Brian got up and walked about in the pine needles as if he had only one arm. He looked back at the trees he passed, and smiled as Mr Lascelles had done. Without realising it he walked with a limp, for he found it difficult to match a gait to having one arm.

The accordionist coughed and began to play, the families sang, and the boy stood still at the edge of the trees to see the valley and the bush on the hills. Rock of Ages cleft for me, let me hide myself in thee. He felt a tremor almost of wonder, but not wonder. A sense of significance and presence comes to the young, and is neither questioned by them nor given any name. All the people of that place seemed shut in there singing, and he alone outside in the valley. He could see all together the silvered snail tracks across the concrete path, the road in pale snatches, the insect cases of pine needles drawn immensely strong, the bird's wing in the long grass, the glowing Lascelles poppy in the sunlit window. Rock of Ages cleft for me. Brian tipped his head back to see the light through the pines, and the blood ran, or the sky moved, and the great, sweet pines seemed to be falling, and he sat down dizzy, and with his shoulders hunched for a moment against the impact of the trees. The church was an ark with all on board; it dipped and rolled in the swell of the accordion, and he alone was outside amidst the dry grass and shadows, a sooty fantail, gravestones glimpsed through the falling pines of his own life.

He saw cones. The old cones, puffed and half rotted in the needles were ignored. He wanted those heavy with sap and seed, brown yet tinged with green, and shaped as owls. When dislodged they were well shaped to the hand to be hurled as owl grenades against impossible odds across the road, or sent bouncing among the grave stones to wake somebody there. He gathered new stocks by climbing with a stick and striking them from the branches. At first he climbed carefully to keep the gum from his clothes, but it stuck to him anyway, gathered dirt and wouldn't rub away, and lay like birthmarks on his legs and held his fingers.

His father was preaching, for the church was quiet. Brian heaped up a mass of pine needles beneath the trees, working on his knees and bulldozing the needles with both hands out in front. He built a heap as high as himself, and jumped up and down on it. When he lost interest he left the trees and walked into the graveyard to search for skinks. Quietly he bent the grass from the tombstones, like parting a fleece, and after each movement he waited, poised in case of a lizard. He found none. He imagined that they were destroyed by things that came down from the bush at night. He picked at the resin stains on his hands. Deborah Lascelles, 1874–1932, Called Home. Brian forgot about the skinks. 'Called Home,' he said to himself. He thought about it as he went down the tree-lined margin of the small cemetery and on to the road. He was disappointed that there were no new cars, but one at least was a V8. He shaded his eyes by pressing his hands to the door glass, in an effort to see what the speedo went up to. He reasoned that anyway as it had twice as many cylinders as their car, it must do twice the speed.

Old now is Earth, and none may count her days. The final hymn. Brian went back into the trees and stood as king on his pine needle heap. He arced his urine in the broken sunlight as an act of territory and checked the two balls in his pouch with brief curiosity. He jousted against the pines one more time, and brought down a perfect brown-green owl. He ran his hand over the tight ripples of his cone. He hefted it from hand to hand as he went back to the church.

His father stood at the doorway to shake hands and talk with the adults as they left. Those still inside showed no impatience. They talked among themselves, or listened with goodwill to what was said by and to the minister. There were few secrets, and no urgency to leave the only service for two months. Mrs Patchett showed Mr Jenkins the holes beneath the eaves, and he stuffed them with paper as an interim measure, and promised to return and do more another day. Things borrowed were transferred from car to car. Wheelan Lascelles stood unabashed, and on his one arm the white sleeve was brilliant against the tan. 'That poem you used,' he said to the minister. 'What poem was that?'

'One of my own, in fact.' Brian shared his father's pleasure. They smiled together. The boy edged closer to his father so as to emphasise his affiliation.

'Is that so? I thought it a fine poem, a poem of our own country. I'd like some day to have a copy of it.'

From the sheets folded in his Bible the minister took the hand-written poem, and gave it. It was found a matter of interest to those remaining: the minister giving his poem to Wheelan Lascelles. Others wished they had thought to mention it, and strove to recall it.

'We're going to the Jenkins' for lunch,' Brian's father told him when everyone had left the church. The Jenkins lived twelve miles up the valley. The minister preferred having lunch with a family living past the church, for then in the afternoon the trip to Sutherland's was made that much shorter. He let the Jenkins drive on ahead because of the dust, and followed on. 'Mr and Mrs Jenkins eat well,' he said to his son with satisfaction.

On a terrace above the river were the house and sheds of the Jenkins' farm, and a long dirt track like a wagon trail leading in, and a gate to shut behind. 'What have you got on yourself?' said the minister, as he checked appearances before entering the house.

'Gum.' Brian rubbed at it dutifully, but knew it wouldn't come off.

'And what's in your pocket?'

'Just a pine cone,' he said. His father flipped a hand as a sign, and Brian took the owl and rolled it away. It lay still warm from his body on the stones and earth of the yard.

'You realise old Mrs Patchett died, of course, and wasn't there today,' said Mrs Jenkins when they sat down. Brian thought some day he might return and find his pine cone grown far above the Jenkins' home. 'Her mind went well before the end. She accused them of starving her, and used to hide food in her room. The smell was something awful at times.' Mr Jenkins smiled at Brian and skilfully worked the carving knife.

'She wasn't at the services the last time or two,' the minister said. 'I did visit her. As you say, her mind seemed clouded, the old lady.' Mr Jenkins carved the hot mutton with strength and delicacy.

'She was a constant trial to them,' Mrs Jenkins said. Mr Jenkins balanced on the balls of his feet, and gave his task full concentration. Like a violinist he swept the blade, and the meat folded away.

'I saw Mr Lascelles who's only got one arm,' said Brian.

'Yes, Wheelan Lascelles,' said Mr Jenkins without pausing.

'Old Mrs Patchett was a Lascelles,' said his wife, 'They only left her a short time, but she must have tried to walk back up to where the first house on the property used to be. She went through the bull paddock, and it charged, you see. She wouldn't have known a thing of it, though.' With his smile Mr Jenkins held the gravy boat in front of Brian and, when the boy smiled back, Mr Jenkins tipped gravy over his meat and potatoes, and the gravy flowed and steamed.

'The second family in the valley were Patchetts,' said Mrs Jenkins, 'and then Lascelles. Strangely enough, Wheelan's father lost an arm. There must be long odds against that, I'd say. It happened in a pit sawing accident before Wheelan was born.'

Brian stopped eating to consider the wonder of it: two generations of one-armed Lascelles.

On the long sill of the Jenkins' kitchen window were tomatoes to ripen, and a fan of letters behind a broken clock. And he could see a large totara tree alone on the terrace above the river.

'And which was the first European family?' said the minister as he ate.

'McVies. McVies and then Patchetts were the first, and now all the McVies have gone one way or another. McVies were bushmen, of course, not farmers, and once the mills stopped they moved on.'

'I haven't seen a McVie in the valley for thirty years,' said Mr Jenkins, as if the McVies were a threatened species, fading back before civilisation.

'If your father has only one arm then you're more likely to have one arm yourself,' volunteered Brian.

'Play outside for a while,' his father said. 'Until Mr and Mrs Jenkins and I have finished our tea.'

'There's a boar's head at the back of the shed,' said Mr Jenkins. 'We're giving the beggars something of a hurry up recently.'

'There you are then,' said the minister.

The boar's head was a disappointment, lop-sided on an outrigger of the shed. It resembled a badly sewn mask of rushes and canvas. False seams had appeared as if warped from inner decay. Only the tusks were adamant in malice; curved, stained yellow and black in the growth rings. Brian reached up and tried to pull out a tusk, but although the head creaked like a cane basket, the tusk held, and only a scattering of detritus came down. The vision of the bull that murdered old Mrs Patchett was stronger than the defeated head of a pig. The boy sat in the sun and imagined the old lady escaping back to her past, and the great bull coming to greet her.

'What happened to the bull?' he asked his father as the minister topped up the radiator.

'What's that?'

'What happened to the bull that killed Mrs Patchett?'

'I don't know. Why is it you're always fascinated with such things? I don't suppose the bull could be blamed for acting according to its nature.'

As they left amidst the benevolence of Mr Jenkins' smile, and the persistent information from his wife, Brian saw his cone lying in the yard, green and turning brown, and he lined it through the window with his finger for luck, and saw it sprout there and soar and ramify until, like the beanstalk, it reached the sky. 'A substantial meal,' said the minister.

'There was too much gravy,' said Brian.

'I was born in country like this,' said his father. The bush began to stand openly on the hillsides, and on the farmland closer to the road were stumps which gripped even in death. 'It's awkward country to farm,' said the minister. 'It looks better than it is.' There would be a hut in his pine, and a rope ladder which could be drawn up so that boars and bulls would be powerless below. Tinned food and bottles to collect the rain. Mr and Mrs Jenkins wouldn't realise that he was there, and at times he would come down to the lower world and take what he wanted. 'They tried to make it all dairy country, but it didn't work,' his father said. Brian was willing to be an apparent listener as they went up the valley, mile after mile pursued only by the dust.

Dogs barked them in to Sutherland's. The Oliphants and more Patchetts were already waiting in the main room. There was a social ease among them, arisen from a closeness of lifestyle, proximity and religion. The Sutherlands had no children left at home, the last Patchett boy was at boarding school; only the Oliphant twins, six-year-old girls, were there to represent youth. They sat with their legs stuck out rebelliously because they weren't allowed to thump the piano keys. The Sutherlands had a cousin staying who was a Catholic. Brian watched him with interest. There was a mystery and power in Catholicism, he thought, a dimension beyond the home spun non-conformism that he knew from the inside. Surely there was some additional and superstitious resource with which to enrich life. 'Absolutely riddled with cancer,' Brian heard Mr Oliphant tell the minister.

When the minister was ready, the service in the living room began. No more exact timing was necessary. Mrs Sutherland played the piano, and Mr Oliphant enjoyed singing very loudly and badly. The Oliphant twins refused to stand up with the adults, remaining in a sulk with their legs stiff before them. Their eyes followed Brian past the window as he went from the house. He thought the piano disappointing in comparison with the accordion, more inhibited and careful, less suited to the movement of leaves and water, to the accompaniment of birds.

Brian remembered a traction engine from previous visits. Once it had been used in the mills, but since left in the grass: heavy iron and brass, and great, ribbed wheels. It was warm from the sun, and Brian scaled it and sat there. The traction engine had been built to withstand enormous pressures, and before an age of planned obsolescence. It was a weathered outcrop, the rust only a film which didn't weaken, and the brass solid beneath the tarnish. A land train cast there amidst the barley grass and nodding thistle. He shifted what levers were not seized, and rocked to suggest the motion of the engine on the move.

'You get tired of all the services, I suppose?' said the Sutherlands' cousin. He stood in his carpet slippers, and wore a green woollen jersey despite the heat. He was almost bald, with just a rim of coarse, red hair, like the pine needles the boy had heaped up in the morning. Brian came down to talk. It seemed discourteous to remain raised up. 'I'm in charge of the afternoon tea. I'm a Catholic, you see.' His eyes were deeply sunk, like the sockets of a halloween pumpkin. 'I've nothing against your father.' They watched heavy, white geese trooping past the sheds. 'There's cake, of course, but you know there's watercress sandwiches as well. Can you imagine that?' Brian thought it rabbit food, but the cousin was from the city. 'She went and collected it from the creek, just like that. There's wonder still in the world,' he said. 'Did I tell you I'm a Catholic?' The cousin began to cry without making any noise, but shedding tears. Brian gave him some privacy by taking a stick and beating a patch of nettles by the hen-run. But the cousin wiped his tears away and followed him. He didn't seem interested in maintaining an adult dignity any more. 'Is that gum on your legs?' he said. The boy told him that he had been playing in the trees at Hepburn.

'There's graves there. One said "Called Home" on it.'

'"Called Home" — did it really?' The cousin shared Brian's fascination with the phrase. 'Called Home'. He began to laugh: not a social laugh, but a hoarse laugh, spreading downwards and out like a pool. A sound of irony and fear and submission.

Mr Oliphant began shouting 'Earth might be fair, and all men glad and wise'. The cousin listened with his mouth still shaped from the laughter.

'I'd better see to the afternoon tea,' he said. 'There are lesser rendezvous yet. I'll crib another watercress sandwich if I can hold it down.'

'Peals forth in joy man's old undaunted cry,' they heard Mr Oliphant singing.

'These things are at the end of my life,' the cousin said, 'and the beginning of yours. I wonder if they seem any different for that.' The cousin turned back from the house after a few steps, and came past Brian. 'Jesus,' he said. 'I'm going to be sick again.' He rubbed the flat of his hands on the green wool of his jersey as if in preparation for a considerable task, and walked towards the sheds. He gave a burp, or sudden sob.

The Sutherlands, Mr Oliphant and the minister came out in search of him when their afternoon tea wasn't ready. Brian could see the Oliphant twins looking through the window. 'Have you seen Mrs Sutherland's cousin?' Brian's father asked him. The boy told him about the crying and the sheds.

'I hate to think — in his state of mind,' said Mr Sutherland. He and the minister began to run. Mr Oliphant saw his contribution best made in a different talent. He filled his lungs. 'Ashley, Ashley,' he cried: so loud that birds flew from the open sheds, and the Oliphant twins pressed their faces to the window. The echoes had settled and Mrs Sutherland had prevented him from further shouting, when Mr Sutherland came back.

'It's all right,' said Mr Sutherland. 'He's been sick again, that's all. He's got himself into a state.'

'Who can blame him,' said Mrs Sutherland.

'He was going to make the afternoon tea,' said Brian. 'He started to cry.'

'He's a good deal worse today, but the Reverend Willis is with him.' Mr Sutherland was both sympathetic and matter of fact. 'They're best left alone,' he said. 'Come on back to the house.' Mr Oliphant was disappointed that it wasn't the end, not even in a more dramatic approach to the end.

'A sad business,' he said in his lowest voice, which carried barely fifty yards. Brian was left to wait for his father. He thought that in that quiet afternoon he could hear Ashley's sobs and his father's voice. He climbed back on to the throne which was the engine, and rested his face and arms on the warm metal.

A column of one-armed Lascelles was moving back up the valley from the war, each with a poem in his hand, and the accordion played 'Rock of Ages' as they marched. Mr Jenkins deftly knifed a wild pig, all the while with a benevolent smile, and in his torrent voice Mr Oliphant Called Home a weeping Ashley: deep eyes and woollen jersey. A host of pine owls, jersey green and brown, spread their wings at last, while old Mrs Patchett escaped again and accused her kin of starvation as she sought an earlier home. Behind and beyond the sway of the accordion's music, and growing louder, was the sound of the grand, poppy-red bull cantering with its head down from the top of the valley towards them all.

Mumsie and Zip

Mumsie saw the car coming at five, as she had expected. The general noise of homeward traffic was at a distance, but still the desperation was apparent in the pitch of it. Zip always turned off the engine when in the gate, and coasted on the concrete strips until he was parallel with the window. The grass was spiky and blue in the poor light of winter. Mumsie had cacti on the window sill, and the dust lay amid the thorns of *Mammillaria wildii*.

Zip undid his seatbelt, and stepped out. He took the orange nylon cover from the boot, and began covering the car for the night. He spread the cover evenly before he began to tie it down. Zip always started at the same corner and worked clockwise round the car. He didn't bend to tie the corners as a woman would bend, with backside out, but crouched, agile and abrupt, balanced on his toes. Sometimes when Mumsie was close to him as he crouched like that, she would hear his knees pop. Mumsie wondered if there would be a day when she would go out and ask Zip not to cover the car because there was something of significance she had to attend: a premiere perhaps, or an apparently trivial summons which would become This Is Your Life, Mumsie.

Mumsie knew Zip wouldn't look up as he came past the window: they always reserved recognition for the kitchen when Zip came home from work. Zip would go to the lavatory, and then to their bedroom to take off his jacket and shoes. Mumsie heard him flush the bowl, and go through for his other shoes.

Zip came to the stove. He stood by Mumsie's shoulder. 'How's things?' he said.

The mist of the winter evening was strung through the poles and gables, the thinning hair of a very old woman. Toby McPhedron tried to kick free a flattened hedgehog from the surface of the road.

'Fine,' said Mumsie. 'And you?'

'Busy as usual,' said Zip. 'Just the same, Mumsie. You know how it is.'

'Casserole,' said Mumsie as Zip lifted the lid, 'with the onions in chunks the way you like it. Chunky chunks instead of sliced up thin.'

'Good on you, Mumsie, good on you,' said Zip. 'You know what I like all right.' He rubbed his forehead and circled the sockets of his eyes.

'So the usual day?' said Mumsie.

'You know how it is. Busy, of course: always the same.'

'So Mumsie got a casserole,' said Mumsie.

'You know I like a casserole all right,' said Zip. Mumsie noticed how the pupils of his eyes jittered the way they often did, although his face was flat and still. He stood beside her and looked at the casserole while his pupils jittered.

'You know I couldn't get hardly a thing to dry today. There's no wind and no sun. Hardly a thing dried. I had to take most of it off the line again and put it in the good room with the heater.'

'It's that sort of day,' said Zip. He placed the butter and salt and pepper on the table, and cork mats with the picture of a kitten halting a ball of fluffy wool.

'Mr Beresford died,' said Mumsie.

'Mr Beresford?'

'The place with the new roof, two down from the corner. I heard Mrs Rose talking about it in the shop.'

'Ah,' said Zip.

'So nothing of interest at work today.'

'Uh-huh,' said Zip. He sat down at his place, which was facing the stove and the bench. He laid his hands one each side of his cork mat, as a knife and fork are laid.

'They haven't found the murderer yet,' said Mumsie.

'Murderer?'

'Who murdered those two girls in the boatshed in Auckland. Shaved their heads, I think it said. There's a lot of sick things.'

Zip left his hands resting on the table and he looked at the floor by the bench where the pattern on the lino had been worn away. Mumsie's legs plodded this way and that around the kitchen, but always came back to that worn place, on which she shuffled back and forth from stove to table to bench. Zip seemed absorbed: as if that worn patch were a screen and Mumsie's splayed shoes played out some cryptic choreography. But his black eye spots continued to jiggle, and the focus wasn't quite right to hit the worn lino, but aimed deeper, at something behind. Zip sat still, as if conserving energy for a final effort, or as if that final effort had been made to no avail. Mumsie looked at him from time to time. 'Mumsie's done peas shaken in the pot with butter,' she said, 'and baked potatoes in their skins.'

'You're a winner, Mumsie, that's for sure.'

Tears began to form on the windows, and the light outside was fading quickly. 'I like to be in my own house when it gets dark,' said Zip. They could hear persistent traffic noise from the corner, and Toby McPhedron ran a stick along the tin fence next door.

'You don't mind about the heater on in the good room?' said Mumsie. 'There's no drying at all.'

'We can go there ourselves later,' said Zip. 'We'd have to heat one room.'

'Now why would the murderer shave those girls' heads?' said Mumsie.

'Kinky sex, Mumsie. You want to watch out.' Zip watched his casserole with the chunky onions being served, and the potatoes blistered grey-brown, and the peas in butter glistening as emeralds.

Mumsie talked about Mrs Rose's visit to the dentist, about the manner of Mr Beresford's dying third-hand, about the boatshed murderer, and the good room door-knob which just came off in her hand. The tears made tracks down the windows, and those tracks showed black, or spangled back the kitchen light. Mumsie talked of a party at the Smedley's which they weren't invited to, and how either a niece or a cousin of Debbie Simpson's had a growth in her ear which might be pressing on her brain. Zip said, 'Is that right, Mumsie', and nodded his head to show that he was listening, and in satisfaction as he crunched the casserole onions done in chunks as he liked them, and he kept looking at things deeper than the worn lino by the bench. Mumsie wondered if she should take some pikelets along to Mrs Beresford, or whether she would only be thought nosy because she hadn't really known him. A dog had torn Mrs Jardine's rubbish bag open again, and Mrs Jardine had to clean it up in her good clothes when she came home at lunchtime, Mumsie said.

The winter night, the lizard voice of the traffic at a distance, the condensation on the windows, all intensified the artificial light of the kitchen where Mumsie and Zip ate their casserole, until it was a clear, yellow space separate from the rest of life, independent even from the rest of their own experience, and isolating them there — Mumsie and Zip.

'Mumsie,' said Zip, 'now that was a real casserole, and don't worry about the doorknob, because I can get that bastard back on later.'

'I knew you'd like it, being winter and that. And there'll be enough for you tomorrow.'

Zip lit a cigarette as he stood by the bench and waited to help with the dishes. He pulled the smoke in, and his eyelids dropped for a moment as the smoke hit deep in his lungs. In a long sigh he breathed out. The smoke drifted, the colour of the condensation on the window, and Zip had the teatowel folded over his arm like a waiter, and stood before the plastic drip tray as he waited for the dishes. 'I'll put the rest of the casserole in something else,' said Mumsie, 'and then the dish can be soaked. There's always some bubbles out and bakes on the rim.'

'Let it soak then, Mumsie,' said Zip.

'Don't let me miss the start of the news. Maybe they've found the boatshed murderer.' Mumsie liked everyone to be brought to justice. Zip dried the forks carefully, pressing a fold of towel between the prongs. He tapped the ash from his cigarette into *Chamaecereus silvestrii* on the sill.

'It's just as well we're not in the boatshed belt,' he said.

'But it could be anyone, Zip.'

'Except Mr Beresford, Mumsie. I'd say he must be in the clear.'

'No, I meant it could be any woman. It said on the talkback that these things are increasing all the time.'

Zip spread the teatowel over the stove top, and shuffled the cork mats into symmetry so that the images of the kittens and the wool were inline. He stood by Mumsie as she wiped the table, and then he sat there and put down a plastic ashtray. Mumsie told him not to pick at the contact because it was already tatty, so Zip rotated his cigarette packet instead, standing it alternately on end and side, over and over again. His fingers were nimble, and the packet only whispered on the table as it turned. 'We'll go through to the good room soon,' said Mumsie, 'seeing the clothes are already in front of the heater there.'

'That's right,' said Zip. He sighed, and the smoke came like dust from deep in his lungs, and drifted in the yellow light. 'Another day, another dollar,' he said.

'Just another day, you said.'

'That's right. Another day,' said Zip. He tapped with his finger on the cigarette above the ashtray; a column of ash fell neatly and lay like a caterpillar.

'How many of those have you had today?' asked Mumsie.

'Five or six.'

'Mumsie's going to have to hide them, or you'll be up to a packet a day again.'

'You're a tough lady all right,' said Zip.

'Well, Mr Beresford was a heavy smoker, Mrs Rose said, and he wouldn't be told, just kept on. Mrs Rose said in the shop she wouldn't be surprised if that was it.'

'But you don't know it was smoking Beresford died of.'

'It can't have helped,' Mumsie said. Zip continued to turn the packet with his free hand, head over heels it went, again and again. Mumsie said that she'd heard that a lot of drugs had been found in the fire station, but it was all being hushed up. Mumsie enjoyed her delusion of occasionally sharing privileged information. 'It'll all be swept under the carpet because they know each other, all those people, you see if they don't.'

'They'd bloody well come down on you or me though, Mumsie, that's for sure,' said Zip.

Mumsie was talking about the food specials at Four Square when the phone rang. She was comparing for Zip the large coffee with the giant and the standard. Standard meant small, but nothing in supermarkets is labelled small. Zip remained still, apart from turning the cigarette packet. He paid no attention to the phone: he had no hope of it. He was unlucky enough to know his own life. But Mumsie was quite excited. She wondered who that could be, she said, and she tidied her hair as she went into the passage. Zip didn't alter just because Mumsie had gone. He stayed quietly at the table as if relaxed, turning the cigarette packet. He did work his mouth, pulling his lips back first on one side then the other, as a horse does on the bit. Zip looked at the table, and the worn lino by the bench, and Mumsie's cactus plants which could survive her benign forgetfulness, and at the windows decked with tears, and his eyes jiggled.

Mumsie was happy when she bustled back in. She felt things were going on. There were decisions to be made and she was involved, and someone had taken the trouble to phone her. 'It's Irene and Malcolm,' she said. Zip let out a dusty breath. The tears of condensation left black trails on the windows, and a small rainbow bubble winked as Mumsie shifted the detergent flask. 'They're going to stay for a few days next week,' said Mumsie. 'Malcolm's got some management course again.'

'No,' said Zip.

'Why's that?'

'I don't want them here. I don't want them here next week, or next year, or ever. I don't want other people in my house, Mumsie. Got it? I don't want Malcolm and his moustache telling me how well he's doing, and your sister making you look like Ma Kettle all the time.' Zip didn't raise his voice, but there was in it a tone of finality.

'But they're family,' said Mumsie. She turned the water on and off in the sink for no reason.

'They're not coming. You're going to tell them that they can't come, or I'm going to. You'll do it nicer than me.'

'How often do we have people?' said Mumsie. 'We never see anyone.'

'I don't want to see anyone, and I don't want anyone to see me. People are never worth the effort, Mumsie, but you never seem to learn that.'

'I get sick of no one coming. I get sick of always being by ourselves,' said Mumsie.

Zip spread the corners of his mouth in one grimace of exasperation, and then his face was flat again. 'You're stupid,' he said. 'What are you?'

'Maybe I am,' said Mumsie, 'but I've got a life too. I'm not too stupid to have my own sister to stay, am I.'

'You're a stupid, old bitch, Mumsie, and I'm as bad. In a way I'm worse, because I'm just bright enough to see how stupid we both are, and how we're buggered up here like two rats in a dunghill. We've got to keep on living our same life over and over again.'

'Oh, don't start talking like that, and getting all funny.' The windows were black eyes shining with tears, and the custard light of the room grew brighter in contrast with deep winter outside. The table legs cast stalks of shadow across the floor, and high on the cupboard edges the fly dirt clustered like pepper spots. 'Anyway I've told them they can come, and so they can,' said Mumsie. She pretended that by being emphatic she had made an end of it, but her face was flushed and her head nodded without her being aware.

Zip eased from the seat, and took a grip of Mumsie's soft neck. He braced his body against hers and he pushed her head back twice on to the wall. Mumsie's jowls spread upwards because of the pressure of Zip's hand, and trembled with the impact of the wall. Their faces were close, but their eyes didn't meet. The sound of Mumsie's head striking the wall echoed in the kitchen; the mounting for the can opener dug in behind her ear. Mumsie began to weep quietly without any retaliation. 'Now I tell you again they're not coming,' said Zip. He sat back at the table, and began to turn the cigarette packet top over bottom. Mumsie put her hand to the back of her head for comfort, and her fingers came back with a little blood.

'I swept out the storeroom today, Mumsie,' Zip said. 'I swept out the bloody storeroom when I went to that place twenty years ago, and today I swept it out again. I was doing it when the buyers came and they all went past me and into Ibbetson's office. Ibbetson didn't say anything to me, and neither did any of the buyers. I'm the monkey on a stick.'

'I thought you liked my sister,' said Mumsie. She dabbed at the blood with a paper towel, but Zip didn't seem to notice.

'I'd like to screw her, Mumsie, you know that, but she wouldn't let me, and there's nothing else I want to have to do with her apart from screwing her. She's up herself, your sister.'

'You're just saying it.'

'I'm just saying it and it's the truth. We make a good pair, you and me, Mumsie. We don't take the world by storm. Two stupid people, and if we stopped breathing right now it wouldn't mean a thing.'

'It would to me,' said Mumsie.

'We're dead, Mumsie,' said Zip.

'Don't say that.' Mumsie watched Zip, but he didn't reply. He seemed very relaxed. He looked back at the watching windows and his eyes jittered. Mumsie didn't like silences: talk was reassuring evidence of life moving on for Mumsie.

'You're that proud,' said Mumsie. 'You're so proud, and that's the matter with you. You'll choke on your pride in the end.'

'You might be right there, Mumsie,' said Zip. 'Most of us could gag on our own pride.'

'You hurt my head then, you know. It's bleeding.'

'You're all right. Don't start whining. I'll have to hit Ibbetson's head one day, Mumsie, and then there'll be hell to pay.'

'Oh, don't talk about things like that.'

'It's going to happen. Some day it's bound to happen, and there'll be merry hell to pay.'

'Why can't you just be happy, Zip?'

'I'm not quite stupid enough, more's the pity. I can watch myself and I don't bloody want to.'

'Let's go into the good room,' said Mumsie. 'We'll push the clothes out of the way and sit in there in the warm.'

'Sure, but first Mumsie we'll have a cuddle in the bedroom. I quite feel like it, so you get your pants off in there and we'll have a cuddle.'

'It's cold in there,' said Mumsie.

'You get your pants off, Mumsie,' said Zip. 'You know what your murderer did to the boatshed girls — shaved their hair all off, so you want to watch out.'

'It's awful. I meant to watch it on the news to see if they've found him.'

'You can't trust anyone but your family, Mumsie. You've got to realise that.'

'I suppose so.'

Mumsie kept on talking so that Zip would forget to tell her again to go into the bedroom and take her pants off. She told him that after Mr Beresford died the blood came to the surface of his body, so Mrs Rose said, and his face turned black and his stomach too. 'Maybe it was the tarbrush coming out,' said Zip. She told him about Mrs Jardine claiming the family care allowance, even though their combined income was over the limit. She told him again that the doorknob had come off in her hand, and about the niece or cousin of Debbie Simpson's who had a growth in her ear and they might have to operate because it was pressing on her brain and making her smell things that weren't really there. 'What a world,' said Zip. He ran his thumb and forefinger up and down the bridge of his nose, and his eyes jittered, and their focus point was a little beyond anything in the kitchen. He lit another cigarette, and Mumsie didn't say anything about that, but went on talking about who did Mrs Jardine think she was, just because they both worked and she could afford plenty of clothes.

The light was banana yellow and the windows like glasses of stout, beaded with condensation. Mumsie had a magnetic ladybird on the door of the fridge, and the one remaining leg oscillated as the motor came on. Zip had no question on his face, and his hands lay unused on the table before him. 'Mumsie's going to tell you now that I made some caramel kisses today as a treat,' said Mumsie.

'You're a queen,' said Zip. 'You're a beaut.'

'And we'll have another cup of tea, and take it through to the good room with the caramel kisses.' Mumsie brought the tin out and opened the lid to display the two layers of kisses. 'They've come out nice and moist,' she said.

'They look fine, Mumsie,' said Zip. 'You know I like a lot of filling in them.'

'I made them after I'd been to the shop,' said Mumsie. 'It'll be warmer in the good room, and the clothes should be dry.'

When the tea was made, Mumsie put it on a tray. She was pleased to be going at last to the good room. She paused at the door. The blood was smudged dry behind her ear. 'Bring in the caramel kisses for me,' she said.

'Sure thing, Mumsie,' said Zip. He heard Mumsie complaining about there being no knob on the good room door.

'This bloody door, Zip,' said Mumsie. Zip cast his head back quickly and made a laughing face, but without any noise.

'All right, Mumsie,' he said. 'I'll come and do it now,' but he stayed sitting there, his hands on the table, his face still once more, and only his eyes jit jittering as bugs do sometimes in warm evening air.

Trumpeters

The Trumpeters were a family of very tall, very quiet farmers, who had looked down on other people over many generations — not in a patronising manner, but as if in commiseration at the mutual necessity of striking some sort of compromise with life. The Trumpeters were old inhabitants; not wealthy, but with the livelihood of their property beneath their large feet.

Their farm was in Trumpeters' Road; an indication of the family's ties with the district. An unsealed road amongst the downs, white with dust like white pollen in the summer, and a yellow pollen sign at the corner with Trumpeters' Road marked in black. It was limestone country, karst country, with sink holes and ruled limestone outcrops which were weathered grey, or showed pale yellow as a more recent skin. The larger caves had faint, attenuated, Maori drawings, written over with the bolder egotism of Killjoy was here, Wanker, and Pink Floyd.

Neil Trumpeter was my age. My father had taught us both in the two room primary school. Trumpeters were not scholars, but each generation did its time patiently there, and then at the High School: purgatories completely foreign to their natures, but borne as some sort of social exaction before they had earned the right to return to their land. Old Man Trumpeter admitted that there was a need for boys to mix with others for a while. He made it sound a part of his creed of stockmanship. It was difficult however for a Trumpeter to mix — always head and shoulders above anybody else.

Trumpeters were born distinct by both build and temperament. Old Man Trumpeter came to the parents' interviews and sat on a primary chair. My father would try not to smile, and the folds of Trumpeter's best trousers would envelop the little chair. Old Man Trumpeter's hands were like dragons' feet, and he laid them neatly at a distance on his knees. He never began a conversation, and in reply he spoke slowly, almost as if he were watching one word out of sight before releasing the next. His country sentences had gaps for wind and clouds to gather in, for crops to be observed, for memories to well up powerfully behind the eyes. Old Man Trumpeter advanced on to language as he would an untried bridge — with caution and reserve. 'That's about the size of it,' was his persistent idiom of concurrence.

When I was at school with Neil, his grandfather was still alive. I saw him once sitting bowed in the passenger side of the truck cab, his head framed like a Borgia engraving, and once waiting in the sun at the road gate for the rural delivery man. Age had shrunk him to almost human proportions, and his head sat directly on his shoulders, the neck retracted or the shoulders risen. The grandfather lived to be ninety-eight, but Old Man Trumpeter didn't live anything like as long, and died only a few years after his father, leaving Neil and Mrs Trumpeter alone on the property.

Neil was rather progressive for a Trumpeter. He enjoyed sport at High School and did well in the long jump and high jump. He was liked well enough — there was an absence of malice in the Trumpeter character — and his height and reserve gave him an individuality that pleased his peers. He was called Dawk, not because of anything unusual about his genitalia, but because all Trumpeters were called Dawk at the school. The nickname, once coined, was passed on in a serviceable continuity. Neil failed his exams with equanimity and a sense of tradition, and returned to the property in Trumpeters' Road.

Neil and his mother were apparently quite happy to work their land together after Old Man Trumpeter died, but if it had been otherwise they would have seen it as no one's concern but their own. When Neil was in his late twenties Mrs Trumpeter died suddenly, in a hot summer, my father said, and only a few days after she and Neil had been stung by bees when they knocked a hive over with the tractor and trailer. The doctor said that it wasn't the stings that had anything to do with her dying, that it was haemorrhage of the brain, but anyway she'd barely lost the swelling from the stings when she died, and Neil told the beekeeper he wouldn't have hives on his property any more.

With his mother gone, Neil must have become very aware of his bachelorhood, whether for reasons of personal comfort, or the sharper realisation that he was the last Trumpeter, I can't say, but in his deliberate way he began to look for a wife. He was seen standing amidst race-goers, sports supporters, revellers, even committees. A decent, single man of property looking for a wife. He married Tessa Hall within a year. She was a librarian, and quite new to town. She wasn't at all what you'd expect of a librarian, for Tessa was glowing, chatty, impulsive. She sang parts in the local repertory, and entered the Floral Princess competition — and won. Other men envied Trumpeter his wife's looks, and other women endorsed Tessa's wisdom in annexing security. She wasn't tall, but then the height of Trumpeter women had never affected the inexorable gene that persisted through the male line.

I imagine that the routine and isolation of farm life were something of a shock for Tessa Trumpeter. People were the world as far as she was concerned, and the chaffinch flocks above the crops, easterly drizzle caressing the downs, thick flight of grass grub in the night, dark lucerne in the evening light: what could she make of it? And they were drought years, which while not really threatening a debt free and established farm like Trumpeters', nevertheless meant that there wasn't money for shopping trips to Auckland, or major renovations of the farmhouse. I did hear someone say that the marriage was in trouble early on, but you hear that about most marriages at some time, maybe with truth.

Neil sold out after about five years of marriage. He and Tessa moved to town, and Neil bought motels on the main road — the Shangri-la Lodge Motels. Neil joined Lions, and had his photo in the paper several times with a salmon on opening day. Tessa did most of the work at the motel, and the bustle of people, new and familiar, suited her. They were a popular couple. I saw them occasionally on the modest social round of a country town: once or twice at their own place, with Neil standing above his barbecue guests with an expectant smile, even when it was over. Who can say concerning the happiness of others; the greater part of our life is wasted in pretence of one sort or another.

Yet by chance alone, I know something of how it worked out for Neil Trumpeter. I had been staying the weekend with my parents in the schoolhouse, and I went running in the evening — part of a forlorn effort to stave off middle age. The privacy of the country saved me from the derision of town acquaintances. The dust of Trumpeters' Road puffed out beneath my feet as I jogged in the late amber light. I kept to an easy pace, and had time enough to watch the car and tall figure on the roadside. There is a point on Trumpeters' Road, high on the downs, which gives a good view over much of the Trumpeter place and adjoining properties. You can look down and see the thick, Oamaru stone posts at the entrance, the track from the road gate, the farmhouse and outbuildings, the creek course marked with rough growth in the hills. I could see all that; I could see the abandoned machinery in the grass behind the equipment shed, a record of the Trumpeters' modest technological advance over several generations. Each piece of machinery cannibalised of useful parts, and left just thick tines, flaps, rods and springs in a clenched frenzy of rust. Neil Trumpeter could see it all as well. He had a casual shirt in the fashionable fitting cut, and blue with contrasting white collar and cuffs, yet I could sense the indifference to what he wore, so typical of a Trumpeter. His plain face was clean shaven, with just a patch of thick hairs on each cheek above the shaving line. I stopped beside him and had a spell. It's always difficult to avoid feeling small and fussy beside a Trumpeter. 'Looking at the old place, Neil,' I said, and watched the birches at the road gate and the lengthening shadows amongst the downs.

'That's about the size of it,' he said. He had one hand over the head of a wooden fence post as if it were struggling to leave the ground.

'Do you see much of the people who have it now?' I said. Neil didn't answer. From his quiet height he gazed over the farm he knew. There was a sense of enquiry in his look, as if he wished some response from the place itself. He looked on the lost land that slow Trumpeter voices had sounded over for a hundred years.

'Sweet, sweet Jesus,' he said. 'What have I done.'

A Poet's Dream of Amazons

My friend Esler is sick again. His mother rang, and implored me to hurry to the bedside. She spoke in a whisper, not in deference to the sinking Esler, but from fear that her husband might overhear. Mr Esler hates me.

'He says he mightn't see the night out,' said Mrs Esler. 'He's had a dream again about a Big Woman, and she turned out to be a preammunition of death.' Mrs Esler is loyal in her way, but for a mother of that son her vocabulary is less than impressive. 'The doctor's been twice already,' she whispered. I suppose that a really Big Woman, and irrational as women often are in dreams, could quite well be a sinister omen.

I put down my work at once. I knew it was no joke if Esler said he was dying: well rather I knew that he might laugh about it, but die all the same. Esler fights a persistent and terrible battle against the world, but it is a losing battle.

My moped was in the shed, but before opening the door to it, I rattled the neighbours' fence to start their dog barking. A melancholy and majestic sound that dog made: deep bells in the cold air. Why should anyone sleep if Esler was dying? I interspersed the hound's barks with appeals to Odin, the god of my ancestors. I didn't want Esler to die, for he is one who speaks my language in this town.

On my moped I set a course from the forlorn suburb in which I lived, to the forlorn suburb in which Esler lived. Mrs Esler was watching for me: she was at the door when I approached, hoping that she would be able to smuggle me through to the laundry without a confrontation with her husband. I saw half of him in the doorway of the living room, one arm, one side, one leg, one eye looking down the passage to the front door, and half a sneer to have seen a grown man arrive on a 50 cc step-thru. 'It's only you,' said Mrs Esler. She pulled a face. 'The doctor's been twice. Oh, it's bad, it's bad.' She made another sudden face. Pulling faces is the qualifier Mrs Esler uses when her husband is at hand. They are the briefest flashes across her long face, semaphore by tic that hints at the hospitality, gratitude and compassion she can't speak of. They are spasms of emotional intent, and probably quite unconscious. 'You can't stay long,' she said, as we went up the passage, and then a fleeting contortion to nullify her tone. 'Mr Esler and I don't want you coming around really,' she said, and touched my arm. I turned at the laundry door, and went back, and put my head into the living room. I could see the back of Mr Esler's head as he watched sport on the television. There was a worn patch at the crown, as if he had a habit of twisting his head into the pillows at night.

'Mr Esler.'

'Uh,' said Mr Esler.

'I'm going through to see Branwell.' I said it loudly so that it would carry to Esler in his bed.

'Oh, it's you,' said Mr Esler. He didn't turn towards me.

Esler had his blue tartan dressing-gown on in bed. He looked bad enough to be dying, but he was trying to laugh. He flipped his hands on the covers, and further down I could see his feet jerk. 'Branwell, Branwell,' he wheezed. 'I love it.' As well as liquid at the corners of his eyes, there was white gathered there, like a little toothpaste. On his cheeks were patterns from the creases in the pillow. Esler is balder than his father, but in a different way, going back a long way at the temples, and the hair between quite downy. 'Branwell's good,' he said, 'and look!' He put his hand under the pillow and produced a flat bottle of brandy. 'You see before you indeed, the Earl of Northangerland.'

Esler's voice was squeezed out, as if someone was sitting on his chest. The Big Woman perhaps. His wrist buckled with the effort of getting the brandy bottle back under his pillow. I'd thought up the mention of Branwell as I went over, something to give Esler a lift. He becomes depressed without literary allusions from time to time. He began to tell me about his fantasy of the Big Woman. 'As did the Pharoah I have a dream,' said Esler. 'Each night this vast and determined woman comes to wrestle with me.'

'All I get are nightmares of rooms without doors, and sinking ground beneath my feet.'

'Night after night,' said Esler, 'she seeks me out, and we must love and fight.'

Esler's room had been the laundry, but his mother now has an automatic washing machine in the old pantry, alongside the deep freeze. The laundry tubs have been taken out, and Esler's bed moved in, and a small table by the window. Esler's boyhood room has become a guest room, which means it's never used. His father refuses to let Esler keep it, because he is thirty-six years old, a poet, and still at home. Living in the laundry is one of those strange and bitter compromises that families have, and which remain incomprehensible to outsiders.

Mrs Esler came and interrupted her son, just when he was describing to me the body lock that the naked Big Woman put on him in their struggle. All poets have a tendency to pornography. 'Mr Esler says you've started him coughing again. I won't have it.' Her lengthening face, pulled inexorably towards the grave, convulsed to disavow the message she delivered. When she left, Esler continued to tell me of his Big Woman: a giant poster nemesis of sex. It was typical of Esler that even those things threatening his very life could only appear ludicrous.

His room retains a faint smell of soap and washed woollens. A fine mould like candle smoke covers the underside of the window sill, residue from a more tropical climate.

'Is he still there?' shouted Mr Esler. He must have been taking advantage of an injury stoppage on the television.

'Night after night she comes, this immense woman,' wheezed Esler. 'Hair like a waterfall, navel a labyrinth, thighs like a wild mare.' Esler's warm breath had scents of meatloaf, medication and mortality. His gums had shrunk from the palings of his teeth.

Esler's clothes are on plastic hangers on nails along the laundry wall opposite his bed, and his books are heaped beneath on shelves made from bricks and planks. What can I tell you of my friend that won't make you feel contempt or pity. What can I tell you of this man who is better than us, whose interests and principles have made him in a modern world a mockery, whose skills are as little considered as those of a thatcher, or a messiah.

'Waikato have scored again,' shouted Mr Esler, and Mrs Esler made an odd sound of wifely concurrence, like the instinctive response of a duck to another call.

Esler and I have been friends since we ganged up at eleven to beat the second largest boy in the class: a prematurely hairy slob who used to hold us under water during swimming periods. We became one of those braces so common among boys — Brunner and Esler. We heard our names coupled more at school than we heard them separately. I can imagine the staffroom association.

'Caned Brunner today.'

'Who?'

'Brunner. Fair-haired kid, hangs about with Esler. Caned him too.'

Or perhaps, 'That's Esler, isn't it, smashing those milk bottles?'

'No, that's Brunner.'

'Both look the same to me, little buggers. Call him over.'

We fought together, smoked together, marvelled at the sky and stars together, took out the O'Reilly girls together. I have a scar on the underside of my left arm because Esler accidentally shot me with a home-made spear gun. We both saw Bushy Marsden collapse and die in the gym. We began the dangerous experiment of taking words seriously and so resisting the process of attrition by which life betrays us.

'The Big Woman has a scent of almonds and macrocarpa,' said Esler in wonder and dread. His tartan wool dressing-gown is also his lucky writing jacket, ever since he had it on when he wrote his Van Gogh sequence. Constant use without washing, a little lost food and the oils of feverish sweat from his asthma bouts, have taken the nap from it, have buffed it until it shines like silk, and the original tartan pattern is almost lost. 'Read me something to take my mind off breathing,' said Esler. He had a hundred poets to choose from, and I read Seamus Heaney to him. He nodded his downy head and squeaked 'Yes, yes' at the touches which moved him. The liquid and the white gathered at the extremes of his eyes, spread a little to the corner skin.

'Will you stop that never-ending jawing in there!' shouted Mr Esler to me.

'Exactly,' Mrs Esler said. I could almost hear the snap as her face, just for a moment, was contrite, bewildered.

'Read on,' said Esler.

The laundry never seems a bedroom no matter how long Esler is in it, or how many clothes or hooks he lines the wall with. Images of soap flakes linger in the air as a false Christmas, and one corner of the lino always seems to be damp. There is more utilitarian aura than even poetry can dispel. 'That's so,' said Esler as I read. In a paper packet on the second plank are one hundred and seventy-three green copies of Esler's poems, printed by the Whip-poor-will Co-operative Press. I have the dedication by heart: These poems are for Bruce Brunner and Frank Heselstreet, fellow poets and friends who share my belief that emotion is like ours a round world, and as far enough east becomes west, so is laughter to tears and genius to insanity.

I have eighteen copies in the top of my wardrobe. Frank and I buy one from the bookstore when we can afford to, and have our reward later when Esler tells us another green pamphlet sold. Frank says we might end up with the whole edition of Esler's poems: a private joke, but what are friends for. Esler has always been absurd, but it is only one trait of character, as is deceit or shrewdness, composure or ambition. Just one aspect of my friend, but it makes it difficult to decide if he is dying or not. In a way I understand the Grim Reaper concluding that it is below his dignity to come for Esler, and sending a very Big Woman instead, who can laugh in her killing work and not be out of character.

Mr Esler appeared at the laundry door. His face was like that of a rock groper: reactionary and full of low cunning. 'You're doing him no good at all. Leave him alone, can't you. I blame you for a lot of it,' he said. I never resent Mr Esler's antagonism. I see it rather as one of the few remaining signs of concern for his son — this determination to blame me.

'I know you do,' I said.

'How many did Waikato win by?' said Esler in his squeezed voice. His father knew that Esler didn't care, but couldn't deny himself the satisfaction of saying the score out loud.

'Thirty-two, ten,' he said. 'Thirty-two bloody ten.'

'That means a season's tally so far of one hundred and forty-two for, and fifty-three against,' said Esler. 'How many did Mattingly score?'

'Fifteen.'

'That makes him the highest scoring fullback in Waikato provincial rugby apart from Rawiri,' said Esler.

'You don't care. You don't care!' shouted his father.

'It's so, though,' said Esler. He didn't care, but it was so though. He spent fifteen or twenty minutes each day on rugby statistics, so that he could know more than his father and still disregard the game.

Mr Esler knew better than to dispute Esler's facts, instead he looked around the laundry as a rock groper does another's cave. 'This place stinks of idleness,' he said.

'Mattingly has twenty-four points to go before he reaches Rawiri's record, and he's already played three more first class games,' said Esler. His voice became treble with an effort at volume as his father left.

'Shut up,' cried Mr Esler from the passage.

'Each night now she comes, my Amazon,' said Esler. 'Beautiful, but so huge. Dear God. I try to oppose her with intellect and poetry when lust has failed. It's no use. She's killing me, the Big Woman, ending me with breasts and kisses.' Esler cleaned his lips by rubbing them with his fingers, and concentrated on breathing well for a time.

'I've never been afraid of women, or been against women, have I,' he said.

'I know.'

'The power, the weight, yet the subtleness of her. I can't stand it.'

'Take a sleeping pill or something,' I said.

'I can't. Not with my regular medication.'

Esler is loyal and honest, totally without envy or malice in his friendship, perhaps because the only basis he knows for friendship now is poetry. I have watched his other means of communication atrophy. Esler can discuss anthropomorphic imagery with wit and eloquence for hours, but when the grocer questions him of necessities, Esler grips the counter, is helpless before yet another stranger, stumbles to tell of sliced bread, or free flow green beans. People exchange glances and knowing smiles at this evidence of the dangers inherent in any serious scrutiny of the mind. Esler tries to give Frank and me money from his savings account which has less than three figures; he writes to the *Listener* to point out that regional poets Brunner and Heselstreet have not received sufficient recognition. He is ugly, incongruous, annoying, ludicrous, and a true friend.

Esler asked me to bring a packet from the laundry table. 'It's my new poems to go to Australia,' he said. 'I want you to post it for me. You're luckier than me. Bless it before you put it in the box.' He made no mention of the postage charge: such things are incidental when you are dying. 'Send it airmail, and don't let them use any stamps with heads on. They're unlucky for manuscripts, I always feel.' All the seams in the brown paper were traced with sellotape, and the parcel was quartered in string woven of green and red strands. I bet Esler had said a prayer or a curse over his parcel, and sprinkled on some of the lucky dust that he'd collected from beneath Honey McIlwraith's bed. Esler is that sort of intellectual and innocent. He really believes that there could be someone out there interested in poetry, willing to publish or pay for it, someone who will untie Esler's two-tone string, unpick his sellotape — and cry genius.

'If the Big Woman comes again tonight,' said Esler, then trailed off and began wheezing. It became worse until he was flapping his shoulders, and his veins began to swell.

'Puffer, puffer,' called his mother as she ran in. Her face twitched to one side then the other, as if offering her endless Christian cheeks to be slapped. She meant the asthma gadget with the diaphragm, and she and I tugged Esler to a sitting position, and she did his throat thoroughly as if to ensure it would remain free of greenfly.

When he felt easier, Esler lay back again. 'Okay Mum, okay,' he said. 'I'm fine now.' He turned away from us until he could regain the personal distance he required after the ignominy of his attack, his weakness, his mother with the puffer. Mrs Esler touched his downy head once, but he turned more resolutely and she went out, first her dull curls and then the rest of her face, feature by feature, as a freight train curves from view. Esler rested: his skin gleamed with the sweat of illness and puffer liquid. I watched the soap flakes, and the light of the moon through the window without any curtain. 'Where's Frank?' said Esler finally.

'In Wellington at the technicians' course,' I said.

'They'll destroy him in the end, those computers,' he said. 'He left me the last poem in his Scheherazade series. So detached, so nimble. It makes me doubt my own progress. But those computers are the danger for poor Frank.' He picked up his puffer, held it to his mouth, but forgot to use it. Instead he said, 'I wish I could have a civilised life.' Beneath the bottom plank of his bookcase, close to the bricks, are Esler's two pairs of shoes. Brown shoes with roughly sewn seams, and each left heel worn to a slant, and the inside liners curling up. Where the outlets for the tubs had pierced the wall, Esler has fitted wooden plugs covered with muslin to improve the seal.

'Pass the ball, pass it!' cried his father from the living room.

'France,' said Esler, looking at his poets gathered on the planks. 'France has always seemed to me a place where people have a civilised life.'

'A cultivated people. A people who accept without reserve the necessity of art,' I said. I had almost starved to death on my one sojourn there. Having been nowhere, Esler still believed that life can be essentially different in other parts of the world.

He began on the Big Woman again. He was amused by his own recollections of the dreams. It was a tribute to his creative impulse that even the thing he thought was killing him was transmuted into an entertainment for us both. He had his brandy bottle in one hand, his puffer in the other, and he was trying not to laugh. 'You know,' he said, 'the odd thing is that I do feel that I might be dying this time after all. It's more than asthma the doctor said, but he doesn't know about the Big Woman, of course.'

Later he started tossing about. I put his brandy away and called his mother. She began to fuss over him, but he became worse. Mrs Esler called to her husband that he'd have to ring the doctor about Esler needing to go into hospital, and Mr Esler came and stood by the bed. He has a face not wildly dissimilar to our own: eyes facing forward, a two-entry nose, mouth, and teeth still nominally intact. Yet what a gulf of species is there. He might as well have been a rock groper or a pear tree, standing in the laundry.

'Thirty-six years old, writing bloody poetry, still has asthma, and now dirty dreams,' he said. 'Jesus.' The sound of the puffer was loud. 'I blame you,' he said to me.

'So do I,' said Mrs Esler, her face hidden.

'Heckel and bloody jeckel. It was a sorry thing when you two and that Frank Heselstreet met up,' said Mr Esler. He went out to phone the doctor.

I decided to go the back way. Mrs Esler came out with me. At the other end of the hall I could see Mr Esler with the telephone cord drawn tight. That way he could stand at the living room door and watch the television as he waited to get through to the doctor.

'This asthma can't be all that serious, can it?' I asked Mrs Esler. 'I mean he's had bouts before and come through. There's nothing else, is there?' Mrs Esler held her nose to stop herself from crying, and I didn't say any more. She gave a final, ambiguous face, and then turned her interminable chin away. Mr Esler talked at the other end of the passage on his extended line, as Mrs Esler went back into the laundry.

For a time I waited in the moonlight of winter outside the Eslers' back door. What it came down to, I suppose, was that I thought my friend Esler couldn't die because nothing was ready, and because it wasn't just. There was still too much that was ludicrous, and too much confusion. But you and I and Esler can't always rely on an appropriate setting for our deaths. Esler might have to go in a laundry bed, with soap flakes in the air, brandy under the pillow, a puffer in his mouth, and a Big Woman squeezing him in his dreams, with mould like candle smoke beneath the window sill, with one green vanity collection of his poems from the Whip-poor-will Press, with a polished blue, tartan dressing-gown, and no reason for it to be happening at all. And just a friend or two, who can do nothing but remember better times.

As I walked the path at the side of the house, Mr Esler leant excessively from his window to bring his harsh whisper closer to me. 'Murderer,' he hissed. 'Don't come back. Leave him alone. You bloody writers have done for him.' The moon struck down, and held the Eslers' garden in a frost of light. I didn't take the accusation too much to heart. I knew Mr Esler becomes desperate late at night when all the sports programmes end, when he finds himself with hours ahead and no team left to join, and none to hate, just his wife's Greek faces and his son in the laundry with the ailments of asthma and poetry.

'Murderer,' I heard Mr Esler hissing. There were guilty ones, of course: Pound and Olson, Eliot and Larkin, Yeats and Frost, Stevens and Neruda, Lowell and Williams, Turner and Sewell, had all made their attacks on Esler. And Dylan Thomas. Now there's a murderer if ever I read one.

At the end of Te Tarehi Drive, and turning into Powys Street, which lay stark in the moonlight, I couldn't help laughing at the dying Esler. Laughter can be a guise of love; laughter can be helplessness expressed. Perhaps Esler is simply dying of his poet's amazement at the world in which he finds himself.

I let the moped engine run on in the shed for a few minutes, so that the battery would charge up a bit after the light had been on. I shook the neighbours' fence to rouse Cerberus again, and savoured the echoing sound. A deep barking dog suits a full moon. Esler had been dying before, and got over it. We all have to get over a little dying of ourselves in life. Is he dying of the asthma and the other things his mother wouldn't say, or is the Big Woman, that preammunition of death, suffocating him in his dreams with excess of loving?

The Ace of Diamonds Gang

As our past recedes we can see only occasional pennons on the high ground, which represent the territory traversed between. So the Ace of Diamonds Gang seems my full boyhood before the uncertainty of adolescence. I recall no peculiar origin; like the heroes of history it arose when it needed to be there.

Always the special moment was when we put on our masks. The triangle of white handkerchief over the lower face, and the red diamond that we'd stamped on with the oil paints that belonged to Bernie's mother. There was frisson as each known face became strangely divided. Not handkerchiefs with red diamonds smudged did we acquire, but anonymity, confederacy, a clear exception to approved society. After Boys' Brigade was a favourite time, when lanyards and Christianity had been dispensed with, we would rendezvous in the centre of the old macrocarpa hedge to become the Ace of Diamonds Gang. The night would be moonlit perhaps, and we would move off in dispersed formation, keeping in touch by drifting whistles and calls of birds extinct except within the diamond lands. Like wraiths we went, said Bernie once. He read a lot, did Bernie. Like wraiths, the Ace of Diamonds Gang, if Ashley's farting didn't give us all away.

The Ace of Diamonds Gang was rather like that, subject in practice to mundane deficiencies which threatened the ideal. Ashley's wind, Bernie's glasses and Hec Green having to be in by nine o'clock every night, were the sorts of things. A certain power of imagination was necessary, but for thirteen-year-olds the source of such power is inexhaustible. We never spent much time in explicit definition of the gang, however — each had his own motivation, his own vision of the Ace of Diamonds Gang, and when we struck in that small town each of us gloried in a quite separate achievement. Dusty Rhodes insisted that the gang be used to intensify his wooing of Anna Nicholson, who had the best legs in the school. It was love all right. After watching Anna at the swimming sports, Dusty had an attack of lovesickness so severe that he was away for three days. The Ace of Diamonds Gang picketed Anna Nicholson's front garden sometimes, and when she came back from music practices called from the bushes and tossed acorns up to her window. Dusty considered this a normal form of courtship, and the rest of us had not sufficient experience to suggest alternatives. When Anna's father came out with torch and fury, we would drift wraith-like deeper into the shrubbery, not of course from fear, but to give him a taste of the menacing elusiveness of the Ace of Diamonds Gang when true love was thwarted. Dusty could never understand why Anna Nicholson didn't fall for him. The unbearable passion of first love rarely has any relevance to the response of the other party.

For Bernie and me the Ace of Diamonds Gang was more a life warp to escape from being thirteen years old in a provincial town: a chance to conjure heroism, to strike a pose, to create mysteries in which to dwell. We cut the backs off some Christmas cards, and stamped them with the red diamond. We left one at the scene of each of our exploits, just as in the books we read. The senior sergeant would pin them on his incident board we were sure, and his staff would attempt to work out a modus operandi.

So it was something of a let down to return to Seddon Park weeks after we had painted challenges there, and find the Ace of Diamonds card still there, weathered on the side of the cricket shed. 'They've given up, that's what,' said Dusty.

'That's it, all right. They've given up,' said Ashley.

'Perhaps it's still under surveillance,' said Bernie. It was a good word — surveillance, but even it could not impose conviction in that warm morning with the playing fields dipping to the willows, and a harrier club spread in the distance.

'We haven't actually done much lately,' admitted Ashley, who was sitting downwind a little. 'As a gang I mean.' We lay in the grass, shading our eyes with our hands, and attempting to justify the lack of daring in recent excursions of the Ace of Diamonds Gang.

Dusty suggested we spend time drilling a hole in the girls' changing sheds, but the rest of us wanted a cause of greater daring, and less obvious connection with our own interest. 'My father told me Jorgesson poisoned Mrs Elder's Alsatian because it kept him awake at night,' said Ashley. Jorgesson ran the second-hand yard, and his enmity could be relied on. He had cuffed Dusty's head for cheek, and once set the police on us after seeing us on the stacks of the timber yard. And he gave us wretched prices for any lead or copper we scrounged because he had the monopoly as the only scrap dealer in town. Sometimes we retrieved the stuff from his yard and sold it to him twice over to gain a fair price by simple addition, but even retaliatory dishonesty didn't remove our resentment.

'Hey, Jorgesson,' repeated Dusty. To defy Jorgesson was grand enough to be a reaffirmation of the principles of the Ace of Diamonds Gang, and Dusty agreed to hold in abeyance further collective effort to seduce Anna Nicholson, and the spy-hole in the sheds.

'Let's raid the place and leave a calling card,' said Bernie, raising a small, clenched fist. 'Strike and vanish, vengeance accomplished: the Ace of Diamonds Gang.' It was Bernie who usually provided the linguistic motifs for the gang.

'Christ, yes,' said Hec, 'but I'll have to be back by nine, remember.'

In the fastness of the macrocarpa we met on Wednesday evening, looked out into the soft, eternal twilight of summer. We linked thumbs to make our pledge and put on our Ace of Diamonds masks. Just a handkerchief and a change of mind. The mantle of secret brotherhood then fell upon us — oh, it was fish Christians in the catacombs, the Black Hand, Jacobites, the Scarlet Pimpernel. It was the League of Spartacus, the Boxers, it was Kipling's bazaar. I felt a small part of history's perpetual alternative as we ran through the Marlborough evening.

Jorgesson's was in that part of the town which was never very busy, off the main street and down toward the warehouses. On one side of his yard was a panelbeater's, on the other a vacant section, then the timber yard. When night came, all such lands reverted to the domain of the Ace of Diamonds Gang. We scaled the stepped pyramids of the timber yard, and made inventory of Jorgesson Traders. It resembled a field hospital in a desperate war of machines, the corpses and the parts heaped in rough classification as they came in. The ground was toxic and stained with oils, rust and the juices of dismembered machines. There were heaps of taps like discarded hands, radiators, bumpers, fan units, old bricks, used sinks, ceramic fire surrounds, short blocks, coppers, windows, roofing iron, bottle castles in green and brown, heaps of worn tyres like bitter, dark intestines. Amidst all the obsolescence were a few new kitset patio chairs assembled by Jorgesson during his quiet times. Much of the stock was exposed to take its chances beneath the spartan sky, a second category lay in an open-sided shed and its progressively diminishing lean-tos. We knew that the most precious and portable items festooned Jorgesson's army hut, so that it was a labyrinthine progress for him to make the short journey from his desk and cash box to the door.

There seemed a dim light from the hut as we watched from our battlements. 'He must still be there,' said Hec. Ashley perfumed the night in response to heightened and unexpected tension.

'But we'll still go,' I said.

'We should reconnoitre in strength,' advised Bernie. His glasses glinted a moment in the last light of the evening. We steadied ourselves on the timber, and locked our thumbs again in pledge.

So did we move wraith-like across the rough section between the timber yard and Jorgesson's, scouts taking post, then others fading forward. We hand-cupped each other over the fence, drew up Hec as the last, and stood among Jorgesson's darkened possessions. The one window in the army hut showed light like the pale yellow yolk of a battery egg. It was above head height, and we pushed a drill chassis close to the wall — inch by inch to reduce the noise of the high, iron wheels on the gravel and scattered artifacts of Jorgesson's yard.

Jorgesson was lying on the floor by the door, or rather Jorgesson was lying on a woman who was on the floor by the door. It was the only space available: the one strip for the door to open and the clients to stand amidst Jorgesson's plunder. Jorgesson and his love seemed accustomed to the position, for without needing to look behind her, the woman reached an arm to brace herself on the stack of long life batteries, and Jorgesson's trousers hung conveniently on the impressive tines of a wapiti head behind him.

The apparent irrationality of sex is a vast humour to the young. Jorgesson had no electricity in his hut, and the low, angled light from a small Tilly was unflattering, single tendons jerking behind Jorgesson's great knees were picked out, and the wrinkles behind his head, and how flat his backside was in fact. Of the woman there was little more than the one practical arm, and her toes, separate and tumescent as facets in the Tilly light.

'He's doing her,' said Dusty. 'He really is.' His voice had qualities of awe and relief, as if after all the furtive talk, the innuendo, the chapter endings, the fade-outs, he was reassured that the act itself was not a myth. Jorgesson was doing it before his eyes. 'Jesus,' said Dusty.

'Yeah,' said Hec.

Jorgesson was unaware of any need to prolong his performance for our education. He slipped to the side, cleverly angling one leg between a brass fireguard and a Welsh dresser. He drew a rug about his love, and laid his bare arm upon it to stroke her hair. A candle sheen glowed on his arm in the localised Tilly light, and his face was all Punch features as he talked, stark in relief and shadow. Braces were a limp bridle from the wapiti, and the love's toes had coalesced with the passing of ecstasy.

The Ace of Diamonds Gang found an aftermath of restful affection disappointing. Dusty grumbled on the drill perch, and Bernie began hand signals of obscure intrigue. We had come to punish Jorgesson, and his pleasure would provide another cause. We withdrew to the darkness of Jorgesson's open shed to plan our assault. 'Have you got the card?' said Bernie. It was my turn, my turn to spike it, as Bernie said. I could feel it in my top pocket.

They gave me two minutes to creep around to the front of Jorgesson's hut, and there I took the card from my pocket and the brass pin from the side of my shoe. As I fixed it to the centre of Jorgesson's door, fellow partisans began their attack. Stones cascaded upon the roof, Ashley ran towards me down the flank of the hut banging the boards with a length of piping, Dusty and Hec gave their wolf howls, Bernie beat a scoured copper in sonorous rhythm. The Ace of Diamonds Gang had released its terror.

I could hear also a sudden commotion as Jorgesson tried to rise from among his possessions to counter-attack. I had joined the others in a race for the gate when Jorgesson seemed to smite down the door and was behind us, like a black jumping jack with profanity as his sparks. His voice was husky with passion, and rage gave him an initial impetus — but we were prepared. Fled, the white masks and red diamonds flowing in and out of colour as we raced past the streetlights. We were our own audience, struck by the audacity of the Ace of Diamonds Gang. Avengers, raiders, sentinels, even if Bernie had to carry his glasses as he ran and had trouble keeping up. 'Wait on, wait on,' he kept calling, which impaired our wraith-like progress.

Jorgesson gave up, though, once we reached the Sherwood of the timber yard. It was darker amid the stacks and he had no intimate knowledge of the trails there. He halted and sent in a verbal pack of bastards, buggers and sods to harry us on our way.

'Go home, shagger,' shouted Hec.

'Serve him right,' said Dusty, but his tone was one more of envy than impartial justice.

'Remember the Ace of Diamonds Gang,' called Bernie hauntingly. We joined thumbs on one of the stacks when Jorgesson was gone, and enjoyed the exaggeration of what we had done, except Hec, who had to go straight home, and risk being belted.

The depleted Ace of Diamonds Gang maintained its identity through the streets and short cuts from the timber yard to its macrocarpa headquarters, each scout call an echoing clearance. Yet after victory over Jorgesson there was arrogance rather than caution in our progress, and in the macrocarpa, darker than the blue, summer night, we put aside our masks and our greater lives with unspoken dismay.

In my room I folded my mask and placed it within the fuselage of the Spitfire Mk II, the special place. I began to undress, and as I pulled my jersey over my head I could feel my library card still in the shirt pocket from the afternoon. Except that it wasn't the library card, it was the Ace of Diamonds sign made out of the back of a Christmas card and, as I recognised it, there was a flux of all my stomach, and blood pumping up my eyeballs, hair follicles quickening all over my skin, falling electrical cadences of primeval terror through the matter of the brain. It was the library card I had pinned on the door of Jorgesson's army hut in the second-hand yard. The Ace of Diamonds Gang had witnessed his secret love, had interrupted it, had taunted him from the night sky and the timber stacks — and I had left my library card pinned to the centre of his door to avow responsibility.

I dreamt of Jorgesson's retribution during the night, starting up in abrupt horror at each climax revealed. Jorgesson in the headmaster's study when I was sent for, Jorgesson waiting in the shadows with an old sickle from stock, Jorgesson fingering a garroting cord beneath the swaying pines, Jorgesson at the door with my library card and asking to see my father.

That's how it happened. I had just taken a mouthful of toad-in-the-hole when I saw, through the kitchen window, an unnaturally tidy Jorgesson coming past the geraniums. There was a bulge in his pocket which could have been a garroting cord, and his Punch head was tilted to accommodate a paisley tie. Since then I have always hated geraniums and paisley patterns. A geranium is a coarse, disease-ridden plant with a flare of animosity, and paisley resembles a slide of pond water beneath a microscope. Even toad-in-the-hole has never been quite the same again. My father and Jorgesson spent time in sombre conversation and, although I couldn't catch the words, I could see on Jorgesson's face successive expressions of contained outrage, reasonableness, social duty to parents of evil children. My library card passed from Jorgesson to my father, the indisputable proof of a tale too rich to be denied.

My father punished me with the razor strop, and rang the parent of each friend I had unhesitatingly betrayed. It was the end of the Ace of Diamonds Gang. It was the end of wraith-like sorties into the consciousness of our town. It was the end of silhouettes upon the timber stacks, of thumbs clasped to pledge the redress of makeshift grievances. It was the end of free imagination, and of boyhood perhaps.

Lilies

The chalice of each lily flower was disembodied as darkness spread. Broad lily leaves merged with the shadows of the heavy grass and the docks. Arum flowers were luminous, hung in the night, and in the nearest throats each yellow spadix stood. The casual, crowded growth of such beauty amazed him. He knew the place was just a horse paddock in the suburbs. He had seen at dusk on their arrival the leaking trough, tracks amid the grass and lily clumps, uneven fences, and the horses standing apart for privacy. Yet it became a garden in the night, and from his hip height on the groundsheet the arum lilies were ranged depth on depth, a few pale lights in some places, but most massed as if carried in procession.

'My mother would have a fit,' Jenny said. 'Christ, she's got no idea how people can live. All those things owned and folded into the right drawer, or account, all that possession, getting on in the world, is nothing if you haven't found a really close person — a lover. A lover in all respects. A universal lover I suppose. Ha ha. Someone to trust with all of yourself. Don't you think? Don't you think, though?' Her face was itself the milk white of the arum lilies, but alert rather than decorous. She cocked her head and tried to see his expression in the night. Her hand squeezed his, and he could feel the light, individual bones of her fingers.

'I feel the best I have in the whole trip right now,' she said, 'and I don't care if we never find these people to stay with. We don't need help anyway. We don't need anyone else. This afternoon, coming up fast on the main road, it was so warm, wasn't it? I loved being on the back. I almost fell asleep leaning on you, and I could tell, before you turned, if you were going left or right, because the way the muscles of your back moved against me, like part of myself moving. Sometimes when we passed cars, when we were level with them for that moment, I could see couples in their separate seats and knew they envied us pressed together and then accelerating past. I bet they took it out in grudging comments about damn motorbikes. Eh? I think I understand how you feel about the bike now You get this feeling of protection and isolation on a big tourer, don't you think? The faster you go, the more cocooned and invincible you become: the less distinct any threat can be. It's a sort of unity and a sort of detachment, isn't it?'

In the evening the road had sloped down to the bridge, and the Wanganui River was smooth and muddy, lacking the gravel bed of the South Island country he knew. Throttled back, the exhaust had a different note. Jenny pressed her helmet to his, and shouted, 'Keep going straight on, I think. Don't turn right towards the shops.' They were hoping to find a friend of a friend who might have a bed for the night. A friend's friend never met, never warned, but easy about their imposition they hoped.

In a flat suburb by a sports stadium, playing fields and a few paddocks across the road, the motor had died. The way it had gone made him think it was electrical, not mechanical, or a fuel blockage perhaps, but the light wasn't good enough to find the fault, and the warmth of summer, the languor of a day's travel had sapped any sense of urgency. He had pushed the bike into the paddock, and was held in thrall by the profusion of arum lilies there in the dusk. Each fenceline was overwhelmed with deep banks of lilies, and clusters spread into the low, green fields, and the ditches which especially suited them, so that they suckled in the mud. He had never seen lilies as vigorous and free as weeds before. They were multiplied clump on clump to gain an eminence, and the myriad white mouths among the heavy leaves glowed in summer dusk. 'Oh, they grow like weeds round here,' Jenny said. 'They're everywhere between Wanganui and Palmerston North, but you didn't notice. They've spread all over the place, and nobody thinks twice about them.' But he did. He thought twice, thrice, a hundred times, and always that night he was conscious of the lilies spread around them, and the quiet horses standing thigh deep among their flowers.

'Finding someone to trust is what really matters,' she said. The lilies had the whiteness of her breast, and like breasts their hypnotic form was curved into the night. 'You like that, don't you? I know you like me doing that. I know you're smiling; turn your face towards me so that I can see. I don't believe that there's just one perfect partner for each of us in life. As you say it's a pretty odd coincidence that person should just happen to be in our own community ninety-nine percent of the time. But it still seems to me that a lot of people never have a true relationship in their lives, even if they get married and all the rest. Never find someone to talk to as they would talk to themselves: never know someone care for them the way they wished they cared for themselves.'

Their night vision came in time. With his head close to hers, he wondered if the pupils of her eyes had dilated like those of a cat, but as he bent to see, she thought he sought a kiss, whispered assent and drew his mouth to hers. There were moths and flies in the moonlight, and quite loudly a horse blew its vast, flabby lips in derision.

'I like it best when we're alone,' she said. 'When there's just the two of us we never quarrel. Have you realised that? It's always when other people are about, our friends even, that any trouble comes. I know you don't like staying with my parents, because you say I'm different then. Now we only have to please each other. I'm the only woman, you're the only man. Do you like that? Turn over this way. I think we should stay on our own, and be happy like now. It's so warm I guess we could just stay here with the flowers you like, and in the morning you could fix the bike.'

From the centre of the city came the sound of a fire engine, or an ambulance, but it meant nothing to them for they had no house and complete health, and later a car horn started in the suburb beyond the stadium and sounded again and again, fainter as it moved away. When all those sounds had passed, there was Jenny's voice, so earnest and so lover-like. More enduring still, when she stopped, was the gentle whine of the night air through the trees, the fences and the lilies.

'You don't have to worry about me,' Jenny said, 'because I go into everything with my eyes open and don't expect things to be rosy all the time. You'll see that I can hold down a job if I need to. I can hack whatever has to be done. But the imperative I think is to have some part of each day with the one person who lets you be all of yourself, but not by yourself. You see? Someone to guard your back against the appalling triviality of life. It seems to me that you can't win by yourself.'

Jenny took their oranges from the pannier bag and, in peeling them, reproduced in action the level of intensity she experienced as she talked. She dug and tore the thick skin when she was adamant, and eased it from the fruit in a caress when love was spoken of. Her thin fingers were warm, had the fragrance of leather and orange peel, and the orange peel lay in the dimmed frog green of the grass and lily leaves, held up from the ground by the rich growth. Some pieces showed the underside like mushrooms, and others had their colour up, which caught the faint light and glinted orange to counter the lemon parrot tongues of the arum lilies. She drew on her cigarette, a long, wanton breath, and gave a shudder. He held a match and she squeezed peel at its flame, and the essence spat and flared like a rocket's dying burst far away. Her voice was so private, so trusting, so open to inevitable hurt, that he couldn't look at her, but put his head back and saw the lighted houses on the higher ground where people sat with the limits of their expectations and responsibilities clearly marked around them, while he and Jenny had nothing between them and the sky, could feel the night air drawn like a tide through the docks, the fences, the free lily clumps, the shadowed horses, and bearing off the scent of oranges and lilies and leather. Jenny's warmth and the salt smell of her hair too, bearing off sweet promises that could not otherwise be borne. The lilies pressed around them in the night, candles with a pale yellow flame. Something ancient in them survived within the modern city. Something biblical that was dispassionate in its magnificence. We believe beauty is of itself an invitation, when in nature it is a guarantee of nothing that we will ever understand.

'I don't care to look too far ahead,' she said. 'You never met my grandfather Renneck, but he used to say that you're a long time dead. And he had this other saying — take what you want, and pay for it. Do you see what he meant? I told Mum and Dad I can go back to university any time, but there's other things you can't have on lay-by. Hold me closer because it's getting cooler now. A horse won't stand on us in the night, will it? No, but it's true, isn't it, that nothing matters at all in the end, except having someone to love, but people don't want to say it, or admit it, because if they don't reach it then they're a failure, aren't they, and yet their life still has to go on. They won't, will they, walk over us in the night — the horses, I mean?'

He drew her closer, as if he believed that way they could secure themselves. Save them, save them from the fenceposts uneasy in the ground, from the slope of the stadium against the sky. Save them from the arum lilies, and the shadow horses deep in docks and grass and the lovely bog lilies. Save them from her trust, and his knowledge of its conclusion. Save them, save them amid the lilies from that meek, tidal wind of inconsequence.

Iris

Iris, my mother, had this idea that sooner rather than later something marvellous was bound to happen: a lucky break in life if you kept at it. She wasn't selfish about this, everyone had the same chance for something quite undeserved, like being approached out of the blue in the supermarket by a talent scout to become a model, or marrying an accountant as my aunt did, who now spends money like water and has two homes. For my twenty-first Aunt Esther gave me a cream silk dress, but I snagged it at the polytech wine and cheese on a rivet in the plastic chair.

Even when Iris was too old to go on hoping to be approached in the supermarket for anything other than shoplifting, she believed magnificent opportunity was in the offing. She took Golden Kiwis, and then Lotto tickets, and worked out on the backs of envelopes how she would divide and spend the money. I was to come in for some pretty good stuff when she won, according to the lists. Each mailtime was a high, never mind that she hardly wrote to anyone, had jobs without prospects and shifted a lot. Throughout the drizzle of magazine offers, bills, perfunctory greetings, community newsletters, demands on former tenants and coupon books, she kept a fierce hope in miraculous correspondence. An approach concerning political candidature, perhaps, or an invitation from the Max Factor directorate to be a special consultant, gardenias from a secret admirer, or notification that she was meter maid of the year. Iris never did realise that her whole life was unsolicited. She intently examined each special offer and would speculate joyously if her actual name was used. But how would they know my name, she'd say, look, they use my proper name. So that I could be at my best, she would roam the twilight, feeling in her neighbours' boxes for shampoo sachets sent as samples. Needs must, my girl, she would say firmly. Our time will come.

Iris answered an advertisement about Dr Asmunzov, professor of the mind, who came and said he could do a seance on my dad, even though he'd gone off, not died. I was seventeen and the professor of the mind had other interests as well, for he clasped my knee beneath the table. Being naturally blonde and with a good bust, I've always had to deal with that sort of thing. Iris, my mother, said that it didn't necessarily mean anything, and that men were just like that. Hormonal, she said, and nothing in it to blame anyone. When she was going to school in Taranaki, a share milker used to undo his fly each day as the bus passed his milking shed. The association gave her a particular aversion to cholesterol, she said.

Iris did win a Christmas hamper when I had chicken pox in Form Two, from Woolworths, and once initiated a correspondence with a firm of Auckland solicitors acting for an unclaimed British estate. The hamper she unpacked on my bed and found lots of low-cost, bulky items under the more glamorous surface layer: Weetbix, dried lentils, toilet rolls, stuff like that, and the solicitors lost interest when we couldn't provide any evidence that the family on the Bleeker side originated in Dorset. I ate a small tin of sardines cold from the hamper, and with my finger, put their oil on all the chicken pox that I could reach. My second-hand bed head had transfers of Pooh Bear and Cliff Richard that were nothing to me.

For a time, when we lived in Wanganui, Iris thought we had a fortune at our toes, because our Aramaho suburb neighbours said that the house we rented used to belong to a retired Greymouth dentist who must have been worth a packet, but left nothing when he died in my room. I did consider using the untainted third bedroom, but mine was so much sunnier, and I could come and go from the big window without bothering Iris. She said he would have had it all in gold, being able to get it for fillings as a dentist, though other people weren't allowed to buy it. She had a dream of gold-filled Havelock Dark tobacco tins hidden under the brick paving between the back door and the laundry. We dug up the bricks, every one, but found no gold. The bricks remained stacked on the lawn and next winter we got muddy feet going to the laundry. They were a reminder of yet another false lead in the treasure hunt that was my mother's life. It's there all right though, Iris said, he just doesn't want a woman to find it.

My boyfriends seemed possibilities to Iris: opportunities for advantage. Being blonde and with a good figure, as I said, I had plenty of guys coming on to me. You get used to it after a while. Not great, but not unbearable. It's just the effect you have on hormones, I guess. Mum said that she'd been trim herself in her time, but her face had become a bit of a handbag. My father had been an All Black trialist who couldn't get used to his diminished place in life when he got past playing. He had these wonderful hands, though, Iris said, and should really have taken up the saxophone, or the piano. She took it up herself soon after he left, from an easy stage instruction booklet called *Jazz Sax Made Easy*. She didn't find time for much practice, but made herself a black sequin dress to wear when she played in cabarets. I wore it for the leavers' dance at high school and Maurice Prentice told me that I gave him such a hard on that he could only dance stooped.

Maurice wasn't one of those Iris had any hopes of, but Nigel Utteridge and Denzil Smith were. Denzil and I were both keen on roller-skating and won the under sixteen figure skating title in Marlborough, not long after Mum and I shifted down from Horowhenua. Iris saw a magnificent future for us on the international circuit, like Torvill and Dean, with her managing the television interviews and contracts. She cut down the sequin cabaret dress, sewed in bra cups and I wore it for competitions. Nigel Utteridge was later. His parents were both doctors, would you believe. Each worked in a different practice so they could have professional independence. Mrs Dr Utteridge was quite confiding and told me there were no children after Nigel, because Mr Dr Utteridge was injured by the Big Dipper at the Tahuna fairground. Mr Dr Utteridge had the thickest, most muscular neck you can imagine, wider than his head even. He must have taken up the sport of butting at a very young age. Iris imagined me getting married to the son of two doctors and neither of us having to work again, just sit behind the receptionist's desk, lift our heads occasionally and say, Dr Utteridge will see you now, I'm sorry Dr Utteridge has been delayed by an outbreak of anthrax, Dr Utteridge is at present examining your uterine x-rays. Maurice Prentice was probably the best-looking guy I went out with early on, but very hormonal, always talking about cars and he walked with a stoop.

Sooner or later, Iris would say, our ship will come in. Over Kentucky Fried Chicken on her fiftieth birthday, she told me about this Grandma Moses who, at eighty, started painting pictures of her farm and became famous. The Grandma Moses in all walks of life were a marvel of reassurance to my mother. What can happen once, can happen twice, she said, and she was not afraid to work. She formed a co-operative when we were in Palmerston North. Herself and two huge twins called McIntosh, and they supplied hors d'oeuvres at functions. Salmon or crab finger pastries, gherkin, prune and pineapple on toothpicks, cheese balls, home-ground pâté and cinnamon sticks. They made a go of it, too, though Iris said that people didn't appreciate the cost of the fillings, but then the twin five minutes older than the other had an experience when delivering to the town clerk's farewell. A lap dog ran up inside her dress as she was carrying trays into the civic chambers and she went right off the business. Iris said the filthy little beast had ruined what could have been a catering empire, because that twin had the flair and they couldn't carry on afterwards.

I don't want you to think Iris's vision was a mercenary one. Money wasn't an end in itself. What Iris wanted was to force life to yield her something of value, something from the top drawer. She had no belief in a heaven and wanted a greater share of life. We all go down to the grave in the end, she'd say. Behind the library building, and no longer used, was the old cemetery on the slope. When I had the job at Hendry's cosmetic counter we would meet some lunchtimes and walk through the alleys of crushed, white quartz between the tombs. She would sigh, but only to cool the meat pies she liked for winter lunch. Iris was in fact cheerful in the cemetery for, of all the people on that slope, only she and I had any further hope of a shot at life. Died for King and Country she might read for me, her meter maid shoes making a sensible crunch upon the quartz. Iris would eat strips from the top of her pie and the steam would wisp into the winter air.

Meter maiding was only one of Mum's skills. She believed in a variety of jobs to lure good fortune. In Christchurch she was a fish splitter for almost a year. Well, Lyttelton she actually worked in, but we lived at New Brighton. A bach over which the fine, grey sand would whisper when the sea wind blew through the marram grass. A millionaire's view of the ocean, Iris said. I was still young enough to need entertainment and she played the water pipes for me. By turning on the taps to different positions we could hear fog horns, fire engines, the howling jabberwocky. My schoolbag on the lino beside me, the smell of fish all the way from Lyttelton, the millionaire's view over the fritz haircut of the marram dunes, as I crouched by the lion paws of the bath to hear tubas, or what Iris said was the farting of the elephants in the jungle. I wouldn't be surprised if there's a way to make a career from this, she'd say, and the water is all free, she'd say.

Called Home, or Till the Daybreak Comes, she read out in the cemetery of that later town. As I Am Now So You Must Be Prepare

Yourself To Follow Me, as we opened up a bag of crisps, pausing by the dearly loved and much missed husband of Astral Pruitt while I explained the new gloss shades of half-pink, full-pink, mink-pink. Iris said that the pasty man had asked her to go to the trots with him, but she didn't like his lank hair. A man should have some bit of natural wave or curl in his hair, my mother reckoned. I had plenty of offers from men myself by that time and, while Iris never interfered, she did say that men made lousy friends, and that women knew how to stick together. Her own mother was a grand friend, she said, and in one tough year went into the city gardens and lopped off a branch to make a Christmas tree.

Mum was fascinated by those things which defy routine — a locust swarm, footsteps of *Homo erectus*, Halley's comet, which was certainly a fizzer, the Brewster kid who used to run howling round the block in Te Kuiti when his parents were fighting. Iris would take a cold sausage or potato out to him and he would snatch it on the trot with his face gleaming with tears in the streetlights. Iris was a good neighbour, though a temporary one. She babysat scores of kids who we never heard of again. Later she would send me out to do it. We received neighbourly kindness in return, of course. In the Brewster kid's Te Kuiti, I remember sneaking over each night to plug an extension cord into old Mr Hammond's work bench. He was rich and never went out after dark. While we lived there most of our power-intensive activities were late at night. We had an adaptor plug into the water heater, and a large frypan for our main feed at nine or ten at night. When we had to leave Te Kuiti my mother made Mr Hammond a green, double-knit jersey with a V-neck and raglan sleeves. Only it had a narrow yellow band, because she was one green ball short.

From what Iris said, my grandmother must have been the same sort of person, though I never met her because she had Iris late and died in a nursing home somewhere in the North Island while we were living in Tuatapere. Iris was a school cleaner. There was a mill just down the road and the sawdust piles were mountain ranges there: the oldest peaks with the richest colours. Iris said that once I asked for a packed lunch to take to climb them. She couldn't afford to go up for the funeral. Her sister sent some of their mother's things down to her, including a sealed envelope addressed to Iris in her mother's handwriting. For days Iris left it unopened on the mantelpiece, and speculated on the way the contents would change our lives: how it might be the title deed to her father's brick house in Seatoun which she could not remember having been sold, or evidence that she had an illegitimate brother who had become a Cabinet minister in Brazil. The night we opened it we were having curried eggs for tea. The curry coloured the inside of Mum's mouth as she laughed to find clippings about my father's court appearances. This man deserted his wife and daughter, grandmother had written on the newspaper. Men are a different species, Iris told me over the curried eggs. Men are always alone, she said. My father had played squash twice a week for four years with a work-mate, yet never bothered to know where he lived, or how many children he had. Men don't ask anything of each other. It's both their weakness and their strength.

Iris was disappointed by the degeneration that happens to men as they age — hair grew all over my father's shoulders before he left, she said, as if he had died and the mould already begun. The oldest man I ever saw naked myself, was the physiotherapist who took a fancy to me in Putaruru. Being in his line of business he kept himself from the most obvious signs of mould, but he had eerily white, caved-in buttocks and besides, as I lay on my back on the carpet, I grew tired of looking at the unvarnished underside of his desk with the lines of the carpenter's pencil still clear.

My mother did better work than that. When we were in Bulls she saved for my kitset duchess, and spent hours getting the tracks aligned so that you could open and close the drawers with the tips of your fingers. Just radiata, but how she sanded it, then umpteen coats of dark stain and a clear finish. I've still got it, each scratch and

discoloration is a mark of our life. Yet see, the drawers open with
finger tips, the tracks have traces of the candle grease Iris dripped
on with puckered lips of concentration. The wood smell evokes the
rose-hips that in one Marlborough summer were a livelihood for
Iris and me. We spent weeks picking them from the briars growing
wild on the Wairau terraces and riverbed. It must have been my
holidays and my mother had no better job. She picked into the
pocket of a bag apron and, try as I might, I can't remember how we
got out to the riverbed each day. We sold our harvest to the rose-hip
syrup factory. The syrup was a big thing for children's health at the
time. Dry river terraces with their rabbit scrapes, foxgloves, bleached
grass stems and rose briars. Iris with her bag apron, floppy hat,
bloodied knuckles. We're not licked yet, she said. We would have
our sandwiches together on the stones, from a paper bag so often
used that it had the soft creases of a dowager's face. She'd heard on
the radio that the country was poised for great transformation and
growth and she was determined that we would be swept along with
it. The rose-hips were burnished in all that sun, almost ceramic with
a red-yellow sheen. The last time I saw the sequin dress was when
Iris offered it to me for Glenda's wedding dance. It had grown dull
out of its time, as a lurid fish out of its element grows dull. Perhaps
you're right, Iris said.

I'm surprised at all the places I've lived in. Ours was the off-season,
budget sort of view of Wanganui, Blenheim, Lower Hutt and Bulls,
Putaruru and Tuatapere. I never went surfing at Taylors Mistake, or
had trout at Taupo Lodge, but I surely know the panoramic view
of the Redruth tip, low before the sea, the gull flights wheeling like
windmills above the plastic bags massed on the netting. A man putting
tiles on the Oddfellows Hall in Invercargill was struck by lightning,
yet not hurt much at all. Each working day as I went past, I could see
where the spouting was dented as he fell. The windows were small
and high to stop the rest of us from seeing what the Oddfellows were
up to. Sometimes Iris and I walked past the hall together until we

reached the lights, when she would turn right to old Mrs Brody, who gave her one of the last jobs she ever had, and I would walk on to Acme Smallgoods. Mrs Brody left Mum a Victorian washing bowl and jug used before plumbing was invented. Iris said the set would be worth a fortune today, because it was stamped Duenly Pottery, Sussex, underneath, but the jug was broken when our neighbour's tom jumped up at the budgie's cage. I keep a plant in the bowl now. That bowl is big enough to bath a baby, with bruise blue embossed leaves on it and pink roses.

I've had at least two chances to marry rich, apart from the son of the Drs Utteridge — a sheep farmer from the Hakataramea, and the owner of three rest-homes in Mount Eden. By then, though, neither Iris nor I saw marriage as such an easy step to success. The merino farmer never spoke more than seven words at a time, yet Iris said you've got to think hard about marrying. You've a responsibility to ask yourself if you really want someone coughing in the same bed, walking in and out of your house at will, telling you things about his life. She thought that men were best as visitors.

Iris went at sixty-four: only sixty-four, and I was there. I'd come down to visit her in the first and last house she ever owned. A married couple's house in Murchison, where prices were that cheap. Mum had put new iron on the laundry lean-to and, when the rain began, she took me out in delight to prove it didn't leak, Things were good for her, because she was on super by then and had plenty of work at the pub as well. She was a terrier for work. From the lean-to window we could see the rain cloud moving across the dark, native bush of the Murchison hills, and the rain dashed on the new tin roof. Send her down, Hughie, cried Iris, and she pointed out the good second-hand washing machine and the red lino she'd put down. There wasn't a leak, or a spider's web, in the place. Send her down, Hughie. I think it rains a good deal in Murchison, for the grass on the flats below the bush was lush and there were rushes in the dips. She used to say send her down, Hughie, when she comforted me during a winter we spent in a Johnsonville caravan. We're snug as a bug in a rug here, she'd say. I turned to say something of this to my mother in her Murchison laundry, but she was falling backwards with a stopped heart. As if pole-axed she went down, and any murmur against it I certainly didn't hear above the rain that Hughie sent down. I reckon she died still with the satisfaction of her own home, the new red lino, tin laundry roof, and some great thing to come, even if she never made supermarket star, lost family heiress, or became a medium who told the police of a dozen murder sites, like Beryl Judkins' aunt.

Beryl Judkins' parents took her camping to the Coromandel and she raved on at school about moonlight swims, campfires and pohutukawa blooms along the shore. I must have whined at home about our failure to have holidays, as a ten-year-old will, so Iris made a tent in our backyard by putting a sheet over the clothesline and anchoring the sides. We had onion chips and lemonade. We lay rolled in blankets watching the sky through the tent end. My mother told me about the black sequin dress she was planning to wear as a jazz sax player. I heard a hedgehog sorting for grubs in the currant bushes as Iris described the life of a cabaret star. Mr Thompson came out late on to his lawn for a leak and a spit. We were quiet until he was inside again. Sure, it wasn't Beryl Judkins' Coromandel. Mr Thompson once had his photo in the paper, because an ancestor had been killed at the Wairau Massacre, he said, and he wanted compensation from the government on behalf of the family. The fighting can't have been far from the bright rose-hips of years later.

We shifted away before there was any response to his claim, but Iris checked at the library anyway to see if anyone with our name had been massacred there. She said Bleekers had been in New Zealand since before the Treaty. We shifted because she was offered a job as assistant matron at Stanhope Preparatory School in Johnsonville, but when we arrived the assistant matron refused to leave, because her marriage plans had fallen through, and so we lived in a caravan at the motor camp until Iris became car groomer at Crimmond Motors.

It was a shock at the time, of course, Iris going like that, but I came to be glad she'd not suffered any sense of failure. She died in her first home and, although Hughie was sending it down outside, not a drop could get through to her red lino and washing machine. The certificate gave Murchison as the place of death. I just thought it strange as about the only one of all those towns and suburbs that I'd not shared with her. All those uncaring places where she had fed and clothed me, and so much more. We're not finished yet, she'd say. Some of us have to achieve what we can despite our lives, rather than as a consequence of them. So there was no supermarket stardom, no Lotto first division, no Brazilian millionaire, no double doctor marriage, no jazz sax cabarets in the sequin dress, not even my father coming back reformed and freshly shaved to start again. Just Iris, my mother, and me.

The Rule of Jenny Pen

The heavy moonlight gave it all the appearance of quality linen, flattering the exposed walls of the Totara Eventide Home, and the lines of stainless steel trolleys and wheelchairs by the windows glinted like cutlery upon that linen. The moon was more forgiving than the sun, allowing a variety of interpretations for what it revealed. The shadowed places were soft feathered with blue and grey, like a pigeon's breast.

The only sound was Crealy pissing on to Matron's herb garden. The white cord of his striped pyjamas hung down one leg, and his bald head was made linen in the moonlight. 'Had enough?' Crealy asked the sage, basil and thyme. Residents were not supposed to come out and treat the Matron's herbs to such abuse. Crealy felt his life stir as ever at the defiance of rules. He could see the trim, summer lawn, and the garden which paralleled the side path to the slope of the front grounds. The moonlight lay over it all as a linen snowfall.

Crealy had never before lived in a place so pleasant to the eye, or so well organised — and he hated it. Always a big man, he had never done anything with it, lacking the will, the resolution, the brains and the luck. At eighty-one and in Totara Home, he found that time had awarded him a superiority which he had been unable to earn any other way. He had given little, and lasted well.

Crealy's bladder was empty, so he put a large hand over his face to massage his cheeks, while he waited for an idea as to what to do next. Even in the moonlight the kidney spots on the backs of his hands showed clearly. He could think of nothing novel to do, so decided to persecute Garfield. He went back through the staff door of the kitchen, and bolted it carefully behind him. Before seeking out Garfield, Crealy wanted to be sure that Brisson was settled in the duty room. He went slowly through the kitchen and the dining room, through the corridors which were tunnels in the Totara of all their past lives.

Crealy stood in the shadow of the last doorway, and looked into the corridor which led past the duty room. He was like a bear which pauses instinctively at the edge of a forest clearing to assess possibilities of gain or loss. He walked slowly down the corridor of mottled green lino, his breathing louder than the regular shuffle of his slippers. Before the duty room he slowed even further as a caution, but his breathing was as loud as ever. The door was ajar, and Crealy looked in to see Brisson at leisure.

The duty room had a sofa, a chair, a log book with a biro on a string, a coffee pot, a telephone, a typed copy of the fire drill on the wall. It had the worn, impersonal look common to all such rooms in institutions, whether hospitals or boarding schools, army depots or fire brigades. Brisson lay on the sofa, and held up a paperback as if shielding himself from the light. His head was round and firm like a well grown onion, and light brown with the sheen a good onion has too. He wore no socks, just yellow sneakers on his neat feet. Crealy was surprised yet again to see how young some people were. He'll lie there all night and do nothing, thought Crealy.

'Who's that huffing and puffing outside my door?' said Brisson without moving, and Crealy pushed the door and took a step into the doorway. 'Ah, so it's you, Mr Crealy,' said Brisson. He swung the book down, and his legs on to the floor, in one easy movement. 'Why are you wandering the baronial halls?'

In reply Crealy made a gesture with his large hands which seemed more resignation than explanation. Brisson was lazy, arrogant, shrewd — and young. He took in Crealy: the awkward size of him, the sourness of his worn, bald face, the striped pyjamas and, between them and slippers, Crealy's bare ankles with the veins swollen. Brisson gave a slight shiver of joy and horror at his amazing youth, and Crealy's old age.

'Mrs Vennermann said you squeezed the blossom off her bedside flowers,' he said. Crealy itched his neck. His fingers sounded as if they worked on sandpaper, and the grey stubble was clear in the light of the room. 'She said you pick on people. Is that right?'

'She took my Milo,' said Crealy. Brisson picked up the exercise book that served as the log for duty shifts.

'Shall I put that in here then? Shall I? Mr Crealy deprived of his Milo by Mrs Vennermann. For Christ's sake. And someone said that you have been making Mrs Halliday all flustered. Eh?'

'It's just all fuss,' said Crealy. He began to think how he could get back at Mrs Vennermann.

Brisson smiled at his own performance, looking at old Crealy, at the mottled lino like a puddle behind him, at the exercise book with the cover doodled upon, and the biro on a string from it. He considered himself incongruous in such surroundings. He had such different things planned for himself. 'I won't have a bully on my shift, Mr Crealy. If I have to come down to the rooms, then look out. And don't you or the others come up here bothering me.' Brisson hoped to be with Nurse McMillan. What time was it?

'I don't do anything,' said Crealy in his husky voice. 'It's Jenny Pen.'

'What's that?'

'Eh?' said Crealy.

'Go to bed,' said Brisson, and saw the old man turn back on to the puddle lino, heard the shuffle and breath of him as he went back to the rooms of the east wing. Brisson did an abrupt shoulder stand on the sofa to prove age not contagious, then relaxed again with his book and thoughts of Nurse McMillan.

When Crealy reached the room he shared with Garfield, Mortenson and Popanovich he was ready for a little action. Jenny Pen time. Jenny Pen was a hand puppet that Garfield's granddaughter had made at intermediate school. Although christened Jenny Pencarrow, it looked more like Punch, or the witch from Snow White, for its papier mâché nose and chin strove to complete a circle. Jenny Pen had a skirt of red velvet, and balanced all day on the left-hand knob of Garfield's bed. At night, ah torment, she became the fasces of Nero's power, the cloven hoof, the dark knight snouted emblem, the sign of Modu and Mahu, the dancing partner of a trivial Lucifer, a tender facsimile of things gone wrong.

Crealy lifted Jenny Pen from the bed end, and thrust his hand beneath the velvet skirt. He held her aloft, and turned her painted head until all the room had been held in her regard. Garfield began to cry, Mortenson turned the better side of his face aside, and wished his stroke had been more complete. Popanovich was just a shoulder beneath his blankets. Crealy walked Jenny Pen on her hands up Garfield's chest, and she seemed of her own volition to rap Garfield's face. 'Who rules?' said Crealy.

'Jenny Pen,' said Garfield. Garfield had played seventeen games for Wellington as fullback, and later been general manager for Hentlings. It was all too far away to offer any protection.

'Lick her arse then,' said Crealy hoarsely, and Garfield did, and felt Crealy's hand on his tongue. 'You're on Jenny Pen's side, aren't you?' said Crealy.

'Yes.' Garfield's voice barely quivered, although the tears ran down his cheeks. He could scarcely conceive the life he was forced to lead. His soul peeped out from a body which had betrayed him in the end.

Crealy's eyes glittered, and he looked about to share his triumph with others. 'What about you, Judge? Want to do a little kissing?' Mortenson gave his half-smile.

'It's difficult for me,' he said slowly.

'Bloody difficult with only half of everything working.' Crealy walked over to the last bed, and shook Popanovich's shoulder. There was no reaction. 'What sort of a name is that for a New Zealander,' he said. 'Bloody Popanovich!' He banged his knee into Popanovich's back, but there was no defence of the name. It put Crealy in an ill humour again, and he went back to Garfield with Jenny Pen. He began to go through Garfield's locker. 'It's share and share alike here, Garbunkle.'

'Communism has the greatest attraction to those with the least,' said Mortenson in his slurred voice, knowing Crealy was not bright enough to follow.

'Shut up,' said Crealy. He placed a bag of barley sugars and a box of shortbread biscuits on the top of Garfield's locker. 'Is that all, you useless bugger,' he said. He looked at Garfield for a time, letting Jenny Pen rest on the covers, almost basking in the knowledge shared between them of Garfield's weakness and his strength. And even more, the mutual knowledge of Garfield's former strength and superiority, Garfield's achievements and complacency, now worthless currency before Crealy, who had achieved nothing except the accidental husbandry of physical strength into old age.

'What else have you got hidden after all them visitors?' Crealy slid his free hand slowly under Garfield's pillow, and withdrew it empty. 'Come on now, you bugger,' he said.

'Just leave me alone.'

'Make Jenny Pen sing a song,' said Mortenson. Sometimes Crealy would have Jenny Pen sing 'Knick Knack Paddy Whack Give a Dog a Bone', or 'Knees Up, Mother Brown'. It was an awful sound, but better than the beatings.

Crealy listened a while, to make sure that no one was coming who could take Garfield's part, then he pulled the near side of the mattress up and found a packet of figs. 'That's more like it,' he said. He sat on the bed as if he were a friend of Garfield. 'You selfish old bugger,' he said mildly. 'How many figs do you reckon there are here?'

Garfield didn't answer, and Crealy took hold of his near ear and shook his head by means of it until Garfield cried out. 'Don't you start calling out, or you'll get more,' said Crealy. He opened the packet and began to eat. 'For every one you're going to get a hurry up,' he said, and gave Garfield one right away.

So it began. Popanovich remained in hibernation beneath his blankets, Mortenson watched, but tried to keep the true side of his face as expressionless as the other, even though his good leg was rigid. Garfield covered his ears, and Crealy ate the figs, hitting Garfield's face with each new mouthful. 'Figs make you shit, Garfield, old son,' he said, 'but I'll make you shit without them. That's rich, isn't it. I said that's rich, isn't it, Judge?'

'Exactly,' said Mortenson carefully. What time was it? He tried to remember some of the letters of Cicero he had been reading.

The one light from Garfield's locker cast a swooping shadow each time Crealy leant forward solicitously to hit Garfield, and when Crealy held Jenny Pen up in triumph she was manifest as a monstrous Viking prow upon the wall. Mortenson had to accept the realisation that there were underworlds that he had been able until recently to ignore. Now he was part of one, suffering and observing, powerless through reduced capacity and fear.

When he saw a little shining blood beneath Garfield's nose, he could contain his opposition no longer. Yet stress undid his recent progress and Stefan Albee Mortenson, barrister, solicitor, notary public, could produce before the court of Jenny Pen only, 'Creal, youb narlous nan stapp awus nee.'

'Careful, Judge. I don't need your squawk. I might come across and give you more than just this feathering Garfield's enjoying. I'll do the side of you not already dead, you pinstripe squirt.'

Mortenson had nothing more to say, and Garfield sat with his chin on his chest as if in a trance. 'Had enough?' Crealy asked him. 'You're gutless, the lot of you.' Crealy was bored with his immediate subjects and, with Jenny Pen still on his hand as his familiar, he went to wander the night corridors of the home. No conversation began in the room he left. Popanovich feigned the sleep of death, Garfield remained slumped in his bed and Mortenson had no way of travelling the distance between them to offer comfort.

Mrs Munro knew nothing of Totara's netherworld. She had her own room in the separate block before the cottages, and the sun was laid on the polish of several pieces of her own furniture which had accompanied her. Mrs Munro could never understand those who complained of time dragging. She herself delighted in time to spare for all those indulgences a busy life had denied her, all those intellectual and emotional considerations that the slog of a seven-day dairy had prevented her from enjoying. She wore the tracksuit which she had insisted on for a Christmas present. She liked the comfort, the lack of constriction, the zippers at ankle and chest which made it easy to get off. She liked the two bright blue stripes and the motif of crossed racquets, even though she had never played sport.

Despite something of a problem with head nodding, and a lip operation on the way, Mrs Munro was quietly proud that, although she was an old woman, she was not a fat, old woman. She didn't complain about the food, and she drew more large-print library books in a week than anyone else in the home. She rejoiced in an hour to while away over a cup of tea, or in writing to Bessie Inder, or in putting drops in her ear, or measuring her room with the tape from the sewing basket. Miss Hails from the main block did visit too often, it was true, and her repetitions tended to start Mrs Munro's head nodding, but there was always the bedding storeroom as a sanctuary, and Mrs Munro had built a little dug-out in the blanket piles where she could rest in her tracksuit after lunch until Miss Hails had given up looking for her, and gone visiting elsewhere.

For the present, though, she counted the spots of a ladybird on her window sill, and watched sour old Crealy smoking on a bench by the secure recreation area. Crealy was not compulsive viewing, and when Mrs Munro finished her computations concerning the ladybird, she decided she would begin her next romance of the British Raj.

Crealy's cigarette was the last in the packet he had stolen from Popanovich, who was sleeping again. For Crealy, the days were not as enjoyable as the nights, because he was too much under the eye of authority, and the spirit of his fellows was not as easily daunted when the sun shone. He wondered if Mrs Halliday was by the goldfish pond, but couldn't see her, and so he went back indoors to check Mortenson's locker before lunch. In the main corridor he came across Mrs Joyce, who had her blood changed quite regularly at the clinic. Her forearms and elbows seemed forever to have the yellows, purples and blues of ageing bruises. Mrs Joyce had made binoculars of her hands and stood with them pressed to the glass doors, staring out. 'What's out there?' she asked Crealy.

'Herbs and spices, sycamores and young people. And bloody work.'

'I can't see it,' said Mrs Joyce.

'You've gone daft in there.' Crealy rapped on her head with his knuckles, but she kept peering out into the sunshine through the tunnels of her fingers.

'Let me join Jesus,' she said. Crealy looked down at her pink scalp beneath the white hair. Because there was no resistance whatsoever that she could make, because she was not even aware of his malice, Crealy couldn't be bothered hurting her.

'Dozy old tart.'

'Let me come to thee, sweet Jesus,' said Mrs Joyce. Crealy had a chuckle at that, and at how Mrs Joyce was peering through her hands and the glass, although everything outside was perfectly clear to him.

Matron Frew heard the chuckle from the office, and it reminded her that she wanted words with Crealy. She first of all took Mrs

Joyce's arm in hers and walked with her down to the dayroom. She was back before Crealy could quite disappear from sight down the corridor, however, and she told him, with some bluntness, of the indirect complaints she'd been receiving, particularly from staff who had noticed Crealy pestering Mrs Halliday and Mr Garfield.

'Mark my words,' said Matron Frew. 'I will be watching, and also I'm making mention of things in my report to the board this month. You show an unwillingness at times to be a reasonable member of our community.'

As she spoke Crealy hung his head, but not from meekness or contrition. He was counting the number of usable butts in the sandbox by the office door, and when he had done that he imagined himself in the mild, summer night standing over Matron's herb garden, and pissing on the chives, parsley, mint, fennel and thyme. A lifetime in the indifferent, hostile or contemptuous regard of others had rendered Crealy immune to all three. He recognised no value or interest other than his own.

On Wednesday evenings Matron Frew turned off the television in the east wing lounge and organised communal singing. It was not compulsory as such, but absence meant no chocolate biscuits at the supper which followed. As a professionally trained person, Matron knew that a variety of stimulus was important for the elderly.

The committed, the egotistical and the hard of hearing stood close around the piano, the infirm or less enthusiastic were rims at a great distance. Golden oldies they sang, to Matron's accompaniment. 'The Kerry Pipers', 'Auld Lang Syne', 'The Biggest Aspidistra in the World', 'On Top of Old Smokey'.

Matron had begun her career as a physiotherapist and it showed in her playing, the keys kneaded like a string of vertebrae, each tune well gone over and the kinks removed. 'Waltzing Matilda', 'Home on the Range', 'The White Cliffs of Dover', 'Some Enchanted Evening', 'Polly Wolly Doodle'. Matron Frew allowed her charges to respond in their own way and order, but she always had Nurse Glenn or Nurse McMillan guide Mr Oliphant to the uncarpeted area by the door, because the pathos of any Irish tune made him incontinent.

A refrain, particularly with high notes, would sometimes trigger Miss Hails' weakness and she would begin the incessant repetition of a word. It happened, sure enough, during 'Riding Down From Bangor', and for several minutes Miss Hail sang only 'May'. Crealy was present not just for the chocolate biscuits, but because it gave him perverse satisfaction, after the Matron's rebuke, to exercise intimidation almost under her gaze.

He stood on Mrs Dellow's toe during 'Annie Laurie', and stared into her face, daring her to respond. Her thin voice assumed even greater vibrato and her eyes misted. Crealy then leant in comradeship over blind Mr Lewin and sprayed saliva into his face as 'Christopher Robin Went Down With Alice'.

When the chocolate biscuits came at last, Crealy kept himself between them and George Oliphant until they were all gone, then he said, 'Now isn't that a bugger, George, they seem all gone.'

'Silver Threads Among the Gold', they sang, and 'Swing Low, Sweet Chariot'. 'Home, home, home, home, home, home,' Miss Hails continued, until Matron Frew told her to suck her thumb until the cycle was broken. 'Knees Up, Mother Brown' Crealy liked but, because it was his favourite, the others found no pleasure in joining in.

Mortenson enjoyed the association the songs bore, even if not the singing itself. He preferred to be at some remove from the piano and his fellows, for then he could imagine other company and past days. His mouth would twitch and his good hand move to the melodies. 'Some Enchanted Evening' — he would sing it with Deborah as they drove back from skiing, ready for court work during the week. He hadn't realised then, that all roads led to this. 'Roo, roo, roo, roo, roo,' began Miss Hails.

Before midnight, aware of an odd, sighing wind around the home, Crealy made a patrol of his domain. Only his harsh breathing and shuffle gave him away. In his own room everything was as it should be — Garfield was weeping, Popanovich sleeping, and Mortenson in his snores fell every few minutes into a choking death rattle which woke him briefly, then he slept and it all began again.

Further down the corridor Mrs Doone was talking to herself as she strung up nonexistent Christmas decorations. Every night was Christmas Eve for Mrs Doone, and the wonder and frisson of it were freshly felt night after night. 'Compliments of the season, Mr Ah — ah,' she said as Crealy slippered by. Around the corner, Crealy paused outside the room Mrs Oliffe and Miss Hails shared. Miss Hails was doing her thing, of course. For almost an hour she had been repeating the sound tee, while Mrs Oliffe was trying to find nineteen across, which was Breton Gaelic for divine harbinger.

'Oh, stop going tee, tee, tee, tee,' Mrs Oliffe said, but the simple satisfaction of it set her off also, and she joined in. Outside, Crealy could hear them in unison — tee, tee, tee. He found his own head nodding, and his mouth formed the sound. One night it might spread through all of Totara, and capture them in a transport of repetitious senility.

Crealy put his hand to his face to stop himself. He looked carefully down the corridor. 'Mad old tarts,' he said. He considered opening their door and frightening them into silence, but the chances of being caught up in their chant and left nodding with them indefinitely was too great. He went on, still with one hand to his face. Tee, tee, tee, tee faded behind him.

Outside the Matron's office were chairs for visitors, and a varnished box with a sandtray in it for smokers among the visitors. Crealy was able to find several butts worth using again, before he noticed Mrs Joyce standing by the main doors once more. 'Jesus loves me this I know,' she said. She had two overcoats on, and stood with her hand on the catch of the locked door. 'I'm going home,' she said. 'I've been here nearly a fortnight and they're expecting me back now.'

'You've been here for years,' said Crealy.

'Oh no, just a fortnight, and I need to be at home for every special occasion. We've always been a very close family, you see.' Crealy went through her double set of pockets as she talked, but all he could find was a small book of stamps. 'They may well send a car for me,' she said. They both looked through the glass doors for a moment, but there was only empty wind and moonlight: no car was parked on the linen of the drive.

'You can go home this way,' said Crealy, taking Mrs Joyce by the lapel and leading her towards the kitchens.

'Has the car come then?' she said, and 'God will provide, you know. Even Solomon in all his glory.' Crealy led her through the dining room laid for breakfast, and the kitchens, where worn, steel surfaces glinted like new bone. He unbolted the service door and set Mrs Joyce in the gap. 'There you are, then,' he said. 'The main drive's just around the corner.'

'It's a clear path to home, thank Jesus.' The blue second coat would barely fit over the first, and pulled her arms back like the flippers of a penguin. Rather like a penguin she began walking, struck her head on a pruned plum branch, and reeled past the herb garden.

'What's your name again?' said Crealy, but Mrs Joyce didn't answer and, still unsteady from the blow, made the best pace she could around the side path. She had the scent of freedom; she had a promise of home.

Crealy waited until Mrs Joyce was well gone, and there was no sound of pursuit, or return, then he went out himself and stood in the summer night, sniffing the aromatic air of Matron Frew's herb garden. He hung out his cock, and waited patiently for his prostate to relax its grip so that he could enjoy the physical relief and pleasurable malice of watering the herbs. He had both in good time, then he stood under the sycamore by the old garages and had one of the visitors' cigarette ends, after nipping off the filter.

The sycamore creaked and murmured in the night breeze that blew out from the land to the sea. Despite the ache in his joints, Crealy enjoyed being by himself there beneath the branches, and the summer sky, for he knew that he had always been unloved. Even though old age at Totara had given him a mirror image power and significance, while always before he had been subjugated, he liked still to be alone, to have no sources of action or response other than himself. So he stood beneath the sycamore, and enjoyed his cigarette ends guardedly, shading the glow with a palm, and looking out to the better lit parts of the grounds. 'No bastard can see me,' he said. 'No bastard knows I'm here.'

Even a summer's night grows cold for old bones, and Crealy came in and bolted the door behind him. 'Had enough?' he had asked the mint and parsley as he went by them. He inspected Mrs Joyce's stamps in the dim light. He wanted to search her room, but had forgotten her name.

Crealy had never been an intellectual, and at eighty-one he found it difficult to move and think at the same time. So he remained stooped in the semi-light between kitchen and dining room, and he tried to remember what he had been going to do before he met Mrs Joyce.

He went into the pantry beyond the stainless steel moonlight of the kitchen, and lifted out a large tin of golden syrup. He took a thick crust from the toast drawer and, with his fingers as a ladle, spread golden syrup on it. The syrup lay dark in the tin, but silver in glints as it twined from his fingers.

Crealy replaced the tin, and stood with the bread and syrup in his clean hand, sucking his other fingers. He looked into the shadowed dining room: the identical tables, evenly spaced, and an oblong of light across them from the corridor. The golden syrup was rich and energy giving. Crealy began to wonder if Mrs Halliday was having one of her spells in the home. He made such demands on his old mind that his chewing slowly stopped, and his hand no longer held the bread level. He stood in the kitchen doorway as a Neanderthal at the entrance to his cave. The syrup made a silver necklace to the floor. Crealy couldn't remember: couldn't remember at all.

'Bugger me,' he said at last. He was unable to come up with anything, so he stopped thinking, allowed the motor-sensory centres priority again, and moved into the lino tubes which were the Totara corridors.

At the duty room, Crealy decided to check on Brisson in case he was doing the unexpected thing and actually making a round. There was no key for the duty room door, but when Crealy pushed lightly against it, he found that Brisson had set the end of the sofa hard to it. Then he heard voices. Nurse McMillan talked as she and Brisson made love, but her topic was dissatisfaction with conditions of service, not romance. Lovemaking altered the normal rhythm of her words so that odd, accentuated syllables were driven out of her. '*God* we've all thought *of* handing in our resig*nations*,' she said.

'There's nothing in all the world to match it,' Brisson said.

The palm of one of Crealy's large hands still rested on the door, though he pressed no more. He listened to a tune which mocked him, and his arthritis drove him on, shuffling and disgruntled, missing out as usual. Mrs Doone had finished putting up her Christmas decorations for the night, and the corridor was as bare as when she first began. Even Miss Hails was silent, but as Crealy passed Mr Lewin's room he heard a talking clock. 'It is twelve o'clock, midnight,' it said. Like a fox at a burrow entrance, Crealy stood before the door, but the clock didn't speak again, and blind Mr Lewin, who must have activated it, made no sound either.

As he neared his own room Crealy could hear Mortenson's stricken breathing, and remembered with sudden vividness a time more than thirty years before, when he had been a cleaner at the Nazareth Hall and Mortenson had been president of a group that banqueted there. Crealy had looked out from the serving hatch, waiting to begin clearing up, and S.A. Mortenson CBE, barrister, solicitor, notary public, city councillor and party chairman, had been standing at the top table, standing in dinner jacket to give an erudite speech which was buoyed up constantly by delighted applause and laughter from the other tables. The recollection had such strength that Crealy felt again the flat ache of his own inconsequence, but it passed and he was aware of the cream Totara walls again, and the struggle Mortenson had to breathe.

Crealy laid Popanovich's open bottle of lemonade on the bed so that it would wet the sleeping man's feet, and plucked Jenny Pen from Garfield's bed end and held her briefly aloft. 'Wake up, Judge,' he said, and took Mortenson's nose between Jenny Pen's hands.

Mortenson's good side woke with horror. What time was it? 'Let's have poetry tonight,' said Crealy. He made himself comfortable on the bed with his room-mate. 'And I want to see you enjoying it, Judge, getting into the swing of it,' he said.

> *And where the silk-shoed lovers ran*
> *with dust of diamonds in their hair,*
> *he opens now his silent wing*

began Mortenson indistinctly.

Crealy put one of Jenny Pen's fingers into the slack side of Mortenson's mouth and pulled it into the image of a smile. 'Let's not be half-hearted about this. Try something else,' said Crealy. Mortenson wished to disregard the setting his senses made for him, and the only escape was through the words. He did his best with a bit of 'The Herne's Egg'.

> *Strong sinew and soft flesh*
> *Are foliage round the shaft*
> *Before the arrowsmith*

Has stripped it, and I pray
That I, all foliage gone,
May shoot into my joy.

'Eh?' said Crealy. He tired quickly of poetry, even when seasoned with humiliation. 'Had enough,' he said. His thoughts turned to Garfield. There were hours to go, years maybe, before it would be day again.

Blind Mr Lewin was guided by Mrs Munro to the sunroom in the east wing the next afternoon. Mr Lewin loved the warmth, and found that he could sleep easily during the day in full sunlight. Mrs Munro kindly led him down, and Lewin could feel the warmth even as they approached the end of the corridor. Mrs Munro's head nodded companionably as she pulled a cane chair close to the large window: so close that Lewin was able to put out his hands and feel the glass while sitting comfortably. And she gave him his talking clock to cradle, so that he would not be anxious about his meals. Mr Lewin thanked her, and listened to the departing footsteps.

He had never seen the sunroom, and instead of the meek, faded place that it was, poking out over the crocodile paving and lawns in front of the cottages, he imagined it cantilevered high into the sun's eye, and with only the yellow, benevolent furnace of the sun to be seen from the window. Lewin had known far worse times.

While Mr Lewin slept, Crealy elsewhere watched Mrs Halliday. Mrs Halliday was only in her sixties, but subject to Huntington's chorea in recurring spells during which she often came into the Totara Home to relieve her family. Crealy always took a considerable interest in her visits, for her breasts were large, she still had firm flesh and, caught at the right moment, she could be used without much recollection of it.

Towards the end of the long afternoon she was at her most confused, and Crealy watched from outside the television lounge until he saw her talking to herself and constantly folding and unfolding her cardigan. He went in and firmly led her along the trail of mottled lino to the sunroom, which visitors or clergymen sometimes used to have their talks. 'Has the family come? Has Elaine?' said Mrs Halliday. Crealy was quite pleased to see blind Lewin there, close to the window, for he could pass as a chaperone at a distance, but not act as one on the spot. Crealy sat Mrs Halliday with her back to the window.

'Your family are coming soon,' he said, and opened the front of her dress.

'Is that you, Mrs Munro?' asked Lewin.

'Shut up,' said Crealy.

'The family, you say,' said Mrs Halliday. She allowed Crealy to unclip her bra at the back, and he scooped out her breasts so they made two full fish-heads in the flounce of her dress.

Lewin was still groggy from his sleep, but he didn't wish to seem discourteous. 'Where would we be without families,' he said gallantly, and fingered his talking clock for reassurance. Crealy stroked Mrs Halliday's breasts, and clumsily rolled the nipples between thumb and forefinger so that she pursed her lips and put her hands on his wrists.

'You need to get changed for your family,' said Crealy absently.

'What time is it then?' asked Mrs Halliday.

Lewin pressed his clock.

'The time is four forty-two pm,' it said.

Crealy took another minute of satisfaction in the sun, then refilled Mrs Halliday's bra, and with some difficulty fastened it across her back. Matron Frew might come looking for her soon. 'Stay here and talk to Lewin,' he said.

'Am I changed for my family?'

'Good enough,' said Crealy.

'Who is that?' said Lewin, turning an ear rather than an eye for better comprehension.

'Jenny Pen rules,' said Crealy as he left.

The impartial sun that Mr Lewin blindly enjoyed shone on Mortenson who sat in his wheelchair on a landscaped hillock which looked over the SRA — the safe recreation area. Within it the bewildered or fretful, the complacent and serene, could be left in security. Only the staff could manage the latch. Crealy called it the zoo, but it was pleasant enough, more like a kindergarten. There were seats with foam cushions for thin flesh, and raised garden plots which keen Totarans could work on without stooping or kneeling.

The SRA was overlooked by the wide windows of the dining room on one side, but to the warm north side there was a view across the grass and gardens towards the cottages and the spires of the great world. Mortenson could see the goldfish pond in the zoo, and George Oliphant dolefully shaking the back of his trousers because he was in trouble again.

The Matron and Dr Sullivan stopped beside Mortenson on their round, but finished their conversation before greeting him. 'I've no idea how Mrs Joyce managed to leave the block in the first place,' said Matron.

'It can't be helped.'

'It's a puzzle, though.'

'I haven't told her family the actual circumstances of the death, to minimise the trauma, you see. And how are you, Mr Mortenson?'

'Mr Mortenson is brighter every day,' replied Matron. Mortenson gave his half-smile. He could see the exquisite glow on the sunlit tulips, feel the sun's goodwill on his faithful side, and hear Miss Hails practising her word for the day. The word was nell, or perhaps knell. How was anyone to know but her.

'Nell, nell, nell, nell,' said Miss Hails. Like a prayer wheel she gave a benediction over all the zoo, the lawn, the cottages, the totality of Totara and beyond. 'Nell, nell, nell, nell, knell.'

'Well, nice talking to you,' said Dr Sullivan, and they went on their way. Mortenson felt an itching tic begin at the corner of his eye. In all that ground of apparent pleasure he wondered what Crealy was up to. What time was it? It came to Mortenson that his karma had been assessed; that from the best of lives he was in a spiral descent of reincarnation from which he would emerge perhaps a six-spot ladybird, as counted by Mrs Munro, and would clamp the stem beneath the wine glow of the sunlit tulip blooms.

What time was it? Dr Sullivan and Matron were trying to wake Popanovich. 'It's always the same. Ah, well, he seems healthy enough, and sleep can't hurt him.' Dr Sullivan smiled at the other three in the end room, while Matron moved Popanovich in the bed. The doctor was not a dour person. He believed in good spirits and optimism. He looked about for something that would provide an occasion for light-heartedness and rapport.

Matron sensed that the mood had abruptly changed, though at first she didn't see that behind her Dr Sullivan had taken Jenny Pen from Garfield's bed and mounted her on his hand. Garfield began to shiver, and put his hands out, palms uppermost, as if to play pat-a-cake. Crealy hung his head to one side like an old dog, while the whites of his eyes showed as he kept things in his view. Mortenson felt a sweat break out on his good thigh beneath the rug, and his smile was slow to form and slow to fade. He smiled as a Christian might smile who catches the Devil out walking in the daytime.

'What a good life we lead at Totara,' said Dr Sullivan in falsetto for Jenny Pen, and he jiggled her to emphasise his humour. The only responses were those of Matron Frew's crêpe soles on the lino, and at a distance Miss Hails saying her catechism for the day. It drifted to them down the corridor.

'Mi, mi, mi, mi mi, mi.'

'Perhaps puppeteer isn't my calling,' said Dr Sullivan. He was disappointed by his reception and withdrew into professionalism. Matron knew how to keep that patter going.

Crealy's arthritis was giving him gyppo again. To appease it he walked the maze of corridors, and watched from window after window the sunshowers above the grounds. Dramatic clouds were towed across the sky, and when they met the sun they were lit with red and orange embers, which glowed and shifted in the deep perspectives. From the dining room Crealy saw a travelling shower fracture the surface of the zoo pond, so that the goldfish lost their shape, and became just carrots in the shallow weeds.

On his second circuit Crealy noticed that Nurse McMillan had left the office, and that the morning's mail lay partly sorted on the counter. He eased in, and his stiff hands found envelopes addressed to Mortenson, to Oliphant and Garfield. He pocketed them, and was cheered by the petty malice, even though he couldn't see Mrs Halliday in the TV room as he went past. For the life of him he could not remember when he last had a personal letter. Garfield, on the other hand, received far too much kind attention from outside, and Crealy decided to give him a hard time until the weather improved. He began a search for Garfield, but George Oliphant saw him checking the TV room, and afterwards went to the window that could be seen by Mortenson and gave a warning by semaphore, which Mortenson passed on to Garfield.

Garfield began his slow but urgent escape down the corridors of hours towards the bedding storeroom. The door there had a plunger and cylinder to draw it closed without slamming. To Garfield the mechanism seemed to take an eternity to work, and the cylinder hissed as his view of the corridor and bathrooms narrowed. Garfield sat in semi-darkness, content with the little light entering from a glass strip above the door.

The broad shelves had stacks of sheets and pillowcases, and on the floor were piled blankets which rose like wool bales. Garfield sat on a half-bale to wait it out. He didn't trouble himself with the metaphysics of his situation: what he had come to. The former Wellington fullback and general manager for Hentlings sat grinding his teeth in the bedding store-room of Totara Eventide Home, and listening to the perpetual echoing orchestration which his tinnitus inflicted on him.

Crealy found him there.

It was nearly four. The showers had become less frequent, and a rainbow stood clearly behind the cottages, fading up towards the sun. Yet Mortenson couldn't concentrate on his history of Rome. He felt a helpless consideration for Garfield, and a fear of Crealy. He knew that where there are no lions, then hyenas rule.

His chair was very low-geared and, despite the busy noise of its motor, Mortenson moved only slowly along the corridors towards the bedding room. At alternate windows the day's strange weather was displayed as sunlit promise, then skirts of rain from fiery clouds, then blue sky once again. The door took all the thrust his chair could manage and sank closed behind him, so that the failing light and hiss half hid Crealy's torture of his friend.

'Hello, Judge,' said Crealy. Once he found that Mortenson had come alone, he was pleased. He had become almost bored with Garfield. Yet an advantage can be gained or lost quite unexpectedly, and with such an absence of drama that it is easy to miss the significance. Crealy moved to get a better leverage, overbalanced on the soft surface and fell backwards just a couple of feet into the comfortable crevasse fashioned by Mrs Munro between the banded blankets. His old arms and legs moved silently in the shadows, as if he were a beetle on his back there. He was too stiff to turn easily.

Mortenson took a pillow with his better arm and pushed it across Crealy's face.

'Come on,' he said to Garfield. It was more a delaying tactic at first, with neither of them having much hope of success. Even Crealy gave a sort of grin whenever he managed to free his face, as if he recognised his temporary difficulty, but would soon pay them back all right.

But the more Garfield and Mortenson pushed, and the more Crealy twisted, the deeper his shoulders sank between the blankets. He began to pant and jerk. The others saw a chance indeed and their lips drew back in the dark and they pressed for all their lives. Crealy's big arms and legs fell in harmless thuds against the embracing blankets. Mortenson felt strength and justice in his good arm, even though it trembled with exertion, and Garfield was on his knees to use his body weight upon the pillow.

'Had enough. Had enough, Crealy old son,' he kept whispering. The competitive urge in Garfield revived one last time. Crealy's arms and legs moved less, but his body bucked.

'Now let us play Othello,' slurred Mortenson.

'Had enough,' sobbed Garfield.

For a good time after Crealy was still, they continued to hold the pillow over his face. Accustomed to such full tyranny as his, they could hardly believe that they had beaten him so completely. Even when they heard his sphincter muscles relax, and had the smell of him, they held the pillow down. 'Had enough?' said Garfield tenderly.

'Put the pillow back,' said Mortenson finally, and he wiped the tears from Garfield's face. They didn't look again at Dave Crealy, who was a big, stupid man lying well down among piles of blankets. Garfield opened the door a little and, when he saw that there was no one outside, he held it back for Mortenson's chair, and the snake hissed behind them in the dark.

As they went home they met Mrs Munro guiding Mr Lewin to the sunroom. Mrs Munro delighted in being useful, and was thinking also of a nice cup of tea. 'There's a rainbow,' she said, nodding. Mortenson and Garfield could see its thick, childish bands behind the cottage. At the same time the sun was strong enough to cast shadows from the benches in the grounds. Who knows what Lewin saw, but he could hear with them the piping of Miss Hails at a distance.

'Na, na, na, na, na, na, na, na.'

Mr Lewin pushed the button on his clock.

'The time is four nineteen pm,' the clock said.

309 Hollandia

Ruth had an understanding with Gordon at Reception, and he rang and said there was this older guy in 309 who wanted company. Gordon knew her style, and Ruth knew the hotel. She placed a good deal of reliance on the type of hotel she dealt with, because it was a way of saving hassles. So she had a shower, and put on her new yellow. She was able to wear the slingbacks with higher heels. She wouldn't be on her feet much.

It's nice, the Hollandia. The reception area is in black and gold; there's black buttoned leather suites facing the second storey windows from which you can look down into the shopping mall. Guests at the Hollandia don't call out to each other just to draw attention to themselves, or laugh loudly. You can hear the businessmen folding their newspapers when they have finished reading, or when their clients and acquaintances have arrived. Gordon told her that a lot of those at the Hollandia were on delegations, or teams from government departments.

There was no embarrassment of hanging about in the corridor after knocking, or being turned away because of visitors in the room. Gordon would ring through first and Ruth would go on up if it was okay. It was okay right away for 309. So she stopped looking down at the people in Stabey's examining the silver bracelets, and sapphire and diamond cluster rings which are the thing right now, and she went up. There's a sense of discreet privilege at the Hollandia — private and select. After ten o'clock only guests with keys can use the lifts to the accommodation floors. Ruth was of a mind to appreciate the bold hachures on the lift carpet, and the photographs of Leiden and Haarlem.

She was interested to see what her client was like, even if it was business. Many of them put themselves out to be pleasant and entertaining. The man in 309 was impressive to look at in an ordinary sort of way, but Ruth thought he became less ordinary as she noticed things about him, for he dressed well and spoke well. He had an ease of presence which she found relaxing. His name was Hamish Green, and he thanked her for coming and poured drinks. They sat by the drapes partly drawn across the window, and Ruth looked down at his shoes. She knew that a man's shoes spoke of his place in the world. A man might splash out on a shirt or a jacket, but shoes gave the consistent picture. Hamish Green's shoes were European, probably German she thought. The uppers had double stitching and leather toe caps with punched whorls.

'I hope you don't have to dash off?' he said. Ruth warmed to that: the courtesy which made it sound as if their purpose was social, which perhaps it was, and her presence a favour, and that he would miss her company if she had reason to go.

Yet when they finished a second drink, sitting by the window with the Friday night passing below them, there were times when he didn't talk, as if he were thinking of some other place. Yet it was an easy silence, and he spoke well when he wanted to. He talked wryly of his fear of flying which never seemed to abate he said, and the petty humiliations it caused him, comparing the sensation to that he had in a dentist's chair. Even in his humour there was an unemotional tone which suggested a lack of affinity with the things he spoke of, or a belief in the final triviality of any subject that could be named.

'Are you warm enough?' he said. 'Would you like something to eat sent up?' The view was quite different to that which Ruth had in the reception area. The lights and the traffic made colours and angles of competition, and as the shoppers came closer they seemed to dip below until briefly they were reduced to a bird's-eye view of heads, hair, parcels, before gaining a length of body again. Ruth had become accustomed to observation, to waiting, to her own thoughts during the time which could otherwise bring boredom. Most professional people develop the skill and habit of maintaining a social presence quite successfully while all the time another enquiry of experience or reflection is underway.

It suited Ruth to change in the bathroom. On the folded towels was an envelope with two hundred and fifty dollars inside: left privately there, with no need for either of them to mention it. She put in her bag also the small hotel pack of hair conditioner, for she knew men didn't bother with it, and she turned her head in the mirror's reflection as a check without vanity. She had a three pack of condoms for the hand-sewn pocket of her nightdress. She admired the small, well set tiles of the shower, the heated rail, the sheen of new fittings. She remembered her first flat in the city, with a scornful califont over a bath stained dark yellow like an old tusk. She had learnt how to live better.

'Are you coming through, Ruth?' said Hamish Green, and as she did so he turned from the bedside table, and put down the hotel's black and gold biro. 'Very glamorous,' he said. 'I love to see lace on a woman's skin.' It was said with calm admiration, and as Green hung up his suit he talked about doilies as an extension of the topic of lace. He described them without knowing the name, and Ruth supplied it. He said he remembered in his grandmother's house all these things on dressers and polished wood tables. Ruth imagined him as a rather stolid, obedient boy, visiting his grandmother, and then leaving early so that he would be home in time to do his homework. He went into the bathroom in his turn to wash and change. He had large feet with expansive, milky nails on big toes. He came back in navy blue, with his large, soft feet like the paws of a bear across the carpet. 'It's not up to the lace is it,' he said.

'Dark blue is nice.' Actually, he was too pale for it. It drained him.

'I'll get it off soon enough,' he said.

'So you're beginning to feel hot-blooded?'

He continued talking about clothes as he made himself comfortable in bed, saying that because of his work he wore suits almost all the time, and had few sports clothes. His hands smoothed her breasts, and then Ruth massaged the back of his neck. 'That's it,' Hamish Green said. He took his navy blue top off. Their talk ambled from massage to tension to headaches to acupuncture. Ruth was interested in acupuncture after reading an article in which migraine sufferers had claimed relief with its use. Sometimes she had a bad head herself. While Green explained the theory behind acupuncture, Ruth thought of the times when her migraines had caused her embarrassment with men. Clients didn't expect a woman in her position to have a headache. There was even humour in it, although on each occasion neither she nor they could see it. Ruth imagined that Hamish Green would have enough detachment to appreciate such a situation, but she didn't mention it. She joined instead his game of finding improbable anatomical points for acupuncture.

A phone call interrupted them. It was about his work, for he listened for several minutes just saying yes, and hmm, with his eyes on the ceiling, and Ruth looked there also, noticed the nozzles of the automatic sprinkler system which marred the even surface. Each floor of the Hollandia had its own colour scheme, right down to the covers. The bed in 309 had a pattern in black, pink and lilac, and the pink was picked up in the drapes. Green said hmm once more, then he had his turn; talking of the next day and how he expected things to go, and it was the other person who did the listening. 'We don't want to get into the question of funding at all tomorrow,' he said. 'Surely at the moment we're concerned only with agreement in principle. Discussion on funding is another thing again, and for another meeting.' And so on. Twice he made mention of paschal lamb, and Ruth didn't understand what he meant. He ended the conversation by laughing in his deliberate way and saying, 'All right, but I wouldn't prepare the paschal lamb just yet.' Ruth lay beneath the black, pink and lilac and her lips shaped the syllables of paschal lamb so that she would remember to look it up in her son's dictionary.

Green had a good deal of grey chest hair, yet on his arms the hair was black and straight, lying the same way across his wrist and forearm. The cabinet above the small fridge was open, and the miniatures stood in ranks like the contents of a doll's cupboard — whisky, gin, brandy, liqueurs, red wine, all the things which didn't need to be chilled. 'I wouldn't prepare the paschal lamb just yet,' Hamish Green said.

As he had talked, sitting half-turned towards the table and the phone, for a while she had knelt behind him, continuing to relax his neck and shoulders. Next to the phone was the envelope on which she had seen him write when she came to the bed. It was addressed to him, and she felt satisfaction that he had told her his real name. In the corner he had written her name — Ruth. She imagined he had done it to save the embarrassment of forgetting her name, having to ask again perhaps in the midst of their loving. There were things she liked about the man, not his middle-aged neck and bear paws, but there were things, she thought.

'Sorry about that, Ruth,' he said when the call was over. Maybe he looked at her name on the corner of the envelope before saying that, maybe not. She herself never forgot a client's name until business was over, and never once had a man complimented her on that consideration. On the other hand she had been honey to a hundred men, darling or nothing to more. She had been Wilma, baby, hot pants, sister, Chattanooga Choo Choo even. For a weekend in Sydney it was an auctioneer's sense of humour to call her his opening bid.

Hamish Green talked of how tired he'd grown of staying in hotels, despite knowing that as he had no dependent family anymore it made sense that he was often his company's choice. But hotel room after hotel room, he said. 'Well, there's no dishes to do,' Ruth said. She could find little reason to pity the life he led. She had to bite her tongue sometimes when men complained about such things.

'That's true,' he said. 'I suppose it sounds absurdly indulgent to complain about living in hotels. You're quite right.'

'But I can see what you mean. A hotel's not a home.'

He moved a hand to her thigh. 'Where's home?' he said.

'Right here,' Ruth said. 'You don't mind wearing a sheath? It's better these days.' He stroked her shoulder, and enjoyed slipping the strap of her night-dress up and down, and when he started he was content with the usual missionary position. It was fairly practiced and fairly long, but the earth didn't move for either of them. He then lay on his back with his eyes closed, and began to talk to her again. No confidences or revelations, just his half-serious complaints of the effects of travelling long distances, and how to work effectively despite them. He talked also about those interests and ambitions that he had been obliged to slight for the sake of his work and family. Commonplace topics in most respects. As Ruth listened she sensed that behind the even tone of his indifference, and despite his influence, education, his German shoes, he felt headed in a direction not of his own choosing. She responded to that feeling in two ways natural to her, a selfish satisfaction that he had his problems as she did, and a greater sympathy towards him because of it.

He asked her opinion about diets, said hmm and yes when she was talking, and soon fell asleep. He had moved while she was talking, and slept with his hand on the rise of her hip as if it was a posture he had been long used to. He snored, but not in a way exaggerated enough to disturb her as she lay thinking. She wondered if she could keep her son interested in school, so that he could go on and get a degree in law or accountancy. Then surely he would be able to have a job like Harnish Green's: a job that allowed confidence, self-respect and freedom of choice in little, day to day things even though powerless against the general pattern of life. That way her son wouldn't have to be like her, and she didn't see that in the narrowest sense, for she knew from experience that there were plenty of people of both sexes in the same situation, even if their barter was not so direct or categorical. Later, quieter, when Green's light snoring was as regular as the noise of the sea at a distance, Ruth calculated her income and expenses for the week, and was comforted by the outcome. Yet at the back of her practical mind she posed a question as to how many years she could continue to make the sort of money she did, and how far away was the time when Gordon at Reception would begin to call her less and less.

Almost asleep herself, perhaps even woken by it, Ruth heard Green talking in his sleep. He slurred a few words, then clearer and louder through urgency he said, 'Is that you, Dianne? It's you at last. Don't stand on ceremony.' The words were startling not for themselves, or because uttered in sleep, but rather that the voice was so apart from any tone he had used before. The voice was vibrant and full of sudden appeal, as if another man lay there. Green said nothing more, and continued sleeping, but without any snoring for a long time. Ruth was left to wonder. She thought that Dianne must have been his wife's name, and she moved her lips to remember, don't stand on ceremony, the way she had with paschal lamb. She wondered about his voice and what special world of imagination, memory or emotion was its source. Ruth was interested in patterns of speech, the individual differences helped her in her work to pass the time. When the subject of men's conversation was most predictable there was still the variety of expression. Words, like shoes, she considered useful clues, but the words had interest in their own right too. Thinking of Hamish Green's sleep-talking she smiled, and began to sleep herself.

Ruth woke first in the morning. She found that she didn't sleep in when she was working. Green had moved away in the night towards his own side. He still lay on his back, his jaw dropped somewhat, and his breathing a small gasp on the indrawn air and a sigh on the outgoing. Ruth renewed acquaintance with his face, and noticed most the growth of bristles, so that what had seemed one piece the night before had become two faces; pale above, flint grey below the cheeks. A pirate combination. And on the angle of chest exposed, amongst the ash of curled hair was one incongruous nipple like the wasted kernel of a nut. Yet he had a good head. The face although not handsome suggested reason, and wasn't completely animal the way some men's faces were in sleep.

Ruth went from the bed quietly to have her shower, and when she returned, Green was shaving. 'I've asked for some fruit to be sent up,' he said.

'It's time I was on my way.'

'Me too,' he said. 'A quick shower and then to work whatever the day.' She knew to be putting on a little make-up, out of sight in the bathroom, when room service came, and then she sat close to the window while Green made coffee. They talked of what a city had to offer in a weekend. They weren't completely at ease. She found it more difficult with an intelligent man, once the object of the exercise had been accomplished, and rarely stayed the night in any case. She had her son to consider. She half-regretted having stayed, but then it wasn't fun getting up and leaving the hotel at two or three in the morning, demeaning even. Ruth wished she had some better experience to draw on in her conversation with him. If the feeling had an outcome it was only that her comments became knowing, sharp, even at the expense of people they could see in the Saturday street, or issues of mild interest raised between them. 'You're no fool, Ruth,' he said. She had an answer to that too, but didn't make it, just took her bag and prepared to leave.

'Goodbye, Ruth. I'll remember your lace night-dress. Lovely.' He held out twenty dollars. For a taxi he said.

'Oh, I can walk, I can find my own way all right.'

'No friend of mine walks home alone from the hotel,' he said. That was the right thing to say, Ruth thought, and she didn't find any sarcasm in it. Yet behind all he said she felt some malaise, some lack of expectation. She thought of his sleep-talk in the night; the voice of a different man she had heard just that once.

On impulse she said, 'I won't stand on ceremony then,' and Hamish Green smiled at the phrase, but there was no sign it meant anything to him. She had a last glimpse of him and 309, with the black and pinks well caught in the low morning sun, the envelope with her name on the bedside table, Green's quiet suit and the silver watchband on his wrist.

It was nice wasn't it, the Hollandia. The carpet was obsequious beneath her slingbacks, making no distinctions. Even in the mornings at the Hollandia there was a sense of ease — as if all had been paid for, and quality given for that payment. It was nice, she thought, the Hollandia, with photographs of Groningen and Emmen, Amsterdam, Hilversum and The Hague.

The Rose Affliction

Myra was using the orbital polisher in the staff cafeteria at Proudhams when she first saw the rose. She had been working for five hours, her asthma was bad again and her shoulders ached from hauling the polisher from side to side on the brown and yellow mottled lino. The first rose was in the extreme upper left of her vision, and as her head moved with the polisher, so the rose moved, skimming over the cafeteria lino, or rising up the pale walls when she lifted her eyes. At first Myra thought it just a temporary continuation of the patterned whorls on the floor, or of the enamelled manufacturer's crest on the central boss of the polisher. But it was quite clearly a small rose. The petals were flushed pink with the packed effort of escaping the green bud capsule.

Myra took one hand from the polisher to rub her eyes and then blinked several times, but although the rose blurred for a moment, it reformed perfectly. She could see the slightly crimped ends of the small petals, like a delicate, miniature clam, and the deeper tonings of colour towards the centre of the rose. She turned off the machine and opened her mouth to call out to Ruby, who was doing the executive suites not far away. As the whine of the polisher vanished down the empty night corridors, Myra thought how silly it would sound to complain of a rosebud in her eye, and how impossible to prove. She didn't know Ruby all that well, or trust her with personal things.

It was just that she was tired, Myra told herself. She would come right after a good sleep, and at fifty-nine she had experience of the tricks that body and mind could play on you, though menopause couldn't be blamed any longer. Her knees, for example, after all that wear in commercial cleaning, rattled like dredge buckets if she had to get down on to the floor, and her left ankle on a hot day would swell over the rim of her shoe if she had to stand a lot. She had a frozen shoulder, found it an agony to have to work her right arm above the level of her head. Not that she mentioned those things to the supervisor.

But nevertheless, to see a rose was an oddity: like a transfer, or a logo, high left in her vision and superimposed on anything that she looked at there. Even in the bucket of water, milky with disinfectant, that Myra used for the urinals, the pink rose could be seen, and as Myra had a lift home with Ruby, because Wayne was out in her car, the imposition of the rose continued. 'We'll get double time if we do the two extra hours on Sunday at the Super Doop Market,' said Ruby. As Myra looked at her to answer, the pink rosebud glowed in Ruby's straight, brown hair.

The rose was still in her eye when she woke; had gained company in fact, a darker pink, larger bloom, past its best so that the full petals exposed the straw-coloured stamen of the centre — a round cluster like the cleaning brush Myra's dentist used on his drill. 'Weird,' said Wayne, as he asked her for a loan and, without waiting for an answer, began scrabbling in her purse.

'What do you think I should do about it?' she asked her son.

'Does it hurt?' It didn't hurt at all, just the oddity of it concerned her, and what it might represent as a symptom or warning of something going wrong. 'Well, I'd say just keep on normally then,' said Wayne. 'You don't want to miss work unless you have to. Not with double time at the Super Doop coming up.'

Myra was pleased with Wayne's matter-of-fact response, but she didn't say anything to Ruby, or any of the others at work, although there was a steady growth of roses over the following weeks. They massed to the left of her sight, roses of all colours and types, so that when she was cooking or cleaning, at home or at work, the blossoms were imposed on everything she saw. They festooned the cafeteria tables she wiped clean and softened the blatant commercialism of the Super Doop.

Myra developed a rather off-putting habit of cocking her head sideways in an effort to bring those things she wished to view into the clear area of vision that remained. 'What on earth's got into her?' said Ruby to the supervisor.

'You'd better see the quack,' said Wayne reluctantly at home.

'You realise that it isn't actually the image of a rose,' said Dr Neumann. 'Perhaps a vibratory retinal effect, but more likely organic particles in the vitreous or aqueous humour of the eyes. It is in fact quite common for some opaque cells to be there from birth, or to detach in later life from inner surfaces.'

'Oh, they're roses all right,' said Myra.

'Indeed. Are they "Charlotte Armstrong" then, or perhaps "Diamond Jubilee"?' Dr Neumann was not accustomed to being contradicted.

'I don't know one from another,' she said, humbled.

'The images don't drift you say, though. That's the difficult thing to reconcile with cells in the fluid. There's a drifting effect normally in such cases. I think that we had better make an appointment with Mr Hardie. There's nothing to worry about. He will introduce drops to dilate your pupils before the examination, but there's no discomfort.'

No discomfort, but a considerable wait, Myra found. A specialist's appointment can take months for all but the urgent cases. In the meantime the roses multiplied, white, yellow and red, until they were scrolled over much of Myra's sight, and she saw the world through an increasingly profuse floral lattice of glowing petals and frog-green small leaves. The roses obscured the urinals, and the smeared tables and walls that Myra was meant to clean. Instead of stains and accumulated grease, scuffs and carpet fluff with blowflies, all of which had been her responsibility in life, she had a host of roses closing in.

'But no scents at all. That's the queer thing, and a pity really,' Myra told Mr Hardie, who looked up from his examination to smile to the nurse. Myra could see one side of that smile above a cluster of yellow floribunda.

'We'll keep a check on its progress,' he said. For all his kind intentions he could find neither cause nor cure. 'Don't hesitate to contact me if you experience the least pain,' he told her and, later on the phone to Dr Neumann, agreed it was an unusual and rather tragic case.

'She can't see to work anymore,' Ruby said to the supervisor. 'I can't bear to imagine her cut off from us all. Oh, it's so sad, isn't it? And there's no operation will help, they say.'

'We'll have to get you right on to the sickness benefit,' was Wayne's opinion, 'and the car had better be put in my name, as you won't be able to drive anymore.'

The last roses to come were the richest — and the darkest. Though Myra sat in the sunroom with her face to the window, for her the roses were the enduring and exclusive view. The last roses fitted as if completing a cathedral window, and they bloomed so velvet, so red, downy black-red, red-black. The colour of the blood that goes back to the heart.

Heating the World

Tucker Locke wasn't married until he was forty-two. A cheerful woman from the Taieri with good legs and three daughters finally decided to move north for the sun and take him in hand. Before that Tucker was one of a group of bachelor farmers so typical of the New Zealand heartland that they form a sub-species of the population.

After his mother died, Tucker had done for himself, as the saying goes, and with his cooking he just about did for anybody else who called as well. He had lived in traditional rural simplicity rather than poverty. He had an average downland mixed farm worth about half a million in bad years, and camped in his own home — a tartan rug on the porch bed, a laundry that still had a copper, and yesterday's paper as a tablecloth at breakfast as he read today's.

It wasn't that Tucker was a failure as a farmer, not at all, but his financial priorities and lifestyle were congenital. Super and drench, a new post-hole digger, or drill, the best stock and certified seed, were the natural expenses of life, but to buy a new lampshade, or replace the kitchen lino for reason of colour co-ordination, would no more enter his head than to dine at the Victor Hugo restaurant in town when he had food in his own home. A four and a half thousand dollar skeet gun, on the other hand, or an irrigation mule at twenty thousand, were perfectly justifiable purchases.

The sub-species of rural bachelordom is perpetually renewed, of course, by the very process of attrition which reduces its contemporary generation. By the time he was forty even Tucker had become aware that he was no longer typical among his acquaintances, and that there were deficiencies in a comparative sense. At the tables of his married friends he developed a taste for lasagne and apple strudel. His devotion to cold mutton, mashed potato and swede was somewhat undermined, and the sight of children forced him to consider the fact that his farm had no heir. So, advised by his friend Neville O'Doone, who had taken the plunge a few years before, Tucker began the display which indicated that he was willing as well as eligible. He appeared in the retail area of his local town, wore a woollen tie with his sportscoat and attended a few mixed gender events such as the trots and the show.

The community considered Tucker very fortunate in his marriage, and so did Tucker; nevertheless he had no knowledge of modern women, and the marriage brought changes he had not predicted. Neville O'Doone was his counsel in such things, always in the informal and off-hand way that the sub-species deals with the deepest matters of the psyche.

Tucker and Neville were travelling together to an open day on shelter belt trials at Methven when Tucker first sought advice from his friend. They had been commenting on the management and condition of the properties they passed, doubtful of the future for Romney wool, when Tucker abruptly referred to Neville's wife.

'Margaret likes soap, I suppose,' he said.

'Soap?'

'Women like soaps: a variety of soaps and things,' said Tucker. 'I counted seven along the bath last night, and all partly used, you know.' His laugh had good-humoured ease as its intention, but conveyed bewilderment instead. Neville told him that he meant shampoos. 'Shampoos, all different colours,' agreed Tucker. 'One oily, one normal, one dry, a body shampoo, a protein conditioner, an apricot facial scrub, one enriched with the natural oil of some sort of pretzel which grows only in the Orinoco. And soft pink soap which turns to a slush like snow, and vanishes as rapidly.'

Neville could recall Tucker's bathroom before his marriage: one block of yellow soap on which it was easier to work up a sweat than a lather, and with dirt settled into its seams as it weathered so that it was grained like a metamorphic rock. 'It's mostly liquid stuff they buy,' said Tucker sadly. 'It just runs away. You've no idea. It just runs away down the plughole. And women don't like to share a bath, do they? We've put in a shower as well. I could dip a mob of two-tooths in the time my girls take to shower.' In a half-hearted way Neville tried to persuade Tucker that shampoos and conditioners weren't really soaps. 'All do soaps' job,' affirmed Tucker. 'Can you believe seven different bottles, and others besides. Bath salts and that.'

'Oh, yes,' said Neville, but then he'd been married some years before Tucker. He felt a little superior: the sort of superiority you feel when up to your waist in quicksand, but observing someone else in up to his neck. 'But you wouldn't want to go back to being single again would you, Tucker?'

'Oh, no. Hell, no,' said Tucker, but his face was pensive, as if regarding a mountain of expensive saponaceous products degrading in natural atmospheric humidity.

They were together at the gun-club when next Tucker raised his home life. Neville had commented on a flash, wine shirt his friend was wearing. 'Pull,' said Tucker, and fired. 'Yes, Dianne thinks I should have some new things. My clothes seem to be wearing out more rapidly these days.'

'How come?' Neville hadn't noticed Tucker working any harder than usual.

'I reckon my stuff is getting worn away in the washing machine,' said Tucker guardedly. 'Women love to get the clothes from my back.'

'Do they indeed, you old dog.'

'I mean for washing. I've always felt myself it takes a day or two to feel comfortable in what you're wearing, but Dianne has it into the machine before I'm hardly used to it. Continual washing is bad for the stitching, I'd say, and seems to be shrinking the waistbands, but there's no telling her. I'm getting quite a wardrobe now, you know.'

It was true. For twenty years Neville had identified Tucker off his own property by his blue checked sportsjacket, but he was becoming more difficult to spot since marriage, as his colouration varied. 'Women have a good deal of clothes, you know,' said Tucker with some vehemence.

'I know.'

'My daughters have a drawer of pants each. Whole drawers of pants.' Tucker lifted his hands to emphasise the incredibility of it, then let them fall helplessly to his side. Tucker had been accustomed to maintain three pairs of underpants — one to wear, one to wash and one to change into. He couldn't comprehend the necessity of any other regime. 'Scores of them,' he whispered absently. It was axiomatic for Tucker that clothes were used until they were worn out, the same sensible approach he took to cull ewes, or tarpaulins for the hay shed, yet he was confronted with a philosophy which discarded garments because puce was no longer in fashion, or because the pleats had a tendency to accentuate the hips. 'Margaret buys a fair amount of clothes?' asked Tucker.

'From time to time, yes,' said Neville. Tucker's expression lightened. If headlong expense was universal in wives, he was human enough to feel pleased that he had company in being a witness and somewhat reluctant backer.

'You're getting to understand why women look better than men. One reason, anyway,' said Neville.

'I guess you're right,' said Tucker. 'I've got two suits myself now, though I can't see that people are going to die regularly enough for me to need to alternate them.'

Tucker still shot well, however, despite his financial concern, Neville noted ruefully. He has an eye like a stinking eel, Tucker has. He shot everything out of the air with almost vindictive skill and won another top gun sash and a side of hogget. Neither he nor

Neville thought to relate the cost of their day to the conversation.

Tucker and Neville met on sale days at the Dobb Hotel, the only one in town that hadn't put in a barbecue and outdoor seating. Tucker drank draught beer, but slipped in a Glenfiddich every now and again as a chaser. It was in the Dobb that Tucker confided further in Neville concerning his personal life. They had been talking about the Celtic Old Boys' game, and Neville said Ransumeen wasn't talented enough to bring on the oranges at half-time. 'I've rather gone off fruit,' said Tucker, after a pause during which they both watched through the window Gus McPhedron trying to climb into the back of his utility for a nap. Neville found it difficult to follow Tucker's claim, for old Mrs Locke had been a great one for utilising their own orchard, and their pantry had held rows of bottled plums, peaches and quince jam. She had showed them even, in the produce section of the A & P show. There had been boxes of wrinkled autumn apples in the laundry and Tucker normally had one or two in his pocket, or the glove compartment of the truck. He had a kelpie once which liked eating them, but Tucker had shot it for biting his best ram in a costly fashion. Neville said something of all that. 'No, no,' said Tucker. 'You don't understand. There's bought fruit, see.' His tone was one of shocked disclosure. Fruit was nature's bounty, something that arose naturally from one's land without great attention, and with no mercenary aspects. Ah, but since his marriage, Tucker had been introduced to mandarins and melons, pawpaws and peppers, passion fruit, oranges and kiwi fruit.

'Do you know how much a feijoa costs?'

'Well, ah,' said Neville.

'Much more,' said Tucker. 'We have bananas often in a bowl together with oranges and pears.' Tucker was half defiant, half distraught, convinced that such hubris would bring his ruin. 'This morning I looked at the ticket on one of the bananas. They each have their own ticket, you know. It had come from Ecuador. Ec-u-a-dor!' Tucker was silent after his syllabic exclamation, which had drawn looks from other tables. He was considering the number of chargeable exchanges and activities needed to get a banana from the plantations of Ecuador to his wooden fruit bowl in Te Tarehi. Gus McPhedron was asleep in the ute outside, the tail-gate down, the sun glinting on his tan stock boots. 'And the thing is, see, that often fruit goes off before it's eaten and has to be thrown out.' The concept of produce purchased from the ends of the earth, and then thrown out, was arsenic to Tucker's peace of mind. Almost bitterly he downed another Glenfiddich. 'No one bothers to eat a quince, or a plum, these days,' he told a sagely nodding Neville. 'The whole crop lies beneath the trees in the orchard for the wasps and the birds.'

'But what's that against all the advantages of marriage,' asked Neville.

'Oh, you're right there,' said Tucker. 'Of course I wouldn't change for the world.'

Yet at the Town versus Country game, in the first half, when the action was mainly down the other end, Tucker voiced further anxiety. He had picked up his family from town the night before and unfortunately been exposed to some of the prices. 'You know how much a lipstick costs, just one?' he asked. Neville was embarrassed in case some of their mates heard, but they were too busy abusing the town ref. 'Twenty-nine dollars thirty-nine,' said Tucker. 'It's true. It's true. And how often do you see a tube used right up? Answer me that.'

'You're blind and bloody half-witted with it,' shouted Neville.

'And Sarah wanted some shoes for aerobatics,' said Tucker as the Town took their penalty.

'You mean aerobics,' Neville said.

'Right.'

'You see aerobatics is —'

'Okay,' said Tucker.

'So she wanted sports shoes.'

'I went in with her myself,' said Tucker. 'Reddickers had a sale and

I found a decent pair reduced to fifty-five dollars.'

'That's reasonable enough,' said Neville.

'Oh, but they wouldn't do. Not enough heel cushioning for the effects of aerobics, the woman said. A lot of people did structural damage to their feet that way, she said, and Sarah said her friends had different ones. You wouldn't believe what I had to pay before I got out of that shop.'

'Tell me,' said Neville. 'Back up your man, Cecil, for Christ's sake. That boy's all prick.' But Tucker couldn't bear to mention the actual amount in all its grotesque enormity.

'Six lambs at today's schedule prices,' he said, and even the sight of the Town's captain being taken off on a stretcher barely lightened his spirits. 'Six lambs, can you credit it — and all for jumping about in.'

On their way back from the match, Neville and Tucker heard on the car radio that there was progress at the great power summit. 'They're wanting more changes,' said Tucker pensively. Neville thought he was referring to the world leaders, but after some confusion realised that Tucker was meaning his wife and daughters. Perhaps it was just a matter of scale after all, though. 'Interior renovations,' said Tucker, as if giving Neville a medical diagnosis of some significance.

'So?' said Neville.

'First grade Axminster, designer wallpaper, new drapes.' Tucker was marking them off on his fingers as he spoke, and steering with upward pressure of his knees. It seemed that Tucker's wife was determined that the good room get the works. 'Ceiling repainted, pelmets removed, droop light fittings and new fire surround tiles of Tuscan red. We'll use the room a good deal more because of it, of course,' said Tucker to console himself, yet the car shimmied because Tucker's knees were trembling.

'It's improving your asset, Tucker,' said Neville. 'There's that as well.'

'That's true,' said Tucker. Neville's considerate response encouraged him to further revelation. 'We all have duvets now,' he continued, his tone wavering between pride and defensiveness. 'Yes, duvets on all the beds, and now we have a double dozen unused blankets folded in the cupboard.' Tucker had pressed past anxiety to a state almost of awe. The grandeur of the extravagance conditioned him to expect some providential punishment. All those blankets that had provided sensible warmth for generations of Lockes, now stored with good wear still in them, and duvets purchased in their bedstead. It couldn't be right in the view of a Calvinistic God. 'Of course I'm a believer in progress,' said Tucker stoutly.

'A lot of the improvements have been on you, haven't they?' said Neville. 'I mean Dianne's done you up proud since you've been married.'

'True, true,' said Tucker. Neville was thinking of Tucker's wet-weather gear. In the old dairy next to the back door there had been an array of Locke coats going back into rural antiquity. Tucker's favourite had been a sou'wester which must have defied the last ice-age, and although the cuffs were frayed completely away, the coat itself remained so stiff that if Tucker took it off between cloud bursts, it would stand like a tent in the wet grass. And it blended in with the landscape so well that even the wiliest mallard couldn't pick Tucker out in the mai-mai.

'That new nylon parka, for example,' said Neville.

'An anorak,' said Tucker. 'You ever heard of an anorak?'

'Oh yes,' said Neville complacently, as a well-married man.

'A bright, red anorak.'

'Very fetching.'

In frosty July, Tucker and Neville went to a euchre evening at Wally Tamahana's. Afterwards as they stood in the moonlight to enrich the nitrogenous content of the lawn, Tucker spoke with unease of the range of alternative milks with which he was forced to become familiar since he was persuaded to abandon a house cow. Red tops, blue tops, green tops, banded tops, low fat, non-lipid, reduced cholesterol, anti-coagulate, mineral free. Tucker claimed he could see a logical trend in it all: the more things were removed from the milk the more the product cost. 'You know,' he said to Neville, 'soon we'll pay the highest price of the lot for milk with everything extracted — and it'll be water.'

'It's all progress, I suppose,' said Neville, but he too could remember the cream jug of his boyhood in which the spoon would stand upright.

'Right. Right. Of course I wouldn't have it any other way,' said Tucker bitterly.

Neville was deliberately cheerful as he drove Tucker home, but Tucker, having lost fifty-seven dollars at the euchre to Wally Tamahana, was in a mood to resent any hint of extravagance in others. They rattled over the cow-stop at the entrance to Tucker's farm and drove up the track. The median grass not yet brittle with frost whispered beneath the car, and the lights and the moon picked out the massed stinging nettles by the hen-house and sheep yards. Tucker's house was a focus of activity and warmth: every room seemed to be lit, and one of Tucker's new daughters was singing along with her cassette player. Neville thought it grandly welcoming, but Tucker gave a whimper. 'The door. Ah, God.' The back door was open in defiance to the vast, surrounding winter night, and the glow of double bar heaters could be seen. 'Look, look,' said Tucker brokenly. 'We're heating the world.'

Pluto

I saw him first in the pool — a blue, free-standing motel pool set in high duckboards and with a fence of the same boards for privacy, and to stop toddlers from straying in to drown. Wesley Smith was very thin. He gripped the pool ladder and floated like a spider monkey, with his arms and legs spread yet bent. His feet were lunar pale beneath the clear water, and his shins sunburnt. I don't suppose there is a great opportunity to build up a tan in prison administration.

My wife and Jean had taken a liking to each other as soon as they met in the motel laundry. They had been to the gallery together, to the shops. 'Her husband runs a prison,' my wife had told me. It was an indirect introduction to Wesley Smith, and I briefly indulged the fancy that he was the Mr Big who manipulated the occupants and staff of all the cell blocks, although I knew that even such a power would hardly be on holiday in a Tahuna motel. 'Don't be absurd,' Liz said. 'He's the governor, or whatever, there.' And so he was; the head of the largest prison in the nation, and getting away from it all by having a fortnight in Nelson.

'Ah yes, of course,' he said as Jean and Liz introduced us, and from a sense of courtesy he came out of the pool to talk to me. The dense hair of his arms and legs lay in scrolls from the play of the water, the shaving line on his chin was blue-purple, and within his rather taut face the eyes were oddly lustrous, expansive. 'Our wives have decided that we shall be friends,' he said, 'and so we must comply.'

I brought out to the poolside a carafe of the local apple wine, and the four of us got on with friendship. Wesley told a story against himself as a city man getting lost in a shopping mall at Richmond, and in the relaxed mood of holiday we were all able to stretch to an anecdote or two, so putting our best feet forward in acquaintanceship. We were couples of a similar background, outgrown by our children, and without any clash of temperament. It is no disrespect to marriage to say that there are times on holiday when another couple is welcome. My wife was glad of a more knowledgeable shopping companion, and I found that Wesley was a golfer, and not intimidated by silence. It was in fact that casual friendship hoped for while on holiday, and uninhibited by any likelihood that I would fall within Wesley's workday jurisdiction, or he within mine. He already had a competent dentist. I could tell by the quality of his capped upper incisors.

I wouldn't class myself as a particularly curious man, not prying into other people's lives I mean, but it was difficult to be with Wesley Smith without wondering at times about the nature of his job: the responsibilities of it, and the special pressures of the whole criminal and penal aspect of our society. With just a few people it's like that, a poet maybe, or a professional soccer player, and you wonder how their particular frame of mind must affect their view of the day's ordinary experience that you share.

Occasionally when we were walking up to the tee, or tending the motel barbecue, just saying commonplace things, or nothing at all, I would look at thin Wesley and imagine his gaol with its tiers of mezzanine cells, and similarly hierarchical prisoners, exercise areas, security devices, staff with needs for promotion or counselling, and all that bitterness, deceit, despair, malice, pressing outwards. Dentistry certainly isn't an ideal lifestyle. Working in people's mouths all day is a good living financially, but not an easy one, and the figures show the profession has one of the highest suicide rates of any career, but I imagined that Wesley Smith would smile at any stresses I could mention.

Jack Spratt could eat no fat and his wife could eat no lean, the old rhyme says, and I normally expect the close proximity of personality in marriage to highlight differences, but Jean and Wesley Smith seemed similar in essential temperament: both intelligent, self-possessed, slightly rueful. Jean had her weaving, which success had made more an art form than hobby, and Wesley was a wood carver with his work in several important collections.

It was wet on the second Monday of our vacation, and cool as well. The city was swollen with campers with nowhere else to go, and the concrete block cathedral tower at the head of the main street was a fulcrum for an uneasy swirl of cloud. After leaving Jean and Liz at an exhibition of pottery, I drove back towards the beach, and later went over to Wesley's unit to find him carving, his tools on the window sill and the chair as close as possible to seek the light. Wesley's carvings were smaller and more elaborate than I had expected. Two of them stood on a tray by the motel window. One was a wood pigeon in kauri, the painstaking and precise detail of the feathers only partly complete. The other was carved in a macrocarpa canker, Wesley said, and the grain had a wonder of its own. It, too, was incomplete but enough had been done to show that one pygmy had snared another with ropes about a tree trunk, and with exultation, yet caution, leant forward to torment his enemy with a spear. The whole thing no more than ten centimetres high, and yet scores of hours needed to show the two creases on the crouching pygmy belly, or the pattern on the woven twine that held his enemy, whose individual fingers had been carved around the coil he tried in vain to keep from pressing on his throat.

I won't presume to make comment about artistic merit, or the talent of the carver, but fine work is an element of my profession also: almost a worker in ivory, I could say, and I could appreciate the patience and precision that amount almost to a trance to work such detail on such a scale. Wesley had a wooden vice with padded jaws and a suction base, and over this in the window light he bent to carry on his almost oriental art. We talked for some time of the levels of dexterity needed, and he was very interested in the added constraints imposed by working inside somebody's mouth. He had in fact been considering buying one of the old dental service treadle drills, he told me, and he asked me questions concerning them, and also the advanced, high-speed modern drills. Wesley said he often did a model in soap first to check on balance and technical problems before committing himself to wood. He'd done some scrimshaw work, he said, and some in meerschaum, sandstone and jade, but hard wood he loved best of all. Wesley said carving was popular with the long-term prisoners, and that he took a class himself of the three or four who grew to love it: their obsession perhaps to blot out the reasonable, unreasonable world. When Wesley told me of the most skilled prisoner, I had a sense of undeclared envy in his heart that the man had more time than the governor himself to perfect his craft. From the motel window I watched the rain bounce on the road in a sudden fury and the water flow off its curve and fill the hollows of the lawn alongside as Wesley quietly talked.

The leisure of a wet day can be a time for confidences, and the carvings, the discussion of common practices to an extent, had moved us on from our usual trivial subjects. I had a measure of natural curiosity about the prison and his work there. His eminence in an unfashionable career: what it was like to be in charge of the underworld that society wished to see only through safe and entertaining fictions.

'What do you imagine it to be?' Wesley said. He loosened the carving of the pygmies from the suction vice and put it gently aside. He leant back and drew his finger along the blue-purple rasp of his chin. I was close enough to see the grey, downy light reflected in the noticeable curve of his soft eyes.

'I visualise a job demanding a good deal of administrative skill, and judgement as well, and elements of sympathy, even compassion.'

'The system squeezes out compassion,' said Wesley. 'Perhaps you will understand that everything there has to do with responsibility and power. We have all the responsibility and barely enough power, strange as it may seem. They have no responsibility and considerable power. Think of me as a general manager of a firm whose clients are willing it to fail. There's no goodwill, and the best of policies, the most secure of theories, can be destroyed by apathy, by spite and viciousness.' Wesley and I watched the rain, and he twirled the most slender of chisels in his fingers.

'It can't be easy,' I said.

'Not a week passes without a stir of some sort, an effort to screw the system. Not a week without accusations from inmates or their outside supporters, and whatever deceit or animosity is discovered they suffer little and just lapse back sullenly to await another opportunity. But oh, let there be a hint of negligence or oversight on our part, something not done quite by the book, and it's a different story. I can be front-page news then.' Wesley's eyes lit, and his voice, still quiet, had nevertheless a tone of savage fun. 'We're never bored,' he said. He smiled at me, as the veteran smiles at the new chum who cannot know the significance of what he hears.

'I can imagine that,' I said.

'It's a difficult game when only one side is bound by any rules, and when it's only us who have anything much to lose, any character to be discredited. Do you see what I mean? One of my best department heads is fond of saying that we manage the anal end of society. No one else much wants to know how things are in our prisons, our psychiatric wards, our front-line welfare services.'

'You seem able to cope with the pressures well enough.'

'When has the pitcher gone too often to the well, though,' said Wesley. 'That's a question, isn't it.'

I thought about that when we drove back through the cool rain to collect our wives. It was the only talk of that sort we had, for the weather cleared for the remaining days, and Wesley put away his carving and his frankness, for golfclubs, tourism and studied cheerfulness again.

We worked something out for the last day of the Smiths' holiday. They were to drive their rental car through the Lewis Pass and fly out from Christchurch in the evening. Liz and I took our car with them as far as Shenandoah, and we found a picnic spot there with meadow grass on one side of the river and native bush to the water's edge on the other. Wesley loved the bush, Jean said. She and Liz had made a special picnic lunch with fruit and fresh rolls, and I brought a bottle of Barossa red to mark the parting of the ways. It was a hot, blue day and the sunburn was intensified on Wesley's thin legs and the shoulders of our wives.

We got on well till the very last, and it was more than regret at the recognition of another holiday's conclusion that made us sorry to part. Jean said it was time Liz and I moved to the main city, and Wesley said that instead of being content with just one captive at a time in my chair, I could become the official prison dentist with as many patients as I could manage, and paid with no bad debts by the state as well. We talked in an inconclusive way of meeting again during next year's vacation. The Coromandel perhaps, or even Singapore, said Jean hopefully. It could all be worked out in letters, we agreed. Growing sleepy in the sun between the cars, and with the red wine drunk to mark our parting, we allowed our personalities a certain abandon before return to workaday selves.

The Smiths left before two. We waved them out of the meadow grass and bush at Shenandoah. Wesley held up one slender hand and wrist in salute, and Jean smiled back until the corner. There was anti-climax, of course, with their departure, and Liz and I had only two more days ourselves before returning to the world which had caries at the bottom of its garden.

I was asleep on the tartan rug in the shade of the car, and Liz was reading, when Jean came back to Shenandoah alone in the rented car. Liz woke me even before Jean had stopped and, in the stupor of that sudden awakening in the heat, I was at a loss for a moment to realise that Wesley should be with her, and both of them over the

Lewis and on their way to Christchurch. 'I didn't know what else to do,' said Jean, embarrassed by her return. 'Wesley didn't come back and I waited and waited, and then I went into the bush a little way, but you can't see anything, there's no tracks.' Liz put an arm around her shoulders.

'It's all right. You'll see,' she said.

Jean explained that just past Springs Junction the trees crowded the road, almost reached over it for one lovely section of the growing slope before the top of the pass, and Wesley had pulled over to stop and enjoy the bush: a last opportunity before the barren heat of Canterbury on the other side. A last walk in the calm trees, hundreds of years old, before he was back to work. He just walked in, she said, and never came out.

Oh, we said that he'd be waiting on the roadside now sure enough, that he'd be wondering where she'd got to, but I had a feeling of desolation about it right from the start. When has the pitcher gone too often to the well, Wesley had said. I packed up in a hurry, even in those circumstances struck by my own selfish concern at not being able to find the red thermos top.

Jean came with Liz in our car, while I drove the rental after them back towards the pass. Just a few kilometres past the buildings of Springs Junction was the place where Wesley had gone missing, and it was beautiful right enough. The bush was drawn up to the sides of the road and formed a canopy so that the road was part shadow, part dappled sun, in degrees of direct and indirect light. The air was tunnel cool and fragrant, the banks plump with moisture which kept a rich green in the tumbling ferns. Liz pulled over where there was a slightly wider road edge, and Jean was standing among the first trees when I joined her. There was no sign of Wesley. The road ahead wound out of sight towards the summit. The bush was high on our right and undulated away down the valley on the other side.

'He must have lost his way, or twisted his ankle,' I said. 'He's sensible enough to work his way down the watershed if he's got lost, and so come out further down, no worse off and just feeling a bit foolish.' I wasn't convinced: why should Jean be? She must have understood her own husband, had some knowledge of the things which would make Wesley walk into the bush and not return. I walked in myself, so that it might seem I was taking positive action. I followed the direction Wesley had taken, and within a few metres the road was lost above me and the bush closed up in intense scrutiny. The ponga ferns were clumped at head height and great sooty trunks slid up into the shifting forest canopy like the poles of a big top. I called Wesley's name, and heard no reply. There was just the noise of my own feet in the sloping leaf mould, and a chorus of cicadas far louder than I had ever heard before.

Maybe Wesley Smith was watching me, sitting amidst the fern and lancewood with his thin, hairy arms around his knees, and his lustrous eyes wide in the shadows. Maybe he was watching me go through the routine. It wasn't that I didn't care, but that I didn't believe he was lost in the way it would be assumed he was lost, in the way that would be reported in the papers. Prominent penal administrator missing: Dr Wesley Smith lost in Lewis Pass wilderness.

I made my way back up the slope towards the road, and came out fifty metres or so from the parked cars. I stood to catch my breath before walking down to Liz and Jean, before travelling back to the Junction to make the necessary report. Perhaps I rested also so that Wesley would have just that much more time to do what he wished. Within me was a conviction that Wesley would never be found, though God knows what it is makes a person step away from wife or husband like that, from life, and walk into the bush. Afterwards when there was all the speculation about whether he was still alive, still out there, my own interest and sympathy, my own guilt even, was not at all for the consequences of his action: just the motivation.

Supplication for Position

The Staff Clerk
Department of Standard Punitive Levies and Assessable Arrears
Private Bag
Wellington 1.

Dear Staff Clerk,

**Supplication For Position 735/A86 As Advertised In Metropolitan
Newspapers**

I have decided, Staff Clerk, to take a fresh approach in regard to
this position and in respect of our relationship. For this reason I
have ignored form PSI7a, which has failed me in the past, and
which is difficult to obtain here in any case. I have discarded also
the professional detachment and predictability of those former
applications to the tribe of Staff Clerk who are Janus at the portal
of the Civil Service. I'm weary of shaping myself for the minds of
others, attempting to be tailormade for a position as I must imagine
it; to be tested by you, Staff Clerk, as a child's block is tested in the
shaped vacancies, to see if I pass through to the inside. Fain would I
be seen as individual, capable of growth. There is an element of ploy
in this novelty, I must confess, but message there as well.

From my hut, Staff Clerk, overlooking the Te Tarehi lagoon, I can
hear the ocean in lazy play behind the bar, and on the other hand
see thick bush of wonderfully contrasted greens along the estuary,

and crowded back inland. What do you see I wonder, on your left hand and your right, within your typical New Zealand. There is a sort of Spanish moss hangs from the trees here, Staff Clerk, along the river banks. I've not seen it elsewhere. And sometimes at first light the condensation drips from filigrees and branches through the river mist which smokes from the smooth water, and beards up to match the drooping moss.

You see that I have a sincere intention to present myself to you candidly. Let us be truthful, you and I. I am a conventional age for an applicant, 35, and received an education in Auckland, city of my birth. I was in the academic stream in Sledgeham High. In my U.E. year I was not accredited because of a personality clash with the Headmaster (since retired), but in the external exams I achieved marks of 63 in Chemistry and 74 in History. I failed U.E. that year however, because I thought the English exam was in the afternoon, but it was in the morning. Even now, Staff Clerk, the thought of it brings the copper taste of terror to my throat. My conversion to Islam has given me a bulwark against such dependence on worldly things ever again. I completed my U.E. in a second sixth form year at Sledgeham, during which I was canteen monitor and considered unlucky not to be a prefect (the Headmaster had not then yet retired).

As I write this, rain has begun here at Te Tarehi, Staff Clerk. The sky and estuary are fused by the flux of it, the noise drowns the play of the sea. The rain cloud is moving round me from the hills. I am a sort of Crowhurst, drifting here, able to create my own record of the world, for there's no other human observer. The leak by the fireplace has begun again, into the pan I've positioned there. This is a prodigal part of the world, Staff Clerk.

I attended the University of Auckland for two years, and passed Maths and Classics. In addition I took an active part in student affairs, being nominated for the position of student sexual harassment officer, and narrowly missing out at the Vote because of feminist lobbying. Allah meant men to excel: good women are obedient said the Prophet. In 1977 I decided to interrupt university studies on the understanding that I had the inside running for the post of assistant meteorological officer on the New Zealand Antarctic Wintering Over Party of 1978. Unfortunately my landlord's efforts on my behalf were undermined by political favouritism, and despite passing a three week voluntary snow survival course at Mount Cook, I wasn't offered the post. I had also strengthened my professional background by correspondence courses in meteorological methodology. But what do such disappointments matter in the end, Staff Clerk. Our poet Ma'arri said this world resembles a corpse, and we around it dogs that bark.

Today, Staff Clerk, I shall have whitebait for both meals: whitebait fried in egg and dashed with vinegar. Whitebait heaped up on my enamel plate in defiance of conventional poverty. And for one of these meals I'll have a second course as well, my steam pudding recipe with golden syrup sauce. The Prophet taught that occasional physical indulgence is the means to rid ourselves of bitterness.

After meteorology was closed to me, I spent several years in pest eradication. Do you know the Basin at all, Staff Clerk? It is country difficult to forget. It was my living to kill a great many creatures of the Basin. Rabbits, hares, wallabies and the rest of them, but do you know of the vast flocks of Canada Goose in such places, Staff Clerk? And how they're thinned as flappers, or when moulting. Though it should not, the scale of death has always increased its impact. A magnificent and wily bird, the Canada Goose, who has succeeded as a pioneer here. I began reading poetry in the Basin, Irish mainly, and Australian. Down from the tussock ridge-line, out of the direct wind, I would have my lunch beside the issue Yamaha, and feed on words.

I left the Basin to become co-founder of Aorangi Fitch Breeders Ltd. My partner in this venture was Wally Volper, with whom I had much metaphysical discussion. Wally was temperamentally drawn to existentialist thinking. Our philosophical stock increased, but unfortunately the fitch breeding business received a fatal check when lightning struck our shed in October '83 and destroyed nearly 100 on-heat fitch females. Yet all is as Allah wills it, and I had become gradually aware of a fundamental incongruity between my killing occupations and my beliefs. Killing needs to be better paid than I found it, and in more than cash.

Here at Te Tarehi, Staff Clerk, the air is always cooler after rain, and you can hear the water long afterwards still dripping, trickling, running in the bush; evened out so that the last of one day's rain is joined by the first of the next. There are peat and moss bogs here, Staff Clerk, as you would read of in Old Ireland, but no stone fences and no bombs. The fern fronds are brown arms as if from chimpanzees, and there are fantails who pine to be admired like chorus girls stumbled on in exile. Also a plague of evening sandflies to prevent a paradise. At night the moon is a bright bone on the water of the lagoon, and the sea shovels the stones endlessly on the other side of the bar: perpetual navy navvy. In those nights are ancient, indistinct New Zealand shapes and sounds along the estuary.

I joined the Islamic commune at Colenso in 1984, after a spell on the oyster boats from Bluff. Comparative religion fascinates us, Staff Clerk, don't you think, once we begin the reflective phase of our lives. We define ourselves by our beliefs, and only the most wise and most stupid never change. I was in charge of hydroponic vegetable growing at the commune, and had a regular correspondence with the DSIR on the subject. I had success with succulents, but was never able to reach the target of self-sufficiency. That wasn't the reason that I left however. Ideological considerations have always been my priority. I was opposed to the move away from collectivism towards an insidious form of charismatic leadership which was undermining the commune. No one would listen to me. I have remained a Moslem, but grown suspicious of institutional links. More and more, Staff Clerk, it is the mystical tradition of Sufism which appeals to me. Of the five pillars of Islam only the pilgrimage has not been followed by me, but I have time to achieve it.

So I am here at Te Tarehi beside the lagoon: antipodean Walden's Pond for scrutiny both outward and internal. A white heron was in the estuary last week, Staff Clerk, it stood in Japanese simplicity against the dark background of the trees. There are still wild cattle from generations back, small and shaggy. I've seen them burst from the flats into the bush when they're disturbed.

You won't dismiss the general nature of this supplication I hope, Staff Clerk. I want to present a *curriculum vitae* of attitude as well as mere event you see. In my new approach perhaps the hem of bureaucracy can be lifted to let in the Indian summer of Te Tarehi: wasps curled in ecstasy upon the fallen fruits, and recollection of sky broken into blue and golden darts by the partial masking of the leaves above. Don't assume either, that it requires no courage to live calmly and alone and listen to your life passing.

Call for me, Staff Clerk, and I will shave my face and hood my eyes, will place a tie around my neck, will break the days and nights to hours again, will learn whatever sub-paras and sub-sections apply in each case, will be punctilious as well as punctual in all the Department may require. I will combine with you to serve the quaestor of Standard Punitive Levies and Arrears, keeping all criticism to professional confines.

The estuary is mottled, Staff Clerk, with the shadows of the trees, but my fresh whitebait on the bench are still transparent as if of ice. I feel a sense of incipient competence in the tasks you may assign.

Staff Clerk, I wait for your reply.

Bruce Vancelea
(now Harun)
The Wold Jar Hut
Te Tarehi Lagoon
Summer of '86

A View of Our Country

Simon Palliser had spoken to the Blenheim Rotary Club on his experiences as a noted traveller, and I agreed to drive him down to Christchurch so he could see something of the country on the way before flying out to Paris via Singapore. I was going on business anyway, and the President thought that I could do our scenery justice, so Palliser would have an impression of the place to take with him.

As we crossed the high bridge close to Seddon, Simon Palliser looked down to the blue, wild flowers and the pooled water. He asked me if I'd ever been to the Ivory Coast. 'I flew in to Abidjan,' he said. 'Some fifteen years or so I suppose after they got their independence from the French. The heat was killing, and after a few days I decided to move into the hinterland. I hired a car and drove to Yamoussoukro where the President had his palace. I'm telling you this because crossing that river reminded me of the crocodiles of Yamoussoukro. I drove 240 kilometres to get there, through Ouossou and Tomumodi, along a road more and more enclosed by jungle and the red soil the jungle fed on. But at Yamoussoukro itself the jungle had been cleared and a modern city built alongside the President's family village. Great plantations had been laid out too, of mangoes, pineapples and avocados. Down one side of the President's palace an artificial lake had been created and stocked with turtles, catfish and crocodiles. There had been no crocodiles in that district before, I was told.

'The crocodiles were fed late in the afternoon, and the hotel hired a driver from the Baoule tribe to take me to view them. The driver met me on the broad boulevard in front of the foyer entrance. He was a cheerful and talkative man with fair English. He began to tell me about his country as we walked to the carpark.

It was a little cooler than the coast, and a mist gathered in the city of Yamoussoukro; at once such a modern place, yet the site of chiefly power for hundreds of years.

'There was a causeway across the lake to the palace gates lined with coconut palms and iron railings, and at the gate the Presidential Guard stood sentry. The crocodiles waited with their mouths agape, on a shelf of sand between the embankment and the lake, and the feeder came in a pick-up truck and took buckets of meat to feed them. He called lovingly in French as he threw pieces down to the crocodiles who seemed short-sighted and inefficient eaters. It began to rain heavily, and colours came up on the backs of the crocodiles, and more crocodiles and a few turtles came out of the lake. The mist crept closer and the rain dimpled the surface of the lake. The feeder then took a chicken from his truck, and swung it back and forth in the rain above the railings, all the time appealing in French to the crocodiles. Then he tossed the chicken into the air.

'The chicken gained courage from being free in the air and rain. It flapped stoutly and landed over the heads of the crocodiles and in the lake. As it landed a turtle surfaced, as if it had duplicated the flight beneath the water, and the chicken was seized. It was an auspicious thing to happen. The feeder was alarmed and angry; my Baoule driver was glum. The feeder climbed the fence and ran towards the water across the sand to frighten the turtle. Instead one of the largest crocodiles jumped forward like an ungainly rabbit and had the keeper's leg in its mouth. There were perhaps twenty or thirty people watching, and the feeling of all seemed not one of horror, or even active concern, but a deep hopelessness. The crocodile backed into the lake, giving several gulping changes of grip which drew the feeder more firmly to him. The feeder called out once in French, then was silent, and his long robe trailed behind him. One of the guards fired into the air, and the keeper's wide eyes were fixed on us, his audience, even as he disappeared.

'The rain dimpled the lake surface just the same; turtle and chicken, crocodile and man were gone, leaving us powerless in the wet. "Quickly come away with me now," my driver said. I was thinking that there had been no crocodiles at all at Yamoussoukro until the lake had been dug for the President's palace.'

It was a dry year in Marlborough. When we stopped a little past Ward for a thermos of tea, the hills were very brown and the heat confused their outlines. Palliser said it reminded him of Spain. 'Emotionally, Spain was a turning point for me,' he said. 'A woman I was very much in love with, left me to take up a United Nations job in the Mato Grosso, and I drifted south into Andalusia and was very drunk, for several weeks. You know Andalusia I suppose? Of the several weeks I can remember nothing, a blank in my life, then I sobered up in the little town of Baeza in the hills above the Guadalquivir. I can feel the very evening, the air heavy with jasmine and orange blossom, the soil red as a heart. There were prickly pears at the roadside and within some of them the torreo bird had picked out small nests, and their heads watched at the entrances as I passed. My friend took me to the café to hear the gypsies sing the cante jondo, and all through it the more stolid locals sat at the back tables and continued with their dominoes. I didn't drink, and watched the gypsies under the influence of wine move from the plaintive cante jondo to a wild flamenco, all castanets and exclamation. In the midst of it a farmer brought in a lynx he had killed in his fields, and hung it from a beam by the door for his friends to admire, or to attract a buyer for the skin perhaps.

'As the gypsies danced and sang, as the domino players became steadily more absorbed in their own purpose, I sat with the scent of jasmine and orange blossom through the café door, and the Persian gleam of fur upon the lynx. It turned slowly on the cord, first one way then the other, as if its tufted ears still sought some magnetic north of freedom.'

The seaward Kaikouras crowd the main road to the ocean's edge south of the Clarence river and rise abruptly to over 3,000 metres. Simon Palliser had a love of mountains. 'Of course Switzerland has been something of a second home to me,' he said. 'Several times between expeditions I rested at Brunnen on the shores of Lake Luzern. Do you know it? A town of solid, unpretentious houses on a flat strip of land, while beyond it the steep, glaciated slopes descend into the lake like the sides of a fiord. I made a base at the guest-house of the Gotthardt's usually, and from my upstairs room I had a view of the small steamer berths, and the many trees of that part of the town. I remember on one of their election days taking the rack and pinion railway from Brunnen to Axenstein, a high resort with magnificent views across the lake. Because of the elections and the season there were few people travelling, and in my compartment only one other person; a Swedish woman, beautifully dressed, who spoke excellent German. She told me in a gentle, quite unselfconscious way that she had been travelling to overcome her grief at the recent death of her husband, and that her main difficulty was coping with the loss of sexual satisfaction brought about by the abrupt end of her marriage. She had found no opportunity for solace not repugnant to her she said, until seeing me who bore a singular resemblance to her husband.

'It was all so natural, so kind, so tinged with inevitability. We stood close in the corner of the rack and pinion carriage, with her lovely skirt folded up. Her tears were wet on my cheeks, perhaps I cried myself. She clasped her hands at the small of my back and pulled strongly. Past the blonde hair fastened back from her smooth face, the lake seemed quite calm from such a height and pine forests rose up to the snow line on the mountains above the water. She murmured her husband's name through her tears, I recall. Have you travelled to Sweden? Sven is a common Christian name there.'

As we drove down the coast close to Kaikoura, Palliser thought he saw a seal on the rocky shore. He was interested because of the heavy swell also, and the scene reminded him of British Columbia. 'I had a temporary job in conservation there,' he said. 'I was camped in the magnificently unspoiled Pacific Rim National Park on Vancouver Island. My main task was checking on the sea lions which lived in groups on rocky islets off the coast. On the one day in three or four the swell allowed, I would circle the outcrops in the small boat provided, count the sea lions and record the colour of any tags recognised through the binoculars. Most days I couldn't go out, and I would walk through the stands of Sitka spruce which fringed the beaches, or I would push into the rain forest further inland. The garter snakes would sidle under salmonberry bushes as I approached, and in the cathedral quiet of the rainforest could be heard just the organ music echo of the great Pacific rollers breaking on the first American coast to obstruct them.

'It was cool rain forest, without many birds, and often difficult to walk through because of the swampy places and fallen trees. Ferns and mosses thrived on the decay, as did puff balls, stallion heads and frilled fungi which added the only vivid colours: visceral gleams of red, yellow and spotted black orange, powdered horns like those of a myriad snails sprouting electric blue from the cancerous side of a log.

'After storms I would walk the grey sand of the Pacific beach, see the heaped driftwood, whole trees sometimes, and piles of rotting seaweed which were alive with jumpers. Some of the driftwood still had soil and stones in its roots and gum on its branches, other pieces had been fully digested by the sea and were worn and pale like old soap. On one morning I was amazed to see the vast horns of a caribou caught in the cleft of a tree close to the water line. The tips of the tines were four metres apart, and the antlers would make an arch that two men could march through without stooping. I couldn't dislodge it from the driftwood, and overnight everything was carried away again by the tide and the storm. So are opportunities lost and nothing can be done. I've often thought that the only explanation of such size is that the horns and skull that held them must have been a prehistoric find, carried down to the sea at last from Alaska or the Yukon where some great bull died ten thousand years ago.'

Simon Palliser slept for a while then, his head jogging on his shoulder, and woke when we were coming through Parnassus. I was going to explain the origin of the name for him when we saw a small girl and her doll waiting patiently for the rural delivery man on the grassy roadside by her farm mail box. 'She reminds me of a child I met once in Mexico,' said Palliser. 'On my way to Tierra del Fuego I stopped in Mexico and took the opportunity to visit the Mayan ruins at Chichen Itza. I drove out from Mérida after a meal of tamale with black beans. Rather than the pyramids and temples it was the sacred well of sacrifice that interested me. A huge, circular limestone opening, and twenty metres down sheer rock walls to water which is twenty metres deep again. Young men and virgins were sacrificed in full finery there. The remnant of the jutting altar can still be seen. Government divers have recently managed to recover gold masks and skulls from the mud.

'I had my lunch of chocolate and melon by the stones and shadow of the well's lip, and some Indian children squatted around me to beg a share. I could hear the murmur of the visitors and the more assured, single voices of the guides. I could see people clambering up the stepped side of the pyramid. I thought how this setting of absolute tyranny and religious death had become with time a picnic spot and oddity, the stones and pits denied the sacrifice which had given them their significance. When they had eaten my food the children left me, except for one small girl who calculated that I must have something hidden, or that I would tip her for the privilege of being rid of her. She sat by the rim of the well of sacrifice, and childlike twisted her fingers into the cracks of the wall while watching me intently. All in an instant her fingers drew out a ring of gold with blue amethyst centre, which had lain so long so close to all the people passing. While my mouth was still opening, she rolled the ring once in her fingers as a pebble, and still with her eyes fixed on mine, reached her thin hand over the rim of the well and dropped the jewel to the water and mud far below.

'She must have seen something in my face then that dismayed her, for she bounced up and skimmed away through the heat of Chichen Itza to join the other urchins. There was nothing I could do, you see, nothing that would bring back such a chance missed.'

I thought the Canterbury plains a good contrast to the landscape earlier in the day, and I told Palliser that the Waimakariri, which was coming up, was one of our major rivers. 'For me,' he said, 'the river which has my soul is the Okavango, and I've seen both Niles, the Mekong, Mississippi, Rhine, Ganges, Amazon, Yangtze, Congo, Euphrates, the Don and the Orinoco. The Okavango flows away from the sea into the Kalahari, wonderful incongruity. In ancient times there was a huge lake over most of Botswana, but earthquakes altered the courses of the other rivers which fed it, and now only the Okavango continues spreading over 18,000 kilometres into a million channels and lagoons: the inland estuary of a once inland sea. The great Okavango flows into the sand, holds back the shimmering menace of the desert each year. It's one of the most beautiful and luxuriant places in the world, and protected from the worst of modern encroachment by the tsetse fly and sleeping sickness. I've been drawn back again and again, as perhaps you have yourself. On an early visit I was charged by a tusker while hunting zebra, and had to shoot. The authorities made me pay an excessive elephant licence fee despite my protests that I had acted only in self-defence. The ivory was confiscated, although I kept the tail, and later had an ebony stock fitted to it, making a fly swat.

'On that visit to the Okavango old Johannes de Wette was still alive, and living on one of the estuary islands in the south.

He was 87 years old and his brother-in-law had captured Winston Churchill during the Boer War. De Wette was one of the true white hunters and we sat overlooking the papyrus beds, listening to the slap of catfish and myungobis, the ugly cries of the malibu stork, while he told me of the old days on the Okavango. They used to make hippo rafts to navigate the swamps by shooting four hippo in the head and sewing their mouths closed. After twelve hours the heat so blew their bellies up that they had the buoyancy of gigantic corks, and were used one at each corner of a log raft. De Wette and his comrades would drift through the channels raised up on hippo carcases as if on a dais. Among the Botswana in those days they were treated like royalty, and de Wette said that a bed of Botswana maidens was provided for the hunters — 18 or 20 girls, their bodies gleaming with fig oil, would lie with arms and legs intertwined to make a couch for the night. De Wette's seamed, Afrikaner face was impassive as he told me, but his deep eyes were wistful as we watched a magnificent white-necked fish eagle plummet from the sky into the deep channels of the Okavango.'

As we came into the quiet, spread suburbs of Christchurch, Palliser contrasted them with the intensity of Calcutta. He had come down from Tibet to convalesce he said, after suffering from frost-bite, and to avoid the tourist traps had found a room in the Ashin district of Calcutta. 'It's always been my object to take part in the real life of any place I find myself in,' he said. 'You will remember no doubt the typical stench that part of Calcutta has, the cooking fires, exhaust fumes, oil and dung, the smell of the river and of the cremation grounds further out. Part of that smell too is poverty and loss of dignity. All within sight of the domed Victorian Railway Terminus, memorial to the Raj, and not far from the *maidan* — the lungs of Calcutta.

'My room was made of tar paper and the sides of packing cases from the Bala engineering works. As I lay on my sleeping bag at night I could see stamped on the boards above the curtained doorway the words, Store Away From Boilers.

'My small-time landlord liked to entertain me by taking me to the bazaars in the evening, spurning the untouchables from our path with the hauteur of a man of property. Street after street where life went on. Everything is done in the streets because there is no option. Past the pumps in the street for household water, the stall holders and beggars, the people crouched in doorways, the goat boy selling milk as required from his animal's udder, the banana sellers, hooded rickshaws with their drivers squatted between the poles and resting. One night we saw a goldfish and ball-bearing eater outside a flower shop and a potter's. There are no ends to the way a man can be demeaned in search of a living. Up to ten goldfish and ball-bearings I saw him swallow, then sing for a while, then regurgitate them into a plastic bag of water, so that they swam again apparently unharmed. In the narrow alley at the side of the potter's shop were piles of clay and wood, shards of pottery, trays of small images of Kali set out to dry. The sideshow swallower may have noticed me watching with more interest than most of the passing crowd, or perhaps it was just as a European who gave him an American dollar that I received attention. He stood before me with a smooth, handsome face, and swallowed five ball-bearings the size of golf balls and in good English told me that he was a B.A. "You are seeing what a person will be doing for sake of family," he said. "What we are brought to is a terrible thing." Behind his personal misery was all the beauty of the flower shop, garlands of jasmine and marigolds from the red soil, roses even, and a few sacred lotus blooms set further back. The swallower became vehement at his plight, shouting to be heard above the transistors and bazaar noise. In his misery he forgot to maintain muscular control of the ball-bearings in his gut, and they must have moved down, for suddenly he screamed with pain and fell back amongst the marigolds and jasmine. It drew more people and more interest than his former act, and all the watchers loudly gave advice as to the best way to cure him. The flower seller called loudest of all about the dying man. I asked my landlord what he was saying and was told the vendor demanded to know who would pay for the crushed jasmine and roses.'

I left Simon Palliser at his hotel by the Square. He was grateful he said to have had the opportunity to see something of the nature of the country here, and to spend time getting to know me. We could see the Cathedral quite clearly, and Palliser said as I left that it reminded him of a peculiar thing that happened while he was staying in Strasbourg some years before.

The Dungarvie Festival

Ivan and Len worked together for two years, and then by chance got to know each other on the summer day they didn't make it to the Combined Local Bodies Civil Defence Seminar in Dunedin. Each council had to send two representatives, and there was a good deal of duck-shoving to sort out who had to go. Ivan was landed with it because he was a comparative newcomer, and wouldn't be missed anyway. To show that the council was taking civil defence seriously there had to be a chief as well as an Indian, so Len, who was administration officer, had to go.

He came around early to pick Ivan up, so that they could be away in good time, and Ivan saw that they had been given the oldest vehicle in the fleet. They would be the Kettles come to town in Dunedin. The ute's left front guard had been in pink undercoat for years, and in the back was an assortment of road signs and three boxes of poisoned carrots that someone kept forgetting to set out around the treatment ponds. Low on both doors were paint bubbles, showing where the rust was eating through from the inside.

Len knew he looked incongruous. His good suit was already picking up a variety of rubbish from the wool sack which covered the front seat. Neither of them said anything about the ute, though, and Len drove, as befitted a chief, and Ivan sat on the pink wing side as the Indian. Len's manila envelope with the programme for the seminar lay on top of the dash, so Ivan put his there as well. They didn't discuss the programme: it had headings such as statutory responsibilities of local authorities, and counter-disaster logistics for rural communities.

Reticent, I suppose, is a word that you could use for Len, and professional would be another. He did his job from day to day without malice or favour, and without any inclination to pry into the thoughts or lives of colleagues. A working relationship over two years had for Ivan merely confirmed those aspects of Len's nature that he had recognised within the first week.

'We've drawn the short straws,' said Len with a smile.

'It looks that way.'

That's all they said for a while, but to be fair to both of them the ute didn't encourage conversation. The motor laboured and the road signs and poisoned carrots in the back had a disappointing fellowship. Also there was the threat of the Central summer, even at that time of the day. The ground had little cover, and the schist outcrops were bright, scaly, with no sweat to give.

'I don't much like the sound of the old girl,' said Len when they were close to Dungarvie, and as if by speaking of it he gave recognition, even acquiescence, the motor sickened in that instant and then died. They drifted, with just the road noise and the diminishing quarrel of the road signs and carrots, almost to the restricted speed zone of the village, and where they should have reduced speed the ute stopped completely.

'Ah well, Jesus,' said Len.

'At least we're not far from a garage. That's a welcome fluke.'

'That's true.'

There was a garage at Dungarvie. They could see it clearly. In fact all of Dungarvie could be clearly seen ahead. On the left the garage, then a community hall, on the right three stock crates jacked up on a section until needed, then the gap of a lucerne paddock before the store. Past the store was the only separate house they could see for all Dungarvieites. Len tried the starter several times without success, then went to the front of the ute and looked at the engine, more from a sense of responsibility than any hope of finding what was wrong. Ivan stood by him, but looked along the flat road to Dungarvie. He saw no one. Nothing moved, and in the time between the ute stopping and their walk to the garage beginning, only a blue Triumph passed them, paying no heed to them, or the restricted speed zone, disappearing down the road before they had taken many steps.

Len and Ivan took off their ties, and folded them and put them in the pockets of the coats they carried as they walked into Dungarvie. 'I suppose I should have rung up the yard yesterday and insisted on a better vehicle,' said Len. 'I just never thought we'd end up with that ute. I mean they knew we were going through to a meeting in Dunedin. It's poor.'

'I suppose it's mostly bad luck really.' Ivan was more accustomed to being given the ute as council transport.

'Yes, but after all we are going to the city as representatives of the council, aren't we.'

Ivan could feel his lips drying as he walked. He licked them, and moved his coat from his shoulder where it was making him sweat, and let it hang over his wrist. Through the thin soles of his best shoes he could feel the unevenness of the seal. It seemed to take a long time to walk the two hundred metres or so before the garage. Some barley grass heads had attached themselves to his trouser legs. He felt his face screwing up against the glare of the sun.

The garage was wooden: so old and so high that it may once have been a smithy. There was no one amid its workday untidiness, although a transistor radio, hidden like a cicada in the jumble of the side bench, sang on. Ivan and Len were not surprised. They knew that in a country district one mechanic is thinly spread. They kept walking and, even before they reached the hall, the sound of laughter claimed them: laughter despite the few, quiet buildings and the sky burnt to a powder blue. The laughter billowed from the community hall, but then lost its force in all the calm, surrounding space.

Laughter at once natural and engaging, asking to be found out, yet also with defiance perhaps at all that emptiness, all that press of the given moment that there was no movement to disguise.

The hall was representative of a persistent species: outside all cream weather-boards and bleached red tin roof, inside a wooden floor with chairs stacked to one side, and on the walls the district rolls of honour for the Great War 1914–18 and the Second World War 1939–45. At the far end was one door to the committee room, and another, plus a slide, to the 'facilities'. A rolled bowling mat leant like a furled flag in a corner and on top of chair stacks were three jars of dried flowers and an unclaimed cardigan.

The laughter came from the far end of the hall, in the open door of the facilities, but Len and Ivan found it difficult to see the people there at first, because of the alternate shadow then fierce shafts of light from the windows as they walked the length of the floor. Two women and a man sat on chairs and peeled potatoes. One woman had yellow shorts, matching sneakers and the ease of attractiveness, the other had a floral dress and a laugh like a string of firecrackers. Their helper was a Maori, very thin, wearing a green army singlet, shorts and heavy boots. Even carrying their coats and ties, Ivan and Len felt over-dressed. The three had a sack of potatoes and two enamel basins at their feet. They washed and peeled the potatoes in one basin and laid them in the water of the other so they wouldn't brown.

Ivan and Len had found their mechanic it turned out — Charles. Evonne had the Hollywood legs, and Judith the laugh which made every speaker feel a wit. The two of them were mother helpers for a Guide camp being held in the domain next to the hall. It is the way sometimes that the more random the meeting, the more relaxed the mood. They all fitted in: there was not a nark among them. By rights they should never have met up at all. Ivan and Len should have been on their way to the seminar in Dunedin, should have been through Dungarvie too quickly to have heard the laughter from the hall, or to have seen the red crosses by the names of soldiers who had fallen. Yet

Ivan could smell the bowling mats, and old paper lining cupboards, see the withered flowers in their jars, and the table tennis challenge ladder which displayed its champion so aptly as C. Meek.

Ivan sat with Evonne and Judith, offered himself as a replacement potato peeler, while Charles and Len went back to examine the ute. 'Does it matter much if you're late getting to Dunedin?' asked Evonne.

'We're supposed to be going to a civil defence meeting.'

'I don't know much about civil defence,' said Evonne, 'but then I don't know much about Girl Guide camps either, yet I'm here.'

'All camps have certain fundamentals, like peeling potatoes.' Ivan was flattered by Judith's laugh into imagining he had made a joke. She threw a potato into the basin with such force that the droplets as they scattered were caught in the sun from the window and for an instant held all the colours of the rainbow within themselves. Judith and Evonne began their story of all the indiscretions and mistakes they had committed as mother helpers, and of the Guide officers who never failed to discover them. As Charles, Len and Ivan held no rank within Guides, they were seen as reassuring envoys from a more tolerant world.

Carrots had replaced potatoes by the time Len and Charles returned, and Ivan had joined in so completely that the other men returning had to break the circle. 'Charles says it will take a while: probably something electrical,' Len said.

'Could be the distributor,' said Charles. Judith laughed and Evonne joined in. 'Heh,' said Charles, 'I've told you before there's nothing the matter with my name. I bet plenty of mechanics are called Charles.'

'How many Maori ones?' said Evonne. Judith's laugh, so sudden and so complete, drew them all in. Charles looked at Len and Ivan. He tried to make his thin face deadpan.

'These women are trying to offend me,' he said.

'I rang the office,' said Len.

'What do they think?' asked Ivan.

'Well, they want us to go on if we can be on the road again before midday, otherwise we might as well wait here and bring the ute back when it's fixed. Someone would only have to be driven over to get it anyway.'

'Right.'

'I'll tow her in and have a look at things now,' said Charles. 'If you come up in an hour or so, I should know what the story is.' He took a carrot from Evonne's hand, as if she should know better than to grip such a thing, and walked back through the hall. His shoulder blades showed clearly under the singlet and his boots seemed clumsy on the ends of such thin legs.

'Goodbye Charles,' said Judith sweetly. He didn't turn at their laughter, but waggled his fingers with his hand behind his back.

As a break from the vegetables, Len and Ivan were taken through the back door of the hall to be shown the camp. There were no goalposts on the domain because of summer, but at the far end some pony-jumps were still set up, and on the hall side two lines of bell tents with a flagpole in between. Ivan thought the scene like a limited budget set for a Boer War movie, with a minimum authenticity of the grass worn between the two rows of off-white tents, the flagpole, the heat shimmer beginning over the brown landscape, and the blue, hollow infinity of the sky. He thought things might look like that at the end of the world: all people spirited away, and just the props, the objects, left to get on with it.

'Where are they all?' said Len.

'They're on a badge trek in the hills. A six-hour round hike from the dropping off point, and they have to carry their lunch and emergency clothing in case the weather turns. All the qualified people have gone with them, and we're left here to prepare tea,' said Judith, 'and look after Suzie Allenton, who was sick last night and is sleeping now in her tent.'

'We're supposed to make an inspection of the tents sometime

during the day,' said Evonne, 'and give points to the tidy ones, which go towards the top tent competition.'

Ivan was about to ask what happened if the Boer commandos attacked while the camp was undefended, but he remembered he had said nothing to the others about the impression the tents had created. Yet he imagined Botha's or de Wette's horsemen cantering in to surprise the mother helpers and sick, sleeping Suzie Allenton. 'Were you ever in the Scouts, Ivan?' said Len from the back steps of the hall.

'No.'

'It wasn't my thing either. I never had anything to do with Scouts or Boys' Brigade, and although I was roped into National Service the only tents I remember were bivouac things which we had to carry ourselves. They were so small you had to crawl into them.'

'Time for your confessions now,' said Ivan to Judith and Evonne.

'I was brought up on a farm,' said Judith. 'I could never be in group things.'

'I was in the city, but don't remember going to Brownies, Guides or anything like that. I don't think anybody ever invited me.' Evonne looked carefully at the tents and flagpole, as if for the first time. 'Have I missed out on something important, do you think?'

'You can do your penance as mother helper,' said Len. 'Girl Guides, like any other army, march on their stomachs.'

'I'd like to march on the stomachs of a few of them,' said Judith.

The direct sunlight was intense. Len's head lolled back to rest against the door jamb, and his eyes closed. The others rested their heads in their hands, and supported both by propping their elbows on their knees. Ivan wished he had a hat, and found himself breathing through his mouth. 'Should we make a round of the tents now?' said Evonne after a time. The two women lifted their heads enough to see across the grass to the tents, and assessed the effort it would take to visit them all, and compared that with whatever energy and duty they felt.

'Maybe later,' said Judith.

'I'll just check on Suzie then,' said Evonne. She stood up, pulled her shorts down at the back of her thighs, and walked across grass so dry that it crunched beneath her sneakers.

'I could sleep the day away in a tent myself,' said Len. 'The less you do the less you want to do.'

'She's a good sort,' said Judith, watching Evonne as she neared the tents. 'Her husband's wealthy, but she still comes to take her turn. She pitches in just like everybody else. She even cleaned up on the bus when one of the girls was sick after fish and chips. It's not very pleasant then in the confined space of a bus when you're travelling so far.' Ivan and Len watched Evonne at the tents, her banana shorts and sneakers, her graceful, brown legs. The men kept their faces non-committal in Judith's presence, and they made no comment. 'Yes,' said Judith. 'Beaut legs. She's lucky there, don't you think? Mine keep getting thicker year by year.' She pulled her dress up to show her strong legs and big knees with a smiling crease on each. 'What about your legs?' she said to Ivan.

'Skinny and hairy. Not a pretty sight.'

'It's just as well we're both wearing longs,' said Len. 'I've nothing much to offer in the way of legs either.'

'Charles's have a good natural tan, but they're skinny too,' said Judith.

'Evonne will have to win first prize for legs then,' said Ivan. Evonne looked back towards the hall and laid her head to one side on her hands to show that Suzie Allenton was still sleeping.

Len and Ivan didn't wait for Evonne to reach them across the domain, but gave a wave and told Judith they might be back if Charles wasn't able to fix the truck in time.

'Oh, God,' she said. 'Do come back and rescue us.'

'We haven't lost a mother helper yet,' Len said.

Once the habitual responsibility for events had been shifted from him by forces beyond his control, Len became increasingly relaxed. He was in no hurry on their walk back to the garage, and he talked with Ivan of seeing the original subdivision plan of Dungarvie in the council files: two hundred private sections had been surveyed in the flush of colonial enthusiasm, and sites for shops and churches, but even the gold rushes didn't create that Dungarvie, didn't build its churches or fill its cemeteries. Dungarvie had never been much more than they could see. Ivan noted that there was not even a pub in the place, and his interest was not historical. At least the high, red barn of the garage offered some shade.

'She's never been any Rolls-Royce,' said Charles when they joined him. 'However, you shouldn't have any trouble getting to Dunedin and back.' Len and Ivan looked without enthusiasm at the ute, its patch of pink undercoat, soft tyres, and stains weeping from the various rust spots on the body. The carrots in the back were bleached and wrinkled, a sign face-up announced road works ahead. Len thought of the drive to Dunedin in the heat, and the attention that would be drawn to them by their late arrival at the seminar. 'On the other hand,' said Charles as one of life's entrepreneurs, 'we could declare a Dungarvie Festival if you wanted to stay for a while, and give Evonne and Judith some company. I've even got a carton of beer that we could all chip in on.'

Len opened his mouth as if to say no in his role as administration officer, but then was seized by the wonderful implausibility of it all as he stood in the garage doorway. The few ill-hung bell tents he could see not blocked by the hall, the dozing store, the barley grass in the free sections, the sheep crates with dung burnt to an inoffensive crust, the old smithy garage he stood in, Charles smiling from the shadows which matched his skin. 'Well, why not,' Len said and, having said it and not been struck down by conscience or by lightning, he repeated it boldly. 'Well, why not. We're too late to bother going on anyway, don't you think?'

'Yes,' said Ivan and Charles with certainty. Charles hoisted the carton of beer into the rear of the truck, and they drove back slowly towards the hall through the welling shimmer of the road and grass.

The mother helpers had gone inside again, and were preparing a vat of mince and onion to go with the potatoes. The sight of the beer on Charles's shoulder was enough to start them laughing. The sooner the meal was prepared, the sooner they could relax, Judith said, so Ivan and Len chopped carrots directly into the mince while Charles sliced onions. Tears ran down his face, and his brows lifted oddly as he tried to keep his eyes from closing.

'Come on, come on,' said Charles. The women took some apples and apricots, everyone took a mug, and Charles led the way across the domain to the culvert where the road crossed the stream. There was a small, scoured pool where the concrete ended. Charles took the bottles of beer from the carton, and dropped them on to the shingle bottom, reaching down till his shoulder was in the water so that the bottles would land gently. Part of his singlet became bright again with the water, and the drops skated across the oil of his hands. There were small grasshoppers at the pool's edge, and a silver skink for a moment on the concrete of the culvert bridge. Len tasted his share of the first bottle, which was given no time to cool.

'I love the salty taste good beer has,' he said. 'Ah, it's needed in this weather.'

They surrounded the small pool. Len and Judith stepped over the trickle of its outlet and sat on the other side, but that put them hardly any further apart than the others. All of them were soon barefoot. Charles's feet were dainty alongside his work-boots. Judith tucked her floral dress up like pantaloons, and hung her legs in the water so that the effect of refraction had them broken at the calf. Ivan leaned forward to eat a ripe apricot so that the juice would fall on to the grass and not his best shirt or suit trousers. He had knotted the corners of his handkerchief, soaked it, and it lay on his dark head as a first defence from the sun. Occasionally a truck or car went by in the midday heat. The growing whine of any approach gave all five a chance to compose their faces. Sometimes drivers or passengers happened to look down and saw with envy, surprise or condescension the group around the culvert pool celebrating the festival of Dungarvie. But as time went on, the road, its travellers, its starting points and destinations, ceased to be a relevant awareness, and no disguise or provision for them was made at all.

'Let's hope no one breaks down,' said Evonne to Charles, 'otherwise you'd have to leave our picnic and fix the car.'

'Actually I never meant to be a mechanic,' he said. 'I wanted to be a physicist.'

Judith's laugh exploded pod-like in the dry air. She had difficulty in holding her mug of beer. Len's laugh was almost as loud, almost as distinctive: high-pitched and abrupt, it was not the social laugh that Ivan had heard from him in the past, but a new laugh. It was a laugh of instinctive delight and lack of inhibition. 'No, I did, fair go,' said Charles. Laughter feeds on itself, so that they were all drawn in. Charles himself found his voice so collapsed with laughter that it was husky when he managed to carry on. 'Look, look, I was a marvel at physics at school and could have easily gone on, but at Vic I got sidetracked into a heavy metal band, and lost my bursary because I failed everything except physics.'

What a depth of humour and irony there is in actuality. Evonne lay back because her stomach was sore from laughing. There must be a hundred reasonable ways to explain the move from physics and a Wellington rock band to sole charge of the Dungarvie garage in the old smithy. It had the freakish likelihood of truth. 'I wanted to be a wildlife officer,' said Len, sudden in his decision to be confidential as well. He had dipped his hands into the pool, and cooled his face with the water. The hair of his forehead was stuck together. 'I wanted to save the black robin, the takahe, the kakapo and so on.' At his ears amid the short sideburns were the first grey hairs, and on the sides of his nose the sheen where his glasses normally rested. 'More than anything else, that's what I was set on doing, and somehow

I've ended up as an accountant, a council administration officer.'
He was still sufficiently self-conscious to add that of course he had
remained a financial member of the Forest and Bird Society. It set
the others off again, particularly Judith. She considered it a great
one-liner. Her feet jerked beneath the water and her laughter cracked
like a stock whip across the domain. Did any accountant ever dream
of becoming an accountant, any more than the day-shift foreman
of the chicken nugget factory dreamt of his success, or a man sold
his soul to the devil for the right to be caretaker at the Shangri-La
Lodge and Cabin Park? How many shopping reporters, high school
language teachers, rural delivery drivers, one-term politicians, or
Pleasant Valley inmates could point to a constant ambition?

The bottles of beer lay on the gravel bottom of the pool, and
quivered like trout in the ripple of Judith's feet. The stones had a fuzz
of slime because the water was barely flowing, the label from one
bottle had come adrift and undulated like a fin. The pool had a thin
lip of green cress and clover before the brown grass began. 'How can
you work day after day in this heat?' said Evonne to Charles, who
was reaching down into the pool to bring up another prize.

'You tell me,' he said. 'This part of the country is stranger to me
than to most of you, I'd say. I'm Tuhoe, you see, children of the mist,
and so on. This isn't my place.' It was a final incongruity. Len was
delighted with it.

'I don't suppose there are many Tuhoe physicists in Dungarvie
when you come to think of it,' he said.

Everything seemed amusing to them in that afternoon. Sometimes
there is an intoxication of the heart which has little to do with drink:
some combination of circumstances and personalities which slips
past defences and brings a mood of goodwill and acceptance. All of
which may be just another way of saying how hot it was in Central
that day, how influential the beer and fruit on empty stomachs, how
each person felt release in a new role and company, knowing it was
just for one day. Ivan noticed that Len rolled his trousers higher as

time went on, and that his face was almost impetuous. They had left the office, yet not arrived at the seminar. They had shrugged off routine, yet not assumed interim responsibility. They were in a pleasant limbo, and yet with some excuse.

'Me?' Evonne was saying. 'I wanted to be a school dental nurse, and make snowmen with red ink faces from cotton wool wads. The uniform quite suited me, I thought, and as well you had your own special room. Instead, I'm just a rich bitch, I suppose.'

'A toast to the mother helpers,' said Charles amid the talk of Bertie Germ and money, and the mother helpers drank deeply to themselves as a sign that they recognised their worth.

Ivan wondered about himself: what he had intended as distinct from what he had become. The physicist, the wildlife ranger, the dental nurse, and Judith still with her mystery, all wanted to hear of his lost life. Judith shaded her eyes the better to watch him, and her mouth was open for her explosive, benevolent laugh. 'An actor,' he said. There was joy that he had not disappointed them. Charles threw his head back as if to dislodge something in his throat. 'I did a fair bit at school, and then a polytech course. We had a group that toured schools and hospitals but, when the funding was withdrawn, I switched to office management.' As he said it, he was amazed how the exigencies of the moment become, in retrospect, a seamless process of inevitable selection.

'Oh, but you would have been good on the stage,' said Evonne loyally. 'You could be a gentleman caller for Laura, or a rebel in a kitchen-sink play.'

'Or the fool in *Lear*,' said Len, 'who knows more than the king.'

'Give us something now,' said Judith.

'I've forgotten it all.'

'Yes, come on, Ivan,' said Len. He was delighted that his colleague had revealed such an exotic past. A chant began.

'We want Ivan. We want Ivan.'

In any other setting, any other time or people, Ivan would have suspected an edge of vindictiveness, an underlying hope of some humiliation, but the Dungarvie Festival was all goodwill. None of them knew each other well enough to wish for any harm. Ivan stood up to free his breathing, and gave them one of Biff's speeches from *Death of a Salesman* about the dangerous gap between self-image and reality.

As part of his concentration on it, Ivan had an exact awareness of the others listening; their combined physical existence on the grass there, around the culvert pool. A grass stem turned in Len's fingers, and on one pale ankle bone a green vein was looped. Judith's sunburnt face was full on to him to give support, and Charles nodded as he listened and dabbed an insect from his beer. The Boer War tents were in their two rows at a distance, the hall and store and garage becalmed in heat and time. Then Ivan quoted Willie to his friends in the Dungarvie domain, isolated from the rest of the world with a bird singing up high somewhere, one great, strutted pylon glinting on the hill, two lines of sagging tents and, in one of them somewhere, sick, sleeping Suzie Allenton whom he never saw.

Ivan had his immediate appreciation, however, and a stock truck happened to pass at just that time and made a roar of approval upon the little bridge above them. Judith had seen the film version and talked of it with Len and Evonne, while Charles gave Ivan his ideas on the importance of sustaining enthusiasms. Ivan was breathing heavily because of the heat and his nervousness at reciting. He was content to listen for a while. 'You must keep the idea of your life being special,' Charles said. 'Of having nothing to do with any historical generalisations or social trends, but instead as a free-wheeling thing with all the possibilities still there if you want to explore them.'

'There's an underlying feeling of time past,' Ivan heard Judith saying, 'and it's pressing forward into the present and the future more and more.' For a moment Ivan thought that Charles would accept that as an answer in their own conversation, but Charles still waited.

'Sometimes I doubt the depth of what we see,' said Ivan. 'Sometimes, despite the exact, connecting detail before us, I feel it bulging, and just a shimmer at the seams to hint at things quite different beneath.'

'That's it,' said Charles, and he topped another bottle.

'Didn't he marry Marilyn Monroe or something?' asked Len. 'I thought I read that he married Marilyn Monroe.' He picked blemishes from his apple with his fingernail.

'At our last staff meeting,' said Ivan, 'we were discussing the computer training programme, and for an uneasy moment the words spoken didn't fit the movements of the people's mouths, and there was the scent of the open sea that I haven't thought of for years.'

'That's it,' said Charles. 'Last week I took an irrigation pump I'd mended back to a cocky up the valley, and at the gate a dog challenged me. Not a sheepdog either, but a Labrador. The sun was going down, and this old dog stood right before me, barking hoarsely, but it had so little belief in its own threat, or mine, that its eyes turned away as it barked. I had a feeling that it marked something in my life, but I had no way of guessing the significance.'

'Kerouac called Monroe a trash blonde. He met her once and she snubbed him,' said Evonne.

'I've never read any Kerouac,' said Len. 'I come across the name from time to time, but I've never read anything.'

'We'll do our Kerouac dance for you,' Judith said. She and Evonne stood up and swung their hips slowly and undulated their arms. Judith's dress was still tucked in, and her legs were pink with sunburn, only behind the knees still white. Evonne could have been a Marilyn Monroe herself, with smooth muscles on her thighs, and heavy breast. Len gave his new, high-pitched laugh, but much softer than before.

'That's just a hula,' he said.

'Now reincarnation is another thing,' said Charles. The beer had reached his eyes and they had a moist gleam. He lifted the strap of his green singlet, and scratched his shoulder. His thin body was crumpling in the heat and the relaxation of unforced conversation. 'I find myself considering it quite often.'

'You believe in reincarnation?' said Ivan. Evonne and Judith still did their Kerouac dance, and Len clapped in time. It was a leisurely dance because of the heat, and Judith could drink from her mug without interrupting her movement.

'Let me give you an example,' said Charles. 'I had this dream of hunting polar bears from a kayak, and one reared up on an ice-floe, and I felt all the authenticity of detail in an instant: how the water drummed the kayak skin against my hips, and the bear's fur yellowed and disordered in the armpits as it raised great paws.'

'An Eskimo dream. You didn't,' said Ivan.

'What's this?' said Evonne.

'Charles dreamt he was an Eskimo.' The dancing was over, and Evonne and Judith sat down to laugh again.

'You didn't!' said Len.

'Only a few nights ago,' said Charles. 'It was so true that it woke me up. It took a while for the Arctic chill to pass. I got out of bed and went to the window. I could see some of the hill facings full to the moonlight, and a fenceline across them. But there wasn't a polar bear in sight.'

'Perhaps an Eskimo has had a vision of Dungarvie as recompense,' said Ivan. 'The view from your window with the dark gullies and moonlit tussock slopes of the Old Man Range, and a single fenceline to divide one side of emptiness from the other.'

'Or the festival now,' said Judith. 'Us at our picnic here when we're all supposed to be somewhere else. But it's so hot. You'd hardly dream such heat.'

Even reincarnation and the Kerouac dance couldn't protect them all forever. The afternoon was well on, and consciences were stirring. No one voiced it, but they had a small fear that the Guides and qualified instructors might return from training and they would have to see themselves reflected in scornful eyes — five feckless people, moist-faced and idle in the sun from an excess of goodwill and beer.

'I suppose we'll have to go,' said Len, but he continued to lie back, his suit trousers rolled below the knees. 'I haven't enjoyed myself so much in ages.'

'We've still got our inspection to do, and poor Suzie Allenton,' said Evonne.

'And the meal,' said Judith.

'You didn't give the mother helpers any of the carrots from the truck, did you, Charles?'

'Why not?'

'They're poisoned.' Len knew this would set Judith off again.

'That's the sort of lunch issue our council runs to,' said Ivan. Amid the laughter, Len clumsily stood up, but was unable to find his balance. Too many factors were combined against him: dizziness from standing up suddenly in the heat, pins and needles in his left leg from the hard ground, the flattery of beer and laughter, the loss of steadying inhibitions. He began to fall sideways despite whirling his arms, and the laughter increased. He tried to turn his fall into a leap across the pool, easy enough, but hit the far edge with an outstretched leg and half fell in. Had it meant his death, the others could not have stopped their laughter, which went on as Len hobbled in a circle on the grass to get his jarred leg moving properly again.

The incident allowed Ivan and Len to make easy goodbyes, with no scrutiny of the day attempted. Laughter and spontaneous acceptance had been the start of their trivial festival, with laughter and openness they kissed and parted.

Ivan and Len carried their shoes across the domain, and when they reached the truck they opened both doors, but stood outside for a while until the cab was a little less stifling. 'You'd better drive,' said Len. 'I think you drank less than me.' They could see Charles fitting his heavy boots as they pulled away, and when Ivan gave a farewell on the horn, Charles, Evonne and Judith raised their hands and, even at that distance and above the noise of the ute, there seemed an echo of machine-gun fire which might have been Judith's laugh.

Dungarvie fell over the edge of the world behind them. Soon they could see just the top of the high smithy garage. The morning's trip seemed a life away. 'We're not much further ahead on civil defence,' said Ivan.

'The farmers round here say that disaster struck some time ago anyway, and today's seminar was too late for that.' Len was dusting his feet with his socks while Ivan drove, then he rolled down the legs of his suit trousers and began picking out spears of barley grass. 'I never knew you'd been an actor,' he said. 'We should see more of each other and talk about those things.'

'We will.'

'Judith was the only one that didn't tell us what she wanted to be. Did you hear her say that she was going through a break-up with her husband?'

'No.'

'She told me while you were talking to Charles about reincarnation, or his time at Vic, or maybe his Eskimo dreams. Being a mother helper was a chance to step back from normal things and sort herself out.'

'She could laugh anyway.'

'That's true. You meet interesting people by accident at times, don't you? Scores of times I must have been through Dungarvie and I don't think I've ever stopped. Yet today was some sort of fun, wouldn't you say?'

They talked easily in the afternoon sun. The Dungarvie Festival had been one of those oddities — a oncer — like a freak giant hailstorm, or the escape of zoo leopards into the suburbs. Those things which happen once in a blue moon, and which bind those caught up in them with a sharp sense of comradeship, and of life's possibilities after all.

Tomorrow We Save the Orphans

My final voyage, a winter's night, and Dubois accompanies me as a courtesy of farewell. After more than a year at Acme Textiles, I have been appointed a researcher with Statsfact Polling Agency. Dubois is piping me ashore. 'I might do the same at your age,' he says, 'but later you'll see the advantages of night work. Fewer people and more interesting ones.' He's right: they drop through the sieve of daylight employer to a nether world. The most fallible of fools and perverse of the profound.

The breath that forms Dubois' words is a plume in the freezing air as we stand beneath the water tower and check the sacking on the pipes. Appearance is most marked and memorable on the day that we meet a person, and the day we part. Dubois' continental good looks are in some way debased, the casual, toss away features of a circus rouseabout, but his eyes and hands have individual authenticity. Dog-killing hands, strong and supple, with muscle raised between thumb and forefinger, and eyes that will not tolerate deceit.

'I've been reading more about castle development and the influence of the Crusades. Brattices and the advantages of circular masonry,' he says.

I returned from Europe with an innocent bladder infection and a debt of over three thousand dollars to my parents. Acme Textiles was unimpressed with my education, but when I crooked my arm to make a muscle and talked of labouring in Wolverhampton, the personnel manager said okay, I'd got it, night work, but only if the caretaker liked the look of me. I never saw the personnel manager again. He was the Charon who delivered me to the underworld. His name was O'Laughlan. The managing director, whom I never met at all, was called Jim Simm, and the caretaker was N.F. Vincenze Dubois. Life is full of such splendid ironies.

On this last night, a winter round, Dubois seems willing to put aside all except that final cover which is the necessary reserve to keep the glare of other people from our soul. At farewell to comradeship and proximity, it matters little if some confidences are shared which might be awkward if you had to meet again. We all learn to jog along in our relationships, not expecting too much, not admitting ambitions we can afterwards be beaten with. 'Have you really been here fourteen months?' says Dubois. He has a muslin cleaning rag knotted around his neck for warmth and the collar of his tartan jacket turned up against the chill. 'Fourteen months. Fourteen months,' he says, 'and I don't remember more than two or three things in that time, apart from the Middle Ages, that I care a damn about. I hope it's different for you.'

Night has a stark effect. A liposuction that removes the inessential until the bones, the sinew, the organs only of an impartial world remain. The dump skips cast perfect shadows from the moon across the frosted shingle and dirt of the yard. Larger stones are rising up like mushrooms, and cats troop Indian file silhouettes upon the wall at Pine Light Engineering with shoulder bones that undulate against the sky. Grass which grows three storeys up in the gutterings gives a faint, prairie whisper in the barely moving air, and hedgehogs fossick out from weed and fennel corners to feed.

Frontages of industry present the latest faces, but the backsides retain the scars and emblems of old allegiances. Pine Engineering was once the warehouse of Pacific Skins Ltd, and Acme Textiles itself incorporates, among others, the bulk of Aldous D. McManus and Sons, Pastoral Agents and Scourers, estab. 1862. The brave old lettering can be seen behind the fire escapes. Dotty Standish has come to one of the small side-doors to cry, as she does most nights. Her husband died three months ago from cancer of the bowel. Dubois will not fire her yet, as she has been a good cleaner for several years.

'I could have made you assistant caretaker, or night watchman, if you wanted to stay on, even though you're no good with your hands,' says Dubois as we check the loading bay doors. Our steps echo on the hollow wooden ramps and between the echoes is the sound of Dotty snivelling not far away. 'I heard a new dog barking last night,' says Dubois. 'A Labrador, or Labrador cross I reckon, at the refrigeration depot, or perhaps further over at the seed driers.'

Dubois is chunky and middle-aged, but nimble still. In the main machine room he vaults to the top of the spinners to check them. He leaps from one to the next. There are fourteen French Bavantes and six Wisconsin Hammonds, the names in proud red and green bas-relief on the sides of the casings over which Dubois strides. He has come to check on the Hinkles' electrician. As caretaker Dubois has patronage to dispense; not just cleaning for the women of his choice, but suppliers and tradespeople. The Hinkles' man has finished with the freight lifts, and tells us they should get their certificates of worthiness now.

'I meant to say,' says Dubois, 'that my telly is playing up. The sound cuts out every now and then.'

'I'll call in on my way out,' says the Hinkles' man eagerly.

'Would you?'

'No sweat, Jesus, no. If it's anything serious we could let you have a nearly new set we've repossessed.'

'Tell Keith I'll probably need someone out to fit new fluorescent lighting in accounts. I'll know for sure in a week or two.'

'Right. No sweat. See you then,' says the Hinkles' man. Dubois conducts the conversation from the height of the spinners, which accentuates his mastery. He now climbs higher as the electrician leaves. Into the steel rafters he moves to check his rat baits, disturbing delicate colonies of wool fibres built up over the years. Some fall lightly in clumps like varicoloured lichens, others disintegrate and drift for a time before the lights as a haze of green, or gold, or blue.

'The bastards have been at it.' His voice is tight with satisfaction. 'Oh rat, rat, you'll feel thirsty now.' Dubois half swings through the bolted rafters above the machines, leg and arm, leg and arm, careful to protect his head. 'Rat, rat,' he says, 'you feel the thirst of death.'

The factory at night is a titanic; dimly lit and throbbing. A place of many levels and decks, with lives a world apart separated by just a bulkhead, or a narrow stairway that says factory staff only. The boiler pipes are never silent in this season, the air conditioning fans resonate with individual melodies from deck to deck. A persistent vibration gives a sense of movement, of voyaging, so that Acme Textiles is pressing on over the sea of the night.

Vincenze Dubois is more absolute captain of the firm by night than Jim Simm ever is by day. In trading hours the place is subject to the compromise and transactions of the world, taking cognisance of powers of equal, or greater, strength. But Dubois has a concentric empire, a ship of the night that rumbles self-sufficiency, and to which only minions from the outside come. This caretaker knows the place as an extension of himself. The cleaners and the routine of their tasks, the machines in all their variety, rat paths in the ceilings and cellars, the seventh skylight in the warehouse which leaks after hail. He knows the stalagmites of borer dust glinting on the lower beams of the acid store, the folded blankets behind the dye crates where the works supervisor takes Sarah from reception during breaks, the blue pigeons which have pushed past the netting on the east gable, the forgotten box of Chinese silk cocoons above the cupboard in the old boardroom presented by a trade delegation in 1949. Dubois knows Stevens of personnel picks his nose, that the three original doors nailed shut behind boxes in the old storeroom are solid kauri, that the morning sun strikes Acme first on the rusted iron above the blue pigeoned east gable. There is a piebald rat in the boiler house,

Dubois tells me, which eschews all poison, and antique green jars in wickerwork ignored beneath the dust and spiders' lace of the upper gantry. Cannington writes old-fashioned poetry on the firm's paper, and Tess Eggleslee hides stolen lipsticks in the ledge above the toilet cubicles. There is a faint stain on the smooth wooden floor of the press room. Dubois points it out as the blood of Kenny Donald, crushed there seven years before by a forklift carrying the umber bolts of commercial grade which were so popular at the time.

'Remember we talked of mead,' says Dubois. 'I've had some working, several batches, in fact, with different herbs, but it's difficult to control the fermentation. I'm not very hopeful and honey's bloody expensive.'

We are in the first-storey offices, which have imitation wood grain formica desks and vinyl swivel chairs with corrective backs. There is not a cobweb, or a textile thread, in sight. From these windows the freight yard is a bleak field. In the summer the security beams suffuse the penetrable and billowing air, but now their light is fractured, crystalline in the frozen night. The Tuki sisters watch Dubois check behind the wall heater and beneath the photocopiers.

'You won't find anything there, eh,' they say.

'I'll catch you one night,' says Dubois.

'Promises, promises,' they say.

Dubois will miss the Medieval Age, I suppose. As well as women and machines, he likes discussion of the origin of heraldic devices, and how donjon, Norman-French for tower, became corrupted by time and usage into dungeon. Dubois likes me because I am an intellectual and simpleton. I am without authority or skills in the nether world, yet have information he finds interesting. 'There was a Dubois with William at Hastings,' I say, 'and Cardinal Dubois was Premier Minister in 1772 and in effect the ruler of France.'

'I was told that Dubois meant by the wood. My grandmother always said we had property in New Orleans.'

'Edmond Dubois-Crance served in the Royal French guard,

but became a leading Jacobin in the revolution and organised its armies.'

'There's a Negro branch of the Dubois in the States,' Dubois says.

'What did you do before?' I ask him.

'Before?'

'Before becoming a caretaker,' I say. Dubois leans away from me to peer behind the drink dispenser.

'Charlotte, Charlotte,' he calls, and Charlotte comes from one of the corridors. 'There's cardboard cups squashed down the back here. Get one of the girls to poke them out with a broom handle please. Michelle, perhaps: she looks as if she'd be better with that end than the brush.' Charlotte laughs, nods, walks away, says nothing. 'Charlotte,' calls Dubois again a little while after. He has found something else to rectify, but Charlotte is out of earshot. 'Charlotte? Ah, never mind. Do you ask a lawyer or an architect what they did before? Do you ask a headmistress or a mercantile banker what they did before?'

'It's just that . . .'

'It's just that you can't imagine an eighteen-year-old deciding to make a life career as a custodian, right?'

'No, it's not that,' I say, but it is exactly that. Caretaking is something that you end up doing, surely, as a result of compromises and expedients. A wintering over until you line up something more in keeping with your view of yourself. There is something in the concept of caretaker that suggests the pathological poles of murderer or poet.

'It's my life's job,' says Dubois. 'I started out as a primary school caretaker and I've done pretty much all sorts. The more night work the better, though, because I'm interested in freedom, see, which is a form of power.' Dubois hears a hoon car in the alley, and leaps up on to one of the canteen tables so that he can watch the lights pass his domain. We can hear the car back-firing as it slows to turn into Astle Street.

Charlotte comes in to release the *Phantom of the Opera* in volume from the cleaners' transistor. The Tuki sisters, three doors down, start to sing along and, before Charlotte can go back to work, Dubois begins to dance with her. How well they dance on the white and yellow of the cafeteria floor, amid the chair legs upturned on the tables, and spun by the swelling music of the night. Dubois is handsome, and the muslin cloth a cravat at his throat. There is no parody in the care and skill he shows, and Charlotte's calves are well muscled above her working shoes. Faces and voices at the doorways as the other women watch them dance, and when it is over they go back to work the better for it. Dubois is unselfconscious regarding the life he leads.

On our way to the boardroom, Dubois and I are talking of tallage and the earliest practice of paying in kind. And the tax which was a further burden on the serf. The boardroom has 'Boardroom' in gold pretension on the door, in case there may be confusion with other rooms with a fourteen-berth, pale pine table and better than average blue vinyl chairs. Dubois smokes a black cheroot, but we don't sprawl, for it is too cold in this part of the building. Our hands are in our pockets and we shrug our shoulders for warmth. On the wall there hang the managing directors: Jim Simm will be added in good time, but their *doppelgängers* of the night persevere only in the minds and pub stories of casual workers. Even Dubois can remember only the caretaker immediately before him. A 21st Battalion man whose stashes of gin still turn up from time to time. However complete and despotic their reign, caretakers go largely unrecorded. So earls and barons pass into history by virtue of their rank, while butlers who bestrode a world below the stairs are forgotten when their subjects die.

'So heriot was the death tax,' says Dubois. 'Nothing much alters in the state's greed, does it?' I am so close I hear the outside leaf of his cheroot crackle as he draws in and the red rim moves. 'Let's talk of Sir William of Cabagnes who captured King Stephen in battle,' says Dubois, his finger checking a window catch. I am sentient of the subterfuge and interlock of time and place in that instant. The moonlight winking on Dubois' thumbnail at the window, my rather nasal voice pronouncing the vowel in mace, my torso shrunk within the heavy clothes of winter, the words Alistair P. Brigeman beneath his proud black and white face on the wall. A tremor through the carpet from the Phantom's songs beneath. Then time moves with a whisper, and again we bowl on towards our end.

The cleaners are nearly finished for the night. The long watch is an exclusively male affair. They walk past us in the shadowed corridor. Dubois asks me to check the fire-doors on level three. He'll catch me up shortly, he says, and as I go on he steps out to separate Carol from her friends, guiding her towards the switchroom with the pressure of his hip. 'Wait your patience,' Carol says, so as not to seem too amenable while still in view.

The fire-doors are as safe as most excuses. I decide to walk back outside the loading bays. Dubois has told me it is important not to become too rigid in one's routine, for that could be exploited by a thief. I doubt for the moment that he is following his own advice. An angel swish: high on the factory side above me a muffled thump, and a mallard drake falls to the frozen dirt and stones of the moonlit yard. I turn a full circle with a sheepish smile to see who has played this joke, but there is nobody. The drake's sleek head follows me. I don't want the responsibility it brings and try to shoo it away. In response the duck rolls on its side, almost like a cat to have its stomach scratched, but one wing extends in a tremor of departing life and in the soft body feathers where two legs should be, is only one and a little blood. Something terrible has been happening further in the night.

A car without lights is driving slowly down the yard. The gravel crunches sharply in the cold air. It is only Ransumeen who works for Sleaptite Security. Ransumeen is an idle, moaning sod who has been an insulation salesman, grader driver, post tanaliser and now, despite his complaints, will see time out in the security business. 'It's an agony, my back,' he says. He gets out and falls into step beside me, pulling on a balaclava to wear beneath his uniform cap. Ransumeen has no regard for me, but seeks anyone to talk to on a lonely shift. 'It's an agony. Too small for my build. I've a good mind to tell them that I'll have to toss it in unless I get a better car.'

'Right,' I say. Ransumeen has a habit of arriving at the Lintell Street entrance after ten o'clock when the women are leaving. He hopes to entice the younger ones with an offer of a ride home in the security car.

'I could do with a workout for the old mutton gun,' he boasts. But Dubois has warned the women against him, because he considers Ransumeen workshy and unreliable. 'I suppose the cleaners have almost finished now?' says Ransumeen. The balaclava does nothing for his looks. 'That Eileen's got a nice pair on her, a very nice pair.' He sees the women coming from the lighted doorway in twos and threes, and hurries from me to offer them double service.

The full moon this mid-winter night has a round, idiot face. My nose is putty, and all of us are made slump shouldered by the cold This stark, dead duck yard of Acme Textiles has no links with the expansive world in which the same night staff played volleyball last Christmas. On that night the air had rolled languidly amidst us, heavy with fragrance of the chocolate factory, the wheat silos, metallic cinders from the foundry, the sharp tar and salt from the harbour, and the plebeian scents of weeds along the fences of stained factory yards. I was in charge of the beer and fruit juice from the munificent management, and took it from the cafeteria into the summer night, where Charlotte, Carol, Rua, Eileen with such a good pair, the Tuki sisters and the others chased a yellow balloon as their volleyball. It was a mutant version of the office party, or the true one perhaps, with Dubois as seigneur, myself as squire in the medieval sense. The cleaners were boisterous and obscene, because they were all female together, away from their families and knowing they deserved better than the treatment they received.

The world is a thousand worlds and our experience of it is determined by the point of vantage. The history of one moment in one place is a thousand histories, which are horror and joy apart, men and women apart, old and young apart, worlds of temperament and esteem apart, of education and expectation apart. Our own vision is a lie to the rest of the world who jog beside us. Eileen and the Tukis had leapt for the balloon into the tar- and wheat-scented summer night, and Dubois gave gifts of pantyhose purchased from his own wages.

I say nothing to Ransumeen of these recollections. Disappointed in his advances, he heaves phlegm in the moonlight, tells Dotty he's not going her way and complains of the rigours of the job as we head for Dubois' winter headquarters in the boiler room. 'Where is that mad bastard?' says Ransumeen. 'A good Kiwi name, I must say — Dubois. Jesus.' The furnace is now kept going all night. Dubois is there before us, his face cherry red in the glow of the drip-feed and his hands clasped around his enamel mug as if in prayer. There is a low, wooden form that we sit on, and the great pipes lead off above our heads, each one lagged with sacking held by hoops of tin. This is the vibrating engine-room of our night ship and almost I can hear the ocean of the outer world surge past. Dubois has made a line of blue plastic packing tape which stretches between the pipes and dries his jockeys, woollen work socks and heavy shirt.

'I've been thinking about the three-field system,' he says, with only a nod to Ransumeen, 'as the means of maintaining some level of fertility in village soil. It's the tie to the seasons surely, one spring sowing, one autumn, one fallow, that explains its importance more in the north.'

'I suppose so.' Dubois is at his most scholarly in the post-coital glow. The fly of his work trousers is still partly undone and the corner of a green shirt can be seen, yet the collar of the one he wears is grey. Ransumeen is a reluctant audience on the occasions when

Dubois and I discuss feudalism. He is not aware of any connection between the past and the present: those not alive have never lived. His perception of life is reptilian, conscious only of the sun which warms his blood during the day, and the frost which slows him in his night work. He can barely maintain a latitudinal interest in things around him unrelated to his appetites, let alone a longitudinal one in the past and the hereafter. Only the concept of *droit de seigneur* appeals to Ransumeen from talks between Dubois and myself in the boiler house, on our rounds, or in the gully of the roof where we have sat on pigeon-blue summer nights.

'So the big cheese of the district could have every sheila on her wedding night?'

'It was a prerogative not often enforced in practice,' I say. Ransumeen doesn't want to know that.

'They knew how to live in those days,' he says. Ransumeen's response assumes, I suppose, that he himself would have been the big cheese.

The warmth of the boiler room is having an effect. Ransumeen lifts his cap to remove his balaclava. 'There's a bloody vicious Doberman at Fraser's yard,' he says. 'A real goolie cruncher. The police and our guys won't check anything on those premises.'

'Fraser's, Fraser's,' ruminates Dubois.

'Grocery warehouses, down from the coolstores.'

'Of course,' says Dubois. 'A big Doberman, eh? They have tender feet.'

'A real bastard. He tore the cheek off a boy whose bike threw a chain there. He had to have his arm grafted on to his face for ages.' Ransumeen gives me the thumbs up so that Dubois cannot see. He knows the caretaker's interest has been aroused: an odd passion whetted.

'If you're passing again in a couple of hours with a mate who'll take over here, we could pay this Doberman of yours a visit.' Dubois takes up a stick, and thumps along the overhang of the boiler house roof until a deadened sound tells him that Pongo is lying in his coats there for the warmth. 'I know you're there, Pongo. You remember that anything goes missing round here and you're for it.' I have never climbed up to the roof to see Pongo, but passed him once in the yard. He is quiet, gingery and, on winter nights, creeps up to the boiler house overhang in Dubois' fiefdom.

As we begin another round, Ransumeen takes his cue to leave. He complains about his car again. The yard lights and the moon make geometric patterns of the skips and pallets, the high building walls and roofs. All that the day will prove worn and soiled has a bridal veil in the winter frost. How cold it is. Can this be the same ground over which Dubois saunters in summer nights, coming from the staff showers back to his humble rooms by the incinerator? I have seen him with a towel as a skirt, and carrying just his trousers and soap. Parrots and roses climbed on his back: tattoos of green, vermilion and purple. Parrots and red roses while I explained to him that steward was originally sty-ward, to emphasise the importance of swine in medieval times.

With Ransumeen gone we check the west doors and go in again. Dubois continues to give me company on this, my last night. He is thinking of agriculture again. 'Why didn't they use horses to plough with more?'

'Horses were few in number and expensive,' I say. 'The ox was the draught animal for ordinary people: healthier over its life span, giving more work from poor fodder and the people didn't mind eating it at the end. The church then forbade the eating of horse meat.' We talk of medieval stock practices as we patrol the factory. Dubois stops abruptly to feel the air. Niceties of movement and temperature, which I cannot register, tell that a window has been left ajar. Complacent people think that occupations of little status can have no special skills: that any fool can be a lobster catcher, gardener, or poet. The main cleaners' storeroom is ajar, and Dubois' quick instincts lead him to investigate. There lies Dotty with her head on the orbital polisher and her feet among the mop handles. Her thin legs are hairy and her breath comes as quickly as if she were climbing the Matterhorn.

'She's taken all her pills at once again,' says Dubois, and lifts her easily in the fireman's hold to carry her into the cafeteria. 'No. No, Dotty, there's no easy death for you here,' he says, and gives me the daughter's number to ring. It's not the first time, but the last cannot be far off. While we wait and talk of Agincourt, Dotty moans beneath the drug. Dubois has placed a bag of cleaning rags beneath her head, and she smiles fatuously despite the noises she makes. Dotty's daughter and her husband are ashamed of her. They come quickly. Without thanks to us, or more than angry solicitation for Dotty, they bear her away. 'Poor Dotty,' says Dubois. 'She's about come to the end of her tether.'

Ransumeen blows his horn after midnight, and it is sharp in the cutting air. He is back with a friend who will patrol while we go to punish the Doberman who bit off the boy's cheek. Dubois armours himself in his dog fighting kit, which I have seen only once before, in October when he killed a roving Alsatian which kept shitting by the boiler house door. More than anything else he looks like a samurai: black breastplate, wickerwork and elbow guards. The orient had a modern feudal age, I remind Dubois. 'Know your enemy,' says Dubois. 'It's the head and hands you have to be most careful of.' He has tubular steel finger stalls within his fireman's gloves, and tells us that a fully grown Great Dane has a bite that will shear three-millimetre aluminium, while a bull mastiff damages mainly by shaking. 'I come crawling for a big dog,' says Dubois, 'but it's me that walks away. Get past the shock impact and the bite, and dogs rupture internally quite easily really. Sudden, full-body weight even from a kneeling position is too much for them. Rottweilers are sensitive to that, despite their reputation. You see dogs are not meant by nature to be individual fighters.'

Fraser's is well away, among the newer factories on low-lying ground. Ransumeen switches off, and the car glides down the empty street and up to the gates so as not to antagonise the dog until Dubois is ready. There is a straggling, knee-high mist from the sea, and beyond the streetlight is a main pylon with its own barbed wire enclosure. The thick cables droop and glisten between that pylon and the next. From its skeleton, knuckles of insulators hang to grasp each wire, and the electricity crackles and snaps so loudly in the winter air that it is difficult to hear what Ransumeen says in his voice at once ingratiating and confident. 'The mad, mad bastard,' he says. 'No one would believe it, would they?'

Dubois is fighting the Doberman on all fours. Neither of them makes any deliberate noise. The dog has Dubois' left arm in its teeth and shakes its head, wrenches suddenly with an instinct unpleasant to see. All the while it keeps its body away from the caretaker, who shuffles in a circle, attempting to come to it. The sparking of the pylon lines is amazingly loud. The breath rising from man and dog mingles in the broken mist. The fight is difficult to watch because of the many shadows despite the moonlight.

In the entire time the Doberman does not release its first hold. 'Get the bastard. Stick the bastard,' hisses Ransumeen. His greater animosity is expressed towards the dog, I think. He glances behind to check that the street is empty. Dubois and the dog drag and circle their way to the heavy netting of the inner fence. There Dubois is able to get the Doberman side on at last and bring his elbow down with the weight of his body behind it. Abruptly a sound like the first harsh burst from bagpipes. A second time the sound, and the Doberman scrambles lop-sided away with its head low 'The bastard's done for. It'll die soon,' says Ransumeen. I see in my mind's eye the duck again, its iridescent head, and the wing fretting on the yard. I hear Dotty snivelling. I tell myself I should have no sympathy for a dog that bites a boy's face.

Dubois gives no commentary on his actions as we drive back to Acme Textiles, and does not immediately take off his helmet. It is metallic blue, with the half-visor that modern helmets have. Perhaps he wants time for his civilised face to reassemble behind the mask. The leather padding of his left arm is bright with the Doberman's saliva. Ransumeen catches my eye and smirks.

We have coffee and brandy in the boiler room on our return. What envy might Pongo feel, only a thickness of tin, and a world, away. Ransumeen tells his colleague how Dubois got rid of the Doberman, but is cut short by the caretaker. Ransumeen's work-mate, who is a keen Salvation Army man, takes the opportunity to produce three glossy, foolscap posters promoting an orphans' fund, and he asks Dubois if they can go up in the staff canteens. It is little enough return for his surveillance, and Dubois puts them aside with a nod, close enough to the furnace to have the flames flicker on the beseeching faces of the orphans as Ransumeen tells the story about the staff nurse and the elephant. It's not well received: Dubois and I have heard better punchlines, the Salvation Army man doesn't like the genre.

'They can't be regular partners,' says Dubois, as we watch the Sleaptite couple from the boiler room door. The moonlight and the frost grip ever tighter, and the world outside is motionless, except for Ransumeen and the Salvation man squeezing into the small security car. 'There were some twenty-five thousand slaves entered in the Domesday Book,' says Dubois, 'but the numbers gradually diminished.'

'They joined the rank of the half-slaves, the villeins.'

'The luck of birth meant more then.' He seems to have forgotten the posters, but when I remind him that we will be passing the cafeteria he waves a hand. 'This is your last night as castellan,' he says. 'Tomorrow we save the orphans.' So the orphans remain in the glare of the drip-feed, together with the jumble of samurai armour.

We decide to begin through the piece room, whose arched windows cast the dense, quiet light of the moon like cheeses on the concrete floor. 'Did I tell you of Hugh the Brown, Lord of Lusignan?

A wonderful crusader who was victimised by King John,' I begin. Dubois does not answer me. He is lost for a moment behind the curtain of epilepsy. These petit mal attacks come only occasionally, then he picks up again without realising that he is ten seconds behind the rest of the world. Here is matter for metaphysical speculation: the brief loss of synchronisation might, in the puzzle of time and events, either kill or save him. I saw him have a more serious attack only once, after he came from fighting a schnauzer in the docks, and a fierce, spring hailstorm then blocked the gutterings so that the water banked up, flowed down the walls of the computer room and into the switchboard beneath. We were coming back through the nanny presses, having done what we could, when Dubois began soft noises which were no words, took with the urgency of a lover one of the press covers to lie on, as he felt the aura. He sat down and held up the palm of one hand as a sign to me that what was to happen would be over without harm, or revelation, without need of any intervention. Convulsive trembling, harsh breath, the glimpse of a parrot's head upon his shoulder, then calm in which his face was innocent. Soon he had been up again and taken up his command.

'I find the guilds interesting,' says Dubois. He is bending at the grating of the ducts to check the air flow. 'Furriers and glaziers, silversmiths and ironmongers, doublet and hose makers, glovers, cobblers. They were unions in their way.'

'But including employers as well as workers. Setting up standards of the craft, as well as conditions. I suppose more like the Japanese *zaibatsu* than unions on a British model.'

'A personal approach.'

'Things suited the scale of commerce, the scale of population then. The people of London would come out to see their king, or a hanging, quite literally. In William the Conqueror's time London was the size of Oamaru.'

'No,' says Dubois. He slows to consider it.

'It's true. Much of England was forest, and wolves ran in packs through Shropshire.'

'Ah, I can see it,' says Dubois.

Our checks have led us outside again and our faces shrink in the cold. It seems that he is going to see the whole shift out with me. He flashes his torch behind the loading bay door handles. He has put some blacking there as a test of Ransumeen's efficiency. 'That whining bastard's not done a check. I'll have him out.'

Dubois turns to look across the yard. He shows his teeth, and draws his breath deeply in defiance of the temperature. 'This is my weather as a northerner,' he says. 'A people get acclimatised over thousands of years, and function best that way. I can't stand too much heat. A cold day and a stiff wind makes something in me stir. I'm at my most alert and ready. I have this awareness of my origins.'

'It's sound enough reasoning,' I say. 'Clear genetic links with environment are proved. Look at those Andean Indians with special respiratory adaptations for altitude, and Kalahari bushmen who hardly sweat.'

'In this weather my tribe stirs inside me.'

'You might find that you suddenly come out with the words of a Frankish war cry,' I say. I wonder, however, how the boiler room fits Dubois' hypothesis.

'I'm rusty on the Franks,' says Dubois, 'except for Charlemagne. I remember that he could hardly write.'

'Yet he spoke popular Latin as his mother tongue and was also fluent in German and classical Latin.'

'Tell me something else.'

'The Basques had a rare victory over him at the Roncevalles Pass. About 780 — no, I can't remember. Anyway that's where the epic hero Roland died.'

This is the trivial way I can be of help to Dubois, some recompense for lacking the skills of a handyman. I owe my job at Statsfact Polling Agency to the Acme Textiles testimonial Dubois provided. The managing director's stationery was from Jim Simm's office, and

Dubois asked Noreen to do the typing. Noreen was a cleaner, but had been a secretary before she started having children. Dubois suggested the sentiments and in-house detail, Noreen the authenticity of phrase — such as, throughout his successful time with us, and, it is with pleasure and no hesitation that I recommend. I like best of all the part referring to my grasp of corporate sales strategy and my progress in the fast track executive promotion scheme.

'When he was old and sick, he had to campaign against King Godfrid of the Danes and, as the Franks marched north through Saxony, the Emperor's pet elephant, Abbul Abbas, died. It was seen as a terrible omen,' I tell Dubois.

'Abbul Abbas,' says Dubois meditatively.

On our way back to the boiler room, Dubois detours through his maintenance workshop, where his tools line the walls. All have blue paint on their handles and are stamped with the letters VD to lessen the likelihood of theft. I have accustomed myself not to smile, or pass any comment. Through the cavernous main factory we walk and Dubois is contentedly imagining his poison at work above us. 'Rat, rat,' he says, 'you begin to feel the thirst of death.' So might we all in time, of course.

Furnace light flickers on Dubois' clothes strung to dry and the orphans who still await a home. The great pipes rumble in this engine-room which powers Acme Textiles through the night. It is like this with heaven and hell perhaps; no spatial difference, just that Lucifer leads the night shift and employs the same means to different ends. Dubois untucks the muslin from his neck, allowing it to hang as a scarf. 'We'll have a last cuppa, then you might as well go. No sense in two of us hanging on till the last.' Not once during this last night has Dubois said that we might meet again, that any possibility for the continuation of our acquaintanceship exists. He is too honest and too worldly, understanding the contacts of labour. We have spoken more of manors and garderobes than our own lives, but then who wishes to be told the details of other people's problems. It is sufficient comfort merely to know that they have them.

Dubois comes out to see me leave. He challenges the winter air with Merovingian equanimity, and shows the white of his eyes at the offensive sound of a dog somewhere beyond the engineering works. His hair is greying, but only at the edges so that it appears frosted like all else around us. Even the flat surfaces of tin or wood have fine hachures of frost, not shiny at all, but feathered almost, grey-white in the moon and security light like a blossoming mildew. The puddles by the freight entrance, though, do have a crystal surface, and creak beneath our feet. From illogical habit we stand out from the shadow of the factory, although the lighted yard will be no warmer. 'Things will go all right for you,' and Dubois takes a hand from his pocket to shake with. There is music for this white winter night. Pongo is playing his mouth organ. No doubt he has been kept awake by the comings and goings of this last voyage.

For every place there is the official and accredited view, and for every place there is a reverse of which only intimacy allows knowledge. From our lives we can all demonstrate the truth of that. So at Acme Textiles I leave a population known only by those who must board each night. And Vincenze Dubois is its strange captain.

Working Up North

My older brother arranged a job for me as a fish splitter in Nelson and I travelled up to Blenheim by train and then to Nelson by bus the next day. In the Rai Valley an old Bedford truck loaded with pumpkins had run off the road and lay overturned like a beetle amidst the pig fern, with the brilliant orange and yellow pumpkins scattered alongside.

We were the first to come across it and the bus driver posted people to warn traffic, then he and a thickset woman who said she was a physical education specialist decided to comfort the truck driver, who had a broken wrist. The rest of us stood around to appreciate the novelty of it. The truck driver was quiet and self-reliant. I think that having a busload of gawpers at his mishap was the worst thing about it as far as he was concerned.

The pumpkin crash meant that we were late into Nelson and if there had been anyone to meet me, there wasn't any longer. I left my bag and walked down to Golden Seafoods on the waterfront. There was a blue sky, but also a strong wind that put grit in your face and stirred up the shallow water to make a dirty mix which slapped among the jetty piles and broke along the sea wall of the road to Tahunanui.

Golden Seafoods (1974 Ltd), it said on the wooden sign, and there was a picture newly glossed of a crab with its pincers up and what looked like a groper. I went past the small window of the direct to the public sales and further down to the large sliding door of the factory where I got a good whiff of the fish, rubber and damp clothes that made the atmosphere of the place. A small man, with blue gumboots and hair like a dunny brush, was hosing out the place with such force that tides of water washed through the door and ruffled there in the wind. I stepped on a pallet to keep dry till he saw me. He raised a hand to show that he had, then finished off the job.

'Just having a good swill out for the day,' he said. 'This chop has meant there's not much coming in and gives me a chance to catch up. I guess you're another McGarry. You've got the look of your brother.' He spoke loudly into the wind, but the stiff, white crest of his hair moved not a bit with the force of it. 'Another soft-palmed varsity wallah is all we need,' he said with a grin as we went into the big shed of the factory. 'You fixed up for somewhere to stay?'

I knew this must be Mr Trubb, who was Golden Seafoods. I knew that he had five boats and the factory, three retail outlets, some big contracts, a stake in a helicopter safari business on the Coast, and that he expected all his employees to work hard and toiled more than any of them himself. 'I haven't got anything fixed up,' I said. 'I've just got in and my bag's still at the depot, but I don't want to be any trouble.'

Of course I was happy to have his help, so I ended up sitting in the factory to escape the wind, with the concrete floor a glistening shadow, while Mr Trubb finished his cleaning. All the factory staff had gone early, because there wasn't much catch in and he saw the opportunity to have a good dung out. When he'd finished with the water hose he did some of the plant with superheated steam. A nasty way to have an accident, it seemed to me. I did offer to help, but Mr Trubb said I'd have the chance soon enough. He shouted through the steam that my brother used to put in a fair day's work for a fair day's pay and I could see that some sort of benchmark was expected of me. There were stainless steel-rimmed tables, drip trays, trolleys, plastic and waxed boxes, a line of freezers and a rack of rubber aprons like new pelts. I guessed that it would all dwindle to the apparatus of monotony soon enough.

Mr Trubb had the build of a sixteen-year-old and the full head of hair, though grey, added to the impression of youthfulness at a distance. But not so nimble anymore, and close up you saw how lined and worn was his dark skin and how the veins stood out over his arms and neck. He had a green 4.2 Jaguar, and he said that he'd pick up my gear if I liked and take me to Chandler's where several of his casuals stayed. First he had three boxes of fillets to deliver to the Brightwater Hotel, and as we drove he told me that he'd lived all his life in Nelson; left school at fourteen to begin nailing apple boxes and by eighteen had his own truck, which he drove between Nelson and Blenheim most of the day and night. 'You can't do that sort of thing now,' he said.

As an ex-truck driver, Mr Trubb was interested in my story of the Bedford and the pumpkins in the Rai Valley. He thought probably a blowout caused the load to shift. There's a knack to loading a truck, just as there's a knack to building a haystack. Mr Trubb told me a good deal of the way he'd become established in the world. It didn't seem to be so much boastfulness as a wish to show the rest of us what hard slog leads to. He saw himself as no different from anyone else and wanted others to have the satisfaction of getting on through hard yakker. He seemed rather surprised when I told him that my brother had gone overseas for a spell.

At the Brightwater Hotel I helped to carry in the big cartons. 'Duck under a load,' said Mr Trubb, 'rather than lifting it to your own height. It's a good lesson, that.' Mr Trubb was paid in cash and he shouted beer, which we drank inside because of the wind, and when he realised I hadn't had any lunch, he bought chips and pan-fried fish — his own, I guess. 'Go on, go on,' he said. 'We'll sweat it out of you tomorrow. One thing I've learnt is that you've got to eat well to work well. You ever done any real farm work? You can judge a farmer's savvy by the meals he gives his shearers and musterers.'

Mr Trubb had a packet of cheroots, thin and dark like himself, and he'd smoked two of them and eaten his food before I'd finished my fish. 'If you don't mind,' he said, 'we'll just drive a few miles up the Lee Valley. There's this hill property that I might be interested in, though not at the money that's being talked at the moment.'

It was lovely, quiet, up the Lee. The river itself was small and clear in a rock bed, and the hills were being greened up with pine plantings. The no exit road wasn't much wider than the Jaguar and on the small river flats the wind showed itself as muted flurries in the long grass. Mr Trubb stopped the Jaguar in a paddock gateway that had a bit of height over the property he was interested in: quite steep country and some of it gorsed, but with the Lee Stream in a series of small cascades below. 'I reckon there's a different sort of tourism coming,' he told me. 'More people want to stay in the country, not city hotels.'

He had this idea for a lodge above the river and the whole farm around it for privacy — hundreds of hectares. He didn't want to let on to the owners about those plans, of course. 'Keep it under your hat,' said Mr Trubb with easy familiarity, as if I was someone he'd relied on for years. The late afternoon sun slanted down the valley and we went out into the wind and looked across to the terrace where Mr Trubb thought he'd build the lodge, long and single-storeyed to be in keeping. 'What do you think?' he said, and I was close enough to see the veins standing out from his neck and the small skin cancers on his face and arms from years of sweat in the Nelson sun.

I appreciated being treated as an equal, as if I had already proved myself a toiler at Golden Seafoods, but I didn't want to presume. If he had to come into the factory in a day or two and give me a rocket over something then it would make it more embarrassing. 'The Asians,' said Mr Trubb, 'they jump at anything like this. We don't realise how lucky we are to live here. The best air and water in the world.' At the head of the valley was the sheen of old serpentine workings and there was a scattered mob of Hereford steers on the river flat. Among the green of the young pines on the far slope were the rust-coloured branches from the last pruning. There were briars close to us on the roadside and the berries had a summer burnish. Not one vehicle had passed us since we arrived, yet we must have been within half an hour of the city.

Mr Trubb walked back to the Jaguar and stood by the door for a moment. Then he leant forward and said something I didn't catch, before he slipped to his left along the flank of the car, which partly supported him. His body slid, taking the fine dust from the polished paintwork beneath. He lay in the grass by the car, and when I knelt down I could hear his altered breathing, which was oddly similar to the noise that the wind was making in the wheel arch of the car. One of his eyelids was almost closed and a trouser leg snagged on a briar as I lifted him. The suddenness of it made me swear a good deal for relief.

There was a moment, with Mr Trubb belted in the front seat and the Jaguar's automatic roughly sorted out to get me to Brightwater, when I had a sudden, passing amazement that everything in the valley was just the same. The green and brown of the pines unaltered, the steers still filling their guts, the cascade of the Lee, the utterly indifferent whine and pulse of the wind.

A stroke rather than a heart attack, so I was told, and Mr Trubb died a few days afterwards, despite putting in some hard work to stay alive. I couldn't settle at Golden Seafoods, and for the rest of the vacation dug potters' clay at Mapua and then did some fruit picking in the Upper Moutere. When the new term started I was lucky to get offered a ride from Nelson down through the Lewis, and we passed the turn-off to the Lee Valley on the way. I had a glimpse of the Brightwater pub again. I'd been a couple of months in the Nelson district and yet afterwards I always associated the whole time with three things from that very first day — the pumpkin smash in the Rai Valley, Mr Trubb and his vision of the lodge, and that damn, persistent wind.

The Occasion

On their way to the North Island they had one night in the Astle Motels, Picton, before they were to cross over on the ferry. The motels were concrete block, painted cream both inside and out, so that several times that evening it took Mervyn a moment to recall if he'd come inside, or was still standing outside. There was a shower so confined that it felt like a coffin. 'Oh, it's only for one night, isn't it,' his wife said. 'One night won't kill you.'

The owners, the Perrits, had four units near the steep road, then their own home that looked as though it, too, was painted cream inside and out, then a long strip of lawn, with a faded trampoline to justify the phrase, children's play area, in the brochure. Right at the back, by a Japanese box hedge, was a tin garden shed with high windows.

Mervyn had these pills for what ailed him, and after he'd taken a couple he couldn't settle to watch the game show on the television. Whoever was going to win the family sedan, the trip with spending money to Los Angeles, or be dismissed with just the sponsor's products, seemed a long way from the Astle Motels. Mervyn walked past units two, three and four, each resounding with the same game show host, past the Perrits' house. It was dark and the lights of the town glowed below with a spurious magnificence ending abruptly at the sea's edge.

He climbed on to the trampoline, gingerly lest it disintegrate beneath his weight. Much of the elasticity seemed weathered out of it. Rocking gently there, oddly reassured by the movement, he was high enough to see directly into the window of the lit garden shed, where Mrs Perrit was dancing among laundry powders, empty cartons, and heaped net curtains like Kleenex, which had long ago hung in all the units.

Mervyn had never been introduced to Mrs Perrit, had never heard her voice, knew nothing of her life beyond that day, had seen her just the once before, standing behind her husband and sucking her teeth as Mervyn signed in. Yet, oscillating four feet above the lawn in the summer night, Mervyn glimpsed her in some most private transport of euphoria, dancing by herself in the tin shed. She wore a sleeveless print dress, cut unkindly so that the puckered flesh and hair of her armpits were displayed when she raised her hands to place the palms together. She closed her eyes as she spun as if better to establish the consummate surroundings in which her dance was set. Mrs Perrit was a large, clumsy woman in Picton, who apparently wished to be set free. Her hair was lacklustre and her movements of absurd gentility.

The psychiatrist later was at pains to point out to Mervyn that of course everything at the Astle Motels was the occasion of his breakdown, and not in any way the cause. He found it interesting and important to have Mervyn realise that the dancing, the trampoline, all of it, was merely a conjunction of phenomena. Mervyn had not been driven mad by Mrs Perrit's dancing in the back shed. No, there was a complex series of factors going way back that took a good deal of the psychiatrist's time, and a good deal of Mervyn's money, to identify.

Mervyn knew that his doctor was right, that the dancing Mrs Perrit wasn't to blame, but always afterwards when he thought of his illness, or when he felt very low in himself — how are you, in yourself, Mervyn, his wife would say — then he felt again suspended, oscillating in a summer night, while watching poor, desperate Mrs Perrit dancing in the hope of who knows what release. It was a parody that struck deep into Mervyn's heart.

He saw, as if the wind had turned suddenly, that the whole splendid ballet of life casts larger shadows, which are the jig of death.

Mervyn had crept down from the trampoline, walked back to his Ford Falcon by the concrete motel unit, and sat with the door open, reciting in sequence of purchase all the cars that he had ever owned. That's where his wife found him eventually. The first one, he told her gently, the very first, was a second-hand 1936 Morris Eight, older than himself, and it was two-toned, black and a wonderful scarlet, and the doors were hinged behind the seat so that, if they opened while you drove, they could scoop in the whole world.

Cometh the Hour

The sun lay stretched in the evening and summer sky, the weeping elms sighed and rustled in the cat's-paws of the easterly, and Crimmond's Alsatian, like a wine taster, raised its head to the promise of night. James Cumuth paused at the doorway of his wooden sleepout before going in at the end of his working day. Tall and spare he stood there, holding his left arm with his right hand in an odd posture of relaxation. In his urban backpack, as well as items from the Super Doop store, were the latest copy of *International Creative Scientist*, his plastic lunchbox with the Glad Wrap folded ready to reuse, and a piece of driftwood shaped rather less like a dolphin than he had first thought. In his jacket pocket was the half-size manila envelope that held his bonus from Palmer's Product Testing.

Cumuth wasn't insensible to the attractions of the natural world, though his was essentially a life of the mind. He registered the subsiding sun, the elms, his landlady's clumped irises, even the gleam of condition on the Alsatian's pelt as it cast an oblique glance to ensure that he hadn't ventured on to Crimmond property. It was all a banality, though, wasn't it? Cumuth still awaited some mission worthy of him: some palpable need that would justify the cool, implacable resolution he felt inside.

In the neatness of his one room he emptied the bag in a manner that did not lessen the order. It was the neatness of a man who puts no store on possessions: a travelling, on-the-road man who, by whim or principle, could pack in half an hour and blow, leaving nothing of himself behind. He took his one chair to the open door where he sat in the rectangle of amber sun and read from *International Creative Scientist* the Popoffvich article on salinity trends in large European catchment lakes.

Cumuth had not forgotten his bonus envelope, but it remained unopened. A cursory thing. He knew that he was not considered a valued employee, and he knew from experience that Paul Bigelow was right when he said that the rich have a touching faith in the efficacy of small sums. At Palmer's Product Testing, Cumuth's task that week was the determination of epidermal resistal material in Paree Natural Parfume Creme after atmospheric exposure — in other words how thick a skin was likely to form on the top when the lid was left off. A man doesn't establish a personal creed on such things.

Cumuth had a BSc, but more than that he had a pioneer ancestry: lean men who had walked slow and tall through their time, proudly reticent men who could spit a double metre from the side of their mouth, without leaving a trace on their chin, when they heard a personal vanity spoken. Solitary men with a natural focus on mountain peaks, even the stars above them. Such men despise the even tenor of the life of the mass of citizenry and wait with a quiet half-smile for a challenge sufficiently cataclysmic to justify their acceptance. Their progeny are not numerous, for such pioneers are loath to spill their seed recklessly.

Cumuth himself told no one of such things of course, never consciously exalted himself. It was more a disposition, a detachment of view. He knew, however, that his paternal grandfather had done something in the war so special that no one spoke of it. So he sat in the open doorway of his sleepout, letting the dying sun copper his aquiline features and listening to the soughing of the elms.

Mrs Burmeister, his landlady, watched from the kitchen window and talked with her divorced daughter. I reckon he's a sandwich short of a picnic, she said. He's sunning himself with his mouth open. You could fart in his face and he'd still look at the mountains. Nadine gave her low, even laugh, full of knowing derision concerning men. A loser, she said. A loser with bells on. Neither mother nor daughter set much store by taciturn, frontier values.

He always seems to look past you, said Mrs Burmeister.

Always has an idiot half-smile, said Nadine.

James Cumuth was aware of them at the periphery of his line of sight, aware of the tilt of the Alsatian's muzzle also and the pulsation of the Harley Davidson, about two blocks away he reckoned. The magazine had fallen to the floor in the doorway and his hands were relaxed in the dying sun. The hands of a pianist, or a fighter pilot. When the hog was out of earshot it was quiet in the suburb, but not too quiet.

In the labs at Palmer's, Mrs Burmeister's opinion of James Cumuth was unknown, yet shared nevertheless. He was a loner all right. He was the cat that walked by himself. A one man band, that's for sure. Odd ball city, all right. He was a queer fish. He contributed little to the harmless gossip and advantageous obsequiousness of the staff cafeteria. He drank his coffee black, his bourbon neat, and if he was looking out of the third floor lab window at the small people scurrying below when Errol Golightly PhD came around, then he made no pretence to be doing anything but that, watching the small people scurrying.

You can see that he wasn't one for cultivating the approval of other people, and he had this habit of screwing up his eyes a bit and looking into the far distance as if to check for some menace there. One or two women at Palmer's, and one or two men, were initially attracted to his steady silence and his slender hands, but they found he meant no invitation by them. The personnel manager said that there was no reason for family pride; that Cumuth was brought up by an uncle who ran a video parlour, and that he lived in a one-room sleepout over in Kodacks. No truth at all, he said, in the idea that Cumuth was part Easter Island chief on his mother's side. None at all.

And people don't like idiosyncrasy in a quiet person, whereas in a boisterous one they see it as being just hard case behaviour. Now that's the truth. Cumuth wore tan stock boots; always he wore them, when everyone knew that there wasn't any stock for miles and miles around. Even way out of the city what you got was crops, horticulture and stuff. Everyone knew that. Aaron Schoone came from the country. He'd survived out there for years and he said nobody wore stock boots. Glasshouses and orchards and nurseries and poultry farms were the things out there, Aaron told the cafeteria crowd at Palmer's Product Testing.

Once they had this full-day professional motivation course run by Clarence Best Associates and Cumuth came in a full twenty minutes late after lunch and never said as much as a word, but walked slowly to his chair and screwed up his eyes a little and put his left stock boot on his right knee — after he'd sat down of course.

On the fourteenth, Wesley Igor Drom, the notorious garrottist and entrail fetishist, broke out of the maximum security institution at Happy Glades with a body count of twelve. Some papers said more. Drom moved through the pigeon blue summer dusk like a kauri tree stump. He bit a man half to death at the motorway overbridge and even took flowers without paying from a little boutique next to the Bonafide Dance Academy and the waterbed shop. Blazing red roses, the boutique lady said, and when the top psychiatrist being interviewed on television was told that, he said, ooh, red you say, ooh, now that's not a good sign by a long chalk.

The Enderby twins were roller skating at the Kodacks rink on the night of the fourteenth. Normally they'd be safe home, but it was Easter Mulheron's birthday and a whole bunch of them were skating before being picked up. Wesley Drom, irritated by the noise, crippled the gatekeeper with a twist of his left hand and took the Enderby twins as lightweight hostages. Tucked both of them under one arm, it was said, so that their blonde ringlets hung in the night. The armed offenders squads were all over, but no sign, and they had to be careful because of the twins.

To Mrs Drom, Wesley Igor was just her boy who took a wrong turning, I suppose: to the city he was the nation's galvanised degeneracy, and to James Cumuth he was manifest destiny.

Mrs Burmeister and Nadine were woken by the sound of Drom beating the Lewis-Smythes so that they would rustle up a breakfast for him in quick time. Dawn is a good time for screams to carry. Cumuth was at the door of the sleepout when his landlady came out on to the veranda, and she told him all she knew about Drom and the breakout from television. Sweet Jesus, she said, that'll be him all right, murdering someone.

Oh God, he's at it. Right here and he's killing everybody, said Nadine. He's butchering people and there's nothing to be done. She stood in her pink, candlewick dressing-gown and pressed both hands to her throat.

James Cumuth reached back into his sleepout for his boots, and sat on the step to draw them on. There is a bleak, steely quality to the first dawn light and it seemed reflected in JC's eyes as he ran a hand through his hair before going over to the house of the Lewis-Smythes. You can't do anything there, said Nadine. You'll get torn to pieces. Jesus yes, but for the first time there was an uncertain note in her derision. Cumuth looked past her as ever and gave his half-smile redolent with a stoical serenity. He walked across the lawn belonging to the Crimmonds, and the Alsatian bounded towards him with its ears back and lip up, but was checked by some emanation of the man's presence, and began fawning and dragging its head sideways on the grass. Attaboy, said Cumuth softly.

Wesley Igor Drom realised that it was almost the end of the line and was intent on taking a few more down with him. He still had the Enderby twins under one arm like bagpipes so that the sharpshooters wouldn't risk a shot at a distance. The breakfast can't have been to his liking, for he gave both host and hostess their quietus head down in the full sink, and when a brave unarmed combat expert made a rush through a skylight, thinking Drom had his hands full, Drom proved adept with a novelty bottle of peanut butter in the shape of Princess Di. It struck the expert's head with a sound like a greywacke stone on a rotten pumpkin.

A good many people formed a ring behind the police cordon as the light improved. Somehow JC got through both ring and cordon without so much as a word. People felt a need to step aside. They watched him stroll across the dewy grass and pause to trail his relaxed hand in a jasmine bush. He stopped on a nice piece of crazy paving between the back door and the barbecue area and stood balanced there with his hands relaxed by his side and his legs somewhat apart. The morning sun coppered his face in profile, glinted on his tan stock boots. The breeze made hush, and not a bull horn sounded. Nellie Hambinder later swore that there was in the sky a cloud the exact shape of a tombstone. No mistaking it, she said.

How long am I going to be waiting here, Drom? said JC. His voice was even and dispassionate, coming from a long way inside the man.

Then Wesley Igor Drom stepped out of the door to face him, and there was no shouting, no frothing. He saw the green grass, the elms, the summer flowers, the barbecue area, all in the light of a new day. He heard the uncaring birdsong and the water dripping from the overflowing Lewis-Smythes' sink. Tree trunk Wesley saw many of the police and gawpers who crouched at a distance, and he saw as well the one man who stood before him and he dried his hands on the ringlets of the Enderby twins and gave the moment its due.

Put down the Enderbys, said JC, and for once his eyes were focused not on some distant thing, but on the man to whom he spoke. It was a match, you see. It was black and white, day and night, fire and water, it was the Greek guy and the Minotaur, it was the circle of the agonising grace of man's free will to face his destiny. For both of them.

Put down the Enderbys, said JC. And Wesley Drom put the twins aside as you put a pair of fire tongs aside, and in the same movement drew a chromed sawn-off shotgun from beneath his coat and fired, and the police started firing, and when it was all over in slow motion and the birds had flown up from the elms in startled alarm, then the police came forward urgently to check the dead, and Nadine said, he lived with us, in a voice of reverential exultation and Nellie Hambinder began to sing 'Rock of Ages', and Crimmond's Alsatian slunk away into history.

That's just as it happened and just how it's remembered. People still visit the place today.

Growing Pains

When I was fourteen I began suffering cruelly from lovesickness. It was a debilitating and socially unacceptable disease which so ravaged me that I survived it only at the cost of much of my emotional capability. Infatuation, which is simply the imagination uninformed, was torn out of me by merciless experience.

My first coveted love was the wife of the golf professional at Prippen Lea, where I used to caddy and search for balls. Mrs Lassiter. She must have been all of twenty-three and had a toddler around whose soft throat I imagined my hands. Mrs Lassiter liked me: she said I had a cheeky face. With a thrilling freedom of language, she said bugger and shit. There were wisps of pale hair at her neck and she looked at me sideways when she laughed. You men, she said indulgently when her husband joked with me about the girls' team he was coaching — you men. She smelt of silver paper and fabrics dried in the sun. On the occasions when she and the golf professional took me home in their Volkswagen, I imagined him having a collapse at the wheel and myself taking decisive command. I couldn't understand how he could bear to go to work at the golf club and be parted from her. He was a generous man with a quick wit, but I never took to him.

I played football in the seconds with Jeremy Annis who was a Christian, and he invited me to go to a Bible class camp at Kaikoura. I met Ruth Rossons, who lived there, and, after playing charades in the youth hall, I experienced sharp pains in my left side and decided that I must marry her. She was very meek and when discomforted in playing out charades, put her hands to her face. The inside of her knees took my breath away and I thought that I wouldn't live long. In the boldness of this desperation I arranged to pick her up at her place on the Sunday, and walk with her to church. On that morning I walked the several blocks to her house and it began to rain: something that I had made no plans for. Wet and wretched, I hung about outside her gate and then went and sheltered in a phone box a little way down the street. I had so little understanding of courtship that it didn't occur to me to walk up their path in a manly fashion and introduce myself. I imagined that Ruth's parents would be aware of my intentions towards their daughter as plainly as I was myself. So I hid. They went to church in a dark blue Morris Oxford and Ruth gave one long, backward look through the rain to the phone box in which I stood in abject humiliation with hair plastered on my forehead. I've never seen her since and couldn't bear to do so.

My friend Alun, the one with his right-hand little finger as long as all the others, had a brother in the navy. Sometimes when he was home on leave he would deign to answer our questions. These questions were so unimportant to him that he answered them only when he was also occupying his time with more worthwhile pursuits, such as polishing the chisel toes of his immaculate black, Italian shoes, or shaving carefully down to the dark hair at the base of his neck. 'What's it like?' he answered. 'Well, it's like a flock of sparrows flying off your arse.' Alun told me that his brother in the navy had more fucks than hot dinners. It's like that there, he said. More than anything else in the world, I wanted to be part of a profession that had more fucks than hot dinners. A good many have shared that ambition, I imagine, and only grudgingly become reconciled to being brain surgeons, solicitors, software millionaires, physicists and silversmiths of international repute.

Amelia Bennie had the best tits at the girls' school. On her way in the mornings she pedalled past the lower entrance to our school and often we would wait there just to have the pleasant sight of her passing. There was no mockery, no shouts, just an admiring and respectful regard as she went by; rather as dockworkers stop work a while to watch a ship of grand armament glide past them in the channel. After seeing Amelia Bennie, even a double period of mathematics with Bodger could be borne and the bullies by the cafeteria stood up to because of a surfeit of testosterone. I wonder if she was ever aware of the hundred phantom hands upon her in the course of a day.

Travelling up to a family holiday in Nelson, I fell in love with the motelier's daughter in Blenheim when we stopped for one night there. Jasmine Courts. I never knew her name, but she smiled twice at me in the little cabin of a motel office, and I lay awake most of the night in case she came to tap on my window. She must have been able to restrain herself, but for weeks the random recollection of the blonde pony-tail against the tan of her shoulders would cause an ache of despair and loss in my heart.

Albie Joseph's good-looking sister was three years older than us and heavily into narcissism, although then I didn't recognize it as such. Normally she was almost as contemptuous of me as she was of her brother, and surrounded by a galaxy of moth-like friends of both sexes. One very windy, autumn Sunday I went round to the Josephs' two-storeyed brick and roughcast house above the park and found Melissa there alone. She held the door ajar and said nothing when I asked for Albie. She looked hopefully beyond me for a better class of company. 'Oh, come and help me for a minute then,' she said. Her bedroom seemed full of round, soft mats, frilled cushions and mirrors. 'I'm sorting out sets of things for the week,' she said. 'Ensembles.'

She stood, self-consciously unself-conscious, before the largest mirror in bra and pants and held frocks, tops and skirts to herself from time to time. 'Ideally your legs should be longer than your head and torso combined,' she said. 'I'm lucky there. Feel how smooth my skin is.' She moved my hand to her ribs, and watched my face intently, but only so that she could see the wonder of herself reflected in my expression. 'It's hopeless in a town like this, no matter how beautiful you are. I've sent a folio of photos to a modelling school in Sydney and had acknowledgement of receipt already.'

Only her feet spoilt it a bit; quite large feet with several deep creases above the heel of the fashion shoes she tried on. Her feet were asexual, common, rather like my own in their very practical configuration. Her feet lacked those attributes of gender possessed by the features to which I was naturally drawn — the heavy hair as a frame for her face, the flare of her hips, the slight pout of her belly above the waistband of her knickers.

Melissa tired of my few, feeble compliments. Even as a makeshift audience I was unsatisfactory. 'You'd better go now,' she said as the wind blew the small branches of the silver birch against the bedroom window, where they tapped and scrambled like the antennae of lascivious lobsters. I never told anyone of my privileged session, because of my shame at her complete dominance, her sure knowledge that I was utterly without masculine threat.

Towards the end of my fifth form year I had a notable success with Pamela Burridge, who was friends with Samantha Chesterfield, whose older sister, known as Stunner, was so beautiful that Nobby Allidger, halfback for the Firsts, drowned himself in the Rangitata when she dumped him. Albie Joseph and I met Pamela and Samantha at the skating rink one Sunday evening. I didn't dare ask Samantha out, so instead I asked Pamela if she'd go to the end of term rage with me. Afterwards, I heard that the main reason she agreed was that she was taken with the Ivy League shirt I was wearing. It was my brother's and I'd snaffled it while he was in hospital with blood poisoning. What made Pamela's agreement particularly sweet was that Albie aimed too high, asked Samantha, and got refused.

Only later did I realize that the date with Pamela posed something of a difficulty regarding wheels. I had been a licensed driver for seven weeks and knew that my father wouldn't let me have the car at night. It always seems to be that way with young love — the practicalities almost overwhelm the benefit. To admit to Pamela that I wouldn't have a car, to scrounge a ride with someone else, was unthinkable. What has to be done for love, has to be done. It was necessary to steal the family car for the night. Late on the Saturday afternoon of the rage I told my father that I'd wash the Humber Hawk and put it away, as he wouldn't be using it — would he? I cleaned it zealously, particularly the back seat, where I imagined Pamela recumbent, but at dusk I crept out and pushed the car from the drive and partway down the block, where I came to it later when I had dressed for the dance.

All manner of things could have gone wrong, of course, but for once the whole thing was a triumph of dangerous deceit. The adrenalin rush sustained me most of the night, and even assisted me to maintain something of a conversation with Pamela. Although I was a poor dancer she allowed me afterwards to kiss her in the back seat, and I squeezed her so tightly into the corner that she was almost melded into the upholstered junction. I think I could have gone out with her again if I'd shown more interest in her suggestion to take her ice skating at Lake Tekapo the next day, but even theft from one's family has its limits.

As an adolescent, my life within my family was completely apart from my life outside it. More than that, I was a different person in each context; different principles and beliefs, contrary motivations and emotional responses. I think for my brothers and sisters it was just that way too. If I came across them socially, at the dance hall, the beach, or movie theatre, there was only bare recognition between us. This was perhaps the reason for my failure with Prue Golightley, who was my doubles partner when we won the under seventeen title at the Sinjohn Tennis Club. She had coloured pom-poms on the heels of her sports shoes and a very solid forehand volley: in a long game her sweat would slick some of her dark hair to her forehead and neck.

Sometimes, after watching her play, I had difficulty walking. What completely stumped me was how to bridge the gap from discussing service actions and school friends, to a request for her to take off her clothes. What possible form of intermediary communication was there? Often I feared that the tension of it all would send me into a swoon.

One evening when I had been particularly impressive at the net and we were alone in the trophy room, I interrupted her talk of Monty Finchley's ringworm by reaching forward and putting my playing hand down the front of her blouse. It was a madness that I was helpless to contain. Prue and I both waited for a few moments, almost as if we expected some explosion, or some external admonition. Her bra was very confidential and easily defeated me. I think she, too, was disappointed with the experience: she removed my hand. 'Don't ever do that again,' she said. 'If we weren't playing in the final tomorrow, I'd tell your mother.'

I played like a man possessed in the final, hoping that a brilliant victory would save me from a charge of carnal knowledge in the High Court. Prue's mother and mine were friends. Two weeks later my mother came into my room and asked me if I ever wanted to talk any things over with her. 'No,' I said, 'not that I can think of.' She told me that Prue Golightley told her mother everything and not to hesitate if I wanted to talk. Was I sure that there was nothing? I was sure. There was nothing, I said, nothing that I could think of.

In the seventh form, when I was nearly eighteen, I was put out of my misery. I met Sandra Browning, who came down in a Diocesan team to the National Secondary Schools' Netball Tournament. A group of us seniors from Boys' High were invited to the dance at tournament's end in the gardens' hall and Alun's sister introduced Sandra and me. Sandra was tall and strong, with a bandaged graze on her wrist from the semi-final and a straight, dark blue dress. 'Are you much at sport?' she asked me, and as she had little access to the truth, I enlarged my reputation somewhat. All's fair after all. She had a very long face, well chinned, which wasn't unattractive, and she could stand a pause in conversation without uneasiness as we danced. 'I'm going to try for Phys. Ed. School,' she told me.

Towards the end of the dance she came with me from the hall and into the gardens. It was a cold time of the year, but someone had left the door to the hothouse unlocked, and we went into that warm and heavy atmosphere, the narrow path between banks of ferns and orchids, the hanging baskets of tropical and fragrant achimenes, the sinuous hoses lying discarded and barely visible in the moonlight through the glass. We avoided the pain of conversation. Like Adam and Eve, we climbed into the rich, natural profusion of the hothouse gardens and lay down, wasteful of the flowers crushed beneath us. Her breasts were sweeter and more full beneath her dress than I had guessed. The act itself was so explosive that I expected to be bleeding from the ears, but the only wound was a deep cut on my left ankle from a ponga trunk. I had been in such transport that the pain had failed to register.

It never occurred to me that Sandra might be in need of some reassurance. She wept freely on my almost hairless, adolescent chest and then was suddenly cheerful and began to organise our life together. Distantly I could hear the thudding of the band in the hall and was amazed that the world had gone on, that any continuity could have survived what we had experienced. All the world was winter and only Sandra Browning and I lay together in a perpetual summer, or so then it seemed.

Rebecca

Maybe the very worst thing that a woman says to a man is that she feels towards him like a sister, and almost as bad is to want to talk about Our Relationship, as though it's one of a set of abridged novels.

'I need to know where I am,' says Rebecca. She is sitting on the sill of the window in our flat above Montgomery's Kitchen Showroom in Madras Street. Full summer and the warm air brings scents from the park, intimations from the Chinese takeaway, as well as fumes from the traffic. She seems settled, prepared to give time and attention to what it is that explains our presence together here. The late sun glints on the hairs of her tanned forearms, two large top teeth rest on her lower lip, but such things are inadmissible as evidence. She taps a stainless steel table knife on the grey, worn wood of the window sill.

'Don't you have any ambition whatsoever?' she says.

'To get you back into bed,' I say. In a sense this is true.

'Don't you have any long-term plan,' she says, 'and see yourself in five, ten years' time, in the phases of its achievement?'

Rebecca wishes to be a television frontperson. She is quite open about this career and already has a post-graduate journalism diploma and a part-time reporter's job with Peninsula Radio. She has acquired professional training in front of the cameras, and practises the techniques before our mirror. She can retain a direct gaze and small, natural smile indefinitely as a fadeout. It had been remarked on, she once told me, that she had no tendency to rictus.

'I've always thought I'll die young,' I say.

'Why's that?'

'I just do. Whenever I try to imagine myself twenty years on, or whatever, there's just a fog there, grey and damp and dense.'

'That's weakness,' says Rebecca. 'You're this sort of drifter who never imposes himself on life.'

So much is interpretation, isn't it? The emotional climate in which we experience things. Nine months ago, when Rebecca and I began living together, she thought my drifting a positive thing: a refusal to be hog-tied by the conventional. She would lie bare-breasted beside me in the midday sun and eat hard-boiled eggs. Small pieces of yolk, their outer surface gun metal blue, shimmied on her warm skin. Now she has her arms tight about her knees, and she rocks impatiently on the window sill above the kitchen showroom. Even her smile has a slight constraint of impatience. 'Anyway,' she says.

We have spent a good deal of the night on it — Our Relationship — and in that exposition I have realised how unsatisfactory she considers it to be. Most of her grievances cut so deep that I've no reply, but I offer to do something about not having a car. 'I could buy one,' I tell her. 'I could get together the deposit. I think Richie Tomlinson is wanting to sell the veedub.'

'It's not just that, although I'm sick of not having a decent set of wheels. This flat here, four rooms stuck above the shops and still with the cruddy student furniture. A toilet cistern which won't flush properly, yet never stops running.'

What we're talking about hasn't anything to do with cars, or sofas, or the warm aromas from the Chinese takeaway, nothing to do with red diamonds worn from the lino around the stove, or the ice cream pottle substituting for the missing bottom louvre. What we're talking about is the failure of our infatuation with each other. Ambition is a loveless thing. As long as Rebecca was in love she was content to lie eternally naked in the sun and eat boiled eggs. A concern for her future as a television frontperson signalled a change of heart. As soon as she let me go then she saw that I was drifting.

'We can still see each other around,' she says. Everything about this woman is admirable, except her opinion of me. Her big front teeth, the muscles of her shoulders, the faintest stubble of her armpits, are part of the wonder. 'No reason at all we can't still see each other around,' Rebecca says. There is an advertising blimp floating behind her in the blue sky above the city. DOOLEY'S TOYOTA. The moment is there for me to say something that will undercut triviality and strike her soul like an arrow.

'You're right. We're bound to still see each other around.'

I feel hard done by, that's the truth of it. I have established the pleasures of my life on her without thought for any future and now she wishes to be free. What is the use of talking of the north wind when the southerly is blowing?

Rebecca sits in the frame of the window and, although we continue to talk, I can see so clearly that there is a past now, and a future, in her conception. We have separated, she and I, as the holistic present has divided.

'Don't think that I regret any of it, though,' she says.

'Nor I.'

As we talk we are separate and there is the past, the present and the future once again. A consciousness of those divisions is with us when we are out of love, so that in a sensible fashion we order things in the hope of consequences to our benefit.

'I just have to give more time to my work,' she says. 'I've got to get ahead.' What she has to get ahead of is lying in bed until the afternoon sun is in our eyes, not answering the phone because we know we've done nothing deserving of good news, spending the rent money on a Hello Dolly Masquerade Ball.

'Do you remember the Hello Dolly Masquerade Ball?' I ask her.

'So what?'

They had a terrace at the ballroom, just like in the movies, and

Rebecca and I went out and looked over a carpark, but also, in the moonlight, a line of concrete tubs with ornamental conifers. The cooler air made me realise that my shirt was wet with sweat, and Rebecca's hair had started to come down. She was one of the best-looking women there, by anyone's assessment. An older woman who had argued with her partner came out and fell over the small balustrade into the carpark. She broke her collar bone and was in the papers. It happened after Rebecca and I had been standing together with the breeze on our flushed faces, but because I was only a few minutes from being there and have seen the photograph, it has become part of my experience — this heavy woman with puffed sleeves and tears on her cheeks, the thud of her on the asphalt.

'Look,' says Rebecca. 'If it's better for you I can stay for another day or two. I want you to feel that we've talked it through, not just that I'm walking out or something.' The blimp bobs as if in agreement with such counsel. Every time I kissed her I was excited by the smooth, white keys of those two front teeth. 'People are changing, growing all the time.' All such generalisations are perfectly true, but I see no connection between them and what is happening to us. Rebecca drums with the knife on the window sill, holding it loosely in her fingers so that it can reverberate.

'I'd rather not draw it out,' I say.

Less than a year ago I first met her at the final of theatresports in the old town hall. She had a lovebite on her neck and neither of us made any mention of it then, or since. She told me that she'd been invited to apply for the Drama School in Wellington, but wanted to go into journalism.

As she goes down the stairs what we have between us is drawn tight for the last time and then parts. We will indeed see each other around, as she says; will see each other here as she comes for her things. Nothing will be the same. From the window I see her walk past the display of whiteware, microwaves, dual sinks and cupboard units that we live above. We have talked a great deal over two days, and the more intimate the discussion, the more certain was the outcome. When a glance, a kiss, a hand on the shoulder, an old joke half told, can't do the job, then recourse to analysis is bound to fail.

Rebecca doesn't look up and I see, in contrast to a Chinese girl she passes, that her hair isn't black after all, but very dark brown. Maybe in a long time I will find myself, clear of fog, in Dooley's to select a car from the gleaming new models there, and I will get an odd snag in my breathing, unaccountable, as I see the Dooley's sign. Maybe I will sign a contract and think of boiled egg crumbs on her warm skin, her slightly buck teeth, whole glamorous kitchens beneath us as we slept.

Peacock Funeral

A return to the place made Hammond think of life, you see, and death, which is necessary at least to highlight life. And the cry of the peacocks across the grass courts from the gardens, and the small children's cases, almost phosphorescent green, or pink, bobbing like marshmallows to keep the cars away. The hospital on the hill where Hammond had worked, the perfumed gardens between it and the town; enduring trees with name tags to introduce themselves to passing generations, a clearing, too, with Humpty on a wall to supervise the swings and regard with an eternal smile the great plaster bum of the elephant slide. The peacocks strode through the paths, tails rich and dark swept in the leaves, but the cries had always an empty truculence.

The mood was self-imposed, of course. Despite having given no warning, Hammond was well received at the hospital. The one departmental colleague who still recalled him, made time to greet him, to reminisce, to introduce him to the head of the unit, with whom they had herbal tea. Ginny had been fond of such drinks. She had small packs of them, each with a name more wondrously aromatic than the contents could hope to be, and there were always a few small, discarded bags clustered at the plughole of the sink. His mother once told him that the only thing from her childhood which could still move her was the recollection of the blue sky seen through the branches of a yellow plum tree in Motueka.

An offer was made to accompany him around the place, but

Hammond knew the pressures of their work, how much of a nuisance the passer by can be in a busy day. The colleague had become intensely interested in the hospital grounds as an unofficial extension of the gardens; the unit chief, on the other hand, was curious he said, as to how funding was controlled in Hammond's existing job. There were condolences as well.

Structurally there had been little change; it wasn't large as hospitals go. A new ambulance put-down bay at casualty admission, an internal decor of lighter pastels, a lot more signs outside informing people of possible destinations. It had all seemed common sense before. There were still the rose plots before the main block and still they seemed in half bloom, unable to provide a full show at any time of the year. The grass was stiff with drought, the garden clods ash grey. Hammond could see the third-floor window from which Mr Neilson, with good reason, did a header to the carpark. A wind from the sea was persistent on the hill, bowling in from a horizon always flat and far and sad.

Hammond followed the exact way he had always taken to the house in Liebers Street. Some of the mundane landmarks were still there. A plaster lighthouse on the Seddon Street corner; the paua shell porch further on; the home of a woman who was once the mistress of an ex-mayor. At the Bidewell Boarding House there was no old garage any more with a hole cut so that the door could be closed and just the front bumper stick out like a moustache at the other end. The dairy had become gaudy and its produce spilled out into makeshift displays on the footpath. Hammond caught a glimpse of the high counter where his children would wait to hear Mrs Lee say, 'Hokey-pokey, or plain?'

He had been filled with confidence then, believing that, having achieved the qualifications for a professional career, he had passed the greatest test and everything else would come naturally. That experience proved it almost true was the greatest danger.

The house was too far from the gardens for the peacocks to be heard except in the still of night. Then, when the children were asleep and Hammond and his wife lay together, sometimes they had heard those urgent calls. At first Hammond thought them exotic, but as his own life soured the notes became more discordant. Why, after all, should a creature's beauty be any indication at all of benevolence?

The brick house was part of the archaeology of his life, and even without going in, he could see things as significantly and trivially vital as the ossifications, shards and simple beads in site strata. The cracks in the roughcast beneath the main ridge facing he had twice filled with sealant, and once fallen from to lie painfully winded in the hydrangeas. The golden elm that shook leaves into the gutterings, he had heeled in and sequestered with sacking. There was a false bolt hole in the letter-box that perpetuated one of his lesser mistakes, and the concrete lip to the basement garage was never quite enough to prevent water running in during the worst rains of winter.

The things he recognised were overlaid by the habitation of other people, and as he stood on the sunny footpath the house was both painfully intimate and painfully strange to him, and he had a slight taste of copper at the back of his throat. In one year, inspired by some neighbour since forgotten, they'd had a street party — well, a sort of their end of the street party. Trestles, barbecues, lights strung in the trees and the access denied to vehicles by coloured ropes that depended on toleration for obedience. Ginny had been one of the prime movers responsible for a great success, and people had eaten, laughed and talked in the street well into the night. Everyone was filled wth neighbourly bonhomie and vowed to do it again.

And it was never done again.

Hammond walked on back to the church where he had left his car. At the service there had been several invitations to visit people before he left, but the hospital and the house were all he wanted to meet. At the crematorium Michael and Rae had rested their hands on his shoulder to show they understood that not every father was able to make a success of marriage, but they told him little about their own lives, and he was too proud to ask. The three of them had perhaps become accustomed to the detachment of correspondence. Lynley Grath had glanced at Hammond coldly at the crematorium. She had been Ginny's friend and he'd fucked her just once from behind at a midwinter party in the Tilbury Rooms. He remembered the sharp moon like a searchlight and the sharp pleasure. Lynley had remained a loyal friend to Ginny and sent Hammond a letter of contempt after the divorce.

Despite all that, the crematorium meant the least to him of all the things of the day. It was a new place with much stained glass and blond wood. It overlooked some sloping paddocks that must have been close to the farm on which Bruce Mulheron fell from his tractor and had his legs so badly injured in the discs. Bruce told him that as he lay there at first, in the shock before the pain, he was aware how sweet the fresh soil smelled. After the rare rains towards the end of summer the mushrooms would come, especially around the gateways and the tops of mounds. Hammond and Ginny often went to Mulherons' and other farms to gather them. Real mushrooms, not the designer ones sold in the supermarkets. Large and quickly black on the underside: sudden of growth and strong and dank and black and white. The kids wouldn't eat them. Ginny would bake them with bacon and onion in a pastry shell and Hammond would bring up a bottle of pinot noir. The plots at the crematorium were mainly roses. They seemed to do better there than on the high ground of the hospital.

The cost of life is everything you have. Hammond was glad that Michael and Rae were making their way independently north. He looked forward to their company for a day or two. More than he could express, he looked forward to having them with him, but for the moment, driving away from the church, driving past the peacock gardens, the associations and reproaches of the small city, he wanted only his own admonitions.

Maybe at last you can be happy, Ginny had once said. I truly

believe that you meant the best for us all, but you weren't willing to
forgo anything yourself to make sure it happened. At the time he had
assumed that it was requitable malice in the guise of reasonableness.
Later he had admitted it as honesty. Thinking of it again after the
peacocks and the crematorium, he decided it was truth. How does
one find out all the heartfelt emotions that masquerade as love?

How many couples had held each other in the summer nights, in
the arbours and ardours of the ratepayers' gardens, and thought the
peacocks cried just for them.

Hammond's face itched. He found it necessary to draw the flat of
his hand down his cheek again and again. The sun, still powerful, was
at an unkind angle and made him sneeze. Sometimes in the summer,
after a big blow, the kelp would lie in caramel heaps, rotting on the
stones, and the stench would drift into the town centre. Hammond
thought he had a whiff of it as he drove north. Sometimes his wife
had read Larkin to him while he ate a late supper on his return from
the hospital.

Had Hammond stayed until dusk he would have heard the empty
truculence of the peacocks although they had been taken from the
perfumed gardens years before. Their phantom cries were exactly as
the pain a man feels in an amputated leg.

Goodbye, Stanley Tan

We didn't see the Raffles Hotel; it was closed for renovations. Isn't that always the way, and now if ever the trip comes up in conversation with other people, they expect you to have been to Raffles. We saw the merlion at the harbour, though, and the useless gun emplacements on Sentosa Island. We climbed to Fort Canning on the site of the ancient royal palace. We had our photo taken with a black snake at the cable-car terminal and in the Tiger Balm Gardens and in the Orchid Gardens and with pygmy hippos only a fence away. We have a photo emphasising my bulk as I board a bum boat, a photo of my wife boarding the bum boat, a photo of a woman from Tuttle, North Dakota, who for an hour was our best friend in the world, disembarking from a bum boat. We have photos of our hotel bed covered with a day's purchases from plazas twenty storeys high. We have photos in which we can identify nothing, not even ourselves, and for which there seems no earthly or unearthly reason. These photographs tend to cause disagreement as to whether they even belong to the Singapore album, or whether they are of Hong Kong, or Penang, or Bangkok. As if there were any real connection between the settings and ourselves.

But you know all of that. It is part of collective tourist folklore, so let me give you three things that come from a working visit, when I was twenty-seven and had a larger appetite for experience, and a smaller perception of its whereabouts, than my own country suited. Flotillas of scooters and motorbikes at the very start of the day, with riders wearing their jackets back to front as a windbreak; lizards on the walls where the first sun strikes; Thais, muffled like gangsters, spraying weeds and verges and, unmuffled, doing many of the other menial jobs. From that time I have only one photo. Dog-eared and monochrome, it shows me with Stanley Tan outside the illegal pig abattoir in which we worked. Strangely enough, it was my farming background which provided for me in that close pressed city. That more intimate knowledge of Singapore is like a dream now and provides no link with the present place. For some months I lived closely with Stanley Tan as a friend, but even then we knew that it was the fortuitous friendship of circumstance, and not something that could survive once we left the squeals of the abattoir and the concrete room by the old harbour where we slept with the continual noise and smell of the city through the metal bars of the door. There is a sense of free fall in the relationships of youth that is lost in a later regard for security.

The woman from Tuttle, North Dakota, is a different story. An hour on an Asian bum boat seems to have cemented our lives together. She has since sent postcards from Nepal, Denmark, Egypt, Timor and Tuttle, North Dakota. She is planning a trip to New Zealand with her husband largely on our unsuspecting praise of the country.

Her husband, she told my wife, is six foot three and was legal counsel to the previous Governor of North Dakota.

My wife and I stayed at a hotel in Orchard Road that had an atrium designed by the Pharaohs, and a labyrinth of soft, air-conditioned corridors. I slept more poorly there than I had years before in the barred, concrete room by the estuarine harbour. My wife likes hotels, but I lay listening through much of the night to the shouts from the streets. It was as if gangs still fought there, which, Stanley Tan said, was the regular thing before Lee took over.

So safe a city did he make it that Stanley and I, my wife and I, years apart, could wander late at night and feel quite at ease. My wife is a perceptive traveller, whereas I am merely a bewildered one. She pointed out to me that although people drove on the left in Singapore, they tended to walk on the right. Nobody whistles as they go about their business, she said, and she was right. I guess that it's some cultural thing between Singaporeans and ourselves.

Orchard Road was like a drying room into which a community had been herded. The cries began with intensity, but were rendered languid by the hot, moist air as they rose towards our hotel room. When we had finished work, Stanley Tan sometimes took a shower in the flush room where the gutted pigs were given a final hose down and their bristles shaved if the buyers preferred them that way. The naked pigs were similar in colour to the naked Stanley, but carried more fat. If he jostled them as he held the hose with one hand and washed with the other, the carcasses would sway coyly away, then back again. Occasionally I showered there myself; it was cooling, but I disliked the feel of blood clots and fat between my feet and the concrete floor. If he showered at the abattoir, Stanley usually took a head he could buy cheaply and exchanged it for the favours of a very short, smiling mother of two who had a calligraphy stall in the direction of our room.

My wife said that I should attempt to find the places I was accustomed to from those far-off months in Singapore. Long hours and little money had reduced my view of the city. After more than twenty years how was I to find the site of an illegal pig abattoir smaller than a New Zealand family home, the barred apartment cell Stanley Tan and I shared, the parasol shop that twice a day served fried rice and vegetable ends among the umbrellas to a few regulars who worked close at hand? The owner of the abattoir saw no reason for breaks of longer than twenty minutes. I could still find my way to Raffles, of course, although my wife and I couldn't go in. Twice I had been there before. Once with a Canadian girl whom I met lost by the parasol shop; once to have a gin sling with Eddie Gilmore who supervised my thesis. There were the ceiling fans and a good deal of dark wood. There was also an air of self-conscious history. Eddie Gilmore was to give a plenary address at the three-day conference, but knew he wasn't well. 'Would that I were in the abattoir with you,' he said with feeling. 'Killing pigs and young again, or better still that I were here and young again.'

Our American friend from Tuttle told my wife and me on the bum boat that of all the places she had visited, and she seemed well through the places of the world, Singapore was the cleanest and the most orderly. She said that they had the sense to teach everyone English in Singapore, and so put them in the ballgame with everyone else. Certainly it's comforting to have foreign people speak your language in their country. The friend from Tuttle, North Dakota, said that she found it easier to understand the Singaporeans than she did us, though we also were in the same ballgame, I guess.

One morning of lurid skies when Stanley and I arrived for work, the old wooden door was still closed and the cobbled pen at the back empty of porkers. Mr Ng stood with a police officer by the wooden door, but what was going on had nothing to do with the abattoir being illegal: in the whole incident that didn't arise. The police in Singapore were busy people with strict priorities. Two people had fallen, or been pushed, from the top of the old building that had the parasol shop on its ground floor. It had happened in the darkness, but the bodies still lay uncovered, though watched by another policeman with folded arms. Mr Ng was impatient with the time taken by police procedure; he wanted to truck in his pigs, but could hardly do so under the very noses of the authorities.

Gold is very special to the Chinese, and my wife had heard of a manufacturing jeweller in Bukit Timah Road who had lovely stuff, and all twenty-two carat or better. We went there in a taxi and, sure enough, the bracelet chains and necklaces were superb, but my wife wasn't the only one to have heard of them and there were whole busloads of people, from all over the world it seemed to me, crowded into a small showroom. Our friend from Tuttle, North Dakota, seemed the only tourist in Singapore at the time who wasn't there.

After a while I went out and sat on the parapet above the carpark on the shady side. I sweated quietly there and watched an employee from the pottery next door working a pug mill for reconstituted clay. I wished my wife good fortune in finding just the gold chain that she wanted within her budget, and I had a sudden foresight that thereafter, whenever she wore it, whenever it was remarked on, I would again be on that parapet in the hot shade, watching the boy working the pug mill. The clay made a glistening cream right up to his elbows. Several times he looked up and smiled; once he raised an arm richly gloved in clay. I felt a whim to explain to him that years before I had lived in the city, worked with Stanley Tan killing and gutting pigs, eaten in the parasol shop, covered the cheerful woman calligrapher with some considerable goodwill myself while her younger child watched with religious solemnity, been taken by the police to see if I could identify the bodies in the street.

Stanley Tan and I had been regulars for the cheap meals at the parasol shop, and it was thought that we might recognise the dead men, but we didn't. One man was quite plump and much of his chest and stomach was showing from a shirt completely open at the front. There was no sign of injury, but his body was an odd purple-grey that I recall unpleasantly well. Mr Ng was quite sure that they were gamblers who had brought death on themselves and told the police so.

As we went by taxi to the airport my wife and I talked of what we had done in Singapore, so that we could reach agreement on the things to be considered high points, and the incidents of disappointment and bad service that we would retain as criticism. So much experience in between had to be discarded as transient to make room for the next destination. As we talked I half recognised the area through which we moved. Stanley Tan and I had driven out towards Changi sometimes to collect pigs, years before the new airport was built there. We had travelled in an old Bedford truck and usually at night. There had been fish farms down Tampines Road then, and the moon and few artificial lights would flick and scud from the heavy surface of one pond after another.

Stanley Tan had a smile that was all in the eyes and in the crinkles around them, while his mouth stayed the same. As we came back past the fish farm pools one night, the crate sides of the Bedford tight with pigs from the smallholdings, he told me very dirty jokes that I've forgotten, and talked as well about the tigers which his grandfather could remember in the area. 'Forget the lions,' said Stanley. 'Singapore was tiger country, and the Chinese owners of the pepper and gambier plantations had no end of trouble getting coolie workers because of the attacks. You, now, has your family given up anyone to the tigers?'

I began to tell my wife about the tigers and the Tans, but the heat, the noise of the many aircraft overhead and our provincial anxiety to do everything right at the airport distracted us and so there wasn't much pleasure in the telling, or the listening. A kind attendant in the flight lounge, though, took a photo of us both. We are standing close together, both in affection and in accordance with subject grouping, and we have smiles fit for a new destination.

The Birthday Boy

The wooden house on the corner had been built for a successful grocer, long dead and with no later generations remaining. The big house had all the chapters of a slow decline and was eventually divided into three flats so that the place became a mixture of cheap, ad hoc alterations and solid, original carpentry. Gazz and Vicky had four rooms at the front of the house; three were self-contained, but to reach their bathroom they crossed the communal hall with its central strip of raddled carpet, flanking floorboards of mahogany stain, and the dim, green-yellow glow from the front door leadlights.

Gazz was sleeping in the mid-morning. A pink sheet was held across the window with drawing pins. The corner nearest to the bed was often used by Gazz as a napkin. He didn't snore, but lay very quietly with a damp patch by his mouth, and the scar showing in the hairs of his left eyebrow. There was a tartan rug over the wall side of him. The other side was naked apart from his blue underpants. A thin, hairy leg, an arm with no tattoos, a soft stomach, one nipple in the straggling hair of his chest. Gazz was thirty-seven years old that very day, but he'd forgotten it, and no one else would jog his memory with a celebration.

His eyes opened quite suddenly; nothing else changed as a result. Gazz lay just the same except that he took in what he could see of the room. There was someone knocking on the front door, but Gazz was neither interested, nor alarmed. He knew there would never be any good news, that any of his few acquaintances would come again, that Vicky had her own key. It would be the landlord, or a man about starting your life anew with Christ, or a kid selling chocolate eggs out of season.

When Gazz sat up, his clothes were to hand where he had left them on the floor. It took him forty seconds to put them on and to run his fingers through his hair. He then stood by the side of the window, pulled the sheet back a little with one hand, picked his nose with the other. The twitch was almost up to the window sill; the chestnut that the grocer had imagined one day shading his entrance was a broad stump; a large japonica, though, made a blaze of pink. None of these things was of the slightest interest to Gazz.

Vicky came up the path. Her head was like a pear, heavy cheeks and chin towards the bottom of it. A fine, big, white arse, though, when he could get the clothes off it. Their eyes met without message as she passed.

'So you're up at last,' said Vicky.

'Yeah.'

'No joy with dorkface down there. He won't give any credit.'

'Shit.'

'I had to use more rent money.'

'Shit.' Gazz screwed his face right up for a moment as if he had a belly pain. He made a hissing sound through his teeth. 'Shit, another week behind. Any fags?'

Vicky offered him the packet she had already opened.

'Maybe if you went back to Gabites Plywood and told them that you're not sick any more. You're just so slack.'

'Someone was hammering on the bloody door before. That prick for the rent, I reckon.'

Gazz went from the bedroom, across the hall to the bathroom. Further down the hall, Turtle was about to go into his door.

'Morning, Gazz.'

'Yeah.'

Gazz left the bathroom door open so that if he spoke up, Vicky and he could keep talking. He washed his face with his fingers and cold water, brushed his teeth without paste.

'Hey, don't you use my bloody brush,' said Vicky.

'Eh?' said Gazz, as he did just that.

'Do you want to eat soon?' she called.

'What time is it?'

'After eleven.'

'I don't mind.'

'What?'

'I don't care.'

'Eh?'

Gazz turned the water off with a sudden wrench. 'I don't bloody care,' he shouted.

'Well, fuck you too.'

Gazz stood in the hall for a time after he left the bathroom. He listened, then moved through the diminishing green-yellow light towards the back of the house where Turtle and the Tierneys had their flats. He listened at Turtle's door, then the Tierneys'. The Tierneys had external access to their larger flat through the back door, but sometimes they left their hall door unlocked and Gazz could get down on some fags, a few dollars, or a bit of booze. Enough to be useful without stirring up the Tierneys too much. He listened and decided they were at work. He tried the handle. 'Shit.'

He went back into the bedroom and took his electric shaver from the water-stained and lifting walnut veneer of the duchess. He could hear Vicky in the kitchen, so he had a quick flick around the room in search of her cigarettes. 'Shit.' Gazz left the bedroom, eternally darkened by the pink sheet, and went through into the kitchen, which was half an original room with a particle board partition between it and the Tierneys' kitchen. Less plumbing and electrics that way. Gazz stood behind Vicky to shave; he could see a sufficient reflection of his face in that part of the microwave front not covered with insulating tape. Vicky was heating a spring roll. He stretched the thumb and fingers of his left hand apart so that he could get a grip of her backside through the leather skirt. It seemed a long time since he had last had that big arse.

'Bugger off.'

'Come on, Vick. Just a quick one.' Gazz put his other hand, with the razor still buzzing, around her waist and pulled her back.

'No,' she said. 'I've had a shower, and I'm not going to work this afternoon all smelly.'

'Aw, come on, Vick.'

'Bugger off.' Taking his hand from her waist, she took her spring roll from the microwave, sat down at the laminated table by the window and cleared some space for her plate. Gazz was left with his reflection and his shaver.

'I might have one of those,' he said later. She told him to make sure that there was one left for her at night. 'So how long you going to be?' he asked.

'I've got three hours' cleaning at the Richmond. Maybe four at the most, Tracey says.'

'Where's that?'

'By the hospital, Tracey says. Used to be called Aspern, Aspen, something.'

'So you'll be back pretty early.'

'Yeah, I guess so,' said Vicky 'What about you?'

'I might see if the guys in the mart want a hand. Humping stuff off the truck.'

Vicky was idly looking at the newspapers in front of her, but then it was as if she remembered some decision that applied immediately. 'Yeah,' she said and put down her fork to concentrate. Her face was made up for the day: blue eye shadow, heavy powder over her orange peel complexion. Her gloss lipstick was worn away by eating, except at the corners of her mouth. 'Yeah. It's getting pretty shitty around here without even the rent money,' she said. 'It's not on, really.'

'All right,' said Gazz.

'You reckoned you were happy to pay the rent and then we'd share all the other stuff — food and that. You were dead keen then.'

'So I've been short. Jesus, no need to make a thing about it.'

'It's just getting all shitty, that's all I'm saying.'

Tracey leant on the horn when Vicky was touching up her face, and Gazz looked out of the window to check. 'It's that Tracey,' he said. Vicky took her clutch purse and went down the hall, through the leadlighted front door, down the concrete path that was tilted to the side among the weeds because of subsidence over the many years since the grocer's death. The noon sun glinted on the chrome buckles of her leather skirt, and her solid leg muscles showed as she went warily over the camber. Gazz watched her from the top of the path by the door; Tracey watched her from the car.

'See you then,' said Gazz as she went further away.

'Haven't you ditched that loser yet?' said Tracey as she came closer. 'Has he got a feather on the end of it, or bloody something?' It was the direct humour that Vicky liked about working with Tracey.

'Don't tempt me,' she said. 'I've just been giving him a bloody razz-up.'

Gazz stayed outside in the sun while he finished the last cigarette Vicky had given him. He took in the smoke with a very long breath and then allowed it to ease out. He looked over the rank lawn, the chestnut stump, the coral of the japonica, the section of fence that had come down. 'Well, shit,' he said mildly to himself. The smoke drifted with his breath as he spoke.

Back inside, Gazz continued down the hall to Turtle. Turtle had been quite a successful commercial artist until he developed arthritis. With the loss of his one talent he went quickly downhill, but Gazz found that he always seemed to have a few dollars stashed away.

'It's me. Gazz,' he said after knocking. He could hear soft noises. 'Hey, Turtle.' The noises became even softer. 'Open the bloody door, Turt. I know you're in there.'

'What is it?' Turtle's voice came from so close, just behind the door. He must have been standing right there with his face to the wood.

'Let us in,' said Gazz. 'I've got to go to town soon — to work.' Turtle didn't answer, but Gazz could hear him unhooking the safety lock.

Turtle didn't have a hell of a lot going for him once he couldn't draw. He was into his sixties, small, fat, a very slow mover and with a few freckles so big on his pasty face that they were like birthmarks. He once told Gazz that he'd spent a fortune on gold injections. Turtle tried to make up for his delay in opening the door by swaying, smiling, offering coffee.

'Nah,' said Gazz. 'The thing is, see, I need a few bucks to tide me over until the eagle shits.'

'I saw Vicky going off somewhere.' Turtle looked at the vinyl furniture in his living room. It was a tidy room, but not a clean one. He knew that neither changing the subject, nor avoiding Gazz's eyes, would save his money.

'She's got a few hours' work on.' Gazz knew that Turtle was soft on Vicky, that he talked to her when he had a chance, that he would wait with his door ajar for her to walk across the hall in knickers and a top. It was pathetic, wasn't it.

'Aw, come on, Turtle. You won't miss a twenty for a day or two. You can come in later for a drink. I'm late as it is.'

Turtle went through to his bedroom and drew the door behind him. Gazz listened to the slow, soft noises there, imagining Turtle getting the money. Turtle was pretty much a creep, but he had his uses. When Turtle came back he held the twenty out as if he were surprised to discover it and could think of no better use for it than subsidising Gazz. 'Hey, I hope I can help out a friend,' said Turtle, with his voice jollied up.

'Good on you,' said Gazz. 'Well, things to do.'

Gazz walked in the sun for fifteen minutes to reach the Norfolk Hotel, but he thought of nothing around him as he walked, remembered nothing of it, assumed it the same as all the other times he had walked there to save drinking money. He had no curiosity concerning people who walked or drove by, no expectation of recognition. He wore soiled, white sports shoes that were copies of a good brand and a hip-length grey jacket with a black plastic cat hanging from the zip. He spat occasionally, without any shame to make him look around before doing so. Gazz was known to the barman in the Oakleaves Bar of the Norfolk. Not that the barman could remember Gazz's name, but he knew the combination of grey jacket and the scar over Gazz's left eye. 'How you going?' he asked.

'Getting by,' said Gazz.

'That's the ticket.'

'Yeah.'

'Keeping you busy?'

'So, so,' said Gazz.

He took his jug to a blue-topped stool by one of the windows that had a striped awning outside. He passed Norman Rouse, who had worked with him for several weeks on the Parks and Reserves gardening staff. Neither appreciated the other sufficiently to give up his solitude. Gazz settled down to spend his afternoon the best way he knew how. He took a mouthful of his bitter, letting it flush into his cheeks and eddy in his mouth. He looked around the bar to see if anyone had left the day's paper on a stool or table.

Two hours later Gazz stood at the back door of the Norfolk after coming from the lavatory. He enjoyed the sun on his face.

He gave a long yawn without raising a hand to his mouth, and so his slightly yellow side teeth and the dark line of fillings on his lower back ones were plain. He adjusted his trousers at the crotch, moving his cock to the left as he preferred.

A tall man in a brown suit was leaving his Camry in the carpark. When he put the keys into his coat pocket the tag still hung outside so that when he pulled the coat at the front and jerked his shoulders for comfort before walking away, the keys flipped from his pocket to the ground. Gazz saw the quick glint of them, but he made no sound, or movement. His yawn continued to close. He stood by the door and watched the tall man walk through the archway and into Gordon Street.

When the carpark had been quiet for a full minute, Gazz walked over to the Camry, picked up the keys and let himself in. He drove slowly into Gordon Street and then Marsden Road. From there he drove to the old cemetery and parked inside the gates long enough to check the back seat and the boot — only two packets of photocopy paper and a cake mixer with a repair ticket from Nimrod Electrics. Gazz headed into Riverside until he reached the panelbeating shop at the far end of the service lane behind the bakery. He parked the car behind a Telstar that had suffered a nasty frontal.

Gazz walked across the oil-stained gravel to the main building, and looked at the two men working there. He didn't know them and they didn't know him, so he went around the side of the building to a tin, tilt-door garage that served as an office. Bernie Thompson was sorting through files in a carton that had once held twenty-four 190 gram packets of Nacho Style Corn Chips. It took Bernie a while to remember Gazz, but then he smiled and said, 'Gazz. How's things, Gazz?'

'I've got a Camry I don't need.'

Bernie became very matter of fact, very business-like. He pushed the Nacho carton aside and came out with Gazz, and they walked over behind the Ford to look at the car. Bernie assessed it for a full thirty seconds, then he said, 'Nice car.'

'It's yours for five.'

'Come off it, Gazz.'

'Four on the fucken knocker, or I'm off,' said Gazz. 'You know that's fair.'

'It's a nice car,' said Bernie. 'One thing is, we got to get it away pronto and then I'll bring the money. You know I don't have four thou here.'

'Yeah, okay,' said Gazz. He gave Bernie the keys, and then went and sat in the garage office. He had no curiosity about Bernie's business; just sat quietly on the office chair and heard the considerable noise that Bernie's two men were making in the panel shop. Bernie Thompson was back in twenty minutes so Gazz took his envelope of money, walked out of the service lane and began looking for a taxi rank. It was well under an hour since he had left the hotel carpark. 'Well bugger me,' he said as he walked. 'How about that.' A little imagination started up in him as happened in the few times he scored. Money provided options in his life.

When Vicky returned from the Richmond — opened the front door, entered the green-yellow world of that long hall — she could hear Gazz and Turtle laughing. Turtle's laugh was infectious, eager and appeasing at the same time. Gazz laugh was harsh, short, almost as if he were jeering at himself and all else beside. Both of them had been into the hard stuff. Gazz had an impressive collection on the living room table, including two bottles of gin, which was Vicky's favourite. 'What all this then?' she said.

'I came across this guy at the mart who owed me a few hundred,' said Gazz. 'I'd just about given up on it.'

Vicky hadn't much enjoyed four hours of cleaning rooms at the Richmond. She was in the mood for welcome news and relaxation. She let Turtle pour her a really stiff one as an opener before she went through and changed her shoes. She had cleared the letter-box and still carried the bundle in her hand. She dealt the pieces quickly like cards on to the duchess. Supermarket coupons, householder circulars, pre-paid donation envelopes from Corso and the blind, a flyer concerning the Mad Mitch Show in the RSA Hall, a civic explanation of the new refuse scheme, a photocopied slip to let them know that Partietime home caterers was under new management. 'Jesus.'

'What?' said Gazz from the other room.

'Just once. Just once I'd like to get a friggin personal letter. Just once a bloody letter asking how I was and that. Is that so much?'

'Turtle'll write you a letter. Won't you Turt?'

'Sure, if you like.' For a small, soft guy, Turtle could put away a fair bit. Maybe he calculated it the only way he was likely to recoup the money that Gazz chiseled out of him. Vicky, too, drank as if there were a pot of gold at the end of it, but Gazz was steady, persistent, as though it were just the best way he could find to pass the time.

By summer nightfall the three of them were kicking up a fair din. Turtle was attempting a falsetto for 'Bridge Over Troubled Water' when the Tierneys banged on the kitchen partition. Gazz went through and beat on the wall with a pan, yelled 'Shut your fucken hole' seven times. There was no more trouble after that.

Turtle became quite talkative. He kept drinking although he was soon brimful of it: his eyes swam, his lips gleamed wetly, as did his pale face with its great, blotched freckles. Vicky encouraged him to describe some of the odd-ball characters he'd come across in the boarding houses. A woman who had an imaginary husband, and did both voices, even arguments. A retired gold miner who was caught having sex with a pony. Vicky straddled the sofa arm and shrieked. Gazz wondered how Turtle could remember it all, but his reaction was not admiration, only derision. What was the point of anything once it was done with? Turtle's shirt ends had come out the way they usually did; something to do with his belly. They hung outside the green corduroys that he wore even in summer.

Gazz interrupted their laughter. 'Hey, Turtle. I'd say it's about time for a feed.'

'Sure. You're right.' Turtle was reminded not to get above himself.

'That outfit closes at ten, that's all. You don't mind getting some greasies, do you?'

'Right,' said Turtle. 'May I have your order, madam?'

'Why don't you bloody go?' Vicky asked Gazz.

'I don't mind, but Turtle's got a bike. Haven't you, mate? You want to see Turt on that bike. Fucken hell. He's up and down like a whore's drawers.'

Turtle gave an appreciative and lengthy laugh and tried to tuck his shirt in. He wiped his damp face with his hands as he worked out with the others what to buy, then he went into the hall and down to his own room. 'Give him some money,' said Vicky.

'He's into my grog, isn't he?'

'Stop being a tight-arse and give him the money. He shouldn't pay for us.'

'Yeah, okay,' said Gazz. He had a particular reason for wanting Vicky friendly while Turtle was away. He walked down to Turtle's hall door. Turtle had assumed that he was alone and so hadn't fully closed the bedroom door. From the hall doorway, looking across the living room, Gazz could see all of the bedhead and chest of drawers and Turtle wasn't in sight. The soft noise of Turtle retrieving money came from the other end of the room. Gazz stepped back into the hall and didn't show himself until Turtle was on the way out. He walked with Turtle to the front door, stood on the darkening veranda while Turtle unlocked the chain from his wheel. 'No need to rip your guts getting back,' said Gazz. 'Know what I mean?' Turtle wheeled his bike away on the concrete path. Gazz couldn't make out his expression in the dark.

Vicky wasn't all that ready to fall in with Gazz's plans, even though she kept the gin bottle busy, and allowed Gazz to have his hand between her broad thighs in a companionable sort of way. Gazz tried to push her back on the sofa. 'Get off,' she said languidly.

'Aw, come on, Vick.'

'We can have it in bed later on, for Christ's sake.'

'Aw, come on.'

'Turtle will be back in a minute.'

'So what,' said Gazz. He wished that he'd never invited Turtle anyway. He was just an old sod. No use at all.

'Yeah, you'd get a buzz out of that, wouldn't you? Turtle coming back and seeing us. Well, forget it. Did you give him some money?'

'Yeah,' said Gazz. He made the most of feeling her up, and drew her head on to his shoulder with the other hand, but he felt irritation not tenderness. And Vicky had used some sort of hairspray that was unpleasant on his cheek and left a smell that reminded him of the floral air freshener in the staff cafeteria at Gabites Plywood.

'We'll be able to pay some of the back rent, won't we?' said Vicky.

'I suppose so,' said Gazz.

Turtle was something of a gentleman, and made a noise coming in the door and down the hall. He looked sillier than usual, with his corduroys tucked into very short, white socks. 'My hero,' said Vicky and she went into the kitchen to fetch plates and tomato sauce.

'Good one,' said Gazz. He noticed that Turtle put his keys on the mantelpiece of the walled-up fireplace before sorting the food. Gazz handed the second gin bottle to Turtle. 'Get some of this down you while it lasts,' he said.

It was Vicky's habit to become girlish when drunk, giggling and pretending to be shocked by behaviour that she'd exceeded for years. Not that there was anything to shock her about Gazz and Turtle. Gazz drank slowly, saying less and less; Turtle was the reverse on both counts. Vicky and Turtle had a butting contest on the sofa. After the first bout or two, Turtle caught Gazz's eye before starting again, but Gazz gave no sign that he cared. 'Playing silly buggers,' he said. The scar above his eye seemed accentuated by the drinking, and he tipped his head right back to blow smoke at the single light bulb. Turtle began to sing 'Lili Marlene'. He said his father had been an artillery colonel in the war. Vicky joined in, her voice high, penetrating and unmusical.

Vicky was the first to fall asleep, and Turtle pretended to be, because he wanted to stay there on the sofa with his face pushed close to her chest. Gazz went quietly into their bedroom and packed the best of his stuff into the large duffle bag he used instead of a case. When he came out again he could tell that Turtle was really asleep, because his head had rolled out from Vicky's breast a little and his breathing was wheezy. His worn, but oddly boyish face had a sweat of drunkenness on it, and his shirt was nicked up to expose the tunnel of his belly button in the roll of his stomach. Vicky slept with a fatuous but good-humoured smile on the large pear of her face. Gazz could stare at their unprotected faces, which seemed in relaxation to be lumpish, functionally organic — like a head of cauliflower, or a canker on the bole of a cherry tree. 'Completely out the monk,' said Gazz softly to himself, and he made a noise in his nose that sounded like a succession of sniffs, but was a reduced laugh.

Gazz took Turtle's keys from the mantelpiece and closed the door behind himself, as he went into the hall. The light there was no longer green-yellow, but almost grey from the one small bulb at the Tierneys' end. Gazz unlocked Turtle's door and went through to the bedroom. It was drab, but tidy, with just one large Toulouse Lautrec poster as a sign of any other life that Turtle may have had. Gazz knew which end to search, even though it appeared unlikely. There was only a two bar cabinet heater and Gazz soon found the envelope hidden in the back. He counted at least seven hundred dollars. 'Cunning old bugger,' said Gazz. His tone was half admiration, half contempt. He added Turtle's notes to his own, and was so intrigued by the bulk he had in the wallet that he squeezed it several times to feel the wad expand again within the leather. 'Shit,' he said.

On his way to the front door, Gazz didn't check on Turtle and Vicky. He put his duffle bag on his left shoulder and walked carefully down the subsided concrete path, past the stump of the grocer's chestnut tree and the japonica blooms that were colourless in the night. He made no pause at the gateway; he marked his departure in no way whatsoever, not even a glance up at the house. He walked steadily away along the dark, quiet street. What reason was there to look back? There were just the two lights showing. The white light from the room where Vicky and Turtle were sleeping, and the pink light through the sheet pinned over the bedroom window.

A Late Run

'Spruiker?' called the attendant. No one moved, or replied, and the man looked at the slip of paper again. His lips shaped the name to check pronunciation. 'Spruiker?' he said more coarsely.

Reece Spruiker had been watching through the foyer window as a southerly came up. There'd be a fair blow and cold rain as the front moved through. 'That's me,' he said. It was no longer of any real concern to him what the weather did.

'Well, come on, come on.' The attendant took Spruiker's two suitcases that showed cardboard through the wear on their cheap mottled surfaces. He carried them to the mini-van and slid the door open for them and the old man who followed.

'Now, Mr Spruiker,' said the attendant loudly. 'I'll put you on at the depot, right, and your daughter will meet you in Dunedin. Right? Don't wander off at any stop in between except for a quick piss.'

'I know all that.'

'Then why have you been in the bin?'

The attendant didn't find a park close to the depot, and had to carry both cases a fair way. 'Jesus,' he said. 'What you got in here? You murdered somebody or something?'

'Not lately,' said Spruiker.

The attendant didn't feel any need to wait around until the bus left. 'Remember you stay put until Dunedin,' he said and leant forward for the next few words. 'Watch yourself, you old prick,' he said.

'Soft bugger,' replied Spruiker. He waited to make sure that his suitcases were loaded, then climbed into the bus and took a seat as far back as possible.

Some faces are as if carved from soap — sanitised, opaque, all of a part. Others are wonderfully physical, animalistic even, with veins, sprouting hair, blemishes, folds and stains, gleams of linings and liquids and the stench of life. Spruiker's head would look at home on the body of a goat. He watched a woman board who must have been barely forty. She had excellent tits, but instead of taking pride in them her expression was one of discontent.

As the bus journeyed south into the evening, Reece Spruiker watched the farmland and assessed the crops and stock without being aware that he did it. An old man is mainly conditioning. Only the thistles were green in the dry, autumn paddocks. Eventually he could see no more than his own reflection in the dark window. He had been accustomed to sit on the step of his hut at Erewhon in the evenings with a beer and his dog, watching the shadows close in on the Rangitata headwaters, but a new owner can't be expected to inherit goodwill towards an old shepherd who's well past it. Spruiker saw no reason for self-pity in that, or in the fact that, out of five children, only his eldest daughter could be bothered with him. He hadn't gone out of his way for them and expected nothing in return. You had to be prepared to take in life what you dished out.

June and Keith were waiting for him and took him home to the small, weather-board cottage by the old Caversham shops. 'Is any other stuff coming down?' asked June.

'I sold the dogs,' he said.

'Just two cases then,' said Keith, 'and June was wondering where we'd put a load of stuff. Jesus! Good on you.' Keith put the cases in the small, south-facing room. It had a high ceiling and a built-in dark varnished wardrobe with leadlight glass in the door to the hat compartment. Tricky, bubbled paper gave the walls a strange sinuosity.

'A pretty flash place,' said Spruiker, and meant it. He could even catch sight of trees on the hill above the motorway.

'You can't be knocking about by yourself at your age, Dad. You can't do for yourself for ever.' June didn't mention the memory problems he had, the hospital assessment. Spruiker had forgotten all about it.

He wasn't any great trouble, both June and Keith were quick to say that. She did grit her teeth when she heard him spitting phlegm into the basin, and she had to raid his room to get clothes for the wash. He was good at preparing vegetables, doing shopping for her, taking in the washing by four during the winter when she was still at work. Mostly he walked, often down to the various grounds to watch sports teams practising — any sport. Also he liked television; mainly sport again, but also films that often had women's legs and breasts bared for him.

Apart from money for a beer in the evening, he gave his modest universal super to June. In his own odd, selfish way he was a proud man and, faced with the realisation that he might live a good while longer and not be able to maintain his independence, he wondered if he might end up being a nuisance to the only one of his children who didn't treat him with the same cheerful disregard with which he had treated them. Maybe his physical toughness would rebound on him in the end, if the mental side went first. There were special homes, he knew, which charged hundreds a week.

'Dad's always gone his own way. You know that,' Alec had said. 'Tough as old rope.'

'He never interfered; that was the good thing,' Margie had said.

'The bad thing was that he never cared.'

'He wouldn't thank you for doing anything for him. Not a bit of it,' Nigel had said. 'Old people set in their ways are best left alone. I read this article on it somewhere.'

'I've got commitments closer to home, that's for sure,' Louise had said.

But June reckoned that, with nowhere to go and being seventy, her dad needed some help, at least until the latest memory problem sorted itself out. Keith was very fond of his own parents. He could see that June needed to make something of an effort.

'I'm fine. I'm fine,' said Spruiker. 'Jesus, I've looked after myself all my life just about.'

Of the five children, June had the fewest resources to assist her father. Nigel was actually rich, but was cautious about admitting it. June worked in a bakery, and Keith did part-time in the Civic Information Centre, after suffering a breakdown while teaching.

Quite often Keith had time to sit with his father-in-law during the day and watch television, or endeavour to keep up with him as he walked about the city. Keith held no grudge that Spruiker hadn't bothered to give June and him a wedding present years before, though his own parents were very different. He rather enjoyed the old guy's earthy directness, his contempt for his fellows, his emotional reticence.

In the spring a veterans' athletic series from America was shown on afternoon television. Wrinkled people with necks full of tendons, taking themselves seriously in a whole range of events. Some of them were has-beens who couldn't give up gracefully; some were never-beens who found that they could foot it at the end of their lives. Spruiker laughed until his eyes watered at such people making goats of themselves; rejoicing in twilight victories and medal ceremonies; confiding in the interviewers as to their training programmes; sporting their monogrammed gear and warm-up exercises. 'What a load of wankers,' he told Keith. 'A bunch of bloody nellies.'

He stopped laughing when Keith pointed out to him the size of the crowds there to watch and the size of the cash purses. 'It's a fad thing in America at present,' said Keith. 'Something to do with their determination to empower the old and enhance their sociological profile. And money's no problem over there, you know.'

'How much did that old coot get for winning the hurdles?' asked Spruiker.

'Fifteen thousand dollars US. Nearer thirty in our money.'

'Eh!' said Spruiker incredulously.

'Nearly thirty thousand dollars. And that's a regional meet.'

'Jesus George! What about that spindly, hatchet-faced bint who won the long women's race?'

'I think it said not all that much less.'

Spruiker watched the series with less contempt after that. He was amazed that there was a market for all those old people aping the athletics of excellence. He asked Keith to keep a record of the winning fifteen hundred metres times.

'Why, do you think you'll have a go?'

'Don't you tell any bugger.' Spruiker was quite sensitive to ridicule, although he didn't show it.

'There's no money in veterans' athletics here anyway,' said Keith.

'Never you mind.'

On a September Sunday morning when the sun was bright, but without heat, old Spruiker asked Keith to go with him down to the Caversham Oval. 'Don't say anything to any bugger, not even June. I'm not going to be made a laughing stock. Has your watch got a second hand?' Spruiker carried a cheap new pair of tennis shoes in a supermarket bag. 'I haven't the skills for the specialist events,' he told Keith, 'but I reckon I can run as fast as those old bastards there on the television.'

'I think you underestimate them.'

'I was mustering until just a few years ago,' said Spruiker. 'I've never smoked. I've had years and years of high-country air, not like those poor city buggers. And I haven't talked, shagged, boozed, or molly-coddled myself into weakness.'

There wasn't anyone else at the Oval, and that suited Spruiker just fine. He put on the tennis shoes and tucked his trouser cuffs into his grey socks. He took off his green woollen jersey to reveal a grey workshirt with a blue stain at the pocket where a biro had burst. He spat on the ground where the track was marked, and lifted his arms rather awkwardly a few times as a suggestion of limbering up exercises. He was of only average height and he was thin, ugly and seventy years old. He had lines so deep running from both sides of his nose and down past his mouth that his face seemed to have been put together in segments. Years of sun had created a blossom of small cancers on his weathered skin. 'Say go when you're ready,' he told Keith, who tried not to smile. 'Four times around. That's what you said?'

'That's right.'

'Okay then,' said Spruiker.

'Get set, go,' said Keith. He made a show for the old guy by looking keenly at the watch. Spruiker kept his arms low while he ran and his shoulders turned from side to side in what seemed to Keith a poor action. Spruiker's knees didn't come up much either, but he had a surprisingly long stride. He ran round the Caversham Oval four times without any apparent variation in pace, or action, and when he'd finished he'd come within nine seconds of the man from Wabash, Indiana, who had won fifteen thousand dollars at the regional veterans' meet at Tulsa.

'Jesus,' said Keith. 'Jesus, Reece, you did just fine. But maybe I made some cock-up with the watch.'

'No,' said Spruiker. 'As soon as I saw those old pricks on the telly I knew I'd do almost as well. All my life I've had good wind. For years and years I was the top beat musterer on every station I worked on. I reckon there's an opportunity to take some easy money from those soft American buggers who've got so much of it they'll spend it watching geriatrics rupturing themselves.'

'It's not a bad idea, I suppose.'

'It's got to be done in the next year or two, though,' said Spruiker. He put his jersey on again, replaced the tennis shoes in the plastic bag. Keith waited in the cool sun. A tall woman with imperiously piled, grey hair was walking a King Charles spaniel that was sorely in need of exercise. A young guy, cutting across the Oval, had stopped to comb his hair, using the club house window as a mirror. Keith knew that Spruiker was most comfortable when coming out with things in his own way and his own time.

'The first reason,' said Spruiker, 'is that I'm seventy. I'll be among the youngest in the seventy to seventy-five age group. That's a real plus, I reckon. You can go down hill bloody quick at my age. The other thing is that the old grey matter is getting a bit dicey. I could be making chicken noises to myself in the corner any time now.'

Keith and Spruiker talked a good deal about the first point on their way home. The other thing was never mentioned between them again.

'Maybe,' said Keith to June that night, for, as a good husband he told his wife everything in secret, 'maybe your dad's really on to something.'

'One way and another he's been running all his life,' she said.

Keith, who considered that his teaching experience fitted him for both tasks, became coach and manager. As coach he insisted that Spruiker buy some first-rate running shoes; as manager he corresponded with the United States Pan Veterans' Athletics Association and boned up on all the rules and requirements. He began to read a good many books about motivation and metabolism and budget travel, which increased his confidence, but had no other benefit.

Spruiker ran three afternoons a week — around the Oval if it was free, or into the hill suburbs. June pretended to know nothing about it. Keith paced him on the bike if it was road work. 'There's no hills on those athletic tracks,' he said.

'Hills are good for your wind,' said Spruiker. And he enjoyed seeing his son-in-law suffer a bit.

The television series was long over, but Keith was getting all the meet times sent out to him. He even built up files on the most consistent fifteen hundred metre winners and the nature of the different venues. 'Yours is a glamour event,' he told the old guy. 'Top prizes for it.'

Within three months Spruiker was recording times that would have put him in the money if he were running in the States. Keith had spent a lot of time talking to him also about tactics and motivation. 'Visualise yourself passing Dan Swarfest of Shadow Man Falls, Montana; visualise yourself breasting the tape,' he told his father-in-law. Spruiker never bothered to answer. He did agree, however, that he should have the best steak twice a week, and his legs massaged regularly by Mrs Drummhagen who lived next door and used to be a district nurse.

Keith and Spruiker had a meeting after a tea of curried sausages one night. Spruiker said that it was time to go to the States and take some money from the Americans. June pretended to be surprised by the project, but she and Keith had already decided that it was worth-while backing the old guy to have a go. What else did he have? June said. It would take all of Spruiker's small savings and the bulk of June and Keith's. 'I'll win enough to set us up nicely, to more than pay my way in the family, but I don't want anyone getting wind of it. You understand. If anyone asks, it's just a holiday.' Spruiker never overcame a certain self-consciousness, almost shame, about the whole thing. A lot of silly old people flogging themselves in games, taking their laughable performances seriously.

Keith and Spruiker flew to Los Angeles on a Big Top from Christchurch. Spruiker first ran at a qualifying race at the Wachumpba spring festival in Fresno. His first prize barely covered expenses, but enabled him to enter the Pan Veteran indoor event at Sac City, Iowa. He came fourth in the final because he was elbowed in the face at the final turn, but it was a lesson learned. He was never less than third in the thirteen regional meets he competed in after that. He won at Savannah, Lubbuck, Seattle, St Cloud, Saratoga Springs and Troy in Alabama and was a close second to Dan Swarfest in the national final of the United States Pan Veterans' Athletics fifteen hundred metres at Glameen Park, Chicago. He received forty thousand dollars and a citation, and his name was entered on a copper plaque above the members' cocktail bar at Glameen Park, between that of Dan Swarfest and Wesley Boist Smith, who was third.

Keith was amazed and grateful and interested in all around him. He wanted Spruiker to take it easier, to see something of the country and the people while they had the opportunity, but his father-in-law saw it all as a vast sham that might collapse at any minute. Spruiker insisted they stay in modest motels, and the only friend he made was a seventy-six-year-old ex-miner from West Virginia who was doing all right in the hammer throw. They used to watch blue movies and drink Hills pinball beer together after the meets.

One week after Glameen Park, in unit nineteen of the Saddle Sore Motels on the east side of Beaumont, Texas, Reece Spruiker told Keith that it was time to get out, time for a reckoning.

'One of my legs is going,' said Spruiker, 'and I'm fed up with the people. I reckon I've done my dash.' From the motel window they could see a group of young hoods trashing cars in the park of the El Pecho Diner and Bar. The neons were starting to brighten in the dusk. 'What have we got clear?' he asked Keith. 'What can we get back home with?'

Keith got out the laptop that he had purchased from their winnings for managerial purposes. 'In the vicinity of one two five New Zealand,' he said.

'What vicinity? How much clear when we're back home?'

'I'd say a hundred and twenty-six thousand dollars,' said Keith.

'Half for June and half for me,' said Spruiker. Keith assumed charitably that June and himself were seen as indivisible. 'And I don't want any bugger to know more than he needs to.'

In Caversham Spruiker slipped back into his pre-athletic role as if all the rest had never happened. He was happier, though, because he was certain that he wasn't beholden to any bugger, that he wasn't a drag on his daughter. Nothing that the rest of the family could bitch about. He let Keith keep his last pair of expensive running shoes in case his son-in-law developed talent in old age himself. Spruiker reduced his exercise to walking again, watched a lot of television, drank rather more beer — all the same sort of things as before. But he decided that he needed to keep on with the massages from Mrs Drummhagen, and just occasionally came out with a turn of phrase which betrayed his American career and friendship with the West Virginian.

Like when he told the plumber that the new bath was as smooth as a prom queen's thigh.

If anyone ever bothered to ask him what was the best thing he'd managed in his life, he always recalled the time he and Buck had won the Canterbury Huntaway Championship at the Windwhistle dog trials. That dog could walk on water, he said.

The Devil at Bruckners' Pond

No matter how things prosper, a woman can always imagine better times. For Haydon Collins, though, it was heaven gained to be with Alice under the buffalo horns of a new moon. A cool drift of air from Bruckners' Pond, and Alice's gasp from between himself and the coarse weave of the car rug.

Only at such times, rare times, did he feel all of himself alive and free from the lethargies that otherwise laid hold on some part of body, or spirit. The moon's wry smile glittered weakly on the small, dark ruffles of Bruckners' Pond; the willow ends trailed back, whispering of autumn.

Alice's husband never listened to her, and she was entitled to a sympathetic listener. Haydon was an eager confidant, even to the verbatim account of a meter maid, for Alice had no skill of paraphrase, no awareness, in fact, of any such mode of discourse, so all the episodes she cropped from each fortnight of her life were delivered blow by blow. He'd suggested they meet once a week, but she considered it too physical, too taxing, and she was the coach of an under-fifteen softball team that had prospects in its grade and needed to practise twice a week.

'I ticketed the harbourmaster's Landcruiser,' said Alice, 'and his secretary rang me up and said I couldn't do it, not to the harbourmaster in his own precincts. I said to her I could do it in any precincts in the city that has meters: that I could do it to the mayor himself, and I'd ticketed the Civil Defence officer three times in one week, and because no emergency had been declared he had to pay up like anybody else. That's different, she tried to tell me. The Civil Defence officer's different to the harbourmaster in his own precincts. No difference at all, not at all, I says. All's equal under the local regulations and I know it off by heart. She didn't have an answer to that.'

If Haydon raised himself on his elbows he could see the moon fragments dancing on the surface of Bruckners' Pond, and the whips of willow shaking slightly in the night breeze. Miniature waves slapped the mass of root filaments that made the small bank of the pond. There was a morepork calling from the gully upstream, and Haydon was almost overcome by his good fortune to be lying on Alice in such a night, instead of watching television alone, or playing snooker in Paul Barrett's garage.

'You've got guts, Alice. I don't reckon the other meter maids would have the nerve to apply the law so evenly.'

'There's blokes too do the meters,' she said. 'How many of them do you think would ticket the harbourmaster in his own precincts?'

'None of them,' said Haydon. 'You're a bloody marvel. I reckon I should write anonymously to the council and say it too. Someone should do it.'

'I actually should go and see the harbourmaster's secretary again now that I think about it.'

Haydon gave her thigh a light slap, which sounded barely louder than the ripples on the bank, and blew hair back from her face. 'What would you say to her? Tell me exactly what you'd say to her.' In such circumstances he could listen for ever.

'Well,' she said, 'I've come for a bit of a word with you, I'd say, something of a chat about your harbourmaster in his own precincts. I'm not a person who looks to be awkward, you understand —.'

Haydon wished she would divorce her husband so that he could move in with her and make love after the evening meals, while she talked about her day wearing the civic badge, and upholding municipal traffic regulations. Alice was a very warm person: he could feel the fresh heat of her body as she became animated in her hypothetical conversation with the harbourmaster's secretary. 'I'd tell her straight out. Rules is rules I'd tell her, straight out — just stop a minute, there's something hard under the rug: a stone or some damn thing. That's it — no, I'd tell her, in my way of things everybody's equal, whether you're the harbourmaster, or just ordinary Joe Bloggs —'

A noise was coming from the lupins and broom further back from the pond. Haydon could hear it, even though absorbed with pleasure, through the sound of breeze in the weeping willows, and Alice's monologue. It demanded attention not because of volume, but because of eccentricity — it was a noise quite unknown to him. A sound that had something of whirling in it, something of disturbance to natural order, yet also a constituent of powerful personality.

Haydon raised himself from Alice enough to glance behind, and saw the Devil stroll down beside them, nod in a passing sort of way, and then stand on the lip of Bruckners' Pond. He had the goodness to face away for a time, and the moonlight caught his small horns, and the thatch of vigorous, but grey, hair at their base. Haydon and Alice scrambled to uncouple, and then arrange themselves separately on the rug. Alice was very rarely at a loss: she had fronted up to harbourmasters, mayors, media celebrities and Mongrel Mob members in the course of duty. She drew in a full breath to start in on the intruder, but then he turned, could be seen so clearly for who he was, that she let it all out in one long sigh.

'Overall it's a wretchedly poor creation,' said the Devil, 'but I must say that a summer's night at Bruckners' Pond, a warm half wind, a little routine copulation: there are worse places.' He had a voice of blandishment, rich with cynical toleration and forgiveness.

'I beg your pardon!' said Alice, affronted.

'Not at all,' said the Devil. 'Think nothing of it.'

The Devil didn't appear to have any trousers, but he wore a long frock coat of fustian green, mid-calf boots, and there wasn't much gap between. He had side whiskers and a dusky red complexion as if embers glowed within. Despite the night he was quite clearly seen; again the light that made that possible was subtly from within rather than the effect of the moon. He was like one of those unregenerate eighteenth-century squires; bluff, hearty and entirely self-serving in the most natural of ways. The Devil's tail was dark, and heavy on the ground when he moved, and with flukes at its substantial end. Haydon had the odd thought that it would make a great quantity of strong soup.

'I knew the first Bruckner here,' said the Devil, after he had breathed the lake air deeply. 'Old Anton, who bought the place in the 1860s with his wife's money, and had a vision of it as a resort in the European way, all chalets and profit. But of course the family lost it one generation before it became really valuable.' The Devil's humour seemed of an ironic turn, and his smile of reminiscence was dusky and emberish. 'The family were religious, but had a redeeming streak of profligacy,' he said.

'The Reverend David Bruckner's the vicar here, you know,' said Alice, more assured now that she had got her legs together. She wondered whether to introduce Haydon and herself to the Devil, but it was that sort of awkward situation in which you get too far into conversation with a stranger for introductions to be comfortable.

'Quite,' said the Devil, 'and I believe the vestry are at this moment taking a particular interest in the church accounts.'

Haydon feared that he was to be excluded from the conversation with the Devil, and that afterwards his silence would be taken by Alice as a weakness. Remember the time we met the Devil, she might say, and I talked to him, but you had nothing at all to say for yourself did you, nothing at all.

'Bruckners' Pond belongs to the ratepayers now,' he said.

'So it does,' replied the Devil equably, but his smile continued to be for Alice.

'We don't come here often,' she said.

'More's the pity,' said the Devil. 'It's not what you do, but who knows about it, isn't it?'

The three of them considered that, and watched the moon and the willows of Bruckners' Pond for a time, then the Devil wished them well and said that he had to be going. He gave the faintest of bows, but with the assurance of the landed gentry, and his coat was a rich, verdigris green for a moment in the moonlight and his face dusky and glowing, and he walked past them and into the bushes.

As Haydon saw the Devil walking on two legs and with a tail, he realised how fitting and natural it was, and that ordinary people on two legs seemed ungainly and incomplete, while the Devil walked with the grace of a tiger, and his tail made a firm and steadying contact with the ground behind him.

The Devil's departure prompted that of Haydon and Alice. You couldn't just carry on regardless after talking to the Devil. The two of them gathered up the rug and pillows and climbed into the off-roader. 'I'm damned if I know,' said Haydon. 'What can you say that makes sense of that?'

'I wish I'd thought of more to say,' said Alice. It was a feeling foreign to her. 'Anyway, I won't be seeing you again — not like this anyway,' she said clearly. 'The Devil's quite right you know.'

Haydon was so angry that he couldn't get the key into the ignition, but he kept his voice down because he wasn't sure how far the Devil had gone. 'What do you mean, the Devil's right?' he said bitterly, but he knew in his heart the absolute authority of the Devil. The Devil had done for him, no doubt about that, had scotched the greatest of his pleasures. 'What if it had been God, eh?' said Haydon. 'What then?'

'Just the same,' said Alice serenely.

The Language Picnic

Prof Carver Glower was there, Assoc Prof Teems, Dr Podanovich, Dr Johns, Dr Fell and Eileen the department secretary. Only Dr Allis-Montgomery refused to come, because of a vendetta going back seventeen years.

The English department had just that week completed the fourth and final volume of Antipodean English: Growth of a Variant, and Eileen had suggested a picnic. Prof Glower had appropriated the idea, as was his wont and prerogative, and put it to the faculty. 'What do you reckon?'

'Cracker,' said Assoc Prof Teems.

'Bonzer,' said Dr Podanovich.

'Yeah, why the fuck not,' said Dr Fell. 'Out in the boohai, eh. As long as us sheilas aren't expected to bring all the grub.' She preferred not to socialise with her academic colleagues, but knew what was politic in establishing a career. Also she found something generically plaintive in picnics: they reminded her of the desperate efforts her mother had made to placate family disharmony by such occasions. 'We should have Eileen along.'

'Bingo, already come up with that,' replied Prof Glower.

From the carpark amid pine trees the track led down to the beach of black sand. Because the sand was easily kicked out, the track was almost a ditch, and Assoc Prof Teems stumbled. She couldn't recover her balance because of the open basket she carried, and after wild oscillation she tumbled into the heart of a small gorse bush. Her apricot muffins were shaken into the marram grass, and the blue gingham cover she'd had over them caught in the gorse and became a taut pennant in the ripe sea breeze and beneath an effulgent sun. 'Bugger,' she said.

Solicitous as ever, and rendered clumsy by his concern, Dr Podanovich scrambled down to assist her. 'You did a real header,' he said. 'Arse over tip.' He began to pluck the gorse prickles from her pale arm and cheek, his fingers long and nimble from subtle play on the computer keyboard.

'Crapped out badly there,' said Dr Johns, who couldn't disguise that elementary human relief which is a response to the misfortunes of another. He was a small, neat, waxy man, rather like a Belgian detective. 'Come a real greaser all right,' he said, and gave his quick-fire, harsh laugh. Dr Johns was not essentially a malicious man, but he was suffering from an uneasy conscience, and attempting to assuage it by some acerbity towards his colleagues. Within the department he was normally a somewhat devious, and not fully disclosed, ally of Dr Allis-Montgomery, but he'd not had the courage to join him in boycotting the picnic. It was too unequivocal an alignment for him to commit to, but he half despised himself because of his decision.

Prof Glower picked up several of the muffins in a lordly, offhand manner, and shook them free of sand. 'No probs, she'll be jake,' he said. 'Nifty kai, I reckon.' In his heart, though, he was a disappointed man. He led the way down to the beach, and with his fingers combed the remaining long strands of grey hair across the pale luminosity of his head. Already he could feel sand grating there from his hand. Most of his staff were amiable enough, but he had academic respect for none of them, except perhaps Dr Fell, and all the time he felt his leadership under insidious siege by Dr Allis-Montgomery. Prof Glower told himself he should be satisfied with a chair in a New Zealand university, but he yearned for a vice-chancellorship, even more for a professorship at a name overseas institution. Antipodean English was his final play for scholastic distinction, and the first three volumes had received only qualified critical reception. 'Let's find a pearler possie out of the wind,' he said in his falsely jocular tone, and looked over the empty, black beach.

The group set up with their car rugs, baskets and chilly bins in the lee of the last dune before the beach. Assoc Prof Teems was immediately absorbed in removing the remaining gorse prickles; Dr Fell and Eileen caught each other's eye and had a long, exclusive smile at the mismatched socks revealed as Dr Podanovich awkwardly sat down and crossed his lanky legs. 'Just as well we're not wearing our best mocker,' he said. 'Old dungers for the beach I say.' Prof Glower talked to all, and nobody in particular, about the need to leave their offices occasionally, and Dr Johns rather pointedly yawned and lay back with his hands behind his head.

Assoc Prof Teems was an intelligent, gentle woman increasingly buffeted by the winds of change through tertiary education. Her passion was the poetry of Robert Herrick, but that was treated with boisterous derision by first-year students, so she proffered it only to the occasional postgraduate, and even more occasional Herrick conference. She was English, and her interest in the New Zealand vernacular was entirely a reflection of the department's focus. She disliked gorse, lupins and the coastal smell, which made her think some great kipper was rotting out beyond the swell. But she was loyal by nature, and had a strict sense of duty, and so although seventeenth-century English poetry was her spiritual home, she tried to find a place to stand in a new country. No chance of a place of subtlety, of nuanced reflective comment, or classical allusion, she thought wryly, and ran her hand over her skin to check for more thorns and found none. 'Well, here's one pommie who's ready to take a gecko at the friggin' beach,' she said.

'Yeah, let's give it a burl,' said Eileen. 'Maybe there's a bronzed life-saver there.'

'More like a cockie with pig-dogs who hates loopies,' said Dr Johns, but he went with them rather than listen to Prof Glower.

Dr Podanovich untangled his legs and stood up too, but not to go down to the beach. Already he sensed the familiar rifts and indifferences within the group becoming apparent: at least that sardonic Lucifer, Allis-Montgomery, wasn't with them, yet the taint of his eternal bitterness seemed impregnated in their congregation, as the fish-splitter carries always some olfactory reminder of his trade. Dr Podanovich retained an idealistic wish for a professional life of mutual support, respect and effervescent enjoyment. 'I'm going to get a bit of a fire going,' he said. 'I reckon you can't have a dinkum feed without a snarler or two.' Maybe a fire, that ageless symbol of communal gathering, would bring them together happily. Dr Podanovich went off, stooped even more than usual, as he fossicked in the marram grass for driftwood.

'Good on you, mate,' announced Prof Glower, and then in a lower voice to Dr Fell, 'The tight-arse didn't want to cough up for more than supermarket bangers, and now he thinks he deserves a bloody medal.'

Dr Fell permitted herself a knowing smile, but said nothing. She considered Dr Podanovich a sweet simpleton who carried far more than his share of the academic load, and he always topped the students' assessments of their lecturers. On the other hand, she knew she was the professor's favourite, and although she refused to play on that, neither would she deliberately jeopardise the career advantages that might flow from it. She alone was in his confidence regarding his increasing sense of disillusion, and that knowledge mitigated for her his public and empty pomposity. Dr Fell herself was young, had long legs, and professional prospects of even greater extent.

'I was knocked back by East Anglia for visiting prof again,' said Prof Glower. 'No hoper pricks didn't even bother to tell me until I sent an email giving them a rark-up.'

'That's bloody crook,' said Dr Fell. 'It's not on.' The black sand was warm through her fingers, and her bright red toenails glittered in the sunlight. Through a cleavage in the dunes she saw her three colleagues walking the surf line, breaking into a scamper up the beach sometimes to escape the seventh wave. Assoc Prof Teems and Eileen were close together, their heads inclined towards each other. Dr Johns attempted to relax, giving his metallic laugh from time to time, but at a distance his essential self-consciousness and uncertainty were obvious in everything he did. It occurred to Dr Fell that maybe when Allis-Montgomery was present, Dr Johns felt more at ease, because he knew he was then not the most unpopular and isolated person of any group.

'You can bet your arse it was a jack-up anyway,' said Prof Glower. 'Some Nigerian Hausa woman wearing curtain material will have been appointed, and rabbit on to packed bloody halls about the poetry of political dissent.'

'You're not shook on African poetry?'

'Poetry my arse. Everyone's got too bloody windy to say what they really think about post-colonial literature, that's for sure.'

'The new dean of humanities —,' began Dr Fell.

'Effing commel,' said Prof Glower. He realised he had struck a sour note, and promised himself not to allow his inner melancholy to be so obvious, even to Dr Fell. 'Need a bit of old man manuka, eh,' he shouted to Dr Podanovich, who was encouraging the first flames from beneath arabesques of driftwood.

'Nah, she'll be a bottler,' said Dr Podanovich. He took a black and greasy skillet from a supermarket bag and began to lay pink sausages in it.

Walking back towards the picnic spot with Assoc Prof Teems and Dr Johns, Eileen saw a thin wisp wafting from the fire, barely smoke from such dry wood, more a heat distortion like the thermals in boiling water. She knew that Dr Podanovich would be doing all the work, while the other two watched and talked. Eileen had no degree, but often she felt exasperated with the academics she served: their tetchy self-regard and social naïvety coupled with powerful intellects and obsessive interests. During the years most important for learning to relate to others in a diverse society, they had spent their time in libraries, isolated cubicles and, less often, with small intense cabals of people like themselves. Often she felt like an ordinary mother with gifted, but difficult children.

'What's it like down there?' asked Dr Podanovich.

'Pretty nippy round the pippy,' said Eileen, 'but we're getting fit.'

Assoc Prof Teems let herself fall back on the warm slope of the dune. 'I'm knackered,' she said.

Dr Johns came last of the three. He was carrying his black shoes, had rolled his trousers up, and the dark sand clung to his wet legs. He wondered if Dr Allis-Montgomery was working alone at the university, and felt a twinge of guilt. He wished he had brought his own car so that he could have thought of some excuse to go home immediately after the picnic lunch, but then doubted his resolve to carry out something so temerarious. 'Time for tucker, eh,' he said. 'I reckon Paddy's a real gun with them sausies — you can put a ring round that.'

'Yeah, bog in, mate,' said Dr Podanovich. He experienced a sudden, poignant moment of déjà vu. The smell of sausages and burning driftwood, and the astringent fragrance of the sea, occasioned a memory that rose like an ache in his heart: his last fishing trip with his father before the latter's death. Maybe it was an omen that even his father's fishing skills had been unavailing that day, and he'd cooked sausages on the very same skillet. His father had been emaciated by radiation treatment, and although he laughed with his son, he had tragic, imploring eyes.

'Who's for plonk?' said Dr Fell. She took two bottles of Marlborough Sauvignon Blanc from her chilly bin. She had forgone an afternoon of flagrant hedonism with her personal trainer to be with the department, and thought she deserved at least a single pleasure at the picnic.

'Could I effing ever knock back a gargle of that,' exclaimed Prof

Glower. Alcohol was increasingly a solace for him, though he found double malt whisky a more rapid release than wine.

So the English department, minus just the physical presence of Allis-Montgomery, settled with somewhat self-conscious bonhomie to their lunch: al fresco academics ill at ease in a shifting landscape without books, or a dais on which to stand. The contribution of each was a significant reflection of character. Dr Fell's medal-winning white wine and cheese twists; Assoc Prof Teems's apricot muffins and Earl Grey tea; the fresh and sensible club sandwiches brought by Eileen; sherbet trumpets fashioned by Dr Johns in his modern and lonely flat; Prof Glower's salmon and broccoli quiche made by a wife complaisant as to his absence; Dr Podanovich's supermarket sausages and a six pack of Lion Brown.

'Is this good chow or what,' said Prof Glower.

'Monty,' said Assoc Prof Teems. She felt a brief frisson of despair at the thought her life provided no better option than this, and recalled her poet Herrick, driven by lack of congenial company to train a pig to drink wine with him in his vicarage garden.

'Things are cracking up big time,' said Dr Fell. The weather was in sudden change: scudding clouds driven by a building southerly, and the sea, cut off from the sun, turning leaden. The temperature fell quickly; the driven sand scurried in the lupins and grass; the wind made sad orisons along the arc of black beach; the first large drops splattered on sand and foliage, and the spread picnic of the English department.

'Turning real pear-shaped,' said Dr Podanovich. 'I think we'll have to flag it.'

All of them hastened to gather possessions as the southerly storm came upon them. They looked to their own welfare, except benign Dr Podanovich, who offered to carry Assoc Prof Teems's basket and Eileen's thermos. They straggled back up the entrenched path that wound steeply to the carpark through marram grass, gorse, lupins and the soft flanks of black dunes that flinched beneath the heavy rain. Dr Fell, immediately behind Prof Glower, heard several rain pellets strike his balding head with the sound of a kettle drum. Dr Johns experienced a perverse euphoria, for the picnic was ending in disarray, and he'd be home by early afternoon. 'Send her down, Hughie,' he cried, and gave his barking laugh, not noticing one of his shoes fall from his bundle and roll to lie hidden in the lupins. How Dr Allis-Montgomery would enjoy the day recounted with the sardonic delivery of Dr Johns.

'Get your arse into gear up front,' shouted Eileen, impatient at the academics lack of athleticism. 'What drongo's holding us up?'

Prof Glower at the front refused to be hurried. 'Shut your trap,' he said sternly. Eileen was an indispensable secretary, but still a secretary after all. 'You're a bunch of sodding sooks. Wankers, the lot of you.' He strode on, refusing to hunch into the gale, professorial to the last, yet in his heart he felt an irrefutable regret that he had ever abandoned his love of Proust, and taken on the New Zealand vernacular.

End of Term

Even before the final bell kids were drifting away from the classrooms, some with special dispensation because they had buses to catch, others just up and off from teachers whose discipline was weak. Paul Broussard could have named those teachers without bothering to check the rooms, but who wanted to make an issue of it on the last day of term. All through the school there was an unclenching, a slackening, a sense that, ah, things were near enough to over. Among the teachers only the zealots took a grim pride in grinding out a last exercise before the chairs went up. And when the bell rang the students burst from the buildings, swirled briefly at the locker rooms and bikesheds, then as a human tide ebbed away, leaving debris, and within the buildings a scent of packed, reluctant congregation.

Pressure lifted away from the whole institution in a way almost palpable even within Paul's office. Sure, there would be a final flush of administrative tasks for him as teachers completed end-of-term procedures, but he would come back to the school over several quiet days and deal with those without the constant interruptions of school time. Crisis management was his habitual occupation during term, but frequency made it no easier. The stunted glue sniffer brought to his door for the third time in a fortnight, the fifth form Chinese boy lying behind the fives courts with teeth knocked down his throat, the choral singer who had an epileptic seizure, the skinheads from the street refusing to leave the senior girls' common room, the male teacher reduced to tears by the brutal insolence of a fourth form class, the boy who had created a large audience by shitting on the bonnet of the counsellor's car, the shoplifting calls from the supermarket manager, the torching of the twelve, blue outdoor cafeteria tables purchased from school gala funds, the balaclava woman on drugs screaming to see her daughter even though Child, Youth and Family had said it wasn't allowed, the quiet girl found at the back of keyboard skills cutting her legs with broken glass. Such things took precedence over the routine administration of exam timetables, maintenance returns and sports day, which then had to be done late at night, or over his weekends.

Paul intended to go through to the staffroom for a while, have a coffee and wish colleagues a good break. Most would be as eager as the kids to get away, but cheerful as they tidied up final paperwork and told each other of their plans.

It was his custom to have a last walk around the buildings and grounds before leaving the school. Often he found something that needed action before the weekend. He walked down the corridor lined with photographs of laudatory achievement, and the glassed cases of trophies. He passed the open door of Gareth's office and saw the principal stretched back on his chair with the phone to his ear. Gareth lifted the palm of his free hand towards Paul in acknowledgement, and rolled his eyes up to show his exasperation at a call he wished would end. That was another reason Paul liked to take his tour of duty — it took him beyond his office, even if the cellphone accompanied him.

Mary-ann Beale had similar intentions perhaps, because she joined him at the large swing doors to the main entrance. Mary-ann was senior mistress and would have had the deputy principal's job if merit always received its just reward, but she bore Paul no grudge for the male prejudice the majority of the board had exercised in his favour three years before.

'Thank God for the bell,' Mary-ann said.

'Why is it that with four terms now, they still don't seem any shorter?'

'We're getting older,' she said, as they moved out into the main quad which had a showpiece rose garden at its centre. As always she carried her big-format, blue diary with her to record her tasks as they arose. She was a stickler for efficiency, and famous for it. Kids knew that whatever went into Beale's book would in due time have consequence. Her dark hair was always in a page-boy cut, and her lipstick smudged on her soft, shifting face. It was the face of a fat woman, but by discipline she had kept her body from achieving its predilection. 'I've had a cow of a day,' she said. 'One thing after another.'

Paul admired Mary-ann although he never thought to tell her so directly. She fronted up to tough decisions day after day and was slagged off a good deal because of it, but more ex-pupils came back to see her than returned for any other teacher. 'Oh, everybody's twitchy by end of term,' he told her. 'Docky came to me again this morning and said he's resigning. He does it once or twice a year.'

'Accept it, for God's sake. Wouldn't it be a mercy for the kids as well as us.'

'I did, but he never puts it in writing, and withdraws it later anyway. He just wants the satisfaction of telling Gareth and me where we can stick the job. It's a therapy for him, but it winds us up, of course.'

'Docky knows he's not up to it any more, but won't admit it,' said Mary-ann. She felt better for hearing that Paul had been put through Docky's rant. There's more humour to be had in the predicament of others than in your own. She and Paul knew that within the next year they'd have to find some way of easing Docky out.

As Paul and Mary-ann walked past the manual block he thought that she was right, that getting older was as much a reason for their disillusion as anything else. What had amused him about the kids when he was in his twenties and thirties brought only impatience now he was fifty. Year after year they came on with unbounded energy and a sense of their own novelty, constantly renewed, while his finite resources were sapped just that much more by each intake. He could still remember most of the individuals of his first classes, but of later ones just the very best and worst, the majority scarcely registering at all. And from that grey majority a pleasant adult might return and expect to be remembered. Someone for whom there had ever been only one 6B Geography, and who never considered it as one of a long series for Paul.

'I think I'll check the girls' common rooms,' said Mary-ann. 'I had some classes detailed for clean up, but who knows.'

'I'll look in on the boys' ones,' said Paul.

'If you find a mess you might be able to get some of the kids from the final detention. There's a few hardcore still with an hour today, I think.' And that wouldn't be the easiest of jobs — detention supervision on the last day of term. All sorts of possibilities for things to go wrong. Paul tried to remember which staff member had drawn that short straw. And there'd be those kids who didn't show up, obeying that juvenile consciousness of time which considered two weeks an eternity between them and retribution. And when eternity ended, Mary-ann, or Paul, would be waiting.

The senior common room wasn't too bad: attempts had been made, although there were still plenty of textbooks that should have been away in lockers. At least the litter had been taken to the rubbish drums by the cafeteria, leaving just the heavy smell of socks and pastry and hooliganism. The ceiling bore a dark, hachured pattern from the impact of a thousand muddy rugby balls, and the old furniture had been gutted as if in a desperate search for treasure. Everything had been worn back to a fundamental communal minimalism.

Paul walked on through the corridors until he reached the fifth form boys' common room, but even as he went in he heard someone running behind him, and a junior girl with frizzy, pale hair and the tartan school skirt almost to her ankles skidded in the doorway. 'Mrs

Beale wants you to come to the main gym, Mr Broussard.' As she spoke she looked not at him, but at the common room, which was foreign ground to her.

'Okay,' said Paul. He went out into the north quad and cut across the grass, under the wet-weather walkway to the school office and on towards D block. The frizzy girl half walked, half ran beside him. 'Thanks for telling me, ahh —. Thanks for telling me. What's your name?'

'Nadine Troy,' she said, giving a little skip at the disclosure.

'Anyway, thanks, Nadine. You can get away home now.'

'Mrs Beale told me to come back.'

'Okay then.'

Maybe Mary-ann had found a stash of shoplifted stuff, or copped some kids for vandalism. Last year there'd been the discovery of marijuana plants in the ceiling of one of the computer labs, with bulbs rigged up for light and all. How few people outside the system realised the truth of schools — that they weren't cosy and manageable but, like society at large, were places of ambivalence, jostling contradictions, and with a small but powerful criminal fraternity. Many of the druggies, car thieves, intruders and vandals who contested with the police in the weekends, donned uniform themselves on Monday and went off to their classes with their intentions quite unchanged.

'So what's Mrs Beale on about then, Nadine?'

'I dunno.' Nadine trotted up beside him, encouraged by being spoken to. 'I was just going past the gym and she came out and told me to get you from the common rooms.' Nadine's frizzy hair shook like metal filings and he half expected her to jangle. He guessed she was a fourth former, but had no recollection of ever having seen her before, though that was common enough in a large school. He liked her openness and willingness to help. Some kids would be already whining that they had to go, and couldn't someone else do whatever it was that was asked of them.

Paul and Nadine went in the main door of the gym, the shadow there a sudden reduction of light and temperature. The gym was a cool, clean space: the high ceiling, polished wooden floor with court markings in white and blue. No equipment visible at all except the heavy ropes drawn from the centre and secured to the wall bars.

'Mary-ann,' called Paul.

'In here.' Her voice came from one of the storage rooms by the Phys. ed. office. Paul went to the open door and looked in to see the shelves of balls with checker-board markings, the clumped skipping ropes, and Mary-ann kneeling on the floor beside a girl whose head rested on a grey gym mat and whose legs were dark with blood.

'Oh, Jesus,' he said.

Mary-ann looked up at him, the straight hair at the sides of her face finishing at her jaw line. 'I wanted to ring from the office here, but it's locked. Could you use your cellphone for the ambulance?' Paul turned away to dial so that he wouldn't be looking at the girl as he spoke: her heavy, pale legs with the knickers half down, her heavy, pale face with an expression both questioning and oddly resigned.

He had forgotten Nadine, but facing back into the gym he found her close beside him, and as he spoke to the emergency service he tried to position himself between her and the tableau in the equipment room. He held up his hand though she wasn't making any attempt to push through. He felt more immediate pity for Nadine than for the girl on the floor, an irrational feeling, but powerful nevertheless. When he'd finished on the phone he moved out, ushering Nadine back a bit. 'Look, Nadine,' he said, 'Mr Quintock needs to know about this. Would you go to the office and ask him to come over, and then could you please go up to the top gate and guide the ambulance down here? Don't take any notice of the No Vehicle signs — come over the lawns by the swimming pool as a short cut.' Nadine whirled about without speaking, with a final jangle of hair ran noisily through the shadowed body of the gym, was outlined for a moment in the bright rectangle of the door, then was gone.

Paul crouched beside Mary-ann, and his knee popped loudly in protest. 'Have you got a clean handkerchief?' she asked him, and when he gave her the handkerchief, compactly folded, she shook it out with a flourish almost as a conjurer might. Paul took the girl's listless hand in his and could feel the slight sweat on it. Her face was forlorn, as if floating a long way below him.

'It'll be okay,' he said. 'The ambulance will be here in a jiffy. Don't you worry. Everything's fine.'

He thought that he recognised her: not by name, but as the unexceptional sixth former who always had a small, clumsily acted part in the school plays. 'She hasn't been attacked, has she?' he asked Mary-ann, though knowing he shouldn't talk in front of the girl as if she wasn't there.

'She's been pregnant,' said Mary-ann. How well she managed a minimum of specific information.

With relief Paul heard Gareth's loud, enquiring voice in the gym, with relief he went out and motioned him towards the equipment room, where the two of them stood talking in the doorway, Gareth's voice becoming more subdued as he looked past Paul to see Mary-ann and the girl on the floor. 'Right, right,' Gareth said. 'Poor kid.' He hesitated to go closer for it seemed very much the sort of thing women coped with. 'Ambulance?' he said, taking responsibility for lesser matters.

'On its way. I must go out and help Nadine guide them in.'

'Parents?' said Gareth.

'We haven't done anything about that yet,' said Paul.

'I'll see to that now.' Gareth's upper body swayed away, but before his feet moved he remembered he didn't know the girl's name. He swayed back and stepped in to be beside Mary-ann. He leant low and put a hand on her shoulder, gently, as if she were the injured party. 'And this is?' he said softly.

'This is Susan Bates,' said Mary-ann. Susan's face still floated against the grey shadows of the thick mat. Mary-ann was stroking a cheek with the back of her forefinger.

Paul and Gareth walked quickly together across the gym and into the bright sunlight. They saw the ambulance coming across the lawn. 'Jesus, what next, eh?' said Gareth. He lifted his eyebrows very high and puffed out some air through puckered lips. 'I'd better find which hospital they'll go to,' he said. Paul watched him stride off, halt the ambulance briefly with a gesture, send a trio of gawping boys packing, then hurry on to his office.

It was bread and butter stuff for the two ambulance guys. They had Susan Bates in the back, Mary-ann Beale as well at her insistence, and were on their way in just a few minutes. Paul was left in the full, quiet sun outside the gym almost as if nothing had happened at all. But he wasn't alone. There was a seat along the outside wall of the gym, and Nadine had been sitting there since guiding the ambulance in. Her hands were spread each side of her on the warm wood of the bench. She was lifting the heels of her shoes up till her feet rested on the toes and then dropping them again. She did it quickly over and over again.

Paul sat beside her. 'Thanks for helping,' he said. Her heels went up and down, up and down. The sun was warm on their faces. 'She'll be okay now I'm sure.'

'Did she have a miscarriage? My aunt had a miscarriage, but she had children again later.'

'I don't really know,' he said.

It could have been awkward because of who they were in the school, because they didn't know each other, because of what they were talking about, but events had pushed them past all that. 'Look, I'll run you home,' he said. 'I have to go up to the hospital to get Mrs Beale anyway. All this has made you late, hasn't it.'

'I don't live far,' she said. 'Maxwell Street by the park.'

'Mrs Norman lives somewhere there, doesn't she?'

'Sometimes I babysit for her.'

'Good on you anyway,' he said. 'I'm going to have a word to your form teacher.'

'I didn't do much. I'd better go now.' She stood up and he noticed how small her hands were, and that the cuffs of her jersey had been folded back twice because it had been bought for her to grow into. 'What was that girl's name, Mr Broussard?'

'Her name's Susan Bates.' He knew he shouldn't be telling her, but she deserved such a confidence. 'Remember she had a part in the last play. She was the fat witch, but it wasn't a big role.' Nadine nodded and went off down the path with her noisy shoes, and her fair, metallic hair frizzed in the sun. Paul sat and watched until she turned the corner of the science block. He lifted his heels and let them drop again, over and over. He found it oddly relaxing.

How It Goes

Picture this if you will — a silky, summer's night and the porina moths in pale, whiskery candlewick are a clumsy mass intoxication in the warm air. There's the fragrance of the trees gathered in the still night: macrocarpa, pinus radiata and walnut around the yards, more subtle essences from the last of the native bush in the gullies higher up. The boy stands very still, the better to look and listen. He holds the .22 loosely in his right hand, and the long metal torch and a school backpack in his left. The backpack hangs with the weight of three dead possums. Far down the valley lights are winking, glowing and then cutting out, glowing again, as the car, or truck, goes from bend to bend.

The boy stands and listens, watches: at ease in the night. His face is round and smooth, his hair thick and fair and soft, but his body has begun a growth spurt for adolescence so that his arms and legs have a slight clumsiness, although outdoor athleticism is always on the point of catching up.

The lights come closer, pass the turn-off to Heyworths' and Annans'. For the first time he can hear the engine. The sound doesn't carry as well as in the frosty air of winter. He recognises the sound of the ute: his father must be coming home.

The boy begins walking back through the trees and across the yard before the farmhouse. He goes from the shadows through soft moonlight and into pine shadows again. One of the dogs slinks out of its kennel, the chain clinking like coins, but it doesn't bark, perhaps because he has the rifle in his hand. The yard is almost bare of grass, just stones and earth because of the mobs of sheep that have passed, and the movement of machinery, and the scratching of the chooks that now roost hidden in the implement shed, or the lower branches of the pines, maybe even on the perches built for them in their own house.

He throws the possums onto the jutting timber of the tank stand to be skinned tomorrow. He washes blood from his hands in the laundry and goes inside. He puts a small handful of ammunition into the box in the kitchen drawer, and after checking the chamber of the .22 he leans it at the back of the hot water cupboard. He stands in the open back door for a time looking down towards the garage, but the summer night is thick with the flight of moths and the light attracts them so that they come tumbling towards the doorway, like lobbed paper pellets. So he closes the door and stays outside with all around him in the shadows of the night, or the soft, indistinct light of the moon. Picture it. And so he waits for his father with the confidence of one who has rarely been disappointed in affection.

The ute comes up the steep, uneven drive, and its lights flare and glance on the dark mass of the macrocarpas, then break out across the open space of the yards. The ute noses into the open sheds next to the tractor, and when the boy's father turns the engine off, the noise takes time to dissipate, and the small natural sounds take time to resume: the fluffle of a chook in the lower branches, the distant dry cough of a sheep, morepork echo from the far bush. Listen and you will know them.

The father comes carrying supermarket bags, and the boy opens the door for him and follows him inside. 'You okay then?' the father asks, and the son nods. The man puts the bags on the bench without interest in them, and goes through to the lounge with its worn vinyl suite and large television. He sits well down in a chair so that his knees are almost level with his head. He is a tallish man, but most of his height is in his legs, and his bare forearms are burnt to the colour of copper. 'We'll have something to eat soon, eh,' he says.

'Okay.'

'We'll rustle up something from the can tonight.'

'I don't mind,' says the boy. The father has a habit of rubbing his hands on the tops of his thighs, and the sound on the twill fabric is like soft rain on the roof.

'Your mum sends her love.'

'When can she come back?'

'Not for a while yet, I'm afraid,' says the man. He lets his head rest back on the chair, gives a small yawn of discomfort, then sits up ready to say more. The boy is leaning on the back of the sofa, and his father flaps a hand to get him to sit down.

'She's okay, though?' The boy sits and smooths his hair down at the same time. He feels no great apprehension, as his mother talked it all through with him before she went: about the lumps in her breast and the need to get rid of them in case they became a nuisance.

'Look,' says his father, 'it's a matter of things being more serious than the doc first thought, that's all.' He doesn't hesitate much; he's obviously spent some time while driving home getting sorted what he wants to say. 'There's some more tests to be done and that, but he reckons there's no sign of anything really bad. You know that sometimes women get cancer there?' The boy shook his head. 'Well, they do, and that's the worst thing they could find, and it's not that thank God, but the doc still wants some tests to find out why your mum's tired all the time. A night or two at most. It's not worth her coming all the way home and then back again for tests.'

The father waits then, looking at his son, giving time for the boy to ask anything else, but there are no questions. The father gets up purposefully from the chair; he claps his hands together. 'Right,' he says. 'Time for something to eat, or we'll be here all night.'

It is as they leave the room that the man turns the television on. Neither considers it unusual that they should half watch it through the open kitchen door as they make a meal. Neither of them is accustomed to continual conversation, and the lack isn't a source of awkwardness. They have Wattie's baked beans on toast with two poached eggs each as well. The boy has a Coke, which is something of a treat, and his father a beer, which is routine. They take their meal back to the lounge to eat, and watch a movie about gangsters which is set in a country on the other side of the world. They don't bother to draw the curtains: they live three miles from their neighbours, on a country road that is little used. Picture the simple weatherboard house with a red, tin roof set on the river terrace close to the sheds and yards. In the moonlight, of course, the red roof is another colour altogether, and the yellow spill from the lounge window shows the rough lawn, the struggling azaleas and the netting fence that keeps the stock from the garden. And yes, the heavy moths labour through the warm air, attracted to the light. A summer blizzard of insects whirls there in the waning window light, but to the father and his son it's just life, and the soft pattering on the glass is unremarked.

When the gangster movie is over, the man tells the boy that he'd better shoot away to bed. 'Maybe tomorrow you can come in with me to see your mum,' he says. 'If I can get a good run at things tomorrow morning, we'll go in after lunch. I'd like you to help me in the yards.'

'I'll get up when you do,' the boy says. He knows his father will be outside by seven.

'No, that's okay. Just come on over when you're ready. I've got crutching to do.'

The boy is in his room when his father talks to him from the lounge; it's not far away, and with the television off there's no need for the man even to raise his voice. 'I haven't forgotten about us going pig hunting,' he says. 'It's just this thing with your mum is what's important right now.'

'That's okay.'

'We'll go soon and knock a few over. We'll get Geordie and his dogs.'

'I got three possums tonight,' says the boy.

'Good riddance to the buggers,' says his father. 'Goodnight.'

'Night, Dad.'

The boy lies in his bed with a strip of moonlight across his legs and angling across the room. It's so quiet he can hear his father in the lounge rubbing his hands on his knees, and he knows he'll be sitting well down in the soft chair, with his long legs like trestles before him. The boy thinks he'll get up really early in the morning, and be there to help when his father goes outside. He's made such resolutions before and not managed them, but he tells himself this time will be different.

Even with his father so close, there's a sense of absence in the house. The boy is old enough to realise that there are reasons his father might not be telling him all the truth about his mother, and he hopes that's not so. He's briefly shaken by an aching desolation quite new to him, and then feels better again. His father is only a wall away: tomorrow he'll see his mother and she'll maybe come home with them. Things will be okay. He has experienced nothing so awful in his life that he would think otherwise.

Picture him asleep in the small, plain bedroom of the farmhouse, with the moonlight through the window forming a pale, blank screen on the wall, as if some film is about to start and tell us more about his life.

An Indirect Geography

They're gathered up: met here to travel south to help me celebrate my ninetieth birthday, but I couldn't wait any longer. Such decisions are made for us, and death has released me to accompany them on the journey to my funeral. Better they don't know the change of plan.

They cluster ready for departure in this summer morning. Donald's my eldest, and become pompous, though he's family minded and reliable. It's his car they're using and his Aaple Motels they're leaving from. Nigel isn't his, of course. He's Ruth's youngest, and she's my youngest — only forty-six. I never know what to make of Nigel. I can't understand what he says. He talks in an adolescent mumble while he turns his face away. Andrew's my second son. His father always said he was the deep one, but his brains don't seem to have made him happier than anyone else. 'All aboard who's coming aboard then. We'd better be on the road,' says Donald. It's his car and he's the South Islander on his own ground. Nigel asks if he could drive for a while, but Donald says maybe later, on a quiet stretch south of Ashburton perhaps.

'Oh, make no promises that bind us all as passengers,' says Andrew. 'All life hangs by a thread.' He's right there.

'I told Mum not to expect us until this afternoon: that we'd have lunch on the way down,' says Ruth.

'But she'll still be expecting us earlier,' says Donald. 'Whatever time I arrive she says she thought I might have been there earlier.

One day I'll come at daybreak.'

'Mum will have the bed turned down from the night before,' says Andrew.

Ruth will have organised the boys. She will have said they should be coming down to be with me on my ninetieth. She and Nigel flew down to Christchurch yesterday morning and Andrew on a later flight. To be honest, their talk has often bored me, but I think about them a lot. I've had close, special things to say, but rarely said them when the opportunity was there; instead fallen back into the old pattern of trivial, nothing, everyday talk. Sometimes the more you care for people the less risk you take with them.

It's nice, though, that they're gathered up, that they're coming as a family to see me.

Ruth makes herself comfortable in the back with Nigel. It's a long time since she's driven from Christchurch to Oamaru. Her mood is one of family reminiscence and reflection. 'I had a dream about Mum last night. We all gave her our birthday presents, but she wouldn't look at them. She said she wanted to buy back the farm so we could live there again, and she took sets of false teeth out of her mouth one after the other as she talked.'

'It wouldn't take much to buy it back today, by Jesus. I'm glad I got out when I did, that's for sure,' says Donald. Nigel mumbles something about getting out with a packet too, and Donald complains that he can't understand a thing he says.

'All those false teeth in your dream,' says Andrew, 'one set after another, you said. That's an odd thing. Maybe it's a repudiation of age: going back to the good old days of personal virtue and the horse.'

'For all your fancy notions, the age of the horse may well be in front of us as well, the way things are going. Don't write horses off.' Since boyhood, Donald has been impatient with his brother's departure from practical considerations.

So they talk of horses! What do people know or care of horses now. Today they're on the race track, or they're runts of ponies for children to ride. Ralph and I worked in the breath of real horses — draughthorses of strength and even temper, and riding hacks of a decent size. There were drays and traps, waggonettes and sledges. As a girl I went to town on wet days in the gig, when my father couldn't work outside.

The Depression kept horses on, Ralph used to say. Most of us couldn't afford tractors for years and kept the horses going through the thirties. A working horse sweats a lather like sea foam, and at the large concrete troughs, big almost as country swimming pools, they'd stand to drink, and you could hear the water rattling by the gallon down their throats. And after winter work the steam would drift from their great bodies as if they were gradually smouldering away.

Andrew passes the time by gently ragging his older brother. 'When technology fails, you could corner the market in horse transport. You should start secretly now, breeding Clydesdales, and make a killing when the world is desperate. There'd be jobs for all of us too. Nigel as a pooper scooper, for example. A sort of human dung beetle.'

'Keep it in the family, you mean,' says Nigel. He smiles, but continues to watch the houses thinning into the flat farms and orchards south of Christchurch.

It's strange that the ordinary circumstances of your life become novelties with the passing of time. We used to go on school picnics to the top crossing in a wagon. People were admired for skills that aren't known or understood today. Ralph was thought to be the best stacker in the district. He used to go all over the place, from farm to farm in the early days, stacking oats and wheat. Who knows anything of stacking oats before threshing now? Who cares for the skill of the ploughman, the smith, or the water diviner, like Wally Nind who found over forty good wells with a branch of willow.

There was nothing glamorous about it all, God knows, but there were skills that gave livings and personal satisfaction then, that are nothing today. Time gives things a sense of quaintness, and the quaintness disguises the same serious business of living that's always there, so that even your own children are cut off from your early life. In the end you find yourself part of your grandchildren's projects on women in the Great Depression, or the aftermath of the First World War.

They pass Burnham, and Andrew and Donald swap anecdotes of the National Service as eighteen-year-olds. The barracks and the AWOL trips to the city: the regular instructors and the platoon hard cases. They weren't there together, but the experience seems much the same.

Before that there'd been a real war, of course. My young brother, Clem, died at Maleme airfield in Crete, May 1941. Ralph and I had a radio in our bedroom. It had a varnished case almost as big as a grandfather clock. We were tired in the evenings after the farm, but sometimes we would listen for a while, particularly during the war, for news of how things were going.

Ralph would fall asleep before me, especially in the winter. In the winter too, we often lit the fire in the bedroom. The fire would die down during the night. I remember waking up now and then late at night, because there was a sudden last flame behind the guard which lit up the room with flickering patterns, so that the wardrobe would bob, and the varnished radio case and tongue and groove ceiling would glimmer. The last brief flame would soon be exhausted and the dark return, and I'd lie in the warm room waiting for sleep again. There would be the call of a morepork perhaps, or the wind in the woolshed pines like an ocean close at hand, or the rattle of the chains as the dogs slunk in and out of their kennels.

I used to wonder what other people were doing all over the world. I felt for people who were up against it in some way: up against war, or famine, pain, or loneliness, up against sly old age itself.

They're coming to Dunsandel on the plain, and Donald decides he may as well fill up there. He reminds the others that it's the place

Ken Avery wrote the song about, and sings a line or two — 'By the dog dosing strip at Dunsandel . . .' Andrew joins in. 'A dead and alive place really,' says Donald afterwards. 'I remember coming potato picking here one May school holidays, and Dad thought I should have been helping at our place.'

'That's a while now, Donald,' says Ruth.

'Nineteen forty-nine it would be. One of the guys had beer hidden in the water tank, and when he climbed up to get it he gashed his hand, and had to be taken to hospital. Old man Keen told us he'd get lockjaw.'

'Did he?'

'He may have for all I remember. Old man Keen said, "He's a goner, lads, with lockjaw and he's brought it on himself, you see."' Donald pulls up at the pumps, and leaves his story to get out and talk with the pump attendant.

Andrew asks Nigel what job he wants now that he's leaving school, but Nigel is uncommunicative as usual. Andrew looks out at Dunsandel and wonders what makes Nigel tick. His own adolescence is so far behind him. I guess Nigel still thinks there's some special life in store: opportunities to make the changes he dreams of, but won't talk about. He's about to join the dole queue, but won't be doleful either way. Youth is never completely daunted by circumstance.

Keep moving, Nigel. That's the secret. Keep moving. Too many weighty considerations and you're through the thin crust of things and into quicksand beneath. All those supposed meanings, motives, spiritual assessments and the paralysing self-consciousness that nails you down. Keep moving, that's the story. Keep bobbing and weaving, and don't ask for any reason with your rhyme. Keep moving and talking inside: fast talking, sweet talking, soft talking, smooth talking, tall talking. Keep moving, talking, so that the reflex hit men at all the doorways of life don't grow bored and tighten their trigger fingers in their boredom.

Nigel begins to sing what he's picked up of the Dunsandel song, and Andrew joins in more confidently. 'Stop it. They'll hear you,' says Ruth, but she laughs anyway.

'Shut up,' says Donald from outside. 'A couple of bloody humourists,' he tells the attendant. So Andrew returns to his thoughts.

You need to be a humourist here in Dunsandel on the plain. I can't see anyone with lockjaw despite Donald's story. There's no railway station any more; just the compacted gravel and weeds of the yard, just the ramp facing the line. The tracks are rusted on the sides, yet worn shiny on the top despite so few trains passing.

Two garages and the yellow, roughcast tearooms. There's an antique shop, and a thin grey spire of the country church sticks up for its beliefs above the Honda sign, but proves, as it comes closer, to have been taken over for antiques as well. For a young country we are stuffed with antiques.

I look out at Dunsandel, but I'm thinking of Wolverhampton, and the rooms I shared with two art teachers. From my top-storey window I could see the canal's trapped water with its blowfly blue on the oily surface, and an unofficial cycle track among the rubbish on its banks. A quiet Canadian girl and I made love by the window of that view on a wet Monday. I think the dingy threat of the visible world urged us to make a show of defiance: to mimic creation in all that expanse of decay. Lying with her, and just a few post-impressionists, for company, I looked out and saw the rain on the blue-bottle water of the canal and streaking the fences, and the cartons thrown away. She talked of winter in Alberta Province, and I talked of summer in the Mackenzie Country. The two of us drawn close in disillusion with Old England — and camouflaging it as love.

There are Wolverhamptons everywhere, of course. You need to be strong in the Wolverhamptons of Taihape, Gore, Cannons Creek or Remuera, because they're hard on ideals and pretence. You have to pack in all your own spiritual supplies to such places, and not rely on any renewal while you're there.

Ruth is saying that they should take me out to the farm tomorrow, as part of my birthday. Other people own it now, but she thinks they won't mind a visit. I'm quite pleased it won't happen. Other people muck your place around, no matter how pleasant they are. 'If she's well enough,' says Donald. 'You haven't seen her for ages and don't know how frail she's got. You'll find Mum's gone back a lot.'

Of course I've gone back. Who wants to spend their time as a ninety-year-old widow? I've gone back in ways Donald wouldn't dream of. Now I'm free to go back altogether. I don't need any permission now, or any help.

Recently I've never talked much about the past. It's tiresome when you have to keep explaining things that everybody used to know. Like tin-kettling and first-footing. In our district we went first-footing after midnight on New Year's Eve: farm by farm and some of the men getting the worse for drink as it went on. At Tolliger's once before the war, the men shifted the outdoor loo into the vegetable garden. Ray Tolliger lost his rag and threatened to push one of them down the exposed long drop. At least two of those men were killed overseas not long afterwards: killed in places where first-footing in the small hours had greater dangers even than Tolliger's long drop.

Our fun was local and inexpensive. Card evenings, tin-kettling, woolshed dances, A and P shows, weddings and send-offs, were the big things. Ruth talks of progressive dinners, ethnic restaurants, barbecues. I've never been to a barbecue in my life. I waited too long to have a decent kitchen around me, to want to go outside and cook without it.

I worked hard in country schools before I was married, and we slogged on the farm afterwards. Every fine Monday morning for years I lit the copper at six o'clock to heat the water for wash day. The electricity came to the district in time, of course, and I had a washing machine afterwards. Years later Ruth said she'd like the old copper bowl for her plants, and not long before he died, Ralph broke down the concrete casing and took out the copper, and patiently scoured it clean for her. She had a wrought-iron stand made for it, to display her indoor plants. When I visited her in Wellington I sat and looked at that gleaming copper full of dark foliage in her lounge, and I thought of the hundreds of Mondays on the farm I'd stood in the lean-to and stirred clothes in that copper with a broom handle. There it was, after all that time, among Ruth's polished furniture and crystal. I admired the burnished curve of the copper in its stand, and the fronds she cleaned with milk which hung over the sides in green contrast. What's all that in the process of time passing, I wonder?

'I'd forgotten coming down the Showground hill into Timaru like this,' says Ruth. 'I've always had a soft spot for Timaru. Let's have our lunch on Caroline Bay and see what changes there's been.' She sees it all as Donald drives on down and parks by a wooden table on the grass. Recognition mixed with small shocks of change, arouse her recollections.

A lot's still the same. The phoenix palms on the median strip — pineapples we used to call them. The way Donald and Andrew sit waiting while I set out lunch is the same too. The same as Dad used to wait for Mum to provide his food.

The Benvenue Cliffs are still hung with ice-plant and its glassy flowers. There used to be sand dunes between the lawn and the sea, and unpainted, wooden changing sheds. There used to be lupins, marram grass, gorse even, ridges in the dunes and hollows where sunbathers and lovers lay. And in the carnival afternoons there were acts in the sound shell. You sat high on the concrete steps built in the cliff while some local boy sang, 'How much is that doggie in the window'.

'We used to come here often in the long holidays,' she tells Nigel, but it's Donald who answers.

'People don't come the same now. They head inland more, to the lakes.'

'Well, there's no surf here,' says Andrew. 'You need a beach with a good surf, or lakes for water-skiing to get young people today.'

'Young people today!' Donald says. He improves his posture to address a topic that provokes him. 'I'm sick of hearing about young people today, as if they've grown another head. Listen, young people today are the same as young people yesterday, except they've been allowed to get away with too much. After a boot up the jacksie young people today behave a good deal more like the rest of us.'

'Perhaps it would work in reverse,' said Nigel, mumbling, his head turned away to watch the swimmers. 'A boot up the jacksie to make everyone more like young people. A neat experiment, eh.'

'What's that?' says Donald, but Nigel's said all he wants to, and gets up and wanders off over the sand.

'Don't go far,' his mother calls. She starts to tidy up and remembers being on the bay as a girl. We had our last family holiday in Timaru when I was seventeen: Nigel's age now, but I was so much older surely. Girls are, though. For New Year's Eve I wore a full-patterned cotton skirt with a stiff petticoat — they were all in then — and stockings, not pantyhose. And clip-on earrings. I'd met Selwyn Holdaway who had an ivy league shirt which looked great. He used to fold the sleeves up to his elbows, and his brown skin, the muscles moving, the silver watch strap on his wrist, made me think of sex.

You can trust your body at seventeen. The back of your neck isn't wrinkled, your legs don't have swollen veins, and your togs don't ride up over a second crease in your bum. My friend Barbara and I used to wear togs under our dresses to walk down from the motel, and we'd stand in the warm, white-grey sand to undress.

Selwyn Holdaway could talk — he was a great talker. He was fun to be with, and if his legs were slightly bandy it didn't matter because they were brown, muscular legs. He was deputy head boy, or proxime accessit I think, one or the other, and he was going to Canterbury to be a lawyer he told me. On New Year's Eve at the top of the Benvenue Cliffs we stood with a soft bush between us and Barbara and her boy, for privacy. There were still people swimming as the New Year came in, some couples on the anchored raft, the ships' hooters, and a lot of noise from the other side of the bush as Barbara got shirty with her boy.

Between kisses Selwyn talked of going to Canterbury. We agreed to write to each other. He sent me one letter early that year, after he'd started varsity, and I wrote back, but that's all I heard. I blamed still being a schoolgirl. I remember that in his letter he said he'd found great freedom in being away from his family.

If the others weren't here I could walk up the track on the cliffs and look out over the bay again, though it was dark then, of course, that New Year night, and Selwyn Holdaway told me how he was going to write to me about all the things that happened afterwards. He didn't, but all the things happened afterwards just the same.

Nigel has taken off his shirt: his shoulders are red with acne but he doesn't care. Ruth should have him using some of that antiseptic soap, and no chocolate. It's been a long time since Ruth and the boys have been on Caroline Bay, and Andrew is wondering where the years have gone. 'I still feel the same as these young people around us,' he says. 'I could stand up and join in, receive the same quick glances from the girls, but then I see my old, white feet on the sand, or pass my hand over my head and find I've grown bald. "I grow old, I grow old, I shall wear the bottoms of my trousers rolled."'

'You're old, but you never act your age,' says Donald. 'Never had to work hard enough, that's what.'

'Don't start with the bullshit, Donald.'

'Oh, come on you two,' says Ruth.

There they are with the glitter of the sea behind them and the noise of the summer beach around them. The four of them in bright sunshine, which is only a memory of warmth for me now. They wouldn't find it flattering, but they're precious to me because they carry something of Ralph with them as much as for what they are themselves. Donald walks like his dad, and his large, oval thumbs with white moons on the nails are just the same. His shoulders are adopting the same slump of habitual labour. Andrew and Ruth have

Ralph's eyes: the blue irises oddly small so that a full circle of white can often be seen. But Ruth has my skin. The women in my family had wonderful skin.

I look at the four here, and see other characteristics from both sides of the family. A bit of my Uncle Lee in the way Nigel's hair sticks up from the crown, and the thin McCallum lips as Andrew smiles. As my children and grandson walk on the beach I see others, more distant, come forward for an instant through a look, or gesture, signal, then fade away. I've a feeling that the outlines of Donald, Andrew, Ruth and Nigel aren't completely set. There's a jostling aura behind them of generations who want some recognition. And now I've joined them.

The four have a last walk on the sand before they leave, and Andrew and Nigel break into a brief race that only accentuates Andrew's loss of powers. 'Silly buggers,' says Donald amiably.

'Can I drive now?' asks Nigel, as if his winning sprint has made him more competent for the task.

'Oh God,' says Andrew, 'and I'd hoped for just a few years more.'

'Maybe later.' Even Ruth shows no support.

'Maybe on the way back, when you're familiar with the road,' says Donald.

'I could get a bus back, I suppose,' says Andrew.

And so they pile in and drive back to the main road past the phoenix palms again, and close to the cliff track where Ruth stood on a New Year's Eve with Selwyn Holdaway. Donald lectures the others on the regional downturn. 'Listen,' he says, 'I don't know if you realise it, but local government reorganisation and ongoing centralisation will drastically affect places like Timaru. It's make or break for heartland New Zealand over the next few years. Mark my words.'

'Nigel, mark your uncle's words,' says Andrew. 'About three out of ten will do.'

'He really gets into all that stuff, doesn't he.'

The mumble stirs Donald to justify himself. 'Now look, look, you should realise what's important in the long run, and it's not sport, or art, or saving whales, or getting in touch with your individual consciousness, but economics, which means resources, and politics, which means who controls resources. People who think that's boring and can't be bothered with it are handing over their lives to others.' That's Donald's way: as the eldest he's always taken on a role that is practical and responsible. He talks a sort of layman's politics and economics based on newspapers and current affairs programmes, and he picks out those things that agree with his own experience. Things are always cut and dried for him: sometimes he seems cut and dried himself. His thoughts are full of firm, undoubted principles.

I wish they'd have more common sense. Listen, I'd say, there are too many people who want to talk for a living, and not enough prepared to roll up their sleeves and work. Too many people spend their time discussing gender roles, creative dance, post-natal depression and macramé — and then expect someone else to fill their bellies. They scoff at the routines of work, at those who get up each morning, smother their temperament and give a fair day's work for a fair day's pay. Winter and summer, wet or fine, time of the month or change of life, feeling up or feeling down, it's important just to get on with it. Nowadays there are too many people riding on the back of the solid middle class. It's routines and routine people that matter in the end, get things done, not the media ponces, investment counsellors, would-be pianists, solo mums, Maori and lesbian activists. Andrew never understands that.

It's us who carry the can, and get nothing but sneering derision for being fool enough to do it. My old CSM told me that there are two ways in the army: the easy way and the hard way. The easy way isn't easy and the hard way's bloody hard, he said. It's like that for a practical man in New Zealand now, I reckon. The easy way isn't easy and the hard way's bloody hard.

The road south of Timaru is never far from the sea, along the edge of the downs. Ruth and Andrew talk to bring their lives up to date: they've not seen much of each other for years. Nigel sprawls in adolescent languor, a captive in the presence and purposes of his elders.

Glenavy, where the Waitaki is bridged, prompts Andrew to tell Nigel another family story. 'Your Uncle Donald fell in love with a girl here years ago. She had such magnificent knockers that she found it difficult to remain upright. Well, that was one reason.'

'I can see that we're going to have another session of your damn imagination,' says Donald. He's resigned to it.

'Donald told Dad that he was needed on the other farm to help with heading, but he came over here and took Amelia up the valley for the afternoon. Wild oats rather than heading, eh.'

'Yeah?' Nigel begins to show an interest.

'The next day Dad found her bra under the rug in the back seat. I can see him now, bringing it in at morning tea, and Donald's face.'

'It's an old family story,' says Ruth, but laughs all the same.

'You know we'd been swimming and sunbathing, that's all,' says Donald, 'and she kept her togs on to go home. You know that.'

'We know what you told Mum and Dad. Your brain was quicker in those days, among other things.'

'Dad didn't say much, but he seemed impressed by the size of the bra,' says Ruth. She, too, has always played a part in ribbing Donald.

'She was a sizable heifer, certainly, was Amelia,' admits Donald.

Beneath his denial, as always with this story, is a certain embarrassed pride which the others play on. I remember how his father enjoyed the story too; how each of the children starred in their own family anecdotes, as much a part of the family record as the photographs and the collections of small trophies from schools and clubs. Ralph and I would often go over the stories when the children had all gone: a small way to keep them in our lives.

The closer they come to Oamaru the more Andrew is in the grip of the old life, the more what he sees is populated by the past.

We never do completely outgrow our country. Education and travel only make our memories of home more powerful. Not the helicopter views of mountains and waterfalls, but the plain quiet shingle of the Waitaki, say, with the shot of rabbit droppings in the scrapes, or the sight of rugby posts above the fog in winter parks. The corner dairies with the papers piled on the counter, a stainless steel pie-warmer, and a Coca-Cola ad a glossy world away. Uniformed kids on the way home: the greys, blues and greens, the Latin blazer mottos that neither Pakeha nor Maori can understand. Easy country roads through hills contoured with sheep tracks. The long summer beaches with a fragrant breeze coming in and few people to breathe it. The twitch ever creeping out from the fences in to the dry, suburban gardens.

Above all, the committees that meet in community halls and schoolrooms, conference centres and modest boardrooms, vestry rooms, lodges, club lounges and pavilions, civic chambers and staff quarters. The Rabbit Boards, Neighbourhood Watch, Red Cross, Squash Rackets and Indoor Bowls Clubs, PTA and Friends of the School, Women's Auxiliary, RSA, Jaycees, Katherine Mansfield or J.K. Baxter discussion groups, Cactus and Succulent Society, Progressive League, Rape Counselling Centre, Acclimatisation Board, Rotary, Playcentre Management Committee, Guild of Main Street Business-men, VSA Steering Committee, Federated Farmers, Toastmistresses, Masons, Working Men's Club, Friends of the Takahe, Compost Society, Small Bore Rifle Club, Colenso Textile Brass Band, Civil Defence volunteers, Forest and Bird Society, Trampoline and Gymnastics Promotion League, Avalon Marching Club, Repertory Society, Girl Guides' Management Seminar, Embroiderers' and Potters' Fellowship, Alzheimer's and Korsakov's Psychosis Support Group, the committee to organise the Ransumeen family reunion.

All that mister and madam chair, and rising to a point of order, and taking the right of reply, and wishing opposition or abstention to be recorded in the minutes.

Who said we are a taciturn people?

All those hobby-horses ridden assiduously in a hundred rooms and halls of nodding boredom, while outside beneath a leering moon a stray dog savages the sheep in the domain, or glue sniffers twitch in the doorways of the main street.

And they drive on, coming closer to Oamaru. They talk mainly of their own lives, sometimes their conversation is of the places they pass, sometimes of me. Nigel remembers that as a small boy he was promised one of his grandfather's guns, and Donald acknowledges the debt and says there's a good Hollis that would suit him down to the ground. Andrew wonders if Ruth and I will be closer than he ever manages with me. 'Maybe Mum opens up more to you, Ruth, because you're a woman.'

'It isn't any easier,' she says. 'Why should it be easier? Mum was never able to talk to me about being a woman. She was just more afraid for me, and her fear made her angry at times and stopped us becoming close. Being mother and daughter isn't any guarantee of understanding you know.'

She's right. I wanted more for her than I had myself, even though I had everything that mattered. Too much emotion, hope and love is an embarrassment. True feeling for all the family became overlaid with minor irritations and trivial preoccupations — mine and theirs — so that when I should have been grateful for Donald's occasional trips from Christchurch, instead as he talked I was thinking it was time for my television programme, or noticing the dirt from his shoes on the rug.

I should have forgotten sometimes that I'm their mother: put it aside and just talked to them as a person without special responsibility. I should have risked more, but you become more and more aware of the gap between what you feel, and what you can hope to express.

They're nearly home. Cape Wanbrow can be seen above the town, and the downland is pressing towards the sea. The plains are over and cabbage tree country begins.

There'll be no birthday party for me here after all. Let's leave them now before their disappointment, their grief, or their relief. I've recovered all my life now. Still, they're coming to see me — that might still be true. They may come to see me more truly now than they ever have before.

Mr Tansley

Small-scale heroes are enough when you're a kid. Sometimes just conspicuous possession could do it — the man who drove a Ford V8 CustomLine; sometimes just conspicuous loss — the man who lost an arm in a combine harvester. The fish and chip shop owner seemed to me the most fortunate and successful of businessmen. The government deer culler who regularly got sozzled at the Gladstone pub surely had a life of greater excitement than the rest of us.

Mr Tansley was the caretaker at the gasworks, that collection of dark, smudged buildings with storage domes that could rise and fall like cakes in a fitful oven. He rode a black Raleigh bike. When he went to work he wrapped his lunch tin in the jacket of an old pinstripe suit, so the wire spring of the carrier would grip it safely. He took cold tea in a corked beer bottle, which he dangled at the handlebar in a grey woollen sock as he cycled. He pedalled carefully, intent on the road, as if his lunch box, or bottle of cold tea, was at risk. It was no use calling out to him when he rode past on the old Raleigh, because he wouldn't respond, always intent on the road and his slow, persistent pedalling.

He lived in an army hut behind the Loan and Mercantile building, and close to the river. He had a wooden kitchen table with turned legs outside the door of the hut, and there every morning he had his wash and shave. At head height above the table he'd banged a fair-sized nail into the hut wall, and each morning he brought out a metal-framed mirror and hung it up. Also an enamel basin, a green towel, an army mess tin with his shaving gear, and so he'd set up there because there wasn't enough light in the hut, I suppose. The first thing, though, that came out of the hut's security, was his Raleigh bike, and he would press his thumb into the tyres as a test, and always lean the bike in the same way, on the same corner of the shed. I knew the inside of Tansley's shed, and always wondered how he fitted the bike in there last thing at night.

From my bedroom window I could see him most mornings with just a singlet above the waist and his braces hanging beside his trouser legs. In the frost, or drizzle, things were done quick time, but on a fine morning his wash and shave became almost an indulgent ritual, and I sometimes went down before breakfast to join him. He used a cut-throat, and would lift his chin high to tighten the skin of his neck, then slide that long, narrow blade down, and wash the soap and stubble from it in the water of the enamel bowl. The handle, with its split for the blade to fold into, was of ivory yellowed with age and use, and smooth as a horse bit.

'To be clean shaven is a sign of self-respect,' he said once. 'And a man with no self-respect hasn't any respect for others.'

Tansley had been awarded a medal in the desert, fighting against the Desert Fox, my father said. He'd reached the rank of sergeant, but then lost his stripes because he disobeyed an order. My father said that Norman Beal, who was the manager of the Loan and Mercantile Agency and had been an officer in 23 Battalion, maintained that Tansley was morally right, but they broke him to private all the same.

Tansley must have been an older soldier than most, because even allowing for the view of childhood he was surely nearly seventy when he lived in the army hut twenty years after the war. He was a big man, pale despite service in the desert. The muscles of his chest and arms had begun to loosen. The hair on his large chest was grey, and darker hair grew over his shoulders and down his back. Because he spent so much time in his own company, he carried on a sort of conversation with himself at times in a quite unself-conscious way. 'Reckon so,' he'd say. 'I don't doubt there'll be rain before the day's out', and he'd fling the used water from the basin into the river, and stand and look at the sky to find intention there.

On summer evenings he'd sit on the wooden step of his hut and read the afternoon paper — even that's a thing of the past now. 'I see old Joey Wadsworth's dead,' he'd say, or 'Look how they advertise these Jap cars, by Jesus, bold as you like.' You might expect me to say that he and I formed a special bond, that he passed on some principled wisdom to me, and I provided company that mitigated his loneliness, but there was nothing like that. He talked to himself exactly the same whether I was sitting with him or not. From my bedroom window sometimes I could see his lips move. He didn't dislike me; he never told me not to come around; we shared bread and strawberry jam: he just didn't recognise children as the same species as himself.

He had a chrome cigarette-making machine, not much bigger than a tobacco tin, and I often got a glimpse of the simple mechanism when he made one up — rollers and a strip of dark canvas. We're quicksilver as kids, and to me all his actions seemed slow and clumsy. I wondered if his movements had been more adept in the desert when he won his medal. He put a half-choke grip on the loaf to laboriously cut himself a slice, and to do up the buttons of his fly after a piss on the bank was a business of lengthy concentration. The Loan and Mercantile let him use the lavatory at the back of the building, but for just a piss he didn't bother to walk those few yards.

Many afternoons after work he'd walk down Seddon Street and across the bridge to the RSA. He'd have a drink there because I could smell it on him afterwards, but he never came home drunk. It was the company he wanted mainly, I suppose, though he always left his mates behind and came back to the hut alone. There was another man in the town who'd won a medal, but I never saw them together, which surprised me, because I imagined that they would have a lot in common. Mr Lineen the dentist was the other man with a medal, and his left forearm had been hit by mortar fragments, my father said. In summer when he rolled his sleeves up you could see how pitted and thin that arm was.

My father once suggested to Mr Tansley that he apply for a state house. 'This hut here will see me out,' Tansley said, and I heard him say much the same another time about his bike. He was getting ready to go to work at the gasworks, putting the lunch box on the carrier, slipping the cold tea bottle into the grey work sock. He lifted the Raleigh by the centre of the handlebars and spun the front wheel to check for any wobble. 'She'll see me out okay,' he said admiringly.

The bike did see him out, and it wasn't even a close thing, because Tansley was hit by a truck one winter evening when he was biking home in the half dark from his job at the gasworks. He was one day in hospital and then he died. My father said he talked about nothing but locomotives before he died. It seems that as a young man he worked in the railway workshops.

Because my father was both a neighbour and a returned soldier, and Tansley didn't have any family as far as anybody knew, he helped clear out the shed and was a pallbearer. There wasn't any money to speak of in the shed, and no record of a bank account. Someone at the RSA said Tansley used to send all his money in postal notes to Italy, but there are always those stories, aren't there? And how much money do you make as gasworks caretaker anyway?

The town and the RSA didn't care about Tansley's trade, or his lack of savings. The community hadn't forgotten Mr Tansley had won a medal in its service, and so his death deserved to be marked with respect. There were plenty of contributions to do the right thing by him, and the long piece in the paper gave him the rank of sergeant, made no mention of the court martial, and published the citation in full for his military medal. He'd rushed a machine-gun post after its fire had killed two of his mates.

At the funeral Norman Beal of the Loan and Mercantile spoke, and Mr Lineen the dentist who had the other medal in town — the military cross, which was the officers' version of Mr Tansley's medal, my father said. There was a bugler, and it took place in the special RSA part of the cemetery. It all seemed a long way from the old man in a singlet and hanging braces shaving himself outside his shed with a cut-throat razor, or pissing into the river as he debated the day's weather with himself, or setting off on the Raleigh with his lunch box on the carrier and a bottle of cold tea in a sock.

Wake Up Call

Hector Jansen came regularly to Singapore on business. He had his own familiar track through it, but all else remained totally foreign. He knew Changi airport well, how to get to the taxis quickly, how to use Andrew Shih's bank for a decent rate of exchange. He knew several downtown hotels close to the Soong Corporation building. He knew the zoo and Sentosa Island for snatches of relative privacy and the feel of grass beneath his feet rather than concrete. He knew a couple of escort agencies recommended by Andrew Shih. If he kept to his track in the city he seemed quite adept there, but he realised how superficial and restricted his experience was, and that the only thing of significance he had gained over all his visits was some personal credibility with Andrew Shih, and Mr Liang and Mr Yuan-jen at Soong.

On several of his recent visits, Jansen had taken Mervyn Linkiss with him. Jansen had suggested it, and the CEO had wholeheartedly agreed. 'We need you there, though,' said Tony Alexadis. 'I never feel happy about things at that end unless you're on the spot, Hector. You've got the touch with those people.' But they needed to groom someone up for the Singapore side of things. Businessmen there don't like abrupt changes of contact, don't respond well to a strange face over a contract. And Mervyn Linkiss was personable, intelligent and someone Jansen wanted to do well in the corporation.

On the latest trip to Singapore, Jansen felt unwell on the night of their arrival. All his life his health had been good. A passing sickness is soon forgotten, anything that doesn't come to a threatening conclusion, although at the time it worries you. A decade ago Jansen had had evening chest pains over several weeks, which his GP couldn't account for, so Jansen picked up pamphlets on angina and heart irregularities, the cardio-vascular benefits of exercise, and indigestion. But then while he was very busy organising middle management professional development, the pains didn't come any more, and later he hardly remembered why the pamphlets were in his drawer. Even earlier there had been the loud ringing and sharp, spasmodic pain in his left ear while he was holidaying in the Hokianga, so that for several days he didn't go swimming, and rang up a doctor in Whangarei for an appointment. The noises and discomfort stopped suddenly in the night, the appointment was cancelled and recently he had filled in a medical insurance form saying in all sincerity that he'd never had any trouble with his hearing. On his standing CV he described his health as excellent.

The Singapore pain was different, though: it was very central, deep-seated, located somewhere level with the lower ribs, and seeming to need some physical space of its own, so that existing organs there were displaced. When Jansen first woke he thought it was some nausea caused by the heat, but the first movement made him give a sudden cry of distress. Sweat pooled in the hollows beneath his eyes as he lay and wondered what was wrong. He was panting, and gave a small aah with each quick exhalation, which seemed somehow a comfort. With his left hand he reached cautiously, searching for the light switch in the unfamiliar room, then he forgot that in his concentration on his pain. There was enough light from the street anyway, even though the room was several storeys up. It was very early, but already there was traffic noise, particularly the waspish whine of scooters, which for Jansen was always the sound of Asian cities. The hotel was an older one, though still favoured, and the furniture was of massive hardwood. Elephants, surely, must have been needed to move the logs from which such timber originally came.

Jansen straightened himself gently in the large bed, pushed out his legs, so that his stomach had as little constriction as possible, but if anything it made it worse. He remembered the twinges he'd had on the long flight the day before: the sense of his guts being compressed by all that sitting, despite the advantages of business class. The pain flowed and ebbed. It was an acidic pain if such a thing existed. Jansen remembered Mervyn's room number. He had that sort of mind — could still remember the seat numbers of their Singapore flights, and the names of the perfumes he was to buy for his wife, and the exchange rate of the New Zealand dollar against the Euro, the greenback and four Asian currencies.

'Yes?' said Mervyn, his voice husky with sleep.

'It's Hector. I'm sorry to bother you, but I'm feeling really crook. I've just woken up with it and it's giving me absolute gyppo in the guts.'

'I'll come right away. Is your door unlocked?'

'I'll do it now,' said Jansen.

'Okay.'

'Mervyn.'

'Yes.'

'What time is it?'

'Half past five,' said Mervyn.

'Jeez, I'm sorry,' said Jansen.

He found crawling the least painful form of progress, and pulled a face and hissed as he reached up to unsnib the door. He was on all fours back by the bed, gathering strength to climb in, when Mervyn came and helped him. The thin sheet Jansen pulled over himself was unnecessary in the heat, but even with such pain he wanted the decorum of a covering for his grey-haired chest and pale shin bones. He could feel the sweat of sickness and anxiety trickle through the hair above his ears: each pulsebeat flared an aurora around the light source windows.

'Hell,' said Mervyn. 'We're not mucking around here at all. I'm calling the desk for an ambulance.' Jansen gave a tight nod. He didn't say anything because he was afraid of what might come out if he tried. He concentrated on keeping the pain from taking over altogether. The last thing he remembered was his colleague talking forcefully on the telephone, and at the same time patting down his spiky hair with his free hand. Mervyn was a good guy to cope with an emergency. He did have very peculiar hair in the night, though. 'Mr Hector Jansen, Room 453,' said Mervyn. 'Right away. As soon as possible. Whatever emergency procedure you have here. You understand?' He spoke loudly and very distinctly to ensure his English was presented in the most accessible way.

The pain in Jansen's belly was overwhelming.

They'd taken him to a Roman Catholic private hospital close to the harbour. He had his own room with recessed ceiling lights and cream walls. High on the door was a clean, square window through which staff, or visitors, could look in from the corridor. He recognised his suitcase in a corner. Mervyn sat on the only chair in the room. 'Okay, Hector?' he said. Jansen waited a bit to assure himself the pain was much less, and then nodded slightly. Even that movement was enough to make him aware he had a tube up his nose. Mervyn drew his chair closer: it hadn't been seemly somehow to be peering into Jansen's face when he was unconscious. 'You had an emergency operation for something that burst in your stomach,' said Mervyn. Jansen thought of a reply, opened his mouth, but couldn't find the strength to speak. 'I've told the Soong people we'll get back to them tomorrow,' said Mervyn.

Jansen talked to his wife by telephone when he was awake again four hours later. She had been speaking to the doctors and knew a lot more about his condition than he did himself. 'I haven't seen anyone at all,' he said. 'Just Mervyn and flowers sent from Mr Yuan-jen.'

'The doctors have been there, but you've been out to it. They say you'll be fine now, unless there's infection from material that's escaped into your abdominal cavities, but you'll have to stay there several days before you can fly home. I can get tickets to fly over tomorrow, or the day after.'

'No,' he said. 'Thanks, but if everything's okay it doesn't make much sense. You'd just get here and then have to turn round again.'

His wife went on to reassure him that their adult children were fine. It didn't seem inconsiderate to him at all. It had been their way ever since becoming parents. Whatever happened in their own lives was immediately evaluated in terms of its impact on the children. Would his acceptance of promotion disrupt their schooling, or enable them eventually to attend university without taking student loans, or both? Would his wife's absence at the week-long on-campus fine arts course prove a trauma too much for them to bear? And now that both Greg and Samantha were quite grown up, and insistent on their parents pleasing themselves at last, it was too late to alter the focus of their lives. 'Sam wanted to come over and stay with me until you got back,' his wife said, 'but I wasn't having her driving by herself all that way while she's pregnant.'

'No. Quite right,' Jansen said.

'I don't want her to worry in her condition.'

'Quite right,' said Jansen.

'They're both waiting to ring now you're awake more,' his wife said.

Tony Alexadis rang too, saying Jansen was to forget all about business, that the firm was happy to pay for his wife to fly over. He said to pull the plug on the Soong talks for now. They could tee them up again later in the year. Jansen didn't agree. He was sitting up, supported by pillows, and the pain was reduced to a level that allowed him to think about other things if he concentrated. 'Mervyn can handle it with help from Andrew Shih at the table, and me briefing him in the evenings,' he said. 'And Mervyn's been up here several times now, remember. He knows the Soong team, and if we don't get something rolling now we're going to lose a whole year, maybe the project itself grows cold.' The CEO wanted the meeting to go ahead, but only with Jansen's agreement. It was a ritual to show the regard between the two of them, and after a few minutes talk it was decided to carry on, and it had the appearance of being Jansen's decision, though both men knew what the business reality was.

When Andrew Shih came to the hospital, Jansen said the worst thing was being fed by fluids and that he wouldn't have anything near solid for at least another twenty-four hours. Andrew had some misgivings about continuing the talks without Jansen — remember the management faction in the overseas department of Soong working through Mr Hau tong, he said — but Jansen persuaded him that Mervyn was up to it, with their assistance. 'No one's indispensable, Andrew. You know that.'

'Soong like continuity of representation during a deal.'

'So the three of us are still here,' said Jansen. 'It's just that I'm not able to sit at the table.'

'You are able to continue to call the shots though,' said Andrew Shih, pleased with his command of the idiom.

'Tony Alexadis and the board will call the shots. You know that, but we can do a good job at this end.'

'I think you are right,' said Andrew. They had known each other for more than ten years, and done business together in Singapore for several weeks in each of those years. Andrew Shih specialised in assisting overseas firms, and was a model of confidentiality. Jansen knew that Andrew also represented Bridgeport of Australia, Randra and PSR, but never had Andrew said anything to him about the business dealings of those companies, or any others he acted for. Jansen had seen Andrew drunk, heard his best jokes repeatedly, seen him naked with a Thai girl after the '98 deal, but not once had Andrew divulged anything at all. Jansen liked that, and so did Tony Alexadis. 'The best lawyers know when to hold their tongues,' said the CEO.

When Andrew Shih had gone, Jansen rang Mr Yuan-jen at Soong and thanked him for the flowers. Also he apologised for being the cause of the delay in the talks, and said he and Tony Alexadis had full confidence in Mervyn. 'Yet we have become used to your voice on behalf of your board,' said Mr Yuan-jen solemnly.

'Thank you,' said Jansen.

'I know the Catholic hospital. My wife's father had his heart operation done there. All of the doctors are very good. Excellent in fact.'

'Thank you.'

'Yet we will miss your voice,' said Mr Yuan-jen.

Mervyn was excited when Jansen asked him to represent the company at the meetings. The excitement showed itself in the rigorous calm he imposed on himself: the slightly lower and more deliberate speech. It was the response that Jansen expected from his knowledge of his colleague, and it reassured him. He gave Mervyn his own briefing papers, thick with handwritten annotations. 'Perhaps you could spend a couple of hours looking through this,' he said, 'and then come back and we'll go over it. You know it'll all be positioning on the first day anyway. I'll try to sleep for a while, and you come back about eight tonight.'

'I'll put it together with my own notes,' said Mervyn.

'If you can read my writing,' said Jansen.

As he rested, aware of the minor dislocation of having no meal times to mark out his day, he tried to remember his own feelings when he had first taken charge of offshore negotiations for the company. It was unusual for him to search his memory for anything that wasn't strictly applicable to the business needs of the present, but he found the recollection quite clear. He had been sent to Hong Kong to sit in on the preliminary two days of supermarket access talks, with the aim of being able to brief the then CEO when he arrived later. Instead of arriving, the CEO had rung and told Jansen to carry on alone; that they had full confidence in him. Jansen had hardly slept for two days, working on agenda papers until five or six o'clock in the mornings.

It's what Mervyn would do after their talk. He'd go away and cover one hundred percent of everything just to make sure he had the five percent that would come up. That's how a good executive begins, and then with time comes the confidence and judgement which allow selective preparation and some sleep.

When Mervyn came down, he'd read all Jansen's notes, and he asked good questions and was attentive to Jansen's advice. 'Never hesitate to ask for some time to talk to Andrew Shih. Time by yourselves as an extension to lunch, for example. Andrew's so good on the close legal stuff, but also he's great at picking up on any change of tack. And watch Mr Hau tong: that's where any trouble will come from.'

'Maybe I should call in here on my way to Soong tomorrow,' said Mervyn.

'No, you'll be fine. Give me a call when it's all over, but have a cold beer and take off your tie first. And make sure Andrew doesn't send a girl to your room. He's a bugger for that.'

Jansen had a snooze after Mervyn left, and then met his doctors for the first time, including the surgeon who had cut into his stomach. Jansen had come to admire the intelligence and skill of the Chinese: he had no doubt he was in the best of hands. He decided to send the surgeon the company's prestige assorted pack of cheeses. He said how much he appreciated the air-conditioning in his room, and talked with the doctors a little about the amount of snowfall in New Zealand. The Chinese doctors of Singapore found the possibility of a white and frozen landscape interesting and exotic. 'Tomorrow,' said the surgeon, 'you will be able to take some mild food orally, but please don't eat anything visitors bring in without checking with staff. In particular, no fruit. Fruit is in composition bad for you at present.' When they left, the younger doctor looked back through the window in the door, and gave an informal wave and a smile, as if farewelling Jansen at an airport.

He slept less well that night than the one before, and guessed it was because he wasn't so doped up. Twice he eased himself out of the high bed to use the commode, which had a motor for height adjustment. The central heating wasn't calibrated with South Island Kiwis in mind, and even the coolest setting was barely doing the job. He lay on the cover and let his mind wander. It took him to personal things, rather than anything to do with business. The Soong talks seemed a long way from his concern, and instead he began to wonder where he and his wife should live when they retired. They hadn't talked much about it. Jansen thought that was because both sensed that it would prove a sticking point, and in their marriage they preferred to avoid serious disagreement. She enjoyed the opportunities offered by the city; he, although a city man all his life, had a yearning to end up in a small place, by the sea perhaps, or one of the southern lakes.

He knew that it was a notion unfounded on any experience of life in such a place, and not sensible in terms of proximity to the facilities they would increasingly rely on as they got older.

Yet, lying there almost naked in the private room of the Catholic hospital in Singapore, the idea was stronger in him than ever. He told himself that it was just a reaction to the business pressures over the years, this pipedream of a village life with both simplicity and solitude. Maybe even some explicable response to his stomach pain and the operation, which would pass. In the morning common sense would thrive again.

It was a novelty to use a spoon again at breakfast, and, despite the pap, the tastes were strong after being fed intravenously. Even the sensation of food passing down his gullet was briefly unusual. The nurse who brought his tray was youthful and very small. He had a fancy he could see light through her slim hands, and in her presence he felt clumsy and stolid.

Several times during the day he remembered the meeting going on at Soong: Mervyn Linkiss and Andrew Shih working so carefully to secure the right deal. He found it surprisingly easy to move on to other things, however, or just lie and think of nothing much at all. No doubt the pain, and then the operation and drugs, had broken his concentration on business. It occurred to Jansen that all over Singapore there were meetings that were crucial to those involved, but in truth had little significance. All the world was an ant-hill of industrious communication with decision piled on decision, and corporations waxing and waning like the Medes and the Persians.

Despite Jansen's advice, Mervyn came straight from the meeting. He had about him still the whiff of battlefield powder, and went through the happenings of the day with barely suppressed eagerness. He wanted Jansen's advice for the next day, and only just remembered at the end to ask about his health. 'Go back to the hotel and relax for a while. Take it easy,' said Jansen.

Andrew Shih rang soon afterwards to give a more succinct account. Mervyn did better than okay, he said. Tony Alexadis was also in touch. 'I'll give Mervyn a ring, of course,' he said, 'but I wanted to get your feel of things.'

'Andrew Shih says Mervyn's doing fine. And he's been at Soong meetings with me before, remember. I reckon he'll handle it well,' said Jansen.

'You've always been very supportive of him, Hector,' said the CEO. 'That reassures me a good deal.'

For his evening meal Jansen was given sweet fish rice and soft vegetables. The prospect attracted him, but part way through, his appetite left him, and he lay back, conscious of pain. The nurse said that he would probably have such discomfort for a few days, but that it was important that he have solid food passing through the digestive tract as soon as possible. She later changed the dressing on his stomach incision, sprinkling a white powder like icing sugar on the stitched wound.

'How's it looking?' Jansen said.

'Is excellent,' she said.

His room had a television on a swivel bracket, but he didn't turn

it on, although he knew there were English-speaking channels.
There was also a remote, which dimmed the light in the room, and
he used that until there was a soft, half darkness. Activity in the
corridor outside decreased as the night went on, and Jansen lay on
top of the bed with the air-conditioning at maximum coolness. The
pain in his stomach was somehow the pain of recovery, and not the
fearsome thing he'd experienced in the hotel room — was it two,
or three, days ago? He had not the slightest inclination to dwell on
the Soong talks, or Andrew Shih and Mervyn. Thoughts about his
boyhood, his time at university, his two and half years in Canada
were insistent and clear. It's having the scare with the operation and
everything, he told himself in the soft dimness. He'd heard others
talk about the effects of such a shock: the reassessment of your life.
That's what it was.

Until he'd gone to Canada he'd played a lot of badminton,
represented his province even, but he'd never picked it up again on
his return. His job had early begun to push other things from his
life. In his mind's eye he saw the shuttlecock in a perfect arch, and
his quick, athletic leap to meet it. He remembered a men's double
partner who used to bite his own arm to increase concentration, and
a mixed doubles one as expert in blasphemy as in the game, despite
her schoolgirl looks. He was listening to the whispering of the air-
conditioning and trying to remember her full name when Samantha
rang. She wasn't sure of the time over there, she said, and hoped she
hadn't woken him. Jansen was more interested in her health than his
own. 'Oh, Dad, stop worrying about me. I'm pregnant, not sick. I
wanted to go over to Mum's, but she says she's fine. Concentrate on
getting better yourself, for goodness sake. What's the latest from the
doc?' As he reassured his daughter, Jansen wanted to talk about her
as a child: the years when the four of them were the corners of the
family square, and almost everything was shared. He'd experienced
a measure of power and responsibility in business, but not with the
gratification of love that accompanied them in fatherhood. He just

avoided any sentimental mention of that by a switch to badminton, which seemed even to him somewhat random.

'I used to play badminton a lot, Sam. Did you know that?'

'I remember some of your racquets we used to play with as kids. They had very narrow metal shafts, didn't they?'

'That's them. It was my main sport before I went to Canada, and then for some reason I gave it away. Busy, I suppose.'

'Well, you won't be playing badminton for a while now. Are you okay? Are you sure you don't want Mum or Greg to fly over?'

'I'll be home in no time,' said Jansen.

'You're not being bothered with any business stuff while you're in hospital are you?'

'None at all.'

Jansen dozed for a while after his daughter's call and was woken by the slide of his cellphone from his relaxed hand onto his neck. He recognised his surroundings immediately; was not at all disorientated. Mervyn at the Sheraton would be still working almost for sure, but Jansen had no curiosity about that.

Other things had gained in importance since his illness. Sixty-four was an age at which it seemed some balance began to tip, triggered by the failure of his digestion. His father had been chief economist for a bank, but in retirement spent all his time and energy, and a good deal of money, in ridding offshore islands of rats so that native bird species would have a better chance. In old age he derided the profession in which he'd spent most of his life, and which had provided well for him. Economics is a dead language and smells of it, he told his son. And later, when he was diagnosed with Parkinson's disease, he reminded Jansen that old age rarely comes alone. Hector Jansen had loved his father, his mother too, and in thinking of them with a tenderness that surprised him, he drifted off to sleep in the darkened and private room of the Catholic hospital in Singapore.

His pain, if anything, was worse the next day, and both his doctors came back to look at him. His temperature was up a bit. The surgeon said that there was a moderate infection and that they'd go back to intravenous feeding and give him antibiotics. 'It's a dirty operation once the wall of the duodenum has been perforated,' he told Jansen. 'Infections are unfortunately quite a common consequence. You should monitor your own discomfort carefully, and we'll take another x-ray.'

'Will it keep me here any longer?' Jansen asked.

'In another twenty-four hours we'll know how things are,' the Chinese surgeon said. He was a very thin man, and the skin of his head followed the bone structure so closely that he had a slightly mummified appearance.

Andrew Shih rang at the end of the day to say that the second day of talks had gone well. He and Mervyn were on their way to informal drinks with Mr Yuan-jen of Soong. The invitation was a good sign. 'Mervyn did very well again,' said Andrew. 'You'd be proud of him. After lunch Mr Hau tong ambushed us with some in-house memos he'd got hold of, setting out retail margins, but Mervyn was hardly ruffled. He's very well prepared, and has a good rapport with Mr Liang too.'

'That's great, yeah,' said Jansen.

Andrew Shih put Mervyn on, and, during the conversation, Jansen could briefly hear Andrew telling the taxi driver the best way to Mr Yuan-jen's executive club. Jansen had been there several times himself, and remembered the long veranda festooned with wisteria, and the Second World War photographs behind the bar: the thin British general surrendering to the Japanese, and then later the Japanese officer in his turn handing his sword to the British and Americans.

'How are you, Hector?'

'A bit groggy today,' said Jansen.

'Maybe I won't bother you by coming in tonight, then,' said Mervyn. 'Let you get a good rest.'

'Andrew says the day went well. Good on you.'

'I think we're making sound progress. It's a constructive atmosphere, apart from Mr Hau tong, and Andrew's really on the button.'

'Maybe I should give Tony a ring,' said Jansen.

'Actually I've done that. I thought I'd better check in. He especially asked about you, wanted me to pass on his best wishes.'

The circle was closing without him: not with any deliberate exclusion, not with any particular intent, just the pressure of business and the need for the main players to be in direct touch. No one's indispensable. Commerce is a broad pond and the circles form and reform constantly on its surface. Jansen felt only a slightly cynical relief after the call. He hadn't felt up to talking business with Mervyn anyway. Isolated and ineffectual because of his illness, Jansen felt only a benign apathy concerning his career. For the first time he saw past his work to some equally worthwhile life beyond. Sixty-four's not old, not as such, he told himself. He traced with his fingers the perimeter of the dressing on his stomach; massaged gently to test the pain.

Jansen had a vomiting session in the afternoon, bringing up bile and a little blood. The lesser doctor took out the tubes and asked him to sip a thin, white liquid every ten minutes or so. 'This will give you a lining,' he said cheerfully. Jansen saw on the blue name tag that the doctor's name was Lowe. Without the eminent presence of the surgeon, Jansen was more aware of the individuality of the younger doctor. Dr Lowe was darker than most Chinese, and his face was pock-marked from the eyes down. He had an easy, natural smile that made his face attractive despite his complexion. His voice was deeper than most of his fellows: more European in timbre. 'A wash is a pleasant thing after the discomfort of vomiting,' he said. 'I'll arrange it immediately, and just ask if you want something for the pain.'

A male nurse gave Jansen the sponge bath, and recounted his backpacking experiences in Queensland and the Northern Territories. He said the sky was bigger there than in Singapore.

'Has the air-conditioner any cooler setting?' asked Jansen. The nurse looked at the dials carefully, and said it didn't.

Jansen slept for an hour and woke feeling no worse, but for the first time he had the thought that maybe he would die in Singapore: that the end of business for him would be the end of everything. He was angry with himself for not considering the possibility earlier, for not being more searching in his talks with the doctors. He rang the buzzer — he'd not used it before — and when a nurse came, said that he'd like to see Dr Lowe as soon as possible.

Dr Lowe came within fifteen minutes, and his smile was untroubled. He sipped from a white cardboard cup, and pulled the one chair closer to Jansen's bed. 'So,' he said, 'there is something?'

'I'm worse today than yesterday,' said Jansen.

'Yes, you have an infection as we said, and with that a slight fever. It happens quite frequently with acute admission cases such as your own. The abdominal cavity is difficult to cleanse of all intestinal material.'

'But I'll recover, right?' said Jansen.

The young doctor smiled so broadly there was a slight ripple in the dark, bristly hair above his ears. He leant forward, holding the cup loosely on his lap in both hands. 'Would you deal in absolutes in a Catholic hospital?' he said. 'We must remember our fallibility, but what we can say is that nothing in your condition since the operation changes the opinion that you should make a good recovery. Low level post-op infection is quite common in cases such as yours.'

'You'd say if there was real concern?' asked Jansen.

'Yes, absolutely,' replied Dr Lowe. 'You will go back to the snow of New Zealand certainly, I think. Maybe no skiing for a while, though.' He stood up and yawned, and shrugged his shoulders right up to his ears a few times to ease the muscle tension of a long day.

'Thanks.' Jansen wasn't a skier, and he rarely saw any snow, but why bother to challenge the image that Dr Lowe and the surgeon had of him and his country. Dr Lowe leant over and squeezed

Jansen's wrist quickly, and he paused outside the door again to look back through the window and wave, as he had when leaving with the surgeon. He had forgotten his cardboard cup, and the small, pale cone of it was left on the flat of the chair.

Jansen used the dimmer until he was lying in semi-darkness. He still had pain, but accepted it and began to plan the changes he would discuss with his wife. Maybe a trip to begin with — lots of places where he wouldn't need his laptop, his cellphone or his briefcase, where he could wear shorts and a garish top, and even the trivial administration of meals, travel and accommodation would be left to others. He knew that his response to all that had happened was quite predictable and conventional, but accepted it as authentic nevertheless. He had a wake up call in Singapore, his friends and acquaintances would say: a heart attack, or food poisoning, or something, and nearly died. A mixture of vagueness and exaggeration is typical of such second-hand accounts. And he gave it all away, they'd say, and resigned just like that. Why not, good on him, some would say, while others would consider he wasn't going to get right to the top anyway, not at his age.

Maybe his wife was right, he thought. An inner-city apartment with no lawns and the only plants those in pots on a patio that had a view of the harbour. Sam was pregnant, and for the first time he thought not only of her health, but of the child she carried and what part in its life he might play.

Jansen was surprised to feel tears on his face, but without any sobbing. He put it down to the trauma of his illness. The hospital smell of his private room masked the sour base of recent vomit and his crusted dressing. The waspish whine of scooters was at a distance, and the whisper of the air-conditioning close at hand. Life was fragile and there seemed the beating of wings in the tropical night. Home was the thing: Hector Jansen wanted to go home.

Buried Lives

My mother's brother had a farm on the pale loess clay and limestone of North Otago. It was an average farm concentrating on early lambs for the works, and even during his last years my uncle never received any startling offers for it. Its dry hills weren't suitable for dairy conversion, and its soils didn't favour the grapevines that became all the rage in the nearby Waitaki Valley. Yet it was sweet country when it did get rain, and quite free of gorse. The short grassed paddocks in the downs were rilled with sheep tracks: occasional outcrops of limestone were the grey of cigar ash. Almost always there was above it an unclouded egg-blue sky and, although only landscape was visible, in the evenings skeins of seagulls beat their way towards the sea.

I visited a few times as a boy, but I lived there only once for fourteen months after I had a breakdown in my third year at university. My mother preferred to call it a crisis, my father told people I'd hit a rough patch, my mates probably reckoned I'd flunked out as a pothead. I had a breakdown, no matter what you chose to call it. It happened because of a relationship I had with a flatmate and his twin sister. I was getting stoned on prime West Coast shit a lot too. It sounds like a soap opera, I know, but the pain, guilt and confusion of it all finally brought me to an emotional standstill, and I could barely remember to eat, to close the door when I went to the lavatory, or attend the lectures for which I'd enrolled. I felt I lived my life on the bottom of one of those great, sea aquariums with species foreign to me passing as dim shapes soundlessly, and with their own fixed purpose, overhead.

Even in that place, however, I had a conviction that I didn't want any formal treatment — no psychiatrists, no counsellors, no people unknown to me peering and mouthing through the thick glass of my isolation. Maybe a complete change then, my mother suggested, trying to keep anxiety from her voice, and she thought of her brother's farm amid the quiet hills of North Otago. My father, who loved space and solitude, and had been denied both by his career most of his life, was full of supportive agreement. The country was ideal for recovering from a rough patch, he thought, and with typical generosity he offered to buy me a second-hand car so that I could travel between home and farm whenever I liked.

Uncle Cliff and Aunt Sonia were contented people in whose home depression was an unfamiliar visitor. Sonia was the bright and vocal partner, Cliff a stubby, sunburnt man who thought the best of people. They had two daughters of effortless achievement. Evie had already qualified as a doctor when I went to live at the farm; Samantha was completing her architectural degree, and came home a few times while I was there, making me feel even more a failure in comparison, but through no intention of hers.

I was welcomed in the wooden, red-roofed farmhouse and given Evie's room, which was a chrysalis she had discarded, but still exact to the life she had led at home. Blue and yellow banded curtains, a tray of dwarf bottles of perfumes, lotions and nail polishes on the dressing table, sellotape marks on the painted walls where her posters had been, and on the kitset bookcase her gymnastic and debating trophies — including a small greenstone plinth for best summing up at the South Island inter-secondary school championships. Most of the books were from Evie's childhood, which wasn't all that long ago, but some, less read and more dignified, were prizes she had won at high school: *The Works of Jane Austen* published by Spring Books, *History of Rome* by M. Cary, and a hardcover *Moby Dick*. Clothing she no longer needed remained folded in the drawers and hanging in the wardrobe, all with a faint, girlish fragrance. At various times and in flagrant abuse of her privacy I examined all of Evie's life left behind: even the seven letters from Shane Tomlinson which were tied in a small bundle with dental floss, and hidden under a pile of notes for scholarship biology. In the sixth form she had the best legs in the world according to Shane.

Dr Evie's room spoke of normality, cleanliness and achievement. It had no sign of the trivial sordidness of my own life, and in the months I inhabited it I felt like a Visigoth camped in a Roman villa. Even my male clothes and large footwear seemed uncouth and out of place. I masturbated seldom and with great furtiveness, aware of the disgust in the expressions of Evie's dolls ranged behind the trophies. In a strange but powerful way I associated Samantha and Evie and their white, girlish rooms, with Rebecca, twin sister of Richard, and a good part of the reason that I was in my uncle's house at all surrounded by a specific family folklore to which I did not belong. 'What shall we do that's terrible?' Rebecca would say when we'd been drinking, or smoking shit, or just because lectures were over for the week, and by terrible she meant some excess she could laugh at. How different she was from my cousins, yet similar in the ease with which she achieved those things she wanted.

Outside the house was completely different: I belonged there from the first. The yards lay down the slope from the farmhouse, and on the south and west sides were windbreaks of pine and macrocarpa which reached over the implement sheds, the dog cages and the disused concrete dip. The downs rose and fell beyond with paddocks worn to bare dirt at each gateway, and the sheep tracks straggling away over the short, brown pasture. Some of the lower land would be green with lucerne, or in season the low, paler foliage of turnips and chou. From the top hill paddocks you couldn't see the red roof of the farmhouse, or any neighbouring houses, just the grassed hills tumbling towards the Waitaki and back towards the mountains. When I got the shakes, or felt the foreign shapes of the aquarium too oppressive, or Aunt Sonia's cheerful solicitude became too contrary to my own apathy, then I would have a long run, or let out one of the dogs and walk up to the back of the farm. The dogs enjoyed the release, but they never obeyed me. It was only occasionally that I did something useful there — rescued a cast sheep perhaps, or secured a bit of fence washed out in the gully, but Uncle Cliff always thanked me, as if he had sent me there expressly himself. It was a landscape of masculine reticence, which was something of a comfort: perhaps it was the extension of my uncle's temperament beyond himself.

During my time on the farm, Cliff never once mentioned the reason for my presence, and insisted on paying me a small wage. He told the neighbours and friends we met that I'd been kind enough to come and give him a hand for a while. We could work for hours together without words, or awkwardness; at other times he would talk of parts of his life spent crayfishing in the Chathams, and in North Island shearing gangs, before he'd bought the farm. In the winter, bulked up even more with jersey and a frayed parka, he looked almost square: as if he would reach the same height on his side as standing up. Out of the house he allowed himself a few roll-your-owns each day, and there'd be a brief flame at the cigarette's tip as he lit it. His other indulgence was mints, like great white pills, and he always had some in his pocket to share. Whenever we were close, putting in a strainer post perhaps, or bent over a recalcitrant engine, I would have the hybrid tobacco and mint smell of his breath. If I come across those scents now I'm reminded of his straight-grained goodness.

I was able to relieve Cliff of most of the tractor work while I was there. Years of hard slog were catching up on him, and his back played up on the jolting tractor. Harrowing and discing especially are repetitious, undemanding tasks, and I spent hours outwardly circling in the worked paddocks, while inwardly still circling Richard and Rebecca.

Our flat was in the North East Valley, not far from Castle Street, and an easy walk into the university. It was in fact an old cottage, low in the valley so that in winter the sun came only for late lunch and then went away again. Colin, Eric and I lived there in our second year, and when Colin went overseas after the holidays, we put a note on the Stud. Ass. notice board, and Richard came in. He was doing economics, marketing, stuff like that; his twin sister, Rebecca, was easily passing science subjects, and was in Knox College not far from us.

Your flatmates aren't necessarily your best friends. Sometimes in fact you lose your friends by having them as flatmates and finding they're a pain in the arse to live with. Sometimes they're just people who pay their share of the rent and do their own thing. Richard had his own friends, with whom he spent a lot of time in his room. His attitude to his room, and to clothes, should have been a signal to me quite early on, but I was slow to pick up on it. In our rooms Eric and I had a heap of assorted blankets on our beds, and one covering the bare floorboards to stand on in winter. Richard, though, went to the op shop and bought an enveloping green and yellow cover, and later to some other second-hand place and bought curtains which he said had the same yellow in them. Once, when he'd been walking up the path behind me, he said that I should let my hair grow longer: that it would suit me that way. He had a sharp wit that I enjoyed, and was a very generous guy. He had a particular dislike of overweight people, and those who couldn't express themselves cogently.

Rebecca first came round to the flat to help with the curtains. Eric and I decided right away that Richard's room was justifiably the focus of the flat for as long as she wanted it that way. She was short, lithe and dark haired; her skin was very smooth and she had a half, I-know-what-you're-thinking, smile. 'You guys don't really want to help with curtains, do you?' she said.

'I don't mind giving a hand,' I said. She came round more and more after Richard and I clicked. She said she got sick of the routines and restrictions at Knox. Sometimes she cooked a meal; sometimes she got on to Eric and me about doing chores about the place. She and Richard didn't like too much of a mess. Sometimes she'd come very late after a party, or dance, and sleep over in Richard's room, and be wearing some of his pyjamas when she came out bleary in the morning. 'You think they bunk in the bed together,' said Eric, 'or Richard puts pillows and stuff on the floor?'

'I'd invite her in myself,' I said.

'Jesus, so would I,' Eric said.

But then neither of us was Rebecca's brother, which was all the difference surely. I noticed on one of those mornings that she had painted toenails — her small, sallow foot on the cracked lino of the kitchen floor and the pearl-purple hue of her toenails.

There were two nail polishes on the tray on Evie's dressing table in the room on the farm. The plastic tops were the same colour as the thick liquid inside: one was pink and one was red. Both simple, unambiguous colours. Evie's window looked out onto the side lawn of the farmhouse and a large walnut tree with spatulate leaves and the blackening nut cases scattered like sheep shit in the grass underneath. That was one of the jobs I did for my uncle and aunt: I collected up the nuts, shucked them of the tattered, rotting cases, and spread them to dry on the wire of an old bed frame on the veranda. My hands were stained tobacco brown for days, and Aunt Sonia said I shouldn't have bothered, shouldn't have made a mess of myself like that. She knew, though, that it was an attempt to thank them.

Aunt Sonia was one of those central people around whom family and friends revolve. She laughed and talked a lot, and stimulated others to talk while she nodded and smiled as an encouragement to go on. Some women have natural warmth, and she was one. She must have had times of pain and despair, of glum despondency and self-doubt, but I never saw any sign of them. Maybe Cliff was the only witness, maybe she had her black times standing solitary in a closet, the back of the door touching her nose, her face relieved of any need to register optimistic expression.

In the first few weeks I found her kindness and resolute joy in life crushingly unbearable. I would expend all the smiles I had in response to her, until just a rictus remained, and I would excuse myself, and go and sit on Dr Evie's bed, or, more often, go off into the passive indifference of the landscape. Aunt Sonia's emotional energy and eagerness for reciprocation only made me more aware of a chronic malaise within myself. The more outgoing she was, the more difficult any matching emotion on my part.

Like the rainy day when I'd been there only two or three weeks, and Cliff had gone to town to see the bank manager and do other wet weather business. I spent the morning stencilling some of the wool bales, and then came back to the house for lunch. Aunt Sonia had been baking, and the misfits from the batches were my appetising follow-up to an asparagus quiche: misshapen apricot muffins still warm at their fruitful heart, the end slice of ginger crunch, the Afghan made from the last of the mix which had become the runt of the litter. She was packing all that had passed muster into round tins as I ate. She was taller than Cliff, graceful despite the years of physical work, and she vibrated slightly with energy, whereas he toiled with an easy rhythm, or sat quite still with conscious relaxation.

'You know we'll help if we can,' she said. 'You know that.'

I said I did and was thankful for it. 'Sometimes it helps to work through things if you talk them out, use other people as a sounding board,' she said. 'I don't want to pry, or make any judgements,' she said, 'not at all, but if you do want to talk about things then I'm always here.' I said I knew that and appreciated it. I said maybe later I'd feel like doing so, and that there wasn't any big thing to talk about anyway, really. Just sort of getting too tied up with personal relationships at the university. 'Evie and Samantha were just the same,' said Aunt Sonia, putting the Afghans deftly into the blue tin as if they were eggs going back into a nest. 'They had all these problems with boys and body image at the same time as coping with exams. Things get blown up out of perspective when you're under pressure, I think.' I told her they did. I didn't tell her that part of my own problem was a boy, but I told her that I appreciated her offer to talk about things very much, and that having time out on the farm was just the thing I needed right then. Much later I thought it immensely to her credit that, despite her natural disposition to be involved in the lives of all those around her, she never brought up heart-to-heart talks again.

Richard was keen on candid talks too, not believing that anything should be held back in a friendship. He had his own television in his room, and he started inviting me in to watch stuff. We'd sit on the bed, with some of his matched green pillows against the back board to prop us up. He had a real knack for predicting the storylines. I thought maybe he'd seen them all before, but when we went out to films he was just as accurate. 'I bet she kills herself with an overdose, and leaves a note incriminating him,' Richard would say, or, 'It's just soooo obvious, isn't it, that Mr Gendarme is in on it.'

He had this interest in families. He asked me quite a lot about the relationships in mine, and told me a good deal concerning his. His father was the CEO of one of the big power companies, and a wheeler and dealer of shares in a big way as well, Richard said. He supported the family abundantly, but lived three blocks away from them in Thorndon with a younger woman who taught French at the university. 'My mother never talks about it,' Richard said. 'She either believes, or pretends, that it's nothing untoward. They have dinner parties at our house, and Dad stays overnight, and then the next day he goes back to his own place. At Christmas-time his partner goes to her family in Marseilles, and Dad comes to us for a family week of presents and reminiscence. Rebecca and I go between the two houses as we like. She says it all comes down to money, and perhaps she's right. Money allows you to escape convention and yet maintain appearances in a way.'

'Does your father ever talk about it?' I asked.

'Not much. He says take what you want: take what you want, and pay for it.'

Eric never got invited into Richard's room, and I felt a bit guilty. The two of them didn't hit it off somehow. And fewer of Richard's friends came once he was well settled in. Rebecca, though, came more frequently and I was all for that. She'd bang on my door. 'You want coffee?' she'd call. 'Come in and have it with us.' Sometimes the three of us would sit propped on the green and yellow bedcover together; sometimes if it was cold Rebecca would sit on a cushion by the heater and look up at us to talk. I was always aware of her. Even when she wasn't in my field of vision I would know just how she was sitting, or leaning back on the pillows: how relaxed her slim body was, how her dark hair would sway at the side of her face as she talked, how when she was amused a small double crease at the corners of her mouth gave a sudden parenthesis to her smile. She would flip off her blue sneakers and her feet were almost absurdly small, the painted nails winking like gems.

I've got sisters, but I never talked to them the way Richard and Rebecca talked to each other. And I've never heard brothers and sisters talk so unreservedly to each other. Maybe it was because they were twins; maybe it was because they came to treat me almost like themselves. 'You randy little bitch,' Richard might say lightly when she talked of a night out with one of the Knox College guys. 'You make sure you keep those rugby boys out of your pants.'

'What is the smell in this bed?' she might say. 'I hate to think who you've had in here. It should be fumigated before I come round here again. You been shagging an orang-utan or something?'

I never found that smoking shit gave me all that much of a high, and Richard could soak it up and just be mellow, but Rebecca could get really up on it. Maybe it was her lesser body weight or something. After a few tinnies, or time with the spottle, she was most likely to grab me, and ask what we could do that was terrible. At Queen's Birthday weekend the three of us had a session in Richard's room.

Eric had gone home. We went out late for takeaways into a pale, cold drizzle, and Rebecca walked between the two of us with one hand in her brother's coat pocket and one in mine. 'Shit, it's cold, isn't it,' she said loudly. Maybe it was wishful thinking, but I reckon that, as we walked, her hand in the pocket lining pushed down towards my cock several times. 'Jesus, we all need to get warmed up,' she said. The whites of her eyes caught the street lights as she looked up at me.

On the way home we passed one of those wooden houses crammed up to the footpath. We could see a party going on. A group of old people, in their fifties and sixties, all animated and on the go, their faces crowded with gaudy, exaggerated noses, chins and eyebrows like papier mâché heads. To us, pausing in the wet night outside, their gaiety seemed absurd, and they themselves ridiculous in abandonment. 'What a load of wankers,' said Richard, and we stood laughing and unseen in the darkness to watch them.

'Time for a wake up call,' said Rebecca, and in one motion took her hand from my pocket, seized an empty milk bottle from the letter box, and flung it at the window.

The party people shrank back with appalled, vaudeville faces for a moment as the window glass shattered; one or two of them cried out with the shock of it. Half pissed and half high as we were, it seemed both catastrophic and enormously funny. We fled, whooping with laughter, Richard and I dragging Rebecca, who said she wanted to see what the old farts would do.

It wasn't just drink and shit, of course, but the derisive power of being young, and being good-looking, and being sure in your own mind that you would end up doing so much better in life than the adult people around you. We left our coats on kitchen chairs and went into Richard's room, kicking off our shoes before climbing under the cover and setting out the containers of Chinese food to share. Rebecca was in the middle again and her soft breast pressed against me whenever she leaned my way for sweet and sour pork.

'We shouldn't have done it, I know,' she said, 'but they were so gob-smacked, weren't they. People who dress like that, cardigans and all, deserve everything they get anyway. We should send them a fucking note saying that the style police took action against them.' Her jersey was dry, but her black hair was damp, shiny, and the wetness released a strong scent of some shampoo, which mixed with smell of wine and marijuana on her breath when she laughed, and the Chinese food, to make a potion I found strongly erotic.

'Those poor pricks when you smashed the window, though,' I said. 'What the hell got into you all of a sudden?'

'I told you that the world needed something terrible.'

'I hate to think what, or who, gets into her at times. It doesn't pay to ask,' said Richard. He was pushing his shoulder against her playfully so that she pressed more against me.

'Shut up. You can talk.' She was excited rather than offended.

Her words and laughter were quicker, higher. 'But even if you're a criminal we still love you,' and Richard gave her an exaggerated kiss on one side of her face, which was the opportunity for me to kiss her on the other. I wanted to roll right over on her, despite the pottles of food, and kiss her on her lips, feel the length of our bodies together. I wanted to tell Richard to get out of his own room and leave us alone together. Instead he put his arms around both Rebecca and me and started some mock, half-arsed talk about us being three musketeers and facing the world together. I slipped one hand under Rebecca's jersey, but even in the tactile satisfaction of that I had the uneasy awareness that Richard was stroking the back of my neck with two fingers. 'Don't anybody chunder on my bed,' he said, and puffed his cheeks to show he'd overeaten as well as earlier indulgence.

We spent even more time together after that. I often asked Rebecca to come out with just me, and she did sometimes. We went to a few pub band nights and some art films, but she liked best to do things as a threesome, and Richard took offence if he wasn't invited. It was a situation new to me, and I told myself that it arose because of the natural closeness of twins, and that Richard wasn't my competitor for Rebecca in any way that worried me. After all, if it hadn't been for Richard, I'd never have met her at all. Maybe if Rebecca wasn't there, the friendship I had with him may have developed in a quite different way. But that was an uneasy speculation I never dwelt on.

Life turns on such apparently fortuitous things. For if I'd never known Richard and Rebecca, then I wouldn't have spent those months on my uncle's farm, and Cliff and Sonia would have been just one-dimensional relations I'd met occasionally as a kid. The most obvious feature of a person's character may be the salient one, but equally as often you find it quite insignificant when familiarity has been gained. My aunt's warm engagement was the true representation; Uncle Cliff's quiet distance disguised an equal benevolence.

He was aware the old country ways were changing as farming became more technical, new land use replaced pastoralism, and the city populations, growing in both numbers and affluence, pushed their vacationing and holiday homes even into such areas as the Mackenzie Country and the Maniatoto. 'We've been the Celtic fringe,' he said, 'and of course we'll be overrun.' He had an unspoken belief that the satisfaction gained from living in the country diminished in proportion to the increased number with which it was shared. Family was different, of course, and I think he liked having me around. Although he never asked about my state of health, he would suggest tasks we could do together if I'd been quiet and by myself for a long time. 'Would you like to give me a hand dagging and drenching a mob?' he might say, or 'I thought maybe we could do a lambing round together before it gets dark'.

One day in the autumn drought we went out with Caspar Waldren to see if we could find water. Waldren was a retired farmer and water diviner who lived in Oamaru, but still spent a lot of time pottering on the farm he'd relinquished to his son, and on other properties which he'd come to know well during a long life. He had a big reputation for being able to find underground water, sometimes by using a fresh willow wand, sometimes number eight wire bent like a clothes hanger. He had boots worn grey at the toes and an excess of brown, weathered skin on his very thin frame. He was sprouting a lot of hair from nooks and crannies such as his ears and eyebrows, and when I was introduced to him he looked thoughtfully into my face, and said he'd met my mother a couple of times. Despite the heat he wore a tattered pinstriped suit coat. He was an absurd old git really, but my uncle treated him with respect, almost deference.

We took the ute along the lower part of the farm, and when we stopped, Waldren went to one of the willows along the dry creek line, broke off a thin branch and stripped it of bark. As we walked over the short grass in the glare of the sun, the two of them talked mainly about neighbours and local stuff from years before, which meant nothing to me. Caspar Waldren held the willow branch with cocked wrists so it was bent in an arc on his lower chest. Every now and again he would stop, or do a small circle while the willow trembled with a life of its own in his hand, but no mention was made of water and their conversation continued just the same.

We reached a place in the little valley from which the gravel road could just be seen, and close to a fence and gateway where Cliff and I had set up a temporary tailing enclosure some months before. A few tails, shrivelled and dark, were still lying in the grass of the paddock. Waldren was talking of a rare snowstorm that had hit years before. His voice was surprisingly strong for such a slight man, but had the hoarseness of age. The willow in his hand began to buck, and then flipped over and pointed to the ground. 'Whoa, me old beauty,' said Caspar Waldren calmly, and he walked over and around the spot until he stood where the willow branch gave the strongest reaction. 'This'll be it right here, Cliff,' he said.

'Great,' said Cliff. He had a waratah with him, daubed at the top with white paint, and with body weight alone he pushed it as far into the dry ground as he could. 'Thanks for that. Let's go back and have a few beers.' That was the old guy's payment for his divining, that and Cliff's unquestioning acceptance that there was indeed water down there.

We wandered back to the truck, and as I listened to Waldren going on about the things that interested him, I thought how much a world apart he was from my life at the university. As we bumped back along the farm track to have beer on the veranda, Richard and Rebecca might well have been together on the bed in the flat, driving the smoke of some really good shit into the spottle and getting stoned right out of it. 'That's it. Jesus, that's the stuff all right,' Richard would say, and flop back on the pillows and rake his fingers lazily through the rising haze of exhaled marijuana. 'Jesus, that's a lift.' And Rebecca would take just as much and lie back too, and make a noise as if even breathing was a pleasure, and have a smile that was almost post-coital on her small, pale face. How clear her face is still in memory — the thin wings of dark eyebrow, the smooth curve of her cheek, the creases of parenthesis at the ends of her smile. For a slight, non-athletic woman she was strong, the muscles of her neck and shoulders well defined and her breasts high.

The drought that year didn't get quite bad enough for Cliff to spend money drilling at old Caspar's spot, but he had no doubt there was water there all right, and he kept the place marked. Some of the best wells in the district had been found by Caspar Waldren, he told me, and he said that skill was dying out, just like so many country skills before it. I wondered if Rebecca and Richard ever thought of me, and how they'd piss themselves if they could see the life I led on my uncle's farm. I found it hard myself to understand how many ways of life, how many disparate attitudes, can be operating at the same time with no connection at all. During those months I seemed to be in several places at once, unable to get my life together.

Eric left the flat soon after Queen's Birthday weekend. He didn't give much of a reason, but part of it was the threesome thing that had developed with Richard, Rebecca and me. Eric and I had been friends for years and I felt guilty and defensive. When I met him at the pub a couple of weeks afterwards we talked briefly about it. 'Oh, man, you should move on out of there,' said Eric. 'Those two. There's not enough air between them — I don't care if they are twins. And they're always so down on everybody else. Everybody else except them is fucking stupid as far as they're concerned. Let's do something terrible, let's do something terrible: I mean, you have to say there's something pretty weird about her, and they're getting really heavy into smoking shit, aren't they.'

Neither of the twins had taken to Eric, and that was one reason for how he felt, but he was right in much of what he said. If he'd been right in absolutely everything it wouldn't have made any difference to me. It doesn't matter how long a friendship is when you love someone else. There was no person I wanted to be with more than Rebecca; no place more special than Richard's room with his chosen furnishings, the close body scents mixed always with that of marijuana in a slow convection around the two-bar heater, her hand on my chest beneath the shirt, or over my own hand on her inner thigh. The disconcerting thing was Richard, usually lying on the other side of her — or worse, lying on the other side of me: talking with us, laughing with us, ridiculing the rest of the world, when I didn't want him there.

I wanted just Rebecca and me, the natural thing, but how difficult that seemed to be. She liked to be massaged. It would start with her back, and especially she enjoyed her shoulder muscles kneaded and the very top of her vertebrae where I could feel the thick skin gliding on the bone. Richard would join in, and eventually one of us would undo her bra strap so that we could massage down the sides of her chest. It was usually me, even though I tried to conceal my eagerness, and she would ask who was being naughty, without turning her head, and after a bit say 'all right, all right,' and turn over and let us push the bra aside. She would let us draw our hands firmly over her breasts in a pretence of massage, swirl our fingers over the rougher, darker skin circling her nipples. I loved to do it, loved to do it. I have a hundred merging images of it still: the three of us in the dim afternoon light from the flat window, or the buttery glow of the table lamp at night. And the long breathing of the three of us, and her shoulders stretching back, her breasts trembling to our touch, her smile and glances both relaxed and knowing. And Richard would soon transfer his massage from Rebecca to me. 'You shouldn't tighten up so much. Just relax — all of us should just relax and go with the flow.' And in the pleasure of having his hands no longer on her, I could almost ignore that they were on me. 'Just round and round and round,' he'd say. 'It's such a lovely, natural thing to have skin on skin,' as all three of us would move in the ways that pleased us most. 'You naughty boys. You're terrible, that's what you are,' she'd say.

I knew it was some sort of thrall, as well as pleasure I couldn't deny myself. I hadn't had many girlfriends, but I deliberately got in touch with Melanie Faraday again and asked her to come to a Students' Association fancy dress party with me. Hospital was the theme and there were a lot of people in white coats, or bandages; a lot of crutches and stethoscopes. Melanie's giggle as a response to almost all contact, physical or verbal, was just as I remembered it. She had so little subterfuge, so much assumption of goodwill, and I missed the sharp, stimulating awareness Rebecca always had, which was part sexual promise, part gender hostility. Melanie was attractive enough, but despite that she seemed somehow to have a unisex psyche which stressed things in common rather than exciting differences. She danced with cheerful abandon, and giggled at the interruptions that came from friends who cut in to partner her. She drank a lot, but wouldn't have anything to do with weed, or pills. 'I'm behind in my assignments as it is,' she said, as if smoking shit would suddenly take a couple of weeks out of her life. 'I got extensions because I said my father was sick,' and she giggled.

Melanie lived with her parents, and she had her mother's car for the night, so we left the party soon after midnight and I drove down to park overlooking St Kilda Beach. 'So it's watching the submarine races again, is it,' she said. She took off her earrings and put them in the glove box. She was bigger and softer than I'd remembered, and that impression must have been a comparison with Rebecca whom I'd been with more recently. I didn't want to think of the twins: I was glad it was just the two of us in the car at St Kilda, just as our headlights on arrival had shown only couples in the other cars. It was the natural thing, wasn't it. Melanie wore a white nurse's uniform with large buttons and she gave a sighing giggle as I undid them. 'You know the rules,' she said softly. Yes, I knew she didn't actually fuck, but that night I didn't much care. It was some time before I got a hard on, and most of the time I thought of Rebecca in Richard's room: her taut body and uninhibited talk, both of which stoked me to hell. That night with Melanie was a lesson to me that love hasn't much to do with what's comfortable, or natural, or even right. It's about some gut-wrenching imperative that drives you towards a person whatever, or whoever, might be in the way. For me it was Richard who was so often in the way.

As Melanie giggled, or kissed almost as noisily, and we fogged up the windows of her mum's car, and each of us felt the sweat on the body of the other, I knew she wasn't the woman I wanted to be touching, to be listening to, to be smelling.

One of the ways I tried to forget all that on the farm was by running. I'd been into sport at school, but didn't bother at university: all that team ethos and character building shit, and having to turn out for practices no matter how you felt, or how many of the others there you disliked. Running by myself on the farm was different. At first it gave me an excuse to be out of the house when I couldn't face the company even of my uncle and aunt, and then I found that the effort also had a distracting, almost punishing, effect that helped me at the time. My favourite circuit took me up the main gully into the downs, around the limestone bluff which had Maori charcoal drawings in the overhang, and back down the boundary ridge and along the north side of the long pine windbreak. In the winter mornings the grass was white with frost in the shadows and bowed down with droplets in the sun; in the summer evenings the sheep shit rattled like shotgun pellets on the dry ground beneath my feet, and the sheep drowsed in what shade they could find. The bluff had a steep straggle of matagouri and briar. Sometimes I'd take a spell at the top and look over the low hills of the farm, or back to higher ones behind me. I could see part of the snaking gravel road in the valley, and the place where Caspar Waldren had found artesian water.

My uncle had become very economical of physical effort himself since his back had packed up, but he didn't deride my runs. He thought I was getting fit to play rugby and he approved of that. 'No, good on you. Go for it,' he said, and told me that he knew the coach of the local club. He'd played a bit himself years before, and liked to watch the game on television, leaning forward and contorting his worn face with vicarious effort at moments of dramatic achievement.

I was not running to anything, however. I was running from the threesome of Richard, Rebecca and myself, running until the physical effort diminished all else apart from that effort and the strange dazed elation that the metronomic action brought. Sleeping was another thing I did a lot. Sleeping and running were both releases from morbid introspection, and the need to decide a future. How easily I could fall into a deathlike sleep in Dr Evie's innocently fragrant room: sleep that was a dark grave even within the night, and made blank the concerns of life. Running and sleeping were both means of avoidance at different ends of some scale I didn't understand. One involved forcing physical effort to obliterate anxiety and guilt, the other was escape from any consciousness at all. 'Well, at least he sleeps well,' I overheard Sonia telling my mother on the phone. 'And the air is different here on the farm, of course. Yes, he seems to need his sleep.'

I hadn't slept that well at the flat after getting close with Richard. Smoking shit mellows you out, but doesn't give you good sleep. Not me anyway. I looked up the effects of marijuana on the net one time, and it said sleepiness was one of them. Some of the other things, though, I recognised in myself: anxiety, apathy after highs, altered perception of time. And it's supposed to stuff your memory too, and there's a lot about that time which is sort of drifting in my mind. Yet nothing could be clearer to me, less subject to loss, than the times with Richard and Rebecca. I could see it all with a sharpness that was almost an agony.

That was the big thing I tried to work out during my time on the farm: had I gone haywire because of smoking so much shit, or was it because of the twins? I decided maybe it was both, and that I had to make a clean break with both. It was a rational decision that I hadn't been able to make as long as I thought Rebecca would choose me. If she'd rung up, though, when I was on the farm, and asked me to come back, I know I'd have gone, as long as Richard wasn't there. There are things in your life that common sense is helpless against.

In late summer Cliff went up to Wellington for a few days to help Evie move into a house she had bought in Petone. Her big earning years hadn't begun, but as a qualified doctor she had no difficulty getting bank money for a first home purchase, and in addition to her other attributes she was shrewd in business. A wooden house in Petone wasn't where Evie would end up, but it would do as a starting point. Cliff had made an inspection of it, and wanted to replace some rotten weatherboards on the laundry side, and fit a much bigger, aluminium frame window in the lounge. He was appalled at the quotes Evie had received from Wellington tradesmen for the job, and quite capable of doing it himself. I knew the quiet satisfaction he would get from ferreting out sound material at rock bottom prices, and the quality of workmanship his daughter would receive. Uncle Cliff had no formal training in carpentry, motor mechanics, plumbing, or even farming, but like so many practical men of his generation he had picked up these skills of necessity from experience and from his various workmates and neighbours, each of whom had some special expertise.

He wouldn't have been able to go up, he said, if I hadn't been staying on the farm. He said that to make me feel welcome and useful, but it was true as well. It meant Aunt Sonia wasn't alone on the property, and I was there to attend to the outside tasks. It was an opportunity also for her to see what she could do for me. She knew my nature made any cathartic disclosure unlikely, and she didn't press me any longer to talk about my problems. Instead she revealed something from her own past as a sign of trust, and evidence, too, that most of us have false starts in life.

On the third hot evening of Cliff's absence we had an evening meal of cold mutton and salad, and then went out to the veranda and sat on the cane chairs which had weathered grey over years. If my uncle had been at home I may have gone to Dr Evie's room, or had an evening run up to the bluff, but it seemed impolite to leave my aunt without company. The sun hadn't quite gone down, but made reaching shadows from the sheds and trees around the yards, gave a tawny glow to westward slopes of pasture.

'Have I ever told you I studied in Sydney years ago?' Sonia said. I knew very little about her, and felt minimum curiosity because my own tribulations were crushing. 'Yes, I played the viola and studied at Otago's music department. I won a scholarship for strings offered by the Perry Academy, and went over there when I was twenty-one.'

'I never knew you were a musician,' I said.

'I practised several hours a day for years. I was in the junior sinfonia in Sydney, and a member of a chamber group which gave recitals and recorded for radio. I thought music was going to be my life then.'

'So do you ever play now?'

'Never. Haven't for thirty years. I don't even have a musical instrument in the house any more. When you've been able to do something really well, there's no satisfaction in doing it at any lesser level at all. None at all.'

A plausible conclusion, and I didn't question it, although I thought of stories of former sports champions who kept playing on in their sunset decline. 'Not easy, though, to give it all away after that?'

'I didn't even see the two years out. I was so homesick that I used to burst into tears when my folks rang, and I had a boyfriend there which didn't work out.'

We sat there on the grey, cane chairs of the veranda, in the last of the day's sun, and looked down to the yards and the still trees. I remembered I hadn't yet fed the dogs. It was a quiet, ordinary place in which to be talking of concert halls and an artistic career. Sonia's hands were hardened with work, and the knuckles swollen a little. They were not a musician's hands. 'I don't even listen to music much any more,' she said, 'and that does surprise me. But your life takes many turns, doesn't it, and there's always so much to do.'

She didn't seem to be sad about the loss of music in her life, just interested, perhaps slightly puzzled, at the way things turn out. I didn't realise it at the time, but I think she chose to tell me because she hoped in a roundabout way it might suggest to me that things which dominate your life at one point will often loosen their grip with time. However, I was preoccupied with my own concerns: having a bad patch, as my father would say. The glass was thick between me and the rest of the world, and the shapes swimming above me still threatening. I hadn't much curiosity about what had happened to Sonia's aspirations; why she had gone to Sydney to be a professional musician, and come home again to marry Cliff.

I remembered that conversation, and regretted my selfishness, less than three years later when she died suddenly of a stroke. She had been collecting eggs, Cliff said, on a rare rainy day, and when he went looking for her he found the body slumped in the tractor shed with her legs and shoes outside the overhang, sopping wet. Her arm was around the bucket, he said, and not one egg broken. By that time I'd completed my degree, in Christchurch, had a job with the council there, was breathing air again rather than aquarium water and was directly in touch with the world.

The funeral service was held in the small Anglican church of Oamaru stone, which wasn't big enough to seat all the mourners who came. People stood around the christening font, at the back of the church, and spilled out into the bright sunshine. It didn't surprise me that Sonia was so well loved. Old Caspar Waldren was there in his number one suit. He shook his tufted face sorrowfully when I spoke to him, as if he divined my failure to have sufficiently appreciated my aunt. And his surprise was evident when Evie and Samantha went against rural tradition and assisted as pallbearers. As we slid the coffin in the back, the polished top of the hearse gave off heat waves which pulsated through my vision of the paddocks around the church, and Cliff's face was beaded with sweat and tears.

A week later I went down to the farm with my mother to give Cliff a hand with farm jobs, while she helped Evie and Samantha to sort through Sonia's clothes and personal belongings. Without Aunt Sonia the house was like a clock with the spring broken. All at once the place seemed smaller and shabbier, transformed no longer by her energy and warmth. Evie was temporarily in her own room again, and the glimpses of it while passing strengthened the disconcerting mix of feelings I had on my return: gratitude for the acceptance and support I'd received, but also the stirrings of an agony which had been caused elsewhere, but suffered largely there.

Cliff said I could sleep in the little side room, which had filled up over the years with household items no longer needed, but too good to be thrown out. But I took blankets onto the side porch, and slept on the bed wire propped up on beer crates which each year was used to dry the walnuts. The nights were warm and I slept okay there, despite the foraging noises of hedgehogs and of possums, the sudden lighthouse beams of the moon among the passing clouds, and flashes of memory that came as dreams.

Maybe clearing away the personal remnants of someone's life is even sadder than the farewell of the body. My uncle found it impossible to face so the three women combined their fortitude to tackle it. The clothes and shoes with fragrance and signs of wear, and nothing to enclose; the jewellery, trinkets, and mementos of travel; cards and photos which have gained an inexpressible sadness. And those inexplicable possessions of esoteric significance to people we thought we knew. The closest, dearest litter of a person's life open for selection. My mother accepted a silver bracelet, wept over it briefly, then was a comfort to others again. She found a diary Sonia had kept of her time in Sydney on the scholarship, and some letters from an older, married man. 'It all ended most unfortunately,' my mother said. 'A very painful period in her life, I'd say.' She and my cousins had known nothing of Sonia's brief musical career, and I realised too late that I'd been privileged to have her talk of it.

My mother and Evie and Samantha decided not to say anything of it to Cliff, not to show him the diary, or the letters. It didn't matter how much, or how little, he knew, it was better left in the past. It was a buried life, as Sonia herself had suggested to me that evening on the veranda when Cliff was replacing Evie's weatherboards in Petone. It was one of those dead-end roads from which you have to retrace your steps, and find another way, though the journey remains with you always. So memory works on association, not logic. 'The music became part of the pain,' my mother said.

But Sonia had kept the diary, the letters, the scholarship scroll — hidden evidence of the buried life. And she would have had her memories too, which would come unbidden as a visitation to shake her in later life, just as I had my own. Things seep into each other. Back in the farmhouse after Sonia's death I felt her loss, but also the presence of my disturbed, earlier self. While lying on the porch walnut dryer in the warm night, I saw again Richard, Rebecca and myself on another bed that last time.

It was the Monday dusk of a reluctant spring. We'd talked, laughed, smoked shit and ended up, as so often, in that intimate almost naked huddle which was Rebecca's massage. Everything that was the world seemed to move and slide with her; everything that I wanted was there. 'You guys are terrible,' she said, and she arched her back slightly so that her breasts rose further, and she smiled at the ceiling. 'You're always after it, aren't you?'

Richard laughed and put his arms firmly around me, and I felt an intense anger that he was there, that he was touching me, that he was any part of what Rebecca and I did. It was anger and confusion I could no longer repress. 'Will you just fuck off,' I said and pushed at his face with the flat of my hand. He said something; I don't remember what. I do remember Rebecca sitting up abruptly, so that her breasts formed contours of new allure.

'You're always mad keen to be fucking me, but not so keen to be fucked yourself,' she said. 'Ever thought about that? You piss off. You're the one to piss off, right now.'

'Yeah, get the fuck out of it. We've had a gutsful of you,' said Richard.

His voice was suddenly intense, and I picked up my clothes awkwardly while they watched shoulder to shoulder, and I left that room for the last time. As I went through the shabby kitchen, I heard them start talking to each other, quietly, intimately, as if I had never been there. I was shaking so much I had trouble breathing, and I was rendered excessively clumsy and skinned my big toe on a door frame. It came to me that all along there had been no chance of it being just Rebecca and me.

Even after just the four days that I was on the farm after Aunt Sonia's death, I could tell how Cliff was going to live thereafter. He didn't spend more time inside the house than he had to, for it reminded him of a family now all departed, and a life quite changed. He talked briefly of his future on the morning my mother and I were leaving. He and I stood in the sun by the sheds, and in a breeze which had the ends of the branches nodding. 'Work's the best thing, I reckon,' he said. 'I'm glad I've still got the farm. You never know — one of the girls might marry a farmer yet,' and he lit one of his roll-your-owns, which flamed briefly. He knew the chances of that were pretty slim, but he didn't have any hang-up about keeping the property in the family. It would see him out and that was all that mattered. Those quiet, dry hills, the stock he managed, the store of water Caspar Waldren had promised him waiting beneath his land. And when his life was finished there, another, final, dispersal would take place, sweeping away the evidence of Sonia, Evie, Samantha and of himself, except for the physical imprint he made on the land, and except for the different recollections of those who knew him.

The smell of tobacco and peppermints, or prime West Coast shit; the folded North Otago hills, or the narrow North East Valley of Dunedin; Sonia's laughter through the farmhouse, or Rebecca's knowing smile and the flash of the whites of her eyes; the texture of freshly shucked walnut shells, or cold, crumbed lino beneath my feet. All an uneasy mix in which I catch, just rarely now, a glimpse of a former and fugitive self.

Facing Jack Palance

After an ordinary day of selling bathroom fittings, you have a dream in which you must stand against Jack Palance. It wells up through the subconscious, perhaps as a psychic relic of all those matinée films seen in childhood, but its experience now is sober and adult; its issues fundamental and inescapable.

You know without specific recollection that you haven't long been in this small, dusty town, that behind you stretch lonely saddle days in gulches, or high plains drifting, and nights level pegging with a coyote moon. Your lips are chapped, your eyes narrowed to the sun and the horizon, but you walk with the slow ease of a tall, lean man.

The heat rises from the dusty main street, and also presses down from a burnished, implacable sky. So high is the sun that shadows don't lean out from their origins, but crouch close in. Jack Palance is in black, so he and his shadow are as one.

As you walk towards each other, all else seems to draw back to form a dramatic amphitheatre. Townspeople scuttle into doorways and down alleys, the women overawed and tremulous in the face of decisive action beyond the comprehension of their gender, the men furtive, craven, as they slip away. There is the piping, emasculated voice of the fat sheriff as he finds his false duty elsewhere, but no one is listening. The most beautiful of the women bites her lip, and her eyes widen beneath her bonnet.

Black Jack Palance gives a bitter smile, and teeth glint in his wolfish jaw. 'Well lookee here, now,' he says softly. His hands butterfly over the ivory handles of his six shooters which are in sloping holsters for speed of draw, and the belt buckle of Mexican silver glints in the harsh, western sun. Many a man has fallen to the guns of Jack Palance, but you don't let that deter you from what must be done. You remember the advice you had from old Wyatt during a poker night at the Lazy Z, about one gun being enough for any man, and usually one bullet too.

Past the old corral you walk, and the Silver Dollar Saloon with the batwing doors quivering from the mass of cowering people within, who know they see the Titans clash, and will afterwards silence conversations to say — I was there, I was there that day. But the only person you care about is Jack Palance, and you walk real easy with the balance on the balls of your feet, and your gun hand real easy at your side, and you think of the brother and friend you no longer have because of Jack Palance in El Paso, and the lover lost because of Jack Palance in Wichita, and all those sturdy Johnny Reb homesteaders and ranchers' daughters in check shirts, who look to you for justice. And your voice is an even drawl when you say, 'Howdee, Jack. I've been hoping we'd catch up maybe.'

The two of you hold up walking, and stand in the dusty main street beneath the witness of that pitiless sun. Jack Palance, who knows about these things, has you set against the wall of the bank, while his backdrop is the more difficult shimmer of the side street where the barber and coffin maker has a shop. But you don't care about that. There's a faint smell of whisky and saddle leather in the air, and an even fainter one of juniper berries.

'Are you pushing me?' Jack Palance says, and he gives his executioner's chuckle, like the sound of a small scree slide on the mesa's edge.

'I'm pushing, Jack. Why don't you make something of it?' You know your face is saturnine, inscrutable, with a faint, fleeting Mitty smile. All your life has been leading to this point and destiny is writ large in this small town.

There's a long history between the two of you, of course, and although there's no fear in the eyes of Jack Palance, there is acknowledgement that perhaps you are the one: the one sent on this blistering, wind whispering western afternoon to deliver the gift of death. Jack Palance has so often been that emissary, but today for the first time he considers another conclusion. As you face each other there is a sense that despite all that lies as difference between you, there is also an equality in courage and resolve. You and he share something which the ruck of men don't know, but in black Jack Palance it's been traduced and selfishly used.

'Make your play, Jack,' you say evenly, and the only sound is the wind blowing in from the sage brush and tumbleweed country, or is it the indrawn breath of all those invisible watchers, and behind that a faint cosmic music like guitars at the end of a sad, cowboy song. That's how it is all right, and you have a feeling at the inner core of yourself of something both calm and exultant, the serene knowledge that this is the time to do what you have to do, and this is the end of the line for one, or both, of you, clean-cut destiny played out for all to see. Good and evil under the noonday sun. And Jack Palance makes his play with defiance and malice in his dark eyes. His hands are sinuous and devilish quick to the ivory butts of his Colts. Your own gun comes up as naturally and smoothly as a deer's head from a mountain pool.

The sound of those guns blows you right out of your dream, and you sit up abruptly, waking your wife. Almost at once that clean, manly and magnificent resolve begins to fade, though you explain all to her eagerly in an attempt to hold it. 'Weird,' she says agreeably, but then she never was one to wear a bonnet.

She needs your help today, she says, to move the 'Peace' rose from one side of the garden to the other. And you just give your faint, inscrutable, ironic, sardonic, fleeting smile, knowing that although logic and incident in dreams may be bizarre, the emotion is always true. 'I think we can manage that, pilgrim,' you tell her.

Family Circle

Naylor had known since he was five years old that he was adopted. The only mother he knew told him, in the presence of the only father he knew, and because he loved them both it didn't bother him. As far as he could recall, no one during his childhood had accused him of being a bastard on any other grounds than personality, and being adopted was an okay thing. He'd known several kids who were adopted and it was no big deal.

Although older than most, his mother and father seemed much the same as other parents; better than many too. He'd invited mates home feeling quite easy about his position there and his friends' reception. Naylor and his parents ignored his adoption. The three of them were happy with the family the way it was. Naylor didn't spend time in adolescence looking at himself in the mirror and wondering about his genetic inheritance, or whether he was related to someone famous.

He knew he was loved, but even that he thought little about. He just got on with the selfish and absorbing business of growing up — and he was good at it. He did well physically and intellectually. He worked quite hard and got prizes, but not so hard that he isolated himself from his fellows, or aroused animosity. His parents gave support and encouragement without promoting an exaggerated view of him as special. Both of them were achievers, and so achievement was accepted, even expected in a non-demanding way. Opportunity, application, achievement was the natural sequence.

When the crisis came, adoption wasn't the cause, or at the centre of it. His parents, Helen and Greg, became seriously ill together, as they had done most things together and seriously, although their afflictions were different. Helen was diagnosed with leukaemia, and Greg with systemic heart disease two months later.

Naylor received the news of the outcome of his mother's tests while he was at Bristol University doing the postgraduate one-year MSc course in management. 'Your mother's got leukaemia, I'm afraid. We've just come back from the clinic,' said his father, emotion and constraint at odds in his voice. The window of Naylor's second-storey flat faced Wales, he was told, but all he could see was the high façade of a shoe shop with giant advertisements. He watched the colours leach out, the poster expressions become more fatuous as he talked with his father. 'No, we think you should see the year out, Naylor. It's the sensible thing. But your mother looks forward enormously to your return, you know that.' In blatant refutation of Naylor's sense of the world, the early promise of sunlight was on the city.

It was dark, however, and slanting rain glinted multi-tinted in the shifting light of the shoe shop neons, when his mother rang two months later. Naylor stood at the same window to receive the second blow. It occurred to him that was the typical way of it — his father ringing to pass on the bad news about his mother, and then she in turn being emissary for Greg. Both undoubted concern and a desire for control were evident in that perhaps. Was it easier to question an intermediary rather than the sick person personally? 'They think it's a congenital thing,' she said. 'At least that persistent tiredness is explained now. There's a decision to be made concerning the advisability of surgery. The worrying thing, too, is that he insists on looking after me when he's not up to it.'

Nothing truly awful had happened in their lives before, and now two of them faced imminent death, and the third was on the other side of the world in pyjamas, watching sleet machine gun a street slick and gleaming in the night. 'We want you to stick it out over there and finish the course. Only a few weeks to go really, aren't there, and it doesn't make sense to come back so close to completion. Your father's very keen on you finishing and not worrying too much about us.' The typical rationality of it took him closer to tears than any discussion of symptoms, or prognosis, for it was so much part of their natures, and he had benefited from it so often. In his final weeks at the university he began to have powerfully disturbing dreams of childhood, and his academic work suffered. His world was breaking up.

It was not Bristol's fault, but his year there became almost entirely negative in retrospect: pleasant things were overwhelmed by concern for his father and mother, and guilt for staying on, although that was their wish. The city that he had found unpretentious, yet truly cultural, became just a place of exile, and the university course an unwelcome tie. He took no gifts from England to bring home, and instead bought jade turtles for his parents at Singapore airport on his way back. What he would have liked to unwrap for them was good health, but that was beyond him; beyond him also was an adequate expression of his love and gratitude.

He made the attempt on his first evening home, when he and his father sat by his mother's bed, and Helen and Greg told him of the rather precipitate sale they had made of their joint optometry practice, and their hope that his firm wouldn't shift him away from Wellington now that he was back, so that he could live in their home as he had for so many years. The house had been built by Greg's father and had a clear view over Evans Bay, where the planes would come flying low on their descent to the airport when the wind was southerly.

His mother had a special pillow, rather like a massive and inflated bow tie, which both raised and supported her. She was at a stage of her illness which gave her a passing elegance as she thinned. Only too soon that attrition would become monstrous. 'We've decided not to have treatment,' she said. 'The specialists say medical intervention wouldn't gain a great deal of time.' Naylor's father had told him all that in considerable detail, but he realised his mother gained some comfort by being able to go over it all now that he was home, with her again. He held her left hand, which throbbed with a surprisingly strong pulse, and was warm and dry to the touch. 'Your father wants me to be able to stay here as long as possible, and of course I want that, but only if he doesn't insist on trying to do everything himself and jeopardise his own health. I'm going to have someone to help, in addition to the hospital nurse visits. It's expensive, of course, that sort of private care.'

'Naylor doesn't care how much it costs,' remonstrated his father.

'You must have everything that helps,' said Naylor. The term medical intervention still lingered in his mind: one of those expressions that doctors proffer, and patients accept for the small comfort of its precision.

'I'm just being realistic. We have to watch money now that both of us have stopped working, and the clinic's sold,' Helen said.

Both his parents were astute in matters of business, but his mother was the one who had dealt with the financial side of their profession, while his father had concentrated on keeping up to date with advances in optometry. She went over the investment of the sale money with him, and the other main family assets.

Naylor could see what a worthwhile distraction it was for her. She took evident satisfaction in the security she and Greg had built up while still having full lives. Naylor made himself ask questions and keep the topic alive. As the three of them talked, he realised that his mother's concern wasn't entirely that he himself was a beneficiary, but that money was a weapon against her death. Not in any futile effort to defeat that end, or even prolong it, but to preserve dignity and choice; to have the palliatives to avoid some coarse, ignominious farewell. He was ashamed to find he knew virtually nothing of her childhood in which such fear of poverty must have been grounded.

'There'll be money left for you when we're gone,' she told him with evident satisfaction. 'We've always been determined on that.' And Greg nodded, not at all offended by the assumption that his own death was near.

'I don't need any money,' Naylor said. 'I'm fine. My job's fine.' He didn't have any student debt because they had supported him through varsity; he had a good job and even better prospects. 'You and Dad should take every medical advantage, irrespective of cost.'

'Oh, we've paid into insurance for years so at least that's okay,' she said. 'Tell me about your university work. We haven't congratulated you properly about the MSc yet.'

His mother had always had a pale and even complexion, but on her thin face and neck he noticed patches of pink, and the tendons of her neck were evident even though she lay propped and apparently relaxed. She'd had a hairdresser come the day before he arrived home, so that she could look her best.

Naylor told them of his course, his tutors, the New Zealand expat geographer who had befriended him, and whom he'd visited frequently in Bath on a borrowed Vespa scooter, avoiding the motorway. A large plane came up the bay as they talked, and from habit they paused their conversation for the brief time of maximum noise, then resumed quite naturally. His mother had a view across the water towards Miramar and took an interest in yachts and the occasional fuel ship that she'd been too busy to notice before.

'I missed you both a lot,' said Naylor. 'Seeing things over there, the struggle some people have for a decent opportunity, I reckon I've been lucky. You've both made it easy for me.' He had the inclination to say more, but the family wasn't overtly demonstrative, and with both his parents unwell it didn't seem a time to become emotional. He could feel his mother's hand throbbing within the palm of his own. 'By the way,' he said, and stood, held up a finger for patience and mystery, then went to his room to fetch the Singaporean jade turtles. Turtle talk provided a release of sorts, even though death had joined them to make a foursome which wouldn't be broken until Helen left with that new partner.

Naylor worked only mornings for what was left of the year. A nurse visited each day, soon twice each day. Naylor and his father encouraged friends to come in the mornings, because Helen tired quickly. For some time they had a drive in the afternoons to Makara perhaps, or Days Bay and Eastbourne, but that, too, was eventually a labour for her, so the afternoons became a time of rest for both parents: Helen propped in the arms of her encompassing pillow, Greg in his own room with a less exalted view of agapanthus and red hot pokers in the sloping garden. Both of them seemed to sleep more easily in the afternoons with the curtains drawn, than during the nights, when Naylor would hear his father pad clumsily to the lavatory, and not flush it in an unavailing effort to leave others undisturbed. And hear his mother's plaintive, reduced cough, or wake when his own doorway was vaguely illuminated with the last reaches of the light from her room as she sought distraction.

Some of those afternoons he worked in the garden, although it was a task he disliked, because he knew Greg might attempt it himself if the section became unruly. Both his parents loathed neglect and untidiness. Some afternoons he went into the city to a wine bar, whether he had a friend to meet or not. Some afternoons he sat with his mother, who had lost all elegance, except that of her nature.

Several times when she was awake during those afternoons she at last wanted to talk about not being his birth mother, knowing that soon he would be on his own. She said they had hoped having an adopted child would lead to them conceiving one of their own, which happened often, but not in her case. That wasn't the main reason for adopting him, she emphasised. He was wanted very much for himself. 'For years I was afraid of any odd-looking letter which came, in case it was from your mother, or the adoption authorities, and you'd be taken away from us for some reason. I tried not to show that fear, but recently when we were talking about you, Greg said he had exactly the same apprehensions, especially just after the new adoption legislation came into effect in 1986.'

'But I'd be ten then.'

'But we always knew your birth parents would be somewhere, and surely they'd love you.'

'Well, obviously they didn't care enough to make the effort, and it's never really bothered me. You know that.'

That particular afternoon the sky was very blue, and the sea of the bay also. Naylor wore shorts and his Bristol University T-shirt. He sat on one of the wooden kitchen chairs that had become a fixture by his mother's bed. Terminal illness seemed an anomaly on such a day, and his mother, though weak, wanted to talk rather than sleep. 'You know it's all quite straightforward now, finding birth parents. There's a whole website on it. You must have done a search?'

'I haven't,' Naylor said truthfully. 'You and Dad never brought it up, and it never bothered me. What's the point, after all?'

His mother thought there were several points, the most significant that she was dying and that Greg's life was insecure, but she made only oblique reference to what was so self-evident, while the blue sea shimmered, and six or seven small yachts of the same class drew wakes upon it. She told him it could be important some day to have medical knowledge about his parents, and that the longer he put off trying to make contact the more difficult it would be.

'We've got a copy of your birth certificate,' she said. 'We were given it when we adopted you. I don't think many got that.' She took it from a heavy, brown envelope on the bed and passed it to her son. The certificate gave his full name as Naylor Robin Coombes and his mother's as Frances Emily Coombes. There was nothing in the space reserved for the father. 'There'll come a time when you'll want to take it all further,' his mother said. 'I'm sorry now we didn't do something earlier. The more people who love you the better.'

'I don't think I've missed out on anything at all,' Naylor told his mother.

That evening Naylor and his father had a slow walk while the nurse gave Helen a bed wash. An easy walk was good for Greg's heart, the doctors said. Unfortunately Hataitai was mostly up and down and they had only one route that didn't involve exertion. Naylor was tall, but his father was even taller. They had always enjoyed the private joke when people referred to Greg having passed on that gene to his son. Greg had a habit of stooping to other people in conversation which some mistook for condescension but was consideration. Naylor watched his father's tall, slender body sway as he walked, rather as a giraffe sways front to back, not side to side, so that the high body remains in balance. His father was an abstemious man who didn't smoke, ate sparingly and drank good whisky when he drank at all. It certainly wasn't lifestyle that gave him a dicky heart. Maybe it was the asthma that had troubled him, especially when he was younger. Despite himself, Naylor thought of what his mother had said regarding a medical history. He wasn't aware of any particular weaknesses, but who knew what his genes had in store for him.

Naylor kept his pace down, and told his father about the birth certificate and Helen's new-found enthusiasm for him to make some inquiries regarding his birth parents. Greg squeezed his eyes shut momentarily and compressed his lips, as he did when making some concession, some declaration, or coming upon emotion. 'Your birth mother did get in touch,' he said. 'It wasn't long after the new legislation and some counsellor or other approached me with a letter from her. That's the way they do it evidently, or they did then. I accepted the letter, but didn't tell Helen. You know how she feared just that. I accepted it, and replied saying I thought it best that contact wasn't made. You were going off to secondary school and had enough to cope with.'

'What did it say?'

'Just that she didn't wanted to poke in after all those years, but she'd never forgotten you and would appreciate any information. I told her I didn't think it was the right time, and that was it. There weren't any more letters. I don't know what happened to that one, otherwise I'd give it to you even now.'

They stood on the corner that marked the turning point of their walk. The sun had gone beyond the hill and dusk was blurring the sharper demarcations of the day. A steady breeze came in from the sea, which was hidden from view. 'I had to make a decision, and I hope it was the right one,' his father said. 'I admit it was as much for us as for you, especially Helen.'

'You did it for the best — and it probably was.'

His mother almost stopped eating in the last weeks, and died earlier than the doctors, or her family, expected. She went on a morning she was being visited by a relative she'd never much liked, and while Greg was making coffee. He told Naylor maybe she chose to avoid the visitor in that way. It was a form of humour Helen would have enjoyed. The funeral was non-religious and well-attended, and both husband and son spoke, but Naylor felt a dissociation and lack of grief which arose not from any deficiency of love, but an inability to accept that someone so integral in his life was there no more. No reference was made to Naylor being adopted: most people wouldn't have been aware of that.

Afterwards, though, he found himself thinking about it a good deal, and talking about it too with his father. It was not at all that he sought replacement for his mother, but for the first time he felt curiosity, which was partly the consequence of his mother's death: a sense of permission when the inquiry she had encouraged could not possibly threaten her.

Greg was encouraging also, perhaps partly as a self-imposed penitence for stifling that approach by letter many years before. And the mystery of it was a mild intrigue. 'Of course your birth mother may be dead, your father too for all we know, but I think you should consider them as well as yourself. Maybe your birth mother is all alone, or unhappy. Maybe she still wants to know about you. And there's no obligation on either side: that's the good thing, as I see it. Definitely no obligation. None at all.'

They were talking in the lounge on the evening of the day spent helping Helen's sister pack up her things. In time, his father said, he'd move back into the main bedroom with its en suite and view over the sea, but not for a while. Helen's presence was still strong there, and neither wished to diminish it. During the nights immediately after the funeral, Naylor had woken sometimes thinking his mother had turned on her light, thinking he heard her muffled cough. There would be nothing, though his father still padded to the lavatory, still left it unflushed — habit, or a transferred consideration, Naylor wondered. His aunt had suggested some of Helen's jewellery be given to her female relations, nieces in particular, though no such bequests were in the will. Naylor was surprised at the vehemence with which his normally placid father refused to consider that. Naylor was to have it all, he said. They'd talked about it, he said, he and Helen, and just because Naylor was male didn't mean the personal stuff shouldn't be his. And just because he wasn't theirs by blood didn't mean that either, though neither Greg nor his sister-in-law spoke of that. 'Give away the clothes and all that spare linen in any way you like,' Greg had said. 'And take what you like of the dinnerware sets. We're indebted to you for your help.'

In the evening, though, he did talk of adoption and Naylor's options. 'It's completely up to you,' he said. 'You've already got the birth certificate. You can look up the surname in the Telecom White Pages: it's not a very common name. If she's married since then you can check the marriage records. It's up to you, though. Maybe something good could come of it for you and her, maybe not.'

Greg clearly saw the likelihood that he might soon follow Helen, and that Naylor would be left only relatives with whom he had legal connection. Although his father rarely talked of love, he was both sensitive and consistent in its application.

It was a distraction as much as anything else at first, the search for Frances Emily Coombes, and it had as well the element of detection. Naylor was surprised, however, by the comparative ease with which he was able to track his mother down. The changes to the law facilitated it, as did access to official records, and he soon knew Frances was still alive, that she had married and taken the surname of Hollister, and that she lived in Sydney by the zoo. The hard part was deciding if he wanted to make contact after leaving it so long. The satisfaction of his only recently aroused curiosity would be little compensation if any reunion turned out badly, and it wasn't as if he felt any driving need to find Frances, even after Helen's death.

It was a dream that made up his mind. Nothing apocalyptic, or even particularly surreal. He dreamt his father died in the same way as his mother and of the same disease, and that at the funeral, which was held in a very open, paddock-like space, a spiky-haired woman wearing an orange skivvy and grubby tracksuit pants stood up unbidden, and said that the loss of parents was sad but natural, while the loss of a child was unnatural and grievous. Naylor didn't at all think the woman represented his birth mother — rather she reminded him of a mature student in his Bristol University study group whom he'd rather disliked — but the idea that his mother might have suffered in some significant way because she was denied knowledge of him, remained strong.

He said nothing to Greg about the dream. His father would be doubtful of such provenance for any contact with Frances Coombes, or Hollister. Naylor gave instead the rational, commonsense reasons his father had given him, and Greg was satisfied in this way with his own persuasion returned. He agreed, too, with the advice Naylor had been given by the Adult Adoption Central Registry, which was to write to his mother, but have a counsellor in Sydney approach her to see if she wished to receive the letter, and, if so, by what means. Who knew how she might react, or if the husband had been told of Naylor's existence.

The letter said nothing of Helen's death, and not a lot about

Naylor and his life: just that he was now independent and wondered
if Frances still wanted to make contact. The reply was prompt and
came directly from Frances herself. She didn't have any other children,
she said, and made no reference to her husband. After such a long
time, they should meet as soon as possible. She suggested, in what
Naylor took to be a joke, that they toss for which of them should
travel to see the other, 'though maybe it would be awkward for your
family if I came over. I don't want that. Minimum expectation, no
demands, but how I look forward to seeing you.'

Naylor wondered if his father was well enough to be left by himself,
but Greg said he would be fine, and promised not to overdo things.
'I think it's better you go there,' he said. 'If it all gets a bit tricky, you
can choose when to disengage. Not that there's any particular reason
to think it will, but there's the potential for a great deal of emotion,
isn't there,' and he squeezed his eyes closed at the thought of the
heightened feelings a woman could be capable of in such a situation.
'But she said minimum expectations and no demands, didn't she.
Good, good.'

So not long before Christmas, Naylor flew to Sydney, and then
took the ferry across the harbour, and a taxi to his mother's house
close to Taronga Zoo. The day was overcast and hot, the house was
wooden and unexceptional, Naylor's feelings were confused, and
for a moment he considered turning back. Instead he looked at
attractive treetops in the distance, and guessed they were in the zoo,
then he used the wrought iron door knocker which was in the shape
of a woodpecker.

What did he expect there in another country and unfamiliar
surroundings? How, at twenty-six years of age, was he meant to greet
his mother for the first time? At the very second the door opened
there came a single, piercing wail from the zoo. 'It's the bloody
howler monkeys,' the woman said. 'I'm Frances — give me a hug.'
She was short and he was tall, which added to the awkwardness of
the brief embrace. 'Come in, come in,' she said in a consciously

cheerful voice, and led him inside. 'That too,' she said, when he was about to leave his bag.

They walked right through the house and onto wooden decking at the back which looked out to a square of lawn, four rows of vigorous tomato plants, and neighbouring houses on slightly lower ground. In the centre of the lawn a spray hose attachment rotated with a faint protest, and the water made a soft hiss in the air, and a repetitious patter on the grateful grass. Naylor and Frances sat on wooden patio chairs and took stock of each other as they talked.

'It'll be strange for a while won't it,' she said. 'I think we should aim to become friends first, and then let things happen naturally. My God but you're tall. I know you're Campbell now, but it means a lot to me that your first name's still Naylor. I chose it because it was my dad's name, and he never completely gave up on me.'

'Mostly I come across it as a surname,' he said.

Had he expected some genetic frisson on meeting his mother, an instinctive bond immediately apparent between them? Well, it didn't happen, but there was pleasure and goodwill, and curiosity too, beneath the wariness which at least Naylor showed. Both of them were aware of the incongruity — a mother and son who were complete strangers to each other, making rather routine conversation in mundane surroundings. The unseen zoo was the only external sign of any peculiarity, and exotic hoots, shrieks and ambiguous cries occasionally punctuated their conversation. There was so much for each to find out about the other, and such sensitive care not to push interest into interrogation, that peripheral topics took hold. Naylor was told all about the tomatoes in the whispering spray, and their importance for Frances's favourite pastas, long before learning that no longer was there a Mr Hollister on the scene, and Frances heard all about Bristol University in the first hour or so, but not that Helen was dead.

And as they talked they studied each other, letting their gaze fall briefly in consideration, rather than embarrassment, when their eyes met too directly. Naylor could see nothing of himself in his mother, unless it was her hair, which was brown, soft and limp like his own. She was perhaps five foot five and slightly overweight, but Naylor was surprised how young she looked, and realised he had illogically been expecting her to be Helen's age. Her skin was smooth, her bust unaccentuated, and her hands, spread on the wooden armrest of the chair, were small. She was an unexceptional woman, one you would pass in the supermarket aisle without more than a glance, and Naylor was slightly disconcerted by that. He realised he had subconsciously assumed his mother to be different, to be outstanding to him, because of their relationship. That she wasn't, caused not so much disappointment as a faint bewilderment.

'It's an odd situation, isn't it,' he said, realising she might be feeling much the same.

'Jesus, that's certainly right. But it's special too, don't you think, to meet up like this after years and years.' There came a particularly loud trumpeting from the zoo.

'Must be feeding time,' Naylor said.

'For me it's like living next to the railway tracks, or the ocean: the noise becomes so familiar it hardly registers, unless some new creature starts up.' They both listened for a moment, but the zoo didn't proclaim itself further. 'Why don't we ask each other two questions before I get something for us to eat? It might make it easier to relax afterwards.'

'You mean difficult questions?' said Naylor.

'Ones to get out of the way, yes. Short answers now and perhaps the full explanations when we know each other better.'

'Fair enough.'

'You go first then,' she said.

It made a game of the situation, almost, but a game that permitted licence. The zoo was quiet as if even the animals there wished to hear the questions and answers, and the spray from the hose attachment caught the sun briefly in a glitter of rainbow fragments.

'Why did you give me up?' he asked her. 'I'm not at all bitter though.'

'I was nineteen years old, unmarried, and my mother said it would be best for everybody.'

'Who was my father?'

'I knew that would be the next question. He was a tutor at the polytechnic where I started a journalism course. He was in his early forties and married with three daughters. When I told him I was pregnant he gave me $5,000 and the brush-off. I can give you his name if you want it.'

'I've got a name,' said Naylor. 'Anyway, he's probably dead by now, isn't he.'

'I haven't a clue,' said Frances. 'But it wouldn't be hard to find out. But it's not just him to consider — you know now you have half-sisters?'

Naylor asked her if she had more children of her own although he knew the answer, and she smiled and shook her head. 'That's another reason why it's so great you've turned up. I did try to get in touch, you know, years ago now, and Mr Campbell was against it.'

'I know,' Naylor said. 'He thought it best for me and Mum — Helen.'

'He wrote a very kind and thoughtful reply. Although I was disappointed at the time, it made me think he must be a very intelligent man, and I was glad to think of him as your father.'

Naylor knew the opportunity was there to talk of his parents, to say that Helen had recently died, but he was surprised by an almost overwhelming gust of grief, and couldn't at that moment talk of one mother to the other. 'So it's your turn for two free questions,' he said, and Frances smiled again.

'Did you often wonder who your real parents were?'

Naylor had no more sensitivity than was usual in a young Kiwi guy, but he was aware of the need for tact above honesty in answering that question. 'I did quite often,' he said, 'but Mum and Dad never

brought it up and we were happy as we were.' Frances was waiting
for more. 'And I suppose because, as far as I knew, you'd made no
effort to get in touch, I just put it to the back of my mind.'

'I've never wanted to be one of those mothers who give away a
baby to someone else to bring up, then expect to be welcomed back
when the hard work's done.'

'Fair enough.'

'Were you happy — are you happy? When I'd think of you that
was the thing for me. I'd tell myself, he's happy for sure, with people
who love him.'

'Like most kids I had ups and downs,' Naylor said, 'but I was
lucky with my family. It was a very secure place for me, whatever
else happened.'

'And you've done so well — your degrees and that. Everyone's
proud of you, I bet.'

Frances stood up and went down the steps of the deck to turn off
the sprinkler. The last of the water fell with a patter on the lawn and
tomato plants. In the back yard of the house beyond them a guy had
a push bike upended on seat and handlebars for a mechanical check.
'I've got a green salad and some ham on the bone for us,' she said,
'and some blueberry muffins. Do you drink wine, or beer?'

'Beer usually, but I'm easy.'

'You can sit here and listen to the zoo, or you can come inside
while I get it ready and talk.'

'The zoo's pretty quiet now. I'll come in,' said Naylor.

In the small kitchen they continued to talk as Naylor cut ham,
and did what else he could to help. He learnt that Francis hadn't
gone on with journalism, that she was office manager for a sizable
courier firm. She'd had bad luck with men, she said, without giving
details. Now she was happy living by herself, although she still had
friends of both sexes. 'What about yourself?' she asked casually,
without glancing up from the salad she was preparing.

There had been no one special since he left for study in Bristol.

The subject, though, heightened the peculiarity of the situation. He was standing in the kitchen of a stranger, who happened to be his mother and was asking him about his love life. And the thing was, he found it easy enough to answer, because there was no history of emotional intimacy between them: no premises in their lives which both had tacitly accepted as private after years of discourse.

He spent that night in a small, green room with mismatched furniture. The bed-ends were of natural wood, the chest of drawers painted white with ceramic knobs. He occupied the full length of the bed, and could feel the wood with his feet. Maybe it was a young person's bed. For a long time he didn't sleep. He found himself listening for the noises from the zoo and trying to identify them. Although the species were drawn from all over the world, he imagined that most of the individual animals had lived in zoos all their lives, and unlike himself would feel no sense of displacement at all.

He experienced a mixture of emotions from the day. Chief among them, to his surprise, was a sense of sadness and guilt concerning Helen. Meeting and talking with Frances had strangely unlocked his grief concerning the mother he knew: maybe he must farewell one of them before he could draw close to the other.

'What do you think we should do today?' Frances asked him at breakfast. It was a prelude to her idea of visiting friends later in the morning. He had only that full day before flying back home, and considered it strange that she should want to share much of it with other people. At first he thought the motive was to relieve the pressure of being one on one after all the years apart, but he realised Frances wanted to show him to other people: to have the satisfaction, long delayed, of being a public mother. It was a little embarrassing, but also endearing in a way.

Alistair and Jude Soloman had an expensive home out of earshot of the zoo and with a fine view across the harbour. They had their own computer firm, which specialised in developing stocklist software for retailers. Alistair was large, brown and hairy everywhere except the top of his head. He had the direct joviality typical of success. Jude was smaller, browner, less hairy, but equally friendly. Her husband told Naylor with some pride that she was the one in the firm with the brains.

The four of them sat on black leather sofas close to the large lounge window with its view of the sea. 'We've been trying to get Frances to come and work for us,' said Alistair. We need someone like her to organise us — a sort of practice manager. It's all got too big for Jude and me to handle and still push ahead the creative stuff.'

'I can't think of a quicker way to spoil our friendship,' said Frances. 'You both know that.' She had told Naylor that she had known both of them for years: she had been Alistair's girlfriend and Jude's flatmate.

How much they knew about Naylor, however, he wasn't sure; certainly neither Alistair nor Jude showed any great curiosity about his sudden appearance in Frances' life. Most of the talk was of living in Aussie, and business management. Alistair in particular was interested in Naylor's course at Bristol University and whether theoretical business models had a useful translation to actual firms and specific conditions. Naylor enjoyed the discussion. Alistair and Jude were lively challengers without any antagonism at all, and the observations Frances made were full of common sense.

'Stay for lunch,' said Jude Soloman warmly, when it was already past one, and Alistair gave a bushy eyebrow flash of endorsement, but Frances said they'd better get back. When the two women were talking on the way to the car, Alistair took the opportunity to say something personal for the first time. 'That Bryn Hollister,' he said. 'No good at all. A bugger of a man in fact. He ripped your mother off financially as well as everything else. She probably wouldn't tell you that. Anyway, good to meet you, good to see you. We think the world of Frances, and she's been so excited since you got in touch.' He put a very clean, very hairy, hand on Naylor's shoulder briefly.

'Hope to see you again,' he said.

'Did you like them?' asked Frances as they were driving home.

'Yeah, I did. Two people pretty much on the ball, and they've obviously done well. I'm not sure, though, why you wanted me to meet them now.'

'I suppose I wanted some of my friends to see you so that I could talk about you with them later and they'd know who you were. And I suppose I wanted you to see that I'm not all by myself. I was thinking last night how I must seem to you, in my mid-forties and my job isn't very glamorous, and I haven't got a flash house, or a flash car. I'm just getting back on my feet after the marriage thing.'

'As long as you're okay, what does it matter if you haven't got a mansion like your friends,' said Naylor.

'I guess the Campbells had the best of everything when you were growing up. Both of them being professional people and self-employed.'

'We don't live extravagantly,' said Naylor.

They had a walk in the afternoon, and went to the zoo. It seemed a waste to Naylor to be so close, to hear the noise of it, but not enter. Frances hadn't been for ages, she said. The places on your doorstep tend to get overlooked, don't they, until someone comes from outside and is interested. They took the funicular, they viewed the open savannah sections, they appreciated the culturally correct elephant premises, but Naylor enjoyed most the big crocodiles. Their sinister weight as if carved in old iron or pewter, yet those bodies so solid on the banks could, when immersed, hang just below the surface of the water.

The zoo gave them immediate and various topics of conversation when their own inventory failed. It was odd that their second day together was more difficult than the first. Not that they had discovered anything in each other which aroused dislike or distrust, just that the first urgency of meeting was waning and to talk of intimate things was no easier. To admire the silken menace of the

tigers was a relief from any consideration of the future. To watch
the frantic social interaction of monkeys at feeding relieved mother
and son for a time from the quandary of their own relationship. The
awareness of kinship is not enough in itself to allow access to the
heart: Frances and Naylor were well intentioned, but still essentially
strangers.

Most of the evening they filled with explanations of what each
had been doing in all those years apart, and what ambitions each had
for the future. Events and achievements in particular had a protective
rationality: they ended with a sort of curriculum vitae knowledge of
each other. Later, however, in the small green bedroom, with the
bottom of his feet touching the wood, and unable for a second night
to sleep much, Naylor heard Frances crying. It wasn't loud, or high-
pitched, but in the silence of the night he was sure of the sound.
He wanted to ignore it; told himself how intrusive, how awkward,
it would be to make any response. But himself answered back and
said it was his mother weeping, and that tomorrow they would be
separated again as they had been almost all their lives.

To his relief the sobbing stopped, but then he heard Frances walk
quietly through to the kitchen, and faint, yellow rods outlined his
door, which was ajar. She had turned on the kitchen light. Naylor was
reminded of Helen and nights of her illness. He saw from the bedside
digital clock that it was 4.30 in the morning, and he reluctantly
got up and went to the kitchen. Just before he entered he found
himself squeezing his eyes and mouth closed, a quick expression
of unease much in the manner of his father, and his affection and
understanding for Greg flicked out strongly for a moment.

Frances wore a blue towelling dressing-gown, and her feet were
bare. She stood by the sink with a mug in her hands and the window
behind her was darkly reflective. 'I didn't mean to wake you,' she
said.

'I heard you crying and thought I'd better come out.'

'It's what you were afraid of, I suppose. To come over here and find your mother is a flaky woman who blubs in the night.'

'Actually I thought things were going pretty well for a first meeting. I reckoned that we were okay, though of course we're just starting to get to know each other.'

'I promised myself, and you without you knowing it, that I wasn't going to get all emotional. Young guys hate that, I know. Well, all guys do.' Frances came to the table and sat on one of the chairs. Naylor did the same. He had no dressing-gown, and was barefoot as well, but there was warmth in the Australian summer night. He was still pale from his time in England, and his feet were the colour of skim milk. Four thirty in the morning at the kitchen table is a time for straight talking in anyone's understanding of such things. Even the noises of the zoo were temporarily in abeyance.

'You can tell me,' said Naylor.

'There's nothing so special,' said Frances. 'The thing is I feel guilty. I've always felt guilty, and it's stopping me saying the things I want to say. It's stopping me reaching out the way I feel I should. After Mr Campbell wrote and said it was best not to make contact with you, I had counselling on and off for quite a while about the whole business. One of the things the psychologist said was that guilt is incapacitating, and Jesus, is that true. Nothing I can say or do really changes the fact that I ditched you, just as your real father ditched me. Nothing from now on can ever change that.'

'No one blames you,' said Naylor.

'I blame myself,' she said. 'Maybe, though, it's not just guilt, but knowing now I'll never bring a child up. I'll never be a mother to you in that way.'

'You're still my mother.'

They came to it at last, sitting tousled before the dawn: what each thought could come of their meeting. Perhaps it would be the closest, most candid time, they would ever have before they drew back to safe ground; perhaps it was the threshold of some growth of intimacy. They made more coffee and talked as the sky gradually lightened outside, and the cries and calls of the zoo were further herald of the day. Naylor felt at last he was able to tell Frances that Helen was dead: to praise her to his living mother without a sense of betrayal, or competition. He'd half expected to weep at the disclosure, but instead felt relief and gratitude, and went on to speak of Greg as well. In the past there had never been anyone to whom he felt he could praise his parents as they deserved. It was Frances who cried a little as well as smiling and nodding her head to encourage him. It was Frances who took his hand, with neither feeling awkwardness because of it. 'I'll always envy her, though,' she said.

'I lied as well,' she said then.

'Lied about what?'

'About your real father and me. It wasn't true what I said yesterday about that.'

'So who was he really then?'

'Oh, he was the married journalism tutor and all that,' said Frances. 'True enough about the money too, but what I didn't say was that I loved him, and I think he loved me. Maybe I still love him and that's why I'm alone now. Love can be unbearably painful, can't it. Their garage was on the street and we used to meet there at night — sit in the car and talk, make love in the back seat. In all the times I was in that car the engine never started, but Jesus, we went some places. We switched on, Errol and I.

'I'm not just talking about sex. We really talked. Know what I mean? We trusted each other to talk about anything at all: sometimes the first silly things that came into our heads, sometimes the most personal truth we knew. The garage always smelled of fish and macrocarpa, because his fishing gear hung by the door, and one side of the garage was lined with firewood.

'But he wasn't prepared to leave his wife.' Naylor was unsure if he wanted any rehabilitation of his father's reputation. In fact he'd been somewhat relieved to strike him off.

'I was nineteen, he was forty-two and with a family. What future could there be in it? We cried a lot, and although the sex was like a drug there was a sort of desperation about it which we never acknowledged, but which made it sad. Secretly he wanted to be a war correspondent, not a polytechnic tutor. Stuff was going on overseas and he was always talking about it and wishing he was there. He felt his life was on too small a scale, I think: that he could do more if he just got an opportunity.'

'So after the pregnancy and the money you never saw him again?'

'No, but I went to the place one last night without telling him. The garage's back door was always unlocked, and I went in and sat in the car and bawled for a while, with just the smell of fish and macrocarpa to remind me of everything. Then I went home. Put your mistakes behind you: that's what my mother kept telling me. Put your mistakes behind you. Maybe she never was in love. I can't hate him, you know. Even now I don't hate him. I'm not much older now than he was then, and often I'm no more satisfied with my life than he was with his.'

'He'd be an old bugger of seventy now,' said Naylor. 'Have you thought of that? You wouldn't want to run across him now even if he was alive.'

'He was always a good-looking guy.'

'I wondered where I got it from,' Naylor said. He didn't want things to get too heavy. In truth he felt an absence of curiosity regarding this father, rather an increased loyalty to Greg Campbell, who could also be seen as an old bugger of seventy-odd, with heart failure imminent, but whom he loved. The half-sisters were another matter altogether, one too difficult to even consider for the moment — maybe ever.

He would be gone in a few hours. The full sun of the day would come, the zoo would begin its public function, Frances would be cheerfully practical again and he would take the ferry across the harbour and then take to the skies to return home. He would return, having met his birth mother, and with the new knowledge that he had sisters, so rather than things being solved, or finished, they grew more complex and more emotionally demanding. But then that is the nature of a family. In each other they had met something of themselves hitherto missing, and felt strengthened by it, even as they recognised the challenge.

Images

The virtues of my father's character, which I recognised as a boy, became obscured by their familiarity and my arrogance as a youth. Now that he has been dead for quite a time, those virtues are clear to me again, and I realise that he was a fine man. Sometimes in the night I see my father in his prime, and what forms most commonly is the image of him standing on the veranda, with the sleeves of his white shirt half rolled up, and that inward smile on his long face.

My father was a policeman, a detective in fact, in the days when the qualifications for entry were still demanding. He was six foot one, and he never went to fat the way a lot of other policemen did. He ran in the evenings long before that became fashionable: he was the instructor at a fitness class set up for the city police force. He took pride in his physical capability and appearance, not from vanity, but self-respect and because in his job he expected a lot from his body.

I can remember when my father was a uniformed policeman, but more typically I recall him in mufti when he'd been promoted to detective. He was detective inspector in the end, but I was long gone by then. Sometimes he wore grey slacks and a Harris tweed sportscoat, sometimes his dark blue suit, but always a white shirt, and a grey hat when he went out. The hat, I think the style was called fedora, had a dark band and a dint in the top, which my father would sometimes correct with a chopping action of his right hand. Most men and women wore hats in those days when going out, of course. In the image that comes at night of my father on the veranda in his prime, the sleeves of his white shirt are always rolled up in a particular way: not twisted tightly right up onto the biceps, but just two or three folds so that the material lay about halfway between wrist and elbow, and the brown skin of his forearms showed, with the thick, black watchstrap on the left one. When we were together, when he was talking with me, he'd often rest his left hand on my shoulder, and his strong forearm and big, plain watch would be close to my face.

My father was a family man. He and my mother were disappointed, I think, that I was their only child, but that gave me an even greater sense of being loved and being secure. My father often worked long hours, and odd hours too. That's the way it is in the police, but Mum and I always knew how important we were. Once, he promised to take us to see my mother's brother who was sick in Auckland. They told me he was sick, but they knew he was dying, I suppose. Just a couple of hours before we were due to go, the station rang and the superintendent wanted my father to come in urgently, and he wouldn't. The telephone was on a table in the hall, with no chair beside it. People used the phone quite differently then. And I heard my father say that he had expressly asked for this day off, and that it was important for his family, and unless he was given a written order he was going to go. And we did go. My mother saw her brother, and he died of some intestinal thing quite soon after.

My father was very strong like that. He formed his own convictions; he trusted his own judgement, not in a dismissive way without paying heed to the views of others, but because that's how he thought a man should be. A man should be able to form a reasoned and fair view of the world and act accordingly, rather than going along in an unexamined fashion.

My father wasn't a great one for books, although he read the newspaper carefully, listened to radio broadcasts of the news and sport, and encouraged me to read. Immediacy was the priority in his job and his life: he was directly involved with the forces that promoted stable societies and those that threatened them. I think he would have been a good reader if he'd had time. He had a very clear mind and reduced things to order, without forgetting that people have emotions, and that not everything is accessible by logic. He would see things in a month, that the dentist, or city councillor, wouldn't see in a lifetime in the same city. Some must have been awful things and they accounted for the few times when I remember him white faced and silent in the house.

Those of us brought up in a secure and loving home have had one of the great advantages of life, and I'll always be thankful to my parents for that, and make certain allowances because of it. Apart from the few times I remember my father showing particularly the stress from something in his job, he was cheerful, and a good talker. And a good listener as well. He was a positive man who knew all about the malice, deceit, hard luck and cruel desperation out there, yet thought the community had benefits which outweighed them. If people just stood firm for their principles and each other then he believed things would be okay. There was little cynicism in my father, despite his profession being one that encouraged it in some.

When I talk of my father being in his prime, I suppose I mean when I was fourteen or so, and the pensioner murders were all the city talked about, and big national news too. Three old ladies all bashed to death in separate incidents in six weeks of summer, and things done to them that the newspaper reports only hinted at. After killing Mrs Donalds the murderer sat down in the same room with her and cooked himself the fish she'd been saving for her tea.

My father wasn't home very often during that time, so much was going on. They brought in extra detectives from other districts, but my father said local knowledge would be the answer. Almost always there's someone besides the perpetrator who knows enough to make the difference, he said.

Russell Roddick and I talked about it a good deal in the second storey of the old woolstore, overlooking the overgrown river path from the reserve. We'd found a squeeze-through entrance on the railway track side, and had a place among the wool bales for our beer, chocolate, magazines and books. Russell reckoned the murderer wasn't after money because pensioners never have much if they're living by themselves, and he must just like kicking and punching old people to death. Russell asked me if my father had said much about it, and I could honestly say he hadn't, because that would have been unprofessional. He did say that anyone who could do a thing like that, and not just once, was far worse than an animal. But then everyone in the city said that.

Russell was a good mate, and we remained friends right through secondary school. He became a seismologist, of all things, and the last I heard he was in Turkey with plenty to study there. In the old woolstore hiding place we used to talk a lot of rubbish, but also at times we got on to topics that now surprise me to recall — whether our school went on too much about sport instead of academic subjects, whether we should go overseas after university, or stick to New Zealand. Both of us finally made the same choice.

I think my father knew all along who the guy was. In a place that size the police would have a pretty good list of criminals and odd people of one sort or another, and soon narrow the suspects down. It must have been a matter of getting sufficient evidence to justify an arrest.

There was nothing in the paper, nothing official, but not long after school went back, it became known the police were looking for Gil Dipport, who'd been in prison several times, and had bad blood in him, so Russell's father said. I asked my father about it one evening when he, Mum and I were sitting on the veranda after tea. 'Well, he hasn't been seen around since the attacks,' my father said, 'and we need to talk to everyone with a record. Someone must know something.'

'You've got more on him than that though, surely,' my mother said. She understood the code of understatement that was my father's way.

'Well, yes we have,' my father said, but he wouldn't go any further than that, and I don't think he would have said much more to my mother even if I hadn't been there. My parents were close and loving all their lives, but he tried to leave the police work at the door as much as he could. Some families of policemen suffered, he said, because it got about that they knew a lot of what was going on.

'Anyway,' said my mother, 'he'll be well away by now.'

'Gil's never been more than ten miles from this place in his life,' my father said.

There's only one other thing to tell, because all I remember is quite clear and simple really, not a long story. Well, it's absolutely clear and unequivocal in my mind's eye, though perhaps not so simple after all. Two evenings later I went down to meet Russell at our hideout. I ran in the drizzle through the shunting yards and metal scrap yard, and squeezed through the secret entrance. I went up to our place on the second storey. Russell hadn't arrived so I smoked a cigarillo very carefully, because we could easily have set the place on fire, and watched through the dirty window the creek and the track from the reserve which was almost hidden by the clumps of fennel and lupin in some parts, and clear on the creekbed in others.

It gave me a start to see my father walking slowly from the town side. His white shirt showed clearly and he wore no coat, no grey hat. The fine, drifting rain was just beginning to stick the shirt to his shoulders, so he couldn't have come far. He stepped behind one of those half-fallen willows which still continue to grow, and I thought he was going to take a leak. Then I saw a stooped, bald man coming the other way, from the reserve, in and out of view among the lupins. He carried an axe handle, or something similar, and I knew it was Gil Dipport. Why else would my father be waiting there?

And when my father stepped out, Gil Dipport didn't try to run back the way he'd come. I guess he knew my father's capabilities. He just backed into a clear bit of the creekbed and waited with the axe handle, or pick handle, or whatever.

I noticed my father had slipped off his shoes to give him better grip and balance. Maybe they said things to each other, but I was too far away to hear, and almost at once my father began walking up on Gil. He got hit on the arm and the neck, the bruises were there for weeks, but he soon got the better of Gil and wrenched the wooden handle from him, sending him onto the ground where he sat dazed with his legs out in front as if he was at a picnic.

Then my father took a good grip of the axe handle and hit Gil with it the way you would a dog, all the strength of his arms in the last foot or two of the blow. I've never told anybody before. That's the other image I see sometimes at night, as well as my father on the veranda with us in his white shirt with sleeves rolled up, and smiling.

I think my father was a fine man, an exceptional man, I really do. I can't think of a better family man. He's been gone a good many years, and when in the night I have this unbidden memory of him I tell myself it was too long ago to be sure of things now: too long ago and too close to childhood to bear any scrutiny.

Buster

My criminal apprenticeship was served with Buster Marrot, and though I never achieved even journeyman status later in life, and the skills decayed, two trade attitudes have remained strong with me: a proprietorial view of the possessions of others, and a disregard for authority.

Buster was fourteen, and not at all fat despite his nickname. He was dark, smiling and catlike in movement and essential independence. Buster came about the middle of a large Catholic family which lived three houses from us by the bridge on the main road out of town. The Marrots had a gaunt, two-storeyed house all of weatherboard, and fitted in two lodgers as well as seven children. One boarder was always out when I was there; the other was a man called Stokes who had been an alcoholic shearing contractor, but was just an alcoholic by the time he boarded at Buster's. He had so little, and was so easily deceived, that Buster hardly bothered to steal from him. Stokes finally drowned by accident, or design, in the river close by, but that was years after I'd moved, and my recollection is of a quiet, smiling man with washed-out eyes, who would stand with Mrs Marrot in the kitchen and peel vegetables for her. Buster's dad was a casual slaughterman at the works: something of the executioner's presence hung about him, and I always felt my breath constricted when I saw his narrow, sharpened knives laid out on oilcloth on the workshop bench. Buster said his dad could kill easily with just his hands, but still had to slit throats to bleed the sheep.

Buster went to the Catholic school, and was a year older than me. A year is nothing between adults, but it's a clear distinction at fourteen. I don't think Buster would have bothered with me if he'd had any of his school friends living close, and in the weekends I didn't see much of him. Without any discussion between us it was understood it was a 'don't call me, I'll call you' situation. Yet Buster never put me down when we were together, although he was the leader by seniority and nefarious vision. 'You're a bloody quick runner all right,' he'd say after we'd scarpered from some difficult situation. 'You've got a good head on you sometimes,' he said when I suggested selling the eggs we'd stolen from Mrs Philips to the Egg Floor. Mostly I remember him calling in the evenings of summer weekdays, our crimes played out in warm twilights, but there were earnest winter sorties as well.

I never saw any viciousness in Buster, but all his energy went to extort benefit from the world. He was unashamedly amoral and the risk of getting caught was the only consideration and deterrence in any of his plans. He seemed to have bypassed the interests which preoccupied other early teens — Scouts, balsa wood aeroplanes with real engines, rugby — but not yet moved on to sex. Buster was a materialist. Money and possessions were his goals, and he knew them interchangeable. Stolen money bought him what he wanted, and stolen items he didn't want he could flog off for money. He never passed a shop, or a works yard, without casing it for advantage, and he had several regular places that he milked, rather than making just one big hit, which would be noticed.

Borrell's Light Engineering and Metal Scrap in Cook Street was one of them. Borrell's had heaps of roughly sorted iron rusting in their back yard — old stoves, dismembered farm implements, girders, railway tracks — and a wooden barn which had lead and copper piping, brass and bronze fittings, stainless steel taps and basins, laundry coppers, stacks of ornamental wrought iron like that which decorated the Marrots' veranda and ours. Buster knew how to get into the barn through a high window and unbolt the side door. We'd come into the yard from the rough section at the back which had piles of power poles amid the long grass and lupins where we hid Buster's cart. In the dying light we'd sneak out some of the more expensive metals, but nothing that was distinctive enough to be remembered. Copper piping and lead sheet flashings were two of Buster's favourites. Some bits we sold back to Borrell's several times over. I admired Buster's restraint. He knew just how much and how often the trick could be pulled without arousing suspicion. The yard man once said that he liked our enterprise in fossicking stuff out and earning a bit for ourselves. He didn't realise the extent to which his company supported that initiative.

Buster was a bit of an artist in his felonies. He cut a rectangular hole in the pages of the library copy of *The Hunchback of Notre Dame* into which he could slip a packet of Pall Mall, or a chocolate slab, and close the cover. He had a bull-dog clip on his shoulder blades held by a string around his neck, and it was my job in the stationer's to attach a *Wheels* mag or *Batman* issue beneath his jersey, and he'd saunter out, often stopping to talk to the sales girl just for the hell of it.

Sometimes he organised a big heist, like the three yellow railway tarpaulins he stole right off some wagons loaded with boxes of vegetables in the sidings. He sandpapered off the logos, and sold the tarps for over a hundred dollars to the owner of a crayfish boat. No wonder Buster always had money in his pocket and rode a bike with blue metallic paint and gears. I wasn't there when he got down on the tarpaulins, but I was when he burgled Acme, and the outcome is clear in my mind.

Acme Warehouse stored a lot of the bulk supplies for grocery shops and dairies in town. It was a long concrete and corrugated iron building between the RSA and a yard of yellow and red agricultural machinery. Acme were in a different league to Borrell's in terms of both opportunity and security, and Buster was determined to find a way of getting regular access to so much good stuff. We sat in his father's workshop while he made a list of the most desirable and easily disposed of items. The workshop was our usual den, because Buster shared a bedroom with two brothers.

Buster was especially interested in cigarettes. He hoped to be able to take a couple of cartons every fortnight or so without them being missed. That was Buster's calculating and far-seeing nature, even as a fourteen-year-old. At the time I didn't realise his vision of criminal possibility was precocious. Tinned goods were high on Buster's list also: baked beans, pineapple slices, asparagus tips, salmon, tongue. Buster had placement sorted out for them all, and the juvenile anticipation I felt at the chance of gutsing barely registered with him.

The modern Acme building was a considerable challenge to Buster, and he worked on it. He spent a good deal of time in unobtrusive observation, and even went in and spoke to one of the storemen on the pretext that he thought he was able to buy things in bulk for a Christmas Sunday school party. The warehouse had an alarm system on the main doors, Buster said, and no windows. There was a large extractor fan high on the side away from the road, and for a time Buster wondered if we could find a way of removing the fan at will. We did a recce in the early darkness of a July night, carrying a plank surreptitiously through the back streets and then leaning it against the warehouse. I held it while Buster monkeyed up and checked the fan mounts with a torch and crescent. He decided it was too big a job, and besides, there would be too much risk coming and going with goods through such a visible and difficult route.

Buster switched his interest to the dwarfed, glass-fronted office annex to one side of the main doors. It had its own access to the store, and Buster reckoned that, as an add-on, it didn't share the concrete pan underlying the warehouse. We had several sessions sitting around his father's neatly laid out and whetted knives in the workshop, during which we drew in Buster's maths book possible tunnels from the RSA shrubbery and the machinery yard. Reluctantly we decided the plan was too risky and too slow. I suggested somehow getting an imprint of the key on a piece of soap, a comic book fantasy which Buster put aside without ridicule. In fact he said it reminded him that the office had a Yale lock with an inside snib, and this gave him the idea of hiding in the office until after closing time.

We began close planning by taking my father's binoculars down to the RSA shrubbery after school, and lying concealed there on damp, cold ground to spy on the dark-haired office woman. We learnt she spent a good deal of time doing her fingernails, and more time on the phone. She liked to eat white chocolate and take her shoes off when the sun was bright through the armour glass. There were no cash transactions that we observed, although lots of lists from the storemen and delivery drivers. Buster said there would have been lots of cheques in the morning mail which we never saw, and that they'd be in the squat iron safe, the key of which she kept in her purse. We also discovered that the key to the door from the office to the main store was kept beneath a potted cactus on the filing cabinet. The first time Buster saw her through the binoculars take the key from its hiding place to lock up, he gave a long, low whistle. I knew then he'd seen something important. It meant we could move on to the next stage of the plan.

The thing was that the office had only one possible hiding place, and Buster was too big for it. The annex was very small with just the dark-haired woman's desk, two high filing cabinets, the safe in a wooden cupboard, and the shelf with pot plants, vacation postcards and the electric jug. One of the filing cabinets was angled in a corner so that the woman could reach it from her desk, and in the recess of that angle Buster reckoned I could squeeze and hide. I had misgivings, but these were balanced by the pride I felt in being necessary for success, able at last to perform something that was beyond Buster himself.

Buster went to the office and asked if Acme might have a job for him after school. The woman didn't bother to consult anyone and said no, but Buster confirmed that the office door had a Yale snib lock, no alarm that he could see, and that the gap behind the filing cabinet should be big enough for me. That's how I ended up late on a blustery afternoon waiting around the side of the Acme building for Buster to signal from the RSA bushes that the office woman had gone through to the warehouse. It was in some ways the most tricky stage of the whole thing, even though Buster said that most of her absences he'd watched had given enough time for me to get in. Buster told me to pretend I was having a fit if she did come back before I was out of sight. I thought a fit might come quite naturally in those circumstances.

Buster gave the thumbs up from an RSA bush, and I was round the corner to the office without any conscious decision. I stepped onto the desk and then the filing cabinet, for a moment thought the space between it and the wall was insufficient, but then with the energy of fear wedged myself out of sight, my shoulders and head hard in the corner, my knees splayed for room.

On the small patch of blue carpet between my legs was a thin scurf of dust, debris and dead insects, including a bumble bee almost as large as a ping pong ball, dried flower petals, a brass drawing pin, a used tissue. I tried to relax and breathe with my mouth open to make less noise. There was no way I could know if the woman had returned, until I heard her cough at the desk and then take a call from a shopkeeper impatient to receive an order of cereals. To pass the fifteen minutes or so before closing time I imagined the most attractive tinned foods piled high in the warehouse: stacks of fruit salad, corned beef and sweetened condensed milk. And I thought of Buster's praise for my part in the carefully planned operation. I hoped I wouldn't need to sneeze, or fart, tried not to think of the consequences. The dark woman's perfume was heavy in the confined office.

I heard one of the storemen say he was on his way, and soon after there were the sounds of the office woman preparing to go home: the key turning in the door to the warehouse, its scrabble under the cactus pot, the clicking catch of a handbag, and finally the light turned off, the surprisingly loud slam of the office entrance door and a rattle as she checked it was secure. I relaxed mentally, but was so physically constricted that little movement was possible. I decided to count to three hundred before puting my head up. It was almost black behind the filing cabinet once the light was off, and I knew that even outside, a winter night would be coming fast.

After three hundred I gave an awkward push upwards, but nothing happened. Maybe I would be stuck there all night and die, while Buster looked through the window without being able to help. A desperate struggle, and I got my top half out and was able to lift myself over the steel cabinet, and drop beside the desk where I was shielded from the full-length glassed side of the office looking out to an asphalt park and then the road. The RSA bushes were indistinct wind-blown shadow, and I knew the interior of the office would be even darker to anyone outside, yet I hesitated to move about openly. I counted another hundred for good measure, in case the second storeman was slow to leave. I went to the outside door and released the Yale lock so that the door was pushed back strangely on my hands by the invisible wind. I put my left hand out and gave the thumbs up for Buster, not knowing if he'd see in the dusk.

Buster was there almost immediately, breathing heavily not from nervousness, but the sprint across the parking area. 'Bloody great. Well done,' he said, and closed the door behind him. I told him how much of a squeeze it had been. 'I knew you could do it. Shit hot,' he said, and put the binoculars carefully by the door. 'We've got to remember these.'

He took the key from under the cactus, opened the door leading to the warehouse and we went through. Just enough light spilled in from the unlit office to show the outline of two forklifts and the monolithic racks beyond. With a small plastic torch, Buster led the way down the first of the alleys between the store racks. The place was Aladdin's Cave. In the blade of Buster's torch mountains of wealth rose up disguised in sombre cartons and pallets. The racks had printed tags to identify the stores — sanitary products, pet foods, beverages, tinned soups, spices and essences. You could have spent a whole life in there and not wanted for much, I reckoned.

As we came round a corner from brown and icing sugar there was a sound in the dark like a mallet on a wooden peg, and Buster went down in front of me with a hissing cry, the torch skittering away on the bare, concrete floor. 'Shit, shit,' he said in a suppressed, angry voice. 'Just grab the torch,' he said when I knelt down by him, and when I brought it back he snatched it and shone it on his feet. His left foot was in a gin trap which was chained to the rack. The serrated jaws were sunk into Buster's ankle just above his sneakers. It was an old trap, heavily corroded although it had been given a recent oil rub all over.

Buster told me to kneel down close to his foot and take hold of one side of the jaws. He took the other. 'Try not to touch my foot,' he said, 'and pull slowly when I say.' We did it carefully, because I could tell what Buster feared was that one of us would lose grip before there was space for him to get his foot out, and he'd get another dose. When the foot was free, Buster moved it cautiously, saying, 'Shit, shit, shit,' because of the pain. 'I don't think anything's broken,' he said. The sock had soaked up what blood there was, though there was the pearly glint of Buster's round ankle bone. He sat with his back against the rack and rested for a while. I was horrified that the storemen would lay man-traps, but Buster said the gin trap would be for rats he reckoned, big bastards after all the food. I was all for getting out straight away, but with Buster's pain and anger welled up obstinacy as well. 'Take the torch and nick a couple of cartons of cigarettes,' he said. 'I'm sure as fuck not leaving with bloody nothing at all.'

So finally we were back in the little office and with the key replaced beneath the cactus pot. We let ourselves out into the dark, with a cold wind whistling at the warehouse corners. I carried the binoculars and one carton of cigarettes; Buster leant on me and tried to keep pressure off his left foot. There was nobody around in the night, and we went slowly into the RSA grounds and cut across to the river path which would take us home. Buster kept swearing when his foot got a special jolt, but he said that the warehouse people wouldn't have any idea what had sprung the trap, and we could get back in the same way anytime we damn well liked.

We never did, though, for a variety of reasons that are lost to me now, and neither do I remember seeing much of Buster after that night. When we parted close to his place, he said I could have one of the cartons, but a couple of packets was all I wanted. Buster gave me an odd, rueful grin before he limped off into the windy darkness, as if to remind me that you have to expect such things when you go up against the world.

Minding Lear

Money was scarce at the end of the university year. Well, it was always scarce, but then it was just that twitchy time between the end of lectures and the start of exams. My landlady said a friend of hers was wanting someone to look after her old dad for a few days while she and her husband had a break. Fifty dollars a day with food and accommodation, and I could spend most of the time swotting, my landlady said, because no doubt the old guy would mainly be sleeping. Maybe Mrs Lills was keen on me taking it because she'd be sure of her last few weeks' rent. Maybe her motives were altruistic and she wanted to help both me and her friend.

Mrs Lills was a tall woman with skin like a trout's belly, and everything she cooked was stringy like herself, but she set very few rules in her house and didn't interfere in my life. Mr Lills was a diesel mechanic and away most of the time on offshore fishing boats. Occasionally when I came in for a meal he'd be there, his nails ringed with grease, and he never recognised my presence, never spoke a word, as if we were on separate planes of existence, although sharing the same time and space. I wondered sometimes if we would be able to walk through each other with just the whisper of images passing.

Angeline Moffit was the friend's name, and she said if I was interested in the terms, I could come over the next morning, or the one after, to meet her dad, but no later because she had to get someone sorted as soon as possible. Angeline and her husband were going to Nelson for several days. She said the doctor told her it was imperative she have a break, absolutely imperative. I could tell from her voice that she was gratified to be the recipient of such an impressive word. My landlady said that wasn't the all of it: their marriage had been drifting, and Nelson was a second-chance honeymoon.

I went over on the morning after. The Moffits lived in Rosedown, close to the golf course, and seemed to be better off than my landlady. They had ranchslider doors that opened onto a broad concrete patio on which old man Ladd sat in a substantial chair amongst lesser, white plastic ones.

'Dad,' said Angeline Moffit, 'this is Brian who's going to keep you company when we're away.'

'Away?' said Dad.

'To Nelson and Blenheim. We talked about it, and Brian's going to make sure you're okay.'

'Brian?' said Dad. Later I was to realise that Dad was at his best in the mornings, and that's why Angeline Moffit had asked me to call round then.

Mr Ladd was eighty-eight, and suffering some sort of painless physical implosion: a big man, collapsing in on himself so that his shoulders were no longer at right angles to his spine and his head hung like a pendulum in front of his concave chest. His daughter told me he'd been the manager of an engineering firm with two hundred and seventy people, and five branches in the North Island, but what had once been robust and secular appeared to me at first sight mournful, pious and ecclesiastic. His hands were steepled in supplication, his large eyes upturned in abandoned sockets and shadowed by thickets of grey eyebrows.

'Brian's coming back on Sunday, Dad,' Angeline Moffit said, 'and he'll be company for you when we're away.'

Dad didn't say anything, but his eyes rolled at me for a moment, and the bones of his chin worked loosely, like a hand beneath a sheet.

On Sunday after lunch I put a few clothes, my books and swot notes, in my squash bag and went out to Rosedown on my Suzuki. Angeline and her husband were keen to get on their way, enjoy the imperative break from work stress, and achieve the equally imperative repair in their marriage perhaps. She said she'd written everything down on a pad by the phone, but she went over it quickly nevertheless. The first commandment, and underlined, said Dad must never be left alone. So much for squash, I thought. 'Dad's doctor is Dr Morley Smith,' said Angeline. 'I've got the number there, except he's away at present and someone's standing in.' They drove away in a white Corona and, after a quick wave to me, I could see them shrug off care and begin a relaxed conversation.

Dad and I had a little more difficulty gaining rapport. He was convinced I was a spray man come to moss proof the rooftiles, and didn't see why he should have to pay me to watch television with him. 'It's too windy to spray right now,' I told him, and although there wasn't a breath outside, he was mollified. I cottoned on early that it was more productive to debate with Dad on his own terms than appeal to reality.

Women's beach volleyball was the TV programme, and Dad and I sat in the creaking Sunday afternoon and let time pass. The women were powerful, yet shapely, and Dad nodded and blinked, sometimes scratching the top of one hand with the fingers of the other. There are some big dogs which are very lugubrious, ears, lower eyelids and the gleaming sides of their mouths all drawn down. Dad was a bit like that, but his skin in parts was scaled like a dragon's. When the volleyball women had stopped flopping onto their backs in the silky sand, Dad forgot the television and told me it was time for wine and cheese.

I wondered if he was having me on, but the checklist by the phone had no prohibition on wine and cheese. There was one of those round, soft bries in the fridge, and cans of local beer. Dad was interested in the cheese, but waved the beer aside. 'Wine, Mr Mildew, wine,' he said in a tone that implied he was humouring me rather than the other way around. The effort of getting out of the lounge chair gave him hiccups, and when I followed him through the house, rather than discovering wine, we ended in the sunroom, where Dad stood behind the warm glass and looked over the golf course. I discovered a rack of bottles in the cupboard under the stairs, and took a pinot noir back to the sunroom as an incentive for Dad to return back to the lounge. His eyes hardly left the bottle, and he stopped only twice for a hiccup session. 'Now you're talking,' he said. 'Who did you say you were again?'

'Brian.'

'And what do you do in the firm?' he said.

'I'm just here to keep you company till your daughter's back.'

Dad gave a shuddering yawn which ended in hiccups, and after shuffling into a calculated position with his bum towards the big chair, let himself fall back into it. Wine cured his hiccups and took the place of conversation. I watched some European soccer, and soon Dad was dozing with a piece of cheese, like a nub of chalk, in the hand resting on his lap. Awake, or asleep, he breathed always through his mouth, and his lips had an absolute demarcation between the dry, faded outer rind and the gleaming red swell within.

Angeline hadn't left a great deal of prepared food — perhaps she thought I had to earn my money somehow — but there was a large packet of savouries in the deep freeze, and I took some of those for our tea. I wanted to make a good start on my exam revision in the evening. Dad wasn't good at the end of the day, however: that was something I had to learn. He woke up when the sausage rolls and potato-topped miniature mince pies were heating, and bowled the pinot noir bottle with a random sweep of his arm. While I tried to get the stain out of the carpet before it set, Dad began with anxious interrogation. What time was it? Where was his family? Who was I? Who was he? Why hadn't he been asked to sign off the general accounts? When was his left leg to be amputated?

'I didn't know you're going to have a leg off,' I said.

'Who in their right mind would put up with it twitching all the time? The doctor said better to do it at home so that the Inland Revenue and the benefit people don't know. They reduce superannuation payment limb by limb the bastards.'

'Okay.'

I put the plate of savouries between us to cool, but Dad had lost awareness of such mundane things, and bit into a very hot roll, spat it out and cried out in anger and pain. It was an oddly childish error and childish reaction.

'I'm sorry,' I said.

'You're stupid,' he said. 'Who are you anyway? I thought you were going to spray the roof and then piss off. Why don't you go now.' With tears still shining in the nooks and folds of his old face, he began to finger other savouries with a fearful interest. 'What's in these anyway?'

'Sausage, egg and bacon, mince — things like that.'

'That's all right then,' Dad said. 'You need something to put lead in your pencil, not all lettuce leaves and bloody bran. You can't do a day's work on rabbit food.'

'Eat these up then,' I said, and he did, enjoying the flavour once they'd cooled a bit.

But after tea it was still broad daylight at that time of year, and how could you expect a grown man to go to bed. Dad couldn't concentrate on the television, yet was absorbed for almost an hour arranging the loose armrest covers on his armchair. 'Where did you say we are?' he asked finally when he'd lost both sleeves down the squab sides.

'At your place.'

'This rat hole doesn't ring a bell with me,' he said in a voice worn with age, a husky echo like a mournful wind in lakeside reeds.

'Well, it's your daughter's place then, and she looks after you here. It's good to have family for support, don't you reckon.'

Dad drooped his lower lip in silent derision, almost fell asleep, then looked across at me for a time. 'Where do you fit in again?'

'I'm a sort of cousin, on the other side of the family,' I told him.

'I thought you said you're going to spray something.'

'Yeah, that too,' I said.

'Most things could do with a good spray.'

In the summer twilight, almost nine o'clock, I guided Dad to his bedroom, and left the curtains open so that he could see over the golf course. There were just three boys feeling with their feet for balls in the pond, and the blue grey dusk softened their distant outlines. I put Dad's pyjamas beside him on the bed and gave him privacy so that he could undress, but when I went back, he was still sitting there and had taken off just one shoe, which he was holding to his nose like a wine glass. 'These aren't my shoes,' he whispered. 'Not by a long bloody chalk they're not, and I'm hungry, I haven't had anything to eat. If you don't eat you don't shit and if you don't shit you die.'

'What about all the savouries and cheese? What about the wine before you clobbered the bottle?'

'What do you mean?'

'I mean you've had your tea.'

'I'm hungry,' he said.

I got Dad a piece of white bread and honey, and gradually got his clothes off as he passed it from hand to hand. He had a jersey, shirt and singlet on despite summer, and his bones were the only strong lines on his white body. 'There'll be someone in the house tonight, won't there?' he said.

The whole business of getting him off to bed took much longer than I'd thought, and I didn't try to get any swot done after all. I told myself that I'd have a routine for the three days. After watching triceratops and brachiosaurus shaking the earth for half an hour, I switched off the TV, and went to the bedroom Angeline had assigned me, which doubled as her husband's study. The bed was more a settee, and little further than nose distance from the grunty desktop PC and inkjet colour printer. Most of the books were about structural engineering: titles like *Ferro Concrete and Earth Tremors*, *Stress Coefficients in Angular Steel* and *The Place of Design in Practical Construction*. There were a few rugby books, with the photograph pages sticking out slightly from the remainder of the text.

I fell asleep with my face in the eerie green glow of a digital clock, close enough to swallow. A dream of monsters possessed me utterly until a utahraptor reared up and cried, 'I need to shit. Why has this bloody place no lavatory? Rats, rats everywhere, but no lavatory.' The incongruity, and perhaps the scale of consequence, woke me suddenly, and the kiwifruit clock numerals showed almost 3 a.m. Old Mr Ladd swayed in the doorway, half hobbled by his falling pyjama trousers. 'Too late, too late,' he mourned in his stage whisper, and sobbed as he let loose on the floor.

For just a moment I imagined that if I closed my eyes I could return to the lesser terrors of giant carnivores, but the reek of reality was too strong for that. Whatever Angeline was paying me it wasn't enough. I tried to persuade Dad to stay put in the doorway so at least there would be only one clean-up site, but he wandered, desolate and tearful, soiling all as he went. Corralled in the bathroom at last, he reluctantly stepped into the shower, but there somewhat recovered his spirits in warmth and steam.

'Who are you again?' he asked.

'I'm your man Friday,' I said. 'I'm your minder while Angeline's away.'

'She was a wonderful kid, so affectionate. She and my wife were like sisters, and often when I came home from work I'd hear them laughing even as I got out of the car.'

I was almost in the shower with him, reaching through the doorway to make sure he was cleaned up. A situation of intense physical familiarity and yet we were complete strangers. It was easier, though, because I knew that soon he would have quite forgotten his recent humiliation, while his daughter's affection endured in his memory. And she would be a wonderful kid, a glowing and retrospective emblem, no matter how cursory her later regard had become.

In new pyjamas, Dad went obediently to bed, but not to silence. As I cleaned up in the hall and bathroom, he talked on and on about his life in a time before I was born. Awareness of a listener, rather than a partner in conversation, seemed to be his need. 'Are you there?' he'd call from time to time, and a word in reply, or a bang on the plastic bucket, was enough for him to continue. He told me that Angeline had always made his birthday cake after she was eight, that his son, Theo, could have been a world beater in gymnastics if he'd stuck at it.

'Good, was he?' I said, after partly opening the bathroom window and coming to his doorway. 'Where is he now?' It was out before I remembered my landlady telling me that Angeline's brother had died overseas.

Dad didn't reply for a time. His head and shoulders were darker shadows against the bed end. Then, 'You'll be old yourself in time,' he said. 'See how you like it when your turn comes I say. How would you like to go without food for days?'

'We've had plenty to eat, though.'

'Useless prick,' Dad said emphatically.

Half an hour later he was snoring and the smell of shit was growing fainter throughout the house. I weighed up whether I should ring the stand-in doctor the next day and say there was no way I could cope with the old guy. In the few hours sleep that followed, I had another dream: not about dinosaurs, but gymnasts. A whole flock of them performing at once very high on wires, bars and trapeze. All men with cut-away singlets, and superb musculature. All wheeling and spinning and leaping without effort, and all with Dad's head on their young bodies like a lugubrious mask. I could hear the smack of taut equipment, and see the faint drift of chalk from their palms as they prepared for each exercise. Maybe that's how Theo passed the time since his death.

No wonder I slept in. Dad was humming ballads as I made sense of my surroundings. 'Hang Down Your Head, Tom Dooley' was the only one I recognised. My own father sang it sometimes.

'Who are you again?' Dad asked me when I was helping him with his underpants. He was at his best in the mornings.

'I'm your helper.'

'Helper?'

'And maybe I'll spray the roof,' I said.

Dad seemed pleased with something familiar in that. 'Just so,' he said with hollow, echoing satisfaction.

After the grotesque pantomime of the night, the sunlit Canterbury morning promised a conventional sanity. Dad ate toast with ginger marmalade and discoursed on factory management, taking me for a member of his team. 'You see,' he said, 'It's not important now whether I know anything about engineering at all. It's leadership and man management skills that are important to run a company. It's a truth that seems to have to be discovered over and over again. People think the best chemist should run the pharmaceutical company, and the top academic head the university. In fact it's all about motivation and team building.'

'Isn't that American touchy-feely bullshit?' I said. If Dad Ladd was up to coherent discussion in the mornings then why not have intellectual stringency.

'I thought so myself at first, but it's their palaver that's false, not the premise. Take this deal at the moment with the stainless steel casings for Hentlings.' But Dad's voice then lost resolve, as he realised there was some discontinuity between the Hentlings contract and his Monday morning breakfast with a stranger. Bewildered pride stopped him saying more, and he concentrated on his coffee, his head cantilevered far over the table. In the afternoons and evenings when Dad was well away I played anarchic fool to his Lear without scruple, but in the mornings, when he regained something of his original self, I was just an imposter and voyeur, and a sad discomfort was often the tone.

Dad then gazed out across the golf course, his great, loose eyes sliding glances at me when he thought he was unobserved. Defensiveness is a ploy of age, as the mind itself proves unreliable. 'I'm here to keep you company while your daughter's away for a few days,' I said, to spare him the indignity of yet another inquiry as to where he was in the world and with whom.

He nodded firmly, as if he'd been sure of that all along. 'It's good weather here at this time of year,' he said.

I hung out Dad's pyjama bottoms on the line, aware that more articles would have disguised his little accident, but then realised that he had no recollection of such recent things. Some afflictions ameliorate their own effects. A whole day with Dad stretched ahead. For a time I encouraged him to talk more of his management practices and attitudes, but he grew impatient with the lack of sophistication in my questions, and after explaining the professional development system he'd instituted to identify management potential, he fell silent and ignored further promptings.

There was no way I could stand being housebound for three days, and I decided if Dad couldn't be left alone, then he'd have to come with me. I asked him if he played squash and although his answer was noncommittal, I told him that he was bound to enjoy watching anyway. 'We can get a break out of the house,' I said cheerfully, in that positive, sweepalong way that works sometimes with kids. Dad gave a lopsided grin. I rang Martin and told him to meet me there.

I wasn't entirely irresponsible. I put the one helmet on Dad, and even though the sun glittered in the blue, summer sky and the breeze across the golf course was warm to the touch, I buttoned him into his ankle-length, dark, Jack the Ripper coat, and encouraged him to climb onto the Suzuki behind me. The squash bag I held between my thighs and rested on the handlebars. 'Hang on tight, and lean in when I do,' I told him. He did hold on, and as the little bike screamed its way to the squash club, I was aware of Dad's long face at my left shoulder. Did he wonder how it had come to this? A man who had been general manager of an engineering firm employing two hundred and seventy people, trapped on the back of a 125cc Suzuki driven by a stranger who had come perhaps to spray the roof for mildew.

'Sit here,' I told him at the club, and folded his coat to pad the wood of the tiered seating looking down on the court. As Martin and I played, I checked every now and again that Dad was still there. 'Are you okay, Mr Ladd?' and at least once he nodded. A mishit sent the ball into the seating, and despite there being nowhere for it to be lost, we couldn't find it anywhere. I shook Dad's greatcoat and felt the pockets several times, I even patted him down like a policeman searching for weapons. He took it all with equanimity.

'Weird,' said Martin. 'Maybe he's swallowed it.' I wished he hadn't said that, for a squash ball is pretty small, but Dad seemed to be breathing okay and in no discomfort.

'It's not warm here at all, is it,' he said. 'I was wondering if there might be a nice piece of pork for lunch.'

Martin and I played two more games, then I took Dad to the lavatory and togged him up for the trip home. 'Been nice to meet you,' said Martin, whose mother had lots of visitors to the house and was up on manners. I expected Dad to ask who he was again, but he wasn't always predictable and it was still morning. 'Likewise,' he said and compressed his bushy eyebrows in a smile.

Little conversation is possible on a motorbike, unless you shout, but when I stopped at the Ilam Road lights, I could just hear in my left ear Dad humming one of his ballads. It reassured me that riding as pillion passenger had no terrors for him, and that a squash ball wasn't lodged in his windpipe. He was no quick mover any more, but once he got a grip such as that around my waist he held on well.

Dad didn't get any pork for lunch, but I did some cheese on toast, and we sat on the patio. Despite the heat he kept his long coat on, and it didn't worry me. I wanted to insist on having my own way only in issues that mattered. Why shouldn't he sit with a winter coat in the summer sun if he enjoyed it? 'It's a class coat that,' I said.

'I had one like it in the battalion.'

'You were in the war then,' I said.

'Everyone was in the war,' said Dad in the voice Brando used for the Godfather. It was something else I saw no reason to contradict him on. There's all sorts of war, after all. He fell asleep suddenly quite soon afterwards. One moment he was puckering his lips and running a finger on his unshaven neck, the next his head was back on the chair and his nose was casting a shadow like a sundial marker.

For an hour and a half I was able to concentrate on the constitutional effects of the American Civil War. No question came up on that, of course. I had a beer on the quiet too. It seemed to me that I was entitled to keep a little ahead of Dad in regard to alcohol.

Mid-afternoon Dad woke. I looked up from my books to see that he was observing me quizzically. His mouth had fallen open and the sun caught the white stubble on his neck. I knew what he was thinking. 'Who am I again?' I said. 'I'm Brian who's looking after you. Okay?' He nodded with a certain nonchalance to suggest he knew that, then he worked hard at generating a cough strong enough to shift the phlegm accumulated during his sleep. 'Did you enjoy it at the squash courts this morning?'

'Squash?'

'This morning we went down on the bike to the squash courts. Remember?'

'Ah,' said Dad in a guarded and equivocal way. I thought that as he'd forgotten it already I could take him there each morning and it would be a fresh experience each time.

We had a mug of tea, and then I found his triple head shaver at the bottom of his wardrobe and gave him a shave. He quite enjoyed it, moving his head about to tauten the skin at my direction and closing his eyes in the direct sunlight. It had been some time since anyone had taken any care in giving Dad a shave. Long hairs, missed day after day, lay in fold lines of his skin and his upper lip had been neglected. 'I use a cut-throat most times,' said Dad, but that must have been years ago, for there were plenty of moles and blemishes which would have come to a bloody end. I noticed that the skin over his collarbone was very pale, and the fine creases formed small diamond patterns. The tip of his left ear was eaten away slightly by a scaly skin cancer. His cheekbones were pronounced rims beneath his eyes. It was a ravaged face, but strong nevertheless. Dad ran his hand over his features with satisfaction, and two white butterflies tumbled in a courtship dance through the warm air inches from his head. 'You look a new man,' I said.

'I've got very stiff, you know.' He tested his arms by stretching them out, then lifting them above his head slowly. 'You do get stiff with age,' he said. 'Nothing to be done about that. I suppose I'd better be heading home soon.'

'No hurry while it's so warm,' I said. 'Enjoy watching the golfers for a while, then we'll think about things again.'

I did a bit more on the Civil War, but just being aware that Dad was awake made it difficult to concentrate. Even sitting and at rest, the business of living necessitated a range of noises: exhalation was accompanied by a small wheeze, he smacked his lips from time to time, and gave the occasional shuddering and dolorous sigh. And every now and again one of his slightly curled hands flipped suddenly and was still again.

As the sun slipped and the shadows grew from the golf course pines, I began to wonder about Dad and me in the coming night. Maybe the motorbike ride would help him sleep; maybe more physical exertion would help as well. 'How about a walk before tea, Mr Ladd?'

'Eh?'

'We could stretch our legs before tea.'

'Stretch your own legs. Who are you again?'

But with the false, importunate bonhomie that comes so naturally to a carer, I hauled Dad up, gave him his stick and encouraged him off the patio and down the drive. His resistance was expressed by turning a little away from me as we walked and stopping often to explore with his stick any plants to the side.

We began the small, seemingly never-ending block, and I disliked myself for the hope I had that no acquaintance would see me out walking with the old guy, yet maintained that hope just the same. It wasn't a trendy way to spend time on a summer afternoon, especially as he still wore his heavy coat in the last glare of the sun. Dad would stop from time to time to have a good cough, or peer into people's properties if he noticed movement. Self-consciousness is lost with the passing of years. A woman was kneeling on a groundsheet near her letter box to do some weeding, and after watching with interest for some time, Dad turned away, saying in his hollow but penetrating way, 'Women get big arses later in their life, don't you think, Warren?'

'Who's Warren?' I said, urging him roughly on down the street, but without the courage to turn round.

'What's that?'

'Who's Warren?' But Dad just gave his slow, soft smile. Whoever Warren was, and what brief neurological flash had linked him to our day together, was gone for the moment.

When we'd done the circuit and arrived home again, Dad was down to a shuffle. He was interested and somewhat sceptical to be told that was the house he lived in. He had entered that late afternoon free-fall from connectedness which I came to know well. And the fall was into the whirling chaos of each night. 'I'd never buy a house like this,' he said derisively. He was a little ahead of me, and he looked back with his head hung low and the whites of his eyes showing, the way a horse sometimes looks back around its flank.

'It's Angeline's house, and you live with her.' Even in late afternoon his daughter's name struck a chord somewhere, and he didn't contradict me, but came with some reluctance towards the front door.

'And you are again?'

'I'm Warren.' I admit my intention was investigative, a hope that in denial he might reveal this Warren, but Dad's malady was too subtle for my amateur psychology. 'You still haven't sprayed for mildew,' was all he said.

I closed the big glass doors to the patio, but pushed Dad's padded lounge chair close to them so that he was full on to the setting sun. Such comfort activated his appetites. 'Wine and cheese would be very acceptable,' he stage whispered. So I took another red from the cupboard beneath the stairs, but, learning from experience, used a mug for Dad, and kept the bottle well away.

Dad sank so far back into the easy chair that it looked as if some sort of suction was at work, and the sun through the glass on his gunslinger coat must have put his temperature well up, but his face remained pale and he gargled happily in his mug. 'I thought I might cook bangers and mash for tea,' I said. In my second year, when I'd been flatting, it had been my stand-by when rostered for a meal. For visitors my variation was to make a packet gravy and have peas as well. I'd received compliments, not all sarcastic.

'The Germans make a good sausage,' said Dad. 'Here the sausage is a poor man's food, but in Europe they know how to make a sausage, and how to treat it.'

'I thought you hated the Germans. The war and all that.'

'The war. I'm not talking about the war. Who said anything about the war. I thought you said something about sausage.'

'You're right,' I said.

'In the war the food was bloody awful.'

'Mine will be better,' I said.

'War is never better,' said Dad huskily. He looked at me rather belligerently from the depths of the chair, but when I topped up his wine mug his expression softened.

I moved to another topic. 'I wonder how Angeline is enjoying her holiday.'

'She always keeps in touch, always has. Not like some,' said Dad. 'We hardly hear from Theo. What sort of job does she do now?'

'I don't know.'

'It's something to do with work. Some sort of work, I know that.'

'Right.'

I made a good fist of dinner, though I couldn't find any packet gravy. However Dad sank into one of his repetitive spells, and after asking me over and over who I was again, he began complaining that rats were gnawing at him during the nights. 'I don't want to sleep in the rat room again tonight,' he said.

'I don't think there are any rats here,' I said.

'No one can sleep with rats at you all night. The buggers come out of the wardrobe, I reckon.'

'Let's close the wardrobe door then tonight.'

'Oh, they bite to buggery, those buggers.' Dad pushed the coat sleeve up a bit and displayed his pale, waxy skin. 'What's that then,' he said. 'Scotch mist?' There were no bites that I could see, but that didn't mean Dad hadn't suffered: pain can be the consequence of belief.

'No one likes a rat,' I agreed.

'I don't want to sleep in the rat room tonight.'

'No one likes a rat.' Dementia's repetition is so easy to fall into.

I did the dishes while Dad in the lounge railed against the rats, and then I watched a Mafia movie on television with the sound well up. It was hopeless to try and swot while Dad went on. He had dried up by the time the film was over, just nodding to himself and giving the occasional knowing chuckle, which fluttered in his open mouth. There is a cocoon of self-absorption that surrounds the very old and the very young.

For this second night I was determined to be better prepared, and I cajoled Dad into a lavatory visit before he went to bed. Getting the big coat off him was a bit of a test: his affection for it had increased during the day. 'But I'd better have it ready for when I go,' he said testily.

'Where are you going?'

'Back to my own place.'

'Where's that?'

'Same place it's always been.'

'But you won't be leaving during the night.'

'What would you know,' said Dad. I reminded him to wipe himself and flush the bowl, then showed him the way to his bedroom.

'Why are these rooms always in different places?' he said.

'All part of the grand puzzle of life,' I told him.

'I think you're going mad,' he whispered.

Once Dad was tucked up I tried to do more swot, but after the night before I was apprehensive of interruption later in the night, so went to bed at eleven myself. So as not to face the vivid envy of the digital clock face, I lay on my back. Technology was at first a distraction there as well, for on the ceiling was a smoke alarm like a pig's snout, and it cheeped softly to warn that the battery was low. The regular, subdued insistence became finally a lullaby and I fell into a routine anxiety dream of academic failure.

Dad's cries of despair woke me. Piercing, vehement cries, utterly distinct from the echo chamber hoarseness of his everyday voice. 'The rats are here again, the buggers,' he called, and when I went in and put on the light, he was sitting forlornly on his bed with his big hands clasped. He must have been out earlier in the night because he had piled some books against the wardrobe door, and had a maroon blazer on, but no pyjama top. 'Rats are king here,' he said accusingly. Tears glittered on his face. 'Where are my wife and family? Where is my life?'

'Where are the rats?' I asked to appease him. His other questions were too tough for me, and called for a divine answer. 'They've all buggered off,' I said. I pushed books away from the wardrobe and opened the door. 'See. Nothing to worry about.'

Dad didn't answer, but his expression showed he thought my display was mere naivety, and that he and the rats knew a thing or two.

'What is this place?' he said finally.

'It's your daughter's place. You live here.'

'How can it be Angeline's place when she lives with us? She's still at school, so how can she have a place? Why doesn't anyone tell the truth any more? The world's full of liars now. I tell my staff that deceit is the worst failing, and self-deceit the worst of all.'

I thought Dad was bound to query my appearance in his life, but in that night no doubt I was just one more enigma in a pageant of glaring inconsistency. He sat morosely for a time, breathing heavily, as if defeated in one round and having little hope of the next. He looked at the skirting board in front of him with a dull obstinacy. 'I'll get back to my home and family,' he said, 'rats or no rats. You don't know as much as you think you do.'

'You're right there,' I said, with exams in mind.

I got him to lie down again, and didn't bother hassling him about the blazer, or the reason for his wish to leave the light on. I'm sure Dad was a believer in priorities when he was a captain of industry. For me it seemed the way to go in aged care. Food, booze, warmth, light and rats were all important things; what you wore in bed, or said to passing acquaintances, was of little account.

'Leave the light on for the migration of the monarchs,' he said with some dignity. I thought he meant butterflies rather than crowned heads, but the connection to either was obscure.

'Where are they headed?'

'Rings of Saturn,' said Dad with soft assurance.

'Of course.'

I stood on the patio for a while, which was dimly illuminated by the light through Dad's curtains. I could hear him humming to himself in an almost cheerful way, and the golf course across the road was a dark gap bounded by lights of streets and houses. I wondered by what random happenstance old Mr Ladd and I should end up there together, and what small connection it might be with future oddity in which both of us were absent. Maybe his long, dark coat would clothe a jazz musician of the house in time; maybe he'd written a sonnet of censure in regard to rats and folded it in some crevice of the wardrobe from which a buck-toothed child of immigrants would draw it out. Perhaps our tangential conversations would lodge in the Pink Batts, and flap down again decades after into some other verbal banquet of senility.

Dad was asleep when I went back in. The blazer was open and the hair of his chest thick, but almost colourless. I pulled up the sheet, turned out the light, and shook a fist at the wardrobe as a warning to the rats not to start anything. Groggy with bewilderment and fatigue, I lay down on my own bed, pulled my scrotum free from my thighs, and was comfortable. To green numerals and a chirping smoke alarm I was oblivious. Sleep closed on me like the grave.

When I opened my eyes next morning, the clock at the end of my nose showed well after eight o'clock. I spent several minutes working out what was the day of the week, and was amazed that it was only Tuesday. Surely I had been responsible for Dad a week or more. I wondered whether in extreme old age time itself slowed, along with the other functions of life, and if that perception was contagious. To what extent could time drag its feet before halting altogether?

Metaphysics gave place to action when I heard Dad wandering the rooms in search of the lavatory. It lay, of course, behind the one door he hadn't thought to try. 'Hard luck,' I said.

'Bloody place.' He still wore the sports blazer, and his pyjama trousers were wet, but nothing worse had happened. There'd be sheets to wash as well, I reminded myself. He voided with sound like a dredge emptying, and the smell billowed through the house in almost visual intensity. Dad gave a long sigh of relief. It wasn't a bad start to the day. 'Who are you again?' he asked as I helped him dress.

'I am the Panjanmandarin of the Empire of the Rats.'

'No need to get shirty,' said Dad.

'Remember the rats from last night?'

'What rats?' he said, scornful in the comparative logic of morning.

'Anyway,' I said, 'let's have breakfast.'

'What's the chance of an egg?' he asked.

After breakfast Dad started to get ready for work, but I told him that he'd retired years ago, and he agreed and went out to his favourite place on the patio in the morning sun. I took my notes on the poetry of Herrick and joined him. Already there was a ladies' foursome on the fairway closest to us. Their laughter just carried the distance.

'Do you like women?' asked Dad in his soughing voice, and his lantern face hung in their direction.

I said that as a generalisation I was in agreement.

'There weren't many women in the war.'

'No.'

'Women underestimate their anatomical measurements and men exaggerate theirs. That's something I've noticed is a difference.'

I was surprised by Dad's perception, even though it was morning. Every now and again the clouds cleared and the original sharp landscape of Dad's mind was revealed.

'What else do you reckon about women?'

'They're much more reliable as workers,' he said. 'It was my policy to hire women if the jobs were suitable.' Dad enjoyed the sun: kept his face to it even as its summer intensity grew. He had an almost reptilian instinct for heat. Two or three minutes later what he took as a new thought occurred to him. 'There weren't many women in the war,' he said.

'So you said.'

'Did I?'

Throughout the morning I got a little revision done. The high points of our interaction were a couple of trips to the toilet and a shave. The lavatory visits were as laborious as ever, but the shave took a good deal less time than the day before, because we'd done such a good job then. Dad did have another intellectual crescendo, about cars, when we were having a cup of coffee. 'What sort of car do you drive, Warren?' he said. So Warren was with us briefly again.

'I've got a motorbike.'

'One thing that I allow myself in business is a decent car. It gives clients confidence in the firm, but also there's pleasure in the possession of it. Not something posey — no turbo nonsense, or fruit salad colours. A quality six-cylinder three-litre saloon, say, and I prefer manuals. I've never taken to automatics the same.'

'What have you got now?' I asked, knowing he hadn't driven for years.

'A Saab, but I'm not sure where it's kept. Since I've been staying with you here, I'm not sure where it's kept. If you could find out we could take a spin to Feilding, or Taupo. I used to have to drive a fair bit on business and enjoyed it. A long trip on a good road without much traffic, and everything in the car ticking over nicely and the world slipping by without being able to get a grip on you.' Dad's voice was quiet and he was restful in the sun. I imagined him as a busy manager, having a few hours to himself in his company car as he went from one city to another. And not knowing in those rather pleasant interludes that a time would come without any pressure of work at all, without a car, sometimes without a memory.

'Which was the best car you ever had?' I asked him, as a test.

'I had a V8 CustomLine which was a damn good car.'

'What were CustomLines?'

'The big Fords,' said Dad. 'I bought it new and she did over a hundred and fifty thousand miles without missing a beat.' I could see that the recollection of that car was of considerable satisfaction to him: his wrecked face had a half-smile and his hands were at ease in his lap. Maybe he was thinking of the sheen on the CustomLine when he'd just polished it, the burble of the V8 when he fed it the fat, times on holiday with Viv, Angeline and Theo all close to him. Maybe he was rather caught by some glimpse of himself, lithe and on his way up in business.

I opened a tin of sheep's tongues and we had sandwiches for lunch. It was the sort of meat that Dad managed well and it suited summer. I brought out a few lettuce leaves too, but neither of us was great on salad. Small tasks require a good deal of application at Dad's age. Just to get the sandwich to his mouth without losing the tongue filling was for him a task requiring not just tactical hand movements, but a full strategy.

'Would you like to go down to the squash courts again this afternoon?' I asked, but of course yesterday was further from Dad's recall than the Ford CustomLine of history, even at midday.

'Eh?'

'You could watch me play squash, Mr Ladd.'

'Could I,' he said, amiable and uncomprehending.

Martin was keen enough to have a break from study, so I dressed Dad in his full-length Wichita coat again, and left him standing dark and incongruous in the bright sun while I brought round the Suzuki. 'Is it time to go?' he asked as I put his helmet on.

'Into the sunset, pilgrim.'

'It's not sunset yet,' said Dad as, twisting round, I helped him find first the left footrest, then the right. Through the summer streets we went, and the guilt I felt was not for any danger that the old guy faced, but for history and literature neglected.

Despite his visit on the day before, Dad saw everything at the courts afresh: the glass court back and the upper seating, the changing rooms with coffin lockers. He was introduced anew to Martin and found inaugural pleasure in it all. 'You didn't hide the ball yesterday, or swallow it?' asked Martin, but Dad just gave his most quizzical smile to disguise incomprehension. He sat on the top seating for a while, and I forgot him in the concentration on the game, until after losing a close set I looked up and realised he had gone. He wasn't anywhere I looked inside the building, but when I went from the main doors into the carpark, he was sitting on the small concrete wall, his eyes closed in the sun, singing softly to himself. 'I wondered where you'd got to,' I said.

Dad opened his eyes and fell silent. He squinted at me without giving anything away. 'I'm waiting for my wife to pick me up,' he said formally.

'I'm taking you home.'

'Who are you again?'

'Brian. I'm looking after you while Angeline's away.'

'Angeline's away? No one told me that.'

'I'll just get my gear and we'll be off,' I told him. Martin was a bit disappointed we didn't get another few games, but was okay about it. He knew it was a job for me, and thought looking after a very old guy was easy money. I'd started with that idea myself.

On the way back Dad didn't seem so good on the pillion as on the way down, or during the rides the day before. He wasn't hanging on as well, and didn't lean in on the corners. I cut down the speed, and shouted to him to keep a good grip. How would I explain to Angeline if he fell off, or had a seizure of some sort. I made a small, one-sided contract with God that if we got home safely I wouldn't take Dad on the bike again. His left foot did come off the rest and drag on the road, but by then I was down to jogging pace and able to stop before Dad was swung off. He didn't complain, but his increasing bewilderment made me feel all the more guilty, and I was again surprised at how quickly he could change from competence to ineptitude. I apologised to him when we were home, but he had lost the sequence of cause and consequence.

He wouldn't take the coat off, and sat on the patio rubbing his left leg. I gave him a mug of sweet tea, and started on some notes about the Wakefield influence on New Zealand settlement. I hoped the heat of the late afternoon sun, redoubled by the greatcoat, would lull him to sleep for a few hours, but he showed increasing bad humour and fearfulness. He complained about his sore leg, though unable to remember the cause. He complained about being left with a stranger in a house he didn't much like. 'I won't have to spend the night here, will I?' or 'I'm not going to be here when it gets dark am I?' he asked a hundred times, but paid no attention to any of the placating replies I made. I ignored him in the end. Angeline said he'd been a top administrator, but in the bad times all that was left of that serene and calculating efficiency was a querulous anxiety. 'It's a very cold house at night, this,' he said morosely. 'Who are you again?'

'An academic failure in Gotham City,' I said.

'You talk nonsense,' said Dad. His low-slung face turned away from me and he continued the conversation with himself. 'I'm certain we said there was to be underfloor heating right through the living area and the bedrooms. It'll be the rats, the buggers, that have chewed all the wiring. It happens all over the world at night. After the war there was nothing to stop rats spreading at all. In the desert I could always hear them breeding in the night.' Dad peered into the bright sun as if it were blackness over the shifting sand, and cracked his knuckles. The hollow whisper of his voice seemed to be coming from a barren place deep inside.

It was going to be a bad evening. With the exams looming I was desperate to get a decent night's work done. When Dad came out with the predictable request for wine and cheese, I took it as a sign and decided to let him drink enough to enter some Valhalla to which war and rats could not accompany him. For the first time I made a serious inventory of the grog cupboard and found, behind a carton, a bottle of Napoleon brandy which I'm sure Angeline and her husband had forgotten. I brought out also a bottle of shiraz to soften Dad up and provide a glass or two for me. We started on the patio and when the sun had gone down moved into the lounge. We had a mince pie each before I introduced Dad to the brandy. 'Are the others going to have a glass?' he said, all good humour by that time.

'The world has our invitation,' I said.

'Include the orchestra in that.'

'Even the celestial choirs,' I said.

'We'll all be at the start line by 0500 hours,' said Dad.

'Amen to that,' I said.

'Amen.'

For a couple of hours the wine and brandy loosened Dad's tongue and he hummed tunes and talked of his family as if his son and daughter were still children, as if his wife were still alive. Perhaps those years had been the uplands of his life. But then he sagged in his chair, steadily sipped brandy and made small noises with his loose lips. Twice I stopped studying to take him for a leak, and he went meekly, allowing me the first time to get possession of the gunslinger's coat, and lifting his arms without expressing indignity when I worked his zip. I think he would have kept drinking brandy as long as I continued to pour it, but when the bottle was almost empty and the time was after eleven, I put his arm over my shoulder and helped him into his bedroom. It's not easy undressing a very old, drunk man. Dad was all inconvenient elbows, and limp yet recalcitrant feet and hands like dying flatfish. When he was sitting on the bed and I was tugging his pyjama jacket on, he came out with a whispered echo of a conversation long gone. 'There weren't many women in the war.'

'Not many here either,' I said.

'There was one nurse.' Dad's voice had almost disappeared.

'Good on you,' I said.

'Very few women in the war in fact,' and as if this was her cue, Angeline rang from Nelson.

'So how's Dad?' she asked. I told her that he was fine and that he'd just gone off to bed. 'Everything okay then?' Everything was fine I said, and mentioned that he seemed brighter and more active in the mornings. 'Yes, that's the way of it,' she said. 'You're not leaving him alone at all, are you?' I could reply quite truthfully on that, but not to the next rapid interrogation. 'You're making sure he's taking both sets of tablets, green and pink?' I told her there were no problems there, and made a mental note to find the pill bottles and chuck out the number Dad should have taken. I riposted with a question of my own about the undoubted pleasure of her holiday. 'Yes, it's been quite nice, thank you, but I'm sure we haven't had a chance to unwind properly yet.' There was something in her tone which made me think she thought my inquiry overfamiliar. 'Well anyway,' she said, 'do your best until the day after tomorrow and I'll see you then. Don't take too much notice of stuff Dad says at nights. He gets a bit wandery when he's tired.' I told her I thought he'd sleep pretty soundly.

He certainly did that. I checked on him a couple of times before going to bed myself. He could have been dead except for the snoring, and hadn't moved an inch since I put the blankets over him. The snoring was reassuring because at the back of my mind was a fear that he might die in the night, and the post mortem show an exceedingly high blood alcohol level. I took the brandy bottle across the road and flung it into the soft darkness of the golf course, and then, in the exaggerated anxiety that comes late at night, worried about the fingerprints that would be clear upon it. The guilt I felt in drugging the old guy in that way more than undid the scholastic peace that had been my motivation, and eventually I went to sleep with my mind wiped of any revision, and a decision that for the rest of my wardenship I would allow Dad the natural expression of his age, his condition and his metamorphosis of character. At least alcohol had dealt to the rats of dementia, and a deep barking dog was the one animal to inhabit the night.

The only obvious consequence of the binge in the morning was a monumentally soiled bed — a soon forgotten indignity for Dad, and a rightful punishment for me. 'Why is there always a terrible pong in this house?' Dad asked when I had finished getting the worst off the sheets in the tub and then put them in the machine. He showed no signs of a hangover and waited with some impatience for his breakfast.

'I'm going to give the place an airing today,' I said humbly. He was alive and I was so thankful: my vision of the night which saw him stretched out dead drunk in the most literal way was still fresh. 'Tomorrow Angeline comes home and everything needs to be in order. Where are these pills you should be taking anyway?'

'You don't get rid of a stink like this with pills,' said Dad scathingly.

For the first time since I'd been looking after Dad, there wasn't a clear sky. It was still warm, but a high sheet of pale cloud hid the sun. The patio wasn't as attractive without the direct strike of the sun, and after breakfast we stayed in the lounge. Dad was quiet as I shaved him, tilting his head on command and enjoying the busy feel of the electric razor on his skin, but when that was done he wanted to talk about going back to his own home and family. 'I could rent this place out,' he said. 'Investment properties like this can be good little earners if you're not facing on-going maintenance.'

'Angeline's living here though.'

There was a pause. In the mornings Dad had the ability to process some of the things he heard and to notice inconsistencies with his own sense of earlier life. 'How old's Angeline now?' he said cautiously.

'In her forties,' I said, with greater conviction than I felt.

'So she lives here all the time?'

'With you.' I avoided the complication of her husband. Dad nodded, as if he'd known these things all along, his head swaying like that of a Chinese processional dragon. He made a steeple of his big, wrinkled hands, a typical gesture, and his eyes slid behind their sagging lower lids. He was doing his best with some question to himself, but couldn't make anything of it. 'And you are again?' he enquired, almost apologetically.

While I read through my notes on a revisionist history of the New Zealand wars of the nineteenth century, Dad was content to hum and sing to himself while playing with a thread from the band of his thick, blue jersey, but after I went out to collect the mail I found that he had a box of documents on his knee, and he became intent on a scrutiny of them. I tried to concentrate on my work, but after an hour or so I found the obvious repetition of his actions distracting. He would take each envelope, or paper, from the box, manoeuvre it before his face for a time then place it on the coffee table beside him. When all were accounted for, he would replace them in the box and begin all over again, giving just as much concentration to a document on its third or fourth appearance as on its first.

'What have you got there, Mr Ladd?' I said finally, from comradeship rather than curiosity.

'I need everything in order before I go back to my wife and family,' he said.

'Well, that makes sense.'

'I don't seem to be quite on top of things the way I used to be.' His voice was quiet, more self-aware than usual. The limited admission had greater poignancy than his more flamboyant claims. I left the Maori and the colonial militia, and gave Dad the attention he deserved when at his best.

'You're eighty-eight,' I said, 'and I suppose everybody's memory is slipping a bit by then. You're still pretty good on all the early stuff.'

'Things seem different somehow. Why is it that I have to spend so much time by myself these days?'

I had no easy answer to that. In Dad's whirling times I could play a sort of Mad Hatter counterpoint of non sequiturs without belittling him, but when he was in the same world deference to that realisation was due. 'Your wife passed on some years ago and now you live here with your daughter. She's on holiday this week and I'm keeping you company. My name's Brian.'

So much contemporary truth was a shock for Dad. He relaxed back in the chair and his face assumed an added mournfulness. He rubbed the back of each hand in turn and eventually gave a small, wry smile. And there was in his eyes for a moment an ineffable realisation of his own condition. 'That's right. Of course, of course,' he affirmed to himself, 'Viv had a heart attack and she's buried at Padleigh. Yes, of course. And this is Angeline's house.'

But he didn't show any interest in his daughter's home. His voice faded, and he looked out to the uniform, pale cloud high in the summer sky. The revelations of comprehension were of no more joy to him than the perils of senility. Maybe as a natural means of escaping both, he fell asleep soon afterwards, and I worked on through the skirmishes of the 1860s. Dad's mouth hung open and his theatrical, fly-away eyebrows were ludicrously luxuriant. Maybe the wine and brandy from the night before still had some claim on him; might lead him gentle into some good night.

At midday I slipped out of the lounge and assessed Angeline's pantry with lunch in mind. On the one hand was my wish for ease of preparation, on the other the mercenary consideration that food was a part of my conditions of service. Maybe simplicity at noon and indulgence at the end of the day I decided. Baked beans on toast topped with two poached eggs apiece was the outcome. I was pleased all of the yolks were intact, but when I woke Dad he had no flattering comments. 'I suppose there's worse things than beans,' was all he said. 'People don't eat them the same now though, do they. Something to do with roughage, or saturated fats.'

'You don't have to force it down,' I said. I was surprised by the resentment I felt at his criticism. My response gave me an understanding of the greater scale of fury a committed chef would feel if Provençal Braised Pork with Saffron and Truffle Stuffing were disparaged.

'No, no, it's okay.' Dad trailed his knife through the egg yolks. 'I can get through it.'

Dad was not a malicious person. He said he'd help with the washing up, and managed to find a second tea towel and dry one flat plate before I finished everything else. A long afternoon stretched before us and I wanted to move out of the lounge to give some sense of progression to the day, and also get Dad away from his box of documents. The patio was warm and pleasant though the high cloud still reduced the sun to a general and suffusing glow. A small girl on a small trike did endless, intent circles on the neighbour's drive, and on the smooth expanse of the golf course people towed their trundlers and had time for unhurried talk. Dad seemed restless until I remembered his long coat and helped him put it on. Incongruity is of no concern in old age: the weight and texture of the coat must have been pleasing to him and he loved the heat.

'I played a bit of golf myself,' said Dad. 'It wasn't my sport of choice, but in business it's useful to be able to play golf without making a goat of yourself. Especially in Asian countries, you develop a sense of business opportunity and personal trust by playing together.'

'So deals are made on the course.'

'Not so much that, but Japanese and Singaporean businessmen like to get a sense of your personality that way.'

'Were you any good?'

'Not really,' said Dad, 'but it got me to the table without too much embarrassment and I had good products to sell. Do you know anything about mechanical engineering?'

'No.' I thought that was the end of the conversation, because Dad said nothing for a long while and hummed quietly.

'What is it you do know about?' he asked finally, and I almost congratulated him on holding onto one line of thought for so long.

'I'm still at varsity, studying English and History.'

'You do the roof spraying as a part-time thing then?'

'That's it,' I said. Life was too short to tease out absolutely fact and fiction. The end justifies the means when you're talking to someone like Dad, and the thing was to keep him as happy as possible it seemed to me. 'What would you do if you could have your time over again?' I asked him.

'Over again?'

'Would you live your life differently if you had a choice — a different job, different country, stuff like that.'

'I was always a good organiser.' Dad seemed quite interested in the self-analysis. 'My mother and father were muddlers and I reacted against that, I suppose. Logic, systems, the application of reason — that's what I brought to business. People sneer at administrators because they don't understand the skills involved.'

'You did okay, though.'

'People think it's paper shuffling, not real work,' said Dad. He seemed about to say more, but then closed his eyes briefly so I prompted him while he still had a chain of thought.

'So what is important for a manager?'

'People not policy. The best systems in the world are useless if you don't carry your staff. People skills make the difference from the factory floor to the boardroom, that's what I say.' And Dad said it with surprising coherence. It was surely the best I saw him in all the time I was there, and gave me a glimpse of the person he had once been. It was perhaps achieved with some effort, however, for afterwards he concentrated on rubbing his hands, and making sly sheep's eyes at me. 'So are you in some sort of business?' he said finally.

'I'm keeping you company.'

'Ah, yes, that's right.' Dad's voice had the pretence of assurance, but his soft expression was one of increasing bewilderment as his mind moved from the steady recollection of the far past to the morass of the present. 'Yes, of course, that's right, yes,' he said to comfort himself, looking over to the abandoned trike in the neighbouring section. The child had vanished without us noticing.

Dad leant back and closed his eyes; I returned to my swot notes.

No way was I going to risk another squash trip with him on the pillion seat, although I felt stale from lack of physical activity. I was envious of the happy gaggles of golfers who straggled over the well-kept course, and whose laughter carried quite clearly to me. I wondered if any player there ever glanced across at Dad on his patio and had some premonition of their future.

Dad snored for an hour and a half beneath the luminous warm cloud of the summer, and then woke with a good deal of lip-smacking and fidgeting. For another half an hour he hummed and half sang snatches of songs from the forties and fifties, some of which had become popular again. He wasn't conscious of me during this time and I carried on working while the opportunity was there. Finally his awareness circled out and he became quieter, coughed softly in a slightly self-conscious way and regarded me from beneath the thatch of his eyebrows. I said nothing. I wanted the mood and relationship to be of his making, rather than always imposing reality as I saw it on Dad's variable world. I made coffee for us both, and settled in my patio chair again, still without a word. It wasn't a ploy for my entertainment: let Dad kick off, and I'd just run with the ball. Dad began in his own good time.

'Tell me about your time in Ecuador, Warren,' said Dad in his reed-bed whisper. So the sun was over the yard arm, or some such thing.

'It's mostly forest in Ecuador and very hot. They have a lot of insects and bats, but a very shaky economy.'

'Any rats?' asked Dad.

'No rats. It's an odd thing, there's an indigenous tropical lily there and its pollen inhibits the breeding of rats. Ecuador is the only country in the world completely free of rats. They have monkeys with coloured bums, though, and those fish that reduce horses to skeletons in no time at all.'

'But no rats, eh,' said Dad.

'Absolutely not, Mr Ladd. You say that you don't give a rat's arse there, and the locals have no idea what you're talking about. On the other hand there's scorpions as big as saucers and beetles bigger than tortoises to do the scavenging.'

'And are the tortoises any threat?'

'Only to the babies,' I reassured him. 'In Ecuador babies are always left in hammocks, never on the ground where the tortoises can get at them. Even so you notice that a lot of children there have a toe or two missing.'

'How long did you have to stay there, in Whatsit?'

'Oh, I was in Honduras for a couple of years. I had to oversee the establishment of professional development best practice guidelines for the drug cartels.'

'But no rats at all, you say?'

'I brought one of the Venezuelan lilies back, and I'll put it in your room. No rat will come near the place, believe me. The pollen may make you sneeze a bit, but as for the rats it's adios amigo.'

'And the turtles?'

'It's too dry for them here, and MAF won't let you bring them in because of the possible diseases,' I said. 'You should have a really good sleep tonight.'

'Well, the nights seem to be getting longer.' Dad's tone was glum. 'I can't seem to get my joints comfortable for any length of time.'

'Maybe we can suss out where those pills are.'

'I suppose it's always warm in Guatemala?' said Dad.

'But in the rainy season,' I said, 'the water comes so high beneath the pole houses that you can hear the alligators scraping their tails against the piles, and the giant toads cluster on the windows until the light is blocked out.'

'Rats are mighty swimmers, the buggers,' said Dad.

At some stage the little girl next door had reclaimed her trike and was again circling intently: I think the three of us were slightly dizzy. Dad gave a yawn which displayed a lower lip like that of an elephant, and massaged his face. I wondered if Angeline would notice if I took an inch or two off his eyebrows, but then reminded myself that neither he nor I would feel any better as a result. Boredom is not often a productive motivation. I wondered also about the mutual effects of our time together, whether the consequence of the meeting of my youth and his extreme old age would be a more intermediate and beneficial setting for us both: a median view of life.

That day's evening meal was the last I needed to consider, for Angeline and her husband, marriage restored if all went well, were to be back next morning. A sense of closure gave significance to the occasion, and I went out to Angeline's deep-freeze and found a heavy pack of pork slices. A few games of squash and I would burn off the fat from the desirable crackling; in Dad's case surely he didn't have enough time left for cumulative diet-related diseases to be a threat. 'I thought we'd treat ourselves to pork, Mr Ladd,' I said, and got together carrots, potatoes and peas as a counter to that indulgence.

'Ah,' said Dad, 'I could do with a drink.'

'Okay, but we're not having as much as last night.'

'Eh?'

'Nothing. You're just not going to rip into it the way you did last night, though it was my fault.'

'What happened last night?' said Dad.

'Nothing,' I said. 'You slept like a dead man because of the booze.'

'Who's the dead man?' asked Dad.

'We'll have one bottle of red with the pork,' I said, and Dad nodded.

I moved Dad into the lounge, and put a tray on his lap as preparation. There was something on the television about rearing livestock in barns in the American Midwest — all very American Gothic, and Dad had difficulty in getting a handle on it. I tried to keep his interest up as I cooked dinner. I didn't want him getting his papers out again and recycling them endlessly. 'Looks like a pretty big operation they've got going on those farms,' I said, coming in to give him a very moderate top-up.

'What's that?' Dad was gazing at the screen as if it were a box of snakes.

'All those cattle indoors for months, aren't they?'

'Cattle — is that what they are?'

'Aren't they?'

'Look sort of funny,' he said. 'It's dark, isn't it. I reckon there's something wrong with the picture.'

'It's just being inside, I suppose.'

'Who wants to watch cattle inside all the time? What the hell is this all about I want to know,' said Dad. He had a good point arrived at in a roundabout sort of way.

Dad enjoyed his pork. He did take eternity cutting it up, but I resisted the urge to do it for him. Many of the peas escaped him and lay on the tray, his lap, or the carpet around him like green beads. We had a packet of shortbread biscuits for afters, and a cup of coffee.

'Is Viv coming in?' Dad asked. He always spoke fondly of his dead wife.

'No.'

'What about the children?'

'Angeline comes back tomorrow.'

'Tomorrow,' said Dad with surprise and emphasis, as if he had been convinced her return was to be the present day, or any day other than tomorrow. He steepled his hands and worked his long, loose face like a pantomime actor. 'And you are again?' he said.

It was the one day we hadn't had an outing and so without bothering about any confusing preamble of intent or agreement, I stood Dad up in a scatter of peas and we went out into the warm decay of the summer day. The golf course was all vague nature in the twilight. Houses we passed were at their best, blemishes hidden, and weeds not readily distinguished from their invited cousins. It was a slow outing. Dad's walking stick was varnished, and had a rubber stopper on the end, and he lingered as ever to poke at things: unusual letter boxes, shrubs intruding across the footpath, a dog turd. 'How long have I lived here?' he asked. Death can be a sudden fall of the curtain, the cataclysmic closure; it can also be a gradual deprivation of those aspects of consciousness we need to remain in touch with the world. Dad at times seemed in a dinghy drifting further and further out from the rest of us on the shore. 'I'll need to get back to work tomorrow,' he said.

'What's so important?'

'My son, Theo, is joining the board. It's what I've always wanted.'

'That's really great,' I said. 'I bet he'll give you a lot of support.' My landlady said Theo had drowned in Nepal, and hadn't liked his father anyway, so in regard to his son at least, Dad's loss of short-term memory was a blessing for him. 'Well, you haven't got the skills to make a contribution at that level, have you,' he said candidly. 'And no degree.'

'You're right.' I didn't need reminding about such things.

It took us a while to complete the small suburban block and the dusk was more pervasive by the time we reached home again. Dad would have walked right past the gate and begun another slow circuit, but I directed him up the path from which he swung at a few parched flowers with his stick.

'So who are we visiting here?' he asked.

'We live here,' I said.

'Like hell we do,' but nevertheless Dad was willing to come inside and be surprised by every room all over again. 'We've had our dinner, have we?' he wanted to know, and, with rather more diffidence, 'Are you staying the night?'

'I'm Brian, here to keep you company.'

'You'll have to excuse me if I don't entertain you. I've a good deal of work on. Business, you know.'

'That's fine.'

After sundown the bad times came for Dad — well, other world times at least. It showed in his increasing uneasiness and fidgeting. As well as all the stuff with his hands, he pulled strange faces, puckering his lips, or stretching them in an exaggerated and mirthless grin, shooting his bushy eyebrows aloft, and clamping his lower jaw out. All a quite unconscious exhibition of gurning. I wondered if it was a sign of lesser, gremlin personality traits normally suppressed by the deliberate imposition of an integrated character; a sort of geriatric possession having nothing to do with right or wrong. We began the laborious process of getting him ready for bed.

And it was marked not just by mutual effort, but mutual indignity. He wasn't sufficiently supple, or balanced, to soap himself in the shower: arthritis made it difficult for him to raise his arms above his shoulders, or to touch his own feet. I stood in the doorway of the shower to help, lathered his wobbly head, watched the shampoo suds slide over the corrugations of his collapsed chest. Dad gasped happily in the hot jet and the swirling steam, and would have fallen several times had I not gripped his elbow. He was all bone and tendon, and the nails on his big toes were thick, opaque and yellow. As we stood together afterwards in the bathroom and I dried his bum and cock with a lush, blue towel, the incongruity of it all gave me a brief laugh, and Dad chuckled just to follow suit. Two strangers — Dad couldn't even remember my name — so intimate, so innocent, together. 'Is it morning, or night?' he whispered. His hair stood up damply and his eyes roamed in their deep sockets.

'Night,' I said. 'It's night now.'

'Will the rats come for the pomegranate seeds?'

'Not a chance now we've got the Ecuadorian lily,' I said.

'Of course. Of course, and what a relief for all,' he said. 'There weren't many women in the war you know, but I saw a falcon high up above the desert before the tank attack.'

As I swotted in the lounge, I could hear Dad singing to himself in bed. There were some words, some humming, and a good deal of pom pom and pum pum as he entertained himself. He talked to himself too, posing such questions as why the sheet had got caught up, where the wardrobe door led to, and when he'd need to get up to leave in time for the meeting. And he answered each question with interest and patience as one might to a friend. In a moment of wishful thinking I imagined the night was to be peaceful and mercifully swift.

I went to bed with a head full of the battle of Gettysburg: Cashtown Inn, Willoughby's Run and McPherson's Barn, and photographers with the armies for the first time. But barely had the smoke cleared when I was woken by the noise made by Dad barging about in the dark hallway. The slick, green numerals told me it was 3.36 a.m. and Dad was weeping loudly. I went out and lit up the hallway. Dad had taken off his pyjamas and wore dark suit trousers and his beloved long coat. 'Where am I?' he implored brokenly. 'And who the hell are you?'

'I'm Brian.'

'Who?'

'I'm keeping you company,' I said.

'Where's Viv and the kids?'

I began an explanation to bridge some thirty or forty years, but Dad turned away with a hollow moan and wandered back into his bedroom. Nothing related to the present was any consolation to him. There seemed no option but to follow him through the looking glass. I persuaded him to exchange suit trousers for pyjama ones by pointing out he had no underpants, but agreed that the coat of the high plains drifter was useful in protecting him in case he was visited by the rats from the other side. Dad went reluctantly back into bed, and to settle him I sat under the covers beside him, for at four o'clock it was cool enough wandering in my boxers. 'Angeline's coming tomorrow,' I said. 'You'll like that.'

Dad nodded, his lined face glinting with tears. 'What about Viv and Theo?'

'Yep, the whole family.' So could I assume power of life and death, and summon back his wife and the watery Theo. Anything to keep his mind off the rats; anything to help us drift through the darkness without despair.

'Things haven't always been easy, you know, Warren,' Dad admonished me. 'We had a truck load of trouble with Theo. For a while there he just seemed to go from one scrape to another and we were at our wits' end.'

'I suppose most young guys go through a time when they're fooling with drugs and stuff.'

'You don't know the half of it,' said Dad. 'You know he was still stealing money from us when he was nearly thirty years old. He had a baby with a girl in Sydney and he abandoned them both and went trekking in Nepal.' Dad stopped and listened for a time. 'It's very windy outside,' he said, yet everything was still.

'A real southerly buster,' I said.

'Anyway, things haven't always been easy. But they were both great kids and Angeline was never any trouble at all. You worry more about your kids than your own life, do you know that?'

'Absolutely.'

Dad was quiet for a time, but his hands and face twitched and shimmied as the outward show of some inner agitation, a string of Tom Thumb crackers somewhere along his nervous system. I thought maybe a song or two would calm him, and allow me to go back to my own bed. I was tired, and worried about Dad's condition.

'Let's sing a bit,' I said.

'Eh?'

'Sing a bit. You like that.'

'What time is it?' said Dad.

'Time to sing,' I said, but then couldn't think of anything that both Dad and I would know well. I finally came up with 'Waltzing Matilda', and then 'Lili Marlene'. Dad enjoyed that especially, and the singing was more successful than I'd hoped. Only once he stopped singing and put a hand to my mouth, then said, 'Listen to that storm outside.' There was no wind at all. Or maybe winds cracked their cheeks for Dad that I was too young and temporal to hear.

'Maybe it's inside,' I said. 'Let's drown it out.'

We sang 'How Much is that Doggie in the Window', and 'Some Enchanted Evening'. Songs are sung by people and in places never contemplated by their composers, and for reasons quite inexplicable in normal times, and we must have been as odd a juxtaposition as any. Eighty-eight-year-old Mr Ladd and twenty-year-old me, strangers in bed together well before the dawn. When we had sung ourselves out, I told Dad I was going to my own room. 'Do you want the light left on?' I asked him.

'Better had,' he said. 'Maybe it's the swordfish making all that noise outside.'

'They're not doing any harm,' I said.

'Things haven't always been easy, you know, Warren.'

'So you said.'

'Why have I got this coat on in bed?'

'You might have to get up for a piss.'

'Nothing's like it was before,' said Dad and he lay back on the pillows. 'Someone keeps coming in and watching me when I'm asleep,' he whispered.

'How do you know?'

'I can hear them breathing,' Dad said.

I stopped in the doorway for a last check. There he lay with the top of his black coat from the bedclothes and his caricature of a face on the pillow. He was looking back at me, and I bet he was wondering who I was again.

'It'll be morning soon,' I said.

I dropped into my bed as if pole-axed, and into a pit of sleep too deep even for dreams. I awoke to full daylight and the noise made by Dad as he tried to manage himself in the lavatory. I hoped to God he'd taken off the coat, and found my appeal divinely answered. The other things could be washed easily.

'Did you have a good night?' I asked him, wondering what he remembered of the swordfish, the southerly and the songs.

'An okay night, I suppose,' said Dad vaguely. 'It's not as comfortable as my own bed somehow.'

We had our last breakfast together, and Dad was too polite to ask who I was, so I told him anyway. He perked up when I said that Angeline was returning before lunch, and gave me a history of her school achievements, which included awards for physics and impromptu speaking. In the fifth form she gave a reading from the Book of Job at the school prizegiving. 'Theo didn't do himself justice at school,' Dad said.

There was a full, gleaming summer sun for my last morning with Dad. He sat on the patio again in his black coat and seemed to gradually expand in the heat. I had found his best shoes for him to wear in honour of his daughter's homecoming, and their domed, black toes shone at the end of his grey trousers. While I had a clean-up inside the house I could hear Dad talking to himself from time to time, but there was no anxiety in his tone. He seemed to be scrutinising and rearranging bits of his life from long ago. I took particular care to hide the last empty wine bottles well down in the rubbish bag. I packed my gear ready to leave and put it by the Suzuki. 'Are you getting ready to go somewhere?' asked Dad as I came back to the patio with mugs of tea.

'I've got exams in a few days,' I said, and he gave a little chortle as though pleased to be missing out on such things himself. I wanted to wish him well, but wasn't sure how I could do that with sincerity when I knew what was happening to him: the inevitable path before him. 'You look after yourself and don't worry about things,' I said. How could I thank him for not dying on me during my time of supervision.

'Thank you. Thank you,' he replied huskily. 'The nights get longer, don't you think? I suppose I'm not doing much during the day to tire me out.'

Dad was having a snooze when Angeline and her husband returned, but he woke up and knew her immediately, though I thought perhaps he was for a moment surprised to find her so grown up. What a hug they had and then a flurry of questions and answers about their trip and our stay, which bewildered him, and after a minute or two he turned to Angeline's husband and politely asked him who he was again. Welcome to the club. 'Goodness, Dad, you're wearing that greatcoat on a scorcher of a day,' said Angeline and she raised her eyebrows at me.

'He feels good with it on,' I said. 'He likes the heat, doesn't he.'

Angeline called me into the lounge to give me my money in a manila envelope. 'Was everything all right?' she asked, looking at me keenly. She and I knew there was a rich history to my stay, that there had been wild moments on the heath, but that nothing would be served by the rendition of it blow by blow. To talk about it, to admit to such things as we knew, would give them substance and power.

'He wasn't so good at night, but otherwise things were okay.'

'That's the pattern of his dementia,' she said.

It wasn't easy to say goodbye to Dad, for in some ways I never really got to say hello. I wished him well and took his big, loose hand in mine, and he said thank you and that it was a pleasure. But when I was on the motorbike, about to start, with my squash bag balanced on the tank and handle bars, he stood up from his patio chair and called out, 'Warren, Warren.'

'What is it?' I said.

He gaped at me for a moment, gave a rueful smile. 'It doesn't matter,' he said in his hollow voice. 'I'll tell you next time.'

Angeline smiled as apology for her father's confusion, her husband raised a bland hand. As I rode down the drive I had a last view of Dad standing in the hot sun in his black, gunslinger's greatcoat. In all that mundane suburban scene he was the innocent and hapless harbinger of howling winds, swordfish, lilies and rats, womenless wars, and the high cliff before the chasm.

Hodge

I left university with a good degree, but at a time of mild economic recession. I found a job as a vegetable packer at Foley's market, and a south-facing room in a backstreet boarding house in Sydenham. This might seem an introduction to a period of angst and sordid experience, but two things prevented such an outcome. The first was the spontaneous optimism of youth itself, the second was a fellow boarder called Hodge.

Hodge must have been middle-aged, but seemed old to me. He had the room at the end of the hall, and was a run-of-the-mill failure, exceptional only in his infallible bad luck. Hodge was a sort of lightning rod that deflected misfortune from the rest of us. Who knows what it is that makes a man lucky, or the reverse, or why such illogicality exists in a world of just deserts. Maybe it is a proof of karma, and we experience reward for past lives, or must live out expiation. Hodge was a tall man, though incomplete. He had lost his hair naturally, his right big toe in a wood-chopping accident at the Te Awamutu A and P show, and an ear was bitten off some years later by an alpaca which had been eating fermented plums in a paddock next to the Rai Valley store where Hodge stopped to ask directions to some second cousins on his mother's side. His hearing suffered a good deal, and his head tilted towards his remaining ear as if his equilibrium was affected by the loss.

Hodge was surprisingly popular with all of us at the boarding house, for the same reason perhaps that average-looking girls often have a plain friend. No matter how badly things went with us, Hodge was always a consoling comparison. I remember a spring day smoking tinnies among the marram dunes at New Brighton when he was shat on twice by seagulls: now what must be the chances of that, I ask you.

Hodge received only one letter that I know of, a jury summons, and he was delighted at the prospect of being paid to sit in a warm place for several days with free meals, and just send someone to jail. At the selection session, however, not only was Hodge eliminated by challenge of counsel, but a woman present recognised him as the person who came to her neighbourhood the afternoon before the official Salvation Army donation day and collected many of the envelopes.

Even Mrs Thrall, the landlady, took satisfaction in pointing him out as an example of how the male sex ended up. 'There's your own future for you,' she'd say triumphantly to me, or Helmut, or Dylan. 'God won't be mocked, you know.'

Sometimes on a sunny afternoon, when I wasn't at Foley's, Hodge and I would take pillows on to the fire-escape and have a beer and a yarn there. Once his false teeth fell and smashed on the concrete step; another time his heel got wedged between the bars, and Mrs Thrall had to use cooking oil and a mallet to free it. But we had some good hours in the sun. Hodge realised he was sport for the gods, but said that he wasn't as unlucky as most of his family. He told me that his father went right through the war as an infantryman with only shrapnel wounds, shingles and lower rib damage from an encounter with an Italian woman in Tagliacozzo, but then when the returning troopship was in sight of Wellington Harbour, he choked to death on a small bat (*Batis glottum batis*), which escaped from its container and flew into his mouth when he was about to have a beer.

Hodge said his elder brother had seemed the lucky one of the family: a handsome man of prodigious sexual prowess who finally married a stylish Bulgarian woman with substantial investments in natural gas, truffles and Egyptian third dynasty funerary curios. Unfortunately there was a freakish and random accident in which the Bulgarian wife happened to lose control of her Audi, and smash through the side of a suburban house to reveal her husband in bed with a Samoan meter maid. The wife ditched him without a cent, and two of the meter maid's uncles hunted him down to a DOC mangrove swamp reserve in the Hokianga, and castrated him with a boning knife.

Hodge's other brother went to Australia looking for a more propitious citizenship, but after twenty-seven years of unavailing struggle against drought on his outback property, he had to sell it for peanuts, and when leaving the station for the last time was drowned in a flash flood which overturned his Holden ute in the boundary creek. They found him entangled with his faithful kelpie dogs, which had prevented him from opening the door and swimming out. When they buried him on the property, the grave diggers discovered a vein of opal that made the new owners one of the richest families in Australia.

There was one sister in the family. Her name was Prudence, but Hodge said she was always called Guppy. She got all the brains evidently, and was awarded a PhD in computer science by the time she was twenty-two. Unfortunately on the morning of her graduation, while shaving her legs in the bath, she dropped the electric razor in and stopped her heart. The Peeping Tom from next door broke down the door in time to give her the kiss of life, and she was rushed towards the hospital, but the ambulance was hijacked by a stoned whitebaiter from the Coast while slowing at the Colombo Street lights. The whitebaiter — who years later won a category award in the Gore Country Music Festival — left the vehicle outside a cactus and succulent nursery on the outskirts of the city, and Guppy was recovered no worse than before and taken to hospital. She made a complete recovery from electrocution except for a forked scar on her hip, but the Peeping Tom carried a mutated lowland gorilla virus picked up when he was helping tribespeople in Zaïre with livestock breeding advice, and he passed it on to Guppy while saving her life. She lost the motor sensory control of all her limbs and spends her time bedridden, constructing highly successful virtual reality games by blowing into a tube connected to computers. 'She's worth buckets of dough, lucky Guppy,' said Hodge, 'but she doesn't want to have anything to do with me because I'd never give her the top bunk in our bedroom when we were kids.'

Mrs Thrall had a cancer scare the last year I boarded there. She never let on to us just what part of her was under threat, but when the day came for the final outcome of the tests to be announced, she wanted me to persuade Hodge to go with her as a talisman. She promised that she'd cook a big dish of toad-in-the-hole for the night meal if we'd agree. I remember the three of us driving into the city on a summer afternoon. As we left the parking lot, Hodge was nearly run over by a pimpled hoon in a rusted-out Falcon coming at him on his alpaca side, and so almost inaudible. Hodge stumbled back to safety, but did receive a nasty ankle gash from a skateboarder careering past at the time.

The specialist had the best of news for Mrs Thrall, and as far as I know she's still running that two-storeyed boarding house, happily bitching about the male race and fining guys for taking the house pillows out onto the fire-escape, or leaving syringes in the hydrangeas. It was Hodge, of course, who found it a bad day. When reading an old newspaper in the waiting room he discovered that his ninety-three-year-old mum, the last of his relatives, had been par-boiled and sucked under terra firma by a geyser in Rotorua which opened up without warning beneath an inaugural group waiting for the unveiling of a kinetic sculpture in brass, ceramic and poly resin to represent the benevolence of the universal life force.

Hodge told me that after this news he was particularly looking forward to his evening toad-in-the-hole as some sort of counterbalance for the vicissitudes of the day, but it wasn't to be. As we passed the last tall building before the carpark, an eighteen-stone woman cast herself from the window of the Weight No Longer Clinic. She had failed to meet her monthly loss target, but she was spot on as far as Hodge was concerned. The autopsy showed eighty-nine per cent of his bones shattered, but the eighteen-stone woman had a miraculous escape, became a born-again Christian trauma consultant, and is now a much-loved panellist on early evening television. Sometimes in my dreams I have this one freeze frame with Hodge giving a rare smile as he anticipates his toad dinner, and just above his head this vast, pink mass descending.

I miss Hodge, most of all because now he's gone there is nothing to deflect malicious fortune from the rest of us.

Watch of Gryphons

His apartment was on the Corso Cavour, on the south-east side of the old city. He was quite close to the archaeological museum and the garden of the San Pietro church, from which pale Assisi could be seen on the flank of hills across the broad valley. The view from the upstairs apartment, though, was of the street, and the noises were of the street and kept him awake at night until he became accustomed to them.

Dr Luca Matteotti had met him at the station and taken him to the offices of the department responsible for water and power in Perugia. Rather than any personal welcome at the station, Matteotti outlined the hierarchy within the reservoir project organisation and stressed his own overall supervision and responsibility. The director's manner was distant, but on that first day Paul thought it just the effect of formal English as a second language.

Both the station and the offices were in the new part of the city, and nondescript in a way that made them interchangeable with the station and offices of a hundred other cities. But after the coffee and fruit, the introductions to strangers who would become familiar enough, the director drove him up the hill to the old city with its great walls and serenity. 'The gryphon is the symbol of Perugia,' he said, as they passed through one of the gates with that strange hybrid carved above it. Paul was to see stone gryphons many times again. They were on the main buildings of the square, but also reduced and more roughly carved, sometimes mutilated, above low doors in narrow streets and on some of the oldest tombs. They carried, despite absurdity, vestiges of ancient and superstitious power.

'This was an Etruscan city,' said Matteotti, and Paul didn't reply because he knew nothing of the Etruscans except that they were superseded by the Romans. 'There is a great well beneath the city which is nearly two and a half thousand years old. Hydrologists are not new in Perugia, Mr Saville.' The director was smiling, but obviously enjoyed the put-down.

'That's interesting,' Paul said.

It was several days before he first saw the woman from apartment four. As he came up the stairs he heard the loud noise of one of the double turn locks on the apartment doors, and she passed him with a slight smile as a reply to his greeting at the bend in the stairs. Light brown hair she had and a pale skin. 'Buongiorno,' he'd said, and she had smiled and glanced at him without much interest. She'd be nearly forty, he thought, and that was all that occurred to him. Three mornings later he saw her in the bread shop when he was earlier than usual for his breakfast panini. She was supple in movement and spoke quietly to the shopkeeper. 'Buongiorno,' Paul said, and she gave him the same impersonal glance, as if she had never seen him before.

She lived in the apartment one down from him, and always when he saw, or heard, she went in and out alone. Perhaps because there were boisterous families in the other sets of rooms on that floor, and he and the woman lived alone, he wondered about her sometimes.

In the early weeks, though, he was preoccupied with work. Luca Matteotti proved to be an unpleasant and difficult man who saw no reason for Paul and Jeremy to be on the project team for the new reservoir, and accepted them as consultants only because the joint venture British company insisted. Within the first few days he had queried the need for a full series of bore samples to determine if material to be excavated from the site could be used as fill in the earth dam. 'What else would we do with it,' he exclaimed. He had the habit of looking out of the window of his office as he talked, as if Paul's face was repugnant to him, and he accepted outside calls during their discussions, and kept Paul waiting while he did so.

'He hates us both,' said Jeremy.

'Yes, but you he hates just because you're English. Me he hates personally.'

'He hates us both because we know our job and we're here,' said Jeremy. Yet Paul knew Matteotti disliked him not just on the grounds of profession, or nationality, but because their personalities repelled each other. Nothing would alter that; nothing would mitigate it. There was some incompatibility which crackled like electricity between them whenever they were together, and which sometimes surprised the two themselves with its nakedness. Some atavistic emotions were at stake which careful formality could not completely cover. Paul disliked the habitual hauteur of the director's expression, his considered and false laugh, refined dress sense, assumption of cultural superiority, laziness, and his habit of observing the outside world instead of looking at the person he was addressing. He was something of a prick, Paul decided.

Jeremy he liked a lot, but the Englishman had his family with him, and although they were hospitable, Paul didn't want to push that hospitality too far, and he spent most nights working in his apartment, or in the many restaurants of the old city, sometimes with Italian members of the project team. He enjoyed their company, but his lack of Italian made it difficult for him to develop such friendships.

As he spent much time in the apartment, Paul took an interest in people coming and going around him: The Arcottis and Sarzanos were families who seemed similar in their noisy and happy concentration on children, yet they had little to do with each other. They had no time perhaps for anyone beyond the breathless confusion of their own lives. The woman from number four was apart from all that, as Paul was himself. She seemed to have only a fleeting engagement with the world, though outside the apartments must have lain a more substantial life. He grew to know her balanced step in the hall when he was in his own room, and to recognise her from a distance outside by her walk, the cut of her hair and its light brown lustre.

In his mind she was alone always, because he'd never seen her with others, and in that unquestioned, almost unacknowledged, male way he saw little distinction between being alone and being available. So he was surprised, disappointed even, when he came past her door one evening and heard the laughter of a man and a woman in her room. The woman's laughter was quick and unrestrained, at variance with the demeanour he'd witnessed in public; the male laugh was relaxed. Though Paul hadn't paused in the hallway, he felt a moment of aural voyeurism and quickened his pace to his own apartment. Once afterwards he heard the two voices, but never in laughter again, and he never saw anyone coming or going there except the woman. Maybe it was just a visitor, a married lover, or a brother from the other side of the city. A woman like that should have more than a brother's company; should have someone close in the long evenings when Paul himself sat on his balcony, which was little more than a window ledge, and looked over the jumble of orange tiled roofs. They were the gutter-shaped tiles, alternately convex, concave, which Paul was told were originally made by women moulding the clay over their thighs. He had his plans and memos, but often instead of working he would observe the street beneath him, the local people cheerfully walking out to the restaurants, the lift of their voices louder and less guarded than the conversation of New Zealanders. Sometimes he would take the short walk to the high garden of San Pietro church and watch pale Assisi gradually fade behind the dusk that filled the valley. The great stone wall of old Perugia bounded the formal garden, and below it the cars and scooters contested the steep road, becoming visible when night fell, only as white and yellow firefly lights, although the noise remained the same.

By the second month, the feasibility study involved over twenty men at the reservoir site, and Paul worked among them in jeans and an open-necked shirt. Only one or two had any English, but he joked with them using his few words of Italian, mime and laughter. The Italians loved laughter. He wasn't their immediate superior so he relaxed with them. Sometimes, instead of using his cellphone to call for a car, he would ride back to the city with the men in a van. Matteotti was against such blurring of status. He told Paul that he should have a jacket and tie when on-site, and that by fraternising with the men he made it more difficult for the overseer.

Matteotti gave him a ticking off about these things during a routine meeting with Jeremy and several other planners. It was such bad management etiquette that Paul went to his office afterwards and complained. 'You could have asked me to come in and raised these things personally,' he said. 'That's the way it should be in the first instance anyway, not an official blast. I don't appreciate being criticised in front of my colleagues, and in any case all that stuff about clothes and status is incidental to what we're trying to achieve here.'

'It is incidental in your opinion, but not in mine,' said Matteotti. 'On-site relationships have a performance outcome sooner or later.' He was looking at Paul, which was surprising in itself.

'I've no argument with that. It's the nature of the relationship we seem to disagree about.'

'And I told you at the meeting what I expected. That's the whole point, so there will be no further misunderstanding,' said the director. He drew papers towards him as a sign he considered the conversation over. Paul thought it likely that he felt satisfaction in such disagreement, that he saw himself as the bulwark against foreign technocrats who would usurp a legitimate Italian endeavour, and encourage a vulgar popularism. Paul looked at the smooth, dark head of the director bent over his papers, and was tempted to say something about their antagonism, and how they might deal with that in the time they would work together, but he knew that Matteotti would see such openness as an attack, and went out without saying more.

Paul had half agreed to meet a group in the evening at a family restaurant near the Etruscan gate, but after the row he didn't feel like company. He sat on his ledge with a bottle of Trasimeno wine and took less pleasure than usual in the Italians passing beneath him. Because of his own mood, the happiness and laughter of others seemed vacuous and banal, and he wondered why he'd come to work among people so different from his own.

His isolation was broken by knocking on his door, and he went inside and opened it. The woman from number four was there. 'Mi puo aiutare, per favore?' she said. 'Ho bisogno d'aiuto.' Paul didn't understand. 'Help,' she said in English, and beckoned with her hand palm uppermost.

'What's wrong?' he asked.

'Help,' she said again, and went down the hall to her own door, pausing there to gesture to him. When he went in he recognised that the floor plan of her apartment was the same as his, but congested with an abnormal mode of living. The first room had sofas and chairs, but also wood and aluminium contraptions that reminded him of a gymnasium, and a bedroom into which the woman quickly led him had a pipe frame over the special bed, with suspended handgrip and dangling straps.

On the floor was the reason his assistance was needed, and the explanation for his never having heard any man entering, or leaving, the apartment: a naked man of two halves in a twisted sheet. His upper body was well developed in a fleshy way, and his lower half pitifully wasted. 'Did he fall out?' asked Paul, surprised into such a obvious remark.

'Maria doesn't have any English,' the man said. His pronunciation was good, his voice calm. Lying naked and deformed before a stranger, he retained a curious dignity and self-respect. 'Maria was giving me a bed bath and we turned suddenly,' he said.

Even with two of them to lift, it was difficult to get him back onto the bed, and when he was there, Paul noticed the sweat on his face and surmised that he must have felt some pain in the fall, or in being lifted, despite the paralysis. Paul had regained enough composure to address him directly rather than Maria when he spoke next. 'Can I do anything else?'

'I'll be fine now. I'm all right in the bed, or my chair, but if I ever get stranded, as I did now, I'm too heavy for Maria. Pacciale Sarzano would help, but the family is not there tonight.'

They both looked at Maria, and she smiled, hearing her name and seeing them turn to her. For the first time she met Paul's eyes directly.

'My name's Giancarlo,' the man said, and Paul turned and took his outstretched hand while Maria quickly laid the sheet over her partner's hips to cover his cock in its thicket of dark hair.

Giancarlo's clasp was quite strong, and Paul could feel calluses on the underside of the fingers from the handgrip suspended above the bed. The folded sheet emphasised the physical dichotomy: the heavy, white upper body, and the emaciated legs, the shin bones without flesh so that the flat surfaces showed, and the feet permanently curled in and with contorted toes. Maybe Maria shaved his torso, for it was almost hairless, yet on his wasted legs the hair was darkly vigorous as if it benefited from nourishment there which was useful in no other way.

'What is your name?' asked Giancarlo. He had an intelligent, handsome face, though slightly puffy and with unusual creases at the jaw line because of his posture. 'We've been meaning to make contact as good neighbours, and now our laziness has found us out, and we've had to ask your help before introducing ourselves.'

Maria brought another chair through from the other room, and Paul accepted Giancarlo's invitation to have red wine. She helped her partner put on a loose top and covered his legs with a yellow blanket. She took away the large plastic bowl which she'd been using for his bed bath. With her foot she pushed the clean bedpan out of sight. Paul expected her to sit down once she felt the room and Giancarlo were ready for a visitor, but after bringing wine and glasses, she left the room.

'What work are you doing here?' asked the Italian. He seemed eager to hear of anything happening outside the apartment, and yet was to prove well informed also. 'I read everything,' he said, 'but see very little. It's so difficult for me to go outside.'

Of course it was: an apartment on the second floor, for God's sake, when he was wheelchair-bound. It seemed an absurd situation to Paul, but he was a stranger and didn't like to ask why they weren't somewhere more convenient. Giancarlo knew about the reservoir project from the papers, and encouraged Paul to talk about it. When Paul complimented him on his English, he said he'd taken it as a subject for his degree, and he'd taught economics at the university where English was used a lot. He said he still did assignment marking, and Paul was again puzzled for there seemed no reason why he couldn't continue to give lectures. There were vans with devices to load wheelchairs, and there was Maria to wheel him about campus. And this time Paul did ask. 'It's difficult for us as a couple,' said Giancarlo a little vaguely. 'That outside world's not for us.'

Paul didn't stay long despite Giancarlo's friendly interest. He'd entered their apartment as a stranger appealed to in emergency, rather than someone whose company had been sought by choice. Giancarlo thanked him, and called out in Italian to Maria, who came from one of the other rooms to take Paul to the door.

'Grazie,' she said, and held out a box of the local chocolates, which Paul refused to take. They had been closer when lifting the naked Giancarlo onto the bed, but there at the door they were two, not three. She didn't smile: she seemed to look for something in his face, and Paul found in hers sadness, apprehension even, rather than gratitude, or interest. The box sank with her hand; she held it as if she was holding the neck of a goose. 'Grazie,' she said again.

As she closed the door he saw Giancarlo's wheelchair at the far end of the room, and the equipment which had surprised him. He supposed Giancarlo worked on it to keep upper-body strength. He remembered the one time he had heard them laughing. How wrong he'd been in his interpretation of it.

Four days later there was a note from Giancarlo under his door when he came back in the evening. He was invited for a meal on the next Friday. Although he spent many nights alone, Paul at first thought he wouldn't go. The reaction was more clear-cut than any reasons he could give for it. Maybe it was because he knew Maria had a partner, maybe it was Giancarlo's disability and the packed paraphernalia that bore witness to it, maybe it was just the possibility that the invitation came only because he had been of use to them. But he went. He went because he was personally unhappy at his work and had not much to do with his nights; he went because Giancarlo was intelligent and spoke good English; he went because there was something about Maria that drew him.

They ate in the small room opening to the balcony. Paul hadn't seen it on his first visit. It was familiar, however, in being structurally exactly the same as the balcony room in his own apartment — and surprising in its décor. In that room there was nothing at all to hint at Giancarlo's condition except the wheelchair he sat in. The floor had light blue tiles and one wall was crowded with spread book covers. They were not highly pictorial, and all Paul could make out of the titles was that they were scientific.

'It's Maria's job,' said Giancarlo. 'She's a book designer for the university publishers. That's where I met her. It's good because she can work from home most of the time. She uses this table,' and he tapped on the white tablecloth in which fold creases were sharp. He wore a blue shirt not much darker than the tiles, and he gesticulated with his strong, pale hands when he talked. Above the table he was powerful and handsome, and it was easy to forget those useless, clenched, hidden legs.

Giancarlo was a skilful conversationalist. He talked engagingly about himself and his country, but also drew Paul out with genuine warmth and curiosity. Every now and then he'd break off to give Maria a rapid resumé in Italian of what was being said, and she would smile at them both, and make quick comments of which Giancarlo approved. Sometimes she would cheerfully interrupt to offer more food, or wine, then listen again. Late in the evening, when Paul had been enjoying himself by exaggerating Dr Matteotti's faults, and paused to join in laughter with Giancarlo, he realised that he had been talking for a long time and that nothing he had been saying was intelligible to Maria.

'I'm sorry,' he said. 'It's very rude of me to be going on in English all night.'

Giancarlo translated and Maria held up her hands, shrugged.

'She's glad there's someone for me to talk to,' said Giancarlo. 'She grows tired of all my stories over and over.'

'I'm embarrassed that I don't know Italian,' Paul said. 'I should be going to classes, or at least listening to the tapes the company gave me, but all I know are the names of the things I like most in the restaurants, and enough words to buy a ticket.'

'Well, your firm could send you to Turkey next, and you would be back where you started without the local language again. Italy can be breathed, tasted, heard, seen and caressed without an understanding of the language. Maybe, however, I'll teach you just a few special insults to use for your Director Matteotti when next you're in argument.'

The balcony wasn't big enough for Giancarlo's wheelchair, but after the meal Maria and Paul sat close together there, and Giancarlo ran his chair half through the balcony door and was almost with them. While the conversation continued between the two men, and Paul enjoyed it, he was conscious too of Maria's physical presence although she said little. The light from the blue tiled room behind Giancarlo caught the line of her bare shoulder, lit one cheek and made the red wine in her drooping glass glow softly. People were coming past on their way home from the restaurants. As always they didn't think to look up, and so were unaware of being overlooked and overheard. They talked loudly and candidly. Paul thought of the many nights he had sat on his own balcony in such a way, while, unknown to him, Maria would have been on theirs, and Giancarlo as far into the night as his wheelchair would allow.

'People are happy now that they've forgotten work and had good food and wine,' Giancarlo said. 'After the patrons there's a lull and then the restaurant workers come past too: the waiters, cashiers and cooks. They come quietly, singly, because they're tired and it's just been work for them.'

Paul hadn't seen them, and realised that Giancarlo, maybe Maria too, stayed up much later than he did. What did they talk about, he wondered, when even the night workers were going home to bed.

'And I must be on my way, or I'll still be here when they come past tonight,' he said.

Giancarlo wanted him to stay longer, but Paul asked him to thank Maria for more than his 'Grazie, grazie' could convey, and she went with Paul to see him out. Giancarlo had wheeled back to allow them from the balcony, but he didn't follow from the blue-tiled room with book covers and white tablecloth. 'We want you to come again,' he called. Paul and Maria went through the room with Giancarlo's equipment, and Paul thought of all the drudgery associated with that and the specially adapted bed he had seen on his first visit. How often did she have to leave her own room to tend Giancarlo; wash him, prise those twining legs apart, turn and toilet him, dress the pressure points, help him grapple with the exercise machinery they were passing. As he thanked her at the hall door, she looked down so that he saw the sweep of her smooth hair rather than her expression. What sort of a life for her, but then Giancarlo seemed a man worth devotion.

Giancarlo and Luca Matteotti — what poles they represented in the reaches of the Italian character, and increasingly Paul sought the company of the former as a compensation for the perpetual guerilla warfare of his job. Matteotti instigated an audit of Paul's expenses. He held a party, at his house in the countryside outside the walls, to which Paul was expressly not invited, and then spent much of the project managers' meeting talking about it. He sent criticism of the consultants to their London office. None of that seriously threatened Paul's position in the firm, especially as Jeremy and even some Italian scientists were supportive, but it diminished the satisfaction the job otherwise gave him. If you reacted to the director's animosity as a victim you were increasingly treated like one. Paul didn't have a victim mentality: he could cope with Matteotti's dislike as long as he was left alone to do his work.

'Threaten to pack it in,' said Jeremy, who'd talked of doing it himself, even though he was less in the firing line. 'That might smarten him up. Consultants are part of the deal and he can't get the work approved without us.'

'Maybe, but I'm thinking that a crude Kiwi response might be more effective. Something that affects his pride and shows him up in front of others. That's what would hurt him most and make him think twice about knocking me all the time.'

'What, a truckload of sheep shit delivered to his door?'

'Not quite that crude,' said Paul.

'You know, I like to watch his face at meetings,' Jeremy said. 'Each expression is so calculated I think he must practise before a mirror. Don't you think?'

'I bet he does, yes.'

He was in Jeremy's office where they had been assessing computer-generated graphics of water pressure distortion on various natural fills. The view from Jeremy's window was of new Perugia on the flat. It was much the same view as Paul had from his own office, and always if he looked out he thought of the old part on the hill where he had his apartment: the massive gates and walls which had been fortifications in ancient times, the nonsensical alleys, the whisper of the past, and the pigeons resting in the niches of decaying plaster, lizards basking in the morning sun on perpendicular surfaces. The stepped streets which in an afternoon might be crowded with temporary market stalls, and at night cleared again, with just the scents of vegetables, cheeses and cured meats in the warm, lingering air, and leaves and torn ribbon on the cobbles. The orange tiles once moulded on the thighs of women perhaps, and the beaked stone gryphons both worn and fierce. And often he thought of Maria and Giancarlo, citizens of the old city yet rarely venturing into it, the only Italian people whose real life was gradually opening to him.

He invited them for drinks and they accepted. On that Sunday he set out fruit and three cheeses with the wine, all spread on a white tablecloth not unlike Maria's, which he had sought out in the shops, and in the duplicate balcony room too, although there were no lovely blue tiles, just floorboards, and no design work on the walls, just one speckled print of Venice. The difference between an apartment owned and one of casual, transient occupation.

An hour or so before they were to come, Paul found a note pushed under the door. Giancarlo wrote that they were very sorry, but illness prevented them coming, and he hoped Paul would forgive the late notice. Paul noted the wording, which gave no indication which of them was unwell. He surprised himself with the disappointment he felt. He ate the cheeses by himself over a week of evenings, but it was only the Tuesday when Giancarlo came to his door. Paul hadn't seen him out of his own rooms before. He wore a red top promoting the Perugian soccer team. It was close fitting and accentuated the purposeful development of his upper body; his legs were covered by a pale blanket tucked at his waist. The chair seemed all stainless steel and plastic handles; very modern, but without a motor.

'We're embarrassed about Sunday,' he said. 'It was something we looked forward to, but health is a fragile thing in our home.'

'That's okay. We'll arrange it again sometime soon.'

'Maria and I want you to come to dinner again.'

'It's my turn.'

'It was your turn and we let you down, so now it's our turn again. Maria likes me to have company. The only thing is, we hope you won't mind if she works after the meal while we talk. I don't know why she hasn't picked up more English, but she's selective that way.'

'So am I,' said Paul.

He went at least once a week after that. He got used to postponements, assuming Giancarlo had some complication that made it difficult for him, maybe some procedure that depended on the irregular visits of a nurse. Giancarlo liked being seated in the blue-tiled room with the book covers on the wall and the door to the balcony open to the warm, slow-moving air. After the meal Maria would often clear the table and work there, while Paul sat on the balcony and his friend ran his wheelchair into the opening, or, less often, both of them would go into the room Paul didn't like, the one with the special equipment, and he would help Giancarlo into a chest rest with his legs in a sling so that pressure points were relieved.

And always they would talk: about their countries and their lives, about food and wine, about their work and the things they would rather do. They would talk about things quite commonplace to one, but strange to the other. In their conversation they became not only friends, but equals. Paul hardly noticed the wheelchair any more, and was accustomed to Giancarlo suspended in the other room to free him from sitting, the stalks of his legs in loose trousers swaying a little. Sometimes he would do arm and shoulder exercises as they spoke, flexing and swaying while discussing the prevalence of cheating at the university, or asking Paul about time spent in New Mexico and Australia. Often, before he left, Paul would help his friend into his bed, because Maria found the task difficult. Giancarlo would grip the stirrup hanging above his bed and heave himself up, the muscles flexing on arm and shoulder, but someone was needed to assist and guide his useless legs.

Giancarlo had come from a poor family in Rimini. Hardship had sapped the love the family members had for each other and driven them apart. Although he had won through to a university education by talent and application, the early days had scarred him. 'Most people are comfortable to live with comparative failure,' he said, 'but for people like me there is the spectre of absolute failure, dying alone in a dilapidated rat hole behind the shunting sheds.' Because he came from a fortunate country and along an easy path to a professional career, Paul found such a fear hard to imagine. 'My worst dreams are of poverty,' said Giancarlo, 'not my legs.'

'You don't walk in your dreams?' asked Paul.

'Everybody walks in their dreams, or flies. And I'm this way because of an accident, not from birth.'

'What was the accident?' Paul felt able to ask when he'd become a friend, but Giancarlo was vague.

'I was hit by a car,' he said, 'and have little recollection of it.'

Maria was more difficult to get close to. It wasn't just their inability to talk the same language, or that after the meal she often worked at her book design. Usually she seemed glad to see him, and welcoming in her own way. She would laugh when they laughed, and listen when Paul spoke, with a smile on her face, eagerly take the translation from Giancarlo and quickly make some reply for him to pass on. They were the best times, and Giancarlo was never more relaxed and witty than those evenings when the three of them were on song together.

But occasionally there were evenings in which Maria was different, when Paul observed, without her being aware of it, the blank sadness of her expression, and there was unaccountably sometimes an absence in her manner which subtly rebuffed him.

Only once did Paul and Maria go out into the city together.

He had developed nagging toothache, and needed to see a dentist. Giancarlo arranged an appointment with their own dentist who spoke no English, and Maria walked with Paul up the steep, cobbled walkway from Corso Cavour to Corso Vannucci and the cathedral of San Lorenzo. It was mid-morning, warm and still. Perugia was not a prime tourist target, and large enough to absorb those that came without any threat to its identity. Local people maintained their ascendency and their ways without self-conscious display. Paul enjoyed that. He enjoyed, too, walking with Maria in the streets where he was usually alone, and never before with a woman. Despite the ache in his jaw he was conscious of her attractiveness, and the subtle alteration in the way he himself was regarded as a consequence of assumed partnership: such is the Italian way. He allowed himself to imagine that they were going to a café lunch with wine and confidential conversation, rather than he as patient and she as guide, heading to an appointment with the dentist.

The surgery rooms were not far beyond the square, towards the university buildings on the slope, above a chocolate shop in a narrow, uneven street. Atop the entrance were carved crossed keys, an elephant with an improbably long trunk, and a gryphon — all with the detail worn away by the centuries. The waiting room was small, and most of the close-set chairs already occupied.

Paul and Maria sat side by side without being able to carry on a conversation. She read a magazine, and he leant his head back to relax in the heat, conscious of the throbbing of his lower jaw and the flow of Italian from both a mother and son whose knees were close to his own. Any language incomprehensible to him always seemed to be spoken with excessive rapidity.

When it was his turn for treatment, he and Maria went down a long bare hallway and into a surgery, the one window of which looked into a shadowed and confined courtyard packed with dustbins and motor scooters. Above them household washing hung absolutely without movement. The dentist was a young man who listened as Maria passed on to him in turn the description of Paul's toothache which Giancarlo had given her after he had received it from Paul himself. The young dentist and Maria talked a lot as he worked on Paul's tooth, and nothing was asked of Paul except to open his mouth, or rinse. The dentist mimed each of these actions when required, and showed his enjoyment of the little drama by exaggerating the actions, and laughing after each rendition.

On their walk home, Maria took a slightly different route when they were near the square, pointing and saying, 'Il Pozzo Etrusco.' It was the well Luca Matterotti had talked about on the day of Paul's arrival in Perugia. In Maria's company it had much greater attraction for him. The well was hidden in the depths of a building old in itself, yet much younger than the well. Maria and Paul went carefully down the spiral steps until they stood to look down into the ancient pit. Electric bulbs above them cast enough light to show gleaming moss on the curving and chinked brick sides, and scores of coins which had stuck there freakishly, representative of thousands more tossed by tourists, and lost far below in the unseen water. The air was cool: Paul could feel it on his teeth made more sensitive by the recent treatment. The place was a testimony to continuity, and Paul imagined the Etruscan women hauling up their buckets there hundreds of years before Christ. And he was struck with the notion that Maria, whose family had been in Umbria as long as they could trace, may well be related to those women.

'Bellissimo,' he said inadequately, but couldn't understand Maria's reply. They were standing close together on the little platform, and he took her hand as an attempt to thank her for bringing him. Her hand was cool and passive, but she smiled at him, realising he liked the place. There was nothing flirtatious in her smile or manner, yet Paul had to resist a wish to put his arms around her shoulders. More than at any time before he wished he had some command of her language. He felt then no physical encounter was possible without some expression of its origins in talk between them. The moment passed without awkwardness, and Maria and Paul climbed back to the modern level of the city, out into the warm sun, and returned to the apartments.

He continued to feel attracted to Maria, but because of the language thing, her sometimes diffident manner and his deepening friendship with Giancarlo, he only once gave any unequivocal physical signal. And even that was on an impulse more of emotional concern. It happened during one of his many evenings in their apartment. He had left Giancarlo to get more wine, and passing through the short passage to the blue room found Maria's bedroom open to him for the first time. It was a strict little room barely lit by the hall light from behind him, and Maria wasn't there. The white cover on the single bed was tight and bare. As he paused and glanced in, he heard Giancarlo still talking from the equipment room, and he turned his head into the light of the hall and made a flippant reply, but he found the sight of that narrow bed, and the thought of Maria nightly there without a husband, powerfully erotic.

Maria was at the table with no work spread out before her. Her back was towards him and he saw the sheen on her brown hair. She had been withdrawn during the meal, and almost without thinking he put his hand on her shoulder and let it slide a little. 'Are you okay?' he said, yet knowing she wouldn't understand. She gave no reaction to his touch, and then she turned and looked at him briefly with an utter lack of interest; not as any sort of message, but as if he were a stranger a long way off.

Giancarlo was still talking, raising his voice a little to carry down the hall into the balcony room. Paul took away his hand. He went back to the other room, and closed the door of Maria's bedroom as he passed.

'I said you should ask for a car to be assigned to you, so you can drive to places in the weekends. I could make a list of places you would enjoy,' Giancarlo was saying.

'Is Maria all right?' Paul said. 'She's just sitting there at the table without doing anything.'

'She gets overtired sometimes and emotionally not good. Is she crying? If you help me back into the chair, I'll go through to her.'

'Then I'll push off,' said Paul.

'Push off?'

'I'll go, and let you see to Maria,' Paul said. He wondered if it was his fault, if loneliness in Perugia was making him a nuisance to these neighbours, and he wished he hadn't seen into Maria's room; regretted touching her as he had.

Matteotti became attracted by the idea of an economic overview of the project, convinced that politicians and business people weren't able to understand the mass of statistical and scientific information that Paul, Jeremy and the others produced, and therefore there was a place for a more general document in plain language. 'A project manifesto is what we need,' he told them. 'Something soundly reasoned, but not technical, and with artist's impressions showing what the reservoir would look like when completed. People like a picture.' He had a sample at the first meeting on the manifesto, and he brought it up on his PowerPoint screen — the storage lake sparkling, but inaccurately drawn, and attractive parkland developed on the valley sides. Matteotti was enthusiastic, perhaps partly because it was an enterprise in which he would be largely free of the narrow technical dominance exercised by the practical engineers. He sat by the screen and pointed out obvious things to the others. How well he chooses and wears a suit, Paul thought with grudging admiration, and the director's dark shoes shone like obsidian. He was a man of surfaces, and even his considerable intelligence was so often devoted to image and appearance of one sort or another.

The booklet was a surprisingly big budget item, and the contract for it went to a firm in which the director's brother-in-law was a partner, though nothing was said of that. When it was completed, the project managers were given preliminary copies. Paul regarded it as a glossy public relations product and only glanced through it, but Giancarlo noticed it on the table when he and Maria came for drinks. 'Oh, take it away if you like,' said Paul. 'The economic guff in it should make good reading for you.' Giancarlo did take it away and read it with interest, criticising the economic sections with growing delight at their inadequacy. He chronicled the most glaring inconsistencies and falsehoods, and found on the internet original data that had been quite wrongly used in the manifesto.

He knew of the firm to which Matteotti's brother-in-law belonged, he said, and their research and findings were not respected at the university. It was an opportunity to ambush the director in a way to which he might find official retaliation difficult. Giancarlo schooled Paul carefully in each area of weakness in the report and provided him with sources and reasoning. He made a game of the preparation: pretending to be Matteotti, or the representative of the brother-in-law's firm, and making Paul respond to their counter-arguments. In the week before the presentation of the manifesto, Giancarlo had the flu, but his mischievous enthusiasm continued, and Paul sat by his bed for several evenings while his friend went over it all again, twisting his hand in the overhead grip as he damned the most telling examples of confusion of actual with projected figures, or glib assumptions not economically sound. He passed on also criticisms of the booklet's design, which were Maria's contribution to the analysis.

How Giancarlo would have enjoyed that meeting. The director's pride in his initiative encouraged him to invite several journalists and councillors to the function, foreseeing no criticism. He grandly introduced the manifesto and praised its colour illustrations and bullet point summaries. He was unprepared for Paul's deceptively casual but informed criticism. At first he tried to bluff his way out, but when he realised the accuracy of Paul's points, and that he was insufficiently prepared to cope with them, he turned the questions to the representative of the public relations firm and said little. It all had a calm professionalism about it, and the PR rep thanked Paul for his comments, saying they would be helpful in the revision of what all of them realised was still a draft document. Yet Luca Matteotti's

face had a rigidity of anger and affront which Paul allowed himself
to savour as some recompense for the many times the man had given
him a hard time. For the remaining weeks they had together on
the project, the director continued his animosity, but considerably
tempered by his realisation that Paul was capable of striking back.
He had no inkling of what part Giancarlo had played in it all.

Paul wanted to thank his friend for that help, and remembered
his idle comment about a car for weekends: he would offer to take
Maria and Giancarlo away for a day. The outside world's not for us,
Giancarlo had said at their first meeting, but Paul thought they were
cooped up in the upstairs apartment too much. Perhaps that was a
reason for Maria's mood swings.

Paul went to their door and proposed the trip. 'I'm going to take
you both up to the reservoir site, and you can see where the lake will
be,' he said. 'All the times I've been going on about my work and
the place, and you've no idea of it. We'll take lunch and find a spot
somewhere with a good view.'

'I don't know about the chair. The stairs, then getting it in the car,'
said Giancarlo, then quickly spoke to Maria in Italian.

'I'll get one of the vans,' said Paul. He didn't care if the trip
provided an opportunity for Matteotti to criticise him.

'These stairs aren't easy,' said Giancarlo.

'You'd like to see the site, though?'

'I would like that.'

'Why are you living on the second floor with a wheelchair
anyway?' Paul knew him better now.

'We own the apartment. We've been here a long time, since before
the accident. And there's no balcony on any of the lower apartments.'
Maria must have a balcony? Paul could understand that: how many
times she must have finished tending to Giancarlo, even with the
best will in the world, and then had time on the balcony to which
his wheelchair denied him access. No doubt she and Paul often sat
out of sight of each other on separate balconies and watched the

roof tiles lose their colour, the locals drift into the street, and the pigeons crouch in nooks in the stone or plaster walls like blue-grey apostrophes.

On the Friday evening before the planned trip to the project site, Paul went to the vehicle yard and signed out a modern van with both a sliding side door and a back hatch, so that Giancarlo's chair would be bound to fit in one way or another. He drove very little while in Italy, because he had a fear that in an emergency he might instinctively pull over to the wrong side of the road. Once clear of the city, however, he knew there would be little traffic on the way to the reservoir valley, and he wanted his friends for one day at least to be freed from the apartment and be in the sun, in fresh moving air, and among trees and grasses and gardens, and the hills beyond Assisi. It was something he could do before leaving; a token repayment for the many nights of hospitality in the room of blue tiles, and the talk and comradeship.

The weather was promising that Saturday morning, but when Paul went to Giancarlo's apartment, his friend seemed slightly apprehensive. He opened the door himself, which was in itself unusual. 'We had a bad night. Sometimes I get stomach problems and it means a difficult night for us both,' he said. 'She's resting now.'

'Maybe we should call it off?' said Paul.

'Could we just leave it for another hour and see how she feels? Both of us have been looking forward to it.' Giancarlo hadn't shaved, although it was the time at which they'd agreed to leave. Paul had never before seen him in the morning, or unshaven, and his large, handsome face seemed raffish, but older.

Giancarlo was clean-shaven an hour later, and wore a leather jacket of quality and appeal. Paul wondered for a moment what other things he would discover about his friends merely by moving with them beyond the rooms of his apartment, or theirs. Maria was ready to leave too, although the fatigue of the night showed in the passivity Paul had noticed at other times. She made an effort, however, to match Giancarlo's deliberately up-beat tone, and replied to Paul's greeting. They had a small ritual which mocked their mutual language deficiency. Paul would wish her good morning and ask about her work, in Italian, always with the words by rote, and she would reply equally briefly in English with the same enquiry. Giancarlo had almost given up the struggle to interest them in acquiring each other's language.

Giancarlo had predicted difficulty in getting him down the stairs to street level. Paul found he was right. His friend was heavy, the chair awkward and the stairs steep and cramped. Paul placed himself below, and Maria was behind to control the descent. Giancarlo had his own powerful hands on the wheels, yet Paul at times had almost the full weight of both man and wheelchair, and he was relieved when they reached the lower hallway. 'There, nothing to it,' he said reassuringly, and tried to keep his breathing steady. The next challenge was to get Giancarlo from chair to a seat in the van. They chose the front passenger seat for him: although access was more difficult, the seat gave him more support and he could see ahead clearly. As Paul closed the door and stepped back, he thought how handsome Giancarlo was framed in the van window. His longish, black hair was combed straight back in the Italian way, the leather jacket emphasised the bulk of his powerful shoulders, and his face had a calm intelligence. No one would know that he was physically half a man, that he was so dependent on Maria.

They drove through the narrow streets, past the civic buildings with their guardian gryphons — those winged lions with fierce heads of eagles. Paul remarked on them again, and Giancarlo said they were one of the most ancient of all the monsters of antiquity, even appearing on the frescos of Knossos. 'A combination of the greatest power and pride in nature,' he said, 'but even the gryphons couldn't save Perugia from the Romans in the end.' Giancarlo, the underprivileged boy from Rimini, had developed a great sympathy for his adopted city. He said again proudly that Maria came of an old family in Perugia, with so long a history that she might well have Etruscan blood.

He loved the fertile countryside of Umbria too, pointing out the various crops to Paul, the maize, beans, tomatoes, gourds and vines, and tilting his head often to say something to Maria, who said little in reply. There were the old rural homes, a few quite grand, most functional and undecorated, with no gardens. There were new homes too, testimony to the growing prosperity of Euro currency Italy. The new homes were not farmhouses, nor were they gracious mansions. They drew attention to themselves with a spurious exaggeration of the traditional architecture. 'No doubt your favourite, Dr Matteotti, lives in one of those,' said Giancarlo. He had accepted Paul's enemy without question as his own, as friends do. Paul knew, though, that Matteotti, with all his faults, had a genuine sense of his own culture.

As they drew out of the broad valley and into the hills, there were more vineyards and then olives. The olive groves were grey-green, in some lights almost pewter, and the catching nets were spread beneath many of the trees. Some of the ancient stone walls of the terraces had broken down. In small gullies that had no evidence of water flow, grasses and lavenders grew. In one, resting pigs were roughly fenced.

A bluff overlooked the narrow valley in which the reservoir was to be built. Paul had been there often with members of his team, with visiting politicians, or dignitaries, to point out what was proposed for the scheme. From a coarsely grassed parking place a track of fifty or so metres, which Giancarlo's chair should cope with, led upwards. Paul and Maria pushed him, and he kept talking about the fragrances in the country air which had become strange to him because he spent all his time in the apartment. From the lookout Paul could show them where the earth dam would be built, where the lake level would rise to along the hillsides, and where there was an especially porous stratum that was a worry to him.

'What gets flooded?' asked Giancarlo.

'Mainly farmland which has already been bought and the houses removed, but at the top end of the valley are olives which will be cut down after this last harvest, and other full-grown trees around what used to be a small monastery. That was the big argument, really. It's the only building of any historical importance. In the end, though, it was realised that if the lake level were to be kept below the monastery then the whole project wasn't worthwhile.'

They made an odd group there on the bluff. Paul keen to have his friends understand the work he did; Giancarlo responsive not just to the explanation, but to the rare experience of being on a hill in the open air; Maria standing back a pace or two and working with her fingers at the fabric of a small bag she carried, rather than interacting with the other two. Giancarlo relayed to her much of what Paul said, and she nodded almost as a child nods in expected obedience to adults. Paul asked him if she was feeling unwell, and Giancarlo said it was just tiredness and not having the language to join in their conversation. Normally Maria moved gracefully and held herself well, but she stood there a little hunched and downcast, seeming reduced, almost cowed by the reaching country, the drop to the valley floor and the exposed expanse of the sky, hazy at its extremes. When Paul tried his talisman Italian in an attempt at contact, she replied with her rote English and a forced smile.

The two of them guided the wheelchair back down the dirt track. Paul opened the hatch and set out their picnic there on the carpeted floor of the van — bread with salami and tomatoes, cheeses and olives, individual fruit tarts of different flavours, wine in plastic tumblers. The stainless steel surfaces of Giancarlo's chair flashed in the sun; high in the blue sky lengthened the vapour plumes of invisible planes, the moderate wind brought summer scents and summer insects, but no noise from the small valley where the farms had all been sold. The two men began to talk of Matteotti, with Paul telling of the latest test of wills, and Giancarlo offering the most preposterous solutions to the feud.

Neither of them noticed that Maria had left the picnic and wandered away, until Giancarlo suddenly stopped laughing, and looked urgently around for her. She wasn't at the van, and they saw her at the lookout, close to the wooden rail that guarded the edge. She was in an odd pose, almost, Paul thought, like some *Titanic* movie burlesque, and he started to laugh. But Giancarlo gave a gasp as if struck heavily, and lifted his body from the wheelchair by his arms, in sudden, futile urgency. He then fell back. 'Quickly, quickly,' he implored, and without a word Paul took off up the track.

Maria had climbed beyond the rail when Paul reached the lookout. He stopped running, and moved tentatively towards her. 'Hey, Maria, it's me,' he said. 'Don't go any further out there.' Surely the urgency of the situation would enable her to understand English just this once.

She stood on the lip of the bluff, and as Paul stepped over the rail and edged towards her, he was aware that there was an odd wind coming straight up the cliff which held the long grass of the edge in a fluttering free fall. Maria seemed to lean into it, to be held up on its steady insistent breath. 'No, no, Maria,' he said, and he took her left upper arm in his hand and steadied them both on the fluttering edge in the whine of upward wind. He could see her face, and it was the face she had shown him on the night he had passed her open bedroom. It was a face of absence and desolation, of some deep separation from the world. 'Hey, careful now,' he said. As she leant forward, he leant back, neither of them in any struggle, but rather a momentary ballet. Paul's greater weight and strength began to tell and he drew her back from the edge until he could feel the rail behind them. Maria gave a little sigh, and said something in Italian in a low voice. She allowed herself to be drawn back onto the path, and to walk down to the van, with Paul holding her arm as if nothing had occurred.

Giancarlo hugged her waist and talked in Italian soothingly, but she said little. 'We shouldn't have come,' he said. 'I knew she wasn't well and we shouldn't have come.'

'What is it that she suffers from?' asked Paul.

He had for the first time some understanding of the true relationship and dependence the two of them had — the complexity of it, the fragility and the fearful possibility.' His friend looked up at him from the wheelchair, his face close to Maria's side. He was about to speak when his large eyes brimmed with tears, and he looked wordlessly at Paul for a few seconds and then said, 'I can't talk about it. I cannot manage to talk about it now.'

What had begun that morning, at least on the part of the two men, with pleasurable anticipation, ended as a grim ride back to Perugia, though the sun still shone. Giancarlo was strapped in the back so he could hold Maria, who leant on him with a sort of dull fatigue, and said nothing of what had happened at the lookout. Had life become for her a grey monotony, or worse, and a descent against the wind of no more significance than the trailing threads she picked at on her bag?

She was little help back at the apartments in getting Giancarlo up the stairs, and try as he might, Paul was unable to do it safely himself. He went to the door of the Arcottis, and because Signor Arcotti was away, his wife and a woman visitor from Rome came somewhat apprehensively to help. With that assistance the three finally made the upstairs hall — powerful Giancarlo distraught by his concern for his partner and unable to take command, Paul without the language and afraid worse things might yet happen, Maria listless and sad, seeming always half turned away.

They went through to the blue-tiled room, dim because the shutter doors to the balcony were closed, and Maria sat by the table spread with her work, while Giancarlo first gave her two white pills with water, then made coffee.

'I shouldn't have suggested the trip,' said Paul. 'I didn't realise it might be too much for her.'

'No, no. It's a cyclic thing,' said Giancarlo, 'but irregular, and I should have seen the signs, but it seemed a chance for once to be back in the world.' He expertly manoeuvred the chair to put himself as close to her as possible, and put his strong, large hand quite over both of hers on the table. 'She'll be all right. It's part of our life together,' he said simply. He spoke to her in their language, but she made no reply, just put a weary shoulder against his.

'Is there anything I can do?' asked Paul.

'Yes, what we'd like is for you not to be afraid of what happened; not to be afraid of any of this; to come and see us again just as before.'

They sat in an easing silence for a time while Paul and Giancarlo drank coffee, while Maria had her head half bowed and rested on her partner, and the afternoon light bloomed softly through the full-length shutter doors of the balcony. As Paul rose to leave, Giancarlo lifted his hand with one of Maria's within it and touched his friend's arm briefly. 'I'm glad I saw the site before it was flooded for the reservoir,' he said. 'Something will be gained and something gone forever perhaps.'

'I hope Maria feels okay soon.'

Giancarlo spoke to her, and she made the effort to glance up at Paul and spoke in reply. Giancarlo nodded vigorously and clasped her around the shoulder. 'She said not to blame yourself. She will feel better again and again, and worse not so often,' he said.

On the way back to his own apartment, Paul stopped at the Arcotri's door to thank Signora Arcotri. She came out a little warily, but relaxed when she saw he was alone. Her English was adequate to say she was happy to help, but that Giancarlo never went out and perhaps it was better that way. 'She sick,' said Signora Arcotri shaking her head and switching the subject to Maria. 'She run across him in a car, you know that? Yes so. The big, handsome man and she run across him.'

'I didn't know.' Yet somehow it was news of a kind he felt he had been awaiting from one source or another. Signora Arcuti clasped her hands to her breast, gave a shrug and held the pose quite unself-consciously to express her pity, and the powerlessness of us all, then she went back inside to her visitor from Rome.

During the final weeks of his stay, Paul went often to his friends' apartment in the evenings, and there were no more postponements, or misunderstandings on his part of how it was between the couple. When Maria was feeling well, he would stay later, there would be more wine and laughter, and he would often put Giancarlo to bed before leaving. On the bad days he would drop in a paper, talk briefly with Giancarlo over strong coffee while Maria sat lost within herself, and then go.

She was well on the day he left, and kissed him for the first and last time as she and Giancarlo farewelled him at their door. 'Buongiorno Maria, il lavoro, come va?' he said, playing their game to the last, and she replied with her English. He thought of her on the cliff above the reservoir site, and how she had begun to lean into the rising wind. He wondered what terrible world she had to journey through, and how fortunate Giancarlo and she were to have each other, how connected they had become through affliction. 'I'll miss you both,' he said. 'Let's hope we'll all be happy.'

'Happiness is the absence of pain,' replied Giancarlo, and his strong hand tightened on Paul's.

'In bocca al lupo,' said Maria. Paul asked Giancarlo what that meant.

'It's a good luck wish between friends,' he said. 'Being in the mouth of the wolf, and yet unharmed.'

There had been wind and rain in the night. When the taxi paused by the old wall, Paul saw liquidambar leaves stuck to the pavement, their stalks insolently up, small scarlet swans on the dark road. The taxi wound down the hill from the old city, past the gryphons of stone who had witnessed so much pain and so much happiness. Luca

Matteotti had first mentioned the gryphons, but he was nothing to Paul, who remembered rather Giancarlo telling him of those fabulous, threatening creatures that had never existed, yet been powerful in the human imagination for thousands of years. We all have things we cannot do, and sometimes life makes us do them, his friend had said. Maybe in Maria's Etruscan dreams the gryphons still take protective flight against her demons.

Acknowledgements

'Supper Waltz Wilson', 'A Southland Girl', 'The Tsunami' and 'Descent from the Flugelhorn' first published in *Supper Waltz Wilson and other New Zealand stories*, Pegasus, Christchurch, 1979.

'The Master of Big Jingles', 'Mr Van Gogh', 'The Charcoal Burners' Dream', 'Cabernet Sauvignon with my Brother', 'Prince Valiant', 'Thinking of Bagheera' and 'Requiem in a Town House' first published in *The Master of Big Jingles and other stories*, John McIndoe, Dunedin, 1982.

'The Late Call', 'Kenneth's Friend', 'The Divided World', 'The Seed Merchant', 'The Paper Parcel', 'The Fat Boy' and 'The Day Hemingway Died' first published in *The Day Hemingway Died and other stories*, John McIndoe, Dunedin, 1984.

'Lilies' first published in *The Divided World: Selected Stories*, John McIndoe, Dunedin, 1989.

'The Frozen Continents', 'Valley Day', 'Mumsie and Zip', 'A Poet's Dream of Amazons', 'Trumpeters' and 'Another Generation' first published in *The Lynx Hunter and other stories*, John McIndoe, Dunedin, 1987.

'The Ace of Diamonds Gang' first published in *The Ace of Diamonds Gang*, McIndoe Publishers, Dunedin, 1993.

'Iris', 'The Rule of Jenny Pen', 309 Hollandia', 'The Rose Affliction', 'Heating the World', 'Pluto', 'Supplication for Position', 'A View of our Country', 'The Dungarvie Festival' and 'Tomorrow We Save the Orphans' first published in *Tomorrow We Save the Orphans*, John McIndoe, Dunedin, 1992.

'Working Up North', 'The Occasion', 'Cometh the Hour', 'Growing Pains ', 'Rebecca', 'Peacock Funeral', 'Goodbye, Stanley Tan', 'The Birthday Boy' and 'A Late Run' first published in *Coming Home in the Dark*, Vintage, Auckland, 1995.

'The Devil at Bruckner's Pond' 'The Language Picnic', 'End of Term', 'How It Goes', 'An Indirect Geography', 'Mr Tansley' and 'Wake Up Call' first published in *When Gravity Snaps*, Vintage, Auckland, 2002.

'Buried Lives', 'Facing Jack Palance', 'Family Circle', 'Images', 'Buster', 'Minding Leaf', 'Hodge' and 'Watch of Gryphons' first published in *Watch of Gryphons*, Vintage, Auckland, 2005.

The author acknowledges the use of the setting in V S Naipaul's *Finding the Centre: Two Narratives* (Andre Deutsch, 1984) for satirical purposes in the story 'A View of our Country'.

The quote on page 259 in 'The Rule of Jenny Pen' comes from the poem 'Night Owl' by Laurie Lee, published in *My Many-Coated Man* (Andre Deutsch, 1955). The quote on page 259–260 is from W B Years *The Herne's Egg: A Stage Play* (Macmillan, 1938).